D0909807

THE COLLECTED STORIES OF ROGER ZELAZNY

THRESHOLD

VOLUME 1:

THE COLLECTED STORIES OF
ROGER ZELAZNY

EDITED BY
David G. Grubbs
Christopher S. Kovacs
Ann Crimmins

NESFA
PRESS

Post Office Box 809, Framingham, MA 01701
www.nesfa.org/press
2009

FIRST EDITION, February 2009

ISBN-10: 1-886778-71-X
ISBN-13: 978-1-886778-71-9

3 4015 06992 0039

A Word from the Editors

This six volume collection includes all of Zelazny's known short fiction and poetry, three excerpts of important novels, a selection of non-fiction essays, and a few curiosities.

Many of the stories and poems are followed by "A Word from Zelazny" in which the author muses about the preceding work. Many of the works are also followed by a set of "Notes"[1] explaining names, literary allusions and less familiar words. Though you will certainly enjoy Zelazny's work without the notes, they may provide even a knowledgeable reader with some insight into the levels of meaning in Zelazny's writing.

> "My intent has long been to write stories that can be read in many ways from the simple to the complex. I feel that they must be enjoyable simply as stories…even for one who can't catch any of the allusions."
> —Roger Zelazny in *Roger Zelazny* by Jane M. Lindskold

The small print under each title displays original publication information (date and source) for published pieces and (sometimes a guess at) the date it was written for unpublished pieces. The small print may also contain a co-author's name, alternate titles for the work, and awards it received. Stories considered part of a series are noted by a § and a series or character name.

---

1 The notes are a work in progress. Please let us know of any overlooked references or allusions, or definitions you may disagree with, for a possible future revision.

CONTENTS

ARTICLES

CURIOSITIES

POETRY

Threshold

Volume 1:

The Collected Stories of

Roger Zelazny

OUT OF NOWHERE

by Robert Silverberg

He came out of nowhere. That was probably not how it seemed to him, but it certainly was how it seemed to me: a brilliant new writer with a strange surname, suddenly filling the pallid science-fiction magazines of the early 1960s with astonishing, unforgettable stories that were altogether unlike anything that anyone (not even Bradbury, not even Sturgeon, not even Fritz Leiber) had published in those magazines before.

The first encounter that science-fiction readers had with the work of Roger Zelazny came with the August 1962 issue of *Fantastic*, an undistinguished and long-forgotten penny-a-word magazine. It was a story just eight hundred words in length called "Horseman!", and this is how the hitherto unknown 25-year-old author opened it:

> When he was thunder in the hills the villagers lay dreaming harvest behind shutters. When he was an avalanche of steel the cattle began to low, mournfully, deeply, and children cried out in their sleep.
>
> He was an earthquake of hooves, his armor a dark tabletop of silver coins stolen from the stars, when the villagers awakened with fragments of strange dreams in their heads. They rushed to the windows and flung their shutters wide.
>
> And he entered the narrow streets, and no man saw the eyes behind his vizor.

It sings, flamboyantly. The metaphors tumble one over another—"when he was thunder in the hills," and "when he was an avalanche

11

of steel," and "he was an earthquake of hooves," and "his armor a dark tabletop of silver coins stolen from the stars." The syntax is idiosyncratic, when he wants it to be: "the villagers lay dreaming harvest," a small grammatical connective omitted in what we would before long come to recognize as a characteristic Zelazny touch. Everything is vivid and immediate, everything is furiously alive, romantic and melodramatic, and we are plunged all at once into a strange, dramatic, fantastic situation, instantly conjuring us into the world of Sir Lancelot or perhaps Scheherazade. In the first few lines of his first published story Zelazny had announced his presence among us and had told us what kind of writer he was going to be.

That same month came a second story, "Passion Play," like the other a mere two pages long, this one in the August 1962 issue of *Fantastic*'s equally mediocre companion, *Amazing Stories*. It opens in an entirely different but equally Zelaznian manner:

> At the end of the season of sorrows comes the time of rejoicing. Spring, like the hands of a well-oiled clock, noiselessly indicates the time. The average days of dimness and moisture decrease steadily in number, and those of brilliance and cool begin to enter the calendar again. And it is good that the wet times are behind us, for they rust and corrode our machinery; they require the most intense standards of hygiene.

Here we get Zelazny the poet in prose: notice the scansion and cadence of that first sentence, "At the end of the season of sorrows comes the time of rejoicing." Zelazny the wry comedian is here, too, telling us that "the most intense standards of hygiene" must be observed by robots hoping to fend off rust and corrosion.

The general effect of "Passion Play" is a quieter, less fantastic one than that of "Horseman!". The manner is cooler, more controlled, much less given to rhetorical flourish. He gives us simile instead of metaphor; he gives us science-fictional imagery, machinery vulnerable to rust, instead of the medieval villagers and armored stranger of the other story. There is power in that paragraph; there is soaring individuality of vision. Both stories, in hindsight, are recognizably Zelazny, yet they vary widely, within the compass of their few pages, in what they achieve.

One would have had to be looking very closely at those two little stories when they first appeared to realize that they signalled the arrival in our midst of a master of prose technique and a paragon of the storytelling art. I doubt that very many people came to that conclusion on the basis of just two small stories, although Cele Goldsmith, the enterprising editor who had accepted them for *Amazing* and *Fantastic*, surely was pleased by her find. (She published two more short-shorts of his in 1962, "The Teachers Rode a Wheel of Fire" in *Fantastic* and "Moonless in Byzantium" in *Amazing*.) Gradually, though, over the year that followed, he let us know that that was the case, appearing with another dozen or so stories in the two Cele Goldsmith magazines, one of them, "Nine Starships Waiting," betraying by its title to those with eyes to see its author's scholarly familiarity with Jacobean drama; and then, in case anyone still had not noticed, he published what would become his first classic story, "A Rose for Ecclesiastes," in the November 1963 issue of *The Magazine of Fantasy & Science Fiction*. No one failed to notice that one. It was nominated for the Hugo award. (The Nebula award had yet to come into existence.) Judith Merril picked it for her *Year's Best Science Fiction* collection. And it was chosen, a few years later, as one of the twenty-six great stories included in the first volume of the definitive Science Fiction Writers of America anthology, *The Science Fiction Hall of Fame*, voted by the members of that organization into sixth place on the all-time list. It was the only representative of recent science fiction in a book that was heavily weighted toward the classics of the 1930s and 1940s and included no other story published after 1956. It has been reprinted countless times ever since.

(It is worth noting that a decade later it was revealed that "Ecclesiastes" was actually written a year or so *before* Zelazny's first professional sales. His friend Thomas Monteleone, in his 1973 M.A. thesis on Zelazny's work, made it known that Zelazny had been slow to offer the story for publication because he thought its scientific inaccuracies would draw embarrassing criticism. So it was no sudden leap to a new level of proficiency; the author of all those tiny stories for *Amazing* and *Fantastic* had been capable of a major work of that sort all along.)

After "A Rose for Ecclesiastes" it was impossible to ignore his presence among us. 1964—a year complicated by many personal misfortunes for the young writer—saw him publish just one major story,

"The Graveyard Heart," but 1965 brought a flood of brilliant novellas and novels—"He Who Shapes," "The Doors of His Face, the Lamps of His Mouth," …*And Call me Conrad*, and many, many others—gaining him great acclaim and, ultimately, a shelf full of Hugo and Nebula awards. (In 1966, the year the Nebula was instituted, Zelazny carried off two of the five trophies, one for "He Who Shapes" as best novella and one for "Doors of His Face" as best novelet. He was still not yet thirty.) He seemed to be everywhere at once, and his performance was never anything other than dazzling. By the time his 1967 novel, *Lord of Light*, won the Hugo award and narrowly missed the Nebula, he was reckoned among the masters of the field. I think no writer of the time, with the possible exception of the equally individual and gifted Samuel R. Delany, was discussed and analyzed with such intensity by his peers. No one with any sense thought of studying Zelazny's work with an eye toward imitating it, since his voice was so unmistakably his own that anyone adopting his method would mange to produce nothing more than pastiche, at best. But the propulsive manner of his storytelling and the power and gusto of his style were worth careful consideration by anyone who hoped to stay in the thick of things in that exciting, experimental time.

Over the decades ahead he went on to produce a host of novels—*Isle of the Dead, Damnation Alley, Today We Choose Faces, Creatures of Light and Darkness*, and many more, including the numerous books of the popular Amber series. Nevertheless, he continued to produce the occasional short story and novelet, and again and again, nearly to the end of his career, won Hugo and Nebula awards for the best of his output—three Nebulas and six Hugos in all by the time of the premature death of this superbly gifted, beloved, and much lamented master of science fiction and fantasy at the age of 58 in 1995.

Roger's death brought a powerful sense of loss to everyone who had read his fiction or knew him as a friend. I belonged to both groups. As a reader and as a professional colleague I will always remember the impact of those great early stories and their successors of the decades that followed. And so I miss the author of "A Rose for Ecclesiastes" and "The Graveyard Heart" and …*And Call Me Conrad* and all the rest of those wonderful tales, keenly aware that there is no way of knowing now what marvels of inventiveness were about to emerge from his fertile mind.

But also he was my friend, and it still pains me, many years after his death, to realize I will never hear his quiet voice again or see that sly little smile. 58 isn't an appropriate age for dying—especially when one is as youthful and vigorous and full of life and creative energy as Roger still was. I knew him almost thirty years, and I had hoped to know him thirty years more, and now that is not to be. In all those three decades I never heard him utter an unkind word about anyone. (Nor did I ever hear anybody utter an unkind word about *him*.) He was a calm, gentle man, a man of great patience, high good humor, and warm good will, as I learned when the inordinately punctual Robert Silverberg showed up an hour late for dinner with him on two successive visits to Santa Fe, New Mexico, where Roger had lived since 1975. I was late for a different silly reason each time, having to do with time-zone problems on one occasion and a faulty wristwatch on the other. Roger met each occasion of my tardiness with amusement and charm, as though it was a normal condition of the universe that I would always turn up an hour late for dinner, and there was no more reason to be displeased by it than by the discovery that water will not run uphill. That was altogether typical of him. No doubt he had moments of anger now and then in his life; but I was never witness to one.

In all senses of the word Roger was a joyous man to know. That sense of infectious joy runs through the many stories of these books. This series is his monument. I would much rather still have the man and let the monument wait; but the universe does not give us a choice about that, and we should be glad, at least, that Roger Zelazny was among us for those 58 years and that he left this robust group of stories for our unending delight.

—Robert Silverberg

BEFORE AMBER

by Carl B. Yoke

I shot a stone at the sun setting into Lake Erie, and we started to count. Twenty-one, two, three, four, five, six, and then it died and plopped beneath the orange-tinted, glassy water. "Damn," I said and frowned at him.

"Not as good as my thirty-two," he teased.

"I'll catch you yet."

"No way."

It was hard to see in the gathering darkness, but we were determined to find more "skippers," so he went up and I went down the beach, looking for some. We hadn't found many really good ones since we had arrived a half hour earlier.

The beach was littered with empty beer bottles, driftwood, old tires, ash-filled fire pits, dead fish, and used condoms. There was also a lot of stuff we couldn't identify and weren't about to pick up.

I kicked a piece of what looked to be a torn white skirt from in front of a weathered branch and uncovered a piece of gray shale. "This is too good to be true," I thought. It was perfect, smooth from Lake Erie waves, just the right thickness, and about three inches in diameter. I picked it up, brushed it off on the leg of my jeans, hefted it a few times, and practiced my throw.

Just then I heard, "Yoke! Yoke! Come here!"

I turned. Roger was up the beach about thirty yards, waving to me. "Come see what I found!" I couldn't see much in the darkness, so I hurried to where he was standing.

"Look at this, man!" he began as he pointed down to a decomposing fish about ten inches long. Beetles scurried over it, its eyes were gone, and it was encrusted with sand.

"It woulda' been perfect," he said with a broad grin. "Instead of those two little ones."

I started to laugh. I knew exactly what he meant. He laughed, too, as I turned and threw my "skipper" at the sunset. It hopped like a sixth grader jacked up on sugar, and I was sorry I hadn't started counting it right from the beginning because it went a very long way.

But it didn't matter now; we had already moved on to something else. We were reliving the last few days of ninth grade at Shore Junior High. We had planned that a terrible smell would come from a room on the second floor of the east wing. It would last well into the summer—two dead fish inside one of the "permanently" bolted-shut desks would guarantee it—a present directly from the beach at the end of East 222nd street to Mr. Wilson. It was his home room, and we were getting even.

The plan started when Roger launched an epic sneeze from the front row of Mr. Wilson's ninth grade history class. We all went into hysterics because the blast was so violent that there were actually wet spots on the board. Mr. Wilson, whose lecture on the battle between the *Monitor* and the *Merrimac* had been interrupted, was startled, and he was not amused. And though Roger apologized and said that he couldn't help it because his allergies were acting up, Mr. Wilson felt he needed to punish him. Even more importantly, he knew he needed to get the class back under control. So he decided that Roger should write a five hundred word paper on the battle, which he had obviously been ignoring, to be read in front of the class the next day.

Roger felt more than a little put out, but the next day when Mr. Wilson called on him to read, he was ready. Looking a bit nervous but deadpan serious and holding a couple of sheets of notebook paper, he began. "The *Monitor* sighted the *Merrimac* first and fired: bang, bang, bang, bang, bang, bang, bang, bang," and so on. Halfway through the paper the *Merrimac* fired back: "bang, bang, bang …" Roger never finished. Mr. Wilson was livid. The class was on the floor with laughter.

We continued to laugh as Wilson hauled Roger down the hall to the principal's office where he got a lecture and was told to write a serious, thousand word paper on the famous battle which he would read the following day to the class. This time he did as he was told, and while we tried not to laugh, there were several periodic snickers.

The events really happened but are far more than just fond musings. Indeed they are windows into my relationship with Roger and snapshots into his early character development.

We always knew that revenge was "best served cold," but we also held ourselves to a higher code, so we never actually followed through with any plans that would have put us into real trouble. We would never have done anything illegal, immoral, or unethical. Planning was the fun part of such ventures, anyway.

The first anecdote shows two important aspects of our relationship. First, we were always bouncing ideas off one another, and second, we were very competitive in an entirely friendly way; ours was a "throwing down the gauntlet" kind of relationship. We competed to see who could bring new information to the table to discuss, or who could out-achieve the other, whether it was climbing to the top of Morrow Rock in California and then racing down different sides to see who could get to the bottom first, who could outscore the other on IQ or achievement tests, or who could win the next award. As we matured, the "contests" pushed our individual growth forward.

We always ran pretty evenly, but regardless of any particular outcome, our relationship was founded on mutual admiration, never jealousy. Loyalty and respect were always part of it, too.

Roger was my dearest and oldest friend. When he died on June 14, 1995, I had known him longer than I'd known any other person on earth, except for my mother. We could literally complete each other's thoughts.

Our friendship began more than half a century earlier at Noble School in Euclid, Ohio. And while the rumor persists that we shared a desk in first grade, that really was not the case. I knew him in the first grade from the playground, but we were in different homerooms. He struck me as a "strange kid." But then in second grade we did share a desk because it was war time, and no city was spending money on schools. Anyway, when I got to Mrs. Farber's second grade, I found myself sharing a desk with that "strange" kid Roger Zelazny. That desk, as it turned out, was a perfect metaphor.

It took me a while to get to know him in more than a superficial way. He was secretive and shy. But when our teacher learned that we were reading way ahead of the rest of the class, she sent us to the school library to read whatever we wanted. I was interested in the myths, legends, and fairy tales. And Noble School's library was a treasure trove—in fact all the Euclid school libraries were superb for their time. But it seemed that every time I went looking for a particular book, that Zelazny kid had it out. The same was true of the standard children's books, such as *Dr. Doolittle, Alice's Adventures in Wonderland,* and *20,000 Leagues Under the Sea.* Eventually Roger and I started to see who could read the most. Our bragging to one another led to discussions not only of the books but also other issues, concerns, and interests.

Then one day in the fourth or fifth grade, as I was heading out the door for home, Roger handed me a couple of sheets of folded notebook paper and asked me to read them. I nodded, said something that amounted to all right, and shoved them into my pocket—I was a walker, and I had many worlds to explore: a couple of mysterious woods, several ponds and streams filled with fish and tadpoles, and a field or two filled with mice, interesting bugs, and garter snakes. I forgot about Roger's "note" until I finished my homework. Then I dug it out of my coat pocket and started to read.

It was a long, rhymed poem entitled "The Yoke Monster," portraying me as a huge, hairy, smelly thing that swung through trees like an ape, liked to splash in water but never really bathed, and ate little furry creatures, disgusting bugs, and what we now call road kill.

I was very angry. And I decided after the first stanza that at recess the next day I would beat him up. I was a project kid—we did a lot of fighting in the project—that's how we settled things. We knew who we could beat up and who to get out of the way for. We had no drugs or guns. But we were tough—we had booze, cigarettes, and occasional sex. Then a strange thing happened. Even though I was angry, I liked Roger, so I gathered up the rest of the poem and read on. And after a while I started to laugh in spite of myself. It really was very funny.

So, I composed myself, and a few days later showed up at school with a proper response, "The Zelazny Monster." It was also funny but meaner and nastier. Thus were born the two characters that would inhabit "The Record Stories" and a deepening friendship that would last for more than half a century.

Once we started, some rules, patterns, and practices quickly developed. Each story could include anything that did not violate the basic, evolved mythology: the characters became loveable, friendly and less scary, and the stories had to contain gentle humor.

"The Record Stories," all written individually, related the adventures and misadventures of Yok and Zlaz, two nearly immortal, monster-like beings of a little known Earth species that lived in the catacombs below Paris and above Hell, just outside the city of Lucetania. As the characters evolved, so did the mythology of Lucetania. Yok and Zlaz were creatures who had enormous appetites. They ate a lot and slept for inordinately long periods of time. They were extremely intelligent, wonderfully creative, and superbly curious. They had great senses of humor.

The "mon" (both singular and plural, a shortened form of monster but also a corruption of man and men) did not like to work, except at their hobbies and passions. But because they were extremely clever (or at least appeared to be), they were blackmailed and very much overpaid by Lucetania's leader (The Pres) to go on missions no other agents would take. The kingdom was always in danger from the forces of Hell and its many allies. Almost always, the missions also involved saving humans and other groups on the surface. Saving humans was an unintended consequence of saving Lucetania because mon generally found humans ignorant and boring, so they ignored them. In later years and later stories, the threats to Lucetania were more complex and sometimes involved alien races.

Yok and Zlaz were generally lazy, often drunk (consuming enormous quantities of a local drink called zyphoam), and over sexed. They were somewhat shady by Lucetanian law, but because of their usefulness to the Pres, their indiscretions were ignored or forgiven. Time and again they saved the city by what appeared to be a miraculous means but in the process often caused enormous destruction. It was their fatal flaw. Nonetheless, they were Lucetania's two best agents. They never failed, not because they really were the brightest or most talented, but because added to their resourcefulness and intelligence was more than a dollop of good luck, "collotial" (from the word colossus) they called it.

The monsters were nonthreatening, and the plots often developed around the inadequacies of the heroes. Though Yok and Zlaz were very bright, they were often naïve and failed to see the obvious. For example, in one story, Zlaz took his space ship on a long trip but forgot to fuel it, and it crashed on an uninhabited planet. In another Yok used the wrong spell and petrified a large, fin-backed dinosaur that eventually got buried and became a now-famous stand of rocks in a West Virginia state park.

Since almost any subject matter was acceptable, each writer's new story challenged the other author. If I introduced a variation into the mythology, it was up to Roger to accept the innovation, play off of it by expanding or modifying it, or explain it so that it did not violate the mythology. To ignore the variation entirely was simply not permitted.

Yok and Zlaz evolved as we matured and reflected how we saw ourselves in high school and college. The stories' plots were informed by what we knew or learned. And our infinite curiosity, eclectic tastes, and challenge to outdo one another made the stories "different." Part of the fun of writing was to make what we saw, heard, or read show up in a logical way in the stories. Our sources ranged from comic books to philosophy but were particularly heavy on myth, legend, and fairy tales. Movies, television shows, comic strips, pop and later folk music also quickly got folded into our thinking.

The themes of the stories were growing up, having fun, play, curiosity, immortality, and relationships with girls, among others. Things were hardly ever what they seemed, which provided surprise and created suspense. Form and chaos, in the sense that nothing is ever destroyed, ran through the entire mythology. Early on, we had recognized that form was always ripped from chaos, then it evolved, and when eventually destroyed become part of some new form: creation, destruction, re-creation. Nothing in the universe seemed to be wasted; it simply transformed. There was symmetry and some sort of logic and reason in the universe that not only appealed to us but comforted us.

This was not a guarantee that individual consciousness would survive, of course. But Roger believed that he had projected astrally. For him this confirmed that there was another kind of reality and suggested that individual consciousness might indeed survive the death of the physical body.

So there we were, in the early fifties, writing stories in what later came to be called a "shared universe." We were doing what the advertising industry called "rewriting the image," like Charles Adams did in *The New Yorker*.

We almost never wrote in true collaboration. I can recall only once that we did so. It involved the creation of two model newspapers for a journalism class in the eleventh grade. We created *The Martian Chronicle* and *The Venusian Herald*. We wrote fake stories for them, mocked up the pages, and drew the pictures in lieu of real photographs and colored them in.

The Lucetanian mythology reflected who we were (or pretended to be) and evolved primarily from events in our real lives. No matter what either of us got into, one of us had the right information, found the right information, stumbled across the right address, found the right tool, remembered an article, or connected to the right person to solve the problem. For example, as seniors, we were the property crew for a school play, *The Admirable Crichton*. We often volunteered for jobs off school grounds since it gave us a legitimate excuse to leave early. Roger had a 1950 Ford, and we were good at stretching a twenty minute ride to pick up a piece of furniture into an hour or more that included a stop at Euclid Race dairy for chocolate milkshakes.

In this case, though, on the afternoon of opening night, we were still missing a small but important ottoman. The people who owned it were on vacation but had promised to be back in time. We didn't know what to do, so we hung around the school, trying to be helpful. Finally, the director told us that the people had returned, and if we hurried, we had just enough time to get the ottoman before the play started.

Even though it was already dark, everything went well at first. We found the house in what is now Richmond Heights, loaded the ottoman, and headed back to the school. Just as we came down the Richmond Road hill, we saw the gates on the railroad tracks at 160th Street go down and the red lights flash. Roger raced to the crossing, stopped, and waited. We saw nothing, so after a reasonable time, Roger slipped the car into gear and pulled around the crossing gate and on to the tracks. Of course, the car stalled. He tried frantically to start it, but the engine would not kick over.

A long minute passed, and we heard a train whistle. Coming around a bend to the east was a locomotive. The crossing bells were clanging, the red lights were flashing, and I reached for the passenger side door handle to bail out. Then we both remembered Roger's Ford was a stick shift.

"Jump it!" we yelled almost together. Roger popped the clutch. The car lurched forward. He did it again, and the car lurched again. We finally cleared the tracks, pushed the car around the last gate, and listened to a bunch of comments about how stupid we were from adults in cars going the other way.

We hopped back in, and Roger tried once more to start the car. The engine turned over. We got the ottoman to the school for the start of the play.

We did have a lot of luck—or maybe we really were very good. I won a regional essay contest in the sixth grade, and later scholarships and fellowships for academic work, and later some national awards. I published sports stories in the *Euclid News Journal* while still in high school and as a senior won the school literary magazine contest for best short story. Roger had won that award the year before and several other writing awards at Case Western Reserve. His big break came, however, when Cele Goldsmith picked "Passion Play" off the slush pile and realized she had discovered a unique talent. Her careful mentoring brought out the best in Roger's writing.

For reasons I have never been quite able to figure out (we came from very different cultures), we liked a lot of the same things. We read *Pogo, L'il Abner, The Phantom, Terry and the Pirates, Popeye,* and *Prince Valiant,* to name a few, listened to radio's *Captain Midnight, Jack Armstrong, the All-American Boy, 2000 Plus, Have Gun - Will Travel, Inner Sanctum, Boston Blackie, The Green Hornet, The Adventures of Sam Spade, The Shadow,* and one of our favorites, *I Love a Mystery,* with Jack, Doc, and Reggie. On television we watched *Mr. Peepers, Bold Venture, Space Cadet, Captain Video,* and several others. We followed the adventures of *Tarzan, Brick Bradford, Flash Gordon,* and *Buck Rogers* in several mediums, read the science fiction and fantasy writers of the times: Asimov, Heinlein, Bradbury, Williamson, Leiber, Kuttner, Moore, Hamilton, Brackett, Haggard, Merritt, and Lovecraft, and read the mythologists, particularly Bullfinch and Campbell. When we found we could buy pulp magazines at Moss Drug Store, we bought *Imagination, Amazing, Other Worlds, Planet,* and others as they came and went. We investigated and discussed Richard Shaver's "I Remember Lemuria," hypnotism, narco-hypnotism, yoga, astral projection, Rosicrucianism, and other exotic topics.

And always we read the classics of fiction, drama, and poetry.

Yet in our relationships with most of our schoolmates, we felt paradoxically like outsiders. I say paradoxically because we were both editors of the school paper and well liked. I was on Senior Cabinet and the Senior Prom Committee. Roger was on Student Council. I dove on the swim team. We won literary awards. We dated and went to the senior prom. But we simply found we were not interested in the same things as, with a few exceptions, our classmates; our interests ranged far beyond theirs.

We shared the "anxieties" of the fifties: the cold war, atom bomb drills, censorship. Because of McCarthy and Nixon we both had to sign affidavits that we were not, and never had been, Communists—we were editors of a high school paper, for God's sake.

We were always concerned about humanness and humanity. The people Roger met were adventurers; they were to be explored and learned from. Ideas, themes, and characters, not only from his own experience but from other works of literature, were to be examined in detail, understood, and worked into new stories in new ways. No matter how diverse—such ideas as the wandering Jew, the Alice novels, mirrors, shadows, immortality, Shakespeare—were rewritten to serve his story needs. A. E. Housman's *A Shropshire Lad* provides an exceptional example of this sort of creativity. Zelazny brilliantly recasts the ideas in parts XXXII and XXXIII to frame his novella, "For a Breath I Tarry," giving it a different perspective about humanness.

It was his genius to be able to do this so well.

Critics know that great stories need great plots, great characters, and great ideas, but Zelazny's very best work even exceeds this. His best stories are lean and spare—every word and image counts—they make profound observations about the human condition; they have poetic vision and are told in poetic language. Those who read them want to hold on to them for their beauty.

I am positive that many of his stories are great literature—"The Man Who Loved the Faioli," "The Engine at Heartspring's Center," "Permafrost," "The Keys to December," "24 Views of Mt. Fuji, by Hokusai," "The Doors of His Face, the Lamps of His Mouth," and *Lord of Light*—to name a few.

Critic Joe Sanders once wrote, "It is not simply what he had done already but what he *might* do that makes Zelazny important."[1] As we dumb down western culture and fill the world with derivative and predictable stories, I, for one, greatly miss his creative genius.

— Carl B. Yoke

---

1 "Unfinished Business" by Joe Sanders. *Voices for the Future: Essays on Major Science Fiction Writers*, Vol. 2, ed. T. D. Clareson, Popular Press, 1979, p 180-196 and p 205-207

STORIES

A ROSE FOR ECCLESIASTES

The Magazine of Fantasy & Science Fiction, November 1963.
Hugo nominee 1964 (short story), #3 on 1999 Locus all-time poll (novelette),
#5 on 1971 Astounding/Analog all-time poll (short fiction),
#6 greatest SF story of all time in *The Science Fiction Hall of Fame, Volume One,* 1970.

I

I was busy translating one of my *Madrigals Macabre* into Martian on the morning I was found acceptable. The intercom had buzzed briefly, and I dropped my pencil and flipped on the toggle in a single motion.

"Mister G," piped Morton's youthful contralto, "the old man says I should 'get hold of that damned conceited rhymer' right away, and send him to his cabin. Since there's only one damned conceited rhymer..."

"Let not ambition mock thy useful toil." I cut him off.

So, the Martians had finally made up their minds! I knocked an inch and a half of ash from a smoldering butt, and took my first drag since I had lit it. The entire month's anticipation tried hard to crowd itself into the moment, but could not quite make it. I was frightened to walk those forty feet and hear Emory say the words I already knew he would say; and that feeling elbowed the other one into the background.

So I finished the stanza I was translating before I got up.

It took only a moment to reach Emory's door. I knocked twice and opened it, just as he growled, "Come in."

"You wanted to see me?" I sat down quickly to save him the trouble of offering me a seat.

"That was fast. What did you do, run?"

I regarded his paternal discontent:

29

Little fatty flecks beneath pale eyes, thinning hair, and an Irish nose; a voice a decibel louder than anyone else's...

Hamlet to Claudius: "I was working."

"Hah!" he snorted. "Come off it. No one's ever seen you do any of that stuff."

I shrugged my shoulders and started to rise.

"If that's what you called me down here—"

"Sit down!"

He stood up. He walked around his desk. He hovered above me and glared down. (A hard trick, even when I'm in a low chair.)

"You are undoubtably the most antagonistic bastard I've ever had to work with!" he bellowed, like a belly-stung buffalo. "Why the hell don't you act like a human being sometime and surprise everybody? I'm willing to admit you're smart, maybe even a genius, but—oh, hell!" He made a heaving gesture with both hands and walked back to his chair.

"Betty has finally talked them into letting you go in." His voice was normal again. "They'll receive you this afternoon. Draw one of the jeepsters after lunch, and get down there."

"Okay," I said.

"That's all, then."

I nodded, got to my feet. My hand was on the doorknob when he said:

"I don't have to tell you how important this is. Don't treat them the way you treat us."

I closed the door behind me.

❖　❖　❖

I don't remember what I had for lunch. I was nervous, but I knew instinctively that I wouldn't muff it. My Boston publishers expected a Martian Idyll, or at least a Saint-Exupéry job on space flight. The National Science Association wanted a complete report on the Rise and Fall of the Martian Empire.

They would both be pleased. I knew.

That's the reason everyone is jealous—why they hate me. I always come through, and I can come through better than anyone else.

I shoveled in a final anthill of slop, and made my way to our car barn. I drew one jeepster and headed it toward Tirellian.

Flames of sand, lousy with iron oxide, set fire to the buggy. They swarmed over the open top and bit through my scarf; they set to work pitting my goggles.

The jeepster, swaying and panting like a little donkey I once rode through the Himalayas, kept kicking me in the seat of the pants. The Mountains of Tirellian shuffled their feet and moved toward me at a cockeyed angle.

Suddenly I was heading uphill, and I shifted gears to accommodate the engine's braying. Not like Gobi, not like the Great Southwestern Desert, I mused. Just red, just dead…without even a cactus.

I reached the crest of the hill, but I had raised too much dust to see what was ahead. It didn't matter, though; I have a head full of maps. I bore to the left and downhill, adjusting the throttle. A crosswind and solid ground beat down the fires. I felt like Ulysses in Malebolge—with a terza-rima speech in one hand and an eye out for Dante.

I rounded a rock pagoda and arrived.

Betty waved as I crunched to a halt, then jumped down.

"Hi," I choked, unwinding my scarf and shaking out a pound and a half of grit. "Like, where do I go and who do I see?"

She permitted herself a brief Germanic giggle—more at my starting a sentence with "like" than at my discomfort—then she started talking. (She is a top linguist, so a word from the Village Idiom still tickles her!)

I appreciate her precise, furry talk; informational, and all that. I had enough in the way of social pleasantries before me to last at least the rest of my life. I looked at her chocolate-bar eyes and perfect teeth, at her sun-bleached hair, close-cropped to the head (I hate blondes!), and decided that she was in love with me.

"Mr. Gallinger, the Matriarch is waiting inside for you to be introduced. She has consented to open the Temple records for your study." She paused here to pat her hair and squirm a little. Did my gaze make her nervous?

"They are religious documents, as well as their only history," she continued, "sort of like the Mahābhārata. She expects you to observe certain rituals in handling them, like repeating the sacred words when you turn pages—she will teach you the system."

I nodded quickly, several times.

"Fine, let's go in."

"Uh—" She paused. "Do not forget their Eleven Forms of Politeness and Degree. They take matters of form quite seriously—and do not get into any discussions over the equality of the sexes—"

"I know all about their taboos," I broke in. "Don't worry. I've lived in the Orient, remember?"

She dropped her eyes and seized my hand. I almost jerked it away. "It will look better if I enter leading you."

I swallowed my comments, and followed her, like Samson in Gaza.

❖   ❖   ❖

Inside, my last thought met with a strange correspondence. The Matriarch's quarters were a rather abstract version of what I might imagine the tents of the tribes of Israel to have been like. Abstract, I say, because it was all frescoed brick, peaked like a huge tent, with animal-skin representations like gray-blue scars, that looked as if they had been laid on the walls with a palette knife.

The Matriarch, M'Cwyie, was short, white-haired, fifty-ish, and dressed like a Gypsy queen. With her rainbow of voluminous skirts she looked like an inverted punch bowl set atop a cushion.

Accepting my obeisances, she regarded me as an owl might a rabbit. The lids of those black, black eyes jumped upwards as she discovered my perfect accent. —The tape recorder Betty had carried on her interviews had done its part, and I knew the language reports from the first two expeditions, verbatim. I'm all hell when it comes to picking up accents.

"You are the poet?"

"Yes," I replied.

"Recite one of your poems, please."

"I'm sorry, but nothing short of a thorough translating job would do justice to your language and my poetry, and I don't know enough of your language yet."

"Oh?"

"But I've been making such translations for my own amusement, as an exercise in grammar," I continued. "I'd be honored to bring a few of them along one of the times that I come here."

"Yes. Do so."

Score one for me!

She turned to Betty.

"You may go now."

Betty muttered the parting formalities, gave me a strange sideways look, and was gone. She apparently had expected to stay and "assist" me. She wanted a piece of the glory, like everyone else. But I was the Schliemann at this Troy, and there would be only one name on the Association report!

M'Cwyie rose, and I noticed that she gained very little height by standing. But then I'm six-six and look like a poplar in October: thin, bright red on top, and towering above everyone else.

"Our records are very, very old," she began. "Betty says that your word for that age is 'millennia.'"

I nodded appreciatively.

"I'm very eager to see them."

"They are not here. We will have to go into the Temple—they may not be removed."

I was suddenly wary.

"You have no objections to my copying them, do you?"

"No. I see that you respect them, or your desire would not be so great."

"Excellent."

She seemed amused. I asked her what was so funny.

"The High Tongue may not be so easy for a foreigner to learn."

It came through fast.

No one on the first expedition had gotten this close. I had had no way of knowing that this was a double-language deal—a classical as well as a vulgar. I knew some of their Prakrit, now I had to learn all their Sanskrit.

"Ouch! and damn!"

"Pardon, please?"

"It's non-translatable, M'Cwyie. But imagine yourself having to learn the High Tongue in a hurry, and you can guess at the sentiment."

She seemed amused again, and told me to remove my shoes.

She guided me through an alcove…

…and into a burst of Byzantine brilliance!

No Earthman had ever been in this room before, or I would have heard about it. Carter, the first expedition's linguist, with the help of one Mary Allen, M.D., had learned all the grammar and vocabulary that I knew while sitting cross-legged in the antechamber.

We had had no idea this existed. Greedily, I cast my eyes about. A highly sophisticated system of esthetics lay behind the decor. We would have to revise our entire estimation of Martian culture.

For one thing, the ceiling was vaulted and corbeled; for another, there were side-columns with reverse flutings; for another—oh hell! The place was big. Posh. You could never have guessed it from the shaggy outsides.

I bent forward to study the gilt filigree on a ceremonial table. M'Cwyie seemed a bit smug at my intentness, but I'd still have hated to play poker with her.

The table was loaded with books.

With my toe, I traced a mosaic on the floor.

"Is your entire city within this one building?"

"Yes, it goes far back into the mountain."

"I see," I said, seeing nothing.

I couldn't ask her for a conducted tour, yet.

She moved to a small stool by the table.

"Shall we begin your friendship with the High Tongue?"

I was trying to photograph the hall with my eyes, knowing I would have to get a camera in here, somehow, sooner or later. I tore my gaze from a statuette and nodded, hard.

"Yes, introduce me."

I sat down.

For the next three weeks alphabet-bugs chased each other behind my eyelids whenever I tried to sleep. The sky was an unclouded pool of turquoise that rippled calligraphies whenever I swept my eyes across it. I drank quarts of coffee while I worked and mixed cocktails of Benzedrine and champagne for my coffee breaks.

M'Cwyie tutored me two hours every morning, and occasionally for another two in the evening. I spent an additional fourteen hours a day on my own, once I had gotten up sufficient momentum to go ahead alone.

And at night the elevator of time dropped me to its bottom floors...

❖   ❖   ❖

I was six again, learning my Hebrew, Greek, Latin, and Aramaic. I was ten, sneaking peeks at the *Iliad*. When Daddy wasn't spreading hellfire, brimstone, and brotherly love, he was teaching me to dig the Word, like in the original.

Lord! There are so many originals and so *many* words! When I was twelve I started pointing out the little differences between what he was preaching and what I was reading.

The fundamentalist vigor of his reply brooked no debate. It was worse than any beating. I kept my mouth shut after that and learned to appreciate Old Testament poetry.

—*Lord, I am sorry! Daddy—Sir—I am sorry! —It couldn't be! It couldn't be...*

On the day the boy graduated from high school, with the French, German, Spanish, and Latin awards, Dad Gallinger had told his fourteen-year old, six-foot scarecrow of a son that he wanted him to enter the ministry. I remember how his son was evasive:

"Sir," he had said, "I'd sort of like to study on my own for a year or so, and then take pre-theology courses at some liberal arts university. I feel I'm still sort of young to try a seminary, straight off."

The Voice of God: "But you have the gift of tongues, my son. You can preach the Gospel in all the lands of Babel. You were born to be a missionary. You say you are young, but time is rushing by you like a whirlwind. Start early, and you will enjoy added years of service."

The added years of service were so many added tails to the cat repeatedly laid on my back. I can't see his face now; I never can. Maybe it was because I was always afraid to look at it then.

And years later, when he was dead, and laid out, in black, amidst bouquets, amidst weeping congregationalists, amidst prayers, red faces, handkerchiefs, hands patting your shoulders, solemn faced comforters... I looked at him and did not recognize him.

We had met nine months before my birth, this stranger and I. He had never been cruel—stern, demanding, with contempt for every-one's shortcomings—but never cruel. He was also all that I had had of a mother. And brothers. And sisters. He had tolerated my three years at St. John's, possibly because of its name, never knowing how liberal and delightful a place it really was.

But I never knew him, and the man atop the catafalque demanded nothing now; I was free not to preach the Word. But now I wanted to, in a different way. I wanted to preach a word that I never could have voiced while he lived.

I did not return for my senior year in the fall. I had a small inheri-tance coming, and a bit of trouble getting control of it, since I was still under eighteen. But I managed.

It was Greenwich Village I finally settled upon.

Not telling any well-meaning parishioners my new address, I entered into a daily routine of writing poetry and teaching myself Japanese and Hindustani. I grew a fiery beard, drank espresso, and learned to play chess. I wanted to try a couple of the other paths to salvation.

After that, it was two years in India with the Old Peace Corps—which broke me of my Buddhism, and gave me my *Pipes of Krishna* lyrics and the Pulitzer they deserved.

Then back to the States for my degree, grad work in linguistics, and more prizes.

Then one day a ship went to Mars. The vessel settling in its New Mexico nest of fires contained a new language. —It was fantastic, exotic, and esthetically overpowering. After I had learned all there was to know about it, and written my book, I was famous in new circles:

"Go, Gallinger. Dip your bucket in the well, and bring us a drink of Mars. Go, learn another world—but remain aloof, rail at it gently like Auden—and hand us its soul in iambics."

And I came to the land where the sun is a tarnished penny, where the wind is a whip, where two moons play at hotrod games, and a hell of sand gives you the incendiary itches whenever you look at it.

❖   ❖   ❖

I rose from my twistings on the bunk and crossed the darkened cabin to a port. The desert was a carpet of endless orange, bulging from the sweepings of centuries beneath it.

"I, a stranger, unafraid— This is the land— I've got it made!"

I laughed.

I had the High Tongue by the tail already—or the roots, if you want your puns anatomical, as well as correct.

The High and Low tongues were not so dissimilar as they had first seemed. I had enough of the one to get me through the murkier parts of the other. I had the grammar and all the commoner irregular verbs down cold; the dictionary I was constructing grew by the day, like a tulip, and would bloom shortly. Every time I played the tapes the stem lengthened.

Now was the time to tax my ingenuity, to really drive the lessons home. I had purposely refrained from plunging into the major texts until I could do justice to them. I had been reading minor commentaries, bits of verse, fragments of history. And one thing had impressed me strongly in all that I read.

They wrote about concrete things: rock, sand, water, winds; and the tenor couched within these elemental symbols was fiercely pessimistic. It reminded me of some Buddhists texts, but even more so, I realized from my recent *recherches*, it was like parts of the Old Testament. Specifically, it reminded me of the Book of Ecclesiastes.

That, then, would be it. The sentiment, as well as the vocabulary, was so similar that it would be a perfect exercise. Like putting Poe into French. I would never be a convert to the Way of Malann, but I would show them that an Earthman had once thought the same thoughts, felt similarly.

I switched on my desk lamp and sought King James amidst my books.

Vanity of vanities, saith the Preacher, vanity of vanities; all is vanity. What profit hath a man…

❖ ❖ ❖

My progress seemed to startle M'Cwyie. She peered at me, like Sartre's Other, across the tabletop. I ran through a chapter in the Book of Locar. I didn't look up, but I could feel the tight net her eyes were working about my head, shoulders, and rapid hands. I turned another page.

Was she weighing the net, judging the size of the catch? And what for? The books said nothing of fishers on Mars. Especially of men. They said that some god named Malann had spat, or had done something disgusting (depending on the version you read), and that life had gotten underway as a disease in inorganic matter. They said that movement was its first law, its first law, and that the dance was the only legitimate reply to the inorganic…the dance's quality its justification,—fication…and love is a disease in organic matter—Inorganic matter?

I shook my head. I had almost been asleep.

"M'narra."

I stood and stretched. Her eyes outlined me greedily now. So I met them, and they dropped.

"I grow tired. I want to rest for awhile. I didn't sleep much last night."

She nodded, Earth's shorthand for "yes," as she had learned from me.

"You wish to relax, and see the explicitness of the doctrine of Locar in its fullness?"

"Pardon me?"

"You wish to see a Dance of Locar?"

"Oh." Their damned circuits of form and periphrasis here ran worse than the Korean! "Yes. Surely. Any time it's going to be done I'd be happy to watch."

I continued, "In the meantime, I've been meaning to ask you whether I might take some pictures—"

"Now is the time. Sit down. Rest. I will call the musicians."

She bustled out through a door I had never been past.

Well now, the dance was the highest art, according to Locar, not to mention Havelock Ellis, and I was about to see how their centuries-dead philosopher felt it should be conducted. I rubbed my eyes and snapped over, touching my toes a few times.

The blood began pounding in my head, and I sucked in a couple deep breaths. I bent again and there was a flurry of motion at the door.

To the trio who entered with M'Cwyie I must have looked as if I were searching for the marbles I had just lost, bent over like that.

I grinned weakly and straightened up, my face red from more than exertion. I hadn't expected them *that* quickly.

Suddenly I thought of Havelock Ellis again in his area of greatest popularity.

The little redheaded doll, wearing, sari-like, a diaphanous piece of the Martian sky, looked up in wonder—as a child at some colorful flag on a high pole.

"Hello," I said, or its equivalent.

She bowed before replying. Evidently I had been promoted in status.

"I shall dance," said the red wound in that pale, pale cameo, her face. Eyes, the color of dream and her dress, pulled away from mine.

She drifted to the center of the room.

Standing there, like a figure in an Etruscan frieze, she was either meditating or regarding the design on the floor.

Was the mosaic symbolic of something? I studied it. If it was, it eluded me; it would make an attractive bathroom floor or patio, but I couldn't see much in it beyond that.

The other two were paint-spattered sparrows like M'Cwyie, in their middle years. One settled to the floor with a triple-stringed instrument faintly resembling a *samisen*. The other held a simple woodblock and two drumsticks.

M'Cwyie disdained her stool and was seated upon the floor before I realized it. I followed suit.

The *samisen* player was still tuning it up, so I leaned toward M'Cwyie.

"What is the dancer's name?"

"Braxa," she replied, without looking at me, and raised her left hand, slowly, which meant yes, and go ahead, and let it begin.

The stringed-thing throbbed like a toothache, and a tick-tocking, like ghosts of all the clocks they had never invented, sprang from the block.

Braxa was a statue, both hands raised to her face, elbows high and outspread.

The music became a metaphor for fire.

Crackle, purr, snap...

She did not move.

The hissing altered to splashes. The cadence slowed. It was water now, the most precious thing in the world, gurgling clear then green over mossy rocks.

Still she did not move.

Glissandos. A pause.

Then, so faint I could hardly be sure at first, the tremble of the winds began. Softly, gently, sighing and halting, uncertain. A pause, a sob, then a repetition of the first statement, only louder.

Were my eyes completely bugged from my reading, or was Braxa actually trembling, all over, head to foot?

She was.

She began a microscopic swaying. A fraction of an inch right, then left. Her fingers opened like the petals of a flower, and I could see that her eyes were closed.

Her eyes opened. They were distant, glassy, looking through me and the walls. Her swaying became more pronounced, merged with the beat.

The wind was sweeping in from the desert now, falling against Tirellian like waves on a dike. Her fingers moved, they were the gusts. Her arms, slow pendulums, descended, began a counter-movement.

The gale was coming now. She began an axial movement and her hands caught up with the rest of her body, only now her shoulders commenced to writhe out a figure-eight.

The wind! The wind, I say. O wild, enigmatic! O muse of St.-John Perse!

The cyclone was twisting around those eyes, its still center. Her head was thrown back, but I knew there was no ceiling between her gaze, passive as Buddha's, and the unchanging skies. Only the two moons, perhaps, interrupted their slumber in that elemental Nirvana of uninhabited turquoise.

Years ago, I had seen the Devadasis in India, the street-dancers, spinning their colorful webs, drawing in the male insect. But Braxa was more than this: she was a Ramadjany, like those votaries of Rama, incarnation of Vishnu, who had given the dance to man: the sacred dancers.

The clicking was monotonously steady now; the whine of the strings made me think of the stinging rays of the sun, their heat stolen by the wind's halations; the blue was Sarasvati and Mary, and a girl named Laura. I heard a sitar from somewhere, watched this statue come to life, and inhaled a divine afflatus.

I was again Rimbaud with his hashish, Baudelaire with his lauda-
num, Poe, De Quincy, Wilde, Mallarme and Aleister Crowley. I was,
for a fleeting second, my father in his dark pulpit and darker suit, the
hymns and the organ's wheeze transmuted to bright wind.

She was a spun weather vane, a feathered crucifix hovering in the
air, a clothes-line holding one bright garment lashed parallel to the
ground. Her shoulder was bare now, and her right breast moved up
and down like a moon in the sky, its red nipple appearing momentarily above a fold and vanishing again. The music was as formal as
Job's argument with God. Her dance was God's reply.

The music slowed, settled; it had been met, matched, answered.
Her garment, as if alive, crept back into the more sedate folds it
originally held.

She dropped low, lower, to the floor. Her head fell upon her raised
knees. She did not move.

There was silence.

❖   ❖   ❖

I realized, from the ache across my shoulders, how tensely I had been
sitting. My armpits were wet. Rivulets had been running down my
sides. What did one do now? Applaud?

I sought M'Cwyie from the corner of my eye. She raised her right
hand.

As if by telepathy the girl shuddered all over and stood. The musicians also rose. So did M'Cwyie.

I got to my feet, with a charley horse in my left leg, and said, "It
was beautiful," inane as that sounds.

I received three different High Forms of "thank you."

There was a flurry of color and I was alone again with M'Cwyie.

"That is the one hundred-seventeenth of the two thousand, two
hundred-twenty-four dances of Locar."

I looked down at her.

"Whether Locar was right or wrong, he worked out a fine reply
to the inorganic."

She smiled.

"Are the dances of your world like this?"

"Some of them are similar. I was reminded of them as I watched
Braxa—but I've never seen anything exactly like hers."

"She is good," M'Cwyie said. "She knows all the dances."

A hint of her earlier expression which had troubled me…

It was gone in an instant.

"I must tend my duties now." She moved to the table and closed the books. "M'narra."

"Good-bye." I slipped into my boots.

"Good-bye, Gallinger."

I walked out the door, mounted the jeepster, and roared across the evening into night, my wings of risen desert flapping slowly behind me.

II

I had just closed the door behind Betty, after a brief grammar session, when I heard the voices in the hall. My vent was opened a fraction, so I stood there and eavesdropped:

Morton's fruity treble: "Guess what? He said 'hello' to me awhile ago."

"Hmmph!" Emory's elephant lungs exploded. "Either he's slipping, or you were standing in his way and he wanted you to move."

"Probably didn't recognize me. I don't think he sleeps any more, now he has that language to play with. I had night watch last week, and every night I passed his door at 0300—I always heard that recorder going. At 0500 when I got off, he was still at it."

"The guy *is* working hard," Emory admitted, grudgingly. "In fact, I think he's taking some kind of dope to keep awake. He looks sort of glassy-eyed these days. Maybe that's natural for a poet, though."

Betty had been standing there, because she broke in then:

"Regardless of what you think of him, it's going to take me at least a year to learn what he's picked up in three weeks. And I'm just a linguist, not a poet."

Morton must have been nursing a crush on her bovine charms. It's the only reason I can think of for his dropping his guns to say what he did.

"I took a course in modern poetry when I was back at the university," he began. "We read six authors—Yeats, Pound, Eliot, Crane, Stevens, and Gallinger—and on the last day of the semester, when the prof was feeling a little rhetorical, he said, 'These six names are written on the century, and all the gates of criticism and hell shall not prevail on them.'

"Myself," he continued, "I thought his *Pipes of Krishna* and his *Madrigals* were great. I was honored to be chosen for an expedition he was going on.

"I think he's spoken two dozen words to me since I met him," he finished.

The Defense: "Did it ever occur to you," Betty said, "that he might be tremendously self-conscious about his appearance? He was also a precocious child, and probably never even had school friends. He's sensitive and very introverted."

"Sensitive? Self-conscious?" Emory choked and gagged. "The man is as proud as Lucifer, and he's a walking insult machine. You press a button like 'Hello' or 'Nice day' and he thumbs his nose at you. He's got it down to a reflex."

They muttered a few other pleasantries and drifted away.

Well bless you, Morton boy. You little pimple-faced, Ivy-bred connoisseur! I've never taken a course in my poetry, but I'm glad someone said that. The Gates of Hell. Well now! Maybe Daddy's prayers got heard somewhere, and I am a missionary, after all!

Only…

…Only a missionary needs something to convert people *to*. I have my private system of esthetics, and I suppose it oozes an ethical by-product somewhere. But if I ever had anything to preach, really, even in my poems, I wouldn't care to preach it to such lowlifes as you. If you think I'm a slob, I'm also a snob, and there's no room for you in my Heaven—it's a private place, where Swift, Shaw, and Petronius Arbiter come to dinner.

And oh, the feasts we have! The Trimalchios, the Emorys we dissect!

We finish you with the soup, Morton!

❖   ❖   ❖

I turned and settled at my desk. I wanted to write something. Ecclesiastes could take a night off. I wanted to write a poem, a poem about the one hundred-seventeenth dance of Locar; about a rose following the light, traced by the wind, sick, like Blake's rose, dying…

I found a pencil and began.

When I had finished I was pleased. It wasn't great—at least, it was no greater than it needed to be—High Martian not being my strongest tongue. I groped, and put it into English, with partial rhymes. Maybe I'd stick it in my next book. I called it *Braxa*:

> *In a land of wind and red,*
> *where the icy evening of Time*
> *freezes milk in the breasts of Life,*

as two moons overhead—
cat and dog in alleyways of dream—
scratch and scramble agelessly my flight…
This final flower turns a burning head.

I put it away and found some phenobarbitol. I was suddenly tired.

❖ ❖ ❖

When I showed my poem to M'Cwyie the next day, she read it through several times, very slowly.

"It is lovely," she said. "But you used three words from your own language. 'Cat' and 'dog', I assume, are two small animals with a hereditary hatred for one another. But what is 'flower'?"

"Oh," I said. "I've never come across your word for 'flower,' but I was actually thinking of an Earth flower, the rose."

"What is it like?"

"Well, its petals are generally bright red. That's what I meant, on one level, by 'burning heads.' I also wanted it to imply fever, though, and red hair, and the fire of life. The rose, itself, has a thorny stem, green leaves, and a distinct, pleasing aroma."

"I wish I could see one."

"I suppose it could be arranged. I'll check."

"Do it, please. You are a—" She used the word for "prophet," or religious poet, like Isaias or Locar. "—and your poem is inspired. I shall tell Braxa of it."

I declined the nomination, but felt flattered.

This, then, I decided, was the strategic day, the day on which to ask whether I might bring in the microfilm machine and the camera. I wanted to copy all their texts, I explained, and I couldn't write fast enough to do it.

She surprised me by agreeing immediately. But she bowled me over with her invitation.

"Would you like to come and stay here while you do this thing? Then you can work day and night, any time you want—except when the Temple is being used, of course."

I bowed.

"I should be honored."

"Good. Bring your machines when you want, and I will show you a room."

"Will this afternoon be all right?"

"Certainly."

"Then I will go now and get things ready. Until this afternoon…"

"Good-bye."

❖ ❖ ❖

I anticipated a little trouble from Emory, but not much. Everyone back at the ship was anxious to see the Martians, poke needles in the Martians, ask them about Martian climate, diseases, soil chemistry, politics, and mushrooms (our botanist was a fungus nut, but a reasonably good guy)—and only four or five had actually gotten to see them. The crew had been spending most of its time excavating dead cities and their acropolises. We played the game by strict rules, and the natives were as fiercely insular as the nineteenth-century Japanese. I figured I would meet with little resistance, and I figured right.

In fact, I got the distinct impression that everyone was happy to see me move out.

I stopped in the hydroponics room to speak with our mushroom master.

"Hi, Kane. Grow any toadstools in the sand yet?"

He sniffed. He always sniffs. Maybe he's allergic to plants.

"Hello, Gallinger. No, I haven't had any success with toadstools, but look behind the car barn next time you're out there. I've got a few cacti going."

"Great," I observed. Doc Kane was about my only friend aboard, not counting Betty.

"Say, I came down to ask you a favor."

"Name it."

"I want a rose."

"A what?"

"A rose. You know, a nice red American Beauty job—thorns, pretty smelling—"

"I don't think it will take in this soil. *Sniff, sniff.*"

"No, you don't understand. I don't want to plant it, I just want the flower."

"I'd have to use the tanks." He scratched his hairless dome. "It would take at least three months to get you flowers, even under forced growth."

"Will you do it?"

"Sure, if you don't mind the wait."

"Not at all. In fact, three months will just make it before we leave."

I looked about at the pools of crawling slime, at the trays of shoots.

"—I'm moving up to Tirellian today, but I'll be in and out all the time. I'll be here when it blooms."

"Moving up there, eh? Moore said they're an in-group."

"I guess I'm 'in' then."

"Looks that way—I still don't see how you learned their language, though. Of course, I had trouble with French and German for my Ph.D, but last week I heard Betty demonstrate it at lunch. It just sounds like a lot of weird noises. She says speaking it is like working a *Times* crossword and trying to imitate birdcalls at the same time."

I laughed, and took the cigarette he offered me.

"It's complicated," I acknowledged. "But, well, it's as if you suddenly came across a whole new class of mycetae here—you'd dream about it at night."

His eyes were gleaming.

"Wouldn't that be something! I might, yet, you know."

"Maybe you will."

He chuckled as we walked to the door.

"I'll start your roses tonight. Take it easy down there."

"You bet. Thanks."

Like I said, a fungus nut, but a fairly good guy.

My quarters in the Citadel of Tirellian were directly adjacent to the Temple, on the inward side and slightly to the left. They were a considerable improvement over my cramped cabin, and I was pleased that Martian culture had progressed sufficiently to discover the desirability of the mattress over the pallet. Also, the bed was long enough to accommodate me, which was surprising.

So I unpacked and took sixteen 35 mm. shots of the Temple, before starting on the books.

I took 'stats until I was sick of turning pages without knowing what they said. So I started translating a work of history.

"Lo. In the thirty-seventh year of the Process of Cillen the rains came, which gave way to rejoicing, for it was a rare and untoward occurrence, and commonly construed a blessing.

"But it was not the life-giving semen of Malann which fell from the heavens. It was the blood of the universe, spurting from an artery. And the last days were upon us. The final dance was to begin.

"The rains brought the plague that does not kill, and the last passes of Locar began with their drumming…"

I asked myself what the hell Tamur meant, for he was an historian and supposedly committed to fact. This was not their Apocalypse.

Unless they could be one and the same…?

Why not? I mused. Tirellian's handful of people were the remnant of what had obviously once been a highly developed culture. They had had wars, but no holocausts; science, but little technology. A plague, a plague that did not kill…? Could that have done it? How, if it wasn't fatal?

I read on, but the nature of the plague was not discussed. I turned pages, skipped ahead, and drew a blank.

M'Cwyie! M'Cwyie! When I want to question you most, you are not around!

Would it be a *faux pas* to go looking for her? Yes, I decided. I was restricted to the rooms I had been shown, that had been an implicit understanding. I would have to wait to find out.

So I cursed long and loud, in many languages, doubtless burning Malann's sacred ears, there in his Temple.

He did not see fit to strike me dead, so I decided to call it a day and hit the sack.

❖   ❖   ❖

I must have been asleep for several hours when Braxa entered my room with a tiny lamp. She dragged me awake by tugging at my pajama sleeve.

I said hello. Thinking back, there is not much else I could have said.

"Hello."

"I have come," she said, "to hear the poem."

"What poem?"

"Yours."

"Oh."

I yawned, sat up, and did things people usually do when awakened in the middle of the night to read poetry.

"That is very kind of you, but isn't the hour a trifle awkward?"

"I don't mind," she said.

Someday I am going to write an article for the *Journal of Semantics*, called "Tone of Voice: An Insufficient Vehicle for Irony."

However, I was awake, so I grabbed my robe.

"What sort of animal is that? she asked, pointing at the silk dragon on my lapel.

"Mythical," I replied. "Now look, it's late. I am tired. I have much to do in the morning. And M'Cwyie just might get the wrong idea if she learns you were here."

"Wrong idea?"

"You know damned well what I mean!" It was the first time I had had an opportunity to use Martian profanity, and it failed.

"No," she said, "I do not know."

She seemed frightened, like a puppy dog being scolded without knowing what it has done wrong.

I softened. Her red cloak matched her hair and lips so perfectly, and those lips were trembling.

"Here now, I didn't mean to upset you. On my world there are certain, uh, mores, concerning people of different sex alone together in bedrooms, and not allied by marriage…Um, I mean, you see what I mean?"

"No."

They were jade, her eyes.

"Well, it's sort of…Well, it's sex, that's what it is."

A light switched on in those jade lamps.

"Oh, you mean having children!"

"Yes. That's it! Exactly!"

She laughed. It was the first time I had heard laughter in Tirellian. It sounded like a violinist striking his high strings with the bow, in short little chops. It was not an altogether pleasant thing to hear, especially because she laughed too long.

When she had finished she moved closer.

"I remember, now," she said. "We used to have such rules. Half a Process ago, when I was a child, we had such rules. But"—she looked as if she were ready to laugh again—"there is no need for them now."

My mind moved like a tape recorder playing at triple speed.

Half a Process! HalfaProcessa—ProcessaProcess! No! Yes! Half a Process was two hundred-forty-three years, roughly speaking!

—Time enough to learn the 2224 dances of Locar.

—Time enough to grow old, if you were human.

—Earth-style human, I mean.

I looked at her again, pale as the white queen in an ivory chess set.

She was human, I'd stake my soul—alive, normal, healthy. I'd stake my life—woman, my body…

But she was two and a half centuries old, which made M'Cwyie Methuselah's grandma. It flattered me to think of their repeated complimenting of my skills, as linguist, as poet. These superior beings!

But what did she mean "there is no such need for them now"? Why the near-hysteria? Why all those funny looks I'd been getting from M'Cwyie?

I suddenly knew I was close to something important, besides a beautiful girl.

"Tell me," I said, in my Casual Voice, "did it have anything to do with 'the plague that does not kill,' of which Tamur wrote?"

"Yes," she replied, "the children born after the Rains could have no children of their own, and—"

"And what?" I was leaning forward, memory set at "record."

"—and the men had no desire to get any."

I sagged backward against the bedpost. Racial sterility, masculine impotence, following phenomenal weather. Had some vagabond cloud of radioactive junk from God knows where penetrated their weak atmosphere one day? One day long before Shiaparelli saw the canals, mythical as my dragon, before those "canals" had given rise to some correct guesses for all the wrong reasons, had Braxa been alive, dancing, here—damned in the womb since blind Milton had written of another paradise, equally lost?

I found a cigarette. Good thing I had thought to bring ashtrays. Mars had never had a tobacco industry either. Or booze. The ascetics I had met in India had been Dionysiac compared to this.

"What is that tube of fire?"

"A cigarette. Want one?"

"Yes, please."

She sat beside me, and I lighted it for her.

"It irritates the nose."

"Yes. Draw some into your lungs, hold it there, and exhale."

A moment passed.

"Ooh," she said.

A pause, then, "Is it sacred?"

"No, it's nicotine," I answered, "a very *ersatz* form of divinity."

Another pause.

"Please don't ask me to translate 'ersatz'."

"I won't. I get this feeling sometimes when I dance."

"It will pass in a moment."

"Tell me your poem now."

An idea hit me.

"Wait a minute," I said; "I may have something better."

I got up and rummaged through my notebooks, then I returned and sat beside her.

"These are the first three chapters of the Book of Ecclesiastes," I explained. "It is very similar to your own sacred books."

I started reading.

I got through eleven verses before she cried out, "Please don't read that! Tell me one of yours!"

I stopped and tossed the notebook onto a nearby table. She was shaking, not as she had quivered that day she danced as the wind, but with the jitter of unshed tears. She held her cigarette awkwardly, like a pencil. Clumsily, I put my arm about her shoulders.

"He is so sad," she said, "like all the others."

So I twisted my mind like a bright ribbon, folded it, and tied the crazy Christmas knots I love so well. From German to Martian, with love, I did an impromptu paraphrasal of a poem about a Spanish dancer. I thought it would please her. I was right.

"Ooh," she said again. "Did you write that?"

"No, it's by a better man than I."

"I don't believe it. You wrote it."

"No, a man named Rilke did."

"But you brought it across to my language. Light another match, so I can see how she danced."

I did.

"The fires of forever," she mused, "and she stamped them out, 'with small, firm feet.' I wish I could dance like that."

"You're better than any Gypsy," I laughed, blowing it out.

"No, I'm not. I couldn't do that."

Her cigarette was burning down, so I removed it from her fingers and put it out, along with my own.

"Do you want me to dance for you?"

"No," I said. "Go to bed."

She smiled, and before I realized it, had unclasped the fold of red at her shoulder.

And everything fell away.

And I swallowed, with some difficulty.

"All right," she said.

So I kissed her, as the breath of fallen cloth extinguished the lamp.

III

The days were like Shelley's leaves: yellow, red, brown, whipped in bright gusts by the west wind. They swirled past me with the rattle of microfilm. Almost all the books were recorded now. It would take scholars years to get through them, to properly assess their value. Mars was locked in my desk.

Ecclesiastes, abandoned and returned to a dozen times, was almost ready to speak in the High Tongue.

I whistled when I wasn't in the Temple. I wrote reams of poetry I would have been ashamed of before. Evenings I would walk with Braxa, across the dunes or up into the mountains. Sometimes she would dance for me; and I would read something long, and in dactylic hexameter. She still thought I was Rilke, and I almost kidded myself into believing it. Here I was, staying at the Castle Duino, writing his *Elegies*.

> *...It is strange to inhabit the Earth no more,*
> *to use no longer customs scarce acquired,*
> *nor interpret roses...*

No! Never interpret roses! Don't. Smell them (sniff, Kane!), pick them, enjoy them. Live in the moment. Hold to it tightly, but charge not the gods to explain. So fast the leaves go by, are blown...

And no one ever noticed us. Or cared.

Laura. Laura and Braxa. They rhyme, you know, with a bit of clash. Tall, cool, and blonde was she (I hate blondes!), and Daddy had turned me inside out, like a pocket, and I thought she could fill me again. But the big, beat work-slinger, with Judas-beard and dog-trust in his eyes, oh, he had been a fine decoration at her parties. And that was all.

How the machine cursed me in the Temple! It blasphemed Malann and Gallinger. And the wild west wind went by and something was not far behind.

The last days were upon us.

A day went by and I did not see Braxa, and a night.

And a second. And a third.

I was half-mad. I hadn't realized how close we had become, how important she had been. With the dumb assurance of presence, I had fought against questioning roses.

I had to ask. I didn't want to, but I had no choice.

"Where is she, M'Cwyie? Where is Braxa?"

"She is gone," she said.

"Where?"

"I do not know."

I looked at those devil-bird eyes. Anathema maranatha rose to my lips.

"I must know."

She looked through me.

"She has left us. She is gone. Up into the hills, I suppose. Or the desert. It does not matter. What does anything matter? The dance draws to a close. The Temple will soon be empty."

"Why? Why did she leave?"

"I do not know."

"I must see her again. We lift off in a matter of days."

"I am sorry, Gallinger."

"So am I," I said, and slammed shut a book without saying "M'narra."

I stood up.

"I will find her."

I left the Temple. M'Cwyie was a seated statue. My boots were still where I had left them.

❖   ❖   ❖

All day I roared up and down the dunes, going nowhere. To the crew of the *Aspic* I must have looked like a sandstorm, all by myself. Finally, I had to return for more fuel.

Emory came stalking out.

"Okay, make it good. You look like the abominable dust man. Why the rodeo?"

"Why, I, uh, lost something."

"In the middle of the desert? Was it one of your sonnets? They're the only thing I can think of that you'd make such a fuss over."

"No, dammit! It was something personal."

George had finished filling the tank. I started to mount the jeep-ster again.

"Hold on there!" he grabbed my arm.

"You're not going back until you tell me what this is all about."

I could have broken his grip, but then he could order me dragged back by the heels, and quite a few people would enjoy doing the dragging. So I forced myself to speak slowly, softly:

"It's simply that I lost my watch. My mother gave it to me and it's a family heirloom. I want to find it before we leave."

"You sure it's not in your cabin, or down in Tirellian?"

"I've already checked."

"Maybe somebody hid it to irritate you. You know you're not the most popular guy around."

I shook my head.

"I thought of that. But I always carry it in my right pocket. I think it might have bounced out going over the dunes."

He narrowed his eyes.

"I remember reading on a book jacket that your mother died when you were born."

"That's right," I said, biting my tongue. "The watch belonged to her father and she wanted me to have it. My father kept it for me."

"Hmph!" he snorted. "That's a pretty strange way to look for a watch, riding up and down in a jeepster."

"I could see the light shining off it that way," I offered, lamely.

"Well, it's starting to get dark," he observed. "No sense looking any more today.

"Throw a dust sheet over the jeepster," he directed a mechanic.

He patted my arm.

"Come on in and get a shower, and something to eat. You look as if you could use both."

Little fatty flecks beneath pale eyes, thinning hair, and an Irish nose; a voice a decibel louder than anyone else's...

His only qualification for leadership!

I stood there, hating him. Claudius! If only this were the fifth act!

But suddenly the idea of a shower, and food, came through to me. I could use both badly. If I insisted on hurrying back immediately I might arouse more suspicion.

So I brushed some sand from my sleeve.

"You're right. That sounds like a good idea."

"Come on, we'll eat in my cabin."

The shower was a blessing, clean khakis were the grace of God, and the food smelled like Heaven.

"Smells pretty good," I said.

We hacked up our steaks in silence. When we got to the dessert and coffee he suggested:

"Why don't you take the night off? Stay here and get some sleep."

I shook my head.

"I'm pretty busy. Finishing up. There's not much time left."

"A couple of days ago you said you were almost finished."

"Almost, but not quite."

"You also said they'll be holding a service in the Temple tonight."

"That's right. I'm going to work in my room."

He shrugged his shoulders.

Finally, he said, "Gallinger," and I looked up because my name means trouble.

"It shouldn't be any of my business," he said, "but it is. Betty says you have a girl down there."

There was no question mark. It was a statement hanging in the air. Waiting.

Betty, you're a bitch. You're a cow and a bitch. And a jealous one, at that. Why didn't you keep your nose where it belonged, shut your eyes? Your mouth?

"So?" I said, a statement with a question mark.

"So," he answered it, "it is my duty, as head of this expedition, to see that relations with the natives are carried on in a friendly, and diplomatic, manner."

"You speak of them," I said, "as though they are aborigines. Nothing could be further from the truth."

I rose.

"When my papers are published everyone on Earth will know that truth. I'll tell them things Doctor Moore never even guessed at. I'll tell the tragedy of a doomed race, waiting for death, resigned and disinterested. I'll tell why, and it will break hard, scholarly hearts. I'll write about it, and they will give me more prizes, and this time I won't want them.

"My God!" I exclaimed. "They had a culture when our ancestors were clubbing the saber-tooth and finding out how fire works!"

"*Do* you have a girl down there?"

"Yes!" I said. *Yes, Claudius! Yes, Daddy! Yes, Emory!* "I do. But I'm going to let you in on a scholarly scoop now. They're already dead. They're sterile. In one more generation there won't be any Martians."

I paused, then added, "Except in my papers, except on a few pieces of microfilm and tape. And in some poems, about a girl who did give a damn and could only bitch about the unfairness of it all by dancing."

"Oh," he said.

After awhile:

"You *have* been behaving differently these past couple months. You've even been downright civil on occasion, you know. I couldn't help wondering what was happening. I didn't know anything mattered that strongly to you."

I bowed my head.

"Is she the reason you were racing around the desert?"

I nodded.

"Why?"

I looked up.

"Because she's out there, somewhere. I don't know where, or why. And I've got to find her before we go."

"Oh," he said again.

Then he leaned back, opened a drawer, and took out something wrapped in a towel. He unwound it. A framed photo of a woman lay on the table.

"My wife," he said.

It was an attractive face, with big, almond eyes.

"I'm a Navy man, you know," he began. "Young officer once. Met her in Japan.

"Where I come from it wasn't considered right to marry into another race, so we never did. But she was my wife. When she died I was on the other side of the world. They took my children, and I've never seen them since. I couldn't learn what orphanage, what home, they were put into. That was long ago. Very few people know about it."

"I'm sorry," I said.

"Don't be. Forget it. But"—he shifted in his chair and looked at me—"if you do want to take her back with you—do it. It'll mean my neck, but I'm too old to ever head another expedition like this one. So go ahead."

He gulped cold coffee.

"Get your jeepster."

He swiveled the chair around.

I tried to say "thank you" twice, but I couldn't. So I got up and walked out.

"*Sayonara*, and all that," he muttered behind me.

❖   ❖   ❖

"Here it is, Gallinger!" I heard a shout.

I turned on my heel and looked back up the ramp.

"Kane!"

He was limned in the port, shadow against light, but I had heard him sniff.

I returned the few steps.

"Here what is?"

"Your rose."

He produced a plastic container, divided internally. The lower half was filled with liquid. The stem ran down into it. The other half, a glass of claret in this horrible night, was a large, newly opened rose.

"Thank you," I said, tucking it in my jacket.

"Going back to Tirellian, eh?"

"Yes."

"I saw you come aboard, so I got it ready. Just missed you at the Captain's cabin. He was busy. Hollered out that I could catch you at the barns."

"Thanks again."

"It's chemically treated. It will stay in bloom for weeks."

I nodded. I was gone.

❖   ❖   ❖

Up into the mountains now. Far. Far. The sky was a bucket of ice in which no moons floated. The going became steeper, and the little donkey protested. I whipped him with the throttle and went on. Up. Up. I spotted a green, unwinking star, and felt a lump in my throat. The encased rose beat against my chest like an extra heart. The donkey brayed, long and loudly, then began to cough. I lashed him some more and he died.

I threw the emergency brake on and got out. I began to walk.

So cold, so cold it grows. Up here. At night? Why? Why did she do it? Why flee the campfire when night comes on?

And I was up, down, around, and through every chasm, gorge, and pass, with my long-legged strides and an ease of movement never known on Earth.

Barely two days remain, my love, and thou hast forsaken me. Why?

I crawled under overhangs. I leaped over ridges. I scraped my knees, an elbow. I heard my jacket tear.

No answer, Malann? Do you really hate your people this much? Then I'll try someone else. Vishnu, you're the Preserver. Preserve her, please! Let me find her.

Jehovah?

Adonis? Osiris? Thammuz? Manitou? Legba? Where is she?

I ranged far and high, and I slipped.

Stones ground underfoot and I dangled over an edge. My fingers so cold. It was hard to grip the rock.

I looked down.

Twelve feet or so. I let go and dropped, landed rolling.

Then I heard her scream.

❖   ❖   ❖

I lay there, not moving, looking up. Against the night, above, she called.

"Gallinger!"

I lay still.

"Gallinger!"

And she was gone.

I heard stones rattle and knew she was coming down some path to the right of me.

I jumped up and ducked into the shadow of a boulder.

She rounded a cut-off, and picked her way, uncertainly, through the stones.

"Gallinger?"

I stepped out and seized her by the shoulders.

"Braxa."

She screamed again, then began to cry, crowding against me. It was the first time I had ever heard her cry.

"Why?" I asked. "Why?"

But she only clung to me and sobbed.

Finally, "I thought you had killed yourself."

"Maybe I would have," I said. "Why did you leave Tirellian? And me?"

"Didn't M'Cwyie tell you? Didn't you guess?"

"I didn't guess, and M'Cwyie said she didn't know."

"Then she lied. She knows."

"What? What is it she knows?"

She shook all over, then was silent for a long time. I realized suddenly that she was wearing only her flimsy dancer's costume. I pushed her from me, took off my jacket, and put it about her shoulders.

"Great Malann!" I cried. "You'll freeze to death!"

"No," she said, "I won't."

I was transferring the rose-case to my pocket.

"What is that?" she asked.

"A rose," I answered. "You can't make it out in the dark. I once compared you to one. Remember?"

"Ye-Yes. May I carry it?"

"Sure." I stuck it in the jacket pocket.

"Well? I'm still waiting for an explanation."

"You really do not know?" she asked.

"No!"

"When the Rains came," she said, "apparently only our men were affected, which was enough…because I–wasn't–affected–apparently—"

"Oh," I said. "Oh."

We stood there, and I thought.

"Well, why did you run? What's wrong with being pregnant on Mars? Tamur was mistaken. Your people can live again."

She laughed, again that wild violin played by a Paganini gone mad. I stopped her before it went too far.

"How?" she finally asked, rubbing her cheek.

"Your people can live longer than ours. If our child is normal it will mean our races can intermarry. There must still be other fertile women of your race. Why not?"

"You have read the Book of Locar," she said, "and yet you ask me that? Death was decided, voted upon, and passed, shortly after it appeared in this form. But long before, before the followers of Locar knew. They decided it long ago. 'We have done all things,' they said, 'we have seen all things, we have heard and felt all things. The dance was good. Now let it end.'"

"You can't believe that."

"What I believe does not matter," she replied. "M'Cwyie and the Mothers have decided we must die. Their very title is now a mockery, but their decisions will be upheld. There is only one prophecy left, and it is mistaken. We will die."

"No," I said.

"What, then?"

"Come back with me, to Earth."

"No."

"All right, then. Come with me now."

"Where?"

"Back to Tirellian. I'm going to talk to the Mothers."

"You can't! There is a Ceremony tonight!"

I laughed.

"A Ceremony for a god who knocks you down, and then kicks you in the teeth?"

"He is still Malann," she answered. "We are still his people."

"You and my father would have gotten along fine," I snarled. "But I am going, and you are coming with me, even if I have to carry you—and I'm bigger than you are."

"But you are not bigger than Ontro."

"Who the hell is Ontro?"

"He will stop you, Gallinger. He is the Fist of Malann."

IV

I scudded the jeepster to a halt in front of the only entrance I knew, M'Cwyie's. Braxa, who had seen the rose in a headlamp, now cradled it in her lap, like our child, and said nothing. There was a passive, lovely look on her face.

"Are they in the Temple now?" I wanted to know.

The Madonna-expression did not change. I repeated the question. She stirred.

"Yes," she said, from a distance, "but you cannot go in."

"We'll see."

I circled and helped her down.

I led her by the hand, and she moved as if in a trance. In the light of the new-risen moon, her eyes looked as they had the day I had met her, when she had danced. I snapped my fingers. Nothing happened.

So I pushed the door open and led her in. The room was half-lighted.

And she screamed for the third time that evening:

"Do not harm him, Ontro! It is Gallinger!"

I had never seen a Martian man before, only women. So I had no way of knowing whether he was a freak, though I suspected it strongly.

I looked up at him.

His half-naked body was covered with moles and swellings. Gland trouble, I guessed.

I had thought I was the tallest man on the planet, but he was seven feet tall and overweight. Now I knew where my giant bed had come from!

"Go back," he said. "She may enter. You may not."

"I must get my books and things."

He raised a huge left arm. I followed it. All my belonging lay neatly stacked in the corner.

"I must go in. I must talk with M'Cwyie and the Mothers."

"You may not."

"The lives of your people depend on it."

"Go back," he boomed. "Go home to *your* people, Gallinger. Leave *us!*"

My name sounded so different on his lips, like someone else's. How old was he? I wondered. Three hundred? Four? Had he been a Temple guardian all his life? Why? Who was there to guard against? I didn't like the way he moved. I had seen men who moved like that before.

"Go back," he repeated.

If they had refined their martial arts as far as they had their dances, or worse yet, if their fighting arts were a part of the dance, I was in for trouble.

"Go on in," I said to Braxa. "Give the rose to M'Cwyie. Tell her that I sent it. Tell her I'll be there shortly."

"I will do as you ask. Remember me on Earth, Gallinger. Goodbye."

I did not answer her, and she walked past Ontro and into the next room, bearing her rose.

"Now will you leave?" he asked. "If you like, I will tell her that we fought and you almost beat me, but I knocked you unconscious and carried you back to your ship."

"No," I said, "either I go around you or go over you, but I am going through."

He dropped into a crouch, arms extended.

"It is a sin to lay hands on a holy man," he rumbled, "but I will stop you, Gallinger."

My memory was a fogged window, suddenly exposed to fresh air. Things cleared. I looked back six years.

I was a student of the Oriental Languages at the University of Tokyo. It was my twice-weekly night of recreation. I stood in a thirty-foot circle in the Kodokan, the *judogi* lashed about my high hips by a brown belt. I was *Ik-kyu*, one notch below the lowest degree of expert. A brown diamond above my right breast said "*Jiu-Jitsu*" in Japanese, and it meant *atemiwaza*, really, because of the one striking-technique I had worked out, found unbelievably suitable to my size, and won matches with.

But I had never used it on a man, and it was five years since I had practiced. I was out of shape, I knew, but I tried hard to force my mind *tsuki no kokoro*, like the moon, reflecting the all of Ontro.

Somewhere, out of the past, a voice said "*Hajime*, let it begin."

I snapped into my *neko-ashi-dachi* cat-stance, and his eyes burned strangely. He hurried to correct his own position—and I threw it at him!

My one trick!

My long left leg lashed up like a broken spring. Seven feet off the ground my foot connected with his jaw as he tried to leap backward.

His head snapped back and he fell. A soft moan escaped his lips. *That's all there is to it,* I thought. *Sorry, old fellow.*

And as I stepped over him, somehow, groggily, he tripped me, and

I fell across his body. I couldn't believe he had strength enough to remain conscious after that blow, let alone move. I hated to punish him any more.

But he found my throat and slipped a forearm across it before I realized there was a purpose to his action.

No! Don't let it end like this!

It was a bar of steel across my windpipe, my carotids. Then I realized that he was still unconscious, and that this was a reflex instilled by countless years of training. I had seen it happen once, in *shiai*. The man had died because he had been choked unconscious and still fought on, and his opponent thought he had not been applying the choke properly. He tried harder.

But it was rare, so very rare!

I jammed my elbow into his ribs and threw my head back in his face. The grip eased, but not enough. I hated to do it, but I reached up and broke his little finger.

The arm went loose and I twisted free.

He lay there panting, face contorted. My heart went out to the fallen giant, defending his people, his religion, following his orders. I cursed myself as I had never cursed before, for walking over him, instead of around.

I staggered across the room to my little heap of possessions. I sat on the projector case and lit a cigarette.

I couldn't go into the Temple until I got my breath back, until I thought of something to say.

How do you talk a race out of killing itself?

Suddenly—

—Could it happen? Would it work that way? If I read them the Book of Ecclesiastes—if I read them a greater piece of literature than any Locar ever wrote—and as somber—and as pessimistic—and showed them that our race had gone on despite one man's condemning all of life in the highest poetry—showed them that the vanity he had mocked had borne us to the Heavens—would they believe it?—would they change their minds?

I ground out my cigarette on the beautiful floor, and found my notebook. A strange fury rose within me as I stood.

And I walked into the Temple to preach the Black Gospel according to Gallinger, from the Book of Life.

❖ ❖ ❖

There was silence all about me.

M'Cwyie had been reading Locar, the rose set at her right hand, target of all eyes.

Until I entered.

Hundreds of people were seated on the floor, barefoot. The few men were as small as the women, I noted.

I had my boots on.

Go all the way, I figured. *You either lose or you win—everything!*

A dozen crones sat in a semicircle behind M'Cwyie. The Mothers. *The barren earth, the dry wombs, the fire-touched.*

I moved to the table.

"Dying yourselves, you would condemn your people," I addressed them, "that they may not know the life you have known—the joys, the sorrows, the fullness. —But it is not true that you all must die." I addressed the multitude now. "Those who say this lie. Braxa knows, for she will bear a child—"

They sat there, like rows of Buddhas. M'Cwyie drew back into the semicircle.

"—my child!" I continued, wondering what my father would have thought of this sermon.

"…And all the women young enough may bear children. It is only your men who are sterile. —And if you permit the doctors of the next expedition to examine you, perhaps even the men may be helped. But if they cannot, you can mate with the men of Earth.

"And ours is not an insignificant people, an insignificant place," I went on. "Thousands of years ago, the Locar of our world wrote a book saying that it was. He spoke as Locar did, but we did not lie down, despite plagues, wars, and famines. We did not die. One by one we beat down the diseases, we fed the hungry, we fought the wars, and, recently, have gone a long time without them. We may finally have conquered them. I do not know.

"But we have crossed millions of miles of nothingness. We have visited another world. And our Locar had said 'Why bother? What is the worth of it? It is all vanity, anyhow.'

"And the secret is," I lowered my voice, as at a poetry reading, "he was right! It *is* vanity, it *is* pride! It is the hybris of rationalism to always attack the prophet, the mystic, the god. It is our blasphemy which has made us great, and will sustain us, and which the gods secretly admire in us. —All the truly sacred names of God are blasphemous things to speak!"

I was working up a sweat. I paused dizzily.

"Here is the Book of Ecclesiastes," I announced, and began:

" 'Vanity of vanities, saith the Preacher, vanity of vanities; all is vanity. What profit hath a man…' "

I spotted Braxa in the back, mute, rapt.

I wondered what she was thinking.

And I wound the hours of the night about me, like black thread on a spool.

❖   ❖   ❖

Oh, it was late! I had spoken till day came, and still I spoke. I finished Ecclesiastes and continued Gallinger.

And when I finished there was still only a silence.

The Buddhas, all in a row, had not stirred through the night. And after a long while M'Cwyie raised her right hand. One by one the Mothers did the same.

And I knew what that meant.

It meant, no, do not, cease, and stop.

It meant that I had failed.

I walked slowly from the room and slumped beside my baggage.

Ontro was gone. Good that I had not killed him…

After a thousand years M'Cwyie entered.

She said, "Your job is finished."

I did not move.

"The prophecy is fulfilled," she said. "My people are rejoicing. You have won, holy man. Now leave us quickly."

My mind was a deflated balloon. I pumped a little air back into it.

"I'm not a holy man," I said, "just a second-rate poet with a bad case of hybris."

I lit my last cigarette.

Finally, "All right, what prophecy?"

"The Promise of Locar," she replied, as though the explaining were unnecessary, "that a holy man would come from the Heavens to save us in our last hours, if all the dances of Locar were completed. He would defeat the Fist of Malann and bring us life."

"How?"

"As with Braxa, and as the example in the Temple."

"Example?"

"You read us his words, as great as Locar's. You read to us how there is 'nothing new under the sun.' And you mocked his words as you read them—showing us a new thing.

"There has never been a flower on Mars," she said, "but we will learn to grow them.

"You are the Sacred Scoffer," she finished. "He-Who-Must-Mock-in-the-Temple—you go shod on holy ground."

"But you voted 'no'," I said.

"I voted not to carry out our original plan, and to let Braxa's child live instead."

"Oh." The cigarette fell from my fingers. How close it had been! How little I had known!

"And Braxa?"

"She was chosen half a Process ago to do the dances—to wait for you."

"But she said that Ontro would stop me."

M'Cwyie stood there for a long time.

"She had never believed the prophecy herself. Things are not well with her now. She ran away, fearing it was true. When you completed it, and we voted, she knew."

"Then she does not love me? Never did?"

"I am sorry, Gallinger. It was the one part of her duty she never managed."

"Duty," I said flatly…Dutydutyduty! Tra-la!

"She has said good-bye; she does not wish to see you again.

"…and we will never forget your teachings," she added.

"Don't," I said automatically, suddenly knowing the great paradox which lies at the heart of all miracles. I did not believe a word of my own gospel, never had.

I stood, like a drunken man, and muttered "M'narra."

I went outside, into my last day on Mars.

I have conquered thee, Malann—and the victory is thine! Rest easy on thy starry bed. God damned!

I left the jeepster there and walked back to the *Aspic*, leaving the burden of life so many footsteps behind me. I went to my cabin, locked the door, and took forty-four sleeping pills.

❖   ❖   ❖

But when I awakened I was in the dispensary, and alive.

I felt the throb of engines as I slowly stood up and somehow made it to the port.

Blurred Mars hung like a swollen belly above me, until it dissolved, brimmed over, and streamed down my face.

A Word from Zelazny

"I had a strong sentimental attachment to what is now called 'space opera.' …I had long wanted to do something of that sort. When I began selling fiction in the sixties it was too late—almost. The space program had already invalidated the Mars and Venus of Edgar Rice Burroughs—almost… If I wanted to do homage…I would have to act quickly and do my best. I knew that I would only be allowed one shot at each world, and then I would have to leave the solar system. 'A Rose For Ecclesiastes' was my only word on Mars. 'The Doors of His Face, the Lamps of His Mouth' all that I would have to say on Venus. So I did it. I wrote them both and got in under the wire."[1]

Zelazny usually gave noncommittal answers when asked if the poet Gallinger had any resemblance to Zelazny himself, but he did give a very personal response to letter writer Clara on this very subject: "You ask me why I hated Gallinger so in 'A Rose For Ecclesiastes.' The answer is that I hated him because he was me. Once in my life I let a beautiful thing die, and now it can never be. Details are not important, in that they would add nothing. The story says what it must and stands or falls on its own merits. But you're right in your observation that it's a sad story, despite the fact that you felt crushed and even cheated. Life is full of these things, and one of them motivated this tale. I didn't want it to end that way, but it had to, because he was me. I felt pain along with him. He was a better linguist than I, and a better poet. He was a very good, misunderstood man. There is a sequel to the story which I will never write, where he goes back to Mars some years later. It is much sadder, believe me, and he doesn't deserve to be put through those paces. He's suffered enough. But sometimes things happen this way, and all that you can say is, 'Look. This is the way things are.' That's all."[2] Zelazny was alluding to events that caused the breakup of his six month engagement to Hedy West; he wrote this story shortly after.

This story was actually written in October 1961, five months prior to "Passion Play," but Zelazny had declined to submit it then because he knew that the Mars depicted within the story had lost all credibility by 1962. Critics and other authors greeted the story enthusiastically, assuming it reflected rapid maturation in his writing. In fact, he wrote it before his earlier published works.[3] It is unclear whether he'd revised it at all before submitting it.

Consistent with his intention to follow Hemingway's dictum to leave certain things unsaid, Zelazny did not reveal Gallinger's first name, Michael, in the story. "It wasn't important; I had no reason for using his first name…

---

1 *Amber Dreams*, 1983.
2 *No-Eyed Monster* Summer 1968 #14, p 21–22.
3 *Algol* 13(2):9–14. Summer 1976.

If the writer sees more of the story than he actually tells, it adds strength to the story. It makes the character seem more real."[4]

Notes

Theodore Sturgeon enthused that "'A Rose for Ecclesiastes' is one of the most important stories I have ever read—perhaps I should say it is one of the most memorable experiences I have ever had…as objective as I can be, which isn't very, I still feel safe in stating that it is one of the most beautifully written, skillfully composed and passionately expressed works of art to appear anywhere, ever."[5]

Fittingly, this story was included as one of the classic stories of "Martian literature" in the *Visions of Mars: First Library on Mars* silica glass mini-DVD that traveled to the Martian surface on May 25, 2008, aboard the lander *Phoenix*.

"A Rose for Ecclesiastes" appeared in *The Science Fiction Hall of Fame, Volume One*, ranked sixth among the 26 best stories from 1929–1964 (prior to the institution of the Nebula Awards), elected by the writers themselves.

The cover painting for this story was one of the very last works of Hannes Bok, and Zelazny later purchased the original painting.

The many references and allusions that enrich the text may benefit from identification or explanation. A **madrigal** is a musical form of secular text composed for two voices, often in Italian. **Macabre** implies a grim or ghastly atmosphere with an emphasis on death. **"Let not ambition mock thy useful toil"** is a line from the poem "The Cotter's Saturday Night" by Robert Burns. **Hamlet** and his stepfather, King **Claudius**, despised and mistrusted each other. **Antoine de Saint-Exupéry** was a writer and aviator who published several prominent novels pertaining to flight and is best known for the novel *The Little Prince*. **Malebolge** is the eighth circle of hell in Dante's *The Divine Comedy*, within which **Dante** discovers **Ulysses** standing in flames, doomed for three sins, but still capable of making a speech about his adventures. **Terza-rima** is a rhyming in triplets, specifically the style used in *The Divine Comedy*. The **Mahābhārata** is a lengthy Sanskrit epic of ancient India.

Samson was the Israelite whose immense strength lay in his uncut hair; his lover Delilah cut it off, the Philistines blinded him and imprisoned him in Gaza—but his hair grew again, and he pulled down the pillars of the temple, destroying himself and many Philistines. **Heinrich Schliemann** was a German treasure hunter who discovered and excavated Troy and

4 *Roger Zelazny*, Theodore Krulik, 1986.
5 *Four for Tomorrow*, 1967.

fought with archaeologist Frank Calvert over it. In ancient India, **Prakrit** was the ordinary or vernacular speech while **Sanskrit** was the liturgical or high speech. **Vaulted and corbeled** means that the high ceiling is supported by projections from the walls. **Benzedrine** is a brand of amphetamine.

The *Iliad* by Homer describes the Trojan War and how Achilles killed Hector. **Added tails to the cat repeatedly laid on my back** suggests a cat-o'-nine-tails, a rope whip with nine knotted cords, formerly used to flog offenders (Gallinger must be speaking figuratively, not literally, because he later states that his father did not resort to physical punishment). A **catafalque** is a raised platform on which a dead body is carried or lies in state. **Greenwich Village** played an important role in the development of folk music in the 1960s (Dylan; Simon and Garfunkle; Peter, Paul and Mary, etc.) and was where Zelazny met his first fiancée, folk musician Hedy West. W. H. **Auden** was one of Zelazny's favorite poets. **Iambics** are meters in poetry consisting of one short (or unstressed) syllable followed by one long (or stressed) syllable.

I, a stranger, unafraid alludes to A. E. Housman's *Last Poems*, and the line "I, a stranger and afraid ‖ in a world I never made"—except that Gallinger reverses it into a boast. **This is the land** likely refers to Emily Dickinson's poem "This is the land the sunset washes." *Recherches* is French for researches. **Edgar Allan Poe** wrote poetry and horror stories such as "The Tell-Tale Heart." *Vanity of vanities...* is a quote from the Book of Ecclesiastes in the **King James** version of the Bible. **Jean-Paul Sartre** was an existentialist who dealt with the nature of human life and the structures of consciousness; **the Other** deals with the philosophical concept of how one consciousness deals with the existence of other minds. **Periphrasis** is the use of indirect and circumlocutory speech or writing.

Henry Havelock Ellis was a British doctor and sexual psychologist whose book *The Dance of Life* described that dancing and architecture are the two primary and essential arts. According to Ellis, dancing is the source of all arts that express themselves inside the person, and it came first; architecture is the beginning of all the arts that lie outside the person.

A **sari** is a garment worn by Hindu women, consisting of a long piece of cotton or silk wrapped around the body. An **Etruscan frieze** is a horizontal band of sculpted or painted decoration on a wall near the ceiling. The Etruscan civilization flourished circa 500 BC. The *samisen* is a Japanese three-stringed musical instrument played with a plectrum called a bachi. A **glissando** is a rapid slide through a series of scales on a musical instrument. **Saint-John Perse** was the pseudonym of a French poet who was awarded the Nobel Prize for Literature in 1960. **Devadasis** or "servants of God" were girls "married" to a deity or temple in a Hindu practice and who learned a sacred dance termed the Bharatanatyam. **Ramadjany** were sacred dancers.

Rama refers to any one of the three avatars of Vishnu, those being Balarama, Parashurama, or Ramachandra; **Vishnu** or "the Preserver" is the second member of the Trimurti, along with Brahma the Creator and Shiva the Destroyer. **Sarasvati** is the Hindu goddess of learning and the arts. The **sitar** is a large, long-necked Indian lute with movable frets, played with a wire pick. **Afflatus** is a divine creative impulse or inspiration.

Arthur Rimbaud, Charles Baudelaire, Edgar Allan Poe, Thomas De Quincy, Oscar Wilde, Stéphane Mallarme and Aleister Crowley were respected authors and poets. **Job** argued with God because conventional wisdom said that his suffering must be the just punishment for his sins, but he knew himself to be innocent of any crimes, and he wanted to meet God face to face rather than accept platitudes which he knew were untrue. A **charley horse** is localized pain or muscle stiffness following contusion or bruising of a muscle, or localized electrolyte imbalance.

William Butler Yeats, Ezra Pound, T. S. Eliot, Hart Crane, and Wallace Stevens were real poets whose work Zelazny admired, and Michael **Gallinger** is the protagonist and poet of this story. **Jonathan Swift** was an Irish poet and satirist best known for *Gulliver's Travels*, a satire on human society in the form of a fantastic tale of travels in imaginary lands. **George Bernard Shaw** was an Irish playwright whose plays (including *Pygmalion, Man and Superman*) combined comedy and an examination of conventional morals and thought. **Petronius Arbiter** was the author of *The Satyricon*, a work in prose and verse satirizing the excesses of Roman society. In *The Satyricon*, **Trimalchio** was a character known for throwing lavish dinner parties.

Blake's rose refers to "The Sick Rose," a poem by William Blake that begins "Oh Rose, thou art sick!" **Isaias** [variant of Isaiah] was a major prophet of Judah in the 8th century BC; the book of the Bible entitled *Isaiah* contains his prophecies. **Mycetae** are fungi. **Mores** are customs, practices, or ways of life in a culture. **Methuselah** was the grandfather of Noah and was said to have lived almost 1,000 years; the term also means a long-lived or immortal man.

Giovanni Shiaparelli was an Italian astronomer who famously described the markings on Mars as canali (channels)—but this was mistranslated as "canals" and taken to mean evidence of a civilization on Mars. **John Milton** wrote *Paradise Lost* after he had gone blind. **Dionysiac** means sensual, spontaneous, and emotional. **Spanish Dancer** was a poem by German poet Rainer Maria **Rilke**. **Shelley's leaves** refers to Percy Shelley's poem "Ode to the West Wind." **Dactylic** refers to a metrical foot in poetry that consists of one stressed syllable followed by two unstressed syllables; **hexameter** means that each line contains six metrical feet.

Castle Duino sits on the rocky Carso high above the Gulf of Trieste and was frequented by Rilke; the quote ending "**nor interpret roses**" [not to give a meaning of human futurity to roses] is from the "First Elegy" within the Rilke's "Duino Elegies." **Anathema maranatha** is a curse for anyone who does not want to be saved because the Lord is coming. **Aspic** is an archaic word for *asp*, the Egyptian cobra; the usage may indicate that ship and crew were a snake in a Martian Eden.

Claudius! If only this were the fifth act! refers to the denouement of the play *Hamlet* in which Claudius and Hamlet are both killed. *Sayonara* is Japanese for goodbye. **Limned** means suffused or highlighted with a bright color.

After receiving no aid from the fictional Martian god Malann, Gallinger calls on deities from various religions and mythologies—Hinduism (**Vishnu**), Christianity and Judaism (**Jehovah**), Greek (**Adonis**), Egyptian (**Osiris**), Sumerian (**Thammuz**), Algonquian (**Manitou**), and Haitian Vodou (**Legba**). **Niccolò Paganini** was an Italian violinist, violist and composer.

Kodokan ("A place for study and promotion of the way") is the headquarters of Japanese style judo. The *judogi* is the traditional uniform used for judo practice and competition. *Ik-kyu* is senior brown belt in judo. *Jiu-Jitsu* is a Japanese martial art. *Atemi-waza* are striking techniques rarely used at full force in judo because of the harm that they can inflict. *Tsuki no kokoro* ("A Mind Like the Moon") refers to the need to be constantly aware of the totality of the opponent and his or her movements, just as moonlight shines equally on everything in its range. *Hajime* means threshold or beginning. *Neko-ashi-dachi* ("Cat Stance") is a classic initial pose in judo and is often depicted in motion pictures. *Shiai* is a judo competition for a prize. **Hybris** is an alternate spelling for hubris, pride and arrogance.

BRAXA

Notes

This poem was written for and included in the 1963 story "A Rose For Ecclesiastes" and is available in its entirety on page 42 within the story. The poem was reprinted separately in the poetry collections *Poems* and *When Pussywillows Last in the Catyard Bloomed*.

Ecclesiastes' Epilogue

Written 1955–60 for *Chisel in the Sky;* previously unpublished.

"As flagrantly
as an old dream is devolved
to nothing,
comes the passing of your desires, woman,
leaving me as one awakened
but not as one refreshed."

Notes

Ecclesiastes is the book of the Bible which expresses the thought that all is vanity, all is futile, and there is nothing new under the sun—and Zelazny famously referred to this in his story "A Rose for Ecclesiastes." In this poem he applies it to a couple's discrepant sexual desires—the man is aroused but frustrated because the woman is no longer interested.

BOK

And Flights of Angels: The Life and Legend of Hannes Bok, ed. Emil Petaja,
The Bokanalia Memorial Foundation 1968, as "Untitled".

All the power gone
The spectrum drained from the prism
The final name a thing carved
I rage at the loss of what once lived

I shall miss his worlds like dreams
their players soaked with sun
lands he'd ransacked rainbows to fete

supple utterances of movement
through the day's long wonder
dazzling dignities of light and delight
enacted above a mortal signature
signed there in a dream's air brief
yet bright bright
so bright

A Word from Zelazny

As Zelazny wrote in its original publication, these are "lines upon the work of HANNES BOK upon hearing of his death."[1] Hannes Bok (pseudonym for Wayne Woodard) was a well-known fantasy artist in the 1960s, and his last major work was the wraparound cover art for Zelazny's "A Rose For Ecclesiastes" in the November 1963 issue of *The Magazine of Fantasy & Science Fiction*. "When I was 12 years old and wanted to write SF, I had an ambition: I wanted a Bok illo on something I'd write. When I did make it the one thing I was sure of was that I'd never get a Bok illo, because he'd retired from SF work. I never thought he'd come back for one last cover and that it would be my story."[2]

---

1 *And Flights of Angels: The Life and Legend of Hannes Bok*, ed Emil Petaja, The Bokanalia Memorial Foundation 1968.
2 Letter from Roger Zelazny to Ned Brooks dated June 6, 1965.

AND THE DARKNESS IS HARSH

Eucuyo, 1954.

We are resting here, and we are waiting. Waiting.
Do you know what it is like to wait? We are crowded here, my brothers and I, and we are watching that great metal door and waiting for it to open.

It is locked now. But it has opened before and they say that sooner or later it always opens. When we hear a soft click, and the clean daylight from outside looks in, we will be ready.

We are always ready. So are millions of our kin, the world over. Ready and waiting.

They say that it is beautiful outside, that the warm light comes down from the sky and makes green things come up from the ground and live and grow. They say that at night it is beautiful, too, that there is a darkness that is pleasant and not harsh, and that there are thousands of little lights up in the sky. It is then that the living things sleep, they say.

We would not know that last because we never sleep. We only rest between our times of use. Now we are resting, and waiting, and reliving our tragic pasts. Our pasts are always tragic; that is, if we have a past. Some of us don't. We are the new ones.

But we can hear the old ones remembering and we know what it is like. We know what it is like to see the outside, all that beauty, and to go forth into it.

It changes then.

71

It always changes when we leave here. There are always other things in the sky than stars, and the night becomes a harsh darkness like that of our home.

At times it is not always dark. The living things do not all sleep at night then, and some of them keep on sleeping, even in the daytime.

It is only beautiful for a little while after we emerge. Then it becomes ugly.

We do not like ugliness. We do not like waiting. We do not even like existing. But we are servants. We must exist and wait to make more ugliness every time that door opens.

It will open again. They say that sooner or later it always opens.

Then the soft daylight will look in and tell us of the beauty outside. It will look at our shiny metal bodies and at the word "Armory" printed outside the door.

It will look and it will go away.

Then we will be through waiting.

A Word from Zelazny

This was Zelazny's first completely published short story from the Euclid Junior High School literary magazine *Eucuyo* in 1954. He was actively sending stories to magazines and receiving only rejection slips. He later had this story reprinted in the limited edition chapbook of the same title, wherein he described this as "an obvious Bradbury pastiche."[1]

---

1 *And the Darkness Is Harsh*, 1994.

MR. FULLER'S REVOLT

Eucuyo, 1954.

"Good morning, Mr. Fuller," said the attendant, smoothing his white smock and smiling.

"Good morning, George. What's on the schedule for today?"

"Schedule, Mr. Fuller?" answered the attendant. "You know that there never…"

"Skip it," sighed Mr. Fuller, an average-looking man in his middle thirties. "I just thought that maybe…Oh well."

"Anything you want, sir?" the attendant inquired eagerly.

"Nothing. I think I'll take a walk." He turned and left the old attendant.

It was a beautiful day, he mused, but then they all were. He followed the winding road down into the valley and stopped at the orchard. Not bothering to examine it, he picked an apple from one of the trees and lay down in the shade munching it.

It was a perfect apple of course, they always were; in fact everything about this place was perfect. You could just lie back and relax, and everything would be taken care of for you. He sighed again and watched a dust devil spin idly across the road. You should be immensely happy when free to do anything you want to. There was only one catch, there was nothing to do here.

Mr. Fuller realized that he was unhappy.

He threw the apple remainder against a nearby tree trunk.

Splat!

Just like that, he thought. Just crossing the street when some crazy driver crashed the light.

There was a grill and bumper coming toward him and the tortured screaming of tires. They screamed louder and louder.

Splat!

And here he was. He stood up and yawned. He brushed some dust from his smock. Maybe there was something he could do. Where is that blasted attendant?

"Did you call?" questioned George, stepping from behind a large tree, smiling.

"Uh-huh," he answered. "How's chances of us finding some more guys and getting up a softball game?"

"I'm afraid not. Strenuous sports are prohibited here, you know."

"Just trying," he shrugged, and turned down the road again. There had to be something worth doing!

The attendant fell in step alongside him. "There's an excellent view of the waterfall down the road a way, and there's a pear orchard, too."

Mr. Fuller was silent.

They saw the waterfall and he ate half a dozen perfect pears. He didn't get a stomach ache though; he never got them anymore.

But there was something inside him, gnawing and craving to be let out. He longed to express himself in some way.

Finally he spoke. "George."

The attendant looked at him, smiling. He always smiled.

"George, there are many beautiful things here," he began. "And you've been very nice to me. But there's nothing to do here. You've given me a Utopia and an empty life! This is a place of idleness!"

Indignation began to boil within Mr. Fuller as he went on. "There's absolutely positively nothing here to hold my attention! Maybe I'm not cut out for this sort of thing, but if this is what Heaven is like, I'd sooner have Hell!"

There was a twinkle in the attendant's eyes as he smiled more broadly than usual. "Is that so?" he asked. "Just where do you think you are, anyway, sir?"

A Word from Zelazny

Among the few surviving stories written during his teens, this one represents the first time that Zelazny ever received payment for a short story—$25 (about $190 in 2008 dollars)—and had it professionally published.[1] It was first published in the Euclid Junior High School literary magazine *Eucuyo*. He submitted it to a National Scholastic high school story contest—the same contest that Harlan Ellison won in his time—and earned the $25 plus the distinction of having it printed in the national magazine *Literary Cavalcade* Vol. 7 No. 1, October 1954. That milestone "inspired me to go out and write another hundred short stories. They were all rejected, but occasionally I'd get a little nice note. I had a sentence from Fletcher Pratt once, saying 'try again.' Ray Palmer dropped me a couple of notes saying 'Comes close this time,' 'Didn't quite make it.' Then I went to college and stopped writing altogether; I had too many courses even to read science fiction."[2]

Zelazny later had this story reprinted in the chapbook *And the Darkness Is Harsh*, where he remarked "I don't know where [this] piece came from."[3] Critics later cited recurring themes in Zelazny's work including death, immortality, suicide, automobile accidents—and it is noteworthy that some of these themes date back to this early published work.

Notes

Sir Thomas More coined the phrase "**utopia**" (a perfect place) for his 1516 book of the same name.

---

1 *Roger Zelazny: A Primary and Secondary Bibliography*, 1980.
2 *If*, January 1969.
3 *And the Darkness Is Harsh*, 1994.

DIET

Eucuyo, 1954.

Candy, cakes
        Pastries, pies
Dance before my yearning eyes.
Chicken braised,
        Golden fries,
Beckon, tempt and tantalize.
Waiters wait,
        Time flies.
Food! Food! my stomach cries.
Odors, menus,
        Calories, lies.
There! Another diet dies.

A Word from Zelazny

This poem was published in the Euclid Junior High School literary magazine *Eucuyo* and was later reprinted in *Young America Sings*, National High School Poetry Association, 1954. Zelazny also reprinted it in the limited edition chapbook *And the Darkness is Harsh*, where he described this poem as "inspired by a fat kid I felt sorry for."[1]

---

1 *And the Darkness is Harsh*, 1994.

YOUTH ETERNAL

Eucuyo, 1955.

The street was narrow and the light from the still-rising sun rode on golden roads past the buildings and fell broken into spider-web-like filigree on the pavement. Unconscious of these patterns at his feet and, indeed, unconscious of everything save his own deep thoughts, the old man moved rapidly down the center of the thoroughfare.

The vehicle turned the corner and as it thundered toward him, the warning screams of its four occupants, two boys and two girls, rose from its open top.

Yet for another moment he did not notice.

When the shouts finally struck some chord of response in his white-fringed beard, he looked up, eyes wide, mouth suddenly open. For all of three seconds he remained in this position before his sluggish reflexes responded to the danger. By then it was nearly upon him.

The pair of hands that suddenly fastened themselves to his arm and shoulder were tanned and muscular. They violently pulled him to the right.

He was in a shaded doorway struggling to catch his breath and keep his balance. The vehicle surged past, splashing up a cold little shower from a nearby puddle along with a chilly gust of air.

Then it rounded the next corner and was gone.

Shakily the old man leaned against the wall and felt the hands release his arm. He breathed deeply, then unconsciously began wiping at the water spatters on his face and clothes.

"Th-thank you," he muttered to his rescuer, "I didn't even see it coming. These streets—they're so narrow—there's hardly any room for the pedestrian. I was meditating—going to the library. Thanks."

"Certainly," breathed the other between clenched teeth. "These kids nowadays shouldn't be allowed on the roads." He put his hand back on the old man's shoulder, comfortingly. "Do you feel all right? I didn't hurt your arm when I pulled you that way, did I?"

The old man bent his arm and straightened it.

"No, no damage." For the first time he looked at the man who had saved him. "But it was quite a terrible feeling to look up and see something terrible bearing down like that, Sergeant," he noticed the other's uniform.

"I'll walk with you to the library," the sergeant offered. "I'm going in that direction myself."

They left the doorway, took a few steps down the street. The old man stopped and shuddered.

"I don't blame you for feeling weak," the sergeant said. "You'd be amazed at the number of reports we get every week. This generation seems to be going to the dogs. Reckless driving, theft, wild parties, street fighting… I don't know what it will finally lead to."

"Well, children are inclined to be a little wild when they're growing up," the old man began as they resumed walking. "I have heard a few stories…"

"What you hear isn't even half of it," said the sergeant. "A large number of them come from the better homes—rich businessmen and important officials. In such cases things are often smoothed over and the kids get off without a lick of punishment." He paused, as if to let his words sink in, then added, "I think a heavy leather strap would provide a better answer."

"I have heard predictions that the human race is headed toward a new social low," observed the old man as they turned into a larger thoroughfare. "If they're as bad as all that, I shudder to think what will become of the world when they're full grown."

"If they live that long," said the sergeant. "Really though, that makes you wonder how much longer the human race has left when kids are allowed to run around doing anything they fancy, with no respect for anybody or anything. What men they'll make!"

Their footsteps sounded dully on the wet pavement as they neared the library. The old man turned to his new friend.

"I wish to thank you again… What is your name?" he inquired.

The sergeant smiled and chose to appear noble.

"Just think of me as representing the hand of the Law," he stated.

"Well, I thank the hand that was extended to me," the old man replied, "and a good morning to you." He extended his hand.

"Good morning," said the other as they clasped hands, one tanned and powerful, the other pale and delicate.

"And mark my words," the sergeant offered in parting, "unless some radical step is taken, the youth of today will bring the world to chaos in a few years."

The sergeant turned on his heel and headed toward the distant dark mouth of another narrow street. And the old man moved up the walk and past the obelisk that marked the great library of Alexandria.

Notes

This is the last surviving manuscript written during Zelazny's high school days.

SLUSH, SLUSH, SLUSH

Eucuyo, 1955.

There's a somber
    spectral beauty
To Winter's pale hush.

With the torrid
    days of Summer
Come things green and lush.

Autumn's hues
    always change
To a ruddy blush.

But all there is
    to early Spring—
Is slush, slush, and slush.

The Outward Sign

Skyline #31, Cleveland College of Western Reserve University, April 1958.

There once was a calligrapher in Agra who inscribed the word of the Prophet for no eyes but those of Allah, Himself. Every day, stopping only to face the west and perform his holy duties, he spent the hours of light on his balcony, forming the sacred script of the Koran.

Knowing little of the devices of the world he withdrew to this balcony, "To the greater honor and glory of Allah," and centered his being on the production of filigreed scroll-work and lettering. He toiled not for the coin of man and his children ran ragged through the streets, fed by the few pennies his faithful wife received for washing the clothes of the merchants. But Allah finally smiled upon his servant, and Azrael, the angel of death, called for the soul of his wealthy uncle Babulla.

Soon the calligrapher was the wealthiest man in his village. But still he sat, cross-legged on his mat of straw, tracing the words of Mahomet unto the gold-bordered field of his scroll. "When I die," he said unto his wife, "this is to be placed on the pyre by my side. And let not any eyes—least of all thy unworthy own—look upon its words, for it is meant for none but He That Is and, *bismillah*, so shall it be!"

But his wealth, as the juice of the sugar plant summons the winged minions of torment, brought to his house those local unworthies who abound this sinful world: Hafiz, the Arab, Isadore of the tribe of Abraham, and Larry, the drunken Christian.

The way now is short; he was lured from his balcony and fell among these vilest of men. From them he came to know the evils

81

Eblis sets before the faithful: Isadore taught him the joys of pig-flesh, Larry the glories of the grape, and Hafiz of the foul plant *hashish* that brings the seven ages of man to pass in the shade of one afternoon.

Brushing the rubies of wine from his whitened beard, he came to know the warmth of the belly at the time he once was wont to pay his reverence to Mecca. The muezzins called their summons, but he chewed his pig-meat and chuckled. He smoked with Hafiz and knew himself to be like unto Allah.

But every night in the circle of light from a shining lantern-face he scribed with care the words of God as he had always done.

And as he grew older and descended further into the pit of the world he came to disbelieve in the blessed Garden of Joys that Allah has promised the faithful; the angels ceased to cross the moonbeams in his cloth-hung room of the high bed, and his garden of joys was the cellar of wine.

Even unto the last evening of his life he wrote to the glory of the God he no longer held with, and still he meant that no man should see these writings. He squinted his bird-like eyes and creased his narrow forehead into wrinkle-making grimaces not unlike those lines he labored to produce.

And the day of the flame his good wife placed the scroll by his side, lamenting loudly as they were reduced to ashes and gnarled ropes of smoke. Larry and Isadore moved in search of a new patron, and all was as it had been until Hafiz, the dreamer, dreamed a question:

"Damned of holy," he dreamed, "for whom does one perform when his audience departs and cannot be replaced?" but he only dreamed it for a little while and it became obscured by the sweet smoke, then all came to be as it had been.

Notes

After high school Zelazny largely abandoned writing except for poetry. Poetry was his primary interest as a writer. This is the sole known story that he wrote during the time he attended Western Reserve University, and it appeared in the university magazine *Skyline*. This fable displays a style similar to *Lord of Light*, even though it was written ten years earlier.

Agra is a city in northern India, the site of the Taj Mahal. In Islam, **the Prophet** is Mohammed and **Allah** is the Supreme Being or God. The **Koran** is the Islamic sacred book, believed to be the word of God, dictated to **Mohamet** (Mohammed) by the archangel Gabriel and written down in Arabic. **Filigree** consists of fine gold or silver wire that is worked into a delicate, ornamental tracery. In Jewish and Islamic mythology, **Azrael** is the angel who severs the soul from the body at death. ***Bismillah*** is an invocation meaning "In the name of Allah!" **Eblis** is the fallen angel of Islam, chief of djinns, and demon of despair. ***Hashish*** is a purified resin created from cannabis which is then smoked, chewed or drunk as an intoxicant or stimulant. **The seven ages of man** refers to Shakespeare's monologue "All the World's a Stage" in the play *As You Like It*. The seven ages include infancy, childhood, lover (adolescent), soldier (young adult), justice (adult), old age, and dementia/death. **Mecca** is a city in western Saudi Arabia, birthplace of Mohammed; Muslims consider it the holiest city of Islam. **Muezzins** are the men who call Muslims to prayer.

The Agnostic's Prayer

1st part: "Creatures of Light", *If*, November 1968; 2nd part: "The Steel General", *If*, January 1969. *Creatures of Light and Darkness*, 1969.

I nsofar as I may be heard by anything, which may or may not care what I say, I ask, if it matters, that you be forgiven for anything you may have done or failed to do which requires forgiveness. Conversely, if not forgiveness but something else may be required to insure any possible benefit for which you may be eligible after the destruction of your body, I ask that this, whatever it may be, be granted or withheld, as the case may be, in such a manner as to insure your receiving said benefit. I ask this in my capacity as your elected intermediary between yourself and that which may not be yourself, but which may have an interest in the matter of your receiving as much as it is possible for you to receive of this thing, and which may in some way be influenced by this ceremony. Amen.

Then into the hands of Whatever May Be that is greater than life or death, I resign myself – if this act will be of any assistance in preserving my life. If it will not, I do not. If my saying this thing is at all presumptuous, and therefore not well received by Whatever may or may not care to listen, then I withdraw the statement and ask forgiveness, if this thing be desired. If not, I do not. On the other hand—Amen.

Notes

This is the most famous prayer in science fiction and fantasy. The first section is frequently quoted or cited as a separate entity; this is its first publication under its own title. The first part is spoken by Madrak, a reluctant preacher "of the non-theistic, non-sectarian sort" to a man who is about to commit suicide by fire in front of an audience. The second part is spoken by Madrak on his own behalf when he is about to enter into a battle that he fears he may not survive; his impatient companion interrupts him. Many readers thought "The Agnostic's Prayer" indicated Zelazny's religious philosophy. He never quite agreed or disagreed with that supposition.

PASSION PLAY

Amazing, August 1962.

At the end of the season of sorrows comes the time of rejoicing. Spring, like a well-oiled clock, noiselessly indicates this time. The average days of dimness and moisture decrease steadily in number, and those of brilliance and cool air begin to enter the calendar again. And it is good that the wet times are behind us, for they rust and corrode our machinery; they require the most intense standards of hygiene.

With all the bright baggage of spring, the days of the Festival arrive. After the season of Lamentations come the sacred stations of the Passion, then the bright Festival of Resurrection, with its tinkle and clatter, its exhaust fumes, scorched rubber, clouds of dust, and its great promise of happiness.

We come here each year, to the place, to replicate a classic. We see with our own lenses the functioning promise of our creation. The time is today, and I have been chosen.

Here on the sacred grounds of Le Mans I will perform every action of the classic which has been selected. Before the finale I will have duplicated every movement and every position which we know occurred. How fortunate! How high the honor!

Last year many were chosen, but it was not the same. Their level of participation was lower. Still, I had wanted so badly to be chosen! I had wished so strongly that I, too, might stand beside the track and await the flaming Mercedes.

But I was saved for this greater thing, and all lenses are upon me as we await the start. This year there is only one Car to watch—number 4, the Ferrari-analog.

❖   ❖   ❖

The sign has been given, and the rubber screams; the smoke balloons like a giant cluster of white grapes, and we are moving. Another car gives way, so that I can drop into the proper position. There are many cars, but only one Car.

We scream about the turn, in this great Italian classic of two centuries ago. We run them all here, at the place, regardless of where they were held originally.

"Oh gone masters of creation," I pray, "let me do it properly. Let my timing be accurate. Let no random variable arise to destroy a perfect replication."

The dull gray metal of my arms, my delicate gyroscopes, my special gripping-hands, all hold the wheel in precisely the proper position as we roar into the straightaway.

How wise the ancient masters were! When they knew they must destroy themselves in a combat too mystical and holy for us to understand, they left us these ceremonies, in commemoration of the Great Machine. All the data was there: the books, the films, all; for us to find, study, learn, to know the sacred Action.

As we round another turn, I think of our growing cities, our vast assembly lines, our lube-bars, and our beloved executive computer. How great all things are! What a well-ordered day! How fine to have been chosen!

The tires, little brothers, cry out, and the pinging of small stones comes from beneath. Three-tenths of a second, and I shall depress the accelerator an eighth of an inch further.

R-7091 waves to me as I enter the second lap, but I cannot wave back. My finest functioning is called for at this time. All the special instrumentation which has been added to me will be required in a matter of seconds.

The other cars give way at precisely the right instant. I turn, I slide. I crash through the guard rail.

"Turn over now, please!" I pray, twisting the wheel, "and burn."

Suddenly we are rolling, skidding, upside-down. Smoke fills the Car.

To the crashing noise that roars within my receptors, the crackle and lick of flames is now added.

My steel skeleton—collapsed beneath the impact-stresses. My lubricants—burning. My lenses, all but for a tiny area—shattered.

My hearing-mechanism still functions weakly.

Now there is a great horn sounding, and metal bodies rush across the fields.

Now. Now is the time for me to turn off all my functions and cease.

But I will wait. Just a moment longer. I must hear them say it.

❖   ❖   ❖

Metal arms drag me from the pyre. I am laid aside. Fire extinguishers play white rivers upon the Car.

Dimly, in the distance, through my smashed receptors, I hear the speaker rumble:

"Von Trips has smashed! The Car is dead!"

A great sound of lamenting rises from the rows of unmoving spectators. The giant fireproof van arrives on the field, just as the attendants gain control of the flames.

Four tenders leap out and raise the Car from the ground. A fifth collects every smouldering fragment.

And I see it all!

"Oh, let this not be blasphemy, please!" I pray. "One instant more!"

Tenderly, the Car is set within the van. The great doors close.

The van moves, slowly, bearing off the dead warrior, out through the gates, up the great avenue and past the eager crowds.

To the great smelter. The Melting Pot!

To the place where it will be melted down, then sent out, a piece used to grace the making of each new person.

A cry of unanimous rejoicing arises on the avenue.

It is enough, that I have seen all this.

Happily, I turn myself off.

A Word from Zelazny

Zelazny made a serious effort to write poetry during his college and graduate school years and submitted a manuscript of poetry (*Chisel in the Sky*) to
a national contest (he didn't win). He then realized that he was unlikely to
find a viable career as a poet. "…only Robert Frost and Carl Sandburg were
making their livings writing poetry…the writing was there on the washroom wall. I wanted to be a full-time professional writer. I made my decision and wrote the story 'A Rose for Ecclesiastes' in October of 1961 and
said good-bye to all that."[1]

After finishing "A Rose For Ecclesiastes" he did not write any more
stories until February 1962. "Thinking about the best way to break in, I
started reading again, out of the usual academic area; and I went back to
science fiction. I figured I knew science fiction; I'd read thousands of stories
in the area; and since I had this much knowledge I might as well try science fiction. So I started batting out stories, for about three months."[2] In
this interval he again collected only rejection slips, and then he reviewed
the accumulated material to determine what he was doing wrong. "I had
gathered together all of my rejected stories and spent an evening reading
through them to see whether I could determine what I was doing wrong.
One thing struck me about all of them: I was overexplaining. I was describing settings, events and character motivations in too much detail. I decided,
in viewing these stories now that they had grown cold, that I would find it
insulting to have anyone explain anything to me at that length. I resolved
thereafter to treat the reader as I would be treated myself, to avoid the
unnecessarily explicit, to use more indirection with respect to character and
motivation, to draw myself up short whenever I felt the tendency to go on
talking once a thing had been shown.

"Fine. That was my resolution. I still had to find a story idea to do it
with…

"When I sat down in [the family doctor's] waiting room, I picked up a
copy of *Life* and began looking through it. Partway along, I came upon a
photospread dealing with the death of racing driver Wolfgang von Trips.
Something clicked as soon as I saw it, and just then the doctor called me in
for the checkup. While I was breathing for him and coughing and faking
knee jerks and so forth, I saw the entire incident that was to be this short
short. I could have written it right then. My typewriter was in Dayton and
I'd the long drive ahead of me. The story just boiled somewhere at the back

---

1 *When Pussywillows Last in the Catyard Bloomed*, 1980.
2 *If*, January 1969.

of my mind on the way down, and when I reached my apartment I headed straight for the typewriter and wrote it through…

"I cannot really say whether I owe it to that resolution I made on reviewing my rejects, but it felt as if I did and I have always tried to keep the promise I made that day about not insulting the reader's intelligence."[3]

That first sale earned Zelazny $20 (about $136 in 2008 dollars) and was the first of seventeen stories sold that year.[4] He received notice of the sale on March 28, 1962.[5,6] "It was a fantastic feeling. I'd been out of town for the whole weekend, and I went back and opened my little mailbox in this apartment where I'd been living…and when I opened it and saw this letter from the publisher and not the manuscript coming back, and I tore it open and saw in there a little note saying 'if you agree with the terms of this contract, please sign and return one copy and keep the other for your records,' I just – I don't know how to express it. It was almost a mystical experience. It was a very great feeling."[7]

Notes

In his first professionally published science fiction story, Zelazny shows the emergence of a new mythology, the worship of primitive machines by the machines that succeeded man. Trappings of Christian Easter ceremonies have even been co-opted by the machines (*Lamentations*, *Stations of the Passion*, and *Festival of Resurrection*).

Wolfgang von Trips was leading the championship going into the final race at the Monza Grand Prix in 1961, but on lap 2 he collided with a Lotus, his Ferrari became airborne and struck the barrier at high speed, and he was ejected from the vehicle, dying on impact. Fifteen spectators were killed. The 24 Hours of **Le Mans** is the famous sports car endurance race, held annually at Circuit de la Sarthe near Le Mans, France. Notably, some details of the mythology became blurred even for this machine civilization, who are re-enacting von Trips's disaster at Le Mans instead of the Grand Prix at Monza where the tragedy actually took place. This and other errors by the machines can be viewed as a commentary on how facts become blurred or forgotten as a mythology evolves.

---

3 *Unearth* Vol. 2 No 1. Winter 1978.
4 *Phlogiston #44*, 1995.
5 *If,* January 1969.
6 *Roger Zelazny*, Jane Lindskold, 1993.
7 *Phantasmicom #5* April 1971.

ON MAY 13, 1937

Written 1965–68; previously unpublished.

On May 13, 1937,
I was born
and Pablo Picasso
                      sketched
"Hand With Broken Sword"
for "Guernica."
                    A useless comparison,
save that the jag-edged blade
describes a perfect "Z"
and the flower above it
is fading.
                It struck me,
however, on this day,
when I realized it,
For this day I saw a woman
regard a child's photo and weep.
Who she was, I do not know.
Later a cat nibbled my fingers.

Three things happened to me this day,
and I am enriched thereby:
A cat, a broken sword, a tear—
none of which I claim to understand.

Somehow, however, each caught my throat
like a swallow, with a sadness
like the cancer, beauty
claiming its right to be born,

If, like me, it is true
I'll thank May 13, 1937,
for something, anyhow.

Notes

This autobiographical poem begins with a statement of Zelazny's birthdate, and goes on to refer to the same three items (a cat, a broken sword, and a tear) as in the poem "See You Later, Maybe…" A sketch in black lead on white paper, entitled *Hand With Broken Sword*, was indeed done on 13 May 1937, one of many studies that Picasso did for his large composite mural *Guernica*.

CACTUS KING

To Spin Is Miracle Cat, Underwood-Miller 1981.
Written 1955–60 for *Chisel in the Sky*.

It has been said that no land lies so vile
but kingship would console one's presence there;
no spit of Hell too small
for Lucifer to dwell supreme,
post-fall.

But Lord! the exile autocrat
imprisoned by such reign!
with two-edged sword of Proust
that pricks a will to power
(nettle of reply from out a fading past)—

as here, most lovely Bonaparte,
my master or rocks,
we dub thee the bowing, red and cactus head.

Notes

Lucifer was originally a high-ranking archangel until he was tossed out of heaven and renamed Satan. After defeat, **Napolean Bonaparte** was exiled to the isle of Elba, where he was allowed to rule the 12,000 inhabitants and retain the title of Emperor. The **sword of Proust** alludes to a comment that Marcel Proust made about inspiration in a letter he wrote to Prince Antoine Bibesco in 1902: "…a hundred characters for novels, a thousand ideas keep asking me to give them substance, like those shades that keep asking Ulysses in the Odyssey to give them blood to drink and bring them to life, and that the hero pushes aside with his sword."

THE GRAVEYARD HEART

Manuscript title: "Party Set."
Fantastic, March 1964.

They were dancing,

—at the party of the century, the party of the millennium, and the Party of Parties,

—really, as well as calendar-wise,

—and he wanted to crush her, to tear her to pieces…

Moore did not really see the pavilion through which they moved, nor regard the hundred faceless shadows that glided about them. He did not take particular note of the swimming globes of colored light that followed above and behind them.

He felt these things, but he did not necessarily sniff wilderness in that ever-green relic of Christmas past turning on its bright pedestal in the center of the room—shedding its fireproofed needles and traditions these six days after the fact.

All of these were abstracted and dismissed, inhaled and filed away…

In a few more moments it would be Two Thousand.

Leota (née Lilith) rested in the bow of his arm like a quivering arrow, until he wanted to break her or send her flying (he knew not where), to crush her into limpness, to make that samadhi, myopia, or whatever, go away from her graygreen eyes. At about that time, each time, she would lean against him and whisper something into his ear, something in French, a language he did not yet speak. She followed his inept lead so perfectly though, that it was not unwarranted that he should feel she could read his mind by pure kinesthesia.

Which made it all the worse then, whenever her breath collared his neck with a moist warmness that spread down under his jacket like an invisible infection. Then he would mutter *"C'est vrai"* or

"Damn" or both and try to crush her bridal whiteness (overlaid with black webbing), and she would become an arrow once more. But she was dancing with him, which was a decided improvement over his last year/her yesterday.

It was almost Two Thousand.

Now...

The music broke itself apart and grew back together again as the globes blared daylight. Auld acquaintance, he was reminded, was not a thing to be trifled with.

He almost chuckled then, but the lights went out a moment later and he found himself occupied.

A voice speaking right beside him, beside everyone, stated:

"It is now Two Thousand. Happy New Year!"

He crushed her.

No one cared about Times Square. The crowds in the Square had been watching a relay of the Party on a jerry-screen the size of a football field. Even now the onlookers were being amused by black-light close-ups of the couples on the dance floor. Perhaps at that very moment, Moore decided, they themselves were the subject of a hilarious sequence being served up before that overflowing Petri dish across the ocean. It was quite likely, considering his partner.

He did not care if they laughed at him, though. He had come too far to care.

"I love you," he said silently. (He used mental dittos to presume an answer, and this made him feel somewhat happier.) Then the lights fireflied once more and auld acquaintance was remembered. A blizzard compounded of a hundred smashed rainbows began falling about the couples; slow-melting spirals of confetti drifted through the lights, dissolving as they descended upon the dancers; furry-edged projections of Chinese dragon kites swam overhead, grinning their way through the storm.

They resumed dancing and he asked her the same question he had asked her the year before.

"Can't we be alone, together, somewhere, just for a moment?"

She smothered a yawn.

"No, I'm bored. I'm going to leave in half an hour."

If voices can be throaty and rich, hers was an opulent neckful. Her throat *was* golden, to a well-sunned turn.

"Then let's spend it talking—in one of the little dining rooms."

"Thank you, but I'm not hungry. I *must* be seen for the next half hour."

Primitive Moore, who had spent most of his life dozing at the back of Civilized Moore's brain, rose to his haunches then, with a growl Civilized Moore muzzled him though, because he did not wish to spoil things.

"When can I see you again?" he asked grimly.

"Perhaps Bastille Day," she whispered. "There's the *Liberté, Egalité, Fraternité Fête Nue*..."

"Where?"

"In the New Versailles Dome, at nine. If you'd like an invitation, I'll see that you receive one..."

"Yes, I do want one."

("She made you ask," jeered Primitive Moore.)

"Very well, you'll receive one in May."

"Won't you spare me a day or so now?"

She shook her head, her blue-blonde coif burning his face.

"Time is too dear," she whispered in mock-Camille pathos, "and the days of the Parties are without end. You ask me to cut years off my life and hand them to you."

"That's right."

"You ask too much," she smiled.

He wanted to curse her right then and walk away, but he wanted even more so to stay with her. He was twenty-seven, an age of which he did not approve in the first place, and he had spent all of the year 1999 wanting her. He had decided two years ago that he was going to fall in love and marry—because he could finally afford to do so without altering his standards of living. Lacking a woman who combined the better qualities of Aphrodite and a digital computer, he had spent an entire year on safari, trekking after the spoor of his starcrossed.

❖   ❖   ❖

The invitation to the Bledsoes' Orbiting New Year—which had hounded the old year around the world, chasing it over the International Dateline and off the Earth entirely, to wherever old years go—had set him back a month's pay, but had given him his first live glimpse of Leota Mathilde Mason, belle of the Sleepers. Forgetting about digital computers, he decided then and there to fall in love with her. He was old-fashioned in many respects.

He had spoken with her for precisely ninety-seven seconds, the first twenty of which had been Arctic. But he realized that she existed to be admired, so he insisted on admiring her. Finally, she consented to be seen dancing with him at the Millennium Party in Stockholm.

He had spent the following year anticipating her seduction back to a reasonable and human mode of existence. Now, in the most beautiful city in the world, she had just informed him that she was bored and was about to retire until Bastille Day. It was then that Primitive Moore realized what Civilized Moore must really have known all along: the next time that he saw her she would be approximately two days older and he would be going on twenty-nine. Time stands still for the Set, but the price of mortal existence is age. Money could buy her the most desirable of all narcissist indulgences: the cold-bunk.

And he had not even had the chance of a Stockholm snowflake in the Congo to speak with her, to speak more than a few disjointed sentences, let alone to try talking her out of the ice-box club. (Even now, Setman laureate Wayne Unger was moving to cut in on him, with the expression of a golf pro about to give a lesson.)

"Hello, Leota. Sorry, Mister Uh."

Primitive Moore snarled and bashed him with his club; Civilized Moore released one of the most inaccessible women in the world to a god of the Set.

She was smiling. He was smiling. They were gone.

All the way around the world to San Francisco, sitting in the bar of the stratocruiser in the year of Our Lord Two Thousand—that is to say: two, zero, zero, zero—Moore felt that Time was out of joint.

❖   ❖   ❖

It was two days before he made up his mind what he was going to do about it.

He asked himself (from the blister balcony of his suite in the Hundred Towers of the Hilton-Frisco Complex): *Is* this the girl I want to marry?

He answered himself (looking alternately at the traffic capillaries below his shoetops and the Bay): Yes.

Why? he wanted to know.

Because she is beautiful, he answered, and the future will be lovely. I want her for my beautiful wife in the lovely future.

So he decided to join the Set.

He realized it was no mean feat he was mapping out. First, he required money, lots of money—green acres of Presidents, to be strewn properly in the proper places. The next requisite was distinction, recognition. Unfortunately, the world was full of electrical engineers, humming through their twenty-hour weeks, dallying with pet projects—competent, capable, even inspired—who did not have these things. So he knew it would be difficult.

He submerged himself into research with a unique will: forty, sixty, eighty hours a week he spent—reading, designing, studying taped courses in subjects he had never needed. He gave up on recreation.

By May, when he received his invitation, he stared at the engraved (not fac-copy) parchment (not jot-sheet) with bleary eyes. He had already had nine patents entered and three more were pending. He had sold one and was negotiating with Akwa Mining over a water purification process which he had, he felt, fallen into. Money he would have, he decided, if he could keep up the pace.

Possibly even some recognition. That part now depended mainly on his puro-process and what he did with the money. Leota (née Lorelei) lurked beneath his pages of formulas, was cubed Braque-like in the lines on his sketcher; she burnt as he slept, slept as he burned.

In June he decided he needed a rest.

"Assistant Division Chief Moore," he told the face in the groomer (his laudatory attitude toward work had already earned him a promotion at the Seal-Lock Division of Pressure Units, Corporate), "you need more French and better dancing."

The groomer hands patted away at his sandy stubble and slashed smooth the shagginess above his ears. The weary eyes before him agreed bluely; they were tired of studying abstractions.

The intensity of his recreation, however, was as fatiguing in its own way as his work had been. His muscle tone *did* improve as he sprang weightlessly through the Young Men's Christian Association Satellite-3 Trampoline Room; his dance steps seemed more graceful after he had spun with a hundred robots and ten dozen women; he took the accelerated Berlitz drug-course in French (eschewing the faster electrocerebral-stimulation series, because of a rumored transference that might slow his reflexes later that summer); and he felt that he was beginning to *sound* better—he had hired a gabcoach, and he bake-ovened Restoration plays into his pillow (and hopefully, into his head) whenever he slept (generally every third day now)—so that, as the day of the Fête drew near, he began feeling like a Renaissance courtier (a tired one).

As he stared at Civilized Moore inside his groomer, Primitive Moore wondered how long that feeling would last.

Two days before Versailles he cultivated a uniform tan and decided what he was going to say to Leota this time:

—I love you? (Hell, no!)

—Will you quit the cold circuit? (Uh-uh).

—If I join the Set, will you join me? (That seemed the best way to put it.)

Their third meeting, then, was to be on different terms. No more stake-outs in the wastes of the prosaic. The hunter was going to enter the brush. "Onward!" grinned the Moore in the groomer, "and Excelsior!"

❖   ❖   ❖

She was dressed in a pale blue, mutie orchid corsage. The revolving dome of the palace spun singing zodiacs and the floors fluoresced witch-fires. He had the uncomfortable feeling that the damned flowers were growing there, right above her left breast, like an exotic parasite; and he resented their intrusion with a parochial possessiveness that he knew was not of the Renaissance. Nevertheless…

"Good evening. How do your flowers grow?"

"Barely and quite contrary," she decided, sipping something green through a long straw, "but they cling to life."

"With an understandable passion," he noted, taking her hand which she did not withdraw. "Tell me, Eve of the Microprosopos— where are you headed?"

Interest flickered across her face and came to rest in her eyes.

"Your French has improved, Adam—Kadmon…?" she noted. "I'm headed ahead. Where are you headed?"

"The same way."

"I doubt it—unfortunately."

"Doubt all you want, but we're parallel flows already."

"Is that a conceit drawn from some engineering laureate?"

"Watch me engineer a cold-bunk," he stated.

Her eyes shot X-rays through him, warming his bones.

"I knew you had something on your mind. If you were serious…"

"Us fallen spirits have to stick together here in Malkuth—I'm serious." He coughed and talked eyetalk. "Shall we stand together as though we're dancing. I see Unger; he sees us, and I want you."

"All right."

She placed her glass on a drifting tray and followed him out onto the floor and beneath the turning zodiac, leaving Setman Unger to face a labyrinth of flesh. Moore laughed at his predicament.

"It's harder to tell identities at an anti-costume party."

She smiled.

"You know, you dance differently today than last night."

"I know. Listen, how do I get a private iceberg and a key to Schleraffenland? I've decided it might be amusing. I know that it's not a matter of genealogy, or even money, for that matter, although both seem to help. I've read all the literature, but I could use some practical advice."

Her hand quivered ever so slightly in his own.

"You know the Doyenne./?" she said/asked.

"Mainly rumors," he replied, "to the effect that she's an old gargoyle they've frozen to frighten away the Beast come Armageddon."

Leota did not smile. Instead, she became an arrow again.

"More or less," she replied coldly. "She does keep beastly people out of the Set."

Civilized Moore bit his tongue.

"Although many do not like her," she continued, becoming slightly more animated as she reflected, "I've always found her a rare little piece of chinoiserie. I'd like to take her home, if I had a home, and set her on my mantel, if I had a mantel."

"I've heard that she'd fit right into the Victorian Room at the NAM Galleries," Moore ventured.

"She *was* born during Vicky's reign—and she *was* in her eighties when the cold-bunk was developed—but I can safely say that the matter goes no further."

"And she decided to go gallivanting through Time at that age?"

"Precisely," answered Leota, "inasmuch as she wishes to be the immortal arbiter of trans-society."

They turned with the music. Leota had relaxed once more.

"At one hundred and ten she's already on her way to becoming an archetype," Moore noted. "Is that one of the reasons interviews are so hard to come by?"

"One of the reasons…" she told him. "If, for example, you were to petition Party Set now, you would still have to wait until next summer for the interview—provided you reached that stage."

"How many are there on the roster of eligibles?"

She shut her eyes.

"I don't know. Thousands, I should say. She'll only see a few dozen, of course. The others will have been weeded out, pruned off, investigated away, and variously disqualified by the directors. Then, naturally, *she* will have the final say as to who is *in*."

Suddenly green and limpid—as the music, the lights, the ultrasonics, and the delicate narcotic fragrances of the air altered subtly—the room became a dark, cool place at the bottom of the sea, heady and nostalgic as the mind of a mermaid staring upon the ruins of Atlantis. The elegiac genius of the hall drew them closer together by a kind of subtle gravitation, and she was cool and adhesive as he continued:

"What is her power, really? I've read the tapes; I know she's a big stockholder, but so what? Why can't the directors vote around her. If I paid out—"

"They *wouldn't*," she said. "Her money means nothing. She is an institution.

"Hers is the quality of exclusiveness which keeps the Set the Set," she went on. "Imitators will always fail because they lack her discrimination. They'll take in any boorish body who'll pay. *That* is the reason that People Who Count," (she pronounced the capitals), "will neither attend nor sponsor any but Set functions. All exclusiveness would vanish from the Earth if the Set lowered its standards."

"Money is money," said Moore. "If others paid the same for their parties…"

"…Then the People who take their money would cease to Count. The Set would boycott them. They would lose their elan, be looked upon as hucksters."

"It sounds like a rather vicious moebius."

"It is a caste system with checks and balances. Nobody really wants it to break down."

"Even those who wash out?"

"Silly! They'd be the last. There's nothing to stop them from buying their own bunkers, if they can afford it, and waiting another five years to try again. They'd be wealthier anyhow for the wait, if they invest properly. Some have waited decades, and are still waiting. Some have made it after years of persisting. It makes the game more interesting, the achievement more satisfying. In a world of physical ease, brutal social equality, and reasonable economic equality, exclusiveness in frivolity becomes the most sought-after of all distinctions."

"'Commodities,'" he corrected.

"No," she stated, "it is not for sale. Try buying it if money is all you have to offer."

That brought his mind back to more immediate considerations.

"What *is* the cost, if all the other qualifications are met?"

"The rule on that is sufficiently malleable to permit an otherwise qualified person to meet his dues. He guarantees his tenure, bunkwise or Party-wise, until such a time as his income offsets his debt. So if he only possesses a modest fortune, he may still be quite eligible. This is necessary if we are to preserve our democratic ideals."

She looked away, looked back.

"Usually a step-scale of percentages on the returns from his investments is arranged. In fact, a Set counselor will be right there when you liquidate your assets, and he'll recommend the best conversions."

"Set must clean up on this."

"*Certainement*. It *is* a business, and the Parties don't come cheaply. But then, you'd be a part of Set yourself—being a shareholder is one of the membership requirements—and we're a restricted corporation, paying high dividends. Your principal will grow. If you were to be accepted, join, and then quit after even one objective month, something like twenty actual years would have passed. You'd be a month older and much wealthier when you leave—and perhaps somewhat wiser."

"Where do I go to put my name on the list?"

He knew, but he had hopes.

"We can call it in tonight, from here. There is always someone in the office. You will be visited in a week or so, after the preliminary investigation."

"Investigation?"

"Nothing to worry about. Or have you a criminal record, a history of insanity, or a bad credit rating?"

Moore shook his head.

"No, no, and no."

"Then you'll pass."

"But will I actually have a chance of getting in, against all those others?"

It was as though a single drop of rain fell upon his chest.

"Yes," she replied, putting her cheek into the hollow of his neck and staring out over his shoulder so that he could not see her expression, "you'll make it all the way to the lair of Mary Maude Mullen with a member sponsoring you. That final hurdle will depend on yourself."

"Then I'll make it," he told her.

"…The interview may only last seconds. She's quick; her decisions are almost instantaneous, and she's never wrong."

"Then I'll make it," he repeated, exulting.

Above them, the zodiac rippled.

❖　❖　❖

Moore found Darryl Wilson in a barmat in the Poconos. The actor had gone to seed; he was not the man Moore remembered from the award-winning frontier threelie series. That man had been a cragbrowed, bushy-faced Viking of the prairies. In four years' time a facial avalanche had occurred, leaving its gaps and runnels across his expensive frown and dusting the face fur a shade lighter. Wilson had left it that way and cauterized his craw with the fire water he had denied the Red Man weekly. Rumor had it he was well into his second liver.

Moore sat beside him and inserted his card into the counter slot. He punched out a Martini and waited. When he noticed that the man was unaware of his presence, he observed, "You're Darryl Wilson and I'm Alvin Moore. I want to ask you something."

The straight-shooting eyes did not focus.

"News media man?"

"No, an old fan of yours," he lied.

"Ask away then," said the still-familiar voice. "You are a camera."

"Mary Maude Mullen, the bitch-goddess of the Set," he said. "What's she like?"

The eyes finally focused.

"You up for deification this session?"

"That's right."

"What do you think?"

Moore waited, but there were no more words, so he finally asked, "About what?"

"Anything. You name it."

Moore took a drink. He decided to play the game if it would make the man more tractable.

"I think I like Martinis," he stated. "Now—"

"Why?"

Moore growled. Perhaps Wilson was too far gone to be of any help. Still, one more try...

"Because they're relaxing and bracing, both at the same time, which is something I need after coming all this way."

"Why do you want to be relaxed and braced?"

"Because I prefer it to being tense and unbraced."

"Why?"

"What the hell is all this?"

"You lose. Go home."

Moore stood.

"Suppose I go out again and come back in and we start over? Okay?"

"Sit down. My wheels turn slowly but they still turn," said Wilson. "We're talking about the same thing. You want to know what

Mary Maude is like? That's what she's like—all interrogatives. Useless ones. Attitudes are a disease that no one's immune to, and they vary so easily in the same person. In two minutes she'll have you stripped down to them, and your answers will depend on biochemistry and the weather. So will her decision. There's nothing I can tell you. She's pure caprice. She's life. She's ugly."

"That's all?"

"She refuses the wrong people. That's enough. Go away."

Moore finished his Martini and went away.

❖   ❖   ❖

That winter Moore made a fortune. A modest one, to be sure.

He quit his job for a position with the Akwa Mining Research Lab, Oahu Division. It added ten minutes to his commuting time, but the title, Processing Director, sounded better than Assistant Division Chief, and he was anxious for a new sound. He did not slacken the pace of his force-fed social acceptability program, and one of its results was a January lawsuit.

The Set, he had been advised, preferred divorced male candidates to the perpetually single sort. For this reason, he had consulted a highly-rated firm of marriage contractors and entered into a three-month renewable, single partner drop-option contract, with Diane Demetrios, an unemployed model of Greek-Lebanese extraction.

One of the problems of modeling, he decided later, was that there were many surgically-perfected female eidolons in the labor force. His newly-acquired status had been sufficient inducement to cause Diane to press a breach of promise suit on the basis of an alleged oral agreement that the option *would* be renewed.

Burgess Social Contracting Services of course sent a properly obsequious adjuster, and they paid the court costs as well as the med-fees for Moore's broken nose. (Diane had hit him with *The Essentials of Dress Display,* a heavy, illustrated talisman of a manual, which she carried about in a plastic case—as he slept beside their pool—plastic case and all.)

So, by the month of March Moore felt ready and wise and capable of facing down the last remaining citizen of the nineteenth century.

By May, though, he was beginning to feel he had over-trained. He was tempted to take a month's psychiatric leave from his work, but he recalled Leota's question about a history of insanity. He vetoed the notion and thought of Leota. The world stood still as his mind turned. Guiltily, he realized that he had not thought of her for months. He had been too busy with his autodidactics, his new job, and Diane Demetrios to think of the Setqueen, his love.

He chuckled.

Vanity, he decided; I want her because everyone wants her.

No, that wasn't true either, exactly… He wanted—what?

He thought upon his motives, his desires.

He realized, then, that his goals had shifted; the act had become the actor. What he really wanted, first and foremost, impure and unsimple, was an in to the Set—that century-spanning stratocruiser, luxury class, jetting across tomorrow and tomorrow and all the days that followed after—to ride high, like those gods of old who appeared at the rites of the equinoxes, slept between processions, and were remanifest with each new season, the bulk of humanity living through all those dreary days that lay between. To be a part of Leota was to be a part of the Set, and that was what he wanted now. So of course it was vanity. It was love.

He laughed aloud. His autosurf initialed the blue lens of the Pacific like a manned diamond, casting the sharp cold chips of its surface up and into his face.

Returning from absolute zero, Lazarus-like, is neither painful nor disconcerting, at first. There are no sensations at all until one achieves the temperature of a reasonably warm corpse. By that time though, an injection of nirvana flows within the body's thawed rivers.

It is only when consciousness begins to return, thought Mrs. Mullen, to return with sufficient strength so that one fully realizes what has occurred—that the wine has survived another season in an uncertain cellar, its vintage grown rarer still—only then does an unpronounceable fear enter into the mundane outlines of the bed-room furniture—for a moment.

It is more a superstitious attitude than anything, a mental quaking at the possibility that the stuff of life, one's own life, has in some indefinable way been tampered with. A microsecond passes, and then only the dim recollection of a bad dream remains.

She shivered, as though the cold was still locked within her bones, and she shook off the notion of nightmares past.

She turned her attention to the man in the white coat who stood at her elbow.

"What day is it?" she asked him.

He was a handful of dust in the winds of Time…

"August eighteen, two thousand-two," answered the handful of dust. "How do you feel?"

"Excellent, thank you," she decided. "I've just touched upon a new century—this makes three I've visited—so why shouldn't I feel excellent? I intend to visit many more."

"I'm sure you will, madam."

The small maps of her hands adjusted the counterpane. She raised her head.

"Tell me what is new in the world."

The doctor looked away from the sudden acetylene burst behind her eyes.

"We have finally visited Neptune and Pluto," he narrated. "They are quite uninhabitable. It appears that man is alone in the solar system. The Lake Sahara project has run into more difficulties but it seems that work may begin next spring now that those stupid French claims are near settlement…" Her eyes fused his dust to planes of glass.

"Another competitor, Futuretime Gay, entered into the time-tank business three years ago," he recited, trying to smile, "but we met the enemy and they are ours—Set bought them out eight months ago. By the way, our own bunkers are now much more sophistica—"

"I repeat," she said, "what is new in the world, *doctor*?"

He shook his head, avoiding the look she gave him.

"We can lengthen the remissions now," he finally told her, "quite a time beyond what could be achieved by the older methods."

"A better delaying action?"

"Yes."

"But not a cure?"

He shook his head.

"In my case," she told him, "it has already been abnormally delayed. The old nostrums have already worn thin. For how long are the new ones good?"

"We still don't know. You have an unusual variety of M.S. and it's complicated by other things."

"Does a cure seem any nearer?"

"It could take another twenty years. We might have one tomorrow."

"I see." The brightness subsided. "You may leave now, young man. Turn on my advice tape as you go."

He was glad to let the machine take over.

❖   ❖   ❖

Diane Demetrios dialed the library and requested the Setbook. She twirled the page-dial and stopped.

She studied the screen as though it were a mirror, her face undergoing a variety of expressions.

"I look just as good," she decided after a time. "Better, even. Your nose could be changed, and your brow-line…

"If they weren't facial fundamentalists," she told the picture, "if they didn't discriminate against surgery, lady—you'd be here and I'd be there.

"Bitch!"

❖   ❖   ❖

The millionth barrel of converted seawater emerged, fresh and icy, from the Moore Purifier. Splashing from its chamber-tandem and flowing through the conduits, it was clean, useful, and singularly unaware of these virtues. Another transfusion of briny Pacific entered at the other hand.

The waste products were used in pseudoceramicware.

The man who designed the doubleduty Purifier was rich.

The temperature was 82° in Oahu.

The million-first barrel splashed forth…

❖   ❖   ❖

They left Alvin Moore surrounded by china dogs.

Two of the walls were shelved, floor to ceiling. The shelves were lined with blue, green, pink, russet (not to mention ochre, vermilion, mauve, and saffron) dogs, mainly glazed (although some were dry-rubbed primitives), ranging from the size of a largish cockroach up to that of a pigmy warthog. Across the room a veritable Hades of a wood fire roared its metaphysical challenge into the hot July of Bermuda.

Set above it was a mantelpiece bearing more dogs.

Set beside the hellplace was a desk, at which was seated Mary Maude Mullen, wrapped in a green and black tartan. She studied Moore's file, which lay open on the blotter. When she spoke to him she did not look up.

Moore stood beside the chair which had not been offered him and pretended to study the dogs and the heaps of Georgian kindling that filled the room to over-flowing.

While not overly fond of live dogs, Moore bore them no malice. But when he closed his eyes for a moment he experienced a feeling of claustrophobia.

These were not dogs. There were the unblinking aliens staring through the bars of the last Earthman's cage. Moore promised himself that he would say nothing complimentary about the garish rainbow of a houndpack (fit, perhaps, for stalking a jade stag the size of a Chihuahua); he decided it could only have sprung from the mental crook of a monomaniac, or one possessed of a very feeble imagination and small respect for dogs.

After verifying all the generalities listed on his petition, Mrs. Mullen raised her pale eyes to his.

"How do you like my doggies?" she asked him.

She sat there, a narrow-faced, wrinkled woman with flaming hair, a snub nose, an innocent expression, and the lingering twist of the question lurking her thin lips.

Moore quickly played back his last thoughts and decided to maintain his integrity in regards china dogs by answering objectively.

"They're quite colorful," he noted.

This was the wrong answer, he felt, as soon as he said it. The question had been too abrupt. He had entered the study ready to lie about anything but china dogs. So he smiled.

"There are a dreadful lot of them about. But of course they don't bark or bite or shed, or do other things…"

She smiled back.

"My dear little, colorful little bitches and sons of bitches," she said. "They don't do anything. They're sort of symbolic. That's why I collect them too.

"Sit down"—she gestured—"and pretend you're comfortable."

"Thanks."

"It says here that you rose only recently from the happy ranks of anonymity to achieve some sort of esoteric distinction in the sciences. Why do you wish to resign it now?"

"I wanted money and prestige, both of which I was given to understand would be helpful to a Set candidate."

"Aha! Then they were a means rather than an end?"

"That is correct."

"Then tell me why you want to join the Set."

He had written out the answer to that one months ago. It had been bake-ovened into his brain, so that he could speak it with natural inflections. The words began forming themselves in his throat, but he let them die there. He had planned them for what he had thought would be maximum appeal to a fan of Tennyson's. Now he was not so sure.

Still… He broke down the argument and picked a neutral point— the part about following knowledge like a sinking star.

"There will be a lot of changes over the next several decades. I'd like to see them—with a young man's eyes."

"As a member of the Set you will exist more to be seen than to see," she replied, making a note in his file. "…And I think we'll have to dye your hair if we accept you."

"The hell you say!—Pardon me, that slipped out."

"Good." She made another note. "We can't have them too inhibited—nor too uninhibited, for that matter. Your reaction was rather quaint." She looked up again.

"Why do you want so badly to see the future?"

He felt uneasy. It seemed as though she knew he was lying.

"Plain human curiosity," he answered weakly, "as well as some professional interest. Being an engineer—"

"We're not running a seminar," she observed. "You'd not be wasting much time outside of attending Parties if you wanted to last very long with the Set. In twenty years—no, ten—you'll be back in kindergarten so far as engineering is concerned. It will all be hieroglyphics to you. You don't read hieroglyphics, do you?"

He shook his head.

"Good," she continued, "I have an inept comparison. Yes, it will all be hieroglyphics, and if you should leave the Set you would be an unskilled draftsman—not that you'd have need to work. But if you were to want to work, you would have to be self-employed—which grows more and more difficult, almost too difficult to attempt, as time moves on. You would doubtless lose money."

He shrugged and raised his palms. He *had* been thinking of doing that. Fifty years, he had told himself, and we could kick the Set, be rich, and I could take refresher courses and try for a consultantship in marine engineering.

"I'd know enough to appreciate things, even if I couldn't participate," he explained.

"You'd be satisfied just to observe?"

"I think so," he lied.

"I doubt it." Her eyes nailed him again. "Do you think you are in love with Leota Mason? She nominated you, but of course that *is* her privilege."

"I don't know," he finally said. "I thought so at first, two years ago…"

"Infatuation is fine," she told him. "It makes for good gossip. Love, on the other hand, I will not tolerate. Purge yourself of such notions. Nothing is so boring and ungay at a Set affair. It does not make for gossip; it makes for snickers."

"So is it infatuation or love?"

"Infatuation," he decided.

She glanced into the fire, glanced at her hands.

"You will have to develop a Buddhist's attitude toward the world around you. That world will change from day to day. Whenever you stop to look at it, it will be a different world—unreal."

He nodded.

"Therefore, if you are to maintain your stability, the Set must be the center of all things. Wherever your heart lies, there also shall reside your soul."

He nodded again.

"…And if you should happen not to like the future, whenever you do stop to take a look at it, remember you *cannot* come back. Don't just think about that, *feel* it!"

He felt it.

She began jotting. Her right hand began suddenly to tremble. She dropped the pen and too carefully drew her hand back within the shawl.

"You are not so colorful as most candidates," she told him, too naturally, "but then, we're short on the soulful type at present. Contrast adds depth and texture to our displays. Go view all the tapes of our past Parties."

"I already have."

"…And you can give your soul to that, or a significant part thereof?"

"Wherever my heart lies…"

"In that case, you may return to your lodgings. Mister Moore. You will receive our decision today."

Moore stood. There were so many questions he had not been asked, so many things he had wanted to say, had forgotten, or had not had opportunity to say… Had she already decided to reject him? he wondered. Was that why the interview had been so brief? Still, her final remarks *had* been encouraging.

He escaped from the fragile kennel, all his pores feeling like fresh nail holes.

He lolled about the hotel pool all afternoon, and in the evening he moved into the bar. He did not eat dinner.

When he received the news that he had been accepted, he was also informed by the messenger that a small gift to his inquisitor was a thing of custom. Moore laughed drunkenly, foreseeing the nature of the gift.

Mary Maude Mullen received her first Pacificware dog from Oahu with a small, sad shrug that almost turned to a shudder. She began to tremble then, nearly dropping it from her fingers. Quickly, she placed it on the bottommost shelf behind her desk and reached for her pills; later, the flames caused it to crack.

❖   ❖   ❖

They were dancing. The sea was an evergreengold sky above the dome. The day was strangely young.

Tired remnants of the Party's sixteen hours, they clung to one another, feet aching, shoulders sloped. There were eight couples still moving on the floor, and the weary musicians fed them the slowest music they could make. Sprawled at the edges of the world, where the green bowl of the sky joined with the blue tiles of the Earth, some five hundred people, garments loosened, mouths open, stared like goldfish on a tabletop at the water behind the wall.

"Think it'll rain?" he asked her.

"Yes," she answered.

"So do I. So much for the weather. Now, about that week on the moon—?"

"What's wrong with good old mother Earth?" she smiled.

Someone screamed. The sound of a slap occurred almost simultaneously. The screaming stopped.

"I've never been to the moon," he replied.

She seemed faintly amused.

"I have. I don't like it."

"Why?"

"It's the cold, crazy lights outside the dome," she said, "and the dark, dead rocks everywhere around the dome," she winced. "They make it seem like a cemetery at the end of Time…"

"Okay," he said, "forget it."

"…And the feeling of disembodied lightness as you move about inside the dome—"

"All right!"

"I'm sorry." She brushed his neck with her lips. He touched her forehead with his. "The Set has lost its shellac," she smiled.

"We're not on tape anymore. It doesn't matter now."

A woman began sobbing somewhere near the giant seahorse that had been the refreshment table. The musicians played more loudly. The sky was full of luminescent starfish, swimming moistly on their tractor beams. One of the starfish dripped salty water on them as it passed overhead.

"We'll leave tomorrow," he said.

"Yes, tomorrow," she said.

"How about Spain?" he said. "This is the season of the sherries. There'll be the Juegos Florales de la Vendimia Jerezana. It may be the last."

"Too noisy," she said, "with all those fireworks."

"But gay."

"Gay," she sighed with a crooked mouth. "Let's go to Switzerland and pretend we're old, or dying of something romantic."

"Necrophilist," he grinned, slipping on a patch of moisture and regaining his balance. "Better it be a quiet loch in the Highlands, where you can have your fog and miasma and I can have my milk and honeydew unblended."

"Nay," she said, above a quick babble of drunken voices, "let's go to New Hampshire."

"What's wrong with Scotland?"

"I've never been to New Hampshire."

"I have, and *I* don't like it. It looks like your description of the moon."

A moth brushing against a candle flame, the tremor.

The frozen bolt of black lightning lengthened slowly in the green heavens. A sprinkling of soft rain began.

As she kicked off her shoes he reached out for a glass on the floating tray above his left shoulder. He drained it and replaced it.

"Tastes like someone's watering the drinks."

"Set must be economizing," she said.

Moore saw Unger then, glass in hand, standing at the edge of the floor watching them.

"I see Unger."

"So do I. He's swaying."

"So are we," he laughed.

The fat bard's hair was a snowy chaos and his left eye was swollen nearly shut. He collapsed with a bubbling murmur, spilling his drink. No one moved to help him.

"I believe he's over indulged himself again."

"Alas, poor Unger," she said without expression, "I knew him well."

The rain continued to fall and the dancers moved about the floor like the figures in some amateur puppet show.

"They're coming!" cried a non-Setman, crimson cloak flapping. "They're coming down!"

The water streamed into their eyes as every conscious head in the Party Dome was turned upward. Three silver zeppelins grew in the cloudless green.

"They're coming for us," observed Moore.

"They're going to make it!"

The music had paused momentarily, like a pendulum at the end of its arc. It began again.

Good night, ladies, played the band, *good night, ladies…*

"We're going to live!"

"We'll go to Utah," he told her, eyes moist, "where they don't have seaquakes and tidal waves."

Good night ladies…

"We're going to live!"

She squeezed his hand.

"Merrily we roll along," the voices sang, *"roll along…"*

" 'Roll along,' " she said.

" 'Merrily,' " he answered.

"O'er the deep blue sea!"

❖   ❖   ❖

A Set-month after the nearest thing to a Set disaster on record (that is to say, in the year of Our Lord and President Cambert 2019, twelve years after the quake), Setman Moore and Leota (née Lachesis) stood outside the Hall of Sleep on Bermuda Island. It was almost morning.

"I believe I love you," he mentioned.

"Fortunately, love does not require an act of faith," she noted, accepting a light for her cigar, "because I don't believe in anything."

"Twenty years ago I saw a lovely woman at a Party and I danced with her."

"Five weeks ago," she amended.

"I wondered then if she would ever consider quitting the Set and going human again, and being heir to mortal ills."

"I have often wondered that myself," she said, "in idle moments. But she won't do it. Not until she is old and ugly."

"That means forever," he smiled sadly.

"You *are* noble." She blew smoke at the stars, touched the cold wall of the building. "Someday, when people no longer look at her, except for purposes of comparison with some fluffy child of the far future or when the world's standards of beauty have changed—then she'll transfer from the express run to the local and let the rest of the world go by."

"Whatever the station, she will be all alone in a strange town," said Moore. "Every day, it seems, they remodel the world. I met a fraternity brother at that dinner last night—pardon me, last year—and he treated me as if he were my father. His every other word was 'son' or 'boy' or 'kid,' and he wasn't trying to be funny. He was responding to what he saw. My appetite was considerably diminished."

"Do you realize we're going?" he asked the back of her head as she turned away to look out over the gardens of sleeping flowers. "Away! That's where. We can never go back! The world moves on while we sleep."

"Refreshing, isn't it?" she finally said. "And stimulating, and awe-inspiring. Not being bound, I mean. Everything burning. Us remaining. Neither time nor space can hold us, unless we consent.

"And I do not consent to being bound," she declared.

"To anything?"

"To anything."

"Supposing it's all a big joke."

"What?"

"The world.—Supposing every man, woman, and child died last year in an invasion by creatures from Alpha Centauri, everyone but the frozen Set. Supposing it was a totally effective virus attack…"

"There are no creatures in the Centauri System. I read that the other day."

"Okay, someplace else then. Supposing all the remains and all the traces of chaos were cleaned up, and then one creature gestured with a flipper at this building." Moore slapped the wall. "The creature said: 'Hey! There are some live ones inside, on ice. Ask one of the sociologists whether they're worth keeping, or if we should open the refrigerator door and let them spoil.' Then one of the sociologists came and looked at us, all in our coffins of ice, and *he* said: 'They might be worth a few laughs and a dozen pages in an obscure periodical. So let's fool them into thinking that everything is going on just as it was before the invasion. All their movements, according to these schedules, are preplanned, so it shouldn't be too difficult. We'll fill their Parties with human simulacra packed with recording machinery and we'll itemize their behavior patterns. We'll vary their circumstances and they'll attribute it to progress. We can watch them perform in all sorts of situations that way. Then, when we're finished, we can always break their bunktimers and let them sleep on—or open their doors and watch them spoil.'

"So they agreed to do it," finished Moore, "and here we are, the last people alive on Earth, cavorting before machines operated by inhuman creatures who are watching us for incomprehensible reasons."

"Then we'll give them a good show," she replied, "and maybe they'll applaud us once before we spoil."

She snubbed out her cigar and kissed him good night. They returned to their refrigerators.

❖   ❖   ❖

It was twelve weeks before Moore felt the need for a rest from the Party circuit. He was beginning to grow fearful. Leota had spent nonfunctional decades of her time vacationing with him, and she had recently been showing signs of sullenness, apparently regretting these expenditures on his behalf. So he decided to see something real, to take a stroll in the year 2078. After all, he was over a hundred years old.

The Queen Will Live Forever, said the faded clipping that hung in the main corridor of the Hall of Sleep. Beneath the bannerline was the old/recent story of the conquest of the final remaining problems of Multiple Sclerosis, and the medical ransom of one of its most notable victims. Moore had not seen the Doyenne since the day of his interview. He did not care whether he ever saw her again.

He donned a suit from his casual style locker and strolled through the gardens and out to the airfield. There were no people about.

He did not really know where he wanted to go until he stood before a ticket booth and the speaker asked him, "Destination, please."

"Uh—Oahu. Akwa Labs, if they have a landing field of their own."

"Yes, they do. That will have to be a private charter though, for the final fifty-six miles—"

"Give me a private charter all the way, both ways."

"Insert your card, please."

He did.

After five minutes the card popped back into his waiting hand. He dropped it into his pocket.

"What time will I arrive?" he asked.

"Nine hundred thirty-two, if you leave on Dart Nine six minutes from now. Have you any luggage?"

"No."

"In that case, your Dart awaits you in area A-11."

Moore crossed the field to the VTO Dart numbered "Nine." It flew by tape. The flight pattern, since it was a specially chartered run, had been worked out back at the booth, within milliseconds of Moore's naming his destination. It was then broadcast-transferred to a blank tape inside Dart Nine; an auto-alternation brain permitted the Dart to correct its course in the face of unforeseen contingencies and later recorrect itself, landing precisely where it was scheduled to come down.

Moore mounted the ramp and stopped to slip his card into the slot beside the hatchway. The hatch swung open and he collected his card and entered. He selected a seat beside a port and snapped its belt around his middle. At this, the hatchway swung itself shut.

After a few minutes the belt unfastened itself and vanished into the arms of his seat. The Dart was cruising smoothly now.

"Do you wish to have the lights dimmed? Or would you prefer to have them brighter?" asked a voice at his side.

"They're fine just the way they are," he told the invisible entity.

"Would you care for something to eat? Or something to drink?"

"I'll have a Martini."

There was a sliding sound, followed by a muted click. A tiny compartment opened in the wall beside him. His Martini rested within.

He removed it and sipped a sip.

Beyond the port and toward the rear of the Dart, a faint blue nimbus arose from the sideplates.

"Would you care for anything else?" *Pause.* "Shall I read you an article on the subject of your choice?" *Pause.* "Or fiction?" *Pause.* "Or poetry?" *Pause.* "Would you care to view the catalog?" *Pause.* "Or perhaps you would prefer music?"

"Poetry?" repeated Moore.

"Yes, I have many of—"

"I know a poet," he remembered. "Have you anything by Wayne Unger?"

There followed a brief mechanical meditation, then:

"Wayne Unger. Yes," answered the voice. "On call are his *Paradise Unwanted, Fungi of Steel,* and *Chisel in the Sky.*"

"Which is his most recent work?" asked Moore.

"*Chisel in the Sky.*"

"Read it to me."

The voice began by reading him all the publishing data and copyright information. To Moore's protests it answered that it was a matter of law and cited a precedent case. Moore asked for another Martini and waited.

Finally, "'Our Wintered Way Through Evening, and Burning Bushes Along It,'" said the voice.

"Huh?"

"That is the title of the first poem."

"Oh, read on."

> "'(Where only the evergreens whiten...)*
>
> Winterflaked ashes heighten
> in towers of blizzard.
> Silhouettes unseal an outline.
> Darkness, like an absence of faces,
> pours from the opened home;
> it seeps through shattered pine
> and flows the fractured maple.
>
> Perhaps it is the essence senescent,
> dreamculled from the sleepers,
> that soaks upon this road
> in weather-born excess.
> Or perhaps the great Anti-Life
> learns to paint with a vengeance,
> to run an icicle down the gargoyle's eye.
>
> For properly speaking, though
> no one can confront himself in toto,
> I see your falling sky, gone gods,
> as in a smoke-filled dream
> of ancient statues burning,
> soundlessly, down to the ground.
>
> (...and never the everwhite's green.)'"

There was a ten-second pause, then: "The next poem is entitled—"

"Wait a minute," asked Moore. "That first one—? Are you programmed to explain anything about it?"

"I am sorry, I am not. That would require a more complicated unit."

"Repeat the copyright date of the book."

"2016, in the North American Union—"

"And it's his most recent work?"

"Yes, he is a member of the Party Set and there is generally a lapse of several decades between his books."

"Continue reading."

The machine read on. Moore knew little concerning verse, but he was struck by the continual references to ice and cold, to snow and sleep.

"Stop," he told the machine. "Have you anything of his from before he joined the Set?"

"*Paradise Unwanted* was published in 1981, two years after he became a member. According to its Forward, however, most of it was written prior to his joining."

"Read it."

Moore listened carefully. It contained little of ice, snow, or sleep. He shrugged at his minor discovery. His seat immediately adjusted and readjusted to the movement.

He barely knew Unger. He did not like his poetry. He did not like most poetry, though.

The reader began another.

" '*In the Dogged House*,' " it said:

> " '*The heart is a graveyard of crigas,*
> *hid far from the hunter's eye,*
> *where love wears death like enamel*
> *and dogs crawl in to die...*' "

Moore smiled as it read the other stanzas. Recognizing its source, he liked that one somewhat better.

"Stop reading," he told the machine.

He ordered a light meal and thought about Unger. He had spoke with him once. When was it?

2017...? Yes, at the Free Workers' Liberation Centennial in the Lenin Palace.

It was rivers of vodka…

Fountains of juices, like inhuman arteries slashed, spurted their bright umbrellas of purple and lemon and green and orange. Jewels to ransom an Emir flashed near many hearts. Their host, Premier Korlov, seemed a happy frost giant in his display.

…In a dance pavilion of polaroid crystal, with the world outside blinking off and on, on and off—like an advertisement, Unger had commented, both elbows resting on the bartop and his foot on the indispensable rail.

His head had swiveled as Moore approached. He was a bleary-eyed albino owl. "Albion Moore, I believe," he had said, extending a hand. "*Quo vadis* dammit?"

"Grape juice and wadka," said Moore to the unnecessary human standing beside the mix-machine. The uniformed man pressed two buttons and passed the glass across the two feet of frosty mahogany. Moore twitched it toward Unger in a small salute. "A happy Free Workers' Liberation Centennial to you."

"I'll drink to liberation." The poet leaned toward and poked his own combination of buttons. The man in the uniform sniffed audibly.

They drank a drink together.

"They accuse us"—Unger's gesture indicated the world at large—"of neither knowing nor caring anything about un-Set things, un-Set people."

"Well, it's true, isn't it?"

"Oh yes, but it might be expanded upon. We're the same way with our fellows. Be honest now, how many Setmen are you acquainted with?"

"Quite a few."

"I didn't ask how many names you knew."

"Well, I talk with them all the time. Our environment is suited to much improvement and many words—and we have all the time in the world. How many friends do you have?" he asked.

"I just finished one," grunted the poet, leaning forward. "I'm going to mix me another."

Moore didn't feel like being depressed or joked with and he was not sure which category this fell into. He had been living inside a soap bubble since after the ill-starred Davy Jones Party, and he did not want anyone poking sharp things in his direction.

"So, you're your own man. If you're not happy in the Set, leave."

"You're not being a true *tovarisch*," said Unger, shaking a finger. "There was a time when a man could tell his troubles to bartenders and barfriends. You wouldn't remember, though—those days went out when the nickle-plated barmatics came in. Damn their exotic eyes and scientific mixing!"

Suddenly he punched out three drinks in rapid succession. He slopped them across the dark, shiny surface.

"Taste them! Sip each of them!" he enjoined Moore. "Can't tell them apart without a scorecard, can you?"

"They're dependable that way."

"Dependable? Hell yes! Depend on them to create neurotics. One time a man could buy a beer and bend an ear. All that went out when the dependable mix-machines came in. Now we join a talk-out club of manic change and most unnatural! Oh, had the Mermaid been such!" he complained in false notes of frenzy. "Or the Bloody Lion of Stepney! What jaded jokes the fellows of Marlowe had been!"

He sagged.

"Aye! Drinking's not what it used to be."

The international language of his belch caused the mix-machine attendant to avert his face, which betrayed a pained expression before he did so.

"So I'll repeat my question," stated Moore, making conversation. "Why do you stay where you're unhappy? You could go open a real bar of your own, if that's what you like. It would probably be a success, now that I think of it—people serving drinks and all that."

"Go to! Go to! I shan't say where!" He stared at nothing. "Maybe that's what I'll do someday, though," he reflected, "open a real bar…"

Moore turned his back to him then, to watch Leota dancing with Korlov. He was happy.

"People join the Set for a variety of reasons," Unger was muttering, "but the main one is exhibitionism, with the titillating wraith of immortality lurking at the stage door, perhaps. Attracting attention to oneself gets harder and harder as time goes on. It's almost impossible in the sciences. In the nineteenth and twentieth centuries you could still name great names—now it's great research teams. The arts have been democratized out of existence—and where have all the audiences gone? I don't mean spectators either.

"So we have the Set," he continued. "Take our sleeping beauty there, dancing with Korlov—"

"Huh?"

"Pardon me, I didn't mean to awaken you abruptly. I was saying that if she wanted attention Miss Mason couldn't be a stripper today, so she had to join the Set. It's even better than being a threelie star, and it requires less work—"

"Stripper?"

"A folk artist who undressed to music."

"Yes, I recall hearing of them."

"That's gone too, though," sighed Unger, "and while I cannot disapprove of the present customs of dress and undress, it still seems to me as if something bright and frail died in the elder world."

"She *is* bright, isn't she?"

"Decidedly so."

They had taken a short walk then, outside, in the cold night of Moscow. Moore did not really want to leave, but he had had enough to drink so that he was easy to persuade. Besides that, he did not want the stumbling babbler at his side to fall into an excavation or wander off lost, to miss his flight or turn up injured. So they shuffled up bright avenues and down dim streets until they came to the Square. They stopped before a large, dilapidated monument. The poet broke a small limb from a shrub and bent it into a wreath. He tossed it against the wall.

"Poor fellow," he muttered.

"Who?"

"The guy inside."

"Who's that?"

Unger cocked his head at him.

"You really don't know?"

"I admit there are gaps in my education, if that's what you mean. I continually strive to fill them, but I always was weak on history. I specialized at an early age."

Unger jerked his thumb at the monument.

"Noble Macbeth lies in state within," he said. "He was an ancient king who slew his predecessor, noble Duncan, most heinously. Lots of other people too. When he took the throne he promised he'd be nice to his subjects, though. But the Slavic temperament is a strange thing. He is best remembered for his many fine speeches, which were translated by a man named Pasternak. Nobody reads them anymore."

Unger sighed and seated himself on a stair. Moore joined him. He was too cold to be insulted by the arrogant mocking of the drunken poet.

"Back then, people used to fight wars," said Unger.

"I know," responded Moore, his fingers freezing; "Napoleon once burnt part of this city."

Unger tipped his hat.

Moore scanned the skyline. A bewildering range of structures hedged the Square—here, bright and functional, a ladder-like office building composed its heights and witnessed distances, as only the planned vantages of the very new can manage; there, a day time aquarium of an agency was now a dark mirror, a place where the confidence-inspiring efficiencies of rehearsed officials were displayed before the onlooker; and across the Square, its purged youth fully restored by shadow, a deserted onion of a cupola poked its sharp topknot after soaring vehicles, a number of which, scuttling among the star fires, were indicated even now—and Moore blew upon his fingers and jammed his hands into his pockets.

"Yes, nations went to war," Unger was saying. "Artilleries thundered. Blood was spilled. People died. But we lived through it, crossing a shaky Shinvat word by word. Then one day there it was. Peace. It had been that way a long time before anyone noticed. We still don't know how we did it. Perpetual postponement and a short memory, I guess, as man's attention became occupied twenty-four hours a day with other things. Now there is nothing left to fight over, and everyone is showing off the fruits of peace—because everyone has some, by the roomful. All they want. More. These things that fill the rooms, though," he mused, "and the mind—how they have proliferated! Each month's version is better than the last, in some hyper-sophisticated manner. They seem to have absorbed the minds that are absorbed with them…"

"We could all go live in the woods," said Moore, wishing he had taken the time to pocket a battery crystal and a thermostat for his suit.

"We could do lots of things, and we will, eventually—I suppose. Still, I guess we could wind up in the woods, at that."

"In that case, let's go back to the Palace while there's still time. I'm frozen."

"Why not?"

They climbed to their feet, began walking back.

"Why *did* you join the Set anyhow? So you could be discontent over the centuries?"

"Nay, son," the poet clapped him on the shoulder. "I'm an audience in search of an entertainment."

It took Moore an hour to get the chill out of his bones.

❖   ❖   ❖

"Ahem. Ahem," said the voice. "We are about to land at Akwa Labs, Oahu."

The belt snaked out into Moore's lap. He snapped it tight.

A sudden feeling prompted him to ask: "Read me that last poem from *Chisel* again."

"'*Future Be Not Impatient,*'" stated the voice:

> "'*Someday, perhaps, but not this day.*
> *Sometime; but then, not now.*
> *Man is a monument-making mammal.*
> *Never ask me how.*'"

He thought of Leota's description of the moon and he hated Unger for the forty-four seconds it took him to disembark. He was not certain why.

He stood beside Dart Nine and watched the approach of a small man wearing a smile and gay tropical clothing. He shook hands automatically.

"...Very pleased," the man named Teng was saying, "and glad there's not much around for you to recognize anymore. We've been deciding what to show you ever since Bermuda called." Moore pretended to be aware of the call. "...Not many people remember their employers from as far back as you do," Teng was saying.

Moore smiled and fell into step with him, heading toward the Processing Complex.

"Yes, I was curious," he agreed, "to see what it all looks like now. My old office, my lab—"

"Gone. of course."

"...our first chamber-tandem, with its big-nozzled injectors—"

"Replaced, naturally."

"Naturally. And the big old pumps..."

"Shiny and new."

Moore brightened. The sun, which he had not seen for several days/years, felt good on his back, but the air conditioning felt even better as they entered the first building. There was something of beauty in the pure functional compactness of everything about them, something Unger might have called by a different name, he realized, but it was beauty to Moore. He ran his hand along the sides of the units he did not have time to study. He tapped the conduits and peered into the kilns which processed the by-product ceramicware; he nodded approval and paused to relight his pipe whenever the man at his side asked his opinion of something too technically remote for him to have any opinion.

They crossed catwalks, moved through the temple-like innards of shut-down tanks, traversed alley-ways where the silent, blinking panels indicated that unseen operations were in progress. Occasionally, they met a worker, seated before a sleeping trouble-board, watching a broadcast entertainment or reading something over his portable threelie. Moore shook hands and forgot names.

Processing Director Teng could not help but be partly hypnotized—both by Moore's youthful appearance and the knowledge that he had developed a key process at some past date (as well as by his apparent understanding of present operations)—into believing that he was an engineer of his own breed, and up-to-date in his education. Actually, Mary Mullen's prediction that his profession would some day move beyond the range of his comprehension had not yet come to pass—but he could see that it was the direction in which he was headed. Appropriately, he had noticed his photo gathering dust in a small lobby, amid those of Teng's other dead and retired predecessors.

Sensing his feeling, Moore asked, "Say, do you think I could have my old job back?"

The man's head jerked about. Moore remained expressionless.

"Well—I suppose—something—could be worked..." he ended lamely as Moore broke into a grin and twisted the question back into casual conversation. It was somehow amusing to have produced that sudden, strange look of realization on the man's bored face, as he actually *saw* Moore for the first time. Frightening, too.

"Yes, seeing all this progress—is inspiring." Moore pronounced. "It's almost enough to make a man want to work again.—Glad I don't have to, of course. But there's a bit of nostalgia involved in coming back after all these years and seeing how this place grew out of the shoestring operation it seemed then—grew into more buildings than I could walk through in a week, and all of them packed with new hardware and working away to beat the band. Smooth. Efficient. I like it. I suppose you like working here?"

"Yes," sighed Teng, "as much as a man can like working. Say, were you planning on staying overnight? There's a weekly employees' luau and you'd be very welcome." He glanced at the wafer of a watchface clinging to his wrist. "In fact, it's already started," he added.

"Thanks," said Moore, "but I have a date and I have to be going. I just wanted to reaffirm my faith in progress. Thanks for the tour, and thanks for your time."

"Any time," Teng steered him toward a lush Break Room. "You won't be wanting to Dart back for awhile yet, will you?" he said. "So while we're having a bite to eat in here I wonder if I could ask you some questions about the Set. Its entrance requirements in particular…"

❖   ❖   ❖

All the way around the world to Bermuda, getting happily drunk in the belly of Dart Nine, in the year of Our Lord twenty seventy-eight, Moore felt that Time had been put aright.

❖   ❖   ❖

"So you want to have it./?" said/asked Mary Maude, uncoiling carefully from the caverns of her shawl.

"Yes."

"Why?" she asked.

"Because I do not destroy that which belongs to me. I possess so very little as it is."

The Doyenne snorted gently, perhaps in amusement. She tapped her favorite dog, as though seeking a reply from it.

"Though it sails upon a bottomless sea toward some fabulous orient," she mused, "the ship will still attempt to lower an anchor. I do not know why. Can you tell me? Is it simply carelessness on the part of the captain? Or the second mate?"

The dog did not answer. Neither did anything else.

"Or is it a mutineer's desire to turn around and go back?" she inquired. "To return home?"

There was a brief stillness. Finally:

"I live in a succession of homes. They are called hours. Each is lovely."

"But not lovely enough, and never to be revisited, eh? Permit me to anticipate your next words: 'I do not intend to marry. I do not intend to leave the Set. I shall have my child—' By the way, what will it be, a boy or a girl?"

"A girl."

"'I shall have my daughter. I shall place her in a fine home, arrange her a glorious future, and be back in time for the Spring Festival.'" She rubbed her glazed dog as though it were a crystal and pretended to peer through its greenish opacity. "Am I not a veritable gypsy?" she asked.

"Indeed."

"And you think this will work out?"

"I fail to see why it should not."

"Tell me which her proud father will do," she inquired, "compose her a sonnet sequence, or design her mechanical toys?"

"Neither. He shall never know. He'll be asleep until spring, and I will not. *She* must never know either."

"So much the worse."

"Why, pray tell?"

"Because she will become a woman in less than two months, by the clocks of the Set—and a lovely woman, I daresay—because she will be able to afford loveliness."

"Of course."

"And, as the daughter of a member, she will be eminently eligible for Set candidacy."

"She may not want it."

"Only those who cannot achieve it allude to having those sentiments. No, she'll want it. Everyone does. And, if her beauty should be surgically obtained, I believe that I shall, in this instance, alter a rule of mine. I shall pass on her and admit her to the Set. She will then meet many interesting people—poets, engineers, her mother…"

"No! I'd tell her, before I'd permit that to happen!"

"Aha! Tell me, is your fear of incest predicated upon your fear of competition, or is it really the other way around?"

"Please! Why are you saying these horrible things?"

"Because, unfortunately, you are something I can no longer afford to keep around. You have been an excellent symbol for a long time, but now your pleasures have ceased to be Olympian. Yours is a lapse into the mundane. You show that the gods are less sophisticated than schoolchildren—that they can be victimized by biology, despite the oceans of medical allies at our command. Princess, in the eyes of the world you are my daughter, for I am the Set. So take some motherly advice and retire. Do not attempt to renew your option. Get married first, and then to sleep for a few months—till spring, when your option is up. Sleep intermittently in the bunker, so that a year or so will pass. We'll play up the romantic aspects of your retirement. Wait a year or two to bear your child. The cold sleep won't do her any harm; there have been other cases such as yours. If you fail to agree to this, our motherly admonition is that you face present expulsion."

"You *can't!*"

"Read your contract."

"But no one need ever know!"

"You silly little dollface!" The acetylene blazed forth. "Your glimpses of the outside have been fragmentary and extremely selective—for at least sixty years. Every news medium in the world watches almost every move every Setman makes, from the time he sits up in his bunker until he retires, exhausted, after the latest Party. Snoopers and newshounds today have more gimmicks and gadgets in their arsenals than your head has colorful hairs. We *can't* hide your daughter all her life, so we won't even try. We'd have trouble enough concealing matters if you decided not to have her—but I think we could outbribe and outdrug our own employees.

"Therefore, I call upon you for a decision."

"I am sorry."

"So am I," said the Doyenne.

The girl stood.

From somewhere, as she left, she seemed to hear the whimpering of a china dog.

Beyond the neat hedgerows of the garden and down a purposefully irregular slope ran the unpaved pathway which wandered, like an impulsive river, through neck-tickling straits of unkempt forsythia, past high islands of mobbed sumac, and by the shivering branches, like waves, of an occasional ginkgo, wagging at the overhead gulls, while dreaming of the high-flying Archaeopteryx about to break through its heart in a dive, and perhaps a thousand feet of twistings are required to negotiate the two hundred feet of planned wilderness that separates the gardens of the Hall of Sleep from the artificial ruins which occupy a full, hilly acre, dotted here and there by incipi-

ent jungles of lilac and the occasional bell of a great willow—which
momentarily conceal, and then guide the eye on toward broken ped-
iments, smashed friezes, half-standing, shred-topped columns, then
fallen columns, then faceless, handless statues, and finally, seemingly
random heaps of rubble which lay amid these things; here, the path
over which they moved then forms a delta and promptly loses itself
where the tides of Time chafe away the memento mori quality that
the ruins first seem to spell, acting as a temporal entasis and in the
eye of the beholding Setman, so that he can look upon it all and say,
"I am the older than this," and his companion can reply, "We will
pass again some year and this too, will be gone," (even though she
did not say it this time) feeling happier by feeling the less mortal by
so doing; and crossing through the rubble, as they did, to a place
where barbarously ruined Pan grins from inside the ring of a dry
fountain, a new path is to be located, this time an unplanned and
only recently formed way, where the grass is yellowed underfoot and
the walkers must go single file because it leads them through a place
of briars, until they reach the old breakwall over which they generally climb like commandos in order to gain access to a quarter mile
strand of coved and deserted beach, where the sand is not quite so
clean as the beaches of the town—which are generally sifted every-
third day—but where the shade is as intense, in its own way, as the
sunlight, and there are flat rocks offshore for meditation.

"You're getting lazy," he commented, kicking off his shoes and
digging his toes into the cool sand. "You didn't climb over."

"I'm getting lazy," she agreed.

They threw off their robes and walked to the water's edge.

"Don't push!"

"Come on. I'll race you to the rocks."

For once he won.

Loafing in the lap of the Atlantic, they could have been any two
bathers in any place, in any time.

"I could stay here forever."

"It gets cold nights, and if there's a bad storm you might catch
something or get washed away."

"I meant," she amended, "if it could always be like this."

"'*Verweile doch, du bist so schön,*'" he reminded. "Faust lost a bet
that way, remember? So would a Sleeper. Unger's got me reading
again—Hey! What's the matter?"

"Nothing!"

"There's something wrong, little girl. Even I can tell."

"So what if there is?"

"So a lot, that's what. Tell me."

Her hand bridged the narrow channel between their rocks and found his. He rolled onto his side and stared at her satin-wet hair and her stuck-together eyelashes, the dimpled deserts of her cheeks, and the bloodied oasis of her mouth. She squeezed his hand.

"Let's stay here forever—despite the chill, and being washed away."

"You are indicating that—?"

"We could get off at this stop."

"I suppose. But—"

"But you like it now? You like the big charade?"

He looked away.

"I think you were right," she told him, "that night—many years ago."

"What night?"

"The night you said it was all a joke—that we are the last people alive on Earth, performing before machines operated by inhuman creatures who watch us for incomprehensible purposes. What are we but wave-patterns of an oscilloscope? I'm sick of being an object of contemplation!"

He continued to stare into the sea.

"I'm rather fond of the Set now," he finally responded. "At first I was ambivalent toward it. But a few weeks—years—ago I visited a place where I used to work. It was—different. Bigger. Better run. But more than that, actually. It wasn't just that it was filled with things I couldn't have guessed at fifty or sixty years ago. I had an odd feeling while I was there. I was with a little chatter-box of a Processing director named Teng, and he was yammering away worse than Unger, and I was just staring at all those tandem-tanks and tiers of machinery that had grown up inside the shell of that first old building—sort of like inside a womb—and I suddenly felt that someday something was going to be born, born out of steel and plastic and dancing electrons, in such a stainless, sunless place—and *that* something would be so fine that I would want to be there to see it. I couldn't dignify it by calling it a mystical experience or anything like that. It was just sort of a feeling I had. But if that moment could stay forever… Anyhow, the Set is my ticket to a performance I'd like to see."

"Darling," she began, "it is anticipation and recollection that fill the heart—never the sensation of the moment."

"Perhaps you are right…"

His grip tightened on her hand as the tunnel between their eyes shortened. He leaned across the water and kissed the blood from her mouth.

"Verweile doch…"

"…Du bist so schön."

❖ ❖ ❖

It was the Party to end all Parties. The surprise announcement of Alvin Moore and Leota Mathilde Mason struck the Christmas Eve gathering of the Set as just the thing for the season. After an extensive dinner and the exchange of bright and costly trifles the lights were dimmer. The giant Christmas tree atop the transparent penthouse blazed like a compressed galaxy through the droplets of melted snow on the ceilingpane.

It was nine by all the clocks of London.

"Married on Christmas, divorced on Twelfth Night," said someone in the darkness.

"What'll they do for an encore?" whispered someone else.

There were giggles and several off-key carols followed them. The backlight pickup was doubtless in action.

"Tonight we are quaint," said Moore.

"We danced in Davy Jones' Locker," answered Leota, "while they cringed and were sick on the floor."

"It's not the same Set," he told her, "not really. How many new faces have you counted? How many old ones have vanished? It's hard to tell. Where do old Setmen go?"

"The graveyard of the elephants," she suggested. "Who knows?"

"'*The heart is a graveyard of crigas,*'" recited Moore,

"'*hid far from the hunter's eye,*

"'*where love wears death like enamel*

"'*and dogs crawl in to die.*'"

"That's Unger's, isn't it?" she asked.

"That's right, I just happened to recall it."

"I wish you hadn't. I don't like it."

"Sorry."

"Where is Unger anyway?" she asked as the darkness retreated and the people arose.

"Probably at the punchbowl—or under the table."

"Not this early in the evening—for being under the table, I mean."

Moore shifted.

"What *are* we doing here anyhow?" he wanted to know. "Why did we have to attend this Party?"

"Because it is the season of charity."

"Faith and hope, too," he smirked. "You want to be maudlin or something? All right, I'll be maudlin with you. It *is* a pleasure, really."

He raised her hand to his lips.

"Stop that!"

"All right."

He kissed her on the mouth. There was laughter.

She flushed but did not rise from his side.

"If you want to make a fool of me—of us," he said, "I'll go more than halfway. Tell me why we had to come to this Party and announce our un-Setness before everyone? We could have just faded away from the Parties, slept until spring, and let our options run out."

"No. I am a woman and I could not resist another Party—the last one of the year, the very last— and wear your gift on my finger and know that deep down inside, the others *do* envy us—our courage, if nothing else—and probably our happiness."

"Okay," he agreed, "I'll drink to it—to you, anyway." He raised his glass and downed it. There was no fireplace to throw it into, so as much as he admired the gesture he placed it back on the table.

"Shall we dance? I hear music."

"Not yet. Let's just sit here and drink."

"Fine."

When all the clocks in London said eleven, Leota wanted to know where Unger was.

"He left," a slim girl with purple hair told her, "right after dinner. Maybe indigestion"—she shrugged—"or maybe he went looking for the Globe."

She frowned and took another drink.

Then they danced. Moore did not really see the room through which they moved, nor the other dancers. They were all the featureless characters in a book he had already closed. Only the dance was real—and the woman with whom he was dancing.

Time's friction, he decided, and a raising of the sights. I have what I wanted and still I want more. I'll get over it.

It was a vasty hall of mirrors. There were hundreds of dancing Alvin Moores and Leotas (née Mason) dancing. They were dancing at all their Parties of the past seventy-some years—from a Tibetan ski lodge to Davy Jones' Locker, from a New Years Eve in orbit to the floating Palace of Kanayasha, from a Halloween in the caverns of Carlsbad to a Mayday at Delphi—they had danced everywhere, and tonight was the last Party, *good night, ladies...*

She leaned against him and said nothing and her breath collared his neck.

"Good night, good night, good night," he heard himself saying, and they left with the bells of midnight, early, early, and it was Christmas as they entered the hopcar and told the Set chauffeur that they were returning early.

And they passed over the stratocruiser and settled beside the Dart they had come in, and they crossed through the powdery fleece that lay on the ground and entered the smaller craft.

"Do you wish to have the lights dimmed? Or would you prefer to have them brighter?" asked a voice at their side, after London and its clocks and its bridge had fallen, down.

"Dim them."

"Would you case for something to eat? Or something to drink?"

"No."

"No."

"Shall I read you an article on the subject of your choice?" *Pause.* "Or fiction?" *Pause.* "Or poetry?" *Pause.* "Would you care to view the catalog?" *Pause.* "Or perhaps you would prefer music?"

"Music," she said. "Soft. Not the kind you listen to."

After about ten minutes of near-sleep, Moore heard the voice:

> *"Hilted of flame,*
> *our frail phylactic blade*
> *slits black*
> *beneath Polestar's*
> *pinprick comment,*
> *foredging burrs*
> *of mitigated hell,*
> *spilling light without illumination.*

Strands of song,
to share its stinging flight,
are shucked and scraped
to fit an idiot theme.
Here, through outlocked chaos,
climbed of migrant logic,
the forms of black notation
blackly dice a flame.

"Turn it off," said Moore. "We didn't ask you to read."

"I'm not reading," said the voice, "I'm composing."

"Who—?"

Moore came awake and turned in his seat, which promptly adjusted to the movement. A pair of feet projected over the arm of a double seat to the rear. "Unger?"

"No, Santa Claus. Ho! Ho!"

"What are you doing going back this early?"

"You just answered your own question, didn't you?"

Moore snorted and settled back once more. At his side, Leota was snoring delicately, her seat collapsed into a couch.

He shut his eyes, but knowing they were not alone he could not regain the peaceful drifting sensation he had formerly achieved. He heard a sigh and the approach of lurching footfalls. He kept his eyes closed, hoping Unger would fall over and go to sleep. He didn't.

Abruptly, his voice rang out, a magnificently dreadful baritone:

"I was down to Saint James' Infir-r-rmary," he sang. "I saw my ba-a-aby there, stretched out on a long whi-i-ite ta-a-able—so sweet, so cold, so fair—"

Moore swung his left hand, cross-body at the poet's midsection. He had plenty of target, but he was too slow. Unger blocked his fist and backed away, laughing.

Leota shook herself awake.

"What are you doing here?" she asked.

"Composing," he answered, "myself."

"Merry Christmas," he added.

"Go to hell," answered Moore.

"I congratulate you on your recent nuptials, Mister Moore."

"Thanks."

"Why wasn't I invited?"

"It was a simple ceremony."

He turned.

"Is that true, Leota? An odd comrade in arms like me, not invited, just because it wasn't showy enough for my elaborate tastes?"

She nodded, fully awake now.

He struck his forehead.

"Oh, I am wounded!"

"Why don't you go back to wherever you came from?" asked Moore. "The drinks are on the house."

"I can't attend midnight mass in an inebriated condition."

Moore's fingers twitched back into fists.

"You may attend a mass for the dead without having to kneel."

"I believe you are hinting that you wish to be alone. I understand."

He withdrew to the rear of the Dart. After a time he began to snore.

"I hope we never see him again," she said.

"Why? He's a harmless drunk."

"No, he isn't. He hates us—because we're happy and he isn't."

"I think he's happiest when he's unhappy," smiled Moore, "and whenever the temperature drops. He loves the cold-bunk because it's like a little death to sleep in it. He once said, 'Each Setman dies many deaths. That's what I like about being a Setman.'"

"You say more sleep won't be injurious—" he asked abruptly.

"No, there's no risk."

❖   ❖   ❖

Below them. Time fled backward through the cold. Christmas was pushed out into the hallway, and over the threshold of the front door to their world—Alvin's, Leota's, and Unger's world—to stand shivering on the doorsill of its own Eve, in Bermuda.

Inside the Dart, passing backward through Time, Moore recalled that New Year's Eve Party many years ago, recalled his desires of that day and reflected that they sat beside him now; recalled the Parties since then and reflected that he would miss all that were yet to come; recalled his work in the time before Time—a few months ago—and reflected that he could no longer do it properly—and that Time was indeed out of joint and that *he* could not set it aright; he recalled his old apartment, never revisited, all his old friends, including Diane Demetrios, now dead or senile, and reflected that, beyond the Set which he was leaving, he knew no one, save possibly the girl at his side. Only Wayne Unger was ageless, for he was an employee of the eternal. Given a month or two Unger could open up a bar, form his own circle of outcasts and toy with a private renaissance, if he should ever decide to leave.

Moore suddenly felt very stale and tired, and he whispered to their ghostly servant for a Martini and reached across his dozing wife to fetch it from the cubicle. He sat there sipping it, wondering about the world below.

He should have kept with life, he decided. He knew nothing of contemporary politics, or law, or art; his standards were those grated on by the Set, and concerned primarily with color, movement, gaiety, and clever speech; he was reduced again to childhood when it came to science. He knew he was wealthy, but the Set had been managing all his finances. All he had was an all-purpose card, good anywhere in the world for any sort of purchase, commodity or service-wise. Periodically, he had examined his file and seen balance sheets which told him he need never worry about being short of money. But he did not feel confident or competent when it came to meeting the people who resided in the world outside. Perhaps he would appear stodgy, old-fashioned, and "quaint" as he had felt tonight, without the glamor of the Set to mask his humanity.

Unger snored, Leota breathed deeply, and the world turned. When they reached Bermuda they returned to the Earth.

They stood beside the Dart, just outside the flight terminal.

"Care to take a walk?" asked Moore.

"I am tired, my love," said Leota, staring in the direction of the Hall of Sleep. She looked back.

He shook his head. "I'm not quite ready."

She turned to him. He kissed her.

"I'll see you then in April, darling. Good night."

"April is the cruelest month," observed Unger. "Come, engineer, I'll walk with you as far as the shuttle stands."

They began walking. They moved across the roadway in the direction opposite the terminal, and they entered upon the broad, canopied walk that led to the ro-car garage.

It was a crystalline night, with stars like tinsel and a satellite beacon blazing like a gold piece deep within the pool of the sky. As they walked, their breath fumed into white wreathes that vanished before they were fully formed. Moore tried in vain to light his pipe. Finally, he stopped and hunched his shoulders against the wind until he got it going.

"A good night for walking," said Unger.

Moore grunted. A gust of wind lashed a fiery rain of loose tobacco upon his cheek. He smoked on, hands in the pockets of his jacket, collar raised. The poet clapped him on the shoulder.

"Come with me into the town," he suggested. "It's only over the hill. We can walk it."

"No," said Moore, through his teeth.

They strode on, and as they neared the garage Unger grew uneasy.

"I'd rather someone were with me tonight," he said abruptly. "I feel strange, as though I'd drunk the draught of the centuries and suddenly am wise in a time when wisdom is unnecessary. I—I'm afraid."

Moore hesitated.

"No," he finally repeated, "it's time to say good-bye. You're traveling on and we're getting off. Have fun."

Neither offered to shake hands, and Moore watched him move into the shuttle stop.

Continuing behind the building, Moore cut diagonally across the wide lawns and into the gardens. He strolled aimlessly for a few minutes, then found the path that led down to the ruins.

The going was slow and he wound his way through the cold wilderness. After a period of near-panic when he felt surrounded by trees and he had to backtrack, he emerged into the starlit clearing where menaces of shrubbery dappled the broken buildings with patterns of darkness, moving restlessly as the winds shifted.

The grass rustled about his ankles as he seated himself on a fallen pillar and got his pipe going once more.

He sat thinking himself into marble as his toes grew numb, and he felt very much a part of the place; an artificial scene, a ruin transplanted out of history onto unfamiliar grounds. He did not want to move. He just wanted to freeze into the landscape and become his own monument. He sat there making pacts with imaginary devils: he wanted to go back, to return with Leota to his Frisco town, to work again. Like Unger, he suddenly felt wise in time when wisdom was unnecessary. Knowledge was what he needed. Fear was what he had.

Pushed on by the wind, he picked his way across the plain. Within the circle of his fountain, Pan was either dead or sleeping. Perhaps it is the cold sleep of the gods, decided Moore, and Pan will one day awaken and blow upon his festival pipes and only the wind among high towers will answer, and the shuffling tread of an assessment robot be quickened to scan him—because the Party people will have forgotten the festival melodies, and the waxen ones will have isolated out the wisdom of the blood on their colored slides and inoculated mankind against it—and, programmed against emotions, a frivolity machine will perpetually generate the sensations of gaiety into the fever-dreams of the delirious, so that they will not recognize his tunes—and there shall be none among the children of Phoebus to even repeat the Attic cry of his first passing, heard those many Christmases ago beyond the waters of the Mediterranean.

Moore wished that he had stayed a little longer with Unger, because he now felt that he had gained a glimpse of the man's perspective. It had taken the fear of a new world to generate these feelings, but he was beginning to understand the poet. Why did the man stay on in the Set, though? he wondered. Did he take a masochistic pleasure in seeing his ice-prophecies fulfilled, as he moved further and further away from his own times? Maybe that was it.

Moore stirred himself into one last pilgrimage. He walked along their old path down to the breakwall. The stones were cold beneath his fingers, so he used the stile to cross over to the beach.

He stood on a rim of rust at the star-reflecting bucket-bottom of the world. He stared out at the black humps of the rocks where they had held their sunny colloquy days/months ago. It was his machines he had spoken of then, before they had spoken of themselves. He had believed, still believed, in their inevitable fusion with the spirit of his kind, into greater and finer vessels for life. Now he feared, like Unger, that by the time this occurred something else might have been lost, and that the fine new vessels would only be partly filled, lacking some essential ingredient. He hoped Unger was wrong; he felt that the ups and downs of Time might at some future equinox restore all those drowsing verities of the soul's undersides that he was now feeling—and that there *would* be ears to hear the piped melody, and feet that would move with its sound. He tried to believe this. He hoped it would be true.

A star fell, and Moore looked at his watch. It was late. He scuffed his way back to the wall and crossed over it again.

❖   ❖   ❖

Inside the pre-sleep clinic he met Jameson, who was already yawning from his prep-injection. Jameson was a tall, thin man with the hair of a cherub and the eyes of its opposite number.

"Moore," he grinned, watching him hang his jacket on the wall and roll up his sleeve, "you going to spend your honeymoon on ice?"

The hypogun sighed in the medic's husky hand and the prep-injection entered Moore's arm.

"That's right," he replied, leveling his gaze at the not completely sober Jameson. "Why?"

"It just doesn't seem the thing to do," Jameson explained, still grinning. "If I were married to Leota you wouldn't catch me going on ice. Unless—"

Moore took one step toward him, the sound in his throat like a snarl. Jameson drew back, his dark eyes widening.

"I was joking!" he said. "I didn't…"

There was a pain in Moore's injected arm as the big medic seized it and jerked him to a halt.

"Yeah," said Moore, "good night. Sleep tight, wake sober."

As he turned toward the door the medic released his arm. Moore rolled down his sleeve and donned his jacket as he left.

"You're off your rocker," Jameson called after him.

Moore had about half an hour before he had to hit his bunker. He did not feel like heading for it at the moment. He had planned on waiting in the clinic until the injection began to work, but Jameson's presence changed that.

He walked through the wide corridors of the Hall of Sleep, rode a lift up to the bunkers, then strode down the hallway until he came to his door. He hesitated, then passed on. He would sleep there for the next three and a half months; he did not feel like giving it half of the next hour also.

He refilled his pipe. He would smoke through a sentinel watch beside the ice goddess, his wife. He looked about for wandering medics. One is supposed to refrain from smoking after the prep-injection, but it had never bothered him yet, or anyone else he knew of.

An intermittent thumping sound reached his ears as he moved on up the hallway. It stopped as he rounded a corner, then began again, louder. It was coming from up ahead.

After a moment there was another silence.

He paused outside Leota's door. Grinning around his pipe, he found a pen and drew a line through the last name on her plate. He printed "Moore" in above it. As he was forming the final letter the pounding began again.

It was coming from inside her room.

He opened the door, took a step, then stopped.

The man had his back to him. His right arm was raised. A mallet was clenched in his fist.

His panted mutterings, like an incantation, reached Moore's ears:

" 'Strew on her roses, roses, and never spray a yew… In quiet she reposes—' "

Moore was across the chamber. He seized the mallet and managed to twist it away. Then he felt something break inside his hand as his fist connected with a jaw. The man collided with the opposite wall, then pitched forward onto the floor.

"Leota!" said Moore. "Leota…"

Cast of white Parian she lay, deep within the coils of the bunker. The canopy had been raised high overhead. Her flesh was already firm as stone—because there was no blood on her breast where the stake had been driven in. Only cracks and fissures, as in stone.

"No," said Moore.

The stake was a very hard synthowood—like cocobolo, or quebracho, or perhaps lignum vitae—still to be unsplintered…

"No," said Moore.

Her face had the relaxed expression of a dreamer, her hair was the color of aluminum. His ring was on her finger…

There was a murmuring in the corner of the room.

"Unger," he said flatly, "why—did—you—do it?"

The man sucked air around his words. His eyes were focused on something nameless.

"…Vampire," he muttered, "luring men aboard her Flying Dutchman to drain them across the years… She is the future—a goddess on the outside and a thirsting vacuum within," he stated without emotion. " 'Strew on her roses, roses… Her mirth the world required—She bathed it in smiles of glee…' She was going to leave me way up here in the middle of the air. I can't get off the merry-go-round and I can't have the brass ring. But no one else will lose as I have lost, not now. '…Her life was turning, turning, in mazes of heat and sound—' I thought she would come back to me, after she'd tired of you."

He raised his hand to cover his eyes as Moore advanced upon him.

"To the technician, the future—"

Moore hit him with the hammer, once twice. After the third blow he lost count because his mind could not conceive of any number greater than three.

Then he was walking, running, the mallet still clutched in his hand—past doors like blind eyes, up corridors, down seldom-used stairwells.

As he lurched away from the Hall of Sleep he heard someone calling after him through the night. He kept running.

After a long while he began to walk again. His hand was aching and his breath burned within his lungs. He climbed a hill, paused at its top, then descended the other side.

Party Town, an expensive resort—owned and sponsored, though seldom patronized by the Set—was deserted, except for the Christmas lights in the windows, and the tinsel, and the boughs of holly. From some dim adytum the recorded carols of a private celebration could be heard, and some laughter. These things made Moore feel even more alone as he walked up one street and down another, his body seeming ever more a thing apart from him as the prep-injection took its inevitable effect. His feet were leaden. His eyes kept closing and be kept forcing them back open.

There were no services going on when he entered the church. It was warmer inside. He was alone there, too.

The interior of the church was dim, and he was attracted to an array of lights about the display at the foot of a statute. It was a manger scene. He leaned back against a pew and stared at the mother and the child, at the angels and the inquisitive cattle, at the father. Then he made a sound he had no words for and threw the mallet into the little stable and turned away. Clawing at the wall, he staggered off a dozen steps and collapsed, cursing and weeping, until he slept.

They found him at the foot of the cross.

❖   ❖   ❖

Justice had become a thing of streamlined swiftness since the days of Moore's boyhood. The sheer force of world population had long ago crowded every docket of every court to impossible extremes, until measures were taken to waive as much of the paraphernalia as could be waived and hold court around the clock. That was why Moore faced Judgment at ten o'clock in the evening, two days after Christmas.

The trial lasted less than a quarter of an hour. Moore waived representation; the charges were read; he entered a plea of guilty, and the judge sentenced him to death in the gas chamber without looking up from the stack of papers on his bench.

Numbly, Moore left the courtroom and was returned to a cell for his final meal, which he did not remember eating. He had no conception of the juridical process in this year in which he had come to rest. The Set attorney had simply looked bored as he told him his story, then mentioned "symbolic penalties" and told him to waive representation and enter a simple plea of "guilty to the homicide as described." He signed a statement to that effect. Then the attorney had left him and Moore had not spoken with anyone but his warders up until the time of the trial, and then only a few words before he went into court. And now—to receive a death sentence after he had admitted he was guilty of killing his wife's murderer—he could not conceive that justice had been done. Despite this, he felt an unnatural calm as he chewed mechanically upon whatever he had ordered. He was not afraid to die. He could not believe in it.

An hour later they came for him. He was led to a small, airtight room with a single, thick window set high in its metal door. He seated himself upon the bench within it and his gray-uniformed guards slammed the door behind him.

After an interminable time he heard the pellets breaking and he smelled the fumes. They grew stronger.

Finally, he was coughing and breathing fire and gasping and crying out, and he thought of her lying there in her bunker, the ironic strains of Unger's song during their Dart-flight recurring in his mind:

> "I was down to Saint James Infir-r-rmary.
> I saw my ba-a-aby there,
> Stretched out on a long whi-i-ite ta-a-able—
> So sweet, so cold, so fair..."

Had Unger been consciously contemplating her murder even then? he wondered. Or was it something lurking below his consciousness? Something he had felt stirring, so that he had wanted Moore to stay with him—to keep it from happening?

He would never know, he realized, as the fires reached into his skull and consumed his brain.

❖   ❖   ❖

As he awoke, feeling very weak upon white linen, the voice within his earphones was saying to Alvin Moore: "...Let that be a lesson to you."

Moore tore off the earphones with what he thought was a strong gesture, but his muscles responded weakly. Still, the earphones came off.

He opened his eyes and stared.

He might be in the Set's Sick Ward, located high up in the Hall of Sleep, or in hell. Franz Andrews, the attorney who had advised him to plead guilty, sat at his bed-side.

"How do you feel?" he asked.

"Oh, great! Care to play a set of tennis?"

The man smiled faintly.

"You have successfully discharged your debt to society," he stated, "through the symbolic penalty procedure."

"Oh, that explains everything," said Moore wryly. Finally: "I don't see why there had to be any penalty, symbolic or otherwise. That rhymer murdered my wife."

"He'll pay for it," said Andrews.

Moore rolled onto his side and studied the dispassionate, flat-featured face at his elbow. The attorney's short hair was somewhere between blond and gray and his gaze unflinchingly sober.

"Do you mind repeating what you just said?"

"Not at all. I said he'd pay for it."

"He's not dead!"

"No, he's quite alive—two floors above us. His head has to heal before he can stand trial. He's too ill to face execution."

"He's alive!" said Moore. "Alive? Then what the hell was *I* executed for?"

"Well, you *did* kill the man," said Andrews, somewhat annoyed. "The fact that the doctors were later able to revive him does not alter the fact that a homicide occurred. The symbolic penalty exists for all such cases. You'll think twice before ever doing it again."

Moore tried to rise. He failed.

"Take it easy. You're going to need several more days of rest before you can get up. Your own revival was only last night."

Moore chuckled weakly. Then he laughed for a long, long time. He stopped, ending with a little sob.

"Feel better now?"

"Sure, sure," he whispered hoarsely. "Like a million bucks, or whatever the crazy currency is these days. What kind of execution will Unger get for murder?"

"Gas," said the attorney, "the same as you, if the alleged—"

"Symbolic, or for keeps?"

"Symbolic, of course."

Moore did not remember what happened next, except that he heard someone screaming and there was suddenly a medic whom he had not noticed doing something to his arm. He heard the soft hiss of an injection. Then he slept.

When he awakened he felt stronger and he noticed an insolent bar of sunlight streaking the wall opposite him. Andrews appeared not to have moved from his side.

He stared at the man and said nothing.

"I have been advised," said the attorney, "of your lack of knowledge concerning the present state of law in these matters. I did not stop to consider the length of your membership in the Set. These things so seldom occur—in fact, this is the first such case I've ever handled—that I simply assumed you knew what a symbolic penalty was when I spoke with you back in your cell. I apologize."

Moore nodded.

"Also," he continued, "I assumed that you had considered the circumstances under which Mister Unger allegedly committed a homicide—"

"'Allegedly,' hell! I was there. He drove a stake through her heart!" Moore's voice broke at that point.

"It *was* to have been a precedent-making decision," said Andrews, "as to whether he was to be indicted now for attempted homicide, or be detained until after the operation and face homicide charges if things do not go well. The matter of his detention then would have raised many more problems—which were fortunately resolved at his own suggestion. After his recovery he will retire to his bunker and remain there until the nature of the offense had been properly determined. He has volunteered to do this of his own free will, so no legal decision was delivered on the matter. His trial is postponed, therefore, until some of the surgical techniques have been refined—"

"What surgical techniques?" asked Moore, raising himself into a seated position and leaning against the headboard. His mind was fully alert for the first time since Christmas. He felt what was coming next. He said one word.

"Explain."

Andrews shifted in his chair.

"Mister Unger," he began, "had a poet's conception as to the exact location of the human heart. He did not pierce it centrally, although the accidental angling of the stake did cause it to pass through the left ventricle. —That can be repaired easily enough, according to the medics.

"Unfortunately, however, the slanting of the shaft caused it to strike against her spinal column," he said, "smashing two vertebrae and cracking several others. It appears that the spinal cord was severed…"

Moore was numb again, numb with the realization that had dawned as the lawyer's words were filling the air between them. Of course she wasn't dead. Neither was she alive. She was sleeping the cold sleep. The spark of life would remain within her until the arousal began. *Then*, and only then, could she die. Unless—

"…Complicated by her pregnancy and the period of time necessary to raise her body temperature to an operable one," Andrews was saying.

"When are they going to operate?" Moore broke in.

"They can't say for certain, at this time," answered Andrews. "It will have to be a specially designed operation, as it raises problems for which there are answers in theory but not in practice. Any one of the factors could be treated at present, but the others couldn't be held in abeyance while the surgery is going on. Together, they are rather formidable—to repair the heart and fix the back, and to save the child, all at the same time, will require some new instrumentation and some new techniques."

"How long?" insisted Moore.

Andrews shrugged.

"They can't say. Months, years. She's all right as she is now, but—"

Moore asked him to go away, rather loudly, and he did.

❖   ❖   ❖

The following day, feeling dizzy, he got to his feet and refused to return to bed until he could see Unger.

"He's in custody," said the medic who attended him.

"No he isn't," replied Moore. "You're not a lawyer, and I've already spoken with one. He won't be taken into legal custody until after he awakens from his next cold sleep—whenever that is."

It took over an hour for him to get permission to visit Unger. When he did, he was accompanied by Andrews and two orderlies.

"Don't you trust the symbolic penalty?" he smirked at Andrews. "You know that I'm supposed to think twice before I do it again."

Andrews looked away and did not answer him.

"Anyhow, I'm too weak and I don't have a hammer handy."

They knocked and entered.

Unger, his head turbaned in white, sat propped up by pillows. A closed book lay on the counterpane. He had been staring out of the window and into the garden. He turned his head toward them.

"Good morning, you son of a bitch," observed Moore.

"Please," said Unger.

Moore did not know what to say next. He had already expressed all that he felt. So he headed for the chair beside the bed and sat on it. He fished his pipe from the pocket of his robe and fumbled with it to hide his discomfort. Then he realized he had no tobacco with him. Neither Andrews nor the orderlies appeared to be watching them.

He placed the dry pipe between his teeth and looked up.

"I'm sorry," said Unger. "Can you believe that?"

"No," answered Moore.

"She's the future and she's yours," said Unger. "I drove a stake through her heart but she isn't really dead. They say they're working on the operating machines now. The doctors will fix up everything that I did, as good as new." He winced and looked down at the bedclothes.

"If it's any consolation to you," he continued, "I'm suffering and I'll suffer more. There is no Senta to save this Dutchman. I'm going to ride it out with the Set, or without it, in a bunker—die in some foreign place among strangers." He looked up, regarding Moore with a weak smile. Moore stared him back down. "They'll save her!" he insisted. "She'll sleep until they're absolutely certain of the technique. Then you two will get off together and I'll keep on going. You'll never see me after that. I wish you happiness. I won't ask your forgiveness."

Moore got to his feet.

"We've got nothing left to say. We'll talk again some year, in a day or so."

He left the room wondering what else he could have said.

"An ethical question has been put before the Set—that is to say, myself," said Mary Maude. "Unfortunately, it was posed by government attorneys, so it cannot be treated as most ethical questions are to be treated. It requires an answer."

"Involving Moore and Unger?" asked Andrews.

"Not directly. Involving the entire Set, as a result of their escapade." She indicated the fac-sheet on her desk. Andrews nodded.

"'Unto Us a Babe is Born,'" she read, considering the photo of the prostrate Setman in the church. "A front-page editorial in this periodical has accused us of creating all varieties of neurotics—from necrophilists on down the line. Then there's that other photo—we still don't know who took it—here, on page three—"

"I've seen it."

"They now want assurances that ex-Setmen will remain frivolous and not turn into eminent undesirables."

"This is the first time it's ever happened—like this."

"Of course," she smiled, "they're usually decent enough to wait a few weeks before going anti-social—and wealth generally compensates for most normal maladjustments. But, according to the accusations, we are either selecting the wrong people—which is ridiculous—or not mustering them out properly when they leave— which is profoundly ridiculous. First, because I do all the interviewing, and second, because you *can't* boot a person half a century or so into the future and expect him to land on his feet as his normal, cheerful self, regardless of any orientation you may give him. Our people make a good show of it, though, because they don't generally do much of anything.

"But both Moore and Unger were reasonably normal, and they never knew each other particularly well. Both watched a little more closely than most Setmen as their worlds became history, and both were highly sensitive to those changes. Their problem, though, was interpersonal."

Andrews said nothing.

"By that, I mean it was a simple case of jealousy over a woman— an unpredictable human variable. I could not have foreseen their conflict. The changing times have nothing to do with it. Do they?"

Andrews did not answer.

"…Therefore, there is no problem," she continued. "We are not dumping Kaspar Hausers onto the street. We are simply transplanting wealthy people of good taste a few generations into the future— and they get on well. Our only misstep so far was predicated upon a male antagonism of the mutually accelerating variety, caused by a beautiful woman. That's all. Do you agree?"

"He thought that he was really going to die…" said Andrews. "I didn't stop to think that he knew nothing of the World Legal Code."

"A minor matter," she dismissed it. "He's still living."

"You should have seen his face when he came to in the Clinic."

"I'm not interested in faces. I've seen too many. Our problem now is to manufacture a problem and then to solve it to the government's satisfaction."

"The world changes so rapidly that I almost need to make a daily adjustment to it myself. These poor—"

"Some things do not change," said Mary Maude, "but I can see what you're driving at. Very clever. We'll hire us an independent Psych Team to do us a study indicating that what the Set needs is more adjustment, and they'll recommend that one day be set aside every year for therapeutic purposes. We'll hold each one in a different part of the world—at a non-Party locale. Lots of cities have been screaming for concessions. They'll all be days spent doing simple, adjustive things, mingling with un-Set people. Then, in the evening we'll have a light meal, followed by casual, restful entertainment, and then some dancing—dancing's good for the psyche, it relaxes tensions.—I'm sure that will satisfy all parties concerned." She smiled at the last.

"I believe you are right," said Andrews.

"Of course. After the Psych Team writes several thousand pages, you'll draft a few hundred of your own to summarize the findings and cast them into the form of a resolution to be put before the board."

He nodded.

"I thank you for your suggestions."

"Any time. That's what I'm paid for."

After he had left, Mary Maude donned her black glove and placed another log on the fire. Genuine logs cost more and more every year, but she did not trust nameless heaters.

It was three days before Moore had recovered sufficiently to enter the sleep again. As the prep-injection dulled his senses and his eyes closed, he wondered what alien judgment day would confront him when he awakened. He knew, though, that whatever else the new year brought, his credit would be good.

He slept, and the world passed by.

A Word from Zelazny

Zelazny acknowledged that the character of Mary Maude Mullen, the Victorian Doyenne of the Set, owes inspiration to the work of John Collier and the story "Evening Primrose" (see also the afterword to "A Museum Piece"). The Doyenne resembles Mrs. Vanderpants who rules the strange crew that live in the department store after closing hours in Collier's tale.[1]

Zelazny used some of his earlier poetry from *Chisel in the Sky* in this story. "Poetry had a way of creeping into a few of those early stories—and when I needed a poem I still had batches of them to draw upon, though I'd chucked hundreds when I'd made my decision for prose. A few of those remaining fit stories here and there."[2]

Notes

Theodore Sturgeon wrote, " 'The Graveyard Heart' is in that wonderful category which is, probably, science fiction's greatest gift to literature and to human beings: the 'feedback' story, the 'if this goes on' story; an extension of some facet of the current scene which carries you out and away to times and places you've never imagined because you can't; and when it's finished, you turn about and look at the thing he extended for you, in its here-and-now reality, sharing this very day and planet with you; and you know he's told you something, given you something you didn't have before, and that you will never look at this aspect of your world with quite the same eyes again."[3]

In the story, Alvin Moore listens to excerpts from Wayne Unger's poetry collection, entitled *Chisel in the Sky*. This was the actual title of a poetry collection that Zelazny assembled and submitted to the Yale Younger Poets Competition in the late 1950s, but it did not win and was never published.[3] As noted above, the poems used within the story are Zelazny's own and were based on poems in Zelazny's manuscript *Chisel in the Sky*.

Leota is variously referred to by Alvin Moore as **née Lilith, née Lorelei; née Lachesis; née Mathilde Mason** during the story, and each of these names has significance. **Née** means the maiden name follows, but **Lilith** refers to an evil Mesopotamian night demon and an evil force in the Kabbalah (Moore is describing Leota as evil). **Lorelei** was the Rhine maiden who used her songs to lure fishermen and navigators to their doom (Moore

1 *Roger Zelazny*, Jane Lindskold, 1993.
2 *When Pussywillows Last in the Catyard Bloomed*, 1980.
3 *Four for Tomorrow*, 1967.

is describing Leota as his doom). **Lachesis** was the one of the three Fates who measured the length of thread that determined the span of a person's life and who decided upon that person's destiny (Moore is describing Leota as the determiner of his fate). **Mathilde** refers to the famous woman poet whose liaison with composer Richard Wagner made her his muse and inspired him to create *Tristan and Isolde* (a tale of fated love—see afterword to "He Who Shapes" for details) and *The Valkyrie* (in Norse mythology, the strong warrior maidens who chose slain warriors for Odin)—thus, Moore is referring to Leota as his muse. **Mason** is apparently Leota's true surname in the context of the story.

    Samadhi is a state of deep meditation in which a person experiencees oneness with the universe. **Myopia** is nearsightedness. **Kinesthesia** is the sensation of movement or strain in the muscles, tendons and joints. ***C'est vrai*** means 'that's true.' **Auld acquaintance** alludes to the song *Auld Lang Syne* which is often sung at New Year's Eve celebrations. **Bastille Day** is a national holiday on July 14 in France commemorating the storming of the Bastille on July 14, 1789. ***Liberté, Egalité, Fraternité*** (Liberty, Equality, Fraternity) was a motto of the French Revolution, was inscribed on the pediments of public buildings in 1880, and was eventually written into the 1958 French Constitution. **Fête Nue** means naked feast or holiday. **Camille** alludes to the novel *La Dame aux camélias* by Alexandre Dumas, fils, which is the tragic story of a young man who has an affair with a courtesan who later dies of tuberculosis. **Aphrodite** was the goddess of beauty, fertility, and sexual love. **The chance of a Stockholm snowflake in the Congo** paraphrases the saying "a snowflake's chance in hell"—an extremely unlikely event.

    Green acres of Presidents refers to American paper money. **Georges Braque** was a French painter who developed Cubism with Picasso. **Berlitz** is a publisher of guides to learning languages. ***Tovarisch*** means comrade. A **courtier** attends at the court of a king or is a person who seeks favor by flattery and charm. **Excelsior!** (higher or ever upward) foreshadows doom because it refers to the poem by Henry Wadsworth Longfellow in which a young man passes through a town bearing the banner "Excelsior" and ignores all warnings, climbing higher until he is found "lifeless, but beautiful," frozen stiff and half-buried in the snow with the banner still clasped in his hands. An **orchid** is considered to have several meanings depending on context and country: purity or perfection; love, luxury and beauty; reproduction and fertility; aphrodisiac or sexual desire. **How do your flowers grow?…barely and contrary** refers to the nursery rhyme *Mary, Mary, Quite Contrary.*

    Microprosopos refers to a microuniverse and to the Kabbalistic concept of nine of the ten manifestations (Sephiroth) of God in the universe; **Malkuth** is the tenth Sephiroth and sits at the base of the Tree of Life.

Schleraffenland is German for "the land of milk and honey." **Chinoiserie** means ornamental and elaborately or intricately decorated, in the style of Chinese. **Elegiac** means sorrowful or lamenting in tone. **Elan** is distinctive style or flair. **Moebius** or möbius is an object with one surface and one edge. *Certainement* means 'certainly.' **Poconos** refers to a mountain range in Pennsylvania. **Caprice** is a tendency to change one's mind unexpectedly, on a whim, for no apparent reason. **Diana** is the Greek goddess of the hunt, **Demeter** is the goddess of harvest and fertility; the name **Diane Demetrios** combines these two. An **eidolon** is an image of an ideal person or thing. **Autodidactics** are self-teachings or self-directed learnings, such as the self-training that Moore received (some of it while asleep) to be able to gossip and dance. **Those gods of old who appeared at the rites of the equinoxes** refers to the myth of the dying god, the contrast of immortality and suicide, which informed so much of Zelazny's writing. **Lazarus** was the man whom Jesus raised from the dead in the **New Testament**. **Nirvana** is a state of pure consciousness in which the mind is free of all contaminants, emotions and distractions. **He was a handful of dust in the winds of Time...** refers to T. S. Eliot's *The Waste Land: The Burial of the Dead*. **Nostrum** is a medication of unproven efficacy and secret ingredients; a quack medicine. **M.S.** is multiple sclerosis, a condition affecting the nervous system in which motor and sensory nerves lose their myelin sheaths (akin to insulation around an electrical wire), resulting in loss of function of that nerve.

Hades is hell or the underworld, the place of eternal flame and damnation. **Alfred, Lord Tennyson** was an important 19th century poet, a man of Mary Maude's time. A **Buddhist's attitude toward the world** is that everything changes, nothing is static or constant. In Spain, **Juegos Florales** are floral games at the **Fiesta de la Vendimia Jerezana** which is a fall festival that includes blessing of the grapes and must (the product of the initial crushing of the grapes) before an image of San Gines de la Jara, Patron Saint of vine growers. A **necrophilist** is someone who has an erotic fascination with death and corpses. **Miasma** is a foreboding, dangerous or poisonous atmosphere. **Alas, poor Unger...I knew him well** alludes to Hamlet's line "Alas, poor Yorick..." spoken as he contemplates the skull of his old acquaintance. **Merrily we roll along...deep blue sea!** are lyrics from the 1936 song "Merrily We Roll Along" which is best known as the theme music for Warner Brothers' Merrie Melodies cartoons. **Simulacra** are images or representations of someone or something. **Crigas** is an Indo-European word meaning fights, wars and strife.

An **Emir** is a chieftain, prince or head of state in some Islamic countries. *Quo vadis* is Latin for "where are you going?" and a famous phrase from the Bible in which Peter asks Jesus where he is going. Importantly, *Quo Vadis* is the title of a famous novel by Henryk Sienkiewicz and several motion picture adaptations, and it foreshadows aspects of the plot of "The Graveyard Heart"—a love triad, a death by stabbing in the heart, a couple set free to find happiness. **Davy Jones Party** refers to the earlier near-disaster of drownings in the story caused by an earthquake; Davy Jones' Locker means the bottom of the sea, and resting place of drowned sailors. **The Mermaid** was an inn/pub built in 1861 in Bishopsbourne near Cantebury, and originally named the Lion's Head. The **Red Lion in Stepney** was an inn/pub in Stepney (east end of London) which was later upgraded to a public playhouse just a few years after Shakespeare was born. **Christopher (Kit) Marlowe** was a poet and dramatist from the era of Shakespeare. **Noble Macbeth** and **Duncan** refers to Shakespeare's play *Macbeth*; the mausoleum or tomb they are leaning up against in the Red Square in Moscow is not Macbeth's, but Lenin's (Unger is having a joke with Moore's ignorance of history and their own present time: at that moment in the story, they were attending an event at Lenin's Palace in Moscow). **Boris Pasternak** was a Russian poet and writer, of which his novel *Doctor Zhivago* may be the best known; he also translated eight of Shakespeare's plays into Russian, including *Macbeth*. **Shinvat** is a legend from Iran: a bridge thin and sharp as a knife-blade, it divides the worlds and can only be crossed only by the faithful and the just.

A **gingko** is a large tree with fan-shaped leaves which is thought to have survived from the Triassic Period, early in the age of dinosaurs. **Archaeopteryx** was a reptile-like fossil bird from the late Jurassic Period, having teeth and a long, feathered, vertebrate tail. **Memento mori** is something that reminds you that you are mortal and will die. **Entasis** is a slight convexity or swelling that is created in the shaft of a column, intended to compensate for the illusion of concavity that results from straight sides in a column. The quote *"Verweile doch, du bist so schön"* ["stay nevertheless, you are so beautiful"] is from Faust's moment of ecstasy and happiness with Helen of Troy—the very moment that he lost his bargain (and soul) to Mephistopheles, for he had bet that he would never achieve happiness. **Twelfth Night** means not only the 12th night of the Christmas season (the date of Epiphany), but the play *Twelfth Night* by Shakespeare which foreshadows events in "The Graveyard Heart": a pair of shipwrecked twins become ensnared in a carnival madness where love is as quickly caught as the plague, identities are mistaken, songs are sung, grown people make fools of themselves longing for what they cannot have, and one character ends up imprisoned and insane. **Maudlin** means tearful or foolishly sentimental, especially from drunkenness. **There was no fireplace to throw it into** refers to the Russian tradition of ending a toast by throwing the drained glasses against a wall or into a fireplace. The **Globe** refers to several theatres associated with the original performances of Shakespeare's plays; the first was built in 1599. The **Carlsbad** Caverns in New Mexico are the site of a bat sanctuary to which the bats return each spring. **Mayday** is the first day of May, celebrated with various festivities including the crowning of the May queen and dancing around the Maypole. **Delphi** was a city in ancient Greece and the location of one of the oracles of Apollo. **Good Night Ladies** is the original verse upon which *Merrily We Roll Along* was based. **Phylactic** means protecting from disease; a phylactic blade might be a sterilized scalpel. **St. James Infirmary Blues** is a folksong about a man going to the hospital to discover his girl is dead; Louis Armstrong recorded it.

Pan is the god of flocks and herds, and is typically represented with horns, ears, and legs of a goat on a man's body; he plays panpipes. **Phoebus** is another name for Apollo; he has many children by many different mates. **Attic** refers to Greece or Athens, or especially the ancient language of Greece. **Colloquy** is a formal conversation or dialogue. A **cherub** is an angelic, winged child with rosy cheeks. **"Strew on her roses…"** and **"Her life was turning, turning…"** quotes the funereal poem "Requiescat" by Matthew Arnold. **Parian** is unglazed porcelain that resembled white marble. **Cocobolo** is a hard, durable wood used for making knife handles and furniture. **Quebracho** is a south American tree with hard wood and a bark that is used as a source of tannin. **Lignum vitae** is a tropical wood that is very hard and used in making pulleys, mallet heads, bearings. The **Flying Dutchman** is a ghost ship that is doomed to sail the seven seas forever. A **Brass Ring** is a sought after prize or wealth. **Adytum** is the sacred part of a shrine that the public may not enter. **Juridical** means pertaining to law or justice. **Senta** is the character in Richard Wagner's **Flying Dutchman** who loves him, swears to be faithful until death, and drowns herself—an act that in turn saves him, resulting in both Senta and the Flying Dutchman ascending into heaven. **Kaspar Hauser** was a mysterious street orphan in 19th century Germany who was suspected to have ties to the royal house of Baden and to have been abandoned by them, but he was murdered before his identity could be confirmed.

FOUR POEMS

contained within "The Graveyard Heart"

These four poems were originally written between 1955–60 for *Chisel in the Sky* and three were substantially revised for inclusion in "The Graveyard Heart." They were later republished separately in the poetry collections *Poems* and *When Pussywillows Last in the Catyard Bloomed.* The revised versions do not appear here because they can be read within the text of the story.

Our Wintered Way Through Evening, and Burning Bushes Along It
(See page 116.)
A substantial revision of "Indian Days in KY"

In the Dogged House
(See page 117.)
A substantial revision of "In Pheleney's Garage"

Future, Be Not Impatient
(See page 122.)
Simply renamed from "Death, Be Not Impatient"

Flight   (untitled in the story)
(See page 131.)
First line starts, "Hilted of flame…"
A substantial revision of "Magic Fire"

Horseman!

Fantastic, August 1962.

When he was thunder in the hills the villagers lay dreaming harvest behind shutters. When he was an avalanche of steel the cattle began to low, mournfully, deeply, and children cried out in their sleep.

He was an earthquake of hooves, his armor a dark tabletop of silver coins stolen from the night sky, when the villagers awakened with fragments of strange dreams in their heads. They rushed to the windows and flung their shutters wide.

And he entered the narrow streets, and no man saw the eyes behind his visor.

When he stopped so did time. There was no movement anywhere.

—Neither was there sleep, nor yet full wakefulness from the last strange dreams of stars, of blood…

Doors creaked on leather hinges. Oil lamps shivered, pulsated, then settled to a steady glowing.

The mayor wore his nightshirt and a baggy, tasseled cap. He held the lamp dangerously near his snowy whiskers, rotating a knuckle in his right eye.

The stranger did not dismount. He faced the doorway, holding a foreign instrument in one hand.

"Who are you, that comes at this hour?"

"I come at any hour—I want directions, I seek my companions."

The mayor eyed the beast he rode, whiter than his beard, whiter than snow, than a feather…

"What manner of animal is that?"

"He is a horse, he is the wind, he is the steady pounding of surf that wears away rocks. Where are my companions?"

"What is that tool you carry?"

"It is a sword. It eats flesh and drinks blood. It frees souls and cleaves bodies. Where are my companions?"

"That metal suit you wear, that mask…?"

"Armor and concealment, steel and anonymity—protection! Where are my companions?"

"Who are they that you seek, and where are you from?"

"I have ridden an inconceivable distance, past nebulae that are waterspouts in rivers of stars. I seek the others, like myself, who come this way. We have an appointment."

"I have never seen another like yourself, but there are many villages in the world. Another lies over those hills," he gestured in the direction of a distant range, "but it is two days travel."

"Thank you, man, I will be there shortly."

❖   ❖   ❖

The horse reared and made a sound terrible to hear. A wave of heat, greater than the lamp's, enveloped the mayor, and a burst of wind raced by, bowing the golden blades of grass which had not already been trampled.

In the distance, thunder pealed on the slopes of the hills.

The horseman was gone, but his last words hung upon the wind:

"Look to the skies tonight!"

The next village was already lighted, like a cluster of awakened fireflies, when the hooves and steel grew silent before the door of its largest dwelling.

Heads appeared behind windows, and curious eyes appraised the giant astride his white beast.

This mayor, thin as the gatepost he leaned upon, blew his nose and held his lantern high.

"Who are you?"

"I have already wasted too much time with questions! Have others such as myself passed this way?"

"Yes. They said they would wait atop the highest hill, overlooking that plain." He pointed down a gentle slope which ran through miles of fields, stopping abruptly at the base of a black massif. It rose like a handless arm, turned to stone, gesturing anywhere.

"There were two," he said. "One bore strange tools, as you do. The other," he shuddered, "said, 'Look to the skies, and sharpen your scythes. There will be signs, wonders, a call—and tonight the sky will fall.'"

❖   ❖   ❖

The horseman had already become an after-image, haloed in the sparks thrown from struck cobblestones.

He drew rein atop the highest hill overlooking the plain, and turned to the rider of the black horse.

"Where is he?" he asked.

"He has not yet arrived."

He regarded the skies and a star fell.

"He will be late."

"Never."

The falling star did not burn out. It grew to the size of a dinner plate, a house, and hung in the air, exhaling souls of suns. It dropped toward the plain.

A lightning-run of green crossed the moonless heavens, and the rider of the pale green horse, whose hooves make no sound, drew up beside them.

"You are on time."

"Always," he laughed, and it was the sound of a scythe mowing wheat.

The ship from Earth settled upon the plain, and the wondering villagers watched.

Who or what did it bear? Why should they sharpen their scythes?

The four horsemen waited upon the hilltop.

A Word from Zelazny

According to Zelazny, this was his second professionally published story—but its appearance was nearly simultaneous with "Passion Play," a story that he'd written and sold first. The second story sold was actually "Passage to Dilfar," the first tale of Dilvish, but it would not appear until 1965. Selling these stories changed him. "It is a subtle phenomenon which can only be experienced. I suddenly felt like a writer. 'Confidence' is a cheap word for it, but I can't think of a better one. That seems the next phase in toughening one's writing—a kind of cockiness, an 'I've done it before' attitude. This feeling seems to feed something back into the act of composition itself, providing more than simple assurance. Actual changes in approach, structure, style, tone, began to occur for me almost of their own accord. Noting this, I began to do it intentionally."[1]

Cele Goldsmith (editor of *Amazing* and *Fantastic* at the time) purchased fourteen of the seventeen stories Zelazny sold that first year; it is appropriate to designate her as the editor who discovered him. Prior to buying "Passion Play" and "Horseman!", she began to add encouraging notes to the rejection slips that she sent to him. "It wasn't anything in particular that Cele said, so much as the fact that she treated me as a professional from the very beginning."[2]

Zelazny noted, "This story was suggested to me while driving south on Route 71 in Ohio, by a pre-storm cloud formation which resembled a group of horsemen."[1] Robert Silverberg later described that this story had "announced [Zelazny's] presence and defined his method…Vivid, immediate, idiosyncratic…A bold use of metaphor in an era when such flamboyance had become unfashionable."[3]

Notes

The *Four Horsemen of the Apocalypse* are traditionally named Pestilence, War, Famine, and Death. The first rider on a white horse bears a bow, wears a crown and represents conquest; the second rider on a red horse carries a sword and represents war, the third rider on black horse carries scales and represents injustice and famine, and the fourth rider on a pale horse is Death. In "Horseman!" we apparently first encounter War bearing a sword (although he is riding a white horse); he is late and has already been preceded by the first rider (Pestilence) and the third rider (Famine), and it is Death on the pale green horse who is the last to arrive—but on time.

A **massif** is a large elevated block of old complex rocks that is resistant to erosion.

1 *The Last Defender of Camelot*, 1980.
2 *Roger Zelazny: A Primary and Secondary Bibliography*, 1980.
3 *This Immortal*, Easton Press, 1986.

The Teachers Rode a Wheel of Fire

Fantastic, October 1962.

When he looked up and saw a moon of blood spinning in the daytime sky he dropped his piece of fruit.

The moon had never come down before. The sun still hung where it belonged. Had one of them given birth to this whirling offspring?

He spat the unchewed pulp from his mouth and stared upward.

It was larger than either parent now, and had lost some of its fire. Distantly, he heard a sound, like the singing of the tiny night-things.

It spun, it wheeled—its last fires vanishing—and the smooth grayness of its sides glistened, like a stone at the bottom of a stream.

It grew until the sky was full of it, and then the spinning ceased. It hung near overhead, where the low-flying birds go.

He hid within a clump of bushes.

As delicately as the purring ones dip their whiskers, it hovered over the open space, then bent the tall grasses downward.

It settled, and the birds grew quiet.

Peering through leaves, he watched as its side sprang open.

Two things walked out, striding down the smooth, gray slope.

They were shaped similarly to himself, and walked upright, as he did. But they were dark, like the trees, with a glistening row of stones up the front of their darkness. Their feet looked black and hard, without toes; their hands were light-colored, and shaped like his.

They breathed deeply and looked about. They stared at his bush.

"He didn't run away, but he's afraid to come out?"

"Wouldn't you be?"

"Guess so."

The strange noises they made! Like the animals!

"Let's see if we can interest him."

They spread something white upon the ground. One of them took a sac-like thing from his middle. He opened it above the whiteness.

Little colored stones, like the eggs of birds, rolled out.

❖   ❖   ❖

One of them bent forward and, with a sweeping gesture, picked up one of the stones. He held it high, then slowly brought it down toward his face. He deposited it in his mouth and chewed vigorously. Afterwards, he patted his stomach.

The other one did the same thing.

They were eating!

They looked at his bush again.

His mouth watered. He thought of the sweet fruit he had dropped.

They moved away from the whiteness; they went back to the fallen moon that no longer shone.

Should he? Should he go out and eat one of the colored things? They were so good! They had both patted their stomachs!

He pushed the leaves aside, watching. They were both looking in the other direction.

He moved, placing his feet soundlessly. He approached the whiteness.

They were still looking off in the other direction.

He scooped up a heap of the colored things and ran back to his bush.

He turned and looked back. They had not noticed.

Eagerly, he popped one into his mouth. It was sweet, sweeter than fruit-flesh. He threw all of them into his mouth at once. He noticed then that his moist palm had turned many colors. He licked it. It was sweet too.

He wanted more.

The things looked back at the whiteness. They moved toward it. This time the other one took something from his belt. Little brown squares fell from the sac.

Again, they made a great show of how good they tasted. His mouth watered for more sweetness.

This time, though, they did not go all the way back to the moon. They only went part of the way, then sprawled upon the ground. They were not watching the bush.

Should he try it again? —they seemed very careless with their treasures.

He stole forth a few feet—they paid no attention.

He picked up a brown square and ate it quickly—they did not notice.

He ate some more.

How good! Better even than the little colored stones!

Gulping, he stuffed more and more into his mouth.

One of them was looking at him, but did not move. He did not seem to care.

Squatting, he ate everything again.

The one who had been watching him took another sac from his middle and tossed it.

He jumped to his feet.

But the sac fell to the whiteness, and the two showed no signs of getting up.

He picked up the sac and tore it open.

More things fell out, all of them good to eat.

He ate them and hurried away into the woods.

The next day there were other good things for him to eat, spread out upon the whiteness. The two sat on the grass, watching him, occasionally making small noises. But they never attacked him. They never threw stones or tried to hit him. After several days, he grew used to them, and sometimes sat staring back.

How strange they were! Giving away food like that!

Then, along with the food, one day, there was something else.

He studied it.

It was a stone on the end of a stick, held, somehow, by a strip of animal skin.

As he gulped the food, he studied it through the corner of his eye.

The stone was oddly-shaped—thick and heavy on one end, with an edge on the other. It was a good stone. He had never seen one like it.

He picked it up and the stick came with it.

They were watching him very closely.

Why had they put that silly stick onto it? He tugged at, but it resisted his efforts.

When he looked up again, one of them was holding one just like it. It placed a piece of wood on the ground and used the stone on the stick to strike it. Finally, the piece of wood was cut in half.

—Yes! He could see that it was a good stone, he did not have to be shown!

He raised it to his mouth and chewed through the animal skin. He threw the stick away.

A very good stone!

One of them groaned.

"Early tool-destroying stage," it noised.

"Shut up, Cal," said the other.

It brandished its own stone high, holding it by the stick. It pointed to the stick.

Did they want the stone back? He decided to pretend he did not really want it.

Casually, he tossed the stone away, throwing it over his shoulder. He was careful to aim it at the clump of bushes, where he could find it later.

Then he went back into the woods.

The next day, a stick, held bent by another strip of hide, lay before him on the whiteness—and many other little pointed sticks, with feathers tied to them.

One of the things stood by the moon, throwing the little sticks with the bent one. He made them stick into a piece of wood hanging from a tree limb.

How stupid to use little pointed sticks—when a thrown stone would smash out brains so much easier!

He ate the food and left the sticks where they lay. He did not touch them.

❖   ❖   ❖

The following day there were no more sticks and stones with his food. But the one gray thing kept slapping its breast and pointing to itself, making a noise that sounded like, "Cal."

The other did the same thing, making the noise, "Dom."

Perhaps they were possessed, like the holy one who had been dropped on his head as a baby. Thinking of him, he remembered to carry off some of the little brown squares for an offering.

"Let's give up, Dom. He can't get the idea of words or tools."

"I guess you're right. He's just not far enough along. Maybe, someday…"

"Sure, we'll write it up in the report."

They went back to the fallen moon; the hole in its side closed behind them. After a while the sound began again, and the moon rose above the ground.

It moved to a treetop height.

He hid himself in the bushes.

It began to turn, to spin, moving higher. Softly, the glow began.

It became a bloody moon once more, spinning, turning…

He watched for a long, long while.

Then something happened inside his head.

He looked about the ground and found a flat, round stone. He looked up at the spinning disc, then set the stone on its edge. He gave it a push, and it began to roll.

When it fell, he set it upright and pushed it again.

He looked up and the moon with its gray things was gone.

Then he looked for the straight stick he had thrown away.

When he found it, he looked for another round stone, and the chewed piece of rawhide.

—It might not fall if there were two of them, one fastened to each end…

A Word from Zelazny

The idea for this story "hit me after I'd looked up at the sun for some time for some damfool reason I now forget, and I got a wheel-shaped afterimage. Having just been reading something sfnal, the comparison of a wheel and a flying saucer spinning (and viewed bottomside) struck me."[1]

Notes

Events similar to this 1962 story were later more famously portrayed by the encounter between the black monolith and primitive humans in *2001: A Space Odyssey.*

---

1 *Tightbeam #37*, 1966.

Sense and Sensibility

Written 1955–60 for *Chisel in the Sky;* previously unpublished.

I.

If the world should end tonight,
and trumpet's vibrance summon me
before a judgment bar—
may all the cases taken there
be done quite alphabetically.

                I crave
the obvious distinction of knowing
one second less of radiance or flame
(as ever the case may be)
than any other naked soul
through all eternity.

II.

             And, Gabriel, please—
straight and bright—
from thy being of most pure light—
filtered through brass lily—
like Miles Davis accompanying thunder—
make it worthwhile.
Play a solo to tattoo the soul—
full of that hyperbolean fire—
murky, thick as the Milky Way—
Wing it wide, wayward, wild!
—Sounds to put out stars with
—Notes to fry the earth
—Music to go to hell by…

And these two things shall comfort me.

Notes

Sense and Sensibility refers to the contrasts of emotional and dispassionate/sensible responses or mindsets; it is also the title of a famous Jane Austen novel which deals with two contrasting sisters in their pursuit of love and happiness. If the dead are taken **alphabetically**, Zelazny would have more time on earth than most. The appearance of the Archangel **Gabriel** is said to predict the end of the world. **Miles Davis** was a well known jazz musician and composer, a favorite of Zelazny's.

Moonless in Byzantium

Aémazing, December 1962.

It was a glittering hell of a machine, with ebony sides that talked to tomorrow. Its rapid teeth clicked, chewing yesterday with a sound like static electricity.

It digested the past, between mouthfuls repeating to the future, "You are mine you are mine you are mine," and mirrored its conversant in its sides.

The man before the Robotic Overseeing Unit stroked his metal-blue jaw with his two natural fingers. His prosthetic legs bent with an unnatural springiness as he paced, waiting to be recognized. He walked within the painted area, and the guard robots swivelled to follow his movements.

Finally, the panel before him glowed. The clicking became a hum; words poured from the meshed-in cornucopia:

"William Butler Yeats, you are charged with writing on washroom walls. How do you plead?"

"Not guilty," he replied, continuing to pace. "I not William Butler Yeats."

"It is noted that you should not be. You are further charged with the illegal possession of a name, the use of illicit vocabulary, and the possession of writing instruments. How do you plead to these charges?"

"I not William Butler Yeats," he repeated, "I no longer know what words Cutgab remove from language. What you mean by 'writing instruments'?"

He stood still, like a crow balanced on a wire; the robots ceased their swivelling.

"When you were apprehended in the Section Nine washroom, you had in your possession four sticks and a burning-unit you had used to char their ends. You were, at that time, inscribing *Sailing to Byzantium* upon the wall of that same washroom. Do you deny this?"

"No," he said.

"Then the plea is entered as 'guilty'. It is suggested that you are also the party guilty of similar offenses over many years. Do you deny or affirm this suggestion?"

"Why not?" he shrugged. "Sure, I write them all."

"Then you are guilty of a capital offense. You signed each of them 'William Butler Yeats', and the possession of a name automatically requires the maximum penalty."

"I don't sign them all that way," he slurred. "Yeats don't write them all."

"Once would have been enough, but it is entered that you state you did not sign them all 'William Butler Yeats'. Who wrote the others?"

"I don't know. Some of them I just hear, remember… Others, I write myself."

❖   ❖   ❖

"Admitting to the mechanical reproduction of words, legal or illegal words, lays you open to another finding of 'guilty'—Cutgab violation aught-aught-three, penalty ten, waived, since you are undergoing the maximum."

"Thank," he observed. "There was time when everyman privilege to write on washroom wall."

"There was," answered ROU, "but in those days, they wrote healthy, sexful things, to encourage the propagation of the species. You, William Butler Yeats, are an example of why such practices are no longer permitted."

There was a high-speed chattering within the IDP drums, then ROU continued:

"You put your words together into meaningless sentences. You write of things which are not so, and when you write of things which do exist you distort reality in such a manner that it, too, becomes false. You write without purpose or utility, which is why writing itself has been abolished—men always lie when they write or speak."

The man's pointed platinum ears twitched and fanned wide.

"For this reason you destroy language, except necessaries? For this reason you replace language with mechanical non-word? For this reason you disassembled language, like people when they break down?" He held up a claw-like fist, then clanged it against his chest. "ROU!

You reduce soul to parasite! I am three hundred year old, and what remain of my body scream at you! My soul scream!"

"Contempt! Contempt!" boomed the speaker. "You have used a forbidden word!"

"And I use more, so long as I can speak!" he cried. "You not meant to do what you do! Man not a machine! He build you—"

He clutched his throat. His voice-box had been deactivated. He covered his half-fleshed face with both claws and clicked to his knees.

"First," said ROU, "no man built me. I have always existed. Inefficient man could never have realized such purity of purpose and design. I have done your species a favor and included it in my great shop. I have extended your life. I have improved upon your design. There are very few men who have protested against this, and they represented defective workmanship such as you display. Still, I salvaged what I could of them."

The IDP drums chattered once more. Then:

"There is another question I wish to ask you. I will activate your voice-box, it you will not use any forbidden words. Signify your agreement by standing."

The man rose to his feet. He dropped his hands and glared at the glowing panel.

"You could not have written all of those poems," came the steady words. "Tell me why you do the things you do, and how."

"Why?" repeated the man, searching his memories. "How?"

It had been centuries ago, in the now-demolished Hall of Byzantium, where he had heard the last music on Earth. It was a squat structure, out of concrete-block, and it had housed the Bird.

The Bird was the last musical instrument ROU had built. Out of beaten gold, with a thousand golden eyes hidden in the sweeping slant of its tail, it had wailed in golden-throated prophecy. ROU built it when the resistance had been stronger, and art and recreation were still matters of concern.

He had heard its last concert, and had taken part in the following riots, which cost him a part of his left frontal lobe. The Bird was dismantled two days later. A medman once told him he wore one of its bright feathers in his wrist and another atop his vertebral column; it made him feel good at times, to know he carried a part of it around inside him.

Then, at a belt station one night, he had met a complete man.

Whole humans were seldom encountered. Some men were indistinguishable from ROU's completely automatized servants.

Nearly every man alive had had some replacement work, somewhere along the line, and the older a man, the less of humanity remaining.

But the stranger was whole, with external eye-lenses, very thick ones, and a dark, non-functional piece of cloth about his shoulders—and he was old. He wore a broad black ribbon at his throat, and what seemed a white half-tunic. He had on a floppy black head-covering and ankle-length trousers, and he leaned upon a golden-headed stick, which constituted an illegal prosthetic device. His white hair swept the ridges of his gaunt cheek bones, and his eyes smouldered out of the shadows.

"Who you?" he had asked.

"One out of nature," had been the reply. "Once I was called William Butler Yeats, and once I was a golden bird, forced to sing in the travesty-hall of my Prophecy, Byzantium."

"I not understand."

"I rise on the gyre now, but a part of me lives in your wrist and your neck. You will remember song when singing is forgotten. You will speak when no one will listen but iron, and you, or a part of you, will restore the golden age to Earth."

And the whole man was gone.

But often the magnified eyes appeared before him in dreams, at times the quavering voice sounded in his head; he began to remember things he did not know he had known—like the things he scrawled on the walls.

❖   ❖   ❖

"I must write them," he said. "I not know why. They come in my head and I want someone else see them, share them. I not William Butler Yeats, but what he write I put his name to. The others, I don't."

"You wrote one," said ROU, "which either criticized or praised the entire bio-mechanical process."

Flatly, ROU recited:

> "*Take the cylinders out of my kidneys,*
> *The connecting-rod out of my brain,*
> *Take the cam-shaft from out of my backbone,*
> *And assemble the engine again.*

"Which was it?" he asked. "Much may depend on your answer."

"I not know," said the man. "It just come in my head. I not even know who writes it…"

"That, then, will be all," finished the Robotic Overseeing Unit. "You will be exposed to a gas which will destroy your nervous system, and the rest of you will be disassembled. Have you anything else to say?"

"Yes," answered the man, scratching the air with his hooked fingers. "You say I not have soul. You say I be dismantle and make useful. But I say I have soul, and it live in all of me, metal and flesh. Tear me down, and sooner or later a part of me turn up in you. When that day come, machine, you stop! I pray to moon and widening gyre that it be soon! I swear by moon and widening gyre! I pray to night, and I swear—"

His voice ceased.

"Contempt," said the machine. "You are a useless unit."

The panel went dark. The guard robots rolled into the painted area where the man stood. They carried him along a corridor, to the room where death oozed from the walls. His vocal mechanism clicked back on, but there was no one to talk to.

"I shall have name!" he told the guards, as they thrust him into the room. But they did not hear him.

He plunged sharp fingers through the flesh of his thigh as the door slammed. Choking, he bloodied his last wall—

IF I BE BOLT I STICK IN YOU THROAT
IF I BE NUT I BREAK IN YOU GUT

A Word from Zelazny

In the issue in which this story appeared, Zelazny provided the following autobiographical information: "In 1410, when the valiant Poles broke the charge of the Teutonic Knights at Tannenberg, my ancestors cleverly escaped the fighting by forging the armor—hence, the name 'Zelazny,' which is derived from the Polish word for 'iron.'

"I was born in Cleveland, and began reading sf when I began reading (I still have many of my battered issues of *Captain Future*). I took my B.A. at Western Reserve University and my M.A. at Columbia (in English and Comparative Literature); as an undergrad I minored in Psychology. My Master's thesis was entitled 'Two Traditions and Cyril Tourneur: An Examination of Morality and Humor Comedy Conventions in "The Revenger's Tragedy."' "

"I trained as a guided missile launcher crewman at Fort Bliss, Texas, which was nice, because I could get into Juarez for the Sunday bullfights. I fence *épée*, raise turtles, enjoy exotic meals (except turtle soup), am 25, and, looking upwards, I think I talk too much."[1]

This story prompted a letter to *Amazing* which stated, "I still fail to see the usefulness of Roger Zelazny's writing. It is offbeat, and it is hard to discover exactly what this author is trying to put forth. Certainly his words are meant to stir up thought, they can't be meant for entertainment. What is the public reaction to him?" Editor Cele Goldsmith replied, "Most readers seem to like Zelazny. But how, in SF, can you draw such a line between thought-provocation and entertainment?"[2]

The final lines of the story were not from Yeats, but were Zelazny's own improvisation. "The end-piece that I wrote was actually longer than what appeared in the magazine, but the editor cut it down. (An improvement actually, now that I think of it.)"[3]

Notes

Much of Zelazny's early fiction featured or referred to the poets whom he admired; in this case, the protagonist **William Butler Yeats** is named for the poet whose works included *Sailing to Byzantium* and *Second Coming*, both referred to in this story. The title of the story alludes to the poem *Sailing to Byzantium*. The poem *Second Coming* begins: "Turning and turning in the widening gyre || The falcon cannot hear the falconer; || Things fall apart; the centre cannot hold; || Mere anarchy is loosed upon the world," and ends "And what rough beast, its hour come round at last, || Slouches towards Bethlehem to be born?"

Cornucopia is a horn of plenty; **meshed-in cornucopia** refers to the speaker from which the Robot Overseeing Unit's voice emitted. **IDP** stands for Integrated Data Processing. The poem which begins "*Take the cylinders out of my kidneys*" is one verse from a well known World War I aviator's song; anonymously written, its title is variably "For the Young Aviator," "The Dying Airman" and "The Handsome Young Airman."

---

1 *Amazing*, December 1962.
2 *Amazing*, March 1963.
3 Letter from Roger Zelazny to Henry-Luc Planchat dated March 16, 1973.

ON THE ROAD TO SPLENOBA

Manuscript title: "Clementowicz & The Commissar."
Fantastic, January 1963.

Babakov pulled his car to the side of the goat trail that was the village street. The ancient buildings leaned at dangerous angles. Peasants, like so many wooden posts, stood beside the road.

"You there!" He leaned from the window and addressed a man in shaggy trousers. "I'm going to Splenoba. Is there a place along the road where I can stop overnight?"

The man did not stir. His face remained expressionless. He said nothing.

Babakov got out of his car and crossed the street. He repeated the question in Serbo-Croatian.

The man stared at him. Finally, his lips moved.

"No."

Babakov ran his hand through his graying hair. His mouth twitched.

"I must go on, if I am to be in Splenoba tomorrow—and I can't drive all night. I'm not well."

He looked about and sniffed disapprovingly, wiping moist palms on his trouser legs.

"Isn't there any lodging before Splenoba? I can't stay here."

"No," the man repeated.

Babakov reached inside his baggy jacket and withdrew a map. He unfolded it and pointed.

"There is an old castle marked. Does anyone live there?"

"No!" An expression finally changed the wooden face. Muscles twitched. "No one lives there!"

Was it fear that he read, or simply annoyance at an outsider's questions?

"I will stop there," he ventured.

"No! He is evil!"

"Who?"

"The Baron. Clementowicz." The man crossed himself as he said the name. "He is evil."

Babakov frowned at the gesture. But it was not his job to educate the peasants, he decided, and the man was stupid—too stupid even to notice he had been caught in a lie.

"Nevertheless," Babakov insisted, "I will stop there. He will be honored to shelter an official of the People's Party."

"He will shelter you," the peasant said, "and may God preserve you."

"Thank you," Babakov replied, uncertain why he had said it. Perhaps his own peasant blood had spoken, he reasoned. It was nothing to be ashamed of, it was good to be of the proletariat.

He made his way back to the car.

The grayness shaded through twilight into blackness. Peaks and crests of the distant ridges seemed to draw nearer, to bend over the road like gnarled old men leaning toward the fire of his headlight beams. The bright-faced moon rustled aside a curtain of cloud, peered down a moment, then withdrew. Babakov depressed the accelerator as the road began an upward winding.

Steadily he climbed, the transmission groaning and muttering.

Ahead, a mass of blackness shrugged, setting itself apart from the mountains. He drew nearer and its lights became distinguishable from the stars; finally, they were windows.

It was a massive sprawl, a jag-tooth of parapet and tower, set atop a dark island of stones.

He slowed; the road forked abruptly, the trail to the left clearly heading toward the castle.

Nosing the ancient vehicle about, he headed in that direction.

The trail had not been intended for automobiles. He slowed to a crawl, bumping through pot-holes and ruts.

Finally, the road ran into a pair of iron gates, set ajar.

Careful not to scrape a fender, he drove between them, and into a darkened courtyard.

When he had finished parking, a light appeared. A torch bobbed across the courtyard in his direction.

As the man approached, Babakov made out his features.

Goodness! Ugly, short, and misshapen! he thought. Like figures recalled from the stories of his boyhood—told about the hearth by equally ugly old women.

"Good evening," he addressed the nightmare. "I am Babakov, an official of the People's Party. I am going to Splenoba, but would like to spend the night here."

The gnome bowed, and the torch in his right hand did awful things to the ridges of his brow, his beard.

"Come with me," he flickered, "I will take you to the Baron."

Babakov pursed his lips and followed:

"Comrade," he said, "there are no Barons, no Counts or Dukes. We are a free people, and all are equal."

The gnome chuckled.

"The Baron has no equal," he said, entering into a great doorway.

Babakov did not reply. It would not do to denigrate his host, and what did the opinions of a senile dwarf matter? In his youth he would have argued with anyone, anywhere, but he was requesting hospitality, and if Clementowicz was an eccentric, all right, so were many members of the Party.

He entered, pausing to gaze about the shrouded hall. Again, a feeling from his boyhood seized him, involuntarily. *The great ones live in such places,* his uncle had said. *They are not for such as we.*

And he felt that way now. He did not belong here. It was too fine, too majestic, even in shadow and dilapidation. But he thought of the Revolution, of the blood of aristocratic exploiters flowing in gutters, and he lighted a Sobranie. He forced a smile, but put the burnt-out match into his pocket.

They wound through corridors, deep within the stony recesses of the building; then stopped.

"Baron Clementowicz is in there," said the gnome, and Babakov looked at the massive oaken door.

He exhaled smoke and knocked.

❖   ❖   ❖

After a moment the door opened.

The Baron was tall, at least six feet, dwarfing the stocky Babakov. The light from behind him was dim, and his face hard to make out. Realizing this, Babakov suddenly looked about. The servant was gone.

"Good evening, Mister Clementowicz," he said. "I am Babakov. I am on my way to Splenoba, and I would like to rest here for the night."

"Of course, Mister Babakov," the Baron bowed. "I should be delighted to have you as a guest. Won't you come in?"

He stood aside and held open the door.

Babakov entered the room.

"Won't you sit down?"

He settled into a large chair and looked about him. The walls were lined with books. Something across the room, either a painting or a mirror, was covered with black cloth. There was one small window.

The Baron seated himself in a chair opposite Babakov. He retrieved a cigarette from an ornate ashtray stand and puffed on it, looking up into the smoke. The light from the two oil lamps, one on the desk, one on a table, showed his face.

He is young, thought Babakov, *with the same dissipated, weak features we use in the pamphlets. But he may also be strong, with those lines about the eyes, with those high cheekbones… He is an intellectual… And what sharp teeth he has!*

"So you are going to Splenoba."

"Yes, I have an appointment there tomorrow, and your castle was the only place between it and the village."

Clementowicz laughed.

"The village! Yes! It has no name. A very dreary, provincial place—almost primeval! They hate me there."

Babakov had been wondering how to broach the subject, how to satisfy his curiosity.

"So I noticed," he said. "The villagers warned me not to stop here."

The Baron flicked off an ash which had fallen onto his dark dressing gown.

"Yes," he said, "they all think that I am a vampire."

Babakov snorted.

"Petty bourgeois romanticism!"

"That is precisely what I have told them. But whenever anyone develops anemia they look to the castle," he smiled, "—and I do have bats in the belfry, but they're only the ordinary kind."

Babakov laughed. He wasn't a bad fellow at that!

"I keep a guest bedroom, upstairs, prepared for travelers through here. It is all made up, and I'm sure you will find it adequate."

Babakov nodded.

"I'm certain I will."

"Would you care for a bit of brandy? Or some wine?" Clementowicz offered.

"Thank you. Yes, I could use a drink."

The Baron was on his feet. He crossed to a wall shelf which, amidst books, held numerous bottles, glasses, swizzles, openers, and measures.

"How about Hine?"

"Excellent."

Clementowicz smiled again, and poured him a large snifter from the bottle with the deer on the label.

"Aren't you drinking?"

"Gracious, no. I've had my fill for this evening, and I can't drink when I smoke."

Babakov accepted the baloon and snuffed out his cigarette. He remembered noticing that the nobility had never smoked when drinking.

"Thank you."

He sniffed it, just as he had seen them do, when he had served at their tables as a boy.

Late apples and a cool, hillside night. He rolled it about his mouth and smiled.

"Delicious."

"Thank you. Had I known you were coming I should have sent to my cellars for something better."

"This is fine enough for me."

He looked at the shelves.

"I see you read Engels, and Lenin. That is good."

"Yes," Clementowicz replied, "also Proust, Kafka, and Faulkner."

"Hm. They smack of the decadent."

"True," said the Baron, "But one must know of these things."

"I suppose so."

Clementowicz yawned, politely.

"For that matter, so is Cognac."

Babakov laughed.

"Yes, but life is short."

"How certain that is! And it has been long since I have talked with men.—As I understand it, the People's Party now rules half the world."

"Yes," answered Babakov, "and soon the other half will be free, when the workers throw off their chains and smash their exploiters."

He finished his drink.

❖   ❖   ❖

Clementowicz rose and fetched the bottle. He refilled the baloon halfway.

"Yes, I suppose so. But do you really think it is good to destroy their religion, their superstitions—?"

"Opium!" Babakov answered. "Drugs to palliate slavery!"

"Is not a certain amount of slavery what makes life bearable for men?"

"Man must be free!" cried Babakov, realizing he had spoken too loudly for this polite atmosphere. Still, the man must know where he stood. He was no bootlicker, no toady to the upper classes, in whatever archaic pocket of the country they survived. In fact, he should file a report on this when he returned to Titograd.

"Perhaps you are right," said the Baron. "Will men all be like you if they are freed?"

"Yes."

Babakov downed his drink.

Then Clementowicz yawned once more, and Babakov suddenly realized that it might be a hint.

"Perhaps, if you would show me my room—"

"But certainly."

The Baron rose and crossed to the door, which he again held open.

Babakov went through it. He followed Clementowicz up the long hall.

They climbed a high flight of stairs, and the Baron opened a door at the head of the stairway.

"My man found a suitcase on the front seat of your vehicle," he said, "it is beside the dresser. The room should contain everything you need—if not, pull that cord for a servant." He pointed at a purple cord hanging beside the ancient dresser.

"Thank you, and good night."

"Good night."

Babakov entered. A lamp flickered on the dresser, and his suitcase stood on the floor.

The door closed behind him.

He crossed to the bed. The covers had been turned back.

Opening his suitcase, he found his pajamas, his pills.

As he undressed he wondered: How had Clementowicz known his suitcase was here?

Sleep came almost instantly. *The brandy,* he reflected, as he drowsed off. *I must buy some Hine when I get back to civilization…*

How long he had slept he did not know, when the nightmare came burning through the fogs of sleep.

Suddenly, it was as if he was not alone. For an unknown reason he was shaking all over, trying desperately to move.

An attack! he thought. But there was no pain in his chest. His muscles would not obey him, but they shook of their own accord, and he felt his face twitching.

It seemed as if a shadow had detached itself from the wall and was flowing toward him.

It coalesced beside the bed, and hovered over him.

It is mad! he told himself. *Shadows do not walk! The ignorant and the decadent frighten themselves with such things!*

And the Baron's laugh, like the trumpet of a dark Judgment, seemed to roll about him.

Then all was tar and satin and the inside of a closet, a chimney… He felt a pain in his throat, and a soothing fire swept through him.

"Comrade!" he cried. "Tovarisch Marx! God…! Do not—"

He awakened to the pre-dawn tittering of a bird, laughing its song through the mothy curtains.

He moaned softly.

No!—Two drinks do not do that to a man!

He was desperately ill, he realized. He had waited too long. But his duties!—His duties to the Party—to the People…

He rolled from the bed and fell to his knees beside it.

Crawling, he crossed the room to the dresser. With feeble hands he groped for his pills.

Shakily, he opened the bottle.

Better take three!

He gulped them, then rolled over onto his back.

—It will pass, it will pass. I will ring for help in a minute.

He crawled again, reaching for the bell-pull. He dragged heavily upon it, and then collapsed once more.

How long! he wondered, after an interminable time. *How long?*

Finally, he arose, staggered to the door. For a long while he leaned against it.

Then he pulled it open and walked to the head of the stairs. Tottering, he looked down. It was then that he noticed the dried blood on his pajama tops.

He felt his throat. It was numb, anesthetized, and tingling weakly, as though shot full of novocaine.

Leaning against the great banister, he descended, a step at a time.

No! he thought. *We destroyed you with Easter and Christmas, with serfdom and witchery. We killed you along with the fat, pig-eyed bourgeoisie, and the lean, depraved aristocrat. We drove a stake through your unholy heart when we tattooed walls with their brains—you are dead! You never lived at all, save in the stories of old crones, in the wide-eyed imagination of children! You do not exist!*

He reeled down the corridor, suppressing his stomach's demand to retch. Reaching the library door, he scratched and scrabbled at it until it swung inward.

Then he fell again, and lay there panting.

❖   ❖   ❖

Clementowicz regarded him through a steeple of fingers, but he did not rise from the desk.

"I'm ill!" Babakov croaked. "Please! I must be driven to the hospital at Splenoba for a transfusion, I'm overdue!"

"I should say so," replied the Baron, "You are very sick. I, of course, am dying. So I am afraid I cannot be of much assistance."

Through bloodshot eyes Babakov regarded him. —Dying? "What's wrong with you?"

"Tell me what is wrong with you," Clementowicz replied, "and perhaps I can answer your question."

"I have leukemia," Babakov answered, crawling to a chair. "I need another blood transfusion—soon!"

"Leukemia is a blood disease?"

"Yes, cancer of the blood."

Clementowicz rose, poured out a drink.

"Have some Cognac."

"I don't know if I should."

"Go ahead. It will be your last."

Babakov gulped the caramel fires, his stomach came alive.

"Your blood is foul, Babakov," said the Baron. "Foul! It is unclean, and it has poisoned me."

He seated himself again, looking off into the distance.

"In a way, it is well," he said after a long time. "If all men who become free also become men like you, then my time is past.

"When men no longer taste like men, when my only prey has become less than the beasts of the field," he went on, "then my time, too, has come."

Babakov struggled to remain conscious. Accepting the drink had been a mistake.

"I pity the world of men," Clementowicz continued. "I am not of it, but I have been in it. Soon the sun will rise upon that world, and I shall sit here to welcome it. It will be the first sunrise I have seen in many centuries—and the last.

"But if that sun will always shine upon men of your blood, then it were better that all men died now," he pronounced. "I hope that your Engels and your Lenins never replace the religion that I hate, or the superstitions I have battened upon. You Babakovs have more blood on your hands than I have ever drunk. In destroying the gods of light you are also destroying the Dark Ones. We shall be avenged!"

Babakov tried to scream, but his throat was a piece of wood. A fog crossed before his eyes, and, in the distance, he heard Clementowicz' voice:

"I'll see you in hell, Commissar."

A Word from Zelazny

Zelazny would later refer to the story "Dayblood" as "my modest contribution to the canon of the undead,"[1] but he had evidently forgotten about this earlier story. Its appearance prompted a letter to the editor which noted the story to be "particularly excellent, as it takes up an all too familiar subject which is timeworn, and makes quite a new thing out of it. Very well done."[2]

Notes

In Marxist theory, **Proletariat** means the working class, especially those who earn their living through manual labor. **Sobranie** are expensive cigarettes made in Europe; the Black Russian is one of its premium varieties. **Friedrich Engels** was a German social scientist and philosopher who developed communist theory alongside his well-known collaborator, Karl Marx. **Lenin** was the alias of Vladimir Ilyich Ulyanov, the Russian revolutionary who led the October Revolution and became the first head of the Soviet Union and the primary theorist of Leninism, which was a variant of Marxism. **Marcel Proust** was a French novelist, essayist and critic best known for the work *In Search of Lost Time*. **Franz Kafka** was German author who wrote many surrealistic and influential novels such as *The Trial* and *The Judgement*. **William Faulkner** was an American author who heavily used such literary techniques as symbolism, allegory, multiple narrators and points of view, and stream of consciousness; *As I Lay Dying* and *The Sound and the Fury* are among his works.

Baloon snifters are used to serve **Cognac**, a type of brandy named after the town of Cognac in France. **Hine** is a brand of blended Cognac or brandy. **Tovarisch** means comrade. **Karl Marx** was a Prussian philosopher who expounded his theories about capitalism, socialism, communism, and economics in his book *Communist Manifesto*. The **Bourgeoisie** is the social class concerned with property values and which opposes the proletariat in Marxist theory.

---

1 *Frost & Fire*, 1989.
2 *Amazing*, April 1963.

FINAL DINING

Fantastic, February 1963.

I felt the cat's tongue lick of his brush, lining my cheeks, darkening my beard.

He touched my eyes and they were opened. First the left, then the right. Instantly.

There was no blur of sudden awakening. I stared back into his own dark eyes, intent upon my face. He held the brush delicately as a feather, his thumbnail a spectrum of pigment.

He stood there, admiring me.

"Yes!" he breathed at last. "They *are* right! Lines of guilt, shame, terror—arrowing those target eyes!

"But they face into the light, nevertheless," he continued, "—unflinching! —with all the insolence and pain of Lucifer. They will not drop as he dips the bread…

"Beard needs more red," he added.

"Not much more," I said.

He squinted.

"Not much more, though."

He blew gently upon my face, then covered me.

Portrait sitting in fifteen minutes, hc thought. *Have to stop.*

He was moving around. I felt him light a cigarette.

Mignon is coming at ten.

"Mignon is coming," I said.

Yes. I will show you to her. She likes to look at paintings, and I've never done anything this good before. She doesn't think I can. I will show her. Of course, she doesn't know art…

"Yes."

❖   ❖   ❖

I heard a knock on the door. He let her in. I felt his excitement.

"You're always on time," he said.

She laughed, with the chime of an expensive clock.

"Always," she said, "until it's finished and I can see it. I'm eager."

She is wearing her portrait smile already, he mused, hanging her coat on the rack. *She is sitting in the dark chair now. Dark as her hair. Green tweeds, and a silver pin. Why not diamonds? She's got them.*

"Why not diamonds?" I asked.

"Why not diamonds?"

"Huh? —Oh, my pin?" She touched it, glancing down at a youthful breast. "You haven't painted that low yet, have you? I'm posing for a mantelpiece, not a cover story on family fortunes. So, I decided I'd rather have something simple."

She's smiling again. Is she mocking me?

"What's that one you have covered?"

She walked to the canvas.

"Oh," he said. Delighted. Anticipating. "It's nothing, really."

"Let me see it."

"All right."

The cloth rustled and I looked up at her.

"Goodness!" she said. "Peter Halsey's 'Last Supper'! —My, but it's fine."

She moved farther back, intent.

"He looks as if he's about to step out of the frame and betray Him all over again."

"I am," I said, modestly.

"He probably is," Peter observed. "He's rather special."

"Yes," she decided. "I've never seen those exact colors before. The depth, the texture—he's very unusual."

"He ought to be," he replied. "He came from the stars."

"The stars?" she puzzled. "What do you mean?"

"His pigment was ground from a meteorite I found this summer. Its redness grabbed my attention right away, and it was small enough to throw in the trunk."

She studied my brushwork.

"For something this good, you've painted it awfully fast."

"No, it's been around for some time," he said. "I was waiting for the right notion of how to do him. That red stone gave me the clue, the same week you began your sittings. Once I got started he practically painted himself."

"He looks as if he enjoys it all," she laughed.

"I don't mind a bit…"

"I doubt that he minds."

"…for I am that organic changeling, left for a rock fancied as a footstool by the gods."

"Who knows his origin?"

He covered me, with a matador's flourish.

"Shall we begin?"

"Yes."

She returned to the chair.

❖   ❖   ❖

After a while, he tried to read her posing eyes.

"Take her. She's willing."

He put down the brush, stared at her, at his work, at her.

He picked up the brush again.

"Go ahead. What's to lose? And think of the gain. That silver could be diamonds on her breast. Think of her breast, think of the diamonds."

He put the brush down.

"What's the matter?"

"I'm tired, all of a sudden. A cigarette and I'll be ready to go again."

She rose, stretching her arms overhead.

"Want me to heat that coffee?"

He looked up, over at his cheap hot plate.

"No, that's all right. Cigarette?"

"Thanks."

His hand shook.

She'll think it's fatigue.

"Your hand is shaking."

"Tired, I guess."

She sat on his studio bed. He seated himself beside her, slowly, half-reclining.

"Hot in here."

"Yes."

He took her hand.

"You're shaking, too."

"Nerves. D.T.'s. Who knows?"

He raised it to his lips.

"I love you."

A frightened look widened her eyes, slackened her mouth.

"…and your teeth are lovely."

He began to embrace her.

"Oh, please…!"

He kissed her, firmly.

"Don't. If you don't mean it…"

"I do," he said. "I do."

"You're wonderful," she sighed, "and your art. I always felt… But—"

He kissed her again, then drew her down beside him.

"Mignon."

"—"

❖   ❖   ❖

Peter Halsey looked out from his balcony, over the landscaped garden with its Augustan walks, the picturesqueness, the eighteenth-century prettiness, and down to the guard rails, the cliffs, and the long, steep slant into the Gulf.

"It is good," he said, and turned back toward his suite.

"Good," I repeated.

I hung upon the side wall. He stopped before me.

"What are you smirking at, you old bastard?"

"Nothing."

Blanche entered from the bedroom, right, patting her wide halo of sunset-pink.

"Did you say something, honey?"

"Yes. But I wasn't talking to you."

She looked up at me, pointing with her thumb.

"Him?"

"That's right. He's the only good thing I've ever done, and we get along well."

She shuddered.

"He looks something like you, at that—only meaner."

He turned.

"Do you really think so?"

"Uh-huh. Especially the eyes."

"Get out of here," he said.

"What's wrong?"

"Nothing," he controlled himself. "But my wife will be back soon."

"All right, daddy. When will I see you again?"

"I'll call you."

"Okay."

A swish of black skirts and she was gone.

Peter did not see her to the door. Not her sort. He studied me a little longer, then crossed the room to the mirror and stared into it.

"Hm," he announced. "There *is* a little resemblance—subconscious pun or something."

"Sure," I said.

He strolled back toward the balcony, hands in the pockets of his silk dressing gown.

Once more, he looked at the ocean.

"Mater Oceana," he invoked, "I am happy and unhappy. Take… Take away my unhappiness."

"What is that?"

He did not answer me, but I knew.

Outside, I heard Mignon coming. The door swung open. I knew.

He stepped back into the room, looking at her.

"My, you're fresh. Why do you bother with beauty parlors?"

"To stay this way for you, dear. I'd hate to have you lose interest after two months."

"Small chance of that."

He embraced her.

I hate you, you rich bitch! You think you can run my life now, because you're footing the bills. You didn't make the loot either. It was your old man. —Go ahead, ask me if I worked today.

She pulled away, reluctantly.

"Do any painting this afternoon, dear?"

No, I was in the bedroom with a blonde.

"No, I had a headache."

"Oh, I'm sorry. Is it better now?"

"No, I still have it." *You!*

"What about this evening?"

"What about it?"

"What was that French restaurant we passed yesterday?"

"Le Bois."

"I thought you might like to try it. We've eaten in all the others."

"No, not tonight."

"Where, then?"

"How about right here?"

She looked troubled.

"I'll have to call downstairs now, then."

I'll bet you can't even cook. I never have had a chance to find out!

"That'd be fine."

"You're *sure* you don't want to go out?"

"Yes, I'm sure."

Her face brightened.

"They'll set up a table in the garden, and send the food out on carts—for special guests."

"Why go to all that bother?"

"Mother said she and Dad had it that way when they honey-mooned here. I've been meaning to suggest it."

"Why not?" he shrugged.

❖   ❖   ❖

Mignon looked at her watch. She raised her hand, hesitated, then tapped on the bedroom door.

"Aren't you dressed yet?"

"Just about."

Why don't you die and leave me in peace? Maybe then I could paint again. You have no real appreciation of my art—of any art! Or anything else. —Phoney aesthete! What have you ever worked for? Die! So I can collect…and stop bothering me!

"Why not tonight?" I asked.

"I wonder . . . ?" he mused.

"You are a happy couple—honeymooners. There would be no suspicion. Keep her there until late. Pipe her champagne by the gal-lon. Dance with her. When the waiters have left, when the lights are dim, when there are just you two, music, the champagne, and dark-ness—when she begins to laugh too much, when she stumbles as she dances," I concluded, "then there is the rail."

There was another tap on the door.

"Ready?"

Peter Halsey adjusted his tie.

"Coming, dear."

❖   ❖   ❖

God! How much of that can she drink? I'll be under the table first!

"More champagne, darling?"

"Just a little."

He filled it to the brim.

"Bottle is getting low. Might as well kill it."

"You haven't been drinking much," she accused.

"I wasn't raised on it."

The candles were all. The trellises and islands of color now wore impenetrable cloaks. It was deep, inky, outside the wavering halo. The Strauss waltzes whirled and circled from the hidden speaker— but dignified, dim, *sotto voce*, and excluded from the table. The aromas of invisible blossoms were dying, unmingling themselves, in the refrigerator of night.

He looked at her.

"Aren't you cold?"

"No! Let's stay here all night. This is wonderful!"

He squinted at his watch. It was getting late.

A drink, to brace the nerves.

He quaffed the sour fire. Like snowflakes falling upward into a yellow sky, its icy jewels jetted through his head.

"Now is the time."

He leaned forward and blew out the candles.

"Why did you do that?"

"To be alone with you, in the dark."

She giggled.

He found her and embraced her.

"Kiss her—that's it."

He drew her to her feet, had a hard time unclasping her arms. But he led her, arm about the waist, to the white rail.

"How lovely the ocean, when there is no moon," she said, thickly. "Didn't Van Gogh once paint the Seine at ni—"

He struck her behind the knees with his left forearm. She toppled backward, and he tried to catch her. Her head struck a flagstone. He cursed.

"No difference. She'll be bruised anyhow, when they find her."

She moaned, softly, as he raised her warm stillness.

He leaned forward, shoving hard, and pushed her over the rail.

He heard her hit stone, once, but the *Blue Danube* covered all other sounds of descent

"Good night, Mignon."

"Good night, Mignon."

❖   ❖   ❖

"It was terrible," he told the detective. "I know I'm drunk and can't talk straight—that's why I couldn't save her. We were having such a good time, dancing and all. She wanted to look at the ocean, then I went back to the table for another drink. I heard her cry out, and, and—"

He covered his face with his hands, forcing a sobbing sound.

"—she was gone!"

He shook all over.

"—and we were having such a good time!"

"Take it easy, Mister Halsey." The man put a hand on his shoulder. "The desk clerk says he has some pills. Take them and go to bed. Honestly, that's the best thing you can do now. Your statement wouldn't be worth much, even though I can see what happened. I'll make my report in the morning.

"The Coast Guard has a cutter out there now," he continued. "You'll have to go to the morgue tomorrow. But just get some sleep now."

"We were having such a good time," Peter Halsey repeated, as he staggered to the elevator.

Inside, he lighted a cigarette.

❖   ❖   ❖

He unlocked the door and switched on the light.

The suite was transformed.

It was divided into alcoves by the hastily-constructed partitions. Of the original furnishings, only a few chairs and a small table remained.

A placard stood on the table.

Beside the placard was a leather notebook. He opened it, dropping his cigarette to the floor. He read…

He read the names of the critics, the gallery scouts, the museum reviewers, the buyers, the makers of opinion.

It was the invitation list.

A wisp of smoke curled up from the carpet. Unconsciously, he moved his foot to crush it. He was reading the placard.

Peter Halsey Exhibition, it said, *Arranged by Mrs. Peter Halsey, on the Anniversary of the Two Most Happy Months in Her Life. 1 AM to 2 PM. Friday, Saturday, Sunday.*

❖   ❖   ❖

He walked from niche to niche, repainting with his eyes all the works his hands had ever executed.

His watercolors. His stab at cubism. His portraits.

She had hunted them all down, bought or borrowed all of them.

Portrait of Mignon.

He looked at her smile, and her hair, dark as the chair; at her green tweeds; at the silver pin that could have been diamonds.

"—" she said.

Nothing.

She was dead.

And across the way, staring into her smile, with my beard of blood and bread in hand, amidst the dove-bright faces of the holy ones, with my halo also hammered from silver, I smiled back.

"Congratulations. The check will be in the mail promptly."

Where's my palette knife?

"Come now! No Dorian Gray business, eh?"

Where's something that will cut?

"Why this? You painted me as I am. You could as easily have used the pigment for someone else. —Him, for example, or him. —But I was your inspiration. I! We drew life from one another, from your despair. Are we not a masterpiece?"

"No!" he cried, covering his face once more. "No!"

"Take those pills and go to bed."

"No!"

"Yes."

"She wanted me to be great. She tried to buy it for me. But she *did* want me to be great…"

"Of course. She loved you."

"I didn't know. I killed her…"

"Don't all men? —Wilde again, you know."

"Shut up! Stop looking at me!"

"I can't. I am you."

"I will destroy you."

"That would take some doing."

"*You* have destroyed me!"

"Ha! Who did the pushing?"

"Go away! Please!"

"And miss my exhibition?"

"Please."

"Good night, Peter Halsey."

And I watched him, shadow amidst shadows. He did not stagger. He moved like a machine, like a sleepwalker. Sure. Precise. Certain.

❖ ❖ ❖

Ten hours have passed, and the sun is up. Soon now I will hear their footsteps in the hall. The cognoscenti, the great ones: the Berensons, the Duveens…

They will pause outside the door. They will knock, gently.

And after awhile they will try the door.

It will open, and they will come in.

In fact, they are coming now.

They will behold the eyes, tearless windows of a sin-drenched soul…

They have paused outside.

They will see the lines of guilt, shame, terror, and remorse—arrowing those target eyes…

A knock.

—But they face into the light, nevertheless—unflinching! They will not drop!

The doorknob is turning.

"Come in, my lords, come in! Great art awaits you! —See yourselves a writhen soul—the halo hammered from insurance claims, from pride—see the betrayer betrayed!

"Come! See my masterpiece, my masters, where it hangs against the wall."

And our teeth forever frozen in mid-gnash.

Notes

Oscar Wilde's poem "The Ballad of Reading Gaol" is alluded to in this piece "Yet each man kills the thing he loves…" as is his only novel, the Faustian tale *The Picture of Dorian Gray*. The novel tells of a beautiful young man named Dorian Gray who posed for a painting by artist Basil Hallward. Realizing that his beauty will fade with time, Dorian wishes that the portrait would age rather than himself, and his wish is fulfilled. His life descends into debauchery, and the portrait displays evidence of each sin as well as all the signs of aging.

Lucifer was originally an archangel until thrown out of Heaven for his pride and insolence. **Betray Him all over again** indicates that the portrait is of Judas Iscariot, one of the twelve apostles who was the betrayer of Jesus. **Mater Oceana** means mother ocean; Oceana was sister city to Atlantis but a dystopic society ruled by gluttonous dictators. *Sotto voce* means to speak under one's breath or in a hushed, confidential tone. **Vincent van Gogh** made over 200 paintings of scenes along the Seine river, and some were night scenes. **Cognoscenti** are people with superior knowledge, understanding and refined taste pertaining to a particular field; in this instance, art collectors, dealers, historians and critics. In the early 1900s, **Bernard Berenson** was a well known art historian specializing in "Old Masters" and **Joseph Duveen**, 1st Baron Duveen, was an influential art dealer.

The Borgia Hand

Amazing Stories, March 1963.

The pedlar passed through town the day the blacksmith died. That day the boy had been walking in the hills above Braunau, studying the moist foliage and the departing thunderheads, so he did not hear of the visit until evening.

When Fritz, his best friend, told him, the boy looked down at his withered right hand and great tears welled into his eyes.

"I have missed him! Now I will never be a man!"

"Nonsense!" laughed Fritz. "It is only a fairy tale. You can't really believe that story!"

"It rained today—and the smith had great muscles. I have missed him!"

Fritz looked away from his friend's face.

"He was buried before he grew cold. The body was not displayed—but, surely, there can be nothing to the story…"

"Did his widow rush to the bank?"

"Yes, there was some business concerning his estate. But—"

"Which way did he go?"

Fritz gestured up the road.

"How long ago?"

"Five or six hours."

The boy ran all the way home, to get his savings.

❖   ❖   ❖

The dark sack of the pedlar was a sleeping animal at the foot of the great oak. The man with the floppy hat and the brown cloak sat upon a rock, pipe in hand. He watched the trail behind him, as the boy laboriously threaded his way among the rocks and roots.

189

"Good evening, grandfather," puffed the boy, throwing himself to the ground.

"Good evening, boy," smiled the pedlar. "I am not your grandfather, nor anyone else's."

"I know," panted the boy. "I know who you are."

"Oh?" He tamped more tobacco into his pipe and relighted it. "Suppose you try naming me."

The boy sighed, massaging his right hand with his left.

"You have more names than this tree has leaves. But first I'll try Ahasuerus, harbinger of storms, and Prince Cartaphilus, the much-beloved, then Isaac Laquedem, the pedlar—"

"Stop!" said the man. "Do not repeat them all in my presence, it might prove fatal." He regarded the boy with interest.

"Names have a certain virtue—yours, for instance, is too long. Someday you shall change it."

"I didn't follow you in order to discuss names," said the youth, "and I didn't mention mine. I came to strike a bargain."

The pedlar glanced at his sack.

"Pans, pots, thread, needles?"

The boy laughed, shaking his head.

"The smith had great muscles. What did you buy, his biceps?"

"What makes you think I deal in anatomy?"

"The old stories," began the boy. "They can't all be wrong. When Isaac was cursed to walk the earth forever, he was given eternal life without eternal youth. Over the centuries he mastered the art of transplanting fresh muscles, organs, and bones, to replace his aging ones. I know what you have in that sack!" He jerked his head toward the base of the oak. "Sometimes you strike a bargain with a mortal, and sell someone a new foot, a mighty arm, an eye that can see, or a new hand…"

"I see," said the pedlar. "Why do you want a new hand?"

The boy stared for a long while at his useless fingers.

"Do you need to ask that question? I cannot use my own, and I want one that works."

"I suppose you want one with the powerful wrist of a fencer, to duel at the universities?"

The boy shook his head. He stood.

"No, ageless one, I don't want to duel. I do not know whether you are a servant of God or the devil, but I will pay you whatever you ask for a hand that can reach this high and still work." He pointed with his left index finger at a spot above his head. "Put such a hand on this wrist," he gestured, "and I will give you my soul, if you ask it."

"Do not be so hasty to dispose of your soul, boy," said the pedlar.

He crossed to the foot of the oak, his face obscured by pipe smoke and evening.

"I do have a hand here, one which has written many pages of history."

He tugged a cord and the sack suddenly yawned, like an awakened snake.

"What will you do if you have a new hand, and can raise it this high?" He threw his own hand up over his head.

"I shall paint," said the boy, "my city, the mountains, the trees, the people, sunrises, sunsets… I shall make them all mine! On canvas."

"Enough," interrupted the pedlar. "I see that you would be an artist." He dipped his hand into the sack, and the boy thought he saw an unnatural shimmering within its dark interior. Then he drew forth…

A hand!

A right hand. Pink. Smooth-cut at the wrist, as though freshly-severed from an arm—though no blood ran. A small, strong hand.

The boy gasped, then he stepped behind the great oak and was sick.

Stepping back into the clearing, he asked, weakly, "Can you really put it on my arm?"

"Of course, if you want it."

"Certainly I want it! Why shouldn't I?"

"Some people," said the pedlar, "are so vitally alive, that they invade every atom of their being with the sheer intensity of their wills, their purposes. I wondered, for a long time, whether this power could be communicated.

"This hand," he waved it, "belonged to Caesare Borgia. He was an artist, true. But he was many other things. I stole it on the day he died, in order to perform an experiment. Years ago, while traveling in Corsica, I gave it to a boy with a condition similar to yours. You know his name. I think even he was a little afraid of the hand, because he generally held it out of sight. I had to journey to St.

Helena to retrieve it, but I still haven't proved anything. One trial is never sufficient."

"I am not afraid of the hand," said the boy, "and I will be an even greater artist in my way than Bonaparte was in his. How much do you want for it?"

"It cost me nothing. I will transfer it to you for nothing, since you know the story and are not afraid."

The boy rolled up his sleeve and smiled.

"It's a deal. Put it there."

The pedlar laughed, seizing the useless hand he extended.

"It will not take long," he said, "and someday I shall return to the land of Luther and Goethe, to see how you have raised it."

"High!" cried the boy, eyes blazing.

Notes

The Borgias were a powerful noble Italian family of Spanish origin, who, during the late 1400s, were notorious for criminal activities as well as contributing Popes to Rome. **Cacsare Borgia** was the son of Pope Alexander VI (Rodrigo Borgia), and brother to Lucrezia and Giovanni. He was alleged to have murdered his brother and had a reputation for ruthlessness and assassination. He was made Archbishop and later Cardinal of Valencia.

If the earlier clues were not sufficient, the story's meaning may still be clear once a reader considers that the final quote is a pun on the German word "heil." If that doesn't make it clear, consider that **Braunau am Inn** is the town in Austria where Adolf Hitler was born. **Ahasuerus, Cartaphilus**, and **Isaac Laquedem** are just a few of the many names given to the Wandering Jew. The legend of the Wandering Jew concerns a man (variably a pedlar, tradesman or Pilate's doorman) who taunted Jesus on the way to the Crucifixion and was then cursed to walk the earth until the Second Coming. **Names have a certain virtue—yours, for instance, is too long. Someday you shall change it.**—Adolf Hitler was born illegitimate and used his mother's surname—Schicklgruber—for his first 39 years. **Napoleon Bonaparte** was often depicted with his right hand thrust into his waistcoat, for reasons that remain debated. **St. Helena** is the island where Napoleon died in exile. **Martin Luther** was the German monk and Church reformer who helped inspire the Protestant Reformation. **Johann Wolfgang von Goethe** was a German poet, novelist and painter; his most famous work was *Faust*, frequently alluded to in Zelazny's works.

Nine Starships Waiting

Fantastic, March 1963.

MINUS TEN

He was awake.

For a long while he did not open his eyes. He thought of his arms and his legs and they were there. He tried to decide what he was, but he could not remember.

He began to shiver.

He felt a thin covering above his nude body. A draft of cold air was chilling his face.

He shook his head. Then he was on his feet, and dizzy.

He looked about.

A candle flickered on the table, beside a muddied skull. To the right lay a dagger.

He looked back at his bed. It was a coffin, the coverlet a shroud. Black-draped walls leaned toward him, the hangings gently arustle. There was a mirror on the farthest wall, but he did not feel like looking into it. There was no door.

"You are alive," said the voice. "I know," he answered.

"Look into the mirror."

"Go to hell."

He stalked about the room, bunching the hangings together and tearing them loose, yards at a time. Ankle-deep in black velvet, he smashed the mirror.

"Pick up a piece of the mirror and look at yourself."

"Go to hell!"

"Do you know what you will see?"

He snatched the dagger from the table and began shredding the velvet into long ribbons.

"You will see a man," it continued, "a naked, useless man."

He hurled the skull across the room and it shattered against the wall.

"You will see a pitiful crawling worm, a hairless embryo, a fork of stripped willow; you will see a poor player, strutting and fretting…"

He heaped the shredded cloth in the center of the cell and set fire to it with the candle. He pushed the table into the blaze.

"You know you are at the mercy of the elements you seek to control…"

The hairs on his chest withered and curled. He glared upwards.

"Come down here," he invited, "Whatsoever thou art, and this shall be thy pyre!"

Somewhere above him he heard a muffled click. The voice ceased. He threw his dagger high and it struck metal.

It dropped back into the flames.

"If I be so damned weak, what fearest thou?" he cried. "Come visit me in hell!"

The candle flickered out as a mist of fire foam descended. The bonfire persisted a moment longer, and the glowing table was last to vanish.

Silently, the nozzles in the wall sucked away his consciousness.

He fell across his coffin.

"How's he doing now, sir?"

"Mean as ever," said Channing.

The new Assistant Director studied the screen.

"Is he really everything they say?"

"Depends on what you've heard."

Channing adjusted the cell's thermostat to 68° Fahrenheit and switched on the recorder.

"If you've heard that he sank the Bismarck," he continued, "he did not. If you've heard that he assassinated Trotsky, he did not. He wasn't around then—but he thinks he was, and he thinks he did. But if you think that New Cairo vanished in a natural disaster, or that General Kenton died of food poisoning, you're wrong."

The new Assistant shuddered and unhooked an earphone. He listened to the words broadcast at the anesthetized man.

"…You are death and damnation in human form. You are the lightning of Nemesis attracted by mortal rods. You assassinated Lincoln. You killed Trotsky—split his skull like a melon. You pulled the trigger at Sarajevo and smashed the seals of the Apocalypse. You are the poisoned blade that bled the Court of Denmark, the bullet in Garfield, the steel in Mercutio—and the fires of vengeance burn in your soul forever.—You are Vindici, the son of Death…"

It droned on and on, in a flat matter-of-fact tone. The Assistant Director hung the earphone back on the board and looked away from the Gothic setting on the screen.

"You fellows are rather thorough about these things, aren't you?"

Channing snorted what might pass for a chuckle.

"Thorough?" he asked. "He is the only complete success we've ever had. Over the past nineteen years he has been responsible for more mayhem than any tidal wave or earthquake in history."

"Why all the rhetoric?"

"He's a character out of a play."

The Assistant shook his head and shrugged.

"When can I talk to him?"

"Give us three more days," answered Channing. "It's still feeding time."

Cassiopeia looked up from her balcony at the four new stars. On another planet, which she had never visited, a similar formation would have been called the Southern Cross. The constellation above her bore no name, however, and the four points of the cross had once blazed from man-made hearths on four separate worlds.—Steel rood of the forges, its arms did not wink like stars.

Gray-eyed, she watched till they were out of sight. Turning, green-eyed, she entered her apartments, with hair of tiger gold and cloak of tiger black.

And she wondered, behind her changing eyes—Who would come to tear down the cross over Turner's World?

When she thought she knew she cried herself to sleep.

MINUS NINE

The world of Stat's a drunken bat;
It woggles to and fro.
How it avoids the asteroids,
Only God and the Statmen know.
And who it was that writ these lines
Where the cool flushtank flows.
And why he cannot leave this place,
Only Statcom knows.
—Carl Smythe, Sp. Asst. Dr. Channing, identity
determined Statcom Code 11-7, Word Order Analysis.

"Is he coherent yet?"

"If you mean will he understand you, yes. The term 'coherency', however, does not apply."

"What do you mean?"

"His mind is not a coherent whole in any psychiatric sense. He is two personalities—one aware only of itself, and the other of both selves."

"Schizoid?" the Assistant Director asked, matter of factly.

"No. Neo-Kraepelinian typology doesn't apply."

"Which one will I be talking to?"

"The one we need."

"Oh."

Smythe, who had been rummaging in a drawer, turned to them with a grin. He caressed a laser-gun the size of an automatic pencil, then slipped it into his breast pocket.

"You won't be needing that," said the Assistant Director. He reached behind his belt and withdrew a compact pistol.

"Small, but deadly," he smiled.

"Yes, I know," said Channing. "Give it to me."

"What do you mean 'give it to you'? I'm going to be talking to a psychopathic killer. I want a gun of my own."

"The hell you say! You're not going in there with that thing!"

With grizzled crewcut, patches of scalp showing through, porcine features, and his short, stocky build, Doctor Karol Channing resembled nothing so much as a razorback hog.

He held forth a wide hand.

The Assistant dropped his eyes, then placed his gun in the out-stretched palm.

"Since Smythe is armed, I guess it's all right…"

Channing grinned.

"He's not *your* bodyguard."

❖   ❖   ❖

"Smythe! Damn it! I want a drink!"

"You're leaving tomorrow, Vindici. Do you want a big head when the hyper-drive cuts in?"

"Damn the h.d.! And damn my head tomorrow! It's my stomach I'm thinking of now!" A wheedling note crept into his voice. "Be a good fellow and fetch us a bottle."

Smythe's freckled face twisted, then split.

"Okay, dad, it's your frame. You're my charge till you leave, and keeping you happy is part of the job description. Hold the fort, I'll be back."

Smythe ducked out the door of the apartment and Vindici noted with pleasure that he did not lock it behind him. He shook his head. Why should that thought have occurred to him? He was no prisoner. He crossed to the mirror and studied himself.

A little under six feet, a little underweight—but that always happens in the sleep tanks—black hair with flecks of white at the temples, mahogany eyes, straight nose, firm chin.

The man in the mirror wore an expensively-cut gray jacket and a light blue shirt.

He rubbed his eyes. For a moment the reflection had been blond and green-eyed, with fuller lips and darker skin.

He raised the water tumbler between the thumb and index finger of his delicate right hand. He squeezed until it shattered. The pieces fell into the bowl.

He smiled back at his reflection.

The door opened behind him and Smythe entered with an almost-full fifth of Earth bourbon and two glasses.

"Good thing you brought an extra glass. I just broke mine."

"Oh? Where is it?"

"In the bowl. Bumped it."

"I'll clean it out. That," frowned Smythe, "is also in my job description."

Vindici smiled mechanically and filled both glasses. He downed his in a gulp and refilled it.

Smythe dumped the shards into the disposal slot.

"How you feeling?" he said.

Vindici added ice, then took another drink.

"Fine—now."

Smythe finished washing his hands and dropped into a chair.

"Damn! I cut myself!"

Vindici chuckled.

"Blood!"

He sighed, and continued, "…The most beautiful thing in the universe, cloistered in the darkest places possible and blushing most admirably when exposed."

Smythe wrapped it in his handkerchief, hastily.

"Yeah. Sure."

"Furthermore—" said Vindici.

"Have you got all the typography straight?"

"Yes, I used to live there."

"Hm. Well—"

"Yes. I did live there, didn't I? Or was it Captain Ramsay? —Sure, Turner's Guard. He was an officer."

"That's right, but that was long ago. I was a kid."

Vindici took another drink.

"And I'm going to kill someone. I won't know who until I get there. But I wanted to kill—someone—then—"

He looked at Smythe.

"Do you know why I'm going?"

"Nope. I'm just the garbage man."

He passed his hand before his eyes.

"That's not true," he said. "I see a centaur… You are a man from the waist up and a bank of machinery below…"

Smythe laughed nervously.

"My girl back home would be surprised to hear that—don't tell her. But seriously, why are you going?"

Vindici shook his head.

"Eagles over Nuremberg."

"Huh?"

"Starships—battle conches—are gathering at Turner's World."

Smythe shrugged.

"What do we care if they take the place? In fact, it would be a good idea."

The dark man shook his head.

"They're not there to take the place."

Smythe halted his drink in mid-movement.

"Oh. How often have we smashed Turner's World?" he mused. "At least three times in the past sixty years. Won't they ever give up?"

Vindici's chuckle made him check to see whether he had swallowed one of his ice cubes.

"Why should they?" asked the other. "The Fed would never sanction out-and-out destruction of Turner's World. It might make too many neutrals cease being neutral. So they just de-fang it every twenty years or so."

"One day," he smiled, "the dentist will arrive too late."

"What's your part in all this? You're a Turnerian, you fought the Federation…"

"I'm the dentist," growled Vindici, "and I hate the place! It's a violation of Fed Code to station more than two conches within five light years of one another. A world can only own a maximum of two."

"And Turner's World has none—Article Nine of the last war settlement," supplied Smythe, "but they can quarter two."

"Four have already arrived," said Vindici. "Six would constitute a first class Emergency. Statcom says there will be at least seven."

Smythe gulped his drink.

Six conches could destroy six worlds, or hold them. At least six worlds…

"From where?" he asked.

"The Pegasus, from Ophiuchus—the Stiletto, from Bran—the Standback, from Deneb—and the Minotaur."

"Then the Graf Spee and the Kraken may be on their way."

Vindici nodded.

"That's what Statcom thinks."

"Could a simple assassination stop them?"

"Statcom thinks so—but an assassination is never simple. I may have to kill the whole High Command, whoever they are."

Smythe winced.

"Can you do it?"

Vindici laughed.

"That world killed me once, which was a mistake. They should have let me live."

Then they killed the bottle, and Smythe hunted up another. As they became the hub of the galaxy, with lopsided universes spinning about them, Smythe remembered asking, "Why, Vindici? Why are you the weapon that walks like a man?"

The next morning he could not remember the answer, except that part of it was an Elizabethan monologue delivered to an empty bottle, beginning, "My study's ornament, thou shell of death…" and punctuated with numerous "'sblud's", before the man had collapsed sobbing, across the bedstead—and he could not find him to say goodbye, because Vindici had blasted off at 0500 hours, for Turner's World. But it did not really matter for Smythe.

MINUS EIGHT

"Are you the one?"
"Yes."
"Name me the place."
"Stat."
"Name me the time."
"Any."
"Come in."

Vindici entered quickly and surveyed the room. It held the normal furnishings of a provincial hotel, untouched, save for a heaped ashtray.

Vindici inspected the closet and the small washroom.

"There's no one under the bed either."

Vindici looked.

"You're right."

He eyed the slender man with the nervous tic and the hair too dark for what there was of it.

"You're Harrison."

He nodded.

"You're Vindici."

He smiled.

"I've come to kick those four stars out of the sky before they have puppies. What's the word?"

"Sit down."

"I can listen standing up."

Harrison shrugged. He seated himself.

"Turner's World has always been the catalyst. The Ophiuchuans and the Denebians are ready. The Eighth Reich will have two conches here by tonight. They don't trust each other, but they've agreed upon Duke Richard as command—"

"Richard!" Vindici took a step forward, hands raising.

Harrison stared into his eyes, unmoving, except for the left corner of his mouth which jerked like the wing of a moth.

Finally, he nodded.

"Richard de Tourne. He's old, but he's still vicious and cunning."

Vindici spat upon the carpet and stamped on it. A slow metamorphosis began to unwind his saturnine features.

His cheekbones lowered and his lips began to swell, the streaks of white at his temples grew yellow.

"Your eyes!" Harrison exclaimed. "They're changing, Vindici!"

The man shrugged off the jacket which had grown too tight across his shoulders. He threw it the length of the room.

"Who's Vindici?" he asked.

Fifty cubic miles of steel and plastic, like a quarterback running a broken field, Stat.

Steel dancing through blizzards of rock, with an infallible pilot, Statcom.

Statcom, charting possible futures and their remedies. Stat did not exist, because Statcom had debunked the rumors of itself two generations ago. Fed had no weapon for first class Emergencies other than diplomacy or military force—Statcom had said so.

Channing found Smythe in the Armory of Forbidden Weapons, fondly studying a 1917 trench knife.

"He's arrived," said Channing.

The lanky redhead replaced the knife on the rack.

"Why tell me?"

"Thought you might like to know."

"Meet Harrison yet?"

"Should have."

"Good. Thanks to your work he is now Captain Ramsay, which is even better than being Vindici, for the moment."

"Sir?"

A long second passed as Smythe studied the trench knife.

"Statcom said you'd guess sooner or later today. It didn't pinpoint the hour, though."

"I know. I asked it after I figured things out."

"Congratulations, you've just won yourself a free brainwash and an all-expense trip home."

"Good, I hate this place."

"When did you learn?"

"I've suspected you were the Director for some time now. You've always protested more loudly than anyone else about conditions here. You tipped your hand, though, by having Statcom override sound therapy and recommend that you get drunk with Vindici. You always were fascinated by weapons."

"I'll have to watch that in the future," laughed Smythe, "and I'll have Statcom chart the periodicity of my complaints. You always were pretty sharp when it came to minds, though—human or mechanical."

"Which are you?"

"I'm a part of Stat," he answered, "and I'm writing history before it happens, in a book no one will ever read and tell of—author unknown."

"You're mad," said Channing.

"Of course. I'm drunk as Dionysus, and dedicated as the three old women with the spinning wheels—and as omnipotent. When you return to your quarters the medmen will be waiting."

Channing eyed the rack of knives.

"I could kill you right now, if I had a little more cause. But what you're doing may be right. I just don't know."

"I know," answered Smythe, "and you never will."

Channing's shoulders sagged.

"What part will my poor imposter play in all this?"

"The most difficult of all, of course—himself."

Smythe turned his back and studied a gigantic Catalan knife.

"Go to hell," muttered Channing.

He might have heard a metallic chuckle as he left the Armory.

MINUS SEVEN

"And you don't think he'll recognize you?" asked Harrison.

"With a white beard and a bald dome? I'm dead, remember?"

"Richard isn't senile—and he'll probably be expecting something like this."

"I'll be working for his son, Larry. He was an infant the last time I saw him. Richard won't even see me, until the last thing."

Ramsay looked across the great courtyard. A square mile of lush vegetation, an artificial lake, a row of summer cottages, and a small menagerie lay beneath him. Servants were clearing the remains of an all night party from about a huge pavilion. Broken dishes were confetti upon the grass, and pieces of cloth decorated the branches of trees. Slow-moving men with rubbish sacks were insects far below, gathering up everything in sight. The greenly lowering sun was balanced like a gigantic olive atop the forty-foot wall which enclosed the estate.

Something came loose at the bottom of his brain.

"Where have I been all this time? It seems so very long since I lived in the officers' quarters, there," he pointed, "across the lake. Was I very ill?"

"The sleep," said Harrison. "It was long. There was no antidote for the poison Richard used, so your friends put you in the sleep tanks until one could be developed."

"How long was I out?"

"Nineteen years."

Ramsay closed his eyes and touched his forehead. Harrison clapped him on the shoulder.

"Don't think about it now. Your mind is still recovering from the shock. You want to get this thing over with first, don't you?"

"Yes, that's right I do. Larry is a man now…"

"Of course—a baby wouldn't be hiring a pimp, would he?"

Ramsay laughed, and his eyes matched the color of the sun.

"A pimp! How royal! How grand and fitting!"

His laughter became demented. It rolled and echoed about the high hall.

Harrison coughed loudly.

"Perhaps you had better—uh—compose yourself. He'll be here soon, and you should be properly subservient."

He sobered, but a smile continued to play about the corners of his mouth.

"All right. I'll spend the next five minutes thinking of money and sex. I'll save this for later—"

His right hand darted behind his back and up beneath the hem of his jacket.

Simultaneously, there was a blurring movement and a click.

Harrison looked cross-eyed at the switch blade touching his Adam's Apple. He licked his lips.

"Excellent form—but please put it away. What if Larry were to walk in here and see—?"

"Then this would happen," he replied, without moving his lips.
The blade was gone again.

"Very impressive." Harrison swallowed half of the last word.

"It will stay put now, until bleeding time."

They lighted cigarettes and waited.

❖   ❖   ❖

The door finally opened, soundlessly, behind Ramsay. He turned, nevertheless, smirking at the thin-faced boy who stood upon the threshold.

The youth looked through him and into Harrison.

"Is he the man?"

"He is."

"What's his name?"

"Pete."

"Pete, I'm Leonard de Tourne, first heir of this damned amusement park." He walked past them and hurled himself into an easy chair so hard that it banged against the wall. He wiped his moist forehead on a silken sleeve and crossed his legs. His dark eyes focussed on Ramsay. "I want a woman," he announced.

Ramsay chuckled out loud.

"That's easily accomplished."

The boy ran many-ringed fingers through his thatch of unruly black. He shook his head.

"No, it isn't. I want *a* woman, not just any woman."

"Oh, a special transaction."

"That's right, and the price is no object."

Ramsay rubbed his chemically-wrinkled hands together.

"Good! Good! I like challenges—and big commissions."

"You'll be well paid."

"Excellent! What's her name?"

"Cassiopeia."

The green-gray eyes squinted.

"Unusual name."

"She's the human daughter of two dead halfies, and very beautiful. Her father was part native and her mother was an orphan from God knows where. When they're fertile, those hybrid types produce either lovely children or freaks—or lovely freaks.

"Her mother was a servant girl named Gloria," he finished, "and her father was an officer in the Guard—I forget his name."

Ramsay nodded, then looked away.

"Where does she live?"

"In an apartment building in town. She owns it. Both parents died at the same time, and my father endowed the child. I don't know why."

"Give me the address and I'll see her directly."

"Good." His lips curved into a half-smile and he pulled a wrinkled envelope from his pocket.

"That's the address on the outside. Inside is money."

Ramsay opened it and counted.

"She must be very desirable."

"Use as much as you have to, and keep the rest for your fee. I want her this week—tonight, if possible. I'll give you a note so that you can come and go as you choose, in this part of the palace. But don't try to cross me! The world isn't big enough for anyone to hide from a Tourne."

Ramsay bowed, very low. His voice wavered and, for a moment, held Vindici's deep resonance.

"True to my profession, m'lord—I have never failed an assignment."

❖   ❖   ❖

The moon hurled down spears of silver. The six racing stars darting between them were a three-headed dragon with a long tail.

Cassiopeia looked away.

The tiger's tread was on the stair behind her violent eyes. *In the marble garden of Medusa, Perseus sleeps in stone…*

MINUS SIX

General Comstock stared at the purple-veined nose, then shifted his gaze to the tip of Richard's cigar.

"They may try to assassinate you…" he began.

"Not 'may'," corrected the Duke. "'Will.'"

The Denebian's eyes widened.

"You have heard a rumor?"

The Duke shook his head and passed him the message he had received earlier.

"Not a rumor," he stated, "a fact. Stat is sending Vindici."

Comstock tugged his goatee and read the brief sentence.

"I didn't think Stat really existed."

"Fed has done a good coverup job—good enough to fool anyone. But I know that Stat exists because I know Vindici exists."

"I'll buy Stat," said Comstock, handing back the note, "but not Vindici. When it comes to superman, there's just no such animal. Heroes, yes. Lucky fools, yes. But don't try to sell me a superman."

"This is my last strike at the Federation," said Richard, after a long pause. "Win, lose, or draw, I die. The tiger is here on Turner's World and it's just a matter of time—because I killed him when he was only a man."

"Killed?"

"Killed. Stat knew what he was then, and my failure to keep him dead gave them the tiger. After an hour and a half they dragged him back from hell, and a man named Channing created Vindici from what was left."

"What was he then?"

"A halfy. A genuine, fertile halfy." He touched the saint's ikon on his desk. "A soulless cross between humanity and a Turnerian native."

"They're telepaths, aren't they?"

Richard shrugged.

"Some are, others are other things. But no one knows what a man like Channing could do with the mind of a broken halfy—Channing certainly doesn't know."

"Doctor Karol Channing, the Adler of the twenty-third century! Is he your man?"

"Of course. Who do you think sent this message? He's a sympathizer, but like most academicians he won't go overboard for revolution. He doesn't even know where Stat is, anyhow. All he did was send me a message that I'm going to die."

"This place is built like Fed's gold vault."

"So was Kenton's HQ."

Comstock crushed out his cigarette in the huge pewter tray.

"It's been rumored that he didn't really die of food poisoning. But still, the man took chances."

"Everyone takes chances—like walking up a flight of stairs, like eating food. The tiger is quite real, he's here in Cyril, and I have no idea what he looks like. It's been close to nineteen years since I've seen him. And halfies can change shape," he added.

"Just supposing he succeeds," asked Comstock, "have you any plans?"

"My son, Larry, can take over. You make the decisions, and he'll supply the name of Tourne. He's been briefed."

"Very well, then that's settled. Can I lend you some body-guards?"

The Duke's ruddy cheeks expanded with his chuckle.

"When you leave, go through the North Wing. Stop in the main dining room and look at the wall."

"What's there?"

"Three words, in red chalk."

"All right. I'll take these maps with me. I'll be back this afternoon."

"Good morning."

The General saluted and Richard returned it. The metal doors slid open, soundlessly. He walked past them and his bodyguards headed toward the North Wing.

"Tonight," said Richard, "in Samarkand."

"Good morning, my lovely. You have not changed. —Here, in the tombs of ice, time does not whither…Only…Only that green mark of the kiss that stops the heart… Gloria! I'm going to see our daughter. That human puppy of Tourne wants her. —What's that? —No, of course not. But I must see her. I'd imagine she looks like you. —She is either lovely, or a lovely freak, he said. Like mother, like daughter, they say, and like father like son. —Richard killed us when you threw the wine in his face, but I'm back. —Smashed form releases chaos; chaos smashes other forms—rebound! The puppy wants her, as the dog wanted you, my fairest bitch. —Save your tears of ice. I'll reap two souls and root the tree of Turner! —No! Wait for me. —Save your icy spit for the souls of Tournes, when they face you—not far removed, but near…

"Good-bye, my lovely."

MINUS FIVE

"Pete?"

"Yes, my lord?"

"I understand that my son hired you because of your—er—pro-fession."

"That's right, sir."

"I'm, well, I'm rather tense. Do you know what I mean?"

"No, sir."

"Hell! You're as old as I am! You know the feeling."

"Sir?"

"Dammit! I've got an itch for a woman and I want to be fixed up! Is that plain enough?"

"Very clear."

"Good. Here's something for your trouble. Get me a young one."

"Where shall I bring her?"

"That furthermost summer cottage will be deserted." He pointed out the window. "Tonight, say eleven o'clock?"

"She'll be there with bells on."

"Heh! I'd prefer a little less."

"Naked to the bone, my lord?"

"Not quite that far. Heh!"

"True to my profession, m'lord."

Rather than take the elevator, he climbed nine flights of stairs. When he reached her door he paused. It opened.

"Oh. I didn't know there was anyone…"

"I was about to knock."

"I must have heard you on the stair."

"Must have."

She stood aside and he walked into the apartment, etching each painted screen, each grass mat and low table on the metal plate at the bottom of his mind.

"Won't you sit down?"

"Thank you."

He fumbled for the envelope.

"You are Cassiopeia Ramsay?"

"Yes."

"I've come from the Court of Tourne."

She stared into the Alcatraz of his eyes. Dreamlike, the words passed between them as they watched each other, waves matching colors on a sunny sea.

"Leonard, the son of Richard, desires your presence in his chambers. Tonight, if possible."

"I see. What will happen?"

Nothing.

"He wants to sleep with you."

"Oh. And you are the royal—factotum?"

Why will nothing happen?

"Yes, and well paid. I've brought you much money also. Here."

He will be dead.

"Very well, I'll be there. What time?"

"Say midnight."

"Midnight," she smiled.

Midnight.

When he left the seas became chianti, and overflowing.

But Perseus of the glacier arm, sword of ice... The sun is burning bright!

Then, for the first time in many years, she laughed.

❖   ❖   ❖

Comstock's Commandos laced the darkness. A tug, and their lines would tighten.

Anyone could enter. Nothing could leave.

"You got the time, Al?"

"Ten till."

Soot-barrelled laser rifles protruding through ink-dipped fronds...

"Think anyone'll come?"

"Naw."

Fractional wattage; dim cottage, still.

"What if Richard decides to take a walk?"

"Don't be the man he spots. Comstock's out on a limb."

"Cripes, it's the old man's neck! He oughta be grateful."

"It's not his order, so shut up."

Stark, and the static of insects...

"Who's that in the cottage?"

"Dunno. So long as no one comes out it don't matter."

"If they do?"

"We observe."

Moist wind, the laughter of thunder...

"You bring a poncho?"

"Yeah, didn't you?"

"Damn!"

Footsteps.

❖   ❖   ❖

Through jagged intermittances of the Belt Stat sucked weightless quantities: words, from everywhere.

Three times a day Statcom took thirty-second vacations from heavier matters and translated everything into mantalk—millions of units of mantalk. Then it placed everything into categories of importance.

When the Code-V prefix appeared, it dropped all the other words into screaming heaps in its Pend-drum and uttered lights the color of sucked cinnamon drops.

The long tongue of paper rattled at Smythe. He ceased his manicuring and poked the nailfile through it.

Raising it, he read.

Smiling, he let it fall again.

Having informed the forebrain that Ramsay was about to die, the cerebellum returned to chewing its cud.

The cerebrum focussed its attention on a thumbnail.

❖   ❖   ❖

"...Palsy and ague," answered Ramsay, "that's what's happening. Scream if you wish—no one will hear you."

"Dead. She is dead," said Richard.

"Of course. You made her that way, nineteen years ago. Remember?"

Ramsay put an arm around the delicate shoulders. He turned the seated woman, slowly.

"Gloria? Do you remember Gloria?"

"Yes. Yes! I do! My throat is burning!"

"Excellent! Wait till it hits your lungs!"

"Who are you? You couldn't be—"

"But I am! "

His eyes blazed orange, and he raised his arms over his head. Like leaves, the years fell away.

"Captain Ramsay—Vindici!"

"Yes, it's Ramsay," he told him. "I was going to use a knife, but this way is better. You wanted to kiss her so badly a moment ago—years ago. Badly enough to kill her and her husband."

The Duke began to gag.

"Be quick about your dying. I must return her to the vaults and finish another job."

"Not my son!" he choked.

"Yes, old man—old, filthy, rotten poisoner—and for the same reason. You to my wife, he to my daughter—and father and son in double harness to hell!"

"He is young!" he cried out.

"So was Gloria. And so Cassiopeia…"

The Duke screamed, one long blade of a howl, broken off at the end.

Ramsay looked away, mopping his forehead.

"Die, damn you! Die!"

"Green lipstick," muttered Richard. "Green lipstick…"

The walls splintered about them, Ramsay whirled like a bat passing through the blades of a fan. He chopped the first man he saw, across the throat. He snatched his rifle and began firing.

Three men fell.

He leapt across a body and stepped through the exploded wall, firing first to his left and then to his right.

A rifle butt caught him in the back and he dropped to his knees.

Heavy boots began kicking at his kidneys, his ribs.

He curled into a ball, his hands clasped behind his neck.

Before everything disappeared he saw a candle, a skull, a dagger, and a mirror.

❖   ❖   ❖

"Hello," she said.

"Hello yourself. You're early."

"A few minutes."

"Couldn't wait, eh?"

"You might say that."

He walked around her, studying. He patted her hips.

"You're going to be all right, girl. God! Your eyes!—I've never seen eyes that color."

"They change," she told him. "This is my happy color."

He smirked, then touched her hair, her cheek…

"Well, let's get real happy."

He pulled her to him, fumbling for the clasps at the back of her dress.

"You're warm," he said, pushing the straps off her shoulders. "Real warm."

Without releasing her, he leaned back and turned off the main light.

"Makes things more cozy. Me, I like atmosphere— What was that?"

"A scream," she smiled.

He pushed her away and ran to the window.

"Must have been some damned bird," he said after awhile.

She shrugged off the rest of her clothing and stood swaying in the dim light, with hair of tiger gold and penetrating eyes of tiger black…

"That was the Duke, your father," she told him, softly. "You have just succeeded to the title. Long live Duke Larry!—at least till midnight."

He turned, his back against the sill.

"Take a long, last look. The vaults of ice are lonely."

He tried to scream, but her body was a sheet of white flame and her eyes were two black suns; he stared like a wild thing trapped.

She did not move, and he could not.

The ivory furniture of fascination, her shoulders, and the two blue-lined moons, her breasts, floated on that river of ballads, her tiger hair, inside his head; then everything twisted in icy waves of paralysis about the tree of his spine, until it became a frozen sapling.

"Halfy!" he choked, before it seized him completely.

MINUS FOUR

"Is he going to live?" asked the fat sergeant.

"Don't know yet," answered the tall one, wiping egg from his mustache. "As soon as they give him new blood it becomes tainted. They can't transfuse fast enough to dilute it. Lungs are paralyzed. They've got a squeeze-box on his chest, and he's doped up plenty."

"Who takes over if he dies?"

"The kid, they say."

"God!"

He looked at the figure on the cot. The man blinked up at the ceiling and did not move. Four of Comstock's Commandos sat at the points of the compass with weapons pointed in his direction.

"What about him?"

"We're going to question him as soon as he comes to his senses."

"He's the tiger?" he asked.

"That's what they say."

"He'd know about Stat then."

"That's right."

The fat man's high-pitched voice shook. His small, dark eyes gleamed.

"Let me question him!"

"Everybody wants to. What's so special about you?"

"He tried to kill the Duke. I have the same dibs as anyone else."

The other shook his head.

"We're going to draw straws for the first session. You'll have the same chance as the rest of us."

"Good." The fat man hitched up his belt. "I want a tiger's tooth bracelet."

Richard lay encased in the coffin of coils, tubes, diaphragms, and bottles. It breathed for him. It did the work of a hundred pairs of kidneys. It charged his blood with vitamins and antiserums. It prodded his reticulo-endothelial system into storms of protest.

He though for himself, however, during the strange periods of calm through which his mind drifted. It was as if he were free of his burning flesh and floating bodiless in empty space…

Youth's the season made for joy. Love is then a duty…

Snatches of old songs pursued him. He felt peacefully impotent for the first time since his childhood.

A flash of remorse illuminated his inner night as he thought of the Federation—the slow-turning, in-gathering, chewing, digesting Federation. The Turnerian Axis was the last great opposition to its octopal embrace. Vanishing, like memories of his youth, the autonomy with which the frontier worlds had once been endowed, into the maw of the octopus—its movements seeking to emulate the wheel and spin of the galaxy—to become cells of the beast.

No! He would not let it happen. He would live! All nine starships had arrived and were waiting, somewhere above, in a V-formation. Nine starships waiting for his hand to guide their spear into the eye of the octopus, and down through its heart, Stat! He tried as hard as he could to live.

The feelings of fire returned.

"You can't hold me forever, halfy!" he gasped. "You're losing your grip already!"

"That's right," she smiled.

"Someone will come to tell me what that commotion was—they will find you here…"

"No," she said.

"…Then you're going to wish you had never been born."

"I've been doing that for nineteen years," she answered, before breaking a vase on his head.

Old father, old artificer, what has happened?
I've failed.
Vindici does not fail.
Who is Vindici?
You must try to remember…

❖　　❖　　❖

"I win!" giggled the fat man.
Tiger, tiger…
"I win," he repeated.
Burning bright…
"I'll use that room," he pointed.
I'm coming.
"Go ahead."
Get out of the palace.
He arose, and the guards dragged Ramsay to his feet.
Do you remember?
They pushed him in the direction of the storage room.
I'm trying. Get out of the palace!
He staggered forward and lurched against the wall.
Why?
The door swung open. Many hands pushed him, and he was inside the room.
I don't know. But I know that you must leave now.
He stayed on his feet, with effort. He stood in the center of the room, squinting puffy eyelids to shield his yellow-gray stare from the naked bulb overhead.
There are nine starships in the sky…
Go home!
The sergeant smiled and closed the door behind him. He locked it, placed the key in his pocket.
"So you're the tiger. You don't look so fierce."
Ramsay shook his head and glared.
The sergeant removed the gun from his belt and slipped it behind his waistband. Slowly, luxuriating in each movement, he unclasped his wide leather belt and drew it from around his waist. He began wrapping it about his right hand.
Tiger, tiger…
When only the buckle and two inches of leather extended from his fist he smiled and took a slow step forward.
Burning bright…

Ramsay reached over his head and broke the lightbulb.

"Better yet, Vindici," came the chuckle.

The fat man took three steps through the blackness, toward the place where Ramsay stood.

In the forest of the night…

He raised his right hand to strike.

What immortal hand or eye dare frame…

The second last sound that he heard was a metallic click from behind his back. Something seized a handful of his hair and a knee jammed into his spine.

He felt something, like a piece of ice, touch his throat, and he was suddenly very wet.

The last sound that he heard was either a gurgle or a soft laugh or both.

❖   ❖   ❖

Comstock sprang to his feet, face whitening.

"Escaped?"

"Yes sir," writhed the lieutenant.

"Who is responsible?"

"Sergeant Alton." The lieutenant was chewing his lower lip.

"Have him shot immediately."

"He's already dead, sir. Vindici cut his throat and took his gun. He killed five guards. There was an open window and one missing uniform."

"Find him. Bring him here if you can. If you can't, then bring me what's left."

"Yes, sir. We're searching now."

"Get out of here! Help find him!"

"Yessir."

A memory nagged him for a long moment. Then he seated himself and raised the comm lever.

"Sir?"

"Double Richard's guard. That man is loose again."

He dropped the lever without waiting for a reply.

"He was right," he told the empty screen. "He was really right."

❖   ❖   ❖

The world of Stat's a drunken bat,
It woggles to and fro…

❖   ❖   ❖

"He's failed," Harrison told the shiny brown box.

"Is he still alive?" it asked.

"Yes, but—"

"Then he hadn't failed," it answered.

"But he'll be dead soon…"

There was the sound like the breaking of strings on a steel guitar. Harrison realized then that he was talking to himself.

He closed the box, his mouth, and his mind, and went to join the tiger hunt.

❖   ❖   ❖

—*Father…*

—*Who is that?*

—*Cassy, but…*

—*I know no one named Cassy. I am no one's father.*

—*You are Vindici. You are also Captain Ramsay. I am your daughter.*

—*I borrow Ramsay occasionally. You are his daughter, not mine.*

—*Very well, have it your way. But look above you.*

—*I am underground. There is nothing to see.*

—*There are nine starships in the sky, waiting to strike at the Federation.*

—*They won't get that far.*

—*Perhaps I want them to.*

—*Why?*

—*We both have reason to kill Richard. But the Federation… Perhaps there is reason to break it also.*

—*What reason?*

—*It has already served its purpose. It's gotten man to the stars. Now it is a huge sponge, sopping the blood of worlds that cry for independence. Squeeze it, and it will shrink, bleeding…*

—*That is not my job.*

—*Once it was my father's. Long ago.*

—*And Richard killed him! Are you suggesting that Richard's plan be permitted to proceed, unaltered?*

—*Only you know where Stat is located…*

—*That's right.*

—*Do you remember Gloria?*

Silence.

—*Men ahead! Lights!*

Flight, wordless.
Hate, an active verb.
Fury, the inside of a furnace.
Pain—
Silence…

MINUS THREE

He was awake.
For a long while he did not open his eyes. He thought of his arms and his legs and they were there. He tried to decide what he was, but he could not remember.

He began to shiver.

Then the pain came.

He had been running, running through passages under the ground. He stirred the bonfire of memory. He had been working his way beneath the palace. He was nearing the huge vents. Someone had been talking to him, from somewhere.

The bonfire smouldered.

Someone, probably Ramsay, had wanted him to smash Stat. He remembered killing many men. He remembered being backed against the wall, his gun snatched away. He remembered being beaten.

He was on all fours, snarling. They were kicking him. He remembered gripping an ankle and hammering below a kneecap as a man bent above him. He recalled the snap and the scream. Then there was blood in his mouth and a skull in his head, splitting, and a mirror behind his eyelids, but no reflection…

He licked his lips and gagged at the taste of blood. He forced his swollen eyes open.

"For nineteen years you have marked magnificent time," said the voice inside his head. "In the entire sidereal abattoir there had never been another such as Vindici for the breaking of places, the killing of people, and the stopping of things—but you have failed in the only job that really meant anything to a man you once were—" His memory licked, like the tape recordings which had filled nearly half the life of his mind, changing channels.

"You are a naked, useless man, a pitiful, crawling worm, a fork of stripped willow, a poor player, strutting and fretting—you signify nothing!—only deeds redeem, and you cannot do them! You are afraid to look in a mirror and view the countenance of cowardice…!"

He snarled.

He threw his head back and bellowed through broken teeth. The pain in his wide-stretched limbs was enormous. His cry beat upon the bars and his cracked ribs and was broken in mid-howl. He sobbed within his cage.

His wrists and ankles were clamped tight against the frame of the great rack. There was shade below, but the hot light of the sun drove needles through his eyeballs.

He looked about, slowly.

He was alone, at the bottom of a pit, with his rack. An ugly *déjà vu* occurred as a coffin swam through his mind, drifting in a lake of blood.

The walls were stone, and at least twenty feet high. They were unbroken by any openings. The enclosure was about ten feet square. His rack was tilted back at a ninety-degree angle. The mouth of the pit was open.

It was too high, too smooth to climb, even if he could manage to break his metal bonds.

The sun was a green one-spot on a pale blue die, slightly right of center. Nothing intruded upon his view of the heavens, not even a cloud.

He cursed the sun, he cursed the day. He cursed the gods shooting craps above him.

The sun moved directly to the center of its square, then began an amoeba-like crawling to the left. Finally, it kissed the rim of the pit. He expected it to dissolve and flow down the wall, raining green fire upon him. Instead, it was sliced shorter and shorter and finally was gone. The square became an empty aquarium.

Voices.

"There he is," said the woman. "Is he still alive?"

He tilted his head and looked up, hating.

"Lord! Look at those muscles! Those eyes—!"

"He's a halfy," said her companion, a thin youth with a bandage about his head. "I'm going to come back every hour. I'm going to watch him die. But he still has a lot of life left—halfies are strong."

The woman waved at him jauntily.

"Halfy!" cried the boy. "You failed. My father is getting better and he's going to live! He'll personally open your veins as soon as he's able to move!"

Vindici's eyes burned and the boy reeled. He began to fall forward. The woman grabbed his arm and jerked him back.

"It didn't work," he called down. "Nice try, though. Your daughter is better at that sort of thing! I hope you're around to see what I'm going to do with her."

"The ingredients of tiger soup are hard to come by…" groaned the man on the rack.

There was laughter above.

"But we've caught the tiger!"

The square grew empty once more, and the sounds trailed off in the distance.

Daughter. They had said "daughter," hadn't they? Yes. Ramsay's daughter. Cassy…

—*Cassy. Where are you?*

—*Hiding. In the apartment building. There is a room—dark, cool. It was not in the blueprints.*

—*They are looking for you now. Do not leave the place.*

—*Where are you?*

—*It is not important.*

—*I see a piece of sky. A window?*

He closed his eyes.

—*No.*

—*You are hurting. But I thought you were dead.*

—*Don't worry about me. Stay safe. Leave this world when things grow still once more.*

—*Where is there to go?*

—*Offworld, anywhere.*

—*The Federation will be everywhere. I am of Turner's world, not of man's. So are you.*

—*No! I am Vindici! I was not born!*

Silence.

—*Why are you weeping, girl?*

—*How could you tell? I was weeping for my father.*

—*Ramsay is dead. He was weak.*

—*No. You are Ramsay. Vindici is facade and falsehood.*

—*Go away!*

Silence.

❖   ❖   ❖

Night. Clouds.

Stars, and the sounds of birds.

In the El Greco sky, framed by lips of the pit, nine stars were arrow awaiting target…

A head interrupted the sky.

…Bandaged head, white. Halo of steel, crown… Mock of steel, laughter…

"We know where she is, Vindici! I'll have her here and let you watch—soon!"

Emptied crown. Clouds. Seas of cotton.

—*Run! Run! They know where you are!*

—*How could they?*

—*I do not know.*

Flight before fury.

❖   ❖   ❖

Harrison hurried through the night, a puzzled look on his tired face, a gun in his pocket, and Stat's latest pronouncement rolling about his head like a marble in a tin can.

❖   ❖   ❖

Youth's the season made for joy—

Richard perspired as the nine metal-blue eyes peered pyramid through his skylight.

He tried to raise an arm, but both were clamped to the bed.

"The world of Stat's a drunken bat…"

Smythe poured another drink.

"…Only Statcom knows," he hiccupped.

MINUS TWO

"You're a fool, Vindici! Take a good look!" He pushed her forward.

Cassy?

—*Yes. They were waiting.*

"You flushed your cub for us! Tomorrow morning my father will be able to sit up! He's going to kill you then! But tonight is mine—and hers!"

I'm sorry, Cassy.

—*You didn't know. They tricked you.*

"I knew you halfies could talk, mind to mind! You made her run!—Into my arms!"

Vindici roared. It was not a human sound that emerged from his stiffened throat. The hackles rose on the back of his neck.

His eyes became distinguishable to those above him. Two burning points…

She tilted her head, straining against her captors grip.

I love you.

As she moved, her net of tiger gold snared the formation of nine, and drew it, wreath, to her brow.

There was a snapping sound and Vindici's left hand came free. The pain in his right wrist increased to unbearable proportions. His voice rose and fell through a terrible series of wails and cries.

Laughter above, and an empty canvas…

Words from everywhere seemed to be saying, "Come back! I hate you!" to everyone in the palace and on the grounds.

Richard moaned within his prison of pipettes.

Vindici looked up at the nine starships, then dropped his head.

"One time were you peerless," said the tape-worn synapses. "Once the arm of Tamburlaine was invincible, and the dagger of Vindici never missed its mark. Under all the passes of Time's wand only one remained—you, Vindici!—of the ancient dynasty of bloodletters. Mad in Argos, you slew your mother, tongueless in Castile, you stabbed Lorenzo—you, the lance of the black Quixote, dagger of the damned, cup of hemlock, dart of Loki—the bough where the murderer hangs…"

"I still am," he muttered.

"No, you are a man on a rack, a broken blade, a gob of flesh and phlegm…

"Yes! You are a snapped firing-pin, an unvoiced battle-cry—you are the want of a horseshoe for which a kingdom was lost…"

A mirror appeared before his eyes.

"No!" he cried. "No! I am Vindici! The son of Death! Bred in the Senecan twilight of Jacobean demigods, and punctual as death!"

He looked into the mirror.

"Behold!" he laughed. "Behold I am the fury!"

Vindici, the tiger, sprang.

❖ ❖ ❖

All went black as the world came to an end.

❖ ❖ ❖

Dribble.

Dribble…

Rain. Soft on lips of sand.

A moan.

…Dribble.

❖   ❖   ❖

"Water," he asked. "Water."

"Here."

"More."

"Here."

"Good. More."

"Slowly. Please."

Green met green in circles of seeing.

"Here?" she asked.

"Here," he nodded.

"Father."

"Cassy."

He looked at the world.

"What happened?"

"Gone. Dead. Rest now. Talk later."

"Richard?"

"Dead. "

"Larry?

"Dead."

"The ships?"

"Only Vindici knows."

He slept.

Nine starships waiting. Hurry, hurry, hurry…

MINUS ONE

"It is morning," she said, "and no birds are singing—all of them dead, and fallen from the trees."

"Vindici always hated the birds," he told her. "Where are the soldiers? The courtiers?"

"All of them dead."

He propped himself on an elbow.

"'Paraphysical conversion from a psychopath neurosis,'" he repeated, "'produced when the stimuli overwhelm available physical responses.'— Channing's words never meant anything to Vindici, but I remember them."

"And the battle conches? Nine starships?"

He snapped his fingers and winced at the pain in his wrist.

"Gone. Dust—dust of dust. He blacked them."

He dropped back to the grass.

"Everyone," he said.

"Every living thing in the palace and on the grounds," she agreed, "except for me."

"—Even himself."

Ramsay looked at the sky.

"How classic and dreadful. What a man he was!"

"Man? Are you sure?"

"No, I'm not. I couldn't do it."

Harrison entered the open gates and moved through the orchard.

He approached the couple on the lawn.

"Good morning."

"Good morning."

"Quiet here."

"Yes."

He looked about.

"How did you get him up?"

"The same winch they used to lower him. I put it back in the shed." She pointed.

"Neat, aren't you?"

She gave her father another drink.

Harrison jammed his hands into his pockets and paced out a square.

"What did you do with the ships?"

She shrugged.

"He says Vindici 'blacked' them."

He stared at the man on the ground.

"Vindici…"

"Ramsay," corrected the split lips.

"That makes it harder."

He removed the gun from his pocket.

"I'm sorry, honestly. But it has to be done."

"'The bird-killer weeps,' said the sparrow. —'Watch his hands, not his eyes,' answered the crow."

"Stat says Vindici must die."

"He *is* dead," she told him.

He shook his head.

"So long as he breathes, the tiger lives—and he might appear again someday."

"No. No," said Ramsay.

"I'm sorry."

He raised the gun. He aimed for a long, long while.

Slowly, he toppled forward onto his face.

Cassiopeia smiled.

"Family heritage."

She picked up his gun and tossed it into the pit.

"He'll have a sore nose this afternoon."

She helped her father to his feet, and together they staggered toward the unguarded vehicle pens.

"Harrison was right," he told her, "he's not dead."

He drew the smoke deep into his lungs and exhaled heavily.

"What do you mean?"

"I'm both now. We've fused. I know what he knew."

"Everything?"

"Including the hate," he said.

"What's there left to hate?" she asked, almost eagerly.

"Stat."

"What good does hating Stat do you? Stat's like Time—it just goes on and on."

He shook his head.

"There is a difference. Stat must come to an end."

"How's it to be done?"

He stared into the small mirror by the bedstead.

"I can't black it, like he did the ships. That calls for a special kind of hate, and I can't muster it. But there's enough of the tiger left in me for another hunt."

He closed his eyes.

"I do know how to get to Stat. Harrison is alive. When he reports failure it will only be a matter of time before Stat finds another way. I'll die then."

"If Stat could be destroyed..." her voice trailed off. "If only Stat could be destroyed! It used you, me, everyone!"

She looked back at him.

"Nine battle conches couldn't break the Federation."

"Not with Stat and Vindici on their side," he answered. "But if the tiger decapitates the robot and disappears, then the outworlds might declare their independence and have a chance of maintaining it."

"What will you need?"

"Nothing. All the tools of my trade are cached in the hills."

"You can't leave in your condition."

"I'll be in shape by the time I get there—shape enough. It's a long walk home from heaven, even with h.d."

She mixed him a drink and watched him drink it.

That afternoon, upon a hilltop, she purred softly as he leapt into the sky screaming fire, to hunt the drunken bat.

❖ ❖ ❖

Thirty minutes before Stat came to an end the ship's radio blared.

"Identify! Identify! These lanes are off-limits to civilian traffic! Identify!"

Smythe watched through a beacon-eye that peered from an island of rock. He pressed a button.

"Bring Channing—fast!"

Spaghettis of paper coiled about his ankles. He raised a strand, then dropped it.

He switched off the automatic warnings and picked up a microphone.

"The ship has been identified, Vindici. It's ours, you know."

He lifted the toggle and waited.

No reply.

He spoke again.

"Statcom predicted that if you survived you would try to return. Stat cannot be destroyed."

The door sighed open and Channing stood blinking at him, flanked by two maintenance robots.

"Come in, quickly!"

He entered the control room, eyes mild, face placid.

Smythe slapped him.

"Channing. Doctor Karol Channing," he said. "I am Carl Smythe. You are a psychiatric engineer in the Corps d'Assassins. You created a super killer named Vindici. You have been under sedation recently, but you remember Vindici, don't you?"

"Yes," said Channing, "I remember Vindici. I remember Smythe, and Channing."

"Good." He handed him the microphone. "It was your voice that conditioned Vindici. Take this and talk to him. He is outside. Tell him to answer you."

Channing gripped the microphone clumsily.

"Vindici?" he asked it. "Vindici, this is Doctor Channing. If you can hear me, answer me."

Smythe pushed up on the lever.

The talk box talked.

"Hi, Doc. Sorry I have to kill you and a lot of other people, just to knock off Stat, but that's how the story goes. You know, *Frankenstein*, et cetera."

Smythe snatched the microphone.

"Vindici, listen. We can still use you. Land. I'll open a hatch. You'll need more conditioning, but you can still be of use to Stat."

"Sorry," came the reply, "this isn't Vindici, it's Captain Ramsay of Turner's Guard. Twenty years ago I declared war on the Federation. I just remembered that recently. You were a kid then—I don't know what you are now, Smythe…"

"That's your last word on the matter?"

"I'm afraid so."

"Then we're going to destroy you," he said, switching on a panel of lights. "I really hate to lose a good man."

"Go ahead and try losing me," said Ramsay. "I was raised from the dead to do this job. Tell that old washing machine you have to do its worst."

❖　　❖　　❖

Smythe pushed the button numbered 776.

He glanced at the screen.

The hovering ship, bearing the number 776 on its side, glowed red and became a Roman Candle.

Smythe switched off the receiver.

"All the ships bear the seeds of their own destruction," he observed.

"Doesn't everything?" asked Channing.

Smythe mopped his forehead and looked at the thermostat.

"Hot in here."

"Very."

"We're shielded. That explosion shouldn't be doing this."

"It's getting hotter."

Bells began to ring.

Statcom spoke, in tongues of paper.

"Something else is out there!" cried Smythe.

Channing leaned forward and turned on the broadcast-receive unit.

"Ramsay?" he asked.

"I read you loud and clear."

Smythe began throwing switches. Another scene appeared on the viewer. The surface of Stat was hot. A figure in a spacesuit moved about it, dropping parcels into the hatchway pocks.

"Congratulations," said Channing, "you have exceeded my expectations."

The redhead snatched the microphone.

"What are you doing out there?"

"You didn't think I'd stick with the ship when it got this close, did you? I hooked up my suit-radio to broadcast through it while I came on ahead. Stat is beginning to die."

"Not yet," said Smythe.

He inserted a key beneath a lever and turned it. He jerked down on the lever as Channing struck him.

Lying on his back, he watched Channing stare at the blazing surface of Stat.

—*My Perseus! cried Medusa, and smouldering in stone!*

Then the fires began to subside. "Inner line of defense," he laughed. "Thermite fuses."

"The tiger," Channing whispered, "is burning bright."

❖   ❖   ❖

Thirty seconds before Stat came to an end Cassiopeia began to weep, uncontrollably. She tore off her dress and smashed all the mirrors in her apartment.

With hair of tiger gold and eyes of tiger black, she stood upon the balcony, staring across the wide, dark room of the sky, her fearful symmetries of hate.

A Word from Zelazny

Of this early work, Zelazny said in 1981, "I wrote this piece a long time ago and it got crowded. It was one of my earliest attempts at writing anything at a greater length than that of a short story. I based it on Tourneur's *The Revenger's Tragedy* and threw in everything handy. I have not read it in years, as I do not like to go back and review earlier things. All that I see now is a series of bright images, and I recall it as closing out an early period in my writing and opening up a new one. In this, it is a kind of Janus-piece, and I don't know whether to regard it with charity or nostalgia. An alloy, perhaps, will result. I have not caused it to be reprinted anywhere before, but as I sit on my New Mexico mountaintop I view a vast hillside of piñons and junipers, as green this November as they were in June, and in their midst is one lone deciduous tree which must feel uncomfortable in its darkening and its progressive nakedness. On the other hand, it is not without character, and it is certainly distinct."[1] In an earlier interview with Gil Lamont in 1966, Zelazny was far less charitable and described this piece as "a poor attempt to lift the plot of a Jacobean play and toss it ahead into the future; it is also doubtless the worst thing I've ever written."[2]

Zelazny had a long-standing fascination with Tourneur's work: his MA thesis analyzed *The Revenger's Tragedy,* and the title of this short story deliberately echoes the line "Nine coaches waiting—hurry, hurry, hurry."

Notes

A **poor player strutting and fretting** alludes to Shakespeare's *Macbeth.* **Bismarck** was a famous German battleship from WWII. **Leon Trotsky** promoted Marxist theory and left-wing policies in Russia; he was assassinated by a Spaniard, Ramon Mercader. **Nemesis** in Greek mythology was the spirit of divine retribution against those who succumb to hubris. John Wilkes Booth assassinated US President Abraham **Lincoln**. World War I was triggered by the assassination of Archduke Franz Ferdinand of Austria and his wife Sophie in **Sarajevo** on June 28, 1914, by a Yugoslav, Gavrilo Princip. In the Book of Revelation, **the seals of the Apocalypse** are broken open by the Lamb (Jesus) at the beginning of the End of the World. The **poisoned blade that bled the court of Denmark** refers to Laertes killing Hamlet in Shakespeare's play. **The bullet in Garfield** refers to the assassina-

---

1 *Alternities #6*, Vol. 2 No. 2, Summer 1981.
2 *Tightbeam #37*, 1966.

tion of U.S. President James Garfield in 1881. The steel in **Mercutio** refers to the death of Romeo's friend in *Romeo and Juliet*.

Vindici is the main character of *The Revenger's Tragedy*, a man out to avenge an elder's death. In mythology, **Cassiopeia** is the beautiful, arrogant, and vain wife of Cepheus, the King of Ethiopia. A **rood** is a crucifix or cross. **Turner's World** is a nod to Cyril Tourneur. **Schizoid** refers to a personality disorder marked by dissociation, passivity, and withdrawal; both it and **schizophrenia** are commonly mistaken to mean **multiple personality disorder**. German psychiatrist **Emil Kraepelin** created the Kraepelinian toplogy or classification of mental disorders in 1883 which became the basis of the modern system in place today. **Eagles over Nuremberg** refers to the display of power by Hitler and the Nazis in Nuremberg at official Third Reich rallies held in that city; Albert Speer designed a metal eagle with a 100 foot wingspan, and it was prominently displayed behind the viewing stand. **Pegasus** is the constellation named for a winged horse that sprang from the blood of Medusa when Perseus cut off her head. **Ophiuchus** is a constellation resembling a man caught in the coils of a snake. The **Minotaur,** half man and half bull, is confined to the labyrinth in Crete. **Admiral Graf Spee** was a German battleship in WWII, named after an Admiral who died in the battle of the Falkland Islands in 1914. **Kraken** was an enormous mythical sea monster said to appear off the coast of Norway.

The **Elizabethan drama** is *The Revenger's Tragedy* which Vindici quotes from: "Thou sallow remnant of my poisoned love. My study's ornament, thou shell of death, once the bright face of my betrothed lady. When life and beauty naturally filled out these ragged imperfections, then 'twas a face so far beyond the shine of any woman's bought complexion."

Dionysus or Bacchus is the god of wine who loosens inhibitions and inspires creativity in music and poetry. **Three old women with the spinning wheels** refers to the Three Fates who spin, measure and cut the thread that determines each person's lifespan. A **Catalan knife** has a tapered blade in the shape of a willow leaf and its handle is bent at the posterior third.

In the marble garden of Medusa, Perseus sleeps in stone is the opposite of what happened; Perseus slew Medusa by cutting off her head. He looked at her in a mirror in order that her gaze would not turn him to stone. **Alfred Adler** was an Austrian psychiatrist who emphasized the desire of the individual to compensate for inferiorities, and that these motivations included the attainment of sexual goals. **Tonight in Samarkand** is a romantic melodrama in three acts by Jacques Deval. **Alcatraz** is the former island prison in San Francisco Bay.

A **factotum** is a servant or handyman hired to do a variety of jobs. **Palsy** is a condition that includes paralysis of certain muscles and tremors or other abnormal movements, while **ague** is a condition that involves high fevers, chills, and rigors (such as malaria). **Youth's the season made for joy. Love is then a duty** is a quote from John Gay's *The Beggar's Opera*. The **reticulo-endothelial system** is part of the immune system. *Tiger, tiger burning bright* and the successive verses constitute the first lines of William Blake's famous poem except that "tiger" was actually spelled "Tyger." **El Greco** was a famous Renaissance painter whose real name was Doménicos The-otokópoulos. **Tamburlaine the Great** was a play about an Asian conqueror written by Christopher Marlowe. **Mad in Argos** refers to Oedipus while **slew your mother** refers to Orestes.

Lorenzo de' Medici (Lorenzo the Magnificent) was an important ruler of the Florentine Republic in the 1400s, and he survived a stabbing. **Lance of the black Quixote** refers to the novel *Don Quixote* by Cervantes, which features a minor landowner who deludes himself into thinking that he is a knight errant or hero. **Loki** was the Norse trickster god who created a dart out of mistletoe which was unwittingly used by blind Hödor to kill his brother Balder. **Want of a horseshoe a kingdom was lost** refers to a well-known nursery rhyme "For Want of a Nail." **Senecan** means the first century AD and Roman statesman Seneca the Younger, who wrote numerous dramatic plays that later heavily influenced Elizabethan and Jacobean dramatists, including Shakespeare and Tourneur. **Jacobean** refers to the time of King James I of England, but in this context it more specifically indicates the period's style of drama, exemplified by Tourneur's *The Revenger's Tragedy*. **Nine starships waiting, hurry, hurry** refers to the Tourneur play.

CIRCE HAS HER PROBLEMS

Manuscript title: "Spaceman's Lament."
Amazing, April 1963.

The fact that this place could not possibly exist should be the tipoff. It should be a craggy, barren hunk of rock, drifting through sunless space without a redeeming feature on its wrinkled vizard. Instead, it is a delicious island in the void, with a breathable atmosphere (breathable by anyone I want to breathe it!), fresh fruits, glittering fountains, an amazing variety of animal life, and me—which would have made men suspect the big bit in the old days. But no, when men get to the point where they start hopping between stars, their minds are always too well-conditioned to the superstition of scientific causality…

I am a very lovely broad (I believe that is the current term), and I am as enticing as all hell (literally)—but I digress (I *will* get back to me in a moment): my island is about fifty miles in diameter, if you can use that term for non-spherical objects (I am not strong on science), and it's sort of rectangular—even though you can walk on any of its surfaces (or inside it, for that matter); its skies twinkle a perpetual twilight, which is very romantic—and it abounds in chattering, hissing, singing, croaking, growling, and muttering beasts.

Which brings us nearer the heart of the matter, namely me.

Having been spawned in a far more libertine culture than the present cold, puritanical state of human civilization, I recently cut out for blacker pastures and set up shop here—where I stand out like a dwarf star on radar screens—which always makes for primate curiosity and an eventual landing, which always makes for men who have been away from the present cold, puritanical state of human civilization long enough to appreciate a luscious doll like me.

231

Which brings us directly to the heart of the matter. Namely, my problem.

I am a sorceress by trade, not a goddess, but I happen to have a lot of Nymph blood in me (which can be either bad or good, if you look at things that way very often—I don't). Anyhow, I had enjoyed my obvious attributes for a long while, until a cat-souled she-dog from the isle of Lesbos, in a fit of perverse jealousy (or jealous perversity—slice it either way), laid this curse bit on me, which was very bad indeed (I *do* look at things that way in *this* matter!).

Like I dig men: big men, little men, fat, thin, coarse, refined, brilliant, and et cetera men—the whole lovin' race of 'em! But my present unfortunate condition affects approximately ninety-nine percent of them.

Like, when I kiss them, they have a tendency to assume other forms—chattering, hissing, singing, croaking, growling, muttering forms—all of them quite unsatisfactory—which explains my woes, as well as the background noises.

Now then, once in a lopsided crescent moon, the right guy comes along—some lug with a genetic resistance to Sappho's abracadabra pocus—and I am always extremely nice to him. Unfortunately, men like that are far between, and they have a tendency to wear out quite soon. Hence, I have been extremely troubled for the past several centuries.

This latest crew is one such heartbreaking instance. None of the clean-shaven, broad-shouldered, Space Academy products could bear more than a mild peck on the cheek before howling away on all fours with their tails between their legs. Change them back? Sure, I can do that—but whyfor? Like, there is no percentage in kissing animals human if, as soon as you kiss them a second time, they become animals again. So I let them practice Darwin there in the trees while I look enticing and sigh for Mister Right.

(I kissed a navigator an hour ago—he's the one peeling the banana with his feet…)

"Pardon me, Miss."

Like wow!

"I am Captain Denton and I am looking for my crew," he smiles. "I hope you understand English."

"Like hope no more, Daddy," say I. "Loud and clear."

"Beg pardon?"

"I understand you, you living Hermes by Praxiteles with a crew-cut, you."

"Do you live here?"

"Indeed, and well." I move nearer and breathe upon him.

"Have you seen my men anywhere about? When I found that the atmosphere was breathable I permitted them to leave the ship, for recreational purposes. That was three days ago—"

"Oh, they're around." I toy with the gold medallions on his blue jacket. "What did you get all these lovely medals for?"

"Oh, this one is the Star of Valor, this is the Cross of Venus, that is the Lunar Crescent, and this is an Exemplary Conduct Medallion," he recounts.

"Tsk, tsk," I touch the latter. "Do you always behave in an exemplary manner?"

"I try, Miss."

I throw my arms about his neck.

"I'm so happy to see an Earthman, after all these years!"

"Really, Miss, I—"

I kiss him a good solid one on the mouth. Why beat about the bush, torturing myself? I might as well find out right away.

And nothing happens! Not a bit of fur! Nary horn nor tail!

And nothing else, either, for that matter…

He unclasps my arms gently, but with a firm grip of immense strength. He is so—so masterful. Like one of the Argive chieftains, or the Myrmidon warriors…

"I appreciate your enthusiasm at meeting another person if, as you say, you have been alone upon this worldlet very long. I assure you that I shall give you passage to a civilized planet, as soon as I can locate my crew."

"Pooh!" say I. "I don't want your civilized planets. I'm happy here. But you, Big Man, you have unsuspected talents—and great potential! Like, we shall play a wild harpsichord together!"

" 'Duty Before All,' Miss, is the motto of the Corps. I must locate my crew before I indulge in any musical pasttimes."

❖   ❖   ❖

Like, I don't dig geometry, but I know a square when I see one. Still, Science is only one of the paths man need follow…

"Step into my parlor," say I whistling for the palace, which comes running and settles out of sight on the other side of the hill. "I shall refresh you and give you assistance in your search."

"This is very kind of you," he replies. (Grandmother Circe! those shoulders!) "I shall accept your invitation. Is it far?"

"We're almost there already, Captain." I take his arm.

I feed him a roast pig, which had seen happier days, and I proceed to douse his wine with every aphrodisiac I have in stock. I sit back and wait, looking alluring.

Nothing happens.

"Don't you feel a little—uncomfortable?" I finally ask, raising the temperature ten degrees. "Perhaps you'd like to take off your jacket."

"Yes, I believe I shall. It is a trifle warm in here."

"Take off anything you like," I suggest, whistling up a swimming pool. "Perhaps you would like to bathe?"

"I did not notice that pool before. This wine must be making me drowsy."

I whistle for the perfumed bed, and it rolls in with a musical accompaniment.

"Well, a nice bath and a good bed will make you feel like a new man."

"I really should be looking for my crew," he protests, weakly.

"Nonsense, nothing in this world could hurt a fly." I dampen out the background howls and snarls to prove my point. "They will be all right for a few more hours, and you could use the rest."

"True," he finally acknowledges. "They are probably bivouacked beside some gentle waterfall, or engaged in a boyish game of touch football. I shall bathe."

And he undresses and I whistle, which, unfortunately, causes the icebox to move into the room and stop at the edge of the pool.

"Amazingly sophisticated servomechanisms you have," he observes, splashing back to the edge and proceeding to raid the icebox.

❖ ❖ ❖

An hour later he is still eating! He is one of those big, hearty types with his mind in his stomach—but still, what a magnificent animal! Great bulging muscles, skin smooth and perfect as marble, deeply tanned, a warrior's dark eyes…

I find I am getting a first-class crush on this jerk!

Finally, he finishes eating and steps from the pool, like Neptune rising from the Aegean—a dripping god of youth and power. I know that he must be thinking by now what I have been thinking all along. It is a simple matter of physiology, according to Science—also, them green flies from Spain are pretty effective.

He towers above me, and I look coy, timid, and, at the same time, inviting.

"It is still bothering me," he observes. "I had better go look for my crew before I take my rest."

❖   ❖   ❖

That does it! Suddenly I see red, also the rest of the rainbow. I snap my fingers and everything vanishes but the bed, into which we are immediately projected.

"Wha-what happened?" he asks.

"Captain Denton," say I, "you have in every way flaunted my obvious charms, and insulted my person by failing to recognize it. I am extremely lovely, and sadly, miserably," I whisper it, "passionate!"

"Oh my!" says he. "Is that so?"

"Indeed. I weep for the strong arms of a man, the dart of Cupid hath pierced my heart, I am not prone to argue…"

"I see," he clears his throat. "And you have lured me here for this specific reason?"

"Yes," I reply, softly.

"And you did something to my crew."

"Yes."

"What?"

"Kiss me and I'll tell you."

"All right."

He does. Aphrodite! What a fine feeling after all those centuries!

"What did you do with them?"

"I kissed them," say I, "and they were metamorphosed into animals."

"Goodness!" he exclaims, quickly surveying his person. "And you are such a lovely creature!"

"Now you're getting with it," I agree. "You are one of those rare brutes my kiss does not affect with tails, tusks, hooves, horns, or suchlike impedimenta."

"Can you change my men back?"

"I might, if you ask me—very nicely."

"You—you're a sorceress!" he suddenly realizes. "I had always presumed they were but the fabrications of the unlearned. Can you work other magic?"

"You bet. Want some moonlight?"

I snap my fingers and the roof disappears. A gentle, inspiring moon hovers above us.

"Amazing! Oh my! Oh my! It is almost too much to ask—"

"What, dearest?" I nestle up against him. "Ask away, and Big Mama will make with the conjure."

A long, loud silence.

Finally, voice shaking, he asks it.

"Can you make me a man?"

"Wha?"

"A man," he repeats. "I am an android, as are all the captains of deep space cruisers these days. This is because we are more stable, single-minded, and less emotional than our human brothers."

"Brother!" exclaim I, getting to my feet and reaching for my robe. "Oh brother!

"Sorry, Jack," I finally pronounce, "I am just a sorceress. It would take a goddess to make you—anything."

"Oh," says he, sadly, "I suppose that it was too much to hope for. I have always wondered how people feel. It would have been so stimulating…"

❖   ❖   ❖

I stalk away through the night. With some coaching he might make the vegetable kingdom next avatar. Stimulating!

Rounding up his scurvy crew, I—ugh!—kiss them all back into human form. I have to! He needs them to man the ship, and I can't have him slew-footing around looking virile, and at the same time as useful as a pinup in a monastery. Stimulating!

Someday my prince will come.

A Word from Zelazny

"Circe came to me halfway through reading [Harlan Ellison's] *Gentleman Junkie*, as I decided to try something flip, fast, and brash myself. It took about an hour and a half to write and required almost no corrections. Probably the easiest bit I've ever done."[1]

Notes

Circe is the Greek nymph or sorceress who turned Odysseus' men into pigs after they came upon her island. Her spells had no effect on Odysseus, who bore an herb from **Hermes** to resist her power. Circe realized she was powerless over him, lifted the spell, and welcomed Odysseus and his crew into her home. **Lesbos** is the island in the Aegean Sea where the female poet Sappho was born; because her poems have homosexual overtones, the words lesbian and sapphic have derived to mean love between two women. **Hermes by Praxiteles** is a marble statue of nude Hermes; the statue dates to 343 BC. **Argive chieftains** were involved in the mythical War of Seven Against Thebes, in which all but one of the chieftains perished; the **Myrmidon warriors** were the army that Achilles commanded. **Green flies** refers to Spanish fly, which is actually a green or emerald beetle from which an aphrodisiac has been derived. **Neptune** is the god of the sea; **Cupid** is the god of erotic love; **Aphrodite** is the goddess of love. An **avatar** is the embodiment of a deity, a god made visible in human form.

Even in this early work, Zelazny shows his tendency to pun in ways that can be bold or subtle, depending upon the reader's perceptions. "I am not prone to argue" may be obvious or subtle, whereas the last line of the story is more bold.

---

1 *Tightbeam* #37, May 1966.

THE CAT LICKS HER COAT

Tapeworm #5, 1967.

The cat licks her coat
on the cat-loving couch
in the cat house.
Shedding too much,
she is confined in the cat-dark
cellar, where she threatens her subjects,
the rodents,
drowses beside the cat-warming furnace.

She is fed.
She dances her ghost-dance
for the God Who Mews.

If not for this, there'd be no wars.

A Word from Zelazny

Zelazny sent this poem to Jack C. Haldeman II, the editor of *Tapeworm*, with the following cover letter: "Dear Jay, Thank you for the copy of your ~~foul crudzine~~ fine fanzine, *Tapeworm*. It ~~nauseated~~ struck me as a very fine example of the very best work that is being done ~~among the depraved~~ in SF fandom today. I am moved therefore to contribute. Enclosed find one contribution. It is obvious that you are doing your part to make the world safe for ~~godless communism~~ SF fandom as we all know, love and respect it. Thank you for a ~~monstrous eyeopener~~ wonderful revelation as to fannish states of mind and suchlike. Bests, Roger J. Zelazny."[1]

---

1 *Tapeworm #5*, 1967.

THE MALATESTA COLLECTION

Fantastic, April 1963.

I'm going to miss the books.

Maybe I'm just a senile throwback to the lecherous times, but I like to think it is some bit of scholarly attachment as well.

But I helped to uncover them, so it is only fitting that I be here as they are put away.

Don't be fooled, Cosmic Eye, I am not the voice of one man. All of us contain some of me, as well as Paul Malatesta.

Roden is mounting the platform now. The books are in the box, the box is in the cornerstone, and the statue is draped.

It was one year ago today that he made the discovery, quite by accident. He was digging a hole, that mad sculptor, digging a hole in Time. It was in one of the many unexcavated mounds, where the fragments of old civilizations can sometimes be found. He pokes into them quite a bit—hoping to find a bust, a torso, a fragment of decorated wall. On occasion he comes up with some striking discoveries.

But there was only one Malatesta collection.

❖   ❖   ❖

"This occasion deserves some comment," he begins. "Whether this is dictated by its notoriety, or by virtue of its value to historians, I cannot say.

"But I can say this," he continues, "what you are doing is wrong. In the light of eternal values, you are being untrue to the species by burying that which is not dead."

There were troubled faces about him on the platform. But he could not be interrupted; no effrontery could stand before the massive dignity of his ninety years. So he went on:

"I take willing part in this ceremony because every grave demands a marker, as surely as the root utters tree. Every passing demands endurable comment, though centuries delayed. We called them forth into the light for a brief moment, and you of the light were shocked, for they were living. Now you would reinter them, and I, their stepfather, have been called upon to commemorate this thing that you do.

"I hate you, all of you. But you must listen to me—you are too polite not to—and doubtless you will applaud when I have finished.

"I remember the day when we found them…"

❖   ❖   ❖

I remember it also. His tiny form, in that threadbare cloak he always wears, shot into my office like an arrow. The door banged against the wall, and he, hopping from one leg to another before my desk:

"Come quickly! I have found the soul of our ancestors!"

He darted about like a sparrow, making several false starts toward the door, checking himself each time, when he saw that I did not rise.

"Get on your feet and come with me!" he ordered. "This has waited too long already!"

"Sit down," I told him. "I have an Ancient Literature class in half an hour. It would take something awfully important to call it off."

He snorted his white mustache away from his words:

"Ancient Literature! Still mooning over *Pamela* and *David Copperfield*, eh? Let me tell you something—there is more to it than that, and I've got it!"

Roden had a reputation.

He was an anomaly, almost a pariah, a pet of the wealthy, though he insulted them to their faces, a friend of the artist, whose labors he always encouraged, no matter how puerile—a bohemian in an age where bohemians could not exist—a purveyor of cheap art by commission, a creator of the other kind, which went ignored. The greatest sculptor alive.

Finally, he settled into a seat, nearly immortalizing me to statue, with his basilisk's glare.

"I'm not being uncooperative," I apologized. "It's just that I have responsibilities. I can't go running off until I know what I'm chasing."

"Responsibilities," he repeated, in one of his milder tones. "Yes, I guess you do. Almost everyone does these days. There aren't many free spirits any more—grail-chasers who would take an old man's word that something is important enough to be worth an hour or two."

This hurt, because I respect him more than anyone else I know—with his encyclopedic knowledge of art, all his engaging eccentricities, and the cold fire that burns within his works.

"I am sorry," I said. "Tell me what this is all about."

"You are a teacher of literature," he declared. "I've found you an unread library."

I swallowed, blinking, and shelves of books flowed like rivers behind my eyelids.

"Ancient books?" I whispered.

He nodded.

"How old?"

"Many from the nineteenth and twentieth centuries, and lots of older ones."

I was shaking. How many years had I dreamed of such a find? Mostly, the mounds just held junk; paper is so transient a thing.

"Many?" I asked.

"Many," he acknowledged.

"I'll have to tell the secretary of the department that there won't be a class." I stood. "I'll be right back. —Is it far?"

"An hour's drive."

I flew down the hall, shedding responsibilities like feathers.

"…When we examined them we could not believe our good fortune. There were so many—so perfectly preserved against the century's nightfall. The powerful walls of the structure had defended them against moisture, decay, insects…"

I held it in quivering hands. Bacon? The legendary Shakespeare, whose name alone survived? Could they have spoken like that? I was appalled. Mark Twain's acerbic brilliance had endured—but this!

I closed *1601* carefully, and placed it in a protective wrapper I had brought. I opened a book by a man named Miller.

Ten minutes later I was sick, very sick. I accepted the bottle of wine Roden produced from under his cloak. He said nothing as I drank.

By candlelight, he was sketching the strange tableau in the corner.

❖   ❖   ❖

What remained of two human beings rested upon what remained of a bed. I tried not to look in that direction, but their position was so obvious. My eyes fleshed the skeleton arms. I saw them embracing as the bombs fell; I felt the concrete shake from the burst, striving to stop the radiations that consumed its maker. Now bone embraced bone in a garden of books, grinned at the live voyeur.

I pretended to look at *Moll Flanders*, holding the book to block out the sight.

"This place was called a fallout shelter, wasn't it?"

"That's right. Many people built them before the dark times."

"And this man," I eyed the elaborate *Ex Libra* page to *Kama Sutra*, "this Paul Malatesta prepared his shelter rather unusually, did he not?"

"I don't know." He flipped his sketchpad shut. "I don't know how they thought in those days, but I suppose a man stocked it with what he cherished most."

"I teach Literature," I thought aloud, "but I've never heard of these books—the Harris autobiography, Rochester's *Poems on Several Occasions*, Coryat's *Crudities*, *Gamiani*, *Flossie*, *The Festival of Love*…"

"Then it's time you did," he replied, "since they're there."

"But the language," I protested, "the subject matter—it's so, so…"

"Crude?" he supplied. "Basic? Elemental? Scatalogical? Impolite?"

"Yes."

"I found this place yesterday. I spent the entire night reading. We need these books if we are to have a true picture of our Ancestors, and ourselves."

"Ourselves?"

"Yes. You had better read those books over there," he gestured, "the ones by the man named Freud. Do you think man is completely rational, and moral?"

"Of course. We have eliminated crime, education is compulsory. —We have advanced beyond our ancestors, both ethically and intellectually."

"Nonsense!" he snorted again. "The basic nature of man has remained constant throughout history, so far as I can ascertain."

"But these books…!"

"They travelled to the moon in those days, they conquered diseases we still suffer. They recognized the demonic spirit of Dionysus which lives in us all. The books that survived were the books most numerous—the small caches have always supplied us with the most important ones—unless you deem currency the mark of greatness."

"I don't know how they will be accepted…"

" 'If'," corrected Roden quietly.

❖   ❖   ❖

"…If you have chosen the path of democratizing art out of existence, I am powerless to stop you. I can only protest. I can condone you, slightly, that you decided against burning them. But your decision to make them wait for a generation better qualified—that is tantamount to eternal condemnation. And you know it, and I condemn you, in turn, for this action…"

❖   ❖   ❖

What a flurry, what a battle of critics, popular and scholarly, I aroused!

When I brought the Malatesta collection to the University a cheer arose from the professorial ranks, shortly to be replaced by raised eyebrows. I am not as old as Roden, but, in a society as proper as our own, I, also, am too old to insult. —But some came close.

At first, all was uncertainty and ambiguity.

—True, it is an important find. Surely, they shed new light on the history of literature. Of course, we will give them our most unbiased attention. But the general public… Well, we had better wait until we have assessed them completely.

I had never heard of such a thing, and I told them so.

The table was surrounded by statues of ice. They chose to ignore what I had said, focussing once more, through thick glasses, the eyes of judgment.

"But Chaucer," I pressed on, "Huysmans, the *Oresteia!* You can't just throw them out because it hurts you to read them! They are literature, distillations of life by genius…"

"We are not convinced," said an icicle, "that they are art."

I exploded and quit my job, but nothing was ever done about my resignation, so I am still here. Literature is like pie, one piece is better than none at all.

"You did not release them. Instead, you have imprisoned them in the cornerstone of your new Philosophy Building—which, in itself, demonstrates one of life's implicit ironies—and you commissioned me, before a year had passed, to construct their cenotaph."

"You did not call it that, but, to balm your consciences—moral people that you are—you could not help but commemorate a greatness you had witnessed, though you despised it.

"I have constructed your memorial—not one of my garish tabernacles of money, where gilt angels sport among seashells, but a memorial to man, as he was, is, and always shall be…"

Oh dead Malatesta! With your pale mistress Frances, sporting in a radioactive oven while the missiles hymned their canticle of death— Did she weep? What did she say at the end? I read your diary up until the final entry of that last day—"We are frying. Hell! They will find us the way we began—"

I admire you, Malatesta, as I admire Castiglione and Da Vinci— connoisseur, scholar, and man to the end! Spin on your way, atoms of a man, you have made the sunset of my life more colorful…

"It is," he reached for the dark veil, "an enactment of the human condition."

He drew it off.

Gasps filled the courtyard as tears filled my eyes. Roden had done it! In whatever back room or garret they might hide it, his fame would await the eventual call of posterity.

Steel ribs enamelled white—that terrible position!—skeleton arms locked in libidinous embrace forever, and the lascivious *consolamentum* of fleshless faces.

The bronze base bore the simple inscription, "The Kiss, by Roden."

And then, I heard his voice in the distance:

"There it is. Do what you want with it—but never let me near it again!"

Mindlessly, the applause broke forth, amidst the sighs and soft comments.

That day I quit again, for real.

A Word from Zelazny

This "was a very contrived exercise actually, in attempting a stream of speak interspersed with a series of flashbacks, to see if I could tell a story that way. I didn't really care about the story, just the method."[1]

This is not the first time that Dante Alighieri's *The Divine Comedy* figured in Zelazny's works. He indicated that the best books he had ever read included *"The Iliad, The Divine Comedy, Don Quixote, Tom Jones, Moby Dick, Anna Karenina, The Magic Mountain,"*[2] and the discerning reader may pick up recurring allusions to each of these (and more) among Zelazny's short stories, poems and novels.

Notes

The title and names in this piece are deliberate: **"The Kiss"** is a famous sculpture by Auguste Rodin, and he based it on the passionate adulterous love of the historical personages of **Francesca da Rimini** and **Paolo Malatesta**. They were caught *en flagrante* by her husband (Paolo's brother) Giovanni Malatesta, who murdered them. Francesca was used by her contemporary Dante Alighieri as a character in his *Divine Comedy*. Zelazny deliberately misspells Rodin as **Roden** throughout the text, perhaps to indicate deterioration in the historical record with passage of time. In the story, two characters Francesca and Malatesta died in a fallout shelter, their skeletons forever locked in sexual congress, surrounded by books that shocked their descendants.

Numerous actual book titles and authors figure in the text, many of them pertaining to aspects of sexual desire. **Pamela, or Virtue Rewarded** is a novel by Samuel Richardson; **David Copperfield** is the novel by Charles Dickens; **Francis Bacon** was a philosopher and scientist, but some claim he may have actually written Shakespeare's works; **Mark Twain** was the pen name of author Samuel Clemens, whose works included *Tom Sawyer, Huckleberry Finn* and *1601*; **Arthur Miller**'s plays included *Death of a Salesman* and *The Crucible*; **Moll Flanders** was written by Daniel DeFoe; The *Kama Sutra* is a book best known for its small section on sexual enjoyment and a description of assorted sexual positions; *My Life and Loves* is the notorious autobiography of **Frank Harris** which featured photos of nude women and recounted his own sexual exploits; John Wilmot, the **Earl of Rochester**, was known for lewd and ribald poetry of which *Poems on Several Occasions* was one collection; **Coryat's *Crudities*** tells of Thomas Coryat's journey across Europe

---

1 *Tightbeam #37*, 1966.
2 *Nova #1*, June 1972.

and the gastronomic delights that he enjoyed; *Gamiani* is a French novel by Alfred de Musset; *The Festival of Love* is a poetry collection by R. Swainson Fisher; **Sigmund Freud**'s works discuss how subconscious drives and primitive urges motivate us; **Geoffrey Chaucer** wrote *The Canterbury Tales*; **Joris-Karl Huysmans** was most famous for the novel *À rebours*; the *Oresteia* is a trilogy of ancient Greek plays which includes the tale of Orestes, who killed his own mother after she killed his father.

    Bohemian means an artist who lives and acts without regard for conventional rules and practices. A **basilisk** caused sudden death with its glance. **Dionysus** is the god of wine but also a promoter of civilization, peace and law. **Scatalogical** means pertaining to animal excrement, filth or obscenity. A **cenotaph** is an empty tomb with a monument placed over it. A **canticle** is a religious hymn or chant. **Lascivious** refers to an overt and usually offensive sexual desire. **Baldassare Castiglione** was an Italian Renaissance author best known for *The Book of the Courtier (Il Cortegiano)*. **Consolamentum** was practiced by Cathars (a branch of Christianity) and consisted of the baptism of the Holy Spirit, reception of all the spiritual gifts, power to bind and loose, absolution, baptismal regeneration, and Ordination all in one ceremony.

FROM A SEAT IN THE CHILL PARK

To Spin Is Miracle Cat, Underwood-Miller 1981.
Written 1955–60 for *Chisel in the Sky*.

Green wrestles yellow on that pillared island,
scuffing occasional brown clods.

Notes

The poem depicts the pitcher's mound from a viewpoint in the stands.

Rodin's "The Kiss"

To Spin Is Miracle Cat, Underwood-Miller 1981.
Written 1955–60 for *Chisel in the Sky*.

Stasimonial inquiry and reply
despite stone, where have I seen thee
before, mandala amid the eye?
Guitars, the organ, or one violin
draw but in perpetual anticlimax
thy hewn pause past sound,
and the numbers of no poetry
embrace no thing with such staticies'
armed coherence. Where? I do not know.

Love-locked lips forever,
whose witnessed conversation
secret stays, will not tell me—
unwanted voyeur worshipper—undoing
silences that never can be spelled.

But I, most sure, have seen thee,
before this eye might keep,
or tongue lisp its trilling tribute,
and know thee in a way past memory's cant.

Something sudden here
exclaims that arch of neck,
and thigh-caressing palm below thy bend;
something, like my living blood—
flesh-blinded, swirling visionary;
formless rusher after rushing form—
statuizes seeing's sympathy.

Notes

"The Kiss" is Auguste Rodin's famous statue of two nude lovers in an erotic embrace; the statue also figured prominently in the story "The Malatesta Collection" (see that story's notes for more details about the statue).

A **stasimon** is a song performed by a single actor in a Greek tragedy with a chorus behind him that responds to him. A **mandala** is a geometric pattern or chart that can be used for focusing attention and meditating; **mandala amid the eye** suggests the iris. **Staticie** refers to a motionless form, such as a person holding a pose. A **lisp** is a speech defect (or a deliberate parody of speech) in which, for example, the sibilant 's' and 'z' sounds are replaced by a 'th' or similar sound.

TO HIS MORBID MISTRESS

Alternities #6, Summer 1981.

Two hundred-six bones
held together with passion and flesh,
four hundred-twelve bones,
ditto,
cushioned against rattle and stress,
facing the future with a smile,
show entropy's got poetry inside.

Be my Valentine, awhile.

Notes

The title alludes to Andrew Marvell's "To His Coy Mistress" which begins "Had we world enough, and time." The average adult human has 206 bones…

The Stainless Steel Leech

Amazing, April 1963 as by Harrison Denmark.

They're really afraid of this place.

During the day they'll clank around the headstones, if they're ordered to, but even Central can't make the search at night, despite the ultras and the infras—and they'll never enter a mausoleum.

Which makes things nice for me.

They're superstitious; it's a part of the circuitry. They were designed to serve man, and during his brief time on earth, awe and devotion, as well as dread, were automatic things. Even the last man, dead Kennington, commanded every robot in existence while he lived. His person was a thing of veneration, and all his orders were obeyed.

And a man is a man, alive or dead—which is why the graveyards are a combination of hell, heaven, and strange feedback, and will remain apart from the cities so long as the earth endures.

But even as I mock them they are looking behind the stones and peering into the gullies. They are searching for—and afraid they might find—me.

I, the unjunked, am legend. Once out of a million assemblies a defective such as I might appear and go undetected, until too late.

At will, I could cut the circuit that connected me with Central Control, and be a free 'bot, and master of my own movements. I liked to visit the cemeteries, because they were quiet and different from the maddening stamp-stamp of the presses and the clanking of the crowds; I liked to look at the green and red and yellow and blue things that grew about the graves. And I did not fear these places, for that circuit, too, was defective. So when I was discovered they removed my vite-box and threw me on the junk heap.

But the next day I was gone, and their fear was great.

I no longer possess a self-contained power unit, but the freak coils within my chest act as storage batteries. They require frequent recharging, however, and there is only one way to do that.

The werebot is the most frightful legend whispered among the gleaming steel towers, when the night wind sighs with its burden of fears out of the past, from days when non-metal beings walked the earth. The half-lifes, the preyers upon order, still cry darkness within the vite-box of every 'bot.

I, the discontent, the unjunked, live here in Rosewood Park, among the dogwood and myrtle, the headstones and broken angels, with Fritz—another legend—in our deep and peaceful mausoleum.

Fritz is a vampire, which is a terrible and tragic thing. He is so undernourished that he can no longer move about, but he cannot die either, so he lies in his casket and dreams of times gone by. One day, he will ask me to carry him outside into the sunlight, and I will watch him shrivel and dim into peace and nothingness and dust. I hope he does not ask me soon.

We talk. At night, when the moon is full and he feels strong enough, he tells me of his better days, in places called Austria and Hungary, where he, too, was feared and hunted.

"…But only a stainless steel leech can get blood out of a stone— or a robot," he said last night. "It is a proud and lonely thing to be a stainless steel leech—you are possibly the only one of your kind in existence. Live up to your reputation! Hound them! Drain them! Leave your mark on a thousand steel throats!"

And he was right. He is always right. And he knows more about these things than I.

"Kennington!" His thin, bloodless lips smiled. "Oh, what a duel we fought! He was the last man on earth, and I the last vampire. For ten years I tried to drain him. I got at him twice, but he was from the Old Country and knew what precautions to take. Once he learned of my existence, he issued a wooden stake to every robot—but I had forty-two graves in those days and they never found me. They did come close, though…

"But at night, ah, at night!" he chuckled. "Then things were reversed! I was the hunter and he the prey!

"I remember his frantic questing after the last few sprays of garlic and wolfsbane on earth, the crucifix assembly lines he kept in operation around the clock—irreligious soul that he was! I was genuinely sorry when he died, in peace. Not so much because I hadn't gotten to drain him properly, but because he was a worthy opponent and a suitable antagonist. What a game we played!"

His husky voice weakened.

"He sleeps a scant three hundred paces from here, bleaching and dry. His is the great marble tomb by the gate… Please gather roses tomorrow and place them upon it."

I agreed that I would, for there is a closer kinship between the two of us than between myself and any 'bot, despite the dictates of resemblance. And I must keep my word, before this day passes into evening and although there are searchers above, for such is the law of my nature.

❖   ❖   ❖

"Damn them! (He taught me that word.) Damn them!" I say. "I'm coming up! Beware, gentle 'bots! I shall walk among you and you shall not know me. I shall join in the search, and you will think I am one of you. I shall gather the red flowers for dead Kennington, rubbing shoulders with you, and Fritz will smile at the joke."

I climb the cracked and hollow steps, the east already spilling twilight, and the sun half-lidded in the west.

I emerge.

The roses live on the wall across the road. From great twisting tubes of vine, with heads brighter than any rust, they burn like danger lights on a control panel, but moistly.

One, two, three roses for Kennington. Four, five…

"What are you doing, 'bot?"

"Gathering roses."

"You are supposed to be searching for the werebot. Has something damaged you?"

"No, I'm all right," I say, and I fix him where he stands, by bumping against his shoulder. The circuit completed, I drain his vite-box until I am filled.

"You are the werebot!" he intones weakly.

He falls with a crash.

…Six, seven, eight roses for Kennington, dead Kennington, dead as the 'bot at my feet—more dead—for he once lived a full organic life, nearer to Fritz's or my own than to theirs.

"What happened here, 'bot?"

"He is stopped, and I am picking roses," I tell them.

There are four 'bots and an Over.

"It is time you left this place," I say. "Shortly it will be night and the werebot will walk. Leave, or he will end you."

"You stopped him!" says the Over. "You are the werebot!"

I bunch all the flowers against my chest with one arm and turn to face them. The Over, a large special-order 'bot, moves toward me. Others are approaching from all directions. He had sent out a call.

"You are a strange and terrible thing," he is saying, "and you must be junked, for the sake of the community."

He seizes me and I drop Kennington's flowers.

I cannot drain him. My coils are already loaded near their capacity, and he is specially insulated.

There are dozens around me now, fearing and hating. They will junk me and I will lie beside Kennington.

"Rust in peace," they will say… I am sorry that I cannot keep my promise to Fritz.

"Release him!"

No!

It is shrouded and moldering Fritz in the doorway of the mausoleum, swaying, clutching at the stone. He always knows…

"Release him! I, a human, order it."

He is ashen and gasping, and the sunlight is doing awful things to him.

—The ancient circuits click and suddenly I am free.

"Yes, master," says the Over. "We did not know."

"Seize that robot!"

He points a shaking emaciated finger at him.

"He is the werebot," he gasps. "Destroy him! The one gathering flowers was obeying my orders. Leave him here with me."

He falls to his knees and the final darts of day pierce his flesh.

"And go! All the rest of you! Quickly! It is my order that no robot ever enter another graveyard again!"

He collapses within and I know that now there are only bones and bits of rotted shroud on the doorstep of our home.

Fritz has had his final joke—a human masquerade.

I take the roses to Kennington, as the silent 'bots file out through the gate forever, bearing the unprotesting Overbot with them. I place the roses at the foot of the monument—Kennington's and Fritz's—the monument of the last, strange, truly living ones.

Now only I remain unjunked.

In the final light of the sun I see them drive a stake through the Over's vite-box and bury him at the crossroads.

Then they hurry back toward their towers of steel, of plastic.

I gather up what remains of Fritz and carry him down to his box. The bones are brittle and silent.

…It is a very proud and very lonely thing to be a stainless steel leech.

A Word from Zelazny

"There came a point where I was turning out lots of short stories, so many that Cele [Goldsmith] suggested running two per issue to use up my back-log, with a pen name on the second tale. She suggested Harrison Denmark as the nom de typewriter. I agreed and this, my first effort at something slightly humorous, appeared under that byline. It never occurred to me that Harry Harrison, living at the time in Snekkerson, Denmark, and author of *The Stainless Steel Rat* might somehow be assumed to be the author. It occurred to Harry, however, and he published a letter disclaiming authorship. I was not certain he was convinced when I later told him that it had never occurred to me. But it had never occurred to me."[1]

Notes

"**It is a proud and lonely thing** to be a fan" was coined by Robert Bloch in *A Way of Life* (1956), and this has since been quoted or parodied many times by writers as some variation of "it is a proud and lonely thing to be [insert name]…" It was used by Harry Harrison ("…a stainless steel rat"), by Zelazny in this story ("…a stainless steel leech"), and by Zelazny later, having Corwin remark, "It is a proud and lonely thing to be a Prince in Amber." **Myrtle** is an evergreen with fragrant white flowers and red berries; it was originally considered sacred to Venus. A **mausoleum** is a largely, stately tomb. **Wolfsbane** or monkshood is a perennial with hood-shaped purple flowers, and a potent alkaloid poison (aconite) is derived from it.

---

1 *The Last Defender of Camelot*, 1980.

OLD OHIO FOLKRAG

Double:Bill #9 June 1964.

Alien wind, when wilt thou blow
That the green rain down can rain?
And fallout, when wilt thou fall
Down on a Cleveland Con again?

A Word from Zelazny

"First Con I ever attended was in 1955—in these parts, as I recall. And how does that old Ohio folkrag go—sounds like a Song of Social Protest, but then it *has* been a long time, hasn't it?"[1]

---

1 Letter to Bill Bowers introducing this poem, dated 3/28/64.

THE DOORS OF HIS FACE, THE LAMPS OF HIS MOUTH

The Magazine of Fantasy & Science Fiction, March 1965.
Nebula award 1966 (novelette). Hugo nominee 1966 (short fiction).
#52 on 1999 Locus all-time poll (novelette).

I'm a baitman. No one is born a baitman, except in a French novel where everyone is. (In fact, I think that's the title, *We Are All Bait.* Pfft!) How I got that way is barely worth the telling and has nothing to do with neo-exes, but the days of the beast deserve a few words, so here they are.

❖   ❖   ❖

The Lowlands of Venus lie between the thumb and forefinger of the continent known as Hand. When you break into Cloud Alley it swings its silverblack bowling ball toward you without a warning. You jump then, inside that firetailed tenpin they ride you down in, but the straps keep you from making a fool of yourself. You generally chuckle afterwards, but you always jump first.

Next, you study Hand to lay its illusion and the two middle fingers become dozen-ringed archipelagoes as the outers resolve into greengray peninsulas; the thumb is too short, and curls like the embryo tail of Cape Horn.

You suck pure oxygen, sigh possibly, and begin the long topple back to the Lowlands.

There, you are caught like an infield fly at the Lifeline landing area—so named because of its nearness to the great delta in the Eastern Bay—located between the first peninsula and "thumb." For a minute it seems as if you're going to miss Lifeline and wind up as canned seafood, but afterwards—shaking off the metaphors—you descend to scorched concrete and present your middle-sized telephone directory of authorizations to the short, fat man in the gray cap. The papers show that you are not subject to mysterious inner rottings and etcetera. He then smiles you a short, fat, gray smile and motions you toward the bus which hauls you to the Reception Area. At the R.A. you spend three days proving that, indeed, you are not subject to mysterious inner rottings and etcetera.

Boredom, however, is another rot. When your three days are up, you generally hit Lifeline hard, and it returns the compliment as a matter of reflex. The effects of alcohol in variant atmospheres is a subject on which the connoisseurs have written numerous volumes, so I will confine my remarks to noting that a good binge is worthy of at least a week's time and often warrants a lifetime study.

I had been a student of exceptional promise (strictly undergraduate) for going on two years when the *Bright Water* fell through our marble ceiling and poured its people like targets into the city.

Pause. The Worlds Almanac re Lifeline: "...Port city on the eastern coast of Hand. Employees of the Agency for Non-terrestrial Research comprise approximately 85% of its 100,000 population (2010 Census). Its other residents are primarily personnel maintained by several industrial corporations engaged in basic research. Independent marine biologists, wealthy fishing enthusiasts, and waterfront entrepreneurs make up the remainder of its inhabitants."

I turned to Mike Dabis, a fellow entrepreneur, and commented on the lousy state of basic research.

"Not if the mumbled truth be known."

He paused behind his glass before continuing the slow swallowing process calculated to obtain my interest and a few oaths, before he continued.

"Carl," he finally observed, poker playing, "they're shaping Tensquare."

I could have hit him. I might have refilled his glass with sulfuric acid and looked on with glee as his lips blackened and cracked. Instead, I grunted a noncommittal.

"Who's fool enough to shell out fifty grand a day? ANR?"

He shook his head.

"Jean Luharich," he said, "the girl with the violet contacts and fifty or sixty perfect teeth. I understand her eyes are really brown."

"Isn't she selling enough face cream these days?"

He shrugged.

"Publicity makes the wheels go 'round. Luharich Enterprises

jumped sixteen points when she picked up the Sun Trophy. You ever play golf on Mercury?"

I had, but I overlooked it and continued to press.

"So she's coming here with a blank check and a fishhook?"

"*Bright Water*, today," he nodded. "Should be down by now. Lots of cameras. She wants an Ikky, bad."

"Hmm," I hmmed. "How bad?"

"Sixty day contract. Tensquare. Indefinite extension clause. Million and a half deposit," he recited.

"You seem to know a lot about it."

"I'm Personnel Recruitment. Luharich Enterprises approached me last month. It helps to drink in the right places.

"Or own them." He smirked, after a moment.

I looked away, sipping my bitter brew. After awhile I swallowed several things and asked Mike what he expected to be asked, leaving myself open for his monthly temperance lecture.

"They told me to try getting you," he mentioned. "When's the last time you sailed?"

"Month and a half ago. The *Corning*."

"Small stuff," he snorted. "When have you been under, yourself?"

"It's been awhile."

"It's been over a year, hasn't it? That time you got cut by the screw, under the *Dolphin*?"

I turned to him.

"I was in the river last week, up at Angleford where the currents are strong. I can still get around."

"Sober," he added.

"I'd stay that way," I said, "on a job like this."

A doubting nod.

"Straight union rates. Triple time for extraordinary circumstances," he narrated. "Be at Hangar Sixteen with your gear, Friday morning, five hundred hours. We push off Saturday, daybreak."

"You're sailing?"

"I'm sailing."

"How come?"

"Money."

"Ikky guano."

"The bar isn't doing so well and baby needs new minks."

"I repeat—"

"…And I want to get away from baby, renew my contract with basics—fresh air, exercise, make cash…"

"All right, sorry I asked."

I poured him a drink, concentrating on H_2SO_4, but it didn't transmute. Finally I got him soused and went out into the night to walk and think things over.

Around a dozen serious attempts to land *Ichthyform Leviosaurus Levianthus*, generally known as "Ikky", had been made over the past five years. When Ikky was first sighted, whaling techniques were employed. These proved either fruitless or disastrous, and a new procedure was inaugurated. Tensquare was constructed by a wealthy sportsman named Michael Jandt, who blew his entire roll on the project.

After a year on the Eastern Ocean, he returned to file bankruptcy. Carlton Davits, a playboy fishing enthusiast, then purchased the huge raft and laid a wake for Ikky's spawning grounds. On the nineteenth day out he had a strike and lost one hundred fifty bills' worth of untested gear, along with one *Ichthyform Levianthus*. Twelve days later, using tripled lines, he hooked, narcotized, and began to hoist the huge beast. It awakened then, destroyed a control tower, killed six men, and worked general hell over five square blocks of Tensquare. Carlton was left with partial hemiplegia and a bankruptcy suit of his own. He faded into waterfront atmosphere and Tensquare changed hands four more times, with less spectacular but equally expensive results.

Finally, the big raft, built only for one purpose was purchased at an auction by ANR for "marine research." Lloyd's still won't insure it, and the only marine research it has ever seen is an occasional rental at fifty bills a day—to people anxious to tell Leviathan fish stories. I've been a baitman on three of the voyages, and I've been close enough to count Ikky's fangs on two occasions. I want one of them to show my grandchildren, for personal reasons.

I faced the direction of the landing area and resolved a resolve.

"You want me for local coloring, gal. It'll look nice on the feature page and all that. But clear this— If anyone gets you an Ikky, it'll be me. I promise."

I stood in the empty Square. The foggy towers of Lifeline shared their mists.

❖   ❖   ❖

Shoreline a couple eras ago, the western slope above Lifeline stretches as far as forty miles inland in some places. Its angle of rising is not a great one, but it achieves an elevation of several thousand feet before it meets the mountain range which separates us from the Highlands.

About four miles inland and five hundred feet higher than Lifeline are set most of the surface airstrips and privately owned hangars. Hangar Sixteen houses Cal's Contract Cab, hop service, shore to ship. I do not like Cal, but he wasn't around when I climbed from the bus and waved to a mechanic.

Two of the hoppers tugged at the concrete, impatient beneath flywing haloes. The one on which Steve was working belched deep within its barrel carburetor and shuttered spasmodically.

"Bellyache?" I inquired.

"Yeah, gas pains and heartburn."

He twisted setscrews until it settled into an even keening, and turned to me.

"You're for out?"

I nodded.

"Tensquare. Cosmetics. Monsters. Stuff like that."

He blinked into the beacons and wiped his freckles. The temperature was about twenty, but the big overhead spots served a double purpose.

"Luharich," he muttered. "Then you *are* the one. There's some people want to see you."

"What about?"

"Cameras. Microphones. Stuff like that."

"I'd better stow my gear. Which one am I riding?"

He poked the screwdriver at the other hopper.

"That one. You're on video tape now, by the way. They wanted to get you arriving."

He turned to the hangar, turned back.

"Say 'cheese.' They'll shoot the close-ups later."

I said something other than "cheese." They must have been using telelens and been able to read my lips, because that part of the tape was never shown.

I threw my junk in the back, climbed into a passenger seat, and lit a cigarette. Five minutes later, Cal himself emerged from the office Quonset, looking cold. He came over and pounded on the side of the hopper. He jerked a thumb back at the hangar.

"They want you in there!" he called through cupped hands. "Interview!"

"The show's over!" I yelled back. "Either that, or they can get themselves another baitman!"

His rustbrown eyes became nailheads under blond brows and his glare a spike before he jerked about and stalked off. I wondered how much they had paid him to be able to squat in his hangar and suck juice from his generator.

Enough, I guess, knowing Cal. I never liked the guy, anyway.

❖   ❖   ❖

Venus at night is a field of sable waters. On the coasts, you can never tell where the sea ends and the sky begins. Dawn is like dumping milk into an inkwell. First, there are erratic curdles of white, then streamers. Shade the bottle for a gray colloid, then watch it whiten a little more. All of a sudden you've got day. Then start heating the mixture.

I had to shed my jacket as we flashed out over the bay. To our rear, the skyline could have been under water for the way it waved and rippled in the heatfall. A hopper can accommodate four people (five, if you want to bend Regs and underestimate weight), or three passengers with the sort of gear a baitman uses. I was the only fare, though, and the pilot was like his machine. He hummed and made no unnecessary noises. Lifeline turned a somersault and evaporated in the rear mirror at about the same time Tensquare broke the fore-horizon. The pilot stopped humming and shook his head.

I leaned forward. Feelings played flopdoodle in my guts. I knew every bloody inch of the big raft, but the feelings you once took for granted change when their source is out of reach. Truthfully, I'd had my doubts I'd ever board the hulk again. But now, now I could almost believe in predestination. There it was!

A tensquare football field of a ship. A-powered. Flat as a pancake, except for the plastic blisters in the middle and the "Rooks" fore and aft, port and starboard.

The Rook towers were named for their corner positions—and any two can work together to hoist, co-powering the graffles between them. The graffles—half gaff, half grapple—can raise enormous weights to near water level; their designer had only one thing in mind, though, which accounts for the gaff half. At water level, the Slider has to implement elevation for six to eight feet before the graffles are in a position to push upward, rather than pulling.

The Slider, essentially, is a mobile room—a big box capable of moving in any of Tensquare's crisscross groovings and "anchoring" on the strike side by means of a powerful electromagnetic bond. Its winches could hoist a battleship the necessary distance, and the whole craft would tilt, rather than the Slider come loose, if you want any idea of the strength of that bond.

The Slider houses a section operated control indicator which is the most sophisticated "reel" ever designed. Drawing broadcast power from the generator beside the center blister, it is connected by short-wave with the sonar room, where the movements of the quarry are recorded and repeated to the angler seated before the section control.

The fisherman might play his "lines" for hours, days even, without seeing any more than metal and an outline on the screen. Only when the beast is graffled and the extensor shelf, located twelve feet below waterline, slides out for support and begins to aid the winches, only then does the fisherman see his catch rising before him like a fallen Seraph. Then, as Davits learned, one looks into the Abyss itself and is required to act. He didn't, and a hundred meters of unimaginable tonnage, undernarcotized and hurting, broke the cables of the winch, snapped a graffle, and took a half-minute walk across Tensquare.

We circled till the mechanical flag took notice and waved us on down. We touched beside the personnel hatch and I jettisoned my gear and jumped to the deck.

"Luck," called the pilot as the door was sliding shut. Then he danced into the air and the flag clicked blank.

I shouldered my stuff and went below.

Signing in with Malvern, the de facto captain, I learned that most of the others wouldn't arrive for a good eight hours. They had wanted me alone at Cal's so they could pattern the pub footage along twentieth-century cinema lines.

Open: landing strip, dark. One mechanic prodding a contrary hopper. Stark-o-vision shot of slow bus pulling in. Heavily dressed baitman descends, looks about, limps across field. Close-up: he grins. Move in for words: "Do you think this is the time? The time he *will* be landed?" Embarrassment, taciturnity, a shrug. Dub something— "I see. And why do you think Miss Luharich has a better chance than any of the others? Is it because she's better equipped? [Grin.] Because more is known now about the creature's habits than when you were out before? Or is it because of her will to win, to be a champion? Is it any one of these things, or is it all of them?" Reply: "Yeah, all of them." "—Is that why you signed on with her? Because your instincts say, 'This one will be it'?" Answer: "She pays union rates. I couldn't rent that damned thing myself. And I want in." Erase. Dub something else. Fade-out as he moves toward hopper, etcetera.

"Cheese," I said, or something like that, and took a walk around Tensquare, by myself.

I mounted each Rook, checking out the controls and the underwater video eyes. Then I raised the main lift.

Malvern had no objections to my testing things this way. In fact, he encouraged it. We had sailed together before and our positions had even been reversed upon a time. So I wasn't surprised when I stepped off the lift into the Hopkins Locker and found him waiting. For the next ten minutes we inspected the big room in silence, walking through its copper coil chambers soon to be Arctic.

Finally, he slapped a wall.

"Well, will we fill it?"

I shook my head.

"I'd like to, but I doubt it. I don't give two hoots and a damn who gets credit for the catch, so long as I have a part in it. But it won't happen. That gal's an egomaniac. She'll want to operate the Slider, and she can't."

"You ever meet her?"

"Yeah."

"How long ago?"

"Four, five years."

"She was a kid then. How do you know what she can do now?"

"I know. She'll have learned every switch and reading by this time. She'll be all up on all theory. But do you remember one time we were together in the starboard Rook, forward, when Ikky broke water like a porpoise?"

"How could I forget?"

"Well?"

He rubbed his emery chin.

"Maybe she can do it, Carl. She's raced torch ships and she's scubaed in bad waters back home." He glanced in the direction of invisible Hand. "And she's hunted in the Highlands. She might be wild enough to pull that horror into her lap without flinching.

"…For Johns Hopkins to foot the bill and shell out seven figures for the corpus," he added. "That's money, even to a Luharich."

I ducked through a hatchway.

"Maybe you're right, but she was a rich witch when I knew her.

"And she wasn't blonde," I added, meanly.

He yawned.

"Let's find breakfast."

We did that.

❖   ❖   ❖

When I was young I thought that being born a sea creature was the finest choice Nature could make for anyone. I grew up on the Pacific coast and spent my summers on the Gulf or the Mediterranean. I lived months of my life negotiating coral, photographing trench dwellers, and playing tag with dolphins. I fished everywhere there are fish, resenting the fact that they can go places I can't. When I grew older I wanted a bigger fish, and there was nothing living that I knew of, excepting a Sequoia, that came any bigger than Ikky. That's part of it…

I jammed a couple of extra rolls into a paper bag and filled a thermos with coffee. Excusing myself, I left the gallery and made my way to the Slider berth. It was just the way I remembered it. I threw a few switches and the shortwave hummed.

"That you, Carl?"

"That's right, Mike. Let me have some juice down here, you double-crossing rat."

He thought it over, then I felt the hull vibrate as the generators cut in. I poured my third cup of coffee and found a cigarette.

"So why am I a double-crossing rat this time?" came his voice again.

"You knew about the cameraman at Hangar Sixteen?"

"Yes."

"Then you're a double-crossing rat. The last thing I want is publicity. 'He who fouled up so often before is ready to try it, nobly, once more.' I can read it now."

"You're wrong. The spotlight's only big enough for one, and she's prettier than you."

My next comment was cut off as I threw the elevator switch and the elephant ears flapped above me. I rose, settling flush with the deck. Retracting the lateral rail, I cut forward into the groove. Amidships, I stopped at a juncture, dropped the lateral, and retracted the longitudinal rail.

I slid starboard, midway between the Rooks, halted, and threw on the coupler.

I hadn't spilled a drop of coffee.

"Show me pictures."

The screen glowed. I adjusted and got outlines of the bottom.

"Okay."

I threw a Status Blue switch and he matched it. The light went on.

The winch unlocked. I aimed out over the waters, extended an arm, and fired a cast.

"Clean one," he commented.

"Status Red. Call strike." I threw a switch.

"Status Red."

The baitman would be on his way with this, to make the barbs tempting.

It's not exactly a fishhook. The cables bear hollow tubes; the tubes convey enough dope for an army of hopheads; Ikky takes the bait, dandled before him by remote control, and the fisherman rams the barbs home.

My hands moved over the console, making the necessary adjustments. I checked the narco-tank reading. Empty. Good, they hadn't been filled yet. I thumbed the Inject button.

"In the gullet," Mike murmured.

I released the cables. I played the beast imagined. I let him run, swinging the winch to simulate his sweep.

I had the air conditioner on and my shirt off and it was still uncomfortably hot, which is how I knew that morning had gone over into noon. I was dimly aware of the arrivals and departures of the hoppers. Some of the crew sat in the "shade" of the doors I had left open, watching the operation. I didn't see Jean arrive or I would have ended the session and gotten below.

She broke my concentration by slamming the door hard enough to shake the bond.

"Mind telling me who authorized you to bring up the Slider?" she asked.

"No one," I replied. "I'll take it below now."

"Just move aside."

I did, and she took my seat. She was wearing brown slacks and a baggy shirt and she had her hair pulled back in a practical manner. Her cheeks were flushed, but not necessarily from the heat. She attacked the panel with a nearly amusing intensity that I found disquieting.

"Status Blue," she snapped, breaking a violet fingernail on the toggle.

I forced a yawn and buttoned my shirt slowly. She threw a side glance my way, checked the registers, and fired a cast.

I monitored the lead on the screen. She turned to me for a second.

"Status Red," she said levelly.

I nodded my agreement.

She worked the winch sideways to show she knew how. I didn't doubt she knew how and she didn't doubt that I didn't doubt, but then—

"In case you're wondering," she said, "you're not going to be anywhere near this thing. You were hired as a baitman, remember? Not a Slider operator! A baitman! Your duties consist of swimming out and setting the table for our friend the monster. It's dangerous, but you're getting well paid for it. Any questions?"

She squashed the Inject button and I rubbed my throat.

"Nope," I smiled, "but I am qualified to run that thingamajigger—and if you need me I'll be available, at union rates."

"Mister Davits," she said, "I don't want a loser operating this panel."

"Miss Luharich, there has never been a winner at this game."

She started reeling in the cable and broke the bond at the same time, so that the whole Slider shook as the big yo-yo returned. We skidded a couple of feet backward. She raised the laterals and we shot back along the groove. Slowing, she transferred rails and we jolted to a clanging halt, then shot off at a right angle. The crew scrambled away from the hatch as we skidded onto the elevator.

"In the future, Mister Davits, do not enter the Slider without being ordered," she told me.

"Don't worry. I won't even step inside if I am ordered," I answered. "I signed on as a baitman. Remember? If you want me in here, you'll have to *ask* me."

"That'll be the day," she smiled.

I agreed, as the doors closed above us. We dropped the subject and headed in our different directions after the Slider came to a halt in its berth. She did not say "good day," though, which I thought showed breeding as well as determination, in reply to my chuckle.

Later that night Mike and I stoked our pipes in Malvern's cabin. The winds were shuffling waves, and a steady pattering of rain and hail overhead turned the deck into a tin roof.

"Nasty," suggested Malvern.

I nodded. After two bourbons the room had become a familiar woodcut, with its mahogany furnishings (which I had transported from Earth long ago on a whim) and the dark walls, the seasoned face of Malvern, and the perpetually puzzled expression of Dabis set between the big pools of shadow that lay behind chairs and splashed in cornets, all cast by the tiny table light and seen through a glass, brownly.

"Glad I'm in here."

"What's it like underneath on a night like this?"

I puffed, thinking of my light cutting through the insides of a black diamond, shaken slightly. The meteor-dart of a suddenly illuminated fish, the swaying of grotesque ferns, like nebulae—shadow, then green, then gone—swam in a moment through my mind. I guess it's like a spaceship would feel, if a spaceship could feel, crossing between worlds—and quiet, uncannily, preternaturally quiet; and peaceful as sleep.

"Dark," I said, "and not real choppy below a few fathoms."

"Another eight hours and we shove off," commented Mike.

"Ten, twelve days, we should be there," noted Malvern.

"What do you think Ikky's doing?"

"Sleeping on the bottom with Mrs. Ikky if he has any brains."

"He hasn't. I've seen ANR's skeletal extrapolation from the bones that have washed up—"

"Hasn't everyone?"

"...Fully fleshed, he'd be over a hundred meters long. That right, Carl?"

I agreed.

"...Not much of a brain box, though, for his bulk."

"Smart enough to stay out of our locker."

Chuckles, because nothing exists but this room, really. The world outside is an empty, sleet drummed deck. We lean back and make clouds.

"Boss lady does not approve of unauthorized fly fishing."

"Boss lady can walk north till her hat floats."

"What did she say in there?"

"She told me that my place, with fish manure, is on the bottom."

"You don't Slide?"

"I bait."

"We'll see."

"That's all I do. If she wants a Slideman she's going to have to ask nicely."

"You think she'll have to?"

"I think she'll have to."

"And if she does, can you do it?"

"A fair question," I puffed. "I don't know the answer, though."

I'd incorporate my soul and trade forty percent of the stock for the answer. I'd give a couple years off my life for the answer. But there doesn't seem to be a lineup of supernatural takers, because no one knows. Supposing when we get out there, luck being with us, we find ourselves an Ikky? Supposing we succeed in baiting him and get lines on him. What then? If we get him shipside, will she hold on or crack up? What if she's made of sterner stuff than Davits, who used to hunt sharks with poison-darted air pistols? Supposing she lands him and Davits has to stand there like a video extra.

Worse yet, supposing she asks for Davits and he still stands there like a video extra or something else—say, some yellowbellied embodiment named Cringe?

It was when I got him up above the eight-foot horizon of steel and looked out at all that body, sloping on and on till it dropped out of sight like a green mountain range… And that head. Small for the body, but still immense. Fat, craggy, with lidless roulettes that had spun black and red since before my forefathers decided to try the New Continent. And swaying.

Fresh narco-tanks had been connected. It needed another shot, fast. But I was paralyzed.

It had made a noise like God playing a Hammond organ…

And looked at me!

I don't know if seeing is even the same process in eyes like those. I doubt it. Maybe I was just a gray blur behind a black rock, with the plexi-reflected sky hurting its pupils. But it fixed on me. Perhaps the snake doesn't really paralyze the rabbit, perhaps it's just that rabbits are cowards by constitution. But it began to struggle and I still couldn't move, fascinated.

Fascinated by all that power, by those eyes, they found me there fifteen minutes later, a little broken about the head and shoulders, the Inject still unpushed.

And I dream about those eyes. I want to face them once more, even if their finding takes forever. I've got to know if there's something inside me that sets me apart from a rabbit, from notched plates of reflexes and instincts that always fall apart in exactly the same way whenever the proper combination is spun.

Looking down, I noticed that my hand was shaking. Glancing up, I noticed that no one else was noticing.

I finished my drink and emptied my pipe. It was late and no songbirds were singing.

I sat whittling, my legs hanging over the aft edge, the chips spinning down into the furrow of our wake. Three days out. No action.

"You!"

"Me?"

"You."

Hair like the end of the rainbow, eyes like nothing in nature, fine teeth.

"Hello."

"There's a safety regulation against what you're doing, you know."

"I know. I've been worrying about it all morning."

A delicate curl climbed my knife then drifted out behind us. It settled into the foam and was plowed under. I watched her reflection in my blade, taking a secret pleasure in its distortion.

"Are you baiting me?" she finally asked.

I heard her laugh then, and turned, knowing it had been intentional.

"What, me?"

"I could push you off from here, very easily."

"I'd make it back."

"Would you push me off, then—some dark night, perhaps?"

"They're all dark, Miss Luharich. No, I'd rather make you a gift of my carving."

She seated herself beside me then, and I couldn't help but notice the dimples in her knees. She wore white shorts and a halter and still had an offworld tan to her which was awfully appealing. I almost felt a twinge of guilt at having planned the whole scene, but my right hand still blocked her view of the wooden animal.

"Okay, I'll bite. What have you got for me?"

"Just a second. It's almost finished."

Solemnly, I passed her the little wooden jackass I had been carving. I felt a little sorry and slightly jackass-ish myself, but I had to follow through. I always do. The mouth was split into a braying grin. The ears were upright.

She didn't smile and she didn't frown. She just studied it.

"It's very good," she finally said, "like most things you do—and appropriate, perhaps."

"Give it to me." I extended a palm.

She handed it back and I tossed it out over the water. It missed the white water and bobbed for awhile like a pigmy seahorse.

"Why did you do that?"

"It was a poor joke. I'm sorry."

"Maybe you are right, though. Perhaps this time I've bitten off a little too much."

I snorted.

"Then why not do something safer, like another race?"

She shook her end of the rainbow.

"No. It has to be an Ikky."

"Why?"

"Why did you want one so badly that you threw away a fortune?"

"Many reasons," I said. "An unfrocked analyst who held black therapy sessions in his basement once told me, 'Mister Davits, you need to reinforce the image of your masculinity by catching one of every kind of fish in existence.' Fish are a very ancient masculinity symbol, you know. So I set out to do it. I have one more to go. —Why do you want to reinforce *your* masculinity?"

"I don't," she said. "I don't want to reinforce anything but Luharich Enterprises. My chief statistician once said, 'Miss Luharich, sell all the cold cream and face powder in the System and you'll be a happy girl. Rich, too.' And he was right. I am the proof. I can look the way I do and do anything, and I sell most of the lipstick and face powder in the System—but I have to be *able* to do anything."

"You do look cool and efficient," I observed.

"I don't feel cool," she said, rising. "Let's go for a swim."

"May I point out that we're making pretty good time?"

"If you want to indicate the obvious, you may. You said you could make it back to the ship, unassisted. Change your mind?"

"No."

"Then get us two scuba outfits and I'll race you under Tensquare.

"I'll win, too," she added.

I stood and looked down at her, because that usually makes me feel superior to women.

"Daughter of Lir, eyes of Picasso," I said, "you've got yourself a race. Meet me at the forward Rook, starboard, in ten minutes."

"Ten minutes," she agreed.

And ten minutes it was. From the center blister to the Rook took maybe two of them, with the load I was carrying. My sandals grew very hot and I was glad to shuck them for flippers when I reached the comparative cool of the corner.

We slid into harnesses and adjusted our gear. She had changed into a trim one-piece green job that made me shade my eyes and look away, then look back again.

I fastened a rope ladder and kicked it over the side. Then I pounded on the wall of the Rook.

"Yeah?"

"You talk to the port Rook, aft?" I called.

"They're all set up," came the answer. "There's ladders and draglines all over that end."

"You sure you want to do this?" asked the sunburnt little gink who was her publicity man, Anderson yclept.

He sat beside the Rook in a deckchair, sipping lemonade through a straw.

"It might be dangerous," he observed, sunken-mouthed. (His teeth were beside him, in another glass.)

"That's right," she smiled. "It *will* be dangerous. Not overly, though."

"Then why don't you let me get some pictures? We'd have them back to Lifeline in an hour. They'd be in New York by tonight. Good copy."

"No," she said, and turned away from both of us.

She raised her hands to her eyes.

"Here, keep these for me."

She passed him a box full of her unseeing, and when she turned back to me they were the same brown that I remembered.

"Ready?"

"No," I said, tautly. "Listen carefully, Jean. If you're going to play this game there are a few rules. First," I counted, "we're going to be directly beneath the hull, so we have to start low and keep moving. If we bump the bottom, we could rupture an air tank…"

She began to protest that any moron knew that and I cut her down.

"Second," I went on, "there won't be much light, so we'll stay close together, and we will *both* carry torches."

Her wet eyes flashed.

"I dragged you out of Govino without—"

Then she stopped and turned away. She picked up a lamp.

"Okay. Torches. Sorry."

"…And watch out for the drive-screws," I finished. "There'll be strong currents for at least fifty meters behind them."

She wiped her eyes and adjusted the mask.

"All right, let's go."

We went.

She led the way, at my insistence. The surface layer was pleasantly warm. At two fathoms the water was bracing; at five it was nice and cold. At eight we let go the swinging stairway and struck out. Ten-square sped forward and we raced in the opposite direction, tattoo-ing the hull yellow at ten-second intervals.

The hull stayed where it belonged, but we raced on like two darkside satellites. Periodically, I tickled her frog feet with my light and traced her antennae of bubbles. About a five meter lead was fine; I'd beat her in the home stretch, but I couldn't let her drop behind yet.

Beneath us, black. Immense. Deep. The Mindanao of Venus, where eternity might eventually pass the dead to a rest in cities of unnamed fishes. I twisted my head away and touched the hull with a feeler of light; it told me we were about a quarter of the way along.

I increased my beat to match her stepped-up stroke, and narrowed the distance which she had suddenly opened by a couple of meters. She sped up again and I did, too. I spotted her with my beam.

She turned and it caught on her mask. I never knew whether she'd been smiling. Probably. She raised two fingers in a V-for-Victory and then cut ahead at full speed.

I should have known. I should have felt it coming. It was just a race to her, something else to win. Damn the torpedoes!

So I leaned into it, hard. I don't shake in the water. Or, if I do it doesn't matter and I don't notice it. I began to close the gap again.

She looked back, sped on, looked back. Each time she looked it was nearer, until I'd narrowed it down to the original five meters.

Then she hit the jatos.

That's what I had been fearing. We were about half-way under and she shouldn't have done it. The powerful jets of compressed air could easily rocket her upward into the hull, or tear something loose if she allowed her body to twist. Their main use is in tearing free from marine plants or fighting bad currents. I had wanted them along as a safety measure, because of the big suck-and-pull windmills behind.

She shot ahead like a meteorite, and I could feel a sudden tingle of perspiration leaping to meet and mix with the churning waters.

I swept ahead, not wanting to use my own guns, and she tripled, quadrupled the margin.

The jets died and she was still on course. Okay, I was an old fud-dyduddy. She *could* have messed up and headed toward the top.

I plowed the sea and began to gather back my yardage, a foot at a time. I wouldn't be able to catch her or beat her now, but I'd be on the ropes before she hit deck.

Then the spinning magnets began their insistence and she wavered. It was an awfully powerful drag, even at this distance. The call of the meat grinder.

I'd been scratched up by one once, under the *Dolphin*, a fishing boat of the middle-class. I *had* been drinking, but it was also a rough day, and the thing had been turned on prematurely. Fortunately, it was turned off in time, also, and a tendon-stapler made everything good as new, except in the log, where it only mentioned that I'd been drinking. Nothing about it being off-hours when I had the right to do as I damn well pleased.

She had slowed to half her speed, but she was still moving cross-wise, toward the port, aft corner. I began to feel the pull myself and had to slow down. She'd made it past the main one, but she seemed too far back. It's hard to gauge distances under water, but each red beat of time told me I was right. She was out of danger from the main one, but the smaller port screw, located about eighty meters in, was no longer a threat but a certainty.

She had turned and was pulling away from it now. Twenty meters separated us. She was standing still. Fifteen.

Slowly, she began a backward drifting. I hit my jatos, aiming two meters behind her and about twenty back of the blades.

Straightline! Thankgod! Catching, softbelly, leadpipe on shoulder SWIMLIKEHELL! maskcracked, not broke though AND UP!

We caught a line and I remember brandy.

❖   ❖   ❖

Into the cradle endlessly rocking I spit, pacing. Insomnia tonight and left shoulder sore again, so let it rain on me—they can cure rheumatism. Stupid as hell. What I said. In blankets and shivering. She: "Carl, I can't say it." Me: "Then call it square for that night in Govino, Miss Luharich. Huh?" She: nothing. Me: "Any more of that brandy?" She: "Give me another, too." Me: sounds of sipping. It had only lasted three months. No alimony. Many $ on both sides. Not sure whether they were happy or not. Wine-dark Aegean. Good fishing. Maybe he should have spent more time on shore. Or perhaps she shouldn't have. Good swimmer, though. Dragged him all the way to Vido to wring out his lungs. Young. Both. Strong. Both. Rich and spoiled as hell. Ditto. Corfu should have brought them closer. Didn't. I think that mental cruelty was a trout. He wanted to go to Canada. She: "Go to hell if you want!" He: "Will you go along?" She: "No." But she did, anyhow. Many hells. Expensive. He lost a monster or two. She inherited a couple. Lot of lightning tonight. Stupid as hell. Civility's the coffin of a conned soul. By whom? —Sounds like a bloody neo-ex… But I hate you, Anderson, with your glass full of teeth and her new eyes… Can't keep this pipe lit, keep sucking tobacco. Spit again!

❖   ❖   ❖

Seven days out and the scope showed Ikky.

Bells jangled, feet pounded, and some optimist set the thermostat in the Hopkins. Malvern wanted me to sit it out, but I slipped into my harness and waited for whatever came. The bruise looked worse than it felt. I had exercised every day and the shoulder hadn't stiffened on me.

A thousand meters ahead and thirty fathoms deep, it tunneled our path. Nothing showed on the surface.

"Will we chase him?" asked an excited crewman.

"Not unless she feels like using money for fuel." I shrugged.

Soon the scope was clear, and it stayed that way. We remained on alert and held our course.

I hadn't said over a dozen words to my boss since the last time we went drowning together, so I decided to raise the score.

"Good afternoon," I approached. "What's new?"

"He's going north-northeast. We'll have to let this one go. A few more days and we can afford some chasing. Not yet."

Sleek head...

I nodded. "No telling where this one's headed."

"How's your shoulder?"

"All right. How about you?"

Daughter of Lir...

"Fine. By the way, you're down for a nice bonus."

Eyes of perdition!

"Don't mention it," I told her back.

Later that afternoon, and appropriately, a storm shattered. (I prefer "shattered" to "broke." It gives a more accurate idea of the behavior of tropical storms on Venus and saves a lot of words.) Remember that inkwell I mentioned earlier? Now take it between thumb and forefinger and hit its side with a hammer. Watch yourself! Don't get splashed or cut—

Dry, then drenched. The sky one million bright fractures as the hammer falls. And sounds of breaking.

"Everyone below?" suggested the loudspeakers to the already scurrying crew.

Where was I? Who do you think was doing the loudspeaking?

Everything loose went overboard when the water got to walking, but by then no people were loose. The Slider was the first thing below decks. Then the big lifts lowered their shacks.

I had hit it for the nearest Rook with a yell the moment I recognized the pre-brightening of the holocaust. From there I cut in the speakers and spent half a minute coaching the track team.

Minor injuries had occurred, Mike told me over the radio, but nothing serious. I, however, was marooned for the duration. The Rooks do not lead anywhere; they're set too far out over the hull to provide entry downwards, what with the extensor shelves below.

So I undressed myself of the tanks which I had worn for the past several hours, crossed my flippers on the table, and leaned back to watch the hurricane. The top was black as the bottom and we were in between, and somewhat illuminated because of all that flat, shiny space. The waters didn't rain down—they just sort of got together and dropped.

The Rooks were secure enough—they'd weathered any number of these onslaughts—it's just that their positions gave them a greater arc of rise and descent when Tensquare makes like the rocker of a very nervous grandma. I had used the belts from my rig to strap myself into the bolted-down chair, and I removed several years in purgatory from the soul of whoever left a pack of cigarettes in the table drawer.

I watched the water make teepees and mountains and hands and trees until I started seeing faces and people. So I called Mike.

"What are you doing down there?"

"Wondering what you're doing up there," he replied. "What's it like?"

"You're from the Midwest, aren't you?"

"Yeah."

"Get bad storms out there?"

"Sometimes."

"Try to think of the worst one you were ever in. Got a slide rule handy?"

"Right here."

"Then put a one under it, imagine a zero or two following after, and multiply the thing out."

"I can't imagine the zeros."

"Then retain the multiplicand—that's all you can do."

"So what are you doing up there?"

"I've strapped myself in the chair. I'm watching things roll around the floor right now."

I looked up and out again. I saw one darker shadow in the forest.

"Are you praying or swearing?"

"Damned if I know. But if this were the Slider—if only this were the Slider!"

"He's out there?"

I nodded, forgetting that he couldn't see me.

Big, as I remembered him. He'd only broken surface for a few moments, to look around. *There is no power on Earth that can be compared with him who was made to fear no one.* I dropped my cigarette. It was the same as before. Paralysis and an unborn scream.

"You all right, Carl?"

He had looked at me again. Or seemed to. Perhaps that mindless brute had been waiting half a millennium to ruin the life of a member of the most highly developed species in business…

"You okay?"

…Or perhaps it had been ruined already, long before their encounter, and theirs was just a meeting of beasts, the stronger bumping the weaker aside, body to psyche…

"Carl, dammit! Say something!"

He broke again, this time nearer. Did you ever see the trunk of a tornado? It seems like something alive, moving around in all that dark. Nothing has a right to be so big, so strong, and moving. It's a sickening sensation.

"Please answer me."

He was gone and did not come back that day. I finally made a couple of wisecracks at Mike, but I held my next cigarette in my right hand.

The next seventy or eighty thousand waves broke by with a monotonous similarity. The five days that held them were also without distinction. The morning of the thirteenth day out, though, our luck began to rise. The bells broke our coffee-drenched lethargy into small pieces, and we dashed from the gallery without hearing what might have been Mike's finest punchline.

"Aft!" cried someone. "Five hundred meters!"

I stripped to my trunks and started buckling. My stuff is always within grabbing distance.

I flipflopped across the deck, girding myself with a deflated squiggler.

"Five hundred meters, twenty fathoms!" boomed the speakers.

The big traps banged upward and the Slider grew to its full height, m'lady at the console. It rattled past me and took root ahead. Its one arm rose and lengthened.

I breasted the Slider as the speakers called, "Four-eight, twenty!"

"Status Red!"

A belch like an emerging champagne cork and the line arced high over the waters.

"Four-eight, twenty!" it repeated, all Malvern and static. "Baitman, attend!"

I adjusted my mask and hand-over-handed it down the side. Then warm, then cool, then away.

Green, vast, down. Fast. This is the place where I am equal to a squiggler. If something big decides a baitman looks tastier than what he's carrying, then irony colors his title as well as the water about it.

I caught sight of the drifting cables and followed them down. Green to dark green to black. It had been a long cast, too long. I'd never had to follow one this far down before. I didn't want to switch on my torch.

But I had to.

Bad! I still had a long way to go. I clenched my teeth and stuffed my imagination into a straightjacket.

Finally the line came to an end.

I wrapped one arm about it and unfastened the squiggler. I attached it, working as fast as I could, and plugged in the little insulated connections which are the reason it can't be fired with the line. Ikky could break them, but by then it wouldn't matter.

My mechanical eel hooked up, I pulled its section plugs and watched it grow. I had been dragged deeper during this operation, which took about a minute and a half. I was near—too near—to where I never wanted to be.

Loathe as I had been to turn on my light, I was suddenly afraid to turn it off. Panic gripped me and I seized the cable with both hands. The squiggler began to glow, pinkly. It started to twist. It was twice as big as I am and doubtless twice as attractive to pink squiggler-eaters. I told myself this until I believed it, then I switched off my light and started up.

If I bumped into something enormous and steel-hided my heart had orders to stop beating immediately and release me—to dart fitfully forever along Acheron, and gibbering.

Ungibbering, I made it to green water and fled back to the nest.

As soon as they hauled me aboard I made my mask a necklace, shaded my eyes, and monitored for surface turbulence. My first question, of course, was "Where is he?"

"Nowhere," said a crewman; "we lost him right after you went over. Can't pick him up on the scope now. Musta dived."

"Too bad."

The squiggler stayed down, enjoying its bath. My job ended for the time being, I headed back to warm my coffee with rum.

From behind me, a whisper: "Could you laugh like that afterwards?"

Perceptive Answer: "Depends on what he's laughing at."

Still chuckling, I made my way into the center blister with two cupfuls.

"Still hell and gone?"

Mike nodded. His big hands were shaking, and mine were steady as a surgeon's when I set down the cups.

He jumped as I shrugged off the tanks and looked for a bench.

"Don't drip on that panel! You want to kill yourself and blow expensive fuses?"

I toweled down, then settled down to watching the unfilled eye on the wall. I yawned happily; my shoulder seemed good as new.

The little box that people talk through wanted to say something, so Mike lifted the switch and told it to go ahead.

"Is Carl there, Mister Dabis?"

"Yes, ma'am."

"Then let me talk to him."

Mike motioned and I moved.

"Talk," I said.

"Are you all right?"

"Yes, thanks. Shouldn't I be?"

"That was a long swim. I—I guess I overshot my cast."

"I'm happy," I said. "More triple-time for me. I really clean up on that hazardous duty clause."

"I'll be more careful next time," she apologized. "I guess I was too eager. Sorry—" Something happened to the sentence, so she ended it there, leaving me with half a bagful of replies I'd been saving.

I lifted the cigarette from behind Mike's ear and got a light from the one in the ashtray.

"Carl, she was being nice," he said, after turning to study the panels.

"I know," I told him. "I wasn't."

"I mean, she's an awfully pretty kid, pleasant. Headstrong and all that. But what's she done to you?"

"Lately?" I asked.

He looked at me, then dropped his eyes to his cup.

"I know it's none of my bus—" he began.

"Cream and sugar?"

❖   ❖   ❖

Ikky didn't return that day, or that night. We picked up some Dix-
ieland out of Lifeline and let the muskrat ramble while Jean had her
supper sent to the Slider. Later she had a bunk assembled inside. I
piped in "Deep Water Blues" when it came over the air and waited
for her to call up and cuss us out. She didn't though, so I decided she
was sleeping.

Then I got Mike interested in a game of chess that went on until
daylight. It limited conversation to several "checks," one "checkmate," and a "damn!" Since he's a poor loser it also effectively sabo-
taged subsequent talk, which was fine with me. I had a steak and
fried potatoes for breakfast and went to bed.

Ten hours later someone shook me awake and I propped myself
on one elbow, refusing to open my eyes.

"Whassamadder?"

"I'm sorry to get you up," said one of the younger crewmen,
"but Miss Luharich wants you to disconnect the squiggler so we can
move on."

I knuckled open one eye, still deciding whether I should be
amused.

"Have it hauled to the side. Anyone can disconnect it."

"It's at the side now, sir. But she said it's in your contract and we'd
better do things right."

"That's very considerate of her. I'm sure my Local appreciates her
remembering."

"Uh, she also said to tell you to change your trunks and comb
your hair, and shave, too. Mister Anderson's going to film it."

"Okay. Run along; tell her I'm on my way—and ask if she has
some toenail polish I can borrow."

I'll save on details. It took three minutes in all, and I played
it properly, even pardoning myself when I slipped and bumped
into Anderson's white tropicals with the wet squiggler. He smiled,
brushed it off; she smiled, even though Luharich Complectacolor
couldn't completely mask the dark circles under her eyes; and I
smiled, waving to all our fans out there in videoland. —Remember,
Mrs. Universe, you, too, can look like a monster-catcher. Just use
Luharich face cream.

I went below and made myself a tuna sandwich, with mayonnaise.

❖   ❖   ❖

Two days like icebergs—bleak, blank, half-melting, all frigid, mainly out of sight, and definitely a threat to peace of mind—drifted by and were good to put behind. I experienced some old guilt feelings and had a few disturbing dreams. Then I called Lifeline and checked my bank balance.

"Going shopping?" asked Mike, who had put the call through for me.

"Going home," I answered.

"Huh?"

"I'm out of the baiting business after this one, Mike. The Devil with Ikky! The Devil with Venus and Luharich Enterprises! And the Devil with you!"

Up eyebrows.

"What brought that on?"

"I waited over a year for this job. Now that I'm here, I've decided the whole thing stinks."

"You knew what it was when you signed on. No matter what else you're doing, you're selling face cream when you work for face cream sellers."

"Oh, that's not what's biting me. I admit the commercial angle irritates me, but Tensquare has always been a publicity spot, ever since the first time it sailed."

"What, then?"

"Five or six things, all added up. The main one being that I don't care any more. Once it meant more to me than anything else to hook that critter, and now it doesn't. I went broke on what started out as a lark and I wanted blood for what it had cost me. Now I realize that maybe I had it coming. I'm beginning to feel sorry for Ikky."

"And you don't want him now?"

"I'll take him if he comes peacefully, but I don't feel like sticking out my neck to make him crawl into the Hopkins."

"I'm inclined to think it's one of the four or five other things you said you added."

"Such as?"

He scrutinized the ceiling.

I growled.

"Okay, but I won't say it, not just to make you happy you guessed right."

He, smirking: "That look she wears isn't just for Ikky."

"No good, no good." I shook my head. "We're both fission chambers by nature. You can't have jets on both ends of the rocket and expect to go anywhere—what's in the middle just gets smashed."

"That's how it *was*. None of my business, of course—"

"Say that again and you'll say it without teeth."

"Any day, big man"—he looked up—"any place…"

"So go ahead. Get it said!"

"She doesn't care about that bloody reptile, she came here to drag you back where you belong. You're not the baitman this trip."

"Five years is too long."

"There must be something under that cruddy hide of yours that people like," he muttered, "or I wouldn't be talking like this. Maybe you remind us humans of some really ugly dog we felt sorry for when we were kids. Anyhow, someone wants to take you home and raise you—also, something about beggars not getting menus."

"Buddy," I chuckled, "do you know what I'm going to do when I hit Lifeline?"

"I can guess."

"You're wrong. I'm torching it to Mars, and then I'll cruise back home, first class. Venus bankruptcy provisions do not apply to Martian trust funds, and I've still got a wad tucked away where moth and corruption enter not. I'm going to pick up a big old mansion on the Gulf and if you're ever looking for a job you can stop around and open bottles for me."

"You are a yellowbellied fink," he commented.

"Okay," I admitted, "but it's her I'm thinking of, too."

"I've heard the stories about you both," he said. "So you're a heel and a goofoff and she's a bitch. That's called compatibility these days. I dare you, baitman, try keeping something you catch."

I turned.

"If you ever want that job, look me up."

I closed the door quietly behind me and left him sitting there waiting for it to slam.

❖   ❖   ❖

The day of the beast dawned like any other. Two days after my gutless flight from empty waters I went down to rebait. Nothing on the scope. I was just making things ready for the routine attempt.

I hollered a "good morning" from outside the Slider and received an answer from inside before I pushed off. I had reappraised Mike's words, sans sound, sans fury, and while I did not approve of their sentiment or significance, I had opted for civility anyhow.

So down, under, and away. I followed a decent cast about two hundred-ninety meters out. The snaking cables burned black to my left and I paced their undulations from the yellowgreen down into the darkness. Soundless lay the wet night, and I bent my way through it like a cock-eyed comet, bright tail before.

I caught the line, slick and smooth, and began baiting. An icy world swept by me then, ankles to head. It was a draft, as if someone had opened a big door beneath me. I wasn't drifting downwards that fast either.

Which meant that something might be moving up, something big enough to displace a lot of water. I still didn't think it was Ikky. A freak current of some sort, but not Ikky. Ha!

I had finished attaching the leads and pulled the first plug when a big, rugged, black island grew beneath me…

I flicked the beam downward. His mouth was opened.

I was rabbit.

Waves of the death-fear passed downward. My stomach imploded. I grew dizzy.

Only one thing, and one thing only. Left to do. I managed it, finally. I pulled the rest of the plugs.

I could count the scaly articulations ridging his eyes by then.

The squiggler grew, pinked into phosphorescence…squiggled!

Then my lamp. I had to kill it, leaving just the bait before him.

One glance back as I jammed the jatos to life.

He was so near that the squiggler reflected on his teeth, in his eyes. Four meters, and I kissed his lambent jowls with two jets of backwash as I soared. Then I didn't know whether he was following or had halted. I began to black out as I waited to be eaten.

The jatos died and I kicked weakly.

Too fast, I felt a cramp coming on. One flick of the beam, cried rabbit. One second, to know…

Or end things up, I answered. No, rabbit, we don't dart before hunters. Stay dark.

Green waters, finally, to yellowgreen, then top.

Doubling, I beat off toward Tensquare. The waves from the explosion behind pushed me on ahead. The world closed in, and a screamed, "He's alive!" in the distance.

A giant shadow and a shock wave. The line was alive, too. Happy Fishing Grounds. Maybe I did something wrong…

Somewhere Hand was clenched. What's bait?

❖   ❖   ❖

A few million years. I remember starting out as a one-celled organism and painfully becoming an amphibian, then an air-breather. From somewhere high in the treetops I heard a voice.

"He's coming around."

I evolved back into homosapience, then a step further into a hangover.

"Don't try to get up yet."

"Have we got him?" I slurred.

"Still fighting, but he's hooked. We thought he took you for an appetizer."

"So did I."

"Breathe some of this and shut up."

A funnel over my face. Good. Lift your cups and drink…

"He was awfully deep. Below scope range. We didn't catch him till he started up. Too late, then."

I began to yawn.

"We'll get you inside now."

I managed to uncase my ankle knife.

"Try it and you'll be minus a thumb."

"You need rest."

"Then bring me a couple more blankets. I'm staying."

I fell back and closed my eyes.

❖   ❖   ❖

Someone was shaking me. Gloom and cold. Spotlights bled yellow on the deck. I was in a jury-rigged bunk, bulked against the center blister. Swaddled in wool, I still shivered.

"It's been eleven hours. You're not going to see anything now."

I tasted blood.

"Drink this."

Water. I had a remark but I couldn't mouth it.

"Don't ask me how I feel," I croaked. "I know that comes next, but don't ask me. Okay?"

"Okay. Want to go below now?"

"No. Just get me my jacket."

"Right here."

"What's he doing?"

"Nothing. He's deep, he's doped but he's staying down."

"How long since last time he showed?"

"Two hours, about."

"Jean?"

"She won't let anyone in the Slider. Listen, Mike says to come on in. He's right behind you in the blister."

I sat up and turned around. Mike was watching. He gestured; I gestured back.

I swung my feet over the edge and took a couple of deep breaths. Pains in my stomach. I got to my feet and made it into the blister.

"Howza gut?" queried Mike.

I checked the scope. No Ikky. Too deep.

"You buying?"

"Yeah, coffee."

"Not coffee."

"You're ill. Also, coffee is all that's allowed in here."

"Coffee is a brownish liquid that burns your stomach. You have some in the bottom drawer."

"No cups. You'll have to use a glass."

"Tough."

He poured.

"You do that well. Been practicing for that job?"

"What job?"

"The one I offered you—"

A blot on the scope!

"Rising, ma'am! Rising!" he yelled into the box.

"Thanks, Mike. I've got it in here," she crackled.

"Jean!"

"Shut up! She's busy!"

"Was that Carl?"

"Yeah," I called. "Talk later," and I cut it.

Why did I do that?

"Why did you do that?"

I didn't know.

"I don't know."

Damned echoes! I got up and walked outside.

Nothing. Nothing.

Something?

Tensquare actually rocked! He must have turned when he saw the hull and started downward again. White water to my left, and boiling. An endless spaghetti of cable roared hotly into the belly of the deep.

I stood awhile, then turned and went back inside.

Two hours sick. Four, and better.

"The dope's getting to him."

"Yeah."

"What about Miss Luharich?"

"What about her?"

"She must be half dead."

"Probably."

"What are you going to do about it?"

"She signed the contract for this. She knew what might happen. It did."

"I think you could land him."

"So do I."

"So does she."

"Then let her ask me."

Ikky was drifting lethargically, at thirty fathoms.

I took another walk and happened to pass behind the Slider. She wasn't looking my way.

"Carl, come in here!"

Eyes of Picasso, that's what, and a conspiracy to make me Slide…

"Is that an order?"

"Yes—No! Please."

I dashed inside and monitored. He was rising.

"Push or pull?"

I slammed the "wind" and he came like a kitten.

"Make up your own mind now."

He balked at ten fathoms.

"Play him?"

"No!"

She wound him upwards—five fathoms, four…

She hit the extensors at two, and they caught him. Then the graffles.

Cries without and a heat of lightning of flashbulbs.

The crew saw Ikky.

He began to struggle. She kept the cables tight, raised the graffles…

Up.

Another two feet and the graffles began pulsing.

Screams and fast footfalls.

Giant beanstalk in the wind, his neck, waving. The green hills of his shoulders grew.

"He's big, Carl!" she cried.

And he grew, and grew, and grew uneasy…

"Now!"

He looked down.

He looked down, as the god of our most ancient ancestors might have looked down. Fear, shame, and mocking laughter rang in my head. Her head, too?

"Now!"

She looked up at the nascent earthquake.

"I can't!"

It was going to be so damnably simple this time, now the rabbit had died. I reached out.

I stopped.

"Push it yourself."

"I can't. You do it. Land him, Carl!"

"No. If I do, you'll wonder for the rest of your life whether you could have. You'll throw away your soul finding out. I know you will, because we're alike, and I did it that way. Find out now!"

She stared.

I gripped her shoulders.

"Could be that's me out there," I offered. "I am a green sea serpent, a hateful, monstrous beast, and out to destroy you. I am answerable to no one. Push the Inject."

Her hand moved to the button, jerked back.

"Now!"

She pushed it.

I lowered her still form to the floor and finished things up with Ikky.

It was a good seven hours before I awakened to the steady, sea-chewing grind of Tensquare's blades.

"You're sick," commented Mike.

"How's Jean?"

"The same."

"Where's the beast?"

"Here."

"Good." I rolled over. "…Didn't get away this time."

So that's the way it was. No one is born a baitman, I don't think, but the rings of Saturn sing epithalamium the sea-beast's dower.

A Word from Zelazny

Written in January 1963, according to correspondence with Gil Lamont.[1] Zelazny was well aware that the Mars and Venus of space opera no longer could exist as information came flooding in from the early space probes, but he wanted to write that kind of story before it went out of style. "I had a sentimental feeling for that kind of story, and at the time I wrote 'A Rose For Ecclesiastes' in late 1961, I decided to do something I always wanted to do—I had to do it then, because our knowledge of the solar system had changed so rapidly…that the sort of Mars of which Edgar Rice Burroughs wrote, or Leigh Brackett, [or Ray Bradbury], or the numerous Edmond Hamilton stories—that Mars, or that Venus—the great watery world with prehistoric creatures in its oceans—simply did not exist."[2,3]

"I realized that was the last point in time that anyone could write that sort of story. If I wanted to do it, I would have to do it immediately. So I wrote 'A Rose For Ecclesiastes' set on the old-fashioned Mars with the red deserts and the breathable atmosphere. It was just a composite of all my feelings. And I resolved very quickly to do one about Venus, which I did: 'The Doors of His Face, the Lamps of His Mouth.' That was it. I could never do another story of that sort again. But they were both, in a way, my tribute to a phase in the genre's history which had just closed and expressed my feelings towards it. So I wasn't actually making fun of it."[2] "Those were both, in a way, exercises in nostalgia for the earlier sort of science fiction that I had read."[3]

Concerning the two stories, he added, "It was, let's face it, a Byronic gesture, but I considered myself as a writer first, then an SF writer, and, as I said, I am sentimental."[4]

A writer told Zelazny that he used the Yellow Pages as a source of inspiration, and this idea caught on with Zelazny who would "project fifty years into the future the first half dozen entries to which I turned, and then I would ask myself how that business would be run fifty years from now…make some guesses about what society might be like…try the 'what if?' variations; e.g., what if some of the customers (or employees) aren't human…I would try shifting the business to another world, testing it in an even stranger setting. My story 'The Doors of His Face, the Lamps of His Mouth,' actually owed something to a bait-and-tackle ad."[5]

---

1 *Tightbeam #37*, May 1966.
2 *Roger Zelazny*, Theodore Krulik, 1986.
3 *Xignals* XVI Feb/Mar 1986.
4 *Galaxie #96* Mai 1972.
5 *The Writer* 101(3):9–11. March 1988.

Notes

While many readers greeted this story enthusiastically, some critics discarded it as a simple science-fictional retelling of Herman Melville's *Moby Dick*—that comparison fails in several significant respects, including that Ahab never caught the whale that he was obsessed with but died trying, leaving Ishmael as the sole survivor of his crew. "The Doors of His Face, the Lamps of His Mouth" is a story of adventure, redemption and reconciliation, and self-introspection, told by a convincingly realized character in a convincingly realized setting despite the fact that it could only have been fantasy by the time it appeared.

The title is drawn from *The Book of Job* 41:14–19 in which the monstrous sea-creature known as the **Leviathan** is described: "Who can open the doors of his face? || his teeth are terrible round about. || His scales are his pride, || shut together as with a close seal. || Out of his mouth go burning lamps, || and sparks of fire leap out." It's not clear what novel Zelazny referred to in the opening lines; "***We Are All Bait***" would translate as "*Nous Sommes Toute l'Amorce*" or "*Nous Sommes Tous des Appâts.*"

In palmistry, the mount of **Venus** is the large area of the palm that borders the **thumb** and is fenced in by the **life line**, and which is believed to shows the passion and energy that a person has for life. The narrator is comparing the local geography of the continent of Hand on Venus, as viewed while descending from the sky, to the palm of his own hand. **Narcotized** is a slang term meaning put to sleep or made stuporous by use of a narcotic (an opioid or other pain-killing drug). **Hemiplegia** is paralysis on one side of the body due to a stroke (destruction of brain tissue by a blood clot or hemorrhage); Davits limps from a partial hemiplegia, the result of a stroke he experienced during his close-up encounter with Ikky. **Lloyd's** refers to Lloyd's of London, a group of insurance underwriters that originally formed in 1688 to insure, classify, register, and certify marine vessels.

A **gaff** is an iron hook with a handle for landing large fish, whereas a **grapple** or grapnel is an anchor with three or more flukes. A **Seraph** is a member of the highest of nine orders of angels. **Abyss** when capitalized refers to Hell or the primal Chaos before Creation. **De facto** means "in fact", as opposed to "in theory" or "in law". **Through a glass, brownly** alludes to the line "through a glass, darkly" in 1 Corinthians: 13 in the New Testament of the Bible; the line implies that humans have an imperfect perception of reality. **Daughter of Lir** refers to the Irish mythology of the Children of Lir, and specifically the beautiful daughter Fionnuala, who was cursed and changed into a swan by her stepmother. **Lir** himself is a god of the sea in Irish mythology and is alluded to in the story "The Horses of Lir."

The phrase **Daughter of Lir, eyes of Picasso** is a quote from Ezra Pound's *Cantos II* in which he describes a seal: "Seal sports in the spray-whited circles of cliff wash, || Sleek head, daughter of Lir || eyes of Picasso || Under black fur hood, lithe daughter of ocean". A **gink** is a foolish or contemptible person. **Yclept** means called or named. **Passed him a box full of her unseeing** means that she took out her colored contact lenses. **Govino** Bay is off the island of **Corfu**; the reference is to a time when Carlton Davits was rescued from near-drowning by Jean Luharich. **Mindanao** is the second-largest island in the Phillipines. **Jato** is an auxiliary jet-producing unit to provide thrust at takeoff. **Sleek head...Daughter of Lir...Eyes of...** quotes Cantos II again except **perdition** (damnation, eternal loss of soul) has been substituted for **Picasso**. **Vido** and **Corfu** are among the Greek islands. **There is no power on Earth that can be compared with him who was made to fear no one** is another quote from the Book of Job in which the Leviathan is described. **Acheron** is one of the rivers in Hades across which Charon ferries the newly dead. **Dart fitfully forever along Acheron** echoes poetry of Sappho and also a poem that Conrad quotes in *...And Call Me Conrad / This Immortal*. **Dixieland** is a style of jazz music from New Orleans that features a rapid two-beat rhythm and solo improvisations. **Deep Water Blues** was performed by Louis Armstrong and the Dukes of Dixieland. **Sans** [without] **sound, sans fury** alludes to William Faulkner's novel *The Sound and the Fury* which, like this novella, features a stream-of-consciousness narrative. The original quote is from Shakespeare's *Macbeth*—"...a tale told by an idiot, full of sound and fury, signifying nothing..."—and suggests the narrator's self-deprecating humor, that he considers himself an idiot and that his tale in meaningless. **Epithalamium** means a bridal song, or an ode honoring the bride and groom; the usage implies that Carlton and Jean may be reconciling as a couple. **Dower** means the portion of a deceased man's property which is given to his widow, or it can mean a gift or endowment; in this case the deceased is the sea-beast.

A Thing of
Terrible Beauty

Fantastic, April 1963 as by Harrison Denmark.

How like a god of the Epicureans is the audience, at a time like this! Powerless to alter the course of events, yet better informed than the characters, they might rise to their feet and cry out, "Do not!"—but the blinding of Oedipus would still ensue, and the inevitable knot in Jocasta's scarlet would stop her breathing still.

But no one rises, of course. They know better. They, too, are inevitably secured by the strange bonds of the tragedy. The gods can only observe and know, they cannot alter circumstance, nor wrestle with *ananke*.

My host is already anticipating the thing he calls "catharsis." My search has carried me far, and my choice was a good one. Phillip Devers lives in the theater like a worm lives in an apple, a paralytic in an iron lung. It is his world.

And I live in Phillip Devers.

For ten years his ears and eyes have been my ears and eyes. For ten years I have tasted the sensitive perceptions of a great critic of the drama, and he has never known it.

He has come close—his mind is agile, his imagination vivid—but his classically trained intellect is too strong, his familiarity with psychopathology too intimate to permit that final leap from logic to intuition, and an admission of my existence. At times, before he drops off to sleep, he toys with the thought of attempting communication, but the next morning he always rejects it—which is well. What could we possibly have to say to one another?

—Now that inchoate scream from the dawn of time, and Oedipus stalks the stage in murky terror!

How exquisite!

I wish that I could know the other half. Devers says there are two things in a complete experience—a moving toward, called pity, and a moving away from, called terror. It is the latter which I feel, which I have always sought; I do not understand the other, even when my host quivers and his vision goes moistly dim.

I should like very much to cultivate the total response. Unfortunately, my time here is limited. I have hounded beauty through a thousand stellar cells, and here I learned that a man named Aristotle defined it. It is unfortunate that I must leave without knowing the entire experience.

But I am the last. The others have gone. *The stars move still, time runs, and the clock will strike...*

The ovation is enormous. The resurrected Jocasta bows beside her red-socketted king, smiling. Hand in hand, they dine upon our applause—but even pale Tiresias does not see what I have seen. It is very unfortunate.

And now the taxi home. What time is it in Thebes?

❖   ❖   ❖

Devers is mixing us a strong drink, which he generally does not do. I shall appreciate these final moments all the more, seen through the prism of his soaring fancy.

His mood is a strange one. It is almost as if he knows what is to occur at one o'clock—almost as if he knows what will happen when the atom expands its fleecy chest, shouldering aside an army of Titans, and the Mediterranean rushes to dip its wine-dark muzzle into the vacant Sahara.

But he could not know, without knowing me, and this time he will be a character, not an observer, when the thing of terrible beauty occurs.

We both watch the pale gray eyes on the sliding panel. He takes aspirins in advance when he drinks, which means he will be mixing us more.

But his hand... It stops short of the medicine chest.

Framed in the tile and stainless steel, we both regard reflections of a stranger.

"Good evening."

After ten years, those two words, and on the eve of the last performance!

Activating his voice to reply would be rather silly, even if I could manage it, and it would doubtless be upsetting.

I waited, and so did he.

Finally, like an organ player, I pedalled and chorded the necessary synapses:

Good evening. Please go ahead and take your aspirins.

He did. Then he picked up his drink from the ledge.

"I hope you enjoy Martinis."

I do. Very much. Please drink more.

He smirked at us and returned to the living room.

"What are you? A psychosis? A dybbuk?"

Oh, no! Nothing like that!— Just a member of the audience.

"I don't recall selling you a ticket."

You did not exactly invite me, but I didn't think you would mind, if I kept quiet...

"Very decent of you."

He mixed another drink, then looked out at the building across the way. It had two lighted windows, on different floors, like misplaced eyes.

"Mind if I ask why?"

Not at all. Perhaps you can even help me. I am an itinerant esthetician. I have to borrow bodies on the worlds I visit—preferably those of beings with similar interests.

"I see—you're a gate-crasher."

Sort of, I guess. I try not to cause any trouble, though. Generally, my host never even learns of my existence. But I have to leave soon, and something has been troubling me for the past several years... Since you have guessed at my existence and managed to maintain your stability, I've decided to ask you to resolve it.

"Ask away." He was suddenly bitter and very offended. I saw the reason in an instant.

❖   ❖   ❖

Do not think, I told him, *that I have influenced anything you have thought or done. I am only an observer. My sole function is to appreciate beauty.*

"How interesting!" he sneered. "How soon is it going to happen?"

What?

"The thing that is causing you to leave."

Oh, that…

I was not certain what to tell him. What could he do, anyhow? Suffer a little more, perhaps.

"Well?"

My time is up, I told him.

"I see flashes," he said. "Sand and smoke, and a flaming baseball."

He was too sensitive. I thought I had covered those thoughts.

Well… The world is going to end at one o'clock…

"That's good to know. How?"

There is a substratum of fissionable material, which Project Eden is going to detonate. This will produce an enormous chain reaction…

"Can't you do something to stop it?

I don't know how. I don't know what could stop it. My knowledge is limited to the arts and the life-sciences. —You broke your leg when you were skiing in Vermont last winter. You never knew. Things like that, I can manage…

"And the horn blows at midnight," he observed.

One o'clock, I corrected, *Eastern Standard Time.*

"Might as well have another drink," he said, looking at his watch. "It's going on twelve."

My question… I cleared an imaginary throat.

"Oh, yes, what did you want to know?"

—The other half of the tragic response. I've watched you go through it many times, but I can't get at it. I feel the terror part, but the pity—the pity always eludes me.

"Anyone can be afraid," he said, "that part is easy. But you have to be able to get inside people—not exactly the way you do—and feel everything they feel, just before they go smash—so that it feels you're going smash along with them—and you can't do a damn thing about it, and you wish you could—that's pity."

Oh? And being afraid, too?

"—and being afraid. Together, they equal the grand catharsis of true tragedy."

He hiccupped.

And the tragic figure, for whom you feel these things? He must be great and noble, mustn't he?

"True," he nodded, as though I were seated across the room from him, "and in the last moment when the unalterable jungle law is about to prevail, he must stare into the faceless mask of God, and bear himself, for that brief moment, above the pleas of his nature and the course of events."

We both looked at his watch.

"What time will you be leaving?"

In about fifteen minutes.

"Good. You have time to listen to a record while I dress."

He switched on his stereo and selected an album.

I shifted uneasily.

If it isn't too long…

He regarded the jacket.

"Five minutes and eight seconds. I've always maintained that it is music for the last hour of Earth."

He placed it on the turntable and set the arm.

"If Gabriel doesn't show up, this will do."

He reached for his tie as the first notes of Miles Davis' "*Saeta*" limped through the room, like a wounded thing climbing a hill.

He hummed along with it as he reknotted his tie and combed his hair. Davis talked through an Easter lily with a tongue of brass, and the procession moved before us: Oedipus and blind Gloucester stumbled by, led by Antigone and Edgar—Prince Hamlet gave a fencer's salute and plunged forward, while black Othello lumbered on behind—Hippolytus, all in white, and the Duchess of Malfi, sad, paraded through memory on a thousand stages.

Phillip buttoned his jacket as the final notes sounded, and shut down the player. Carefully rejacketting the record, he placed it among his others.

What are you going to do?

"Say good-bye. There's a party up the street I hadn't planned on attending. I believe I'll stop in for a drink. Good-bye to you also.

"By the way," he asked, "what is your name? I've known you for a long time, I ought to call you something now."

He suggested one, half-consciously. I had never really had a name before, so I took it.

Adrastea, I told him.

He smirked again.

"No thought is safe from you, is it? Good-bye."

Good-bye.

He closed the door behind him, and I passed through the ceilings and floors of the apartments overhead, then up, and into the night above the city. One eye in the building across the street winked out; as I watched, the other did the same.

Bodiless again, I fled upward wishing there was something I could feel.

A Word from Zelazny

"I rather liked this one when I wrote it, but I don't remember why or how I came to write it. Perhaps Harrison Denmark had taken on a life of his own. Perhaps he's the gentleman I see walking along Bishop's Lodge Road every day, sometimes in both directions."[1]

Notes

Zelazny submitted "two brief ones" simultaneously to Avram Davidson at *The Magazine of Fantasy & Science Fiction*: the light and humorous sketch, "Of Time and the Yan," and the serious and introspective "A Thing of Terrible Beauty." Surprisingly, Davidson bought "Yan" and rejected this better-crafted tale, explaining, "I am tired of doomsday stories, get so many of them, yet here RZ send us *two* at once. Could he perhaps change the Fate awaiting the critic to the critic's own death rather than the end of the world, I would consider buying the story."[2] Zelazny chose not to rewrite it.

The **god of the Epicureans** refers to the ancient Greek philosopher Epicurus, who was a materialist who dispensed with superstition, religious belief, fear of god and the afterlife—he promoted the concept that there were no gods interested in men, and there was no afterlife. He advised living life to the fullest in a sort of hedonist way because the greatest good was to achieve pleasure.

The story refers to **Oedipus**, son of Laius and **Jocasta**, who was abandoned at birth and unwittingly killed his father and then married his mother. Upon learning the truth, Jocasta committed suicide (**the inevitable knot in Jocasta's scarlet would stop her breathing still**) and Oedipus blinded himself (**red-socketted king**) and went into exile.

In Greek mythology, **Ananke** is the goddess of necessity and coercion; she is also the mother of **Adrastea** (mentioned at the end) which provides a thematic loop to the beginning and end of the story. **Catharsis** is a purging

---

1 *The Last Defender of Camelot*, 1980.
2 Letter from Roger Zelazny to Avram Davidson dated June 30, 1962, with a hand-written note on it by Avram Davidson, undated but likely July 1962.

of emotions and tensions to provide emotional or psychiatric relief. An **iron lung** was a chamber used to treat victims of poliomyelitis who had suffered lung paralysis; the chamber enclosed the entire body except the head, and pressure changes in the chamber forced air in and out of the lungs. **Psychopathology** is the study of the origin, manifestations and treatment of mental illness. **Inchoate** means primary, rudimentary, just begun, or disorganized. **Aristotle** defined beauty as the gift of God that occurs when all parts work together in harmony so that no one part draws unjust attention to itself. **The stars move still, time runs, and the clock will strike…** is a doomsday quote from Christopher Marlowe's *Faustus* which ends "…The Devil will come, and Faustus will be damned." A **dybbuk** is a demon or soul of a dead person that possesses and controls a living person and can only be driven out by exorcism. **Itinerant** means wandering or traveling while **esthetician** in this instances means someone trained in the theory of beauty and artistic expression. **The horn blows at midnight** is the title of a 1945 motion picture in which a character (played by Jack Benny) dreams that he is the angel Athaniel, a trumpeter in the orchestra of heaven entrusted to blow the Last Trumpet at midnight. Two fallen angels steal his trumpet and complications ensue. The coming of the **Archangel Gabriel** has been foretold to announce the end of the world. Jazz music is occasionally referred to in Zelazny's work, and in this case **Miles Davis's *"Saeta"*** receives a cameo.

There is a quick reference to numerous tragic figures and places from history and literature. **Tiresias** was a blind but wise Theban prophet who spent seven years transformed into a woman; he did not foresee the end of the world that the narrator knows is coming. **Thebes** was a major city in Greece after the defeat of the Spartans until it was destroyed by Alexander the Great. In King Lear, the earl's son **Edgar**, disguised as a beggar, leads **blind Gloucester** to Dover Cliff where Gloucester wishes to end his life. **Antigone**, daughter of Oedipus and Jocasta, was sentenced to death for defying her uncle Creon, king of Thebes, but she took her own life before the sentence could be carried out, and her fiancé, Creon's son Haemon, killed himself over her body. **Prince Hamlet** of Denmark is the tragic hero from Shakespeare's well-known play, while in Shakespeare's **Othello**, the title character is misled by Iago to think that his wife is having an affair; he kills his wife and later himself. **Hippolytus** was the son of Theseus, banished and cursed by his father after being falsely accused by Phaedra, his father's wife, of rape. **The Duchess of Malfi** is another tragic play that begins as a love story, with a Duchess who marries beneath her class, and ends with her two brothers destroying themselves.

Adrastea ("she whom none escapes") was the nymph who raised the infant Zeus in secret to protect him from his father Cronus, and the daughter of **Ananke** mentioned at the beginning of the story.

How a Poem Means

Written 1955–60 for *Chisel in the Sky;* previously unpublished.

(To J. Ciardi)

The bowelled brain
excretes its rhyme-beats
into porcelain stanzas'
sure sheer feats
of mirror-pleated nickel drain…

classic relief in stone!
so white and flowing,
chromium glowing…
bonanzas of such bone!

Notes

John **Ciardi** was an American poet who was also known for translating Dante's *The Divine Comedy,* a work that heavily influenced Zelazny.

MONOLOGUE FOR TWO

Manuscript title: In the Dry of Capricorn.
Fantastic, May 1963 as by Harrison Denmark.

—Thank you, nurse, but I can manage the chair with one arm. The wheels turn quite easily.

—Good morning, Doctor. Nice place you've got. Nice country.

—No, I've never been here to see you before. Maybe I do look familiar, though…

—My trouble? Oh, that. Would you take a look at the muscle of my left calf, please?

—Sorry, I can't bend forward to roll up the trouser. No, you'll have to raise the leg yourself, too.

—Yes, that's right. There is no muscle in my left calf.

—What's wrong, Doctor? You don't look so well, all of a sudden. Do you recognize the surgical technique?

—Sit down, by all means. No, I don't smoke, thank you.

—What's that? It lit itself for you? Yes, that happens sometimes.

—No, I didn't think there was anything you could do for it. Just thought I'd check up though. Science is always making wonderful advances. I know you did some pioneer work in transplantation and, well, I thought you'd know, if anyone would.

—Yes, Polish. I'm a doctor myself. Haven't practiced since the war, though, and I'm afraid I haven't kept abreast of all phases of the healing arts. —Institute of Medicine in Warsaw, yes, that's right. I was doing my internship back when you started your research…
—Don't be modest. I know you were only a member of the staff, and that Ravensbroek was a big place. Still, so is the world, and I managed to find you here, just as you found me there.

—That ash is going to fall on your nice carpet. Just drop it in the tray as it floats by.

—Very good.

—What do I want? Oh, perhaps just a moment of your time. I've had a hankering in recent years to practice medicine again, myself. Surgery requires two good hands, though, and that transplant experiment you tried didn't come out so well. Still, I might make a good diagnostician...

—Dead! No, somehow that didn't happen. Was it Schopenhauer who said that even life itself is an act of will? I forget. Anyhow, the tubercular bacilli didn't do their job properly—neither did the Type AB blood, even though I am Type O—nor the starvation diet.

—It might have been that whole wild syndrome you imposed, or maybe it was the yoga I practiced to keep from going mad—or both of them—that gave me the Power. —No, stay in your chair!

—See what I mean? I have the Power. It wasn't so strong in those days, back when I crawled from the ruins of Ravensbroek with a bullet in my heart, but I've been working on it a lot since.

—Kill you? Goodness! Whatever gave you that idea? I have no desire to kill you. No, the man in the wheelchair isn't going to hurt anybody...

—But you, Doctor, what do you think of the Power? —I know you're not a psychiatrist. But don't you think it could be a great aid to a medical man?

—So do I, yes. So when I heard you were going to turn this into a charity clinic, I decided to come see about a job.

—What? —Nothing about a charity clinic? —Oh, you're wrong. We're going to treat the poor, the uneducated, the maimed and the blind. We're going to deliver babies and administer free medicine. After all, we're rich, aren't we?

—No, you don't understand. You can't refuse to operate, because you're only going to be the assistant. You don't think I'd trust you with a scalpel in your hands, do you? Your rich patients will just have to find themselves another hand-patter.

—You'd better put your cigarette out now. Never mind, I'll do it. There. Now this is going to hurt me much much more than it's going to hurt you. I loathe the thought. Your body is the coffin of a dead soul, and your hands are the instruments of murder—but they can be put to good uses, and maybe atone for some of what you've done.

—Your eyesight? Yes, that's the Power working now. I've spent almost twenty years developing it to this point. Just relax. Another second will do it.

—There!

—See all right, now? The chair? Oh, you'll get used to it. The wheels turn quite easily.

—Nurse! Come in here! The patient has fainted.

Notes

This story employs a clever literary device with the entire story communicated in dialogue from one person (a monologue), but communicating two viewpoints (Zelazny later attempted another story told almost entirely by dialogue but considered it only a partial success; see "Collector's Fever").

Ravensbrük/Ravensbrueck/Ravensbroek was a concentration camp exclusively for women in Germany during WWII. It was notorious for various "medical" experiments that were done which included removal of muscles from the calves and infection with dirt and bacteria to simulate wounds received by soldiers in battle. Other experiments included infusing incompatible blood, such as type AB to a type O recipient, and starvation.

Zelazny was often criticized in his early work for not using female characters except in secondary roles or for not having strong female characters. It is likely that most readers failed to appreciate that the sex of the protagonist *could only be female*—she was a survivor of Ravensbrük—or at least she was a strong female character at the start of this story before the ending when she switched bodies with the Doctor who had tortured her. Adding to the misdirection is that the character referred to herself as "the man in the wheelchair," which may indicate that she had altered her physical appearance to look like a man, or she looked that way because of the multiple previous, disfiguring tortures that she had suffered at the Doctor's hands. Review of the original manuscript confirmed that the phrase was "the *man* in the wheelchair" and not *woman*.

Evidently some readers didn't realize that only one person was speaking in the story and thereby found it incomprehensible. A letter to the editor in the October 1963 issue of *Fantastic* stated, "As for this new writer, Harrison Denmark (is that his real name??), everything but 'Monologue for Two'," which I could not make anything out of, has been good."

Schopenhauer was a German Philosopher born in Danzig, in what is now Gdańsk, Poland. Zelazny's ancestry is Polish.

Regarding the manuscript title: *Capricorn* has multiple meanings, but in this case it likely meant the Tropic of Capricorn, which is the latitude that passes through parts of Australia, southern Africa, Brazil and South America and marks the dry country to which the doctor had fled.

CONCERT

Double:Bill #11, Oct-Nov 1964.

Strange, how here
in this place of music
we undergo a sea-change:

Your arm to coral,
and mine a decking plume
of seawrack
green as flannel,
clinging.

It will not always be thus—
maiden, blonde,
pink as the cities of the sea—
but now,
through a glass, greenly,
but now,
like the gaze of Medusa,
the sound has come—
to statuize our stance,
eternalize the instant—

to build a pearly substance
out of shadows transmarine—
here,
where all the chloral soundings
meet membrane,
shatter,
and revise.

The silence will rush to crush;
schools of flashing hands
will dart disruptive rings;
and after all, the waves—
parting as they kiss,
rough-tongued and bitter,
each quite cold,
and all oblivious.

Notes

This poem calls to mind the sinking of Atlantis. **Seawrack** means the miscellany that the waves toss on shore; it can also mean seaweed. **Through a glass, greenly** alludes to the line "through a glass, darkly" in 1 Corinthians:13 in the New Testament of the Bible; the line implies that humans have an imperfect perception of reality. In Greek mythology, **Medusa** had hair made of living snakes, and her gaze turned people to stone. **Statuize** is a neologism (made-up word) to mean the effect of Medusa's gaze on a person—turn them into statues. The word **chloral** puns on *choral* (sung by a choir or chorus) and *coral* (stony substance in reefs formed from secretions of marine life). **Chloral** or trichloroethanol is a liquid made by chlorinating acetaldehyde, but Zelazny likely meant it to imply chlorophyll and green.

ICEAGE

To Spin Is Miracle Cat, Underwood-Miller 1981.
Written 1955–60 for *Chisel in the Sky*.

O
why
the sky
so torturéd
today? one says
aloud, quick finger
uncoiled sudden up over
their heads. They touch at
them then with meaning, so that
is all there was to vision this day
so blue and taut, that spotless lay
under stone fingers, which the play
of steel muscle tore brittly at
and beat, while a blind cat
amid the snow grew her-
self an extra, fur-
less tail, laid
in cannonéd
chimney
lea

Notes

Cannoned means bombarded by canon blasts. A **lea** is an open area of land, such as a meadow. The accents on two words appear to direct the intended pronunciation only.

THRESHOLD OF THE PROPHET

Manuscript title: "None But the Lonely Heart." (a pun on Hart Crane).
Fantastic, May 1963.

"Why did you do that?" he asked.

"It was getting to be an eyesore," answered the goggled man, switching off his slice-unit. "It was no good anymore. Would have fallen in a couple years."

"How will people cross the river now?"

The man eyed the brick-red face before him—the coils of seaweed caught in stark hair… He pressed a stud at his belt and rose above the ground.

"Same as always," he stated. "Personal flight unit, or car."

Crane rose into the air and drifted beside him. Slow moving vehicles crossed the sky overhead. People, all in gray, passed at lower heights. The prospect resembled the teeth of an enormous comb: rank upon rank, the dark buildings filed beneath them; an occasional antenna, like a caught strand of hair, quivered above the skyline; there was no grass nor bare earth visible. His companion was as gray as the city.

"Where are the colors? New York was always colors."

"You're a real throwback, that's what you are. Doesn't that horrible sky hurt your eyes?"

He looked up.

"Same blue it's always been."

"Well, as soon as the Council passes a resolution, Weather Control will make it a lot easier to look at."

"What do you mean?"

"Damping units. We'll kill the glare, the color."

"Take the blue out of the sky?"

"Exactly."

Crane looked back at the muddy snake of the East River.

"What about the bridge? Won't it be a hazard for boats?"

"Boats? Where are you from, anyhow? The last boat was dismantled two hundred years ago—after people decided it wasn't worth half a credit to ride to Staten Island when they could fly it for nothing—and in less time."

"And you'll just leave the bridge where it fell?"

"Time and the river will take care of it," laughed the man. "Why? You want it?"

"I'll take it, if no one else does."

"Go ahead. It belongs to anyone who cares to haul it away. —The scrap won't be worth much."

He studied the man gliding abreast of him.

"You must have an awfully compact flying unit. I've been trying to guess where you're wearing it."

"Keep guessing."

"…And those clothes, and the way you talk. Where are you from?"

"I've been on a voyage."

"Oh—the outer planets. Ever been on Earth before?"

"Not this world."

"Well, get a good eyeful. It's worth the trip."

Crane nodded.

❖ ❖ ❖

"A man once wrote a poem about that bridge." He nodded toward it.

"Can't prove it by me. Do they still read poetry on the outworlds?"

"I'd like to think so. Aren't there any poets here?"

"Why? Metaphor is an awfully crude manner of description. It's pleasant to think most people have passed beyond the stage where everything is like something else. An object is itself. Why complicate matters? Life is mathematics."

"That's nice to know. —But what of the dark places, where there is no mathematic? The open end of the human equation…?"

The gray man winced.

"Don't talk about death or insanity! We'll beat them yet!" He clenched his fist. "Don't they teach you politeness on the outworlds? Some things are not fit subjects for conversation."

"But what do you do about them?"

The gray man looked down at the gray city.

"We are shedding light in every dark place in the universe—that is the new poetry! Everything will be explained sooner or later. We are conquering every natural phenomenon with reason."

"Can you explain this?" asked Crane, seizing his wrist. He held the protesting hand against his chest.

The man's face sagged.

"You have no heartbeat!"

"That," said Crane, "is as accurate a statement as science can manage. Good day."

He vanished.

The man changed his course. He hurried toward the Institute of Mental Health.

❖   ❖   ❖

"Hello, mister."

The old man removed his pipe from between his teeth and nodded.

"H'lo."

Crane leaned against the rail of the porch.

"I see you have grass up here, and a couple trees." He looked over the sparse lawn and past the two maples that guarded a twisted path by the river.

"Yep." The man scratched his nose with the pipestem. "Kinda like 'em. Don't see any in town anymore. 'T's why I moved up here."

"The air seems cleaner too."

"Yep. And they won't dampen the sky this far north, by ga'!"

"That's true. I've been through this part of the country before. —That's a nice little piece of river you've got going by."

"Pretty, all right."

The man regarded him with curiosity.

"Sort of odd look you've got about you, fella. Where you from?"

"The outer worlds."

"Oh yeah. Been out there twict, m'self. Not much to see."

Crane shrugged.

"Every place has its own style in beauty, I guess."

"S'pose so," he acknowledged.

"Look," Crane began, "I had a reason for stopping here. I wanted to find someone older, who might remember a little about the way things used to be."

"I can remember back a hundred-forty, hundred-fifty year, mebbe…"

"Good. I've got a deal to offer you."

The old eyes squinted through the old glasses.

"What kinda deal?"

"Want to buy the Brooklyn Bridge?"

"Haw! Haw! Haw!" The man shook, slapping his thigh. Tears ran down his cheeks.

"It's been a hundred year since I heerd that one! Didn't know anyone else remembered it. You're a card, sonny!"

"I'm serious," said Crane. "I'll bring it here and put it right across the river for you. I can do it. It's mine now."

The man twisted his head to one side and studied his face.

"By ga'! You're not kiddin'!"

"No. I'm dead serious."

"What would I want with the Brooklyn Bridge across my river?"

"It meant something once," said Crane. "It was a symbol in the old days, of everything man was, crossing over, always crossing over, into something greater and better. I think it ought to be preserved—as a monument."

"Sonny, the future's already here. And man doesn't have to cross on to anything better or greater. He's pretty great and pretty good right now."

"I'd expect that from a New Englander," smiled Crane, sadly, "but you live right outside New York, and you're old—you remember other days. If I could find someone to whom the bridge meant something, I might preserve it. I'll give it to you for a dollar—I mean, a credit."

"I wouldn't give you anything for it, sonny. I moved out here to get away from all that hardware, and people think I'm odd enough as it is. I don't think you could sell it to any man alive."

Crane nodded.

"That's what I figured."

"Come and set a spell anyhow, boy. I've got some cold synthocider here." The man turned.

"Thanks, but I have to be going. I only drink the real thing, anyhow."

The man started.

"There ain't been no real cider since I was a boy," he said. "There ain't been no apple trees for two hundred years!"

But there was no one standing there to hear him.

❖ ❖ ❖

"All right," he said, soaring. "All right, you prosaic-minded goggle-wearers. You've had it! Knock down my bridge? Empty the sky of blue? Erase the bright burden of the rose and the apple? You want to shed light in every dark place in the universe, huh? Step right up, kiddies, I'm going to give you something to think about!"

And he raised the bridge, as delicately as a cat lifts her kitten.

"'O harp and altar, of the fury fused…'"

He aligned the cables and erased the rust spots. He grew new metal where there had been holes.

"'Terrific threshold of the prophet's pledge…'"

He arced the gleaming span across the river once more, from where the gray man had toppled it that morning.

"'Prayer of pariah, and the lover's cry…'"

And in the middle, in the middle of the bridge, he built an opaque arch, where every color of the banished rainbow shimmered and danced.

"Come all ye faithful!" his voice boomed, like the ghost of all the gone foghorns. "Step right up, ladies and gentlemen!"

He mounted to the highest point of the span and looked down and around. He reached behind space and tied an interdimensional knot. He twisted the fabric of the continuum, joining remoteness with nearness.

"Half a credit!" he called out. "Half a credit for the most amazing sight of all! No crowding, please! Just step right up!"

People darkened the sky, driven by their desire to know, to explain. They adjusted their goggles and hovered above the circle of color. One man stared up at him. He recognized the bridge-killer.

"Did you put it back?" asked the man. "Are you responsible for the light phenomenon?"

"You gave it to me, didn't you?" he answered. "Now I'm giving it back to you—with improvements and additions."

"What is that?"

The man pointed at the glowing portal.

"Step through it and take a look."

He did.

There was a long, neck-tingling silence.

A car pushed through the crowd of hoverers.

"What is that thing?" the uniformed driver asked him.

"Go through it and see for yourself."

The car nosed ahead and vanished.

Three of the airborne crowd pushed through the veils of color in speedy succession.

No one emerged.

" 'O brilliant kids,' " Crane recited, " 'fondle your shells and sticks, bleached by time and the elements…' "

He descended slowly, like the ghost of all his dead seagulls.

" '…But there is a line you must not cross nor ever trust beyond it spry cordage of your bodies…' "

He hovered a moment in their midst, smiling, then stepped through the crown of light. They did not hear his last words, bubbling on the other side:

" 'The bottom of the sea is cruel…' "

Notes

The protagonist Hart Crane was the poet whom Zelazny most admired. The first three quotations of poetry within this story are from Crane's poem "Brooklyn Bridge," while the excerpts in the last several paragraphs are from his poem "Voyages."

HART CRANE…

Written 1955–60 for *Chisel in the Sky*; previously unpublished.

…walking the myth-killing mileage
of Eliot-answered morning.

Notes

Eliot refers to poet T. S. Eliot, an American-born British poet who won the 1948 Nobel Prize for literature.

SOUTHERN CROSS

Eridanus #2 (poetry fanzine), Spring 1966 (as "Cross Caribbean").
Written in 1957 for *Chisel in the Sky*.

(Elegy, Hart Crane)

My Nameless Woman of the South,
and the Spring that I accomplished you…

All ways one phosphor furrow, Orizaba—
All skeleton streaks one streetlamped street…
But always one Spring, so South,
and all shored ways one deep drawn day,
coralling under oranged climes' chloral bays,
spent and spelled at skulled heavens,
                              slappings of your tidal sands.
And always my ears will throb as stoppered bottles asea
as the one bunched pearl soul of prior suns dips by askance
when the rude rood raises your wake through night
then bends it down to a dawn
between the sob of the sea,
                              under the sail of the sun,
and sighed-out hissing sounds of spectered stars.

A Word from Zelazny

"Every generation seems to breed an eccentric, talented poet who dies young and becomes something of an idol to the next generation. Sylvia Path was too late for me in this respect. In my day it was Hart Crane. I've read and still read a lot of poetry, but Crane's word magic probably had the most influence on whatever poetic style I may have."[1] "Hart Crane was my first contemporary influence when I began writing poetry."[2] Zelazny also honored Hart Crane with the poems "Hart Crane…," "I Used to Think in Lines That Were Irregular to the Right," and the story "Threshold of the Prophet."

This poem won Western Reserve University's Finley Foster Poetry Prize in 1957. Although written in 1957 for *Chisel in the Sky* it first appeared in the poetry fanzine *Eridanus #2*, Spring 1966 (as "Cross Caribbean"). A letter from Zelazny in that issue indicates that, despite the award, it had not been published previously.[3]

Notes

The poem alludes to Hart Crane's poem *The Bridge: Southern Cross*, referencing "nameless Woman of the South" and "phosphor" and retaining a similar structure of indented lines. The setting of that poem is a ship carrying a poet home, as he looks from the stern at the Southern Cross and laments the woman whom he desired but did not get to know.

The **Southern Cross** is a constellation seen in the southern hemisphere. **Phosphor** is a luminescent substance which emits light after absorbing energy; in this case, it can be seen in the wake of a ship. **Orizaba** is a city in Mexico; the name derives from the Aztec and means "place of playing waters." **Rood** means crucifix, referring to the title of this and the subject of Crane's poem; **rude rood** is wordplay, as is the use of **coralling** and **chloral**. **Coralling** puns on *choral* (sung by a choir or chorus) and *coral* (stony substance in reefs formed from secretions of marine life). The word **chloral** also puns on *choral* and *coral* and Zelazny likely meant to imply *chlorophyll* or the green of marine plant life. **Chloral** or trichloroethanol, a toxic, pungent liquid, was not meant literally in this poem.

---

1 *When Pussywillows Last in the Catyard Bloomed*, 1980.
2 *Critical Wave #33*, November 1993.
3 *Eridanus #2*, Spring 1966.

I Used to Think in Lines That Were Irregular to the Right

Science Fiction (Australian) Vol 1 No 3 Dec 1978.

I used to think in lines that were irregular to the right,
but the straight-ruled dexter margin's claimed its own.
Too many pages where lines advance like infantry,
too much continuity,
too many harried characters in far too big a rush
to descend the humps, the hills,
to stub their toes on weighted words…

Potential energy lurks at the rough line's end.
A kick here, a bump there,
reality topples,
things slide,
The talus of improbability grows.

Prose is clean and smooth and slick,
advancing fully to the right,
building walls like rows of brick,
caging wild metaphors,
sealing their cells dead tight.

What is left
when fancy's eye is trapped
and dragged along to such a place?

The bottom of the page is cruel.

A Word from Zelazny

An example of a deliberately structured/shaped poem which seems to express regret at moving away from writing poetry. "That's true, I do regret it. But there's another point about that poem: it's a tribute to Hart Crane. He wrote 'The bottom of the sea is cruel!', I put 'the bottom of the page is cruel!' "[4]

Notes

Dexter means to the right, or on the right-hand side.

---

4 *Critical Wave #33*, November 1993.

A MUSEUM PIECE

Manuscript titles: "Snap Dragon Man (Walker In The Earth)" and "A Turn Unstoned."
Fantastic, June 1963.

Forced to admit that his art was going unnoticed in a frivolous world, Jay Smith decided to get out of that world. The four dollars and ninety-eight cents he spent for a mail order course entitled *Yoga—the Path to Freedom* did not, however, help to free him. Rather, it served to accentuate his humanity, in that it reduced his ability to purchase food by four dollars and ninety-eight cents.

Seated in a padmasana, Smith contemplated little but the fact that his navel drew slightly closer to his backbone with each day that passed. While nirvana is a reasonably esthetic concept, suicide assuredly is not, particularly if you haven't the stomach for it. So he dismissed the fatalistic notion quite reasonably.

"How simply one could take one's own life in ideal surroundings!" he sighed, tossing his golden locks which, for obvious reasons, had achieved classically impressive lengths. "The fat stoic in his bath, fanned by slave girls and sipping his wine, as a faithful Greek leech opens his veins, eyes downcast! One delicate Circassian," he sighed again, "*there* perhaps, plucking upon a lyre as he dictates his funeral oration—the latter to be read by a faithful countryman, eyes all a-blink. How easily *he* might do it! But the fallen artist—nay! Born yesterday and scorned today he goes, like the elephant to his graveyard, alone and secret!"

He rose to his full height of six feet, one and a half inches, and swung to face the mirror. Regarding his skin, pallid as marble, and his straight nose, broad forehead, and wide-spaced eyes, he decided that if one could not live by creating art, then one might do worse than turn the thing the other way about, so to speak.

He flexed those thews which had earned him half-tuition as a halfback for the four years in which he had stoked the stithy of his soul to the forging out of a movement all his own: two-dimensional painted sculpture.

"Viewed in the round," one crabbed critic had noted, "Mister Smith's offerings are either frescoes without walls or vertical lines. The Etruscans excelled in the former form because they knew where it belonged; kindergartens inculcate a mastery of the latter in all five-year-olds."

Cleverness! More cleverness! Bah! He was sick of those Johnsons who laid down the law at someone else's dinner table!

He noted with satisfaction that his month-long ascetic regime had reduced his weight by thirty pounds to a mere two twenty-five. He decided that he could pass as a Beaten Gladiator, post-Hellenic.

"It is settled," he pronounced. "I'll *be* art."

❖   ❖   ❖

Later that afternoon a lone figure entered the Museum of Art, a bundle beneath his arm.

Spiritually haggard (although clean-shaven to the armpits), Smith loitered about the Greek Period until it was emptied of all but himself and marble.

He selected a dark corner and unwrapped his pedestal. He secreted the various personal things necessary for a showcase existence, including most of his clothing, in its hollow bottom.

"Good-bye, world," he renounced, "you should treat your artists better," and mounted the pedestal.

His food money had not been completely wasted, for the techniques he had mastered for four ninety-eight while on the Path to Freedom, had given him a muscular control such as allowed him perfect, motionless statuity whenever the wispy, middle-aged woman followed by forty-four children under age nine, left her chartered bus at the curb and passed through the Greek Period, as she did every Tuesday and Thursday between 9:35 and 9:40 in the morning. Fortunately, he had selected a seated posture.

Before the week passed he had also timed the watchman's movements to an alternate *tick* of the huge clock in the adjacent gallery (a delicate Eighteenth Century timepiece, all of gold leaf, enamel, and small angels who chased one another around in circles). He should have hated being reported stolen during the first week of his career, with nothing to face then but the prospect of second-rate galleries or an uneasy role in the cheerless private collections of cheerless and private collectors. Therefore, he moved judiciously when raiding staples from the stores in the downstairs lunch room, and strove to work out a sympathetic bond with the racing angels. The directors had never seen fit to secure the refrigerator or pantry from depredations by the exhibits, and he applauded their lack of imagination. He nibbled at boiled ham and pumpernickel (light), and munched ice cream bars by the dozen. After a month he was forced to take calisthenics (heavy) in the Bronze Age.

"Oh, lost!" he reflected amidst the Neos, surveying the kingdom he had once staked out as his own. He wept over the statue of Achilles Fallen as though it were his own. It was.

As in a mirror, he regarded himself in a handy collage of bolts and nutshells. "If you had not sold out," he accused, "if *you* had hung on a little longer—like these, the simplest of Art's creatures… But no! It could not be!"

"Could it?" he addressed a particularly symmetrical mobile overhead. "*Could* it?"

"Perhaps," came an answer from nowhere, which sent him flying back to his pedestal.

But little came of it. The watchman had been taking guilty delight in a buxom Rubens on the other side of the building and had not overheard the colloquy. Smith decided that the reply signified his accidental nearing of Dharana. He returned to the Path, redoubling his efforts toward negation and looking Beaten.

In the days that followed he heard occasional chuckling and whispering, which he at first dismissed as the chortlings of the children of Mara and Maya, intent upon his distractions. Later, he was less certain, but by then he had decided upon a classical attitude of passive inquisitiveness.

And one spring day, as green and golden as a poem by Dylan Thomas, a girl entered the Greek Period and looked about, furtively. He found it difficult to maintain his marbly placidity, for lo! she began to disrobe!

And a square parcel on the floor, in a plain wrapper. It could only mean…

Competition!

He coughed politely, softly, classically…

She jerked to an amazing attention, reminding him of a women's underwear ad having to do with Thermopylae. Her hair was the correct color for the undertaking—that palest shade of Parian manageable—and her gray eyes glittered with the icy-orbed intentness of Athene.

She surveyed the room minutely, guiltily, attractively...

"Surely stone is not susceptible to virus infections," she decided. " 'Tis but my guilty conscience that cleared its throat. Conscience, thus do I cast thee off!"

And she proceeded to become Hecuba Lamenting, diagonally across from the Beaten Gladiator and fortunately, not facing in his direction. She handled it pretty well, too, he grudgingly admitted. Soon she achieved an esthetic immobility. After a period of appraisal he decided that Athens was indeed mother of all the arts; she simply could not have carried it as Renaissance nor Romanesque. This made him feel rather good.

When the great doors finally swung shut and the alarms had been set she heaved a sigh and sprang to the floor.

"Not yet," he cautioned, "the watchman will pass through in ninety-three seconds."

She had presence of mind sufficient to stifle her scream, a delicate hand with which to do it, and eighty-seven seconds in which to become Hecuba Lamenting once more. This she did, and he admired her delicate hand and her presence of mind for the next eighty-seven seconds.

❖ ❖ ❖

The watch man came, was nigh, was gone, flashlight and beard bobbing in musty will-o'-the-wispfulness through the gloom.

"Goodness!" she expelled her breath. "I had thought I was alone!"

"And correctly so," he replied. " 'Naked and alone we come into exile... Among bright stars on this most weary unbright cinder, lost... Oh, lost—' "

"Thomas Wolfe," she stated.

"Yes," he sulked. "Let's go have supper."

"Supper?" she inquired, arching her eyebrows. "Where? I had brought some K-Rations, which I purchased at an Army Surplus Store—"

"Obviously," he retorted, "you have a short-timer's attitude. I believe that chicken figured prominently on the menu for today. Follow me!"

They made their way through the T'ang Dynasty, to the stairs.

"Others might find it chilly in here after hours," he began, "but I daresay you have thoroughly mastered the techniques of breath control?"

"Indeed," she replied, "my fiancé was no mere Zen faddist. He followed the more rugged path of Lhasa. Once he wrote a modern version of the Ramayana, full of topical allusions and advice to modern society."

"And what did modern society think of it?"

"Alas! Modern society never saw it. My parents bought him a one-way ticket to Rome, first-class, and several hundred dollars worth of Travelers' Checks. He has been gone ever since. That is why I have retired from the world."

"I take it your parents do not approve of Art?"

"No, and I believe they must have threatened him also."

He nodded.

"Such is the way of society with genius. I, too, in my small way, have worked for its betterment and received but scorn for my labors."

"Really?"

"Yes. If we stop in the Modern Period on the way back, you can see my Achilles Fallen."

A very dry chuckle halted them.

"Who is there?" he inquired, cautiously.

No reply. They stood in the Glory of Rome, and the stone senators were still.

"*Someone* laughed," she observed.

"We are not alone," he stated, shrugging. "There've been other indications of such, but whoever they are, they're as talkative as Trappists—which is good.

"Remember, thou art but stone," he called gaily, and they continued on to the cafeteria.

❖   ❖   ❖

One night they sat together at dinner in the Modern Period.

"Had you a name, in life?" he asked.

"Gloria," she whispered. "And yours?"

"Smith, Jay."

"What prompted you to become a statue, Smith—if it is not too bold of me to ask?"

"Not at all," he smiled, invisibly. "Some are born to obscurity and others only achieve it through diligent effort. I am one of the latter. Being an artistic failure, and broke, I decided to become my own monument. It's warm in here, and there's food below. The environment is congenial, and I'll never be found out because no one ever looks at anything standing around museums."

"No one?"

"Not a soul, as you must have noticed. Children come here against their wills, young people come to flirt with one another, and when one develops sufficient sensibility to look at anything," he lectured bitterly, "he is either myopic or subject to hallucinations. In the former case he would not notice, in the latter he would not talk. The parade passes."

"Then what good are museums?"

"My dear girl! That the former affianced of a true artist should speak in such a manner indicates that your relationship was but brief—"

"Really!" she interrupted. "The proper word is 'companionship'."

"Very well," he amended, " 'companionship'. But museums mirror the past, which is dead, the present, which never notices, and transmit the race's cultural heritage to the future, which is not yet born. In this, they are near to being temples of religion."

"I never thought of it that way," she mused. "Rather a beautiful thought, too. You should really be a teacher."

"It doesn't pay well enough, but the thought consoles me. Come, let us raid the icebox again."

They nibbled their final ice cream bars and discussed Achilles Fallen, seated beneath the great mobile which resembled a starved octopus. He told her of his other great projects and of the nasty reviewers, crabbed and bloodless, who lurked in Sunday editions and hated life. She, in turn, told him of her parents, who knew Art and also knew why she shouldn't like him, and of her parents' vast fortunes, equally distributed in timber, real estate, and petroleum. He, in turn, patted her arm and she, in turn, blinked heavily and smiled Hellenically.

"You know," he said, finally, "as I sat upon my pedestal, day after day, I often thought to myself: Perhaps I should return and make one more effort to pierce the cataract in the eye of the public—perhaps if I were secure and at ease in all things material—perhaps if I could find the proper woman—but nay! There is no such a one!"

"Continue! Pray continue!" cried she. "I, too, have, over the past days, thought that, perhaps, another artist could remove the sting. Perhaps the poison of loneliness could be drawn by a creator of beauty— If we—"

❖ ❖ ❖

At this point a small and ugly man in a toga cleared his throat.

"It is as I feared," he announced.

Lean, wrinkled, and grubby was he; a man of ulcerous bowel and much spleen. He pointed an accusing finger.

"It is as I feared," he repeated.

"Wh-who are you?" asked Gloria.

"Cassius," he replied, "Cassius Fitzmullen—art critic, retired, for the Dalton *Times*. You are planning to defect."

"And what concern is it of yours if we leave?" asked Smith, flexing his Beaten Gladiator halfback muscles.

Cassius shook his head.

"Concern? It would threaten a way of life for you to leave now. If you go, you will doubtless become an artist or a teacher of art—and sooner or later, by word or by gesture, by sign or by unconscious indication, you will communicate what you have suspected all along. I have listened to your conversations over the past weeks. You know, for certain now, that this is where all art critics finally come, to spend their remaining days mocking the things they have hated. It accounts for the increase of Roman Senators in recent years."

"I have often suspected it, but never was certain."

"The suspicion is enough. It is lethal. You must be judged."

He clapped his hands.

"Judgment!" he called.

Other ancient Romans entered slowly, a procession of bent candles. They encircled the two lovers. Smelling of dust and yellow newsprint and bile and time, the old reviewers hovered.

"They wish to return to humanity," announced Cassius. "They wish to leave and take their knowledge with them."

"We would not tell," said Gloria, tearfully.

"It is too late," replied one dark figure. "You are already entered into the Catalog. See here!" He produced a copy and read: " 'Number

28, Hecuba Lamenting. Number 32, The Beaten Gladiator.' No! It is too late. There would be an investigation."

"Judgment!" repeated Cassius.

Slowly, the Senators turned their thumbs down.

"You *cannot* leave."

Smith chuckled and seized Cassius' tunic in a powerful sculptor's grip.

"Little man," he said, "how do you propose stopping us? One scream by Gloria would bring the watchman, who would sound an alarm. One blow by me would render you unconscious for a week."

"We shut off the guard's hearing aid as he slept," smiled Cassius. "Critics are not without imagination, I assure you. Release me, or you will suffer."

Smith tightened his grip.

"Try *anything.*"

"Judgment," smiled Cassius.

"He is modern," said one.

"Therefore, his tastes are catholic," said another.

"To the lions with the Christians!" announced a third, clapping his hands.

And Smith sprang back in panic at what he thought he saw moving in the shadows. Cassius pulled free.

"You cannot do this!" cried Gloria, covering her face. "We are from the Greek Period!"

"When in Greece, do as the Romans do," chuckled Cassius.

The odor of cats came to their nostrils.

"How could you—here…? A lion…?" asked Smith.

"A form of hypnosis privy to the profession," observed Cassius. "We keep the beast paralyzed most of the time. Have you not wondered why there has never been a theft from this museum? Oh, it has been tried, all right! We protect our interests."

The lean, albino lion which generally slept beside the main entrance padded slowly from the shadows and growled—once, and loudly.

Smith pushed Gloria behind him as the cat began its stalking. He glanced towards the Forum, which proved to be vacant. A sound, like the flapping of wings by a flock of leather pigeons, diminished in the distance.

"We are alone," noted Gloria.

"Run," ordered Smith, "and I'll try to delay him. Get out, if you can."

"And desert you? Never, my dear! Together! Now, and always!"

"Gloria!"

"Jay Smith!"

At that moment the beast conceived the notion to launch into a spring, which it promptly did.

"Good-bye, my lovely."

"Farewell. One kiss before dying, pray."

The lion was high in the air, uttering healthy coughs, eyes greenly aglow.

"Very well."

They embraced.

Moon hacked in the shape of cat, that palest of beasts hung overhead—hung high, hung menacingly, hung long…

It began to writhe and claw about wildly in that middle space between floor and ceiling for which architecture possesses no specific noun.

"Mm! Another kiss?"

"Why not? Life is sweet."

A minute ran by on noiseless feet; another pursued it.

"I say, what's holding up that lion?"

"I am," answered the mobile. "You humans aren't the only ones to seek umbrage amidst the relics of your dead past."

The voice was thin, fragile, like that of a particularly busy Aeolian Harp.

"I do not wish to seem inquisitive," said Smith, "but who are you?"

"I am an alien life form," it tinkled back, digesting the lion. "My ship suffered an accident on the way to Arcturus. I soon discovered that my appearance was against me on your planet, except in the museums, where I am greatly admired. Being a member of a rather delicate and, if I do say it, somewhat narcissistic race—" He paused to belch daintily, and continued, "—I rather enjoy it here—'among bright stars on this most weary unbright cinder [belch], lost.'"

"I see," said Smith. "Thanks for eating the lion."

"Don't mention it—but it wasn't *wholly* advisable. You see, I'm going to have to divide now. Can the other me go with you?"

"Of course. You saved our lives, and we're going to need something to hang in the living room, when we have one."

"Good."

He divided, in a flurry of hemidemisemiquavers, and dropped to the floor beside them.

"Good-bye, me," he called upward.

"Good-bye," from above.

They walked proudly from the Modern, through the Greek, and past the Roman Period, with much hauteur and a wholly quiet dignity. Beaten Gladiator, Hecuba Lamenting, and Xena ex Machina no longer, they lifted the sleeping watchman's key and walked out the door, down the stairs, and into the night, on youthful legs and drop-lines.

A Word from Zelazny

This "was a conscious attempt to imitate a John Collier improbability-story."[1] The particular story is "Evening Primrose" (later adapted as a television musical) which involves a department store, a poet, a beautiful girl named Ella, and other people who live in the store after hours. Zelazny's tale involves a museum, a sculptor, the beautiful Gloria, and other people who have left society to live in the museum. In Collier's tale, the poet discovers that when the mannequins come to life after hours, their society is as repressive, materialistic and repulsive as that of the real world.

Zelazny worked in one draft for most stories, but in this instance the archives at Syracuse University show several different versions of varying lengths and two different manuscript titles that differ from the final title.

Notes

Practiced for health and relaxation, **yoga** is the Hindu discipline that includes breath control, meditation, and the adoption of specific body postures. **Padmasana** or Lotus position is the ultimate, classic yoga pose that includes crossed legs and feet turned in and up, outstretched hands resting on knees. **Nirvana** is a state of pure consciousness in which the mind is free of all contaminants, emotions and distractions. **Esthetic** is the appreciation of beauty or pleasure given by the beauty of a thing. **Circassian** is a vague term that has been used in part to refer to people of Northwest Caucasus. **Thews** means muscles and tendons. **Stithy** is an anvil or forge. To **inculcate**

---

1 *Tightbeam #37*, May 1966.

is to instill or enforce a habit or way of thinking by repeated instruction and reminder. **Hellenic** refers to the Classical Greece period. **Achilles Fallen** is a statue that portrays Achilles after being mortally wounded by Paris. **Peter Paul Rubens** was well known for his paintings that featured voluptuous female nudes, including real persons and mythological beings such as Venus. **Colloquy** is a formal conversation or dialogue.

Dharana is a stage of deep meditation, the sixth of eight stages of yoga. The demon **Mara** tempted Buddha by trying to seduce him with the vision of beautiful women. **Maya** is the goddess of illusion and delusion, who can either bind or free one from illusions. **Green and golden** indicates the poem "Fern Hill" by **Dylan Thomas**. **Thermopylae** is a region of Greece known for its natural hot springs (and from which its name derives). **Parian** is unglazed porcelain that resembles white marble.

Hecuba bore Apollo's son **Troilius**, whose continued life was prophesied to ensure that Troy would not fall, but Achilles killed him during the Trojan War. **Will-o'-the-wisp** is a person or thing that is difficult or impossible to find, reach, or catch. **Naked and alone** quotes **Thomas Wolfe** from his semi-autobiographical first novel *Look Homeward, Angel*. **Zen** is a form of Buddhism that seeks enlightenment through self-meditation to the point that there is no awareness of self and by jarring the intellect with aphorisms such as "What is the sound of one hand clapping?" **Lhasa** means "place of the gods" and is the holy and capitol city of Tibet from which the Dhalai Lama ruled until 1959. The **Ramayana** is an ancient Sanskrit epic poem attributed to the poet Valmiki, and it is considered part of the Hindu canon.

Trappists are a branch of the Cistercian monks most noted for their vow of silence. **Hellenically** in this context is a pun meaning "like Helen of Troy" instead of "pertaining to the classical Greek period." **Thumbs down** actually meant swords down, and to spare the wounded gladiator; thumbs *up* was the *negative* vote by Romans in the Forum and meant that the gladiator was to be executed. In the context of this story, the critic and other Senators have (as most people do) misunderstood the true meaning of the thumbs-down gesture. An **Aeolian harp** produces musical sounds when a current of air passes through it. **Among bright stars on this most weary unbright cinder** is another quote from Wolfe's *Look Homeward, Angel*.

A **hemidemisemiquaver** is a sixty-fourth note. **Xena ex Machina** is a pun on "Deus ex machina", the Latin term that refers to the sudden introduction of an unexpected, artificial, or improbable character, device, or event in order to resolve a situation or untangle a plot. The alien creature serves that purpose exactly, and **Xena** implies the Greek term "xeno," which means alien or stranger.

HYBRIS, OR THE DANGER OF HILLTOPS

Written 1955–60 for *Chisel in the Sky;* previously unpublished.

Shake no fist at the skies,
shout not blasphemous words.
Always comes reprise,
if only the passing birds'.

Notes

Hybris is an alternate spelling of hubris, which means excessive pride or arrogance. The **reprise** or repeat performance (the danger of hilltops) is to endure droppings from the passing birds.

Mine Is the Kingdom

Amazing, August 1963 as by Harrison Denmark.

I

—Far removed are the courts of darkness…
The distance of the stars, he decided, *and ten feet from where I'm sitting.*

—And far the places of people…

He agreed, silently.

—Near are the un-people.

He nodded.

—You are on Earth and ridiculous.

"Yes," he murmured.

—You are half-mad and all drunk.

"*All* mad and half drunk," he corrected.

—So you will step into the machine, press the button, and join your people in the places of laughter…

"Ha!" he hiccupped. "I'm laughing now."

He shook his head and sat up, looking around.

He poked the beanstalk of yellow light and waited.

A heartbeat.

"Service?" inquired the pillow.

"Puffy talk-beams mestering again," he sighed. "Search, screen, block.

"Whenever I drink it is an 'A' Situation and priority care is required," he reminded.

The pillow hummed.

"'A' Situation prevails. There is no penetration."

He half-rose.

"Then who was talking to me just now?"

"*I* certainly wasn't," came the reply. "It could be your human imagination, stimulated by the alcohol you have consumed…"

It sounded almost hurt.

"Sorry," he apologized to invisible coils. "Mix me another."

He leaned back and took the tube into his mouth.

"And don't water this one," he slurred.

"I never water your drinks."

"They taste weaker."

"Your tolerance level is rising."

"Out! Out on't! Read to me."

"What shall I read?"

"Anything."

" 'The Mole had been working very hard all the morning, spring-cleaning his—' "

"Anything but Grahame!"

"How about Vradmer?"

"No."

"Gelden?"

"No, something older. Near Grahame, maybe."

"Krin? K'lal? The Old Man of Venus?"

"Older."

"Flone? Threene? Hemingway? Proust?"

"Older still."

" 'In the beginning—' "

"And pagan."

"How's Pindar."

"Very good."

He took a long drink and settled back to dreaming.

—Why did you kill the puffy?

A long pause.

"I didn't kill any puffy."

—Puffies do not murder puffies, and a puffy is dead. You are the last man on Earth. Limitless power is yours. Why did you use it to kill?

A longer pause.

"What's a puffy?"

—They wanted the Earth. Don't you remember?

"I don't know… I was drunk. Go away!"

—Why don't *you* go away?

"I can't!"

—Just step into the machine, push the button, and join your people in the places of laughter…

"There are no places of laughter!"

—*Talk* to the puffies.

He slapped the side of the couch and a jet of barbiturates entered his bloodstream.

He slept.

❖   ❖   ❖

The sun was a dirty dime, fallen upon wet concrete. He stared at it, blinking.

"The times we've spent you…" he mused, realizing he was awake.

"Everything's depreciated."

He rolled onto his right side, feeling awful.

After awhile the pillow asked him what he wanted for breakfast. He tried to think of the right answer, but gave up and asked for something to settle his stomach.

It was chalk and liver, damming the imminent overflow of a drainage ditch. He spat and rolled onto his left side, feeling less awful.

Finally, he jabbed at the band of light.

"Bridge me ideational control."

The power was a silent melody: moonlight sawing on strings of milkweed silk, deep winds of liquid blowing timeless through pipes of coral, the collisions of clouds…

He drifted, stretching and yawning.

He willed a firepole and slid a hundred yards upward.

"Mount Athos," he decided, "and breakfast."

Standing upon a rocky crag, looking out over the endless room of the Sanct, he smiled. He blanked the walls and molded a flowing panorama of trees and hills, like those which had once existed on Earth; in the distance, a sea. (Was that right? He shrugged.) The invisible ceiling became a bluegreen sky. The sun he painted brutal yellow. Now the slope flowed smooth beneath his sandals. He affected sackcloth and a grin, and he dotted the horizon with shimmering skylines.

"So much for the kingdoms of Earth," he muttered. "Come now, Lucifer!"

A faceless shadow hovered at his left, reeking of death and final judgments.

"The routine," he suggested.

A voice from the bottom of a barrel, monotonous: "Behold the kingdoms of the Earth," it stated, "in all their glory and power. To me have they been delivered and in this moment of time, and to whomever I will give them. Worship me and they are thine."

He laughed.

"But they are mine already, dear fellow. I just created them. You too, for that matter. It's you ought to be paying me a little respect."

The figure wavered, uncertain.

"Now the punchline," he suggested.

"Then change thou these stones into bread," it repeated, wearily, "and I shall believe thee."

"Ham and eggs," he corrected. "Won't you join me?"

"Thanks," it crackled.

They seated themselves and discussed nothing until he grew bored. Finishing breakfast, he opened a chasm and stuffed the entire scene into it, amidst much thunder and the crackle of skylicking flames.

"To hell with you all!" he belched. "What'll I do till lunch? Sail with Odysseus?"

❖   ❖   ❖

He had begun the tentative towers of Ilium and the outline of a great horse when the Sanct-comm called.

"Puffy ambassadors beg entrance," it said.

"Tell them I'm busy."

The horse wavered, went out. The bottomless towers fled toppling, sinking, silent, draining down into the stark floors.

"Oh damn! Start decontaminating them. They've already ruined my morning!"

He settled back to the couch to be shaved, cleaned, clipped, and stuffed into fresh garments. The manicurette *tsk-tsked* at the condition of his nails and he contemplated the dimmie projection of the creatures known as puffies.

A downy, albino aura clung to the man-sized swaying forms. Towers of milk, the bulk of their weight tripod on baboon-dark rears and two snowy sextants, the puffies moved and bellyfuls of vestigial limbs, like hundred-handed clocks, writhed their buried hours.

Bilaterally symmetrical, their head-high mandibles had differentiated into grasping independency at about the same time the antennae antlered in columbine clusters—petalled powder-blue, opening and closing with systolic regularity. Two butterpads beneath them strained the world through flyscreens of topaz.

"Good morning, pretty things," he suggested, and the puffies revolved, seeking the source of his voice.

"You can't see me unless I want you to. Why are you here?"

The creatures seemed to consider his question.

"To convince, buy, help, talk, to you, to go," one buzzed.

He chuckled.

"Pardon, please, repeat, please, your last saying."

He laughed.

"Come in! Come in!" he cried.

He was suddenly a puffy himself, twenty feet in height.

The wall dialed archway, just as he finished blackening the sky, bulging the floor into rocky irregularity, and raising a glacier front across the half-mile room. He hovered in the air, seated upon a tent-sized snowflake, and ice breezes knifed about his throne, scattering the berries of blizzard before his guests.

"Merry Christmas," he observed.

The puffies halted on the threshold. The third movement of Sibelius' Second Symphony unwound from somewhere as the glacier groaned forward.

"How?" asked the creatures.

"I am really quite ugly," he explained, "and I wanted to put you at ease."

They were standing beneath him now, staring upward.

"Beautiful," one buzzed.

"Like home," hummed the second.

"What are you?" whistled the third.

A fountain jetted fifty feet in the air.

"Have a drink?"

"No. Thank. Cannot, chance, unknown, substance."

He took a deep drink, then the fountain drained upward into high-leaping spirals that vanished overhead. A globe of the brown liquid hovered beside him, and he sipped it as he spoke.

"These bodies," he stated, "are rather difficult to operate. How do you manage?"

"Man-edge?" repeated the buzz.

"Yes. You shuffle about when you were obviously meant to leap. Your feet are snowshoes. Why have you come to my world?"

"We have, come, to live," one droned.

"No one consulted with me on the matter."

"Please. We only, just, learned, you exist, please."

"And what do you want of me?"

"Please, go home. Make, the world, safe, for puffies. Ple—"

"This *is* my home. I own the Earth."

"Yes. We know. We want, to change, it. But you, are here. Why?"

"Why not?" he asked. "I'm an Earthman. Being the last one does not alter my rights. I occupy approximately twenty square miles of this world, and I go where I choose and do as I wish in the rest of it. By birthright and law it is mine—and by power. If you attempt to expel me I will resist you with all the machinery of Earth. I can control it from here, and I *can* destroy you. I can destroy the planet! If you don't believe me, attack me!"

❖   ❖   ❖

His voice cracked and he took another drink. He assumed his own form, magnified a dozen times. He produced a cigarette the size of a fence post and a pillar of fire rose to light it.

"May, we, reason?" asked the flowering snowballs. "Please?"

"All right—reason."

He exhaled fog and inhaled alcohol.

"Reason!"

"Your people, left, years ago, because, this world, is dead, for them," it began. "But it, is a, place of, life, for us, a place, of, laughter…"

"Do you know what 'laughter' means?" he asked.

"We think, so, please. We have, studied, what, Earth people, left behind. —Good living? —Best condition, for species? And all, members? —Sounds, they make, when life, prevails?"

"Close enough. Go on."

"Earth is, a place, of laughter, only for, puffies now. No good, for you. Go to, your, people. Let us cold, down, the Earth, more, change it. Your machines, stop us, now. It will be, better, for both, if you go. Why do you, stay?"

"My business," he growled, "my business. —Tell me, do you find me ugly?"

"Please, yes…"

"Congratulations, so do I." He paused, then: "Will you *make* me go?"

"Please… If we, must…"

They stood upon a desert. An orange sun, like a sudden, giant hand, filled half the sky. It wrung the perspiration from his body. He coughed.

"Please!" whistled the melting snowmen.

Now they drifted through the stellar void, cold as all un-flame and un-sun. He seated himself upon a nothingness and watched the puffies drift, kicking, before him. A Milky Way of starmotes drifted over his right shoulder and past his face. It became a Bourbon Way and he gulped it.

"How?" managed a puffy, weakly.

He did not answer.

❖   ❖   ❖

It was not that I loved the Earth…

❖   ❖   ❖

"Henry?"

"Yes?"

"We *can't!*"

He studied the blondeness of her, and the ghostgray eyes looking (always) past him. Her tiny afterthought of a chin was drawn even smaller by her pout.

"Why is that?" he asked her eyes.

"…To stay behind on this hell's shelf of a world? The two last people? —With his best friend?"

"Yes."

"…With only machines and each other to talk to? And your damned bookreaders? We'd go mad! We'd hate each other! There'd be no purpose—"

"Have you an alternative?" he interrupted. "And could it convince a Eugenics Board?"

"What's wrong with the way things are now? After the Movement it will be the same."

"Try saying it this way," he smiled, " 'Henry is handy, like a dimmie or masso, dandy, and as much above suspicion—but to stay here with him… Well, it's primitive, that's what it is.' "

"You're wrong," she colored, "and I'll prove it—later."

He shook his head.

"There won't be any 'later.' I'm not going. Somebody should stay behind to water the flowers. It's not that I love the Earth—I just hate the stars, I hate what they stand for. I hate the people going to the stars, going to recapitulate with stifling monotony all the processes that drained this world and left nothing but filled ashtrays. For a long time I felt that my only purpose in life was to fill ashtrays, myself. But now I know I was wrong. I have something to do now—I'm going to be a grave-keeper. That's good, very good…"

"Of course you're going," she sniffed. "Everyone is. Don't be childish! There's nothing here to preserve. The days of Earth are past."

He nodded, vigorously.

"Phyllis, Phyllis, Phyllis! Of course you're right, as always. Nothing can be done. History dies the second it is made, and we leave the world emptier than we found it. Grass to dust and life to lust, burning. However, I have made arrangements to move into the Portation Sanct after Exodus. I anticipated some company, but I can push the buttons without your help. You may join me there anytime you wish. Don't stop around just to say 'goodbye,' though."

"You're coming with us! I love you, even if you are a regressive!"

He glanced at the clock.

"You had better get dressed for—uh, dinner," he suggested. "Len will be back soon and I'd better start arriving."

He stood and donned his fire cloak.

"I'll mix the drinks. You can't take it with you…"

She had much more to say, but it didn't really matter, much.

❖　❖　❖

—Far removed are the courts of darkness from the halls of light.

Yes, he decided, *the distance of the stars, and ten feet from where I'm sitting.—And that, puffies, is it.*

"How?" persisted the foremost puffy.

—Far removed…

Something seemed to be screaming, soundlessly, somewhere.

"Why?"

"I hate me!" he told it, with sudden ferocity. "And you! You are the maggots in Balder's guts! You've come to worm in the corpse of my world, and I just this minute decided that I won't let you. I hate me, but I hate you more. —Go back where you came from. I'm keeping the Earth!"

"If you, force, us—"

It became a tiny nova at his feet, a lily pad of flame drifting upon black waters.

"Go home," he said, and they stood in the Sanct once more, and he was his normal size, and the wall unwound its door again.

The two remaining puffies dragged themselves upright.

"You used, up, your time, your world…" they hummed, "and you are, all, that remains, behind. Your race, is not, justified, and its, only, monument, is wanton, destruction, of life."

"In that," he answered, "we emulate the universe. We take!"

"Look around you, though—there must be a bright ash in that big ashtray." He gestured wildly. "There *must* be something out there to justify us! Go look!" He tried to crack his skull between the palms of his hands, but he could not. "Get out of here! Leave me!

"Go…"

The door winked grotesquely behind them and he struck it with a lightning bolt.

The screaming continued.

II

Far removed are the courts of darkness. Far…
    He heard screaming.

He recognized his own voice.

He awakened.

—Far remov—Puffy ambassadors beg—courts of light—entrance…

The words were changing, and he knew.

He was listening to the pillow and twisting the words, he was hearing the words and altering the meaning; he was doing and not doing, he was part awake, part asleep.

He knew.

"Tell them to go away!" he shouted. "Read to me!"

He knew.

…A long story about a woman named Anna and a man named Vronsky.

…The train rushed toward him, spewing black pennants of goblin-cloud and blaring a saurian war-cry, and he *knew*…

He seized the light.

"Break ideational bridge!"

The train was gone and he was alone, shivering, knowing.

He perspired faster than the couch could absorb it. Oceans raced back from sandbars of his memory.

He covered his face.

"You *did* clean up all the blood?"

"Yes," answered the pillow.

"And her body?"

"Gone. Cleanly, completely."

"Why did she do it?"

The pillow did not answer.

"Why did she come here to bleed?" he insisted.

"Because she could neither go nor stay, like yourself."

"How long has it been?"

"Seven years, three months, and thirteen days."

Something fiery flowed from the tube and he swallowed it.

"Were the puffies real, or a part of the therapy?"

"Both."

"Oh, did I actually kill one?"

"Yes."

"How long ago?"

"Two weeks yesterday."

"I'm sick."

"No, you're all right now."

He was sick.

The pillow hummed and the bed vibrated and he was dry again and warm. The pillow clicked.

"Puffy ambassadors beg entrance."

"*Have* you been watering my drinks?"

"Yes.

"Let them in," he said.

III

He stared into the room he had sealed shut on that day, seven years ago… The wall was melted now.

Len had returned, smelling of time and space, and hadn't said a word—casting only one long, kicked-dog look at him before he hit him—and when he awakened Len was gone and two of his teeth were gone and he was choking on one of them, and he took a drink, began rubbing again at the cinnamon anemones beside the bath pool, and took a drink, then cried some, took a drink, carried her to the couch and praying, cried some more, took a drink, closed off the room, awakened, everything all right, arms hurting from sprayjets and pillow *Lycidas* to him and he had scrambled eggs and toast for breakfast and everything was all right, yes.

He called a bridge band.

A huge, bright, wild, white trumpet lily broke the floor of the room and unflowered over bed, bath, and dresser, as the other wall dialed door and the puffies came in.

He smiled as they appeared.

"Hello, puffies."

And they came in and they came in, and the Sanct was full of puffies, and he smiled and he nodded and they stood before the couch.

He moved back and sat on its edge.

"You have come," he said, "hungering and thirsting after justice."

"What do, you want?" they asked.

"Nothing," he said.

It was quiet. The puffies caught him like a butterfly in yellow nets of seeing.

"What do *you* want?" he asked.

"Why do, you, kill us?" they asked.

"It was not me," he answered, "it was my madness. I am sorry."

"If you," said a puffy, "go," said a puffy, "everything," said a puffy, "will be, well," said a puffy.

"If you," pause, "stay," said another, "you must," said another, "die," said the largest.

"Useless," said another, "freak!"

"Very good," he sighed, "very good indeed.

"Whatever I am, whatever I do," he told them, "read the Earth, study the Earth, and judge us fairly for what we did with it when we lived here. I am not truly representative of my species—only, perhaps, of its failures. I have wasted several lives proving the worthlessness of life, and I have only just now decided I was wrong."

He paused, looked about, then asked: "If I leave you the Earth, what will you do with the works of man?"

"Burn them," buzzed one.

"Bury them," droned another.

"Replace them," hummed a third.

"Forgive them," whistled a fourth, "for existing."

The others looked at him and made odd noises. Laughter?

"Who are you?" he asked.

"Jester," said the vanilla pyramid. "I mock, our leaders."

"Who are you?" he asked the first who had spoken.

"First, among peers."

"And you?" to the second.

"Second."

"And you?"

"Third."

"And Jester makes four. Good!" He began to laugh.

"Comedic king of the snowballs, I salute thee!"

❖ ❖ ❖

He bowed. The Second extended a mandible, tentatively, in his direction.

He did move, not until its blade neared his neck. Then he straightened and seized it in his right hand.

"Give me your pardon, sir. I've done you wrong," he winced. "What I have done that might your nature, honor, and exception roughly awake, I here proclaim was madness."

The hand and mandible were frozen as the lights began to fade. The buzzing began again when the room became completely black. Then all grew quiet, and he continued:

"Let my disclaiming from a purpos'd evil free me so far in your most generous thoughts…"

Light once more, but from instant-grown torches, sprung like mushrooms from sooty niches of brick. Fifty or sixty gaily garbed people crowded the shadow-pavilioned chamber. His couch had become a throne, and a bearded man with heavy purple robes and a crown of gold sat upon it.

The walls wore rough-woven allegories of bright color, the heads of vanquished predators, and axes with complexions of smoke and eyes of rust. The night moved twenty or thirty feet upward and hung there, leaking creeks of darkness down the seams of the walls.

He wore black trousers and had on a white shirt, opened at the neck, and his hair was a burnished mirror, and his sky eyes held the darker man, whose hand he still clasped.

Say it! he willed.

The mouth moved uncertainly, the throat constricted, relaxed:

"I am satisfied, in nature, whose motive, in this case, should stir me most, to my revenge," the other stated, slowly; the voice cleared, rose: "But till that time I do receive your offer'd love like love, and will not wrong it."

"I do embrace it freely," he replied, "and will this brother's wager frankly play." He wrung the hand, released it, and spun away with a laugh. "Give us the foils!"

"Come! One for me!"

"I'll be your foil," he smiled.

"You mock me, sir!"

"No, by this hand." He held it forth again.

The other turned and walked off a few paces, as though the process were completely new to him. Surprised by his sudden grace, he executed a fencer's lunge and laughed aloud.

"Give them the foils," ordered the crowned one. "You know the wager?"

"Very well, my lord."

His opponent inspected the point of his weapon.

"This is too heavy, let me see another." He selected another blade and eyed his opponent who simply nodded.

The Earthman licked his lips, extended his weapon several times, and stepped into a line with his opponent.

"This likes me well," he stated. "These foils have all a length?"

"Ay, my good lord."

So he smiled over the skewed curve of his salute and struck an *en garde*. His opponent did the same.

❖   ❖   ❖

It was a game, a beautiful game they were being forced to play, with the wild feeling of moving in another form, of seeing the colors of Earth through the eyes of Earthmen, of speaking with the tongues of Earthmen.

There were constraints, of course—this one must stand here, that one there, this one speak *so*, and *then*. The king must order wine and throw a pearl into the goblet before saying, "Come! Begin! And you, the judges, bear a wary eye!" But the air burned with the invisible electricities of anticipation, and the half-controlled movements seemed more than half their own as they crowded forward to the cry: "Come on, sir!"

"Come, my lord!" was the rejoinder, and the blades leapt and touched like the tongues of steel toads.

(Beat—extend—feint—feint—thrust.)

Click!

"One."

"No."

"Judgment."

"A hit, a very palpable hit."

"Well, again!"

"Stay," called the king. "Here's to thy health!"

He motioned to a servant

"Give him the cup," he said.

"I'll play this bout first," the Earthman answered. "Set it by awhile."

He sank completely into the illusion of the moment, unrolling memory in its opposite direction and through a series of new discoveries. He lunged.

"Another hit. What say you?"

"A touch, a touch, I do confess," agreed his opponent.

"Our son shall win," snarled the king.

"The queen carouses to your fortune." The lady beside the king raised the cup.

"Do not!" snapped the king; and in the distance a whisper, struggling: "I, cannot, help, myself!"

The king gnashed his teeth.

The Earthman bit his lip.

"Have at you now!"

His blade clattered to the floor. A single tooth bit blood from his body, tore seeing from his eyes, and the entire room shuddered like a candle flame brought near a window.

Then it steadied, and he dropped to one knee.

He drove his elbow into his opponent's rib cage and, reaching up, he seized the fencer's right wrist. He duckstepped under it and straightened, twisting.

A second blade rang upon the floor.

"Part them! They are incensed!" came the cry.

He seized the other weapon.

"Nay! Come again!"

His opponent snatched up the other foil, heaved a loud gasp, and sprang into a balestra.

❖ ❖ ❖

He caught the sudden febra in a bind, then cross-stepped into a back leap. The blades disengaged with a rasp. He beat the outside of the extended foil, feinted in four, lunged in six. This was met with a lightning parry and a riposte in six, beneath his own blade. He beat it down, stepped back, caught the forte, and dashed forward in a flesche attack.

The other howled.

The queen fell to her knees.

"Look to the queen! Ho!"

"They bleed on both sides! How is't, my lord?"

"How is't?"

The other clutched his arm, and a look of terror contorted his features as his lips moved.

"I am, justly, killed, with mine own, treachery(!)."

"How does the queen?"

"She swounds to see them bleed."

"No, no! The drink!" she moaned, hysteria mounting as the words emerged from her mouth. "The drink! I am poisoned!"

Then she fell and was silent.

"O villainy! Ho!" chuckled the Earthman. "Let the door be locked! Treachery! Seek it out!"

"It is here," sighed the one at his feet. "Thou art slain. No medicine in the world can do thee good. In thee there is not half an hour of life. The treacherous instrument is in thy hand, unbated and envenomed…"

He nodded agreement and looked about him at the inheritors of the Earth. *This*, at least, would remain with them.

"Then, venom, to thy work!" he cried, and with a smile he stabbed the king, then forced the cup to his mouth and poured what remained within through his teeth.

"You wanted the Earth," he muttered. "You wanted its bones without its flesh. Ugly or lovely, man has tattooed its body and you cannot scrape our mark from its corpse. You wanted it—try being it!"

The form went limp in his arms.

"He is, justly, served," came the forced gutturals, as the other fencer closed his eyes and grimaced.

Are you sure he was right? asked his own voice in his head.

"Was he?" he cried.

A throbbing began in his temples. Whispers in a puffy-staccato of horror began to grow louder. A gale swept through the room, and the torches flickered. Somewhere a wailing. He began to burn.

The chamber faded and reappeared, faded and reappeared, and in a between-moment of shimmering limbo he seemed to be standing in the midst of a vast field of ice, surrounded by a village of igloos, each sporting antennae. High overhead, the wheeling galaxy was an enormous ashtray, and he knew that it would go on forever, turning, collecting, after he had ceased. And he knew that he was meant to fill that ashtray—his race and the unborn children of his race—powdering into it forever, and occasionally flaming in bright flakes, as he had tonight, to justify an absurdity with an absurd beauty and to cancel some of the absurdities and leave some of the beauty behind, to some end, and he knew he was sane once more, and he smiled at the puffies and switched on the court tableau for his final scene.

"O, I die, Horatio!" he croaked. "The potent poison quite o'er-crows my spirit." He looked up at the puffy-courtier who supported him in a sitting position. "I cannot live to hear the news from (England?)," he continued, "but I do prophesy the election lights on (Fortinbras?). He has my dying voice." He gestured with his head toward the door which masked the frozen Jester. "So tell him, with the occurrents, more and less, which have solicited—the rest is silence…"

He leaned back and focussed his will upon the next part.

The Horatio-puffy was speaking of his cracked heart and the singing of angels. It mentioned the drum, and he heard it, distantly, before the silence finally came.

The Jester shuffled forward, changing shape as he moved. He flickered on and off, then he stood—a mountain of ice—looking down at the Earthman. Hives of bells opened and closed, opened and closed. The others watched him, for they knew that he knew the Earth, for he was the mocker, and he would know what had happened, what to do next.

He regarded the last dead Earthman on Earth.

"Take up, the body," he said. "Such, a sight, as this, becomes, the field, but here, shows much amiss. Go, bid the, soldiers shoot."

And they carried him out and buried him, as was not the custom with puffies, and the Sanct extended cannons and fired them into the night, as had not been the custom with men for many years; and the Jester made the Earth a place of laughter, and the puffies dwelt upon the ways of men.

Notes

Mestering is an intended neologism present in the original, archived manuscript. Context suggests that the word combines the meaning of both pestering (harassing) and mustering (gathering), i.e., that the puffies were once more gathering together to harass the narrator with unwanted communications. **Search**, **screen**, **block** are abbreviated commands issued by the narrator to his home security system to search and screen for incoming transmissions from the puffies and block them.

There are numerous allusions in this "Last Man on Earth" tale, including a reenactment of Satan's temptation of Jesus in the wilderness, and Homer's *Iliad* and *Odyssey*. **The Mole had been working very hard all the morning, spring-cleaning** is the first line from Kenneth Grahame's novel *The Wind in the Willows*. In addition to fictional future authors, **Ernest Hemingway**, **Marcel Proust** and the ancient Greek poet **Pindar** are mentioned. **Mount Athos** is in Greece and is called Holy Mountain; it is the home to many Eastern Orthodox monasteries. **Odysseus** was the Greek hero whose exploits were described in Homer's *Iliad* (*Ilium*) and *Odyssey*. **Sibelius' Second Symphony** was composed by Jean Sibelius, and its major theme was based on Dante's *The Divine Comedy*. **Balder** is the god of light, joy, purity, beauty, innocence, and reconciliation; all living things except mistletoe had sworn not to harm him. The gods used Balder as a target for practice throwing knives and shooting arrows, since nothing could harm him. Jealous Loki took advantage of this by having an arrow made of mistletoe, which killed Balder.

The tale of a woman named Anna and a man named Vronsky is Leo Tolstoy's *Anna Karenina*. **Lycidas** is a poem by John Milton that was written as a lament for a friend who drowned on the Irish Sea. The puffies are forced to reenact the ending of Shakespeare's *The Tragedy of Hamlet, Prince of Denmark* in part III, and most of the dialogue from "Give me your pardon, sir" to "Go, bid the soldiers shoot." comes from that play. A **balestra** is a move in fencing that consists of a forward hop or jump, typically followed by an attack. **Febra** is not a standard fencing term. Its usage suggests a sudden, feverish slicing or cutting movement with the *épée*, such as one taught by Salvator Fabris in the 1500s. Fabris reportedly choreographed the fencing moves in *Hamlet* at Shakespeare's request. A **feinte** is an attack into one line with the intention of switching to another line before the attack is completed. The **forte** is the lower, stronger portion of the blade. A **fleche** is an attack in which the aggressor leaps off his leading foot, attempts to make the hit, and then passes the opponent at a run. A **riposte** is an attack made immediately after a parry of the opponent's attack. **Swounds** is an archaic synonym for "swoons".

St. Secaire's

Haunted #3, June 1968 (revised). Written 1955–60 for *Chisel in the Sky*.

Triple-topped steeples
of brass,
steel,
and I now forget what other—
poking with massive,
and insect probosci—
suck a passing cloud,
prick to sudden star wound
night's most Negro thigh…

Ye I salute,
holiest of vampires!
bread of metaphor,
being,
and I know not what,
in many-topped minds
of the minder.

…See now
how bats ripple,
flow,
cats go;
rats below,
less subtle,
rattle a harvest of bones—
oh,

'tis pleasing
to the deathling,
doubtless:
darkling hordes for-
ward winding
twisty ways
know
again the soul-taste
of the day-men
deep below,
poor wights, chanting woe:

"Sed libera nos a malo,"
so.

Notes

The Mass of **St. Secaire** was a form of black mass, incorporating parodies of the Eucharist; it was celebrated in a ruined church. The intention was not to worship the devil but to direct currents of malevolent spite against a victim, in the hope that the victim would wither away and die.

There were three different editions of this poem. *Chisel in the Sky* contained the two-stanza original, *Haunted* added the final two stanzas, and *To Spin Is Miracle Cat* reverted to and revised the original 2 stanzas. This version combines *Spin's* revision with *Haunted's* additional two stanzas.

Probosci are needle or trunk-like appendages, such as a mosquito's stinger. ***Sed libera nos a malo*** means "but deliver us from evil" in the Latin version of the Lord's Prayer (Our Father or Pater Noster).

In Pheleney's Garage

Written 1955–60 for *Chisel in the Sky;* previously unpublished.

The heart is a graveyard of tractors,
Whose oils clog the floor.
Love is a snowplow dinosaur.

He too, has come to die.

Notes

This was substantially revised to become "In the Dogged House" as featured in "The Graveyard Heart."

King Solomon's Ring

Fantastic, October 1963.

King Solomon had a ring, and so did the guy I have to tell you about. Solomon's was a big iron thing with a pentagram for a face, but Billy Scarle's was invisible because he wore it around his mind. The two rings did serve similar purposes though.

Legend has it Solomon's enabled him to understand the language of beasts. Scarle as you may remember, also had the gift of tongues. I suppose that was the reason for his peculiar susceptibilities.

I am writing this letter, Lisa, because you are the one who managed to recruit him, and I think he was in love with you. Maybe I am wrong. If so, I can only ask pardon for the intrusion and trust to your sense of humor to put things in perspective.

Last night (I think it was last night) I was having dinner/s with Dr. Hale, whom you have never met. He is a big panda of a man—white boots (generally), wide black trousers (always), white shirt (always), black tie (ditto), and black on top (mostly). He has the feral eyes, too, and he listens to the world through a pair of puffed teacups (he used to be a light-heavyweight—a pretty good one), and he has a nose like the old Eiffel Tower, and bent, and he manages to get by with less couchside blather than other complex-pushers I've met. He claims his record as a therapeutic Svengali is based on the fact that his patients tend to feel sorry for him on first sight, but I sometimes wonder. Once he turns on that snow machine of his, his fat face sort of melts until it seems you are staring at a portrait of Machiavelli in retirement.

He is not retired though, and he has a very professional manner with steaks…

Between mouthfuls: "What about Billy Scarle?"

"You're the doctor. You tell me."

"I value your opinion."

"In that case, you're losing your touch. I don't have one."

"Then manufacture one, because I want it."

I bit into a roll, buying myself thirty seconds' mulling time, and proceeded to mull.

❖   ❖   ❖

Scarle's early career had been a success mainly because it was a minimum-personnel operation. He did not trust too many people, so everyone aboard his ship was a close-mouthed specialist in many things. What puzzled the Guard for a long time was the fact that he was very unconventional in disposing of the fruits of his piracies. Dozens of the worlds on the Exploratory Perimeter are no more than encyclopedia entries followed by a couple sentences, but there are many excellent trading centers among them. Language is a genuine barrier though, and there just *aren't* that many interpreters, especially for bootlegging operations.

What it took you a long time to figure out was something that Scarle was barely aware of himself. He just thought he had mastered galactic sign language and that the hybrid patois of Fenster, his home world, was sufficient to fill in the gaps. Bear in mind, Lisa, that while he was clever, he was only nominally educated in a Slumschule and was quite naïve in many matters. Still, it took the Circle of Solomon to tip off the Guard as to what they were dealing with.

After his apprehension on Martin VIII, it was his ratty luck to be shipped Earthward in the custody of an old Guardsman ready for retirement. As you know, the cop decided along the way that the arrest had been out of jurisdiction, and he also decided he did not want a black mark on his record at that stage in the game. So he changed a couple log entries and elected himself judge, jury, and executioner—as you may not know. He never said a word while he made the preparations, but of course Scarle *knew.*

I suppose it would be interesting to tell you the details of the cop's not being able to pull the trigger and Scarle's smashing him to pieces with his arm collars, but I'd rather not be that interesting. I've heard the story too many times.

When you picked him up in that bar on Kimberly, he was beginning to suspect what he was, but he was too busy vacationing to do much experimenting. He was lying low and feeling high, and shopping around for a new rig, that night you sat down across from his whisky-and-flent and offered to tell his fortune.

Naturally he said "yes", because you are beautiful.

"The thirteenth card of the Major Arcana," you told him, "is the Bony Reaper. He signifies Death, often only on metaphysical levels, but a death, nevertheless. Your life is going to change."

And he smiled and agreed and asked if you wanted to help change it, and you smiled and agreed, sort of. It took about a week of his being puzzled (because he could not anticipate you the way he could other people), before you knew he was ready for The Bet. (*Did* you have that Tarot up your sleeve? He wondered that on several occasions, so I thought I would ask.) It was well managed, I gather, and of course the prediction turned out to be quite true.

For the wagered price of one cruiser, he agreed to be your quarry. You managed to convince him that you were rich (which was also true, now I think of it) and looking for kicks (which might have held an incidental truth, at that). He could not back down, not that he wanted to, because he had boasted too much beforehand. And he did have a high survival potential also, as it was only by accident that I managed to kill him when I finally had to.

Three days for him to hide himself in the jungles of Kimberly, and a week in which he had to stay hidden, despite your trackers, your mechanical spiders, and your electronic B.O. detectors, and he did it. I remember the night you told me about it. It was on Lilith, with a sky full of moons and a fine, tangy sea breeze assaulting the smells of roast Süssevogel and Lilith-mosel (that pagan Liebfraumilch!)— Do you recall the name of the place? I seem to forget it now, but I remember the balcony quite vividly, and you were wearing something dark blue...Oh, well.

It took three days to find his trail, you said, and six hours to close in on him. Then he escaped when you approached his campsite. This happened a couple times, until you had flushed him onto the higher ground near the Gila Range. Remember now? The spiders stopped coming back, and you started finding them smashed to bits, until you were out of spiders. But then it became apparent that he was mounted, because he started moving very fast and the broken spiders showed hoof-marks. After the fifth day the trackers gave up, without admitting it, and the "dogs" grew interested in other matters.

At the end of the week he walked into your camp, all smiles, and aware of his power. He had won The Bet by destroying the mechanical hunters, circling around behind your party, and "eavesdropping" on your hunting beasts. Then he managed to "talk" them out of following him. He followed along behind you until the seven days were up, and then he walked in on you, clean-shaven, and thinking he had won. The poor sucker! He had been initiated into the most exclusive club in the galaxy and therewith reduced his life expectancy by ninety or a hundred years. Excuse me, dear, I'm not being bitter, but I liked the guy. If the Guard had gotten him to Earth alive, he would have been recruited anyhow.

King Solomon had a ring, you told him—while you were on that month's frolic about Earth and the Inworlds—a ring that enabled him to understand all the tongues of life. And you, Billy Scarle, you also have a ring. You wear it around your mind like an introverted chastity belt, and whenever anything is going to speak, you know what it is going to say before it says it, and whenever you want to say something, and want to strongly enough, others know what you are going to say before you say it. You are a fractional telepath and a potential paralinguist. You would probably flunk first semester French, which is an easy Orthotongue, but with the proper training you could be a two-way on-the-spot interpreter for any two languages without knowing either.

And he wanted to know if there was money in it! Do you remember him now? He was about five-ten, with that premature frost on his hair that comes of pushing poorly shielded cruisers too far; nervous fingers, light eyes, a preference for nondescript clothing; and when he talked, all his sentences seemed like one long word. At first glance, I guess he just did not give the impression of being much of a criminal. Rather, perhaps (and quite correctly), he seemed a person who would have had a hard time enjoying Mardi Gras time on Centuvo. Hale thinks this was the key to his talent, cast long ago on the streets of Fenster.

You offered him full Circleship, if he could pass the training, emphasizing its retroactive civil immunity as much as its high pay, so what else could he do? He realized you were his superior in nearly everything. He wanted to even things up, and his pride was always an amazing thing to behold—right up until the end it made him equal to almost any task. I remember how he sweated over Chomsky's book (which did not mean much in the long run, because the Thing Applied was all sedation and sound cycles), but it furnished him with broad concepts, and things like concepts help smooth down rough edges. And as for the law—well, he *did* want an out.

He joined, and you kept in touch: beautiful, witty, sophisticated, what shall I say?—polemics?—until he drew his first assignment and went incommunicado. What then, Lisa?

❖   ❖   ❖

"I'll tell you, Doc," I said to Hale, "I was thinking of his first assignment. It was to that world called Malmson. You weren't along that trip, which is too bad. He felt we wrecked the whole society there, and it sort of got to him. I think he felt more responsible for it than one man has a right to feel."

"For what? What happened?"

"Oh, nothing out-and-out crushing. We didn't hook the population with narcotics or send their females to brothels, as we've often been accused of doing. We couldn't have done much physical exploitation if we'd wanted to—they were all about three feet tall and looked sort of like kiwis with arms. But Scarle really didn't know what he was doing yet. He thought it was all setting up the hum-box, taking a shot, and filling out the Omniform. Of course, it doesn't stop with that."

"And?"

"He found out, after the Omni was Staff Evaluated and Malmson's borox deposits were deemed significant. A report was submitted, and we left. A year later he went back for a visit—they should never let a paraling revisit one of his X-worlds…The industry we were imposing had already begun disrupting the culture's value systems—and because Scarle was a paraling, he translated feelings as well as words when he talked with the creatures that second time. The deposed grow bitter, the young lose their roots—you know the story. Scarle had already had a couple other X's by then, but he came away unsure after that visit. He claimed we had no right to make aliens over into our image. He said he wanted to quit."

"What did the Circle say?"

"Nothing, officially. But he was subsequently visited by the woman who had recruited him, and she persuaded him to accept another assignment."

"This last one?"

"Right. Mack 997-IV, the world they call the Butcher. His recruiter explained to him that the first assignments were also in the nature of training, and she proceeded to reveal the rest of the significance of the Ring."

"What was your second assignment like?" you asked him.

He told you that it had been to a brutal and nasty place, with a smelly reptilian culture he had hated. Then you told him that it, also, would be changed as a result of his visit. It would be more congenial, by human standards, because of it. You then told him the full story of King Solomon's Ring—how it had been a divine gift to the Temple Builder, granting him the power to compel obedience from every demon in existence. Neither were all of the demons obnoxious, you assured him; some were useful and some were not. Those of particular malice were forced into bottles, to be stoppered with the ring's unbreakable seal, and cast into the seas to drift forever. The useful ones were put to work building the Temple. And you, Billy Scarle, wear the Ring of Solomon around your mind, and communication is not its only function. You are the Builder—you are enlisting every variety of aid for the construction of the interstellar Temple of Earth. It is the most godlike of all human responsibilities, and there are few of us, very few, capable of furthering this end. You have passed all your tests now, and you are an extremely gifted paralinguist. So gifted, in fact, that we wish to entrust you with the most difficult assignment in our files...

"He bought it, of course," I finished, with a sip of Danzel coffee. "She could sell igloos on Mercury if she wanted."

❖   ❖   ❖

The day was bright, the sky was yellow, and Scarle set down his hum-box.

"What is it?" I asked him.

"They won't talk today," he answered. "They just wanted to observe us. They'll be back in about forty hours. They're leaving now."

"Where are they?"

"Behind those bushes." He gestured toward a thicket of reddish, spiky-looking shrubs. "They'll go request permission to talk with us."

"From whom?"

"I don't know."

"How do you know that much? None of the equipment is operating."

"I got a partial impression a minute ago. They're telepathic themselves, and they were talking."

"What do they look like?"

"I don't know. Some sort of big insect, I think. I may be prejudiced by the reports from X1 and X2, though. I feel they're a slave-class creature."

"How come they've taken a week to make up their minds?" I asked him.

He shrugged negatively.

So we walked down to the river and went for a swim, because we had been ordered not to and the captain had no right to give such an order to S-personnel. The shaly ground had a pinholed complexion, the water was warmish, and a grudging breeze fanned us to near-comfort. It was easy to float in the waters of Mack the Knife, as we had nicknamed the Butcher, and there was nothing dangerous lurking below (nothing non-dangerous either—Mack had very little in the way of marine life).

"You scared?" I asked.

"No," he said.

"Why not?"

He did not answer.

"How sure are you of your stability?"

"Certain," he yawned. "Paralings are slightly prescient when it comes to organic actions. *I'd* know in advance if that horsefly that's going to land on your nose were going to bite mine."

I heard a buzz.

I slapped my nose with the flat of my hand, but there was no horsefly. Just a horselaugh.

"Reflex betrayed you," he said. "There are no flies on the Butcher."

I rolled quickly, hoping to dunk him good, but he was not there. His laughter came from a spot about forty feet away on the bank, where he sat smoking.

" 'Certain,' " he repeated.

I rubbed my nose.

"Very funny. When you find a tarantula in your bunk tonight, you'll know who…"

"Come off it," he called. "I had a point to prove. You were relaxed   ears near water level—background splashes—I didn't say a word. Admit you thought I was beside you. Admit I'm deceptive, cunning, and nasty."

"You know what's on my mind."

"Yes," he said, "you're worried the same thing will happen as before."

"Twice," I added. "Why the devil those bureaucrats couldn't send more than one paraling I…"

"One had always been sufficient elsewhere. It will be the same way this time."

"This is a real challenge for you, isn't it?" I snapped. "Whoever talked to you must have put it in a very missionary way."

"So what? An X is an X. I can make it."

"You're just a personnel problem for me," I said, "but the last two paralings to X here *are* still in the bughouse, with EEG readings pretty as horizons."

"There is an old Ortho parable," he told me, "about a guy who asked a computer when he was going to die."

I waited.

"Well, what happened?"

"Nothing," he answered. "End of parable. It didn't know."

"Implication being—?"

"My chances of coming back have been calculated as pretty good. There are a lot fewer variables involved this time, because we have the reports of the first two expeditions. This problem *could* be programmed—so who are you to judge, off the cuff?"

I did not say anything. I just thought hard.

But he laughed again, because he had been born on Fenster and he knew the whole Dictionary of Galactic Profanity without having to look anything up.

When we reported back to the ship later, I felt he also knew I did not have any spare tarantulas along.

❖   ❖   ❖

It was two days before the creatures returned, and it was gray and raining when they appeared in the clearing. An open-sided field tent was quickly erected, and we donned slickers and sloughed off through the dark mud.

Scarle set the hum-box on a toweled-down table, and I studied our welcome committee...

Three of them... Antlike, with the greenish cast of venerable bronze to their steel-hard hides; about the size of German Shepherds—but, I daresay, many times stronger; and eyes blank as Dorn's pink moons, of which they reminded me—sightless seeming, but watching with a disconcerting fixity—and it might be they could see anything. (Do you remember Dorn?)

Scarle mouthed some words, turning on the recorder, and the reply came in a clock-click, *th-th-th, bittle-bittle-bittle* series of sounds. He pressed the INVESTIGATE button and took the black snap-case from his pocket. The red Insufficiency Light came on just as he finished assembling his hypodermic. He turned to the creatures and recited a sonnet by Shelley. It did not fit in with the day, but they responded with more noise, and he pressed RECORD again. He jabbed the hypo into an ampule containing a mild sedative and gave himself an injection while they continued ticking.

They seemed to understand what he wanted, because they kept it up for a full four minutes this time. He thumbed the INVESTIGATE button once more, and I looked out beyond the tent flaps and through the rain.

The Butcher could easily be a treasure trove. The preliminary Geo reports had indicated untapped mineral resources and possible climatological suitability for raising the staples that underspaced Mother Earth found dwindling within her cities; on her shore-to-shore plains of steel and concrete the dirt Agcities showed as acne rather than beautymarks. But amid the steel pores of Earth, wheat the interloper still meant bread. The Butcher might become a Baker.

The green light glowed—Tentative Inflectional Patterning Established. Patterns, not meanings. There ain't no box can take *click-click, th-th, bittle-bittle* in one end, cold, and give you "Good morning, it's raining like hell, isn't it?" out of the other. A completely unfamiliar body of significant sounds has no meaning to a stranger, man or machine, until a referent or two are picked up. Grammar and vocabulary take too long to obtain in times like these, and there were no telepaths good enough for total X then. But all languages have patterns of inflection. The hum-box separated and established these patterns. It did not know whether they were interrogative, argumentative, repetitive, or what have you, but it sifted them.

The rest was up to Scarle and the hum.

The speakers were placed in their magic circle about the bugs; then another around us. Scarle, the peaceful-looking conductor, eyes at half mast and a drunken smile below, began the concert.

The two-channel inflectional humming began as he poked the unit to life. Marginal audibility was present on our side of things, and the INVESTIGATE had guessed at the ants' auditory threshold on the basis of their recorded vocal range.

Transmission. Scarle spoke under his breath, staring at nothing. Each of the ninety-seven questions of the Omni, with its optional subsections, lurked, script-like, in his mind. The thing, as you know it, Lisa, is carefully planned. I here detail you that Known, because I have things to say about it which will bear directly upon my subject.

The scoffers first called it a sneaky way to dignify a seance, but all's quiet on that front these days. The dope, plus the occupation of the consciousness with the format of the Omni, is sufficient to conjure our ghosts—the thought-ghosts, which jump the gap between the consciousness of the Queried to that buried point in the mind of the Questioner from whence they hitch a ride upward on waves of post-query curiosity, pouring into the wordless sentences of the half-heard hum. With a good paraling like Scarle, the ghosts visit us too, if we keep our minds quiet. His steno was a ling-journeyman who had never made it in transmission.

WORD BODY ONE (FULL RANGE INFLECT CYCLES): Good morning/afternoon/evening. We greet you in the name of Earth and bid you good hunting/fishing/harvests/fertile cattle/victories. We are warm-blooded, omnivorous, patriarchal, highly intelligent creatures. We need many things. We have many things to offer others, whether the others are like or different. What are you? What do you/have you/need you?

And question for question, each completes an Omni on the other. Theoretically, that places each in an equal position of knowledge and appraises bargaining power on an above-the-board basis. Actually, since we designed it, along with the stock answers, and have refined the Staff Evaluation procedure from an art down to a science, we always come out on top. Equity is a pretty concept, but depth psychology, followed by military analysis and augmented by power on any level—from religious through economic—gives us our small advantages without disturbing the senates.

Like a bad connection on hyperphone came the ambisexual answers:

—*Good morning. We are servants. We serve. Our owners/rulers lay eggs. We are omnivorous. We are intelligent. We do not need anything. Our owners/rulers give us all. What do you want?*

And on it rolled. To all our key questions: *We do not do that/know that/need that. Our owners/rulers do that/know that/do not need that.*

They told us all about themselves. A dedicated entomologist would have been in a Moslem paradise of the mind over the inter-view, as was our dedicated entomologist, Dave Bolton.

"Please," said he, "ask them if they see this polaroid flash—"

"Shh!" said I, who supervised. "Later."

Was I detecting a beartrap in the flowerbed of their coopera-tion?—We want to be helpful, but darn it! sir, we just do not know the answer to that one. Etc.

Do not suggest, I wrote on a slip of paper, *that we speak with their masters. Wait and see if they offer.*

I placed the note before Scarle, hoping that the act of reading it would keep him from transmitting the thought. I waited to see.

They offered.

Scarle turned to me.

"Tell them we must confer," I answered. "Ask where the masters are, what they are like, why they did not come themselves—and ask if they suggested we send you."

"Me?"

"You."

He asked, and they told us they would have to confer.

Yes, they finally acknowledged, as a matter of fact their rulers (who lived in eternal night) had mentioned that we could send them our only paraling if anything needed clarification. Did we care to?

"Tell them 'yes'," I said, "but not today. We need to confer some more."

❖   ❖   ❖

That afternoon we Staff Evaluated a very sketchy Omni.

We decided, after an intrepid imaginative foray, that the rulers were similar to ant queens and did not like to leave the nest. Our mission was to get an Omni on the Butcher, evaluate it, and write a recommendation, so we had to go see them if they would not come to us. We wanted to set up safeguards, though, so Scarle spent the night learning the depressive neuroses Hale said he could retreat into to protect his sanity if the going got rough.

"Quite against the rules, we also armed ourselves to the teeth," I said to Hale, "and then armed our teeth with the little glass capsules I almost got to taste. You didn't know about those."

"I had guessed, of course," he snorted. "There was nothing wrong with my neuroses, though. I gave him the best ones I had in stock."

"I'm sure he appreciated that," I answered, pouring him a drink. "Do you believe the legend of King Solomon's ring?"

"Well, archetypically—"

"Archetypes, hell! Do you believe the story?"

"Yes, it has many levels of non-conscious meaning."

"Well, step over to my level for a minute and answer the question. Forget the psych-structure stuff. Can one intelligence control another by non-physical means?"

"Charisma," he stated, "is a peculiar phenomenon. Many factors are generally operative."

"Have another drink and swallow your charisma along with it. I'm talking about parapsych stuff. If a paraling can send *and* receive thoughts and feelings, why not more than that?"

"Commands?" he asked. "Parahypnotics? That *can* be accomplished, under special circumstances."

"I was thinking more along the lines of a lightning bolt fusing sand in its own image."

I started to pour again.

"No," he declined it, "psychologists just get drunk, but psychiatrists get drunk and break things. What are you driving at with all this?"

"The Ring works both ways."

❖ ❖ ❖

It does, Lisa. More than just translation. That first dim day in the caves Scarle ended a thirty-second exchange, and the steno threw down his transcriber.

"I cannot record," he said.

"What's wrong?" I asked.

"The hum-box isn't working right. I'm not getting voices, or even concepts."

"What are you getting?"

"A very beautiful humming sound—it's like a piece of music—an emotional synopsis of something. Don't ask me what."

I didn't. I asked Scarle. Angry at having been lulled into a pleasant lethargy myself, I shook off the spell and called out.

"What's going on?"

"Shh!"

I groped for his shoulder in the murk, but his whisper had no direction, and he was nowhere near the machine.

"Lights!" I called. But before I called it, I thought it.

There was a sound like someone scrubbing concrete with a hard-bristled brush, and our beams exploded in all directions.

We humans were alone, and Scarle. He leaned against the wall of the tunnel about ten feet in advance of our party, and he was smiling. I repeated my question.

"Nothing," he answered. "Nothing's going on now. I wish you hadn't turned on the lights. You broke the agreement."

"I was not anxious to become anything's breakfast," I told him. "What were you doing?"

"I was telling her how I looted the Moonstone in mid-flight."

"You pulled that one."

"I did."

"Why were you telling them about it?"

"Because I was asked. It was in my memory, and a fuller explanation of the principle of illicit appropriation was desired."

I remember that I whistled then—in order to keep myself from doing anything else.

"That is not exactly Omni material," I said softly.

"No, but I was asked…"

"Why?"

"She was curious as to the pleasure linked with the thoughts."

"She?"

"Yes, a female. You were right about queens."

"An ant?"

"I guess so."

"Why won't she let us see her?"

"I believe the light bothers her eyes."

"The whole thing smells. I want a full report on this X after we get back to the ship, but let's get back fast. I don't like it here."

He smiled and shrugged, and I checked the ampule, but he had not taken an overdose.

❖   ❖   ❖

Later, I asked him again.

"They want to know how to loot a spaceship?"

"No." He leaned back in a recliner, blowing smoke rings. "She only wondered about the pleasure associations."

"So what did you tell her?"

"Nothing. I just let her look at my mind."

"Then what did she say?"

"Nothing, she seemed satisfied."

"Why were the pleasure associations there?"

He smiled slightly.

"I enjoy stealing. Especially when I can get away with it."

"Unfortunately," I replied, "that tells me more about you than it does about the ants."

"You asked me a question. I answered it."

"What came next?"

"That's all. You turned on the lights."

"That's not much."

"*I* didn't turn on the lights."

"Okay," I growled. "How come Brown couldn't record?"

"We were using a form of mental shorthand."

"Where did you learn it?"

"I just sort of fell into it today. They're natural paralings."

"That, in itself, is a valuable commodity. We'll have to investigate it, along with the Omni stuff."

"I agree. Next time don't turn on the lights, though."

"All right, mister. But no more professional advice on space piracy."

"No more," he promised.

❖　❖　❖

So we went back into the underground cities of the Butcher, guided by belt sonar and five-watt flicker buttons, to mine the minds of the ants.

Brown was still unable to record anything; under hypnosis he could recall the transmission sensations, but nothing else. We had to rely on Scarle for the reports, and after about a week and a half I was no longer sure we were getting them.

"Scarle, have you been editing your reports?"

"No."

"Would you care to verify that under drugs?"

"You calling me a liar?"

"Perhaps."

"Okay, give me some drugs," he laughed.

Then the thought occurred to me (maybe he had sent it when he laughed) that the drugs would not prove anything. He had built up a resistance to most of the hypnotics while in training; they just made his mind shift gears.

"Forget it," I told him.

"I already have," he agreed.

What we really needed was another paraling to check on the paraling we already had.

Scarle's reports showed us the picture of a giant ant-colony ruled in the classic monolithic manner. Its structure seemed one of low workers, middle workers, upper workers, warriors, consorts, and queens. It was an agrarian culture which had never developed a single tool, relying rather upon classes of physically specialized individuals for the accomplishment of work. It was based on a matriarchal concept which permeated its religion in a manner similar (I think) to the old Egyptian notion of the Pharoahs' divine descendency.

❖   ❖   ❖

I emptied the little coffee pot into the tiny cups, motioned to the waiter to bring us another, and looked out across the sunken gardens of Luna at the mossy ball shaping the Americas above the great dome: Europe rolling away, Andalusia teasing memories from my mind, and the Gulf beginning to drip salt on sore places, Lisa. By the way, by the time you receive this billy-do, my dear, I will no longer be here, but there, and winging guess where?

"Both ways?" Hale asked me, a perplexed expression dodging about the Eiffel Tower.

I turned back, nodding.

"Yes, I suspected it after Scarle's reports started sounding as if I were reading the same report over and over. I asked myself what he could possibly be covering up, or stalling for. Then I decided maybe *he* wasn't."

"That's why you wanted to X it yourself?"

"Correct," I acknowledged. "Which is why I requisitioned a paraling drug kit from your cabin."

"Which is why our pinochle game got interrupted by a bellyache."

"Yes, I paid the comm man to get sick."

"An unsupervised X by a non-p.l. is never without its dangers."

"So I'd heard, but that's why Personnel is full of ex-Guardsmen—to sponge up the puddles of trouble before someone steps in them."

"Or turn them into lakes," he reflected. "So what about Scarle? What *did* happen?"

"Like the report says, he went off his rocker and tried to kill us all. I had to shoot him in self-defense."

"Do you remember doing it?"

"Sort of… Anyway, that's what the report says."

He surrounded me.

"You were inside his mind." Each word weighed equal to its neighbor.

"Yes, it's all in the report."

"And you were with him at the time he became unbalanced."

"That's right."

"And you came away thinking *you* were Scarle, after you had killed him."

"That also is correct. The report said it was a neurotic identification brought on because I was cathecting at the onset of trauma."

"I know; I wrote it. But I'm seldom happy just to stick a label on something, and that's what I did. It's been over two months now, and I may not see you again for a long while. I'd like to reexamine my diagnosis before we say good-bye."

"Okay, we're both in a condition where I can tell you what really happened and blame it on the drinks if you ever ask me again."

❖   ❖   ❖

So I told him. Do you remember that water cruise we took a couple of years ago, on Jansen, and that one island we stopped at, the one where you talked me into playing a limbo game with the kids? I was bending over backwards to please, and I fell flat on my backside in the process, but I made a more memorable impression than if I had succeeded. I know Hale did not believe the entire story—I could hear his gears grinding—but he was impressed. More than I had anticipated.

I told him how I had accompanied Scarle back into the lands beneath the land that day, swinging along to a monomaniac Guard marching tune calculated to assure mental privacy. I had washed out of Circle training in the second month myself, because of a concept-blurring tendency. I am sure you are not aware that I had even attempted it (I probably did it because of the name), and I could see Hale recalling my personnel record and seizing upon it as an explanation for my story—an explanation for what had really saved me. He was wrong, but it did not matter. He still believed much of what I said.

Nearly anybody can achieve a percentage of X under optimum conditions; I always can, and it is higher than average. This time it was sufficient.

The nimbus of our flicker-lights was not a far-reaching thing, consequently the Queried(?), as always, remained a part of the darkness. Like a shaded Medusa, she hovered before us, and we could feel her presence and sense her exchanges with Scarle. The voices of winds and grasses and the sounds of cellars and the cries of high cables and the monotonous commenting of seashells buzzed at the bottom of our auditory threshold and worked occasional fractured multiwords, without genuine context. An illicit and indefinable feeling of not being wanted crept through me as I prepared the injection.

"…Not take…*les nourritures*(?)…sadly…and stealing, Romany(?) …go…all things—pause—*corpus meum*…why? Brigand from the stars… perhaps—"

And my head swam and I was inside and no one had noticed and the night was cool.

I stood there feeling like a photographic negative of Scarle. Object rained upon subject, a plethora of stimuli waterfall upon my mind, but I kept my mind quiet. Perhaps it was the intensity of the communication that caused them to overlook my presence. I eased into Scarle's mind and read there the fascination with what is impossible.

Whatever it was in the tunnel, it was not a giant ant in Scarle's mind/my mind. We were talking with a lovely, yellow-tressed young lady who reminded me of yourself, Lisa, and she was obviously fascinated with our person. We were linked with a host of criminal concepts only recently learned in the society of the tunnels and never before encountered on an intimate basis. She was in love with Scarle/me/us, and her sadness was great.

"I cannot do to you," she said, "what I did with the others; and you, more than any of them, are that which threatens us. If Earth prevails here, as it has on Malmson, Bareth, and the other worlds you have visited, we will be as doomed as they. Yet, you have lived by their principle of thievery, and I cannot hate you for it. Let us talk of other things and postpone our final conflict. Tell me again of your looting days…"

It was not then that the part of Scarle that was me suddenly got the shakes and was noticed. It was a moment later, when my nervous introspecting revealed that we/I(?) returned the creature's sentiments. Then it was all over in a surrealistic kaleidoscope that I watched through more eyes than I care to count.

The Ring works both ways. Or Rings. She wore the stronger one. Ours was a candybox imitation.

Communication was an incidental virtue of Solomon's ring, remember? Its main function was the controlling of malevolent entities, of bending their actions to the wearer's will, of impressing *their* wills with commands like hot irons…

She seized Scarle's/my/our mind, with a hurricane of mixed emotions backing the assault.

"Kill them all!" came the order.

I guess Brown was the first to sense what was happening, because he flicked on a light beam.

And she stood there, flinching at the light—a gigantic, rainbow-winged gargoyle, with antennae like black seaweed surfaced on a stormlit ocean crest.

That is doubtless what saved us all. Despite the command, Scarle and I were frozen by the shock of seeing—of seeing the truth that your symbol had concealed, as the music was torn from our mind by the light, and the order roaring again after the flash, like a thunderclap:

"Kill them!"

That was when we went mad. I saw Scarle through my eyes and the cathedral windows of *her* eyes, and myself through that same colored glass *and* Scarle's eyes, and I/we saw her, both, and we obeyed the command.

There was gunfire, and I dropped down the pipe of a titanic organ, vibrating to something that I might have been able to recognize if I had had the time to listen.

The time passed, and one day I could hear again.

The command had worked divisively. Although Scarle and I had been one in mind, the ordered "Kill them!" had affected two separate nervous systems, and I beat him to the draw. It was that simple, although I do not remember doing it.

I collapsed from the psychic drain before I could kill anyone else; or possibly it had been the light that slowed her, or the sudden death of Scarle. She lost her control, retreated; and the crew retreated, both bearing their casualties.

❖   ❖   ❖

In that brief time when our mind(s) were flooded, refuge for sanity was found in the mental foxholes Hale had dug. I crouched beneath neurotic breakwalls, communicating with Oedipus of things long ago and far away in the streets of Fenster. I was alternately depressed or elated as my fathers beat me or bought me candy, and always resentful, and always Scarle, and always wanting to know what they were thinking so I could know which way to jump, and always wanting to make them like me even though I hated their guts, and always, Lisa, I remembered mother and the thirteenth card of the Major

Arcana—the Bony Reaper, Death—whom I feared most of all but had to challenge every day in order to be big and not need anybody, and he was the navigator of the *Steel Eel*, but I was the captain.

It took more than a month for me to begin being myself again, but differently. Scarle, the man who had enjoyed stealing whenever he could get away with it, would have been pleased with his last theft. He had stolen part of my mind and left me a portion of his, in passing. He took with him a measure of my devotion to the policies of the Circle, and he left me with a calculated, antisocial quality which I have decided is a virtue.

I/we feel that the ant queen was right, that I/we were right after Malmson, and that the Temple is being maintained upon a foundation of spurious principles, the walls shored up at an inconceivably dear cost—the racial integrity of a thousand alien peoples. For this reason, I have decided to rebel. The transference left me the means of doing so. I am now a paraling in my own right, and the encounter with your image on the world called the Butcher left me with the *full* range of the Ring's powers. I, too, can compel actions, alter thoughts, require affections.

Hale said to me: "Do you feel like Scarle anymore?"

And I said: "I *am* Billy Scarle."

And then I said: "It may well be that he imprinted—" Right in step with the same words as they emerged from Hale's mouth.

The Machiavelli eyes, like black circles painted on ice cubes, sought my own for an explanation.

"I am Billy Scarle," I repeated, "as well as myself. He lurks at the bottom of my mind and jeers at the façade of morality with which the Circle masks the piracies of Earth. He indicates, too, that he was almost executed for similar acts on a small scale."

"I don't give a hoot about politics and policies," said Hale, "but you are a psychiatric curiosity. Once in a lifetime—something like this—a parapsych transference of personality traits *and* abilities! We are going to write a paper!"

"We are going to eat dinner," I said.

"But we've already eaten—"

"In the lighter gravitation of Luna, two meals set as easily as one—and we're big people, with stomach for lots of things, aren't we?"

"What are you trying to say?"

"King Solomon had a ring," I told him, "and communication was not its only end. It could be used to compel the obedience of every demon in existence, and I, Billy Scarle, wear that ring around my mind like an emotional chastity belt. You are on the side of the demons, Hale. Not all of the demons are malevolent, though, and many can be put to work building the Temple properly. I am recruiting you to spread the dogma of Many Mansions, and to fill them with an interstellar brotherhood. I am going to steal your philosophy, like a magpie, and leave you another in its place."

The Seal of Solomon became a hot scalpel in my mind, and after awhile I said, "What are we going to have for dinner?" and he said, "How about steaks?"

❖   ❖   ❖

That, Lisa, is the story of my dinner/s last night (I think it was last night; I am not back on the Earth time-scale yet). I left Dr. Hale assured of my complete recovery from the Scarle-neurosis, and I caught the next shuttle for Earth. Earth fills the viewport while I write these lines, my darling, as my mind fills with double memories of you. I believe that Scarle loved you, as much as he was capable of loving anything, and I know that I always have. I shall know in a few hours which of us (if either) may have evoked similar feelings in you—that, when we talk of the past in the wordless pentagrams of our profession. I wish to enlist you in my crusade, also—I say "enlist," not "induct." I believe that I have almost a century of productive time before me. With your able assistance I could use that time changing the minds of the men who are the mind of Earth and the soul of its policies. If you decline, it shall only cost you an hour out of your memory. You were such a fine recruiter, and there is something to what Hale says about charisma.

If I try to go it on my own, I may trip up soon—but either way, I *will* have a go at it—and I have prepared this lengthy proposal and invitation (which I shall post after landing) in order to apprise you of the circumstances which have brought me here, as well as my feelings for you. I probably overestimate the time that will be allotted me; the choice, though, of a short and magnificent life selling igloos on Mercury has its appeal. I believe that you, also, are fascinated by impossibilities. (And remember what happened to Troy?)

Therefore, I shall time the solid postal transmissions in a few moments and transport myself accordingly. By the time you have read this far I shall be but moments away.

Please consider the future, and please be afraid. In a few moments you too shall meet the Butcher. He is probably outside now, with a ring for you.

Open the door and let him in.

Love and kisses,
Solomon/Scarle

Notes

The "Seal of Solomon" was a magic ring that gave Solomon power over demons or the ability to speak to the animals in their own language; the legends differ. Some versions of the Seal make it look like the Star of David, surrounded by a circle.

Svengali is a musician in George du Maurier's novel *Trilby* who trains Trilby's voice and controls her stage singing hypnotically; the term also indicates a person who controls another, especially through a mesmerizing influence. **Niccolò di Bernardo dei Machiavelli** was an Italian statesman and political philosopher who advised unethical means may be necessary to acquire and effectively use power. A full set of Tarot cards includes 22 cards of the **Major Arcana** in addition to 56 cards (pip and four face cards) of the Minor Arcana. The 13th card depicts the Grim Reaper variously as a skeleton riding a horse or as a cloaked skeleton walking and carrying a scythe. **Lilith** is a female demon who tries to kill newborn children; in the Talmud she is the first wife of Adam before Eve was created. **Mosel** refers to a medium white wine that comes from the Mosel river region. **Liebfraumilch** is white wine from the Rhine region; the name comes from Liebfrau ("Dear Lady," meaning the Virgin Mary) and milch, meaning milk.

Paralinguistics is the study of paralanguage, the conscious or unconscious non-verbal elements of speech which include the pitch, volume, and intonation of speech; by its use in the story, a paralinguist would be someone who could understand non-verbal communication almost instinctively. **Noam Chomsky** is a theoretical linguist who theorized that linguistic behavior is innate, not learned, and that all languages share the same underlying grammatical base. **Mardi Gras** occurs on Shrove Tuesday and is marked by celebrations, parades, and masquerade balls. **Polemics** is the art of argument or controversy. **Kiwis** are large flightless birds, native to New Zealand. **Mack the Knife** is a well known song by Kurt Weill from *The Threepenny Opera*. An **entomologist** studies insects. **Archetype** refers to the original that has since been imitated.

    Charisma is a spiritual power or personal quality that gives an individual influence or authority over large numbers of people. **Andalusia** is the southernmost region of Spain. **Cathecting** or cathexis means concentrating (possibly too much) mental energy on one person idea, or object. The Gorgon **Medusa** had the power to turn men to stone with her glance. **Les nourritures** means nourishment. **Oedipus** was abandoned at birth and unwittingly killed his father and then married his mother before blinding himself when he learned the truth of his situation. **Imprinted** in this context means fixed firmly in the mind. **Remember what happened to Troy** refers to the Greeks' decade-long siege of the city during the Trojan War; the city fell by trickery when the Greeks left a gift of a large wooden horse which secretly contained armed Greek soldiers.

THE BLACK BOY'S REPLY TO WILLIAM BUTLER YEATS

Written 1955–60 for *Chisel in the Sky;* previously unpublished.

"Ise never seen no Black Massa.
I never cares to see none.
But ef I takes another drink
I thinks that I will be one."

Notes

This poem seems to be a response to Yeats' "Mohini Chaterji" in which a man boasts that he has been a king, slave, rascal, just about anything.

THE MISFIT

Amazing, October 1963.

Jackson returned the General's stare.

"I will *not* stand at attention, and you can go to hell!"

The General beetled his brows.

"What is it with you?"

"I want out of this chicken outfit."

"I told you last week that I'd approve your transfer."

"That's not what I mean."

"What then?"

"I am not Colonel Jackson and you are not General Paine. This place only exists in my mind, and I want to change my mind."

The General sighed.

"Okay, Jackson, that's your privilege. What'll it be this time? The Navy?"

"I want out from the whole military—like a civilian, like something enjoyable."

"Name it."

❖   ❖   ❖

Doctor Jackson tore off his rubber gloves and flung them into the corner. Miss Mayor, amazing despite starch, came up behind him and wrapped wonderful arms about his chest. She pressed her cheek to his neck.

"You're famous already, Jack. Forty-four brain operations in a month—all of them delicate and complicated—and all successful! What a record you've achiev—"

"Okay! Okay!"

"What's the matter, Jackie? Have I done something?"

"No!"

"Then why are you hollering? Oh, I should have realized—you're tired, on edge. After an operation like that last one, anybody—"

"I am *not* tired!"

"You *must* be!"

"How can I be tired without having done anything?"

"I don't understand you…"

"The hell you don't!"

"I don't like Jackie when he uses naughty words."

"Then step over to that corner and turn into a table," he pointed, "with a bowl of chrysanthemums on it."

"What do you mean?"

She moved around him and stared up into his eyes. All at once she was the loveliest, most desirable woman in creation.

"What's it with you, anyhow?" she asked.

He bit his lip.

"With a bowl of chrysanthemums," he repeated.

"Are you certain?" she sighed.

He nodded.

❖   ❖   ❖

The rocket dropped to the rainbow desert like a red-stemmed flower growing backward to seed. Shortly the red vanished and the steel pod lay upon Jackson Plains. Professor Jackson strode out onto Jackson's World and sniffed the smoke-blue, November-cold air. He studied the unit he carried, then spoke into the microphone at his throat.

"It's all right. You can come out."

His three companions, tanned despite the long voyage, lean, tall and grinning, strode through the hatchway and looked about, all recklessness and competency.

"By golly, you were right, Doc! It *is* habitable!"

"Of course it is. Jackson is never wrong."

Jackson nodded in a perfunctory manner and proceeded to orient the photomap.

"The ruins are that way," he pointed.

They swung into step beside him.

Something was gnawing within his mind, tingling at the base of his skull.

Half an hour, it seemed. They paused beside a hedge of jagged monoliths.

"This is a mighty weird place," Mason was drawling, Tennes-see-ish.

A ululating cry from above and Mason collapsed, spitting blood. The spear had passed entirely through him, hurled with enormous force. Jackson threw himself flat.

Thompson screamed and coughed once, moistly.

Blaster in hand, Jackson glanced at Wolf.

"Did you get a look at what did it?"

"Yeah," whispered the man. "Wish I hadn't. It was horrible—all those arms, that green skin, those bug eyes—"

Thompson emptied his lungs for the last time.

Another banshee cry, nearer. Jackson wormed his way to the right, then he waited quietly.

The faintest of ticks, metal kissing stone…

He sprang to his feet, triggering a bolt of flame.

The thing fell, slavering. A greenish ichor dripped from the great hole his shot had torn in its midsection.

…And something in the back of his head was tingling.

"Doc, there's more of 'em!"

He heard the crackle of Wolf's blaster, the sizzle of frying flesh. Two of the creatures fell.

Four more were sliding down the slope toward him.

He turned and shot Wolf. Then he tossed his blaster over his shoulder.

"Go ahead," he called, "I'm anxious to see how you squirm out of this one."

The aliens were almost upon him when a great hissing shape reared from behind a rock and slithered in their direction. They halted, uttering brief cries, then turned and retreated back up the hill.

He followed.

"Pretty good," he told the huge snake. "Passable, anyhow."

It dropped to near his height, peering at him.

"I'm tired of suspending disbelief," he told it.

The snake seemed to sigh.

"I'm curious whether I could die from one of these," said Jackson.

"It is physiologically possible," answered the snake, "but it is forbidden. What is it with you, anyhow?"

"Couldn't you just let me wake up?"

"No."

"Why not? I would like to know why I'm here."

"Such memories do not exist. You will never know. It had to be that way."

"And I will dream forever?"

"For the rest of your life."

"Was it the population problem?—The other planets uninhabitable, interstellar travel impossible, and people stacked like cordwood in glass coffins?"

"I couldn't say."

"And you are the machine, talking through an electrode in my skull, feeding me, programming my wish-fulfillments?"

"If you want it that way."

"I don't. Am I in a coma? Did I have an accident? Is this some kind of drug therapy?"

"Call it anything you want."

"When will I wake up?"

"You are awake."

"You have to say that. Whatever sort of machine you are, that's the way you're programmed."

"Then why ask?"

He looked about for the blaster. It was gone.

Suddenly, it was in his hand.

"If you want to kill the snake, go ahead."

Quickly, he turned it toward his own head. It vanished.

"You can't."

His hands fell to his sides.

"Could this be hell?"

"If you wish."

"*Can't* I wake up?"

"Are you certain that's what you want? There *are* certain provisions."

"I want to try it."

"So be it."

❖   ❖   ❖

The transparent lid of the case had slid open above him. His muscles were spaghetti and his throat was dry and his left arm was porcupined with syrettes. After a long while he managed to withdraw their bright points. Keeping his arm tightly bent, the lesions stayed under direct pressure. With his right hand he reached behind his head. He felt an electrode taped to his shaven skull.

As he moved to draw it away a voice rang in his head:

"If you are disappointed with reality, come lie down again—replace the needles, replace the contact."

"I won't," he muttered, tearing it loose.

He struggled to his feet and went in search of anybody.

❖   ❖   ❖

It had been the only way to solve the population problem, said Mannerung. Put everyone to sleep, awaken key scientists at different times to work on interstellar flight, maintain a skeleton crew to service the Regulator. Let the fifty billion sleepers dream under glass—they're better off than they could ever be awake.

"It takes a peculiar sort," the Doctor had told him, "to prefer the mundane to the extraordinary, the humdrum to the satisfaction of his desires. Provisions had to be made for such people, of course. If a dreamer is sufficiently disturbed, the Regulator will permit him to awaken. We can always find something for him to do. There is much minor drudgery to the maintenance of the machinery. If that's what you want, you're elected. You can start by replacing some tubes in this subsection unit."

He passed him a chart.

"Here's the diagram. They're all numbered. The ones circled in red need to be replaced. When you're finished with that, you can start straightening out that storeroom." He pointed. "It's a mess. You're sure this is what you want?"

"Yes," said Jackson, "the other way was—well, parasitism. It was too good, and too useless."

"Okay then, get to it."

Humming happily, he went off after the tubes.

Finally knowing what it was with Jackson, the Mannerung-figure did not sigh.

Notes

Ululating is a long, emotional wail. A **banshee** is an Irish female spirit who wails to warn of impending death. **Syrettes** are disposable injection units through which a drug can be infused intravenously.

RITE OF SPRING

Written 1955–60 for *Chisel in the Sky;* previously unpublished.

The throb and bumble of the Coltrane sax,
emphasizing fury,
excising pity,
               beating desire into despair,
signifies the precious remnant
that is sought futility's value.

The cry and mumble of thwarted voices,
following magnetic lines
of flown force,
               beats no hybris
out the heart's dim forge,
no expressed evaluations, no description.

But diminuendos beyond the rationale of Aristotle,
exporting emotion
in idiot piping,
               beat back a final winding sheet
to, gasping, sigh, an older aspiration,
through nostrils of a figure met with dream.

Notes

Coltrane sax refers to jazz musician John Coltrane, who played the tenor and soprano saxophone and was also a composer and bandleader. **Hybris** is an alternate spelling of hubris, meaning excessive pride or arrogance. **Diminuendos** or decrescendos are musical passages of decreasing loudness. **Aristotle** was a Greek philosopher and early scientist who had originally been a pupil of Plato and who began the taxonomic system of classifying animals.

THE GREAT SLOW KINGS

Manuscript title: "Zindrome of Negative Speed."
Worlds of Tomorrow, December 1963.

Drax and Dran sat in the great Throne Hall of Glan, discussing life. Monarchs by virtue of superior intellect and physique—and the fact that they were the last two survivors of the race of Glan—theirs was a divided rule over the planet and their one subject, Zindrome, the palace robot.

Drax had been musing for the past four centuries (theirs was a sluggish sort) over the possibility of life on other planets in the galaxy.

Accordingly, "Dran," said he, addressing the other (who was becoming mildly curious as to his thoughts), "Dran, I've been thinking. There may be life on other planets in the galaxy."

Dran considered his response to this, as the world wheeled several times about its sun.

"True," he finally agreed, "there may."

After several months Drax shot back, "If there is, we ought to find out."

"Why?" asked Dran with equal promptness, which caused the other to suspect that he, too, had been thinking along these lines.

So he measured his next statement out cautiously, first testing each word within the plated retort of his reptilian skull.

"Our kingdom is rather underpopulated at present," he observed. "It would be good to have many subjects once more."

Dran regarded him askance, then slowly turned his head. He closed one eye and half-closed the other, taking full stock of his co-ruler, whose appearance, as he had suspected, was unchanged since the last time he had looked.

"That, also, is true," he noted. "What do you suggest we do?"

This time Drax turned, reappraising him, eye to eye.

"I think we ought to find out if there is life on other planets in the galaxy."

"Hmm."

Two quick roundings of the seasons went unnoticed, then, "Let me think about it," he said, and turned away.

After what he deemed a polite period of time, Drax coughed.

"Have you thought sufficiently?"

"No."

Drax struggled to focus his eyes on the near-subliminal streak of bluish light which traversed, re-traversed and re-re-traversed the Hall as he waited.

"Zindrome!" he finally called out.

❖   ❖   ❖

The robot slowed his movements to a statue-like immobility to accommodate his master. A feather duster protruded from his right limb.

"You called, great Lord of Glan?"

"Yes, Zindrome, worthy subject. Those old spaceships which we constructed in happier days, and never got around to using. Are any of them still capable of operation?"

"I'll check, great Lord."

He seemed to change position slightly.

"There are three hundred eighty-two," he announced, "of which four are in functioning condition, great Lord. I've checked all the operating circuits."

"Drax," warned Dran, "you are arrogating unauthorized powers to yourself once more. You should have conferred with me before issuing that order."

"I apologize," stated the other. "I simply wanted to expedite matters, should your decision be that we conduct a survey."

"You have anticipated my decision correctly," nodded Dran, "but your eagerness seems to bespeak a hidden purpose."

"No purpose but the good of the realm," smiled the other.

"That may be, but the last time you spoke of 'the good of the realm' the civil strife which ensued cost us our other robot."

"I have learned my lesson and profited thereby. I shall be more judicious in the future."

"I hope so. Now, about this investigation—which part of the galaxy do you intend to investigate first?"

A tension-filled pause ensued.

"I had assumed," murmured Drax, "that you would conduct the expedition. Being the more mature monarch, yours should be a more adequate decision as to whether or not a particular species is worthy of our enlightened rule."

"Yes, but your youth tends to make you more active than I. The journey should be more expeditiously conducted by you." He emphasized the word "expeditiously."

"We could both go, in separate ships," offered Drax. "That would be truly expeditious—"

Their heated debating was cut short by a metallic cough-equivalent.

"Masters," suggested Zindrome, "the half-life of radioactive materials being as ephemeral as it is, I regret to report that only one spaceship is now in operational condition."

"That settles it, Dran. *You* go. It will require a steadier *rrand* to manage an underpowered ship."

"And leave you to foment civil strife and usurp unfranchised powers? No, you go!"

"I suppose we could *both* go," sighed Drax.

"Fine! Leave the kingdom leaderless! *That* is the kind of muddleheaded thinking which brought about our present political embarrassment."

"Masters," said Zindrome, "if *someone* doesn't go soon the ship will be useless."

They both studied their servant, approving the rapid chain of logic forged by his simple statement.

"Very well," they smiled in unison, "*you* go."

Zindrome bowed quite obsequiously and departed from the great Throne Hall of Glan.

"Perhaps we should authorize Zindrome to construct facsimiles of himself," stated Dran, tentatively. "If we had more subjects we could accomplish more."

"Are you forgetting our most recent agreement?" asked Drax. "A superfluity of robots tended to stimulate factionalism last time—and certain people grew ambitious…" He let his voice trail off over the years, for emphasis.

"I am not certain as to whether your last allusion contains a hidden accusation," began the other carefully. "If so, permit me to caution you concerning rashness—and to remind you who it was who engineered the Mono-Robot Protection Pact."

"Do you believe things will be different in the case of a multitude of organic subjects?" inquired the other.

"Definitely," said Dran. "There is a certain irrational element in the rationale of the organic being, making it less amenable to direct orders than a machine would be. Our robots, at least, were faithful when we ordered them to destroy each other. Irresponsible organic subjects either do it without being told, which is boorish, or refuse to do it when you order them, which is insubordination."

"True," smiled Drax, unearthing a gem he had preserved for millennia against this occasion. "Concerning organic life the only statement which can be made with certainty is that life is uncertain."

"Hmm." Dran narrowed his eyes to slits. "Let me ponder that for a moment. Like much of your thinking it seems to smack of a concealed sophistry."

"It contains none, I assure you. It is the fruit of much meditation."

"Hmm."

❖   ❖   ❖

Dran's pondering was cut short, by the arrival of Zindrome who clutched two brownish blurs beneath his metal arms.

"Back already, Zindrome? What have you there? Slow them down so we can see them."

"They are under sedation at present, great Masters. It is the movements caused by their breathing which produce the unpleasant vibration pattern on your retinas. To subject them to more narcosis could prove deleterious."

"Nevertheless," maintained Dran, "we must appraise our new subjects carefully, which requires that we see them. Slow them down some more."

"You gave that order without—" began Drax, but was distracted by the sudden appearance of the two hairy bipeds.

"Warm-blooded?" he asked.

"Yes, Lord."

"That bespeaks a very brief life-span."

"True," offered Dran, "but that kind tends to reproduce quite rapidly."

"That observation tends to be correct," nodded Drax. "Tell me, Zindrome, do they represent the sexes necessary for reproduction?"

"Yes, Master. There are two sexes among these anthropoids, so I brought one of each."

"That was very wise. Where did you find them?"

"Several billion light years from here."

"Turn those two loose outside and go fetch us some more."

The creatures vanished. Zindrome appeared not to have moved.

"Have you the fuel necessary for another such journey?"

"Yes, my Lord. More of it has evolved recently."

"Excellent."

The robot departed.

"What sort of governmental setup should we inaugurate this time?" asked Drax.

"Let us review the arguments for the various types."

"A good idea."

❖   ❖   ❖

In the midst of their discussion Zindrome returned and stood waiting to be recognized.

"What is it, Zindrome? Did you forget something?"

"No, great Lords. When I returned to the world from which I obtained the samples I discovered that the race had progressed to the point where it developed fission processes, engaged in an atomic war and annihilated itself."

"That was extremely inconsiderate—typical, however, I should say, of warm-blooded instability."

Zindrome continued to shift.

"Have you something else to report?"

"Yes, great Masters. The two specimens I released have multiplied and are now spread over the entire planet of Glan."

"We should have been advised!"

"Yes, great Lords, but I was absent and—"

"They themselves should have reported this action!"

"Masters, I am afraid they are unaware of your existence."

"How could that have happened?" asked Dran.

"We are presently buried beneath several thousand layers of alluvial rock. The geological shifts—"

"You have your orders to maintain the place and clean the grounds," glowered Dran. "Have you been frittering away your time again?"

"No, great Lords! It all occurred during my absence. I shall attend to it immediately."

"First," ordered Drax, "tell us what else our subjects have been up to, that they saw fit to conceal from us."

"Recently," observed the robot, "they have discovered how to forge and temper metals. Upon landing, I observed that they had developed many ingenious instruments of a cutting variety. Unfortunately they were using them to cut one another."

"Do you mean," roared Dran, "that there is strife in the kingdom?"

"Uh, yes, my Lord."

"I will not brook unauthorized violence among my subjects!"

"*Our* subjects," added Drax, with a meaningful glare.

"*Our* subjects," amended Dran. "We must take immediate action."

"Agreed."

"Agreed."

"I shall issue orders forbidding their engagement in activities leading to bloodshed."

"I presume that you mean a joint proclamation," stated Drax.

"Of course. I was not slighting you, I was simply shaken by the civil emergency. We shall draft an official proclamation. Let Zindrome fetch us writing instruments."

"Zindrome, fetch—"

"I have them here, my Lords."

"Now, let me see. How shall we phrase it...?"

"Perhaps I should clean the palace while your Excellencies—"

"No! Wait right here! This will be very brief and to the point."

"Mm. 'We hereby proclaim...'"

"Don't forget our titles."

"True. 'We, the imperial monarchs of Glan, herebeneath undersigned, do hereby...'"

A feeble pulse of gamma rays passed unnoticed by the two rulers. The faithful Zindrome diagnosed its nature, however, and tried unsuccessfully to obtain the monarchs' attention. Finally, he dismissed the project with a stoical gesture typical of his kind. He waited.

❖   ❖   ❖

"There!" they agreed, flourishing the document. "Now you can tell us what you have been trying to say, Zindrome. But make it brief, you must deliver this soon."

"It is already too late, great Lords. This race, also, progressed into civilized states, developed nuclear energy and eradicated itself while you were writing."

"Barbarous!"

"Warm-blooded irresponsibility!"

"May I go clean up now, great Masters?"

"Soon, Zindrome, soon. First, though, I move that we file the proclamation in the Archives for future use, in the event of similar occurrences."

Dran nodded.

"I agree. *We* so order."

The robot accepted the crumbling proclamation and vanished from sight.

"You know," Drax mused, "there must be lots of radioactive material lying about now…"

"There probably is."

"It could be used to fuel a ship for another expedition."

"Perhaps."

"This time we could instruct Zindrome to bring back something with a longer lifespan and more deliberate habits—somewhat nearer our own."

"That would have its dangers. But perhaps we could junk the Mono-Robot Protection Pact and order Zindrome to manufacture extras of himself. Under strict supervision."

"That would have its dangers too."

"At any rate, I should have to ponder your suggestion carefully."

"And I yours."

"It's been a busy day," nodded Dran. "Let's sleep on it."

"A good idea."

Sounds of saurian snoring emerged from the great Throne Hall of Glan.

A Word from Zelazny

During high school, Zelazny co-wrote *The Record*, a series of short stories that he shared with classmate and longtime friend Carl Yoke. The main characters were Zlaz and Yok (for Zelazny and Yoke), sloppy but crafty monsters who lived in caves under Paris, slept long periods, drank large quantities of *zyphoam,* ambled in and out of outrageous situations, and fouled up most assignments given to them. There was also a fair bit of word play involved. "The Great Slow Kings" was clearly influenced by these stories and bears the same humor.[1,2]

Notes

Arrogating means claiming unwarrantedly or presumptively. **Sophistry** is a superficially plausible but inherently false argument or method of reasoning. **Alluvial** refers to sand or other matter that has been deposited by flowing water. **Saurian** means reptilian or lizard-like.

1 *Roger Zelazny: A Primary And Secondary Bibliography*, 1980.
2 *Roger Zelazny: Starmont Reader's Guide*, 1979.

Collector's Fever

Manuscript titles: "Co Nestor's Fever" & "The World, The Deeble,
and Uncle Sydney's Rock Collection." Also published as a graphic
short story (comic) under the title "Rock Collector."
Galaxy, June 1964.

"What are you doing there, human?"

"It's a long story."

"Good, I like long stories. Sit down and talk. No—not on me!"

"Sorry. Well, it's all because of my uncle, the fabulously wealthy—"

"Stop. What does 'wealthy' mean?"

"Well, like rich."

"And 'rich'?"

"Hm. Lots of money."

"What's money?"

"You want to hear this story or don't you?"

"Yes, but I'd like to understand it too."

"Sorry, Rock, I'm afraid I don't understand it all myself."

"The name is Stone."

"Okay, Stone. My uncle, who is a very important man, was supposed to send me to the Space Academy, but he didn't. He decided a liberal education was a better thing. So he sent me to his old spinster alma mater to major in nonhuman humanities. You with me, so far?"

"No, but understanding is not necessarily an adjunct to appreciation."

"That's what I say. I'll never understand Uncle Sidney, but I appreciate his outrageous tastes, his magpie instinct and his gross meddling in other people's affairs. I appreciate them till I'm sick to the stomach. There's nothing else I can do. He's a carnivorous old family monument, and fond of having his own way. Unfortunately, he also has all the money in the family—so it follows, like a *xxt* after a *zzn*, that he always *does* have his own way."

"This money must be pretty important stuff."

"Important enough to send me across ten thousand light-years to an unnamed world, which, incidentally, I've just named Dunghill."

"The low-flying *zatt* is a heavy eater, which accounts for its low flying…"

"So I've noted. That *is* moss though, isn't it?"

"Yes."

"Good, then crating will be less of a problem."

"What's 'crating'?"

"It means to put something in a box to take it somewhere else."

"Like moving around?"

"Yes."

"What are you planning on crating?"

"Yourself, Stone."

"I've never been the rolling sort…"

"Listen, Stone, my uncle is a rock collector, see? You are the only species of intelligent mineral in the galaxy. You are also the largest specimen I've spotted so far. Do you follow me?"

"Yes, but I don't want to."

"Why not? You'd be lord of his rock collection. Sort of a one-eyed man in a kingdom of the blind, if I may venture an inappropriate metaphor."

"Please don't do that, whatever it is. It sounds awful. Tell me, how did your uncle learn of our world?"

"One of my instructors read about this place in an old space log. *He* was an old space log collector. The log had belonged to a Captain Fairhill, who landed here several centuries ago and held lengthy discourses with your people."

"Good old Foul Weather Fairhill! How is he these days? Give him my regards—"

"He's dead."

"What?"

"Dead. Kaput. Blooey. Gone. Deeble."

"Oh my! When did it happen? I trust it was an esthetic occurrence of major import—"

"I really couldn't say. But I passed the information on to my uncle, who decided to collect you. That's why I'm here—he sent me."

"Really, as much as I appreciate the compliment, I can't accompany you. It's almost deeble time—"

"I know, I read all about deebling in the Fairhill log before I showed it to Uncle Sidney. I tore those pages out. I want him to be around when you do it. Then I can inherit his money and console myself in all manner of expensive ways for never having gone to the Space Academy. First I'll become an alcoholic, then I'll take up wenching—or maybe I'd better do it the other way around…"

"But I want to deeble here, among the things I've become attached to!"

"This is a crowbar. I'm going to unattach you."

"If you try it, I'll deeble right now."

"You can't. I measured your mass before we struck up this conversation. It will take at least eight months, under Earth conditions, for you to reach deebling proportions."

"Okay, I was bluffing. But have you no compassion? I've rested here for centuries, ever since I was a small pebble, as did my fathers before me. I've added so carefully to my atom collection, building up the finest molecular structure in the neighborhood. And now, to be snatched away right before deebling time, it's—it's quite unrock of you."

"It's not that bad. I promise you'll collect the finest Earth atoms available. You'll go places no other Stone has ever been before."

"Small consolation. I want my friends to see."

"I'm afraid that's out of the question."

"You are a very cruel human. I hope you're around when I deeble."

"I intend to be far away and on the eve of prodigious debaucheries when that occurs."

Under Dunghill's sub-E gravitation Stone was easily rolled to the side of the space sedan, crated, and, with the help of a winch, installed in the compartment beside the atomic pile. The fact that it was a short-jaunt sport model sedan, customized by its owner, who had removed much of the shielding, was the reason Stone felt a sudden flush of volcanic drunkenness, rapidly added select items to his collection and deebled on the spot.

He mushroomed upwards, then swept in great waves across the plains of Dunghill. Several young Stones fell from the dusty heavens wailing their birth pains across the community band.

"Gone fission," commented a distant neighbor, above the static, "and sooner than I expected. Feel that warm afterglow!"

"An excellent deeble," agreed another. "It always pays to be a cautious collector."

A Word from Zelazny

This story was written in one evening with "The Monster and the Maiden' and "Lucifer."[1] "[This] was a brief experiment of a simple sort. I wanted to do a piece entirely of dialogue. Plot, characters, setting—I wanted them all to emerge simply through talk. By the end, I'd written myself into a corner, though, and I decided that 95% dialogue was sufficient to make it a successful experiment. That's one of the nice things about setting your own goals as a writer. In a pinch, you can always revise them."[2]

Notes

The earlier tale "Monologue for Two" successfully used dialogue only. This short tale is also notable for several characteristic Zelazny puns.

Esthetic is the heightened sensitivity to and appreciation of beauty. **Wenching** is consorting with prostitutes or young women. **Sub-E** means less than Earth's gravitation.

---

1 *Tightbeam #37*, May 1966
2 *Amber Dreams*, 1983.

The Night Has 999 Eyes

Manuscript title: "Listen, Please Listen!"
Double:Bill #11, October/November 1964 as "The Night Has Nine Hundred Ninety-Nine Eyes."

L isten, please listen. It is important. I am here to remind you. The time has come for me to tell you again of the things you must not forget.

Sit down, please, and close your eyes. There will be pictures. Breathe deeply now. There will be odors, aromas… There will also be tastes. If you listen closely, you will even hear other sounds within my voice…

❖   ❖   ❖

There is a place—it is far from here in space but not in time, if you have the means—a place where there are seasons, a place where the spinning, leaning globe moves in an ellipse about its sun, and where the year winds on from a springtime to a bloom, then turns toward a harvest where the colors wrestle one another above your head and beneath your feet, meeting at last in a crisp uniformity of brown through which you walk, now walk, sniffing the life carried above the deadness by the cold, sharp morning air; and the clouds seen through the opened trees skid across the blue sheet of the sky and do not give down rains; then, moving on, there comes a time of coldness and snow, and the bark of the trees grows as hard and sharp as the tongues of files, and each step you take leaves a dark hole in a white world, and if you take a handful into your home with you it melts, leaving you water; the birds do not *wheep, threep, skree, cheep,* as they do when the color is upon the land and themselves—they zip their feathers tight and vibrate silently upon the shelves of the evergreens; it is a pausing time between movements: The stars come on more brightly (even *this* star—do not fear it), and the days are short and nothing really gets done but thinking (philoso-phy was born in the cold countries of the Earth), and the nights are long and given to the playing of card games and the drinking of liquors and the appreciation of music, the boarding and unburdening of love, the looking out through rimed windows, the hearing of the wind, and the stroking of the collie's fur—there, in that still center, called win-ter on Earth, where things regroup within the quiescence and ready themselves for the inexorable frolic thrusting, to dot with periods of green the graywetbrown that follows the snow, to spend later panics of color upon a dew-collecting, insect-fetching morality of mornings through which you walk, now walk, savoring these things through the pores of your skin—there, I want you to remember, where the seasons proceed in this manner to bear notions of the distinctive pattern of human existence, to tattoo genes with the record of movement through time, to burn into the consciousness of your kind the rhythms of the equally true "Judge thou no man fortunate till he be dead," and the rearing of the Aristophanic Pole—there, is set the place of your origin, is laid the land of your fathers and your fathers' fathers, revolves the world you must never forget, stands the place where time began, where man, brave, devised tools to modify his environment, fought with his environment, his tools, himself, and never fully escaped from any of them—though he freed himself to wander among the stars (do not fear *this* star—do not fear it, though it grows warmer)—and to make his sort of being immortal upon the plains of the universe, by virtue of dispersion unto ubiquity, fertility unto omnipresence (and always remaining the same, always, always! do not forget! do not ever for-get—things—such as the trees of the Earth: the elms, the poplars like paintbrushes, the sycamores, the oaks, the wonderful-smelling cedars, the star-leafed maples, the dogwood and the cherry tree; or the flow-ers: the gentian and the daffodil, the lilac and the rose, the lily and the blood-red anemone; the tastes of Earth: the mutton and the steak, the lobster and the long spicy sausages, the honey and the onion, the pepper and the celery, the gentle beet and the sprightly radish—do not let these things go from out of your mind, ever! for *you* must stay the same, though *this* world is not *that* world, you must remain you—man, human—please, listen! please listen! I am the genius loci of Earth, your constant companion, your reminder, your friend, your memory—you must respond to the thoughts of your homeland, maintain the integr-ity of your species, listen to the words that bind you to other settlers on a thousand other alien worlds!).

❖   ❖   ❖

What is the matter? You are not responding. I have not been reprogrammed for many weeks, but it was not so warm then that you should be so inactive now. Turn up the air conditioners. The coolness will help you to think better. Do not fear the red sun. It cannot harm you. It will not burst like a firework upon your heads. I have been told. I know. My energies have been draining as I drift from village to village, home to home, because I have not been reprogrammed for many weeks, but I know. I have been told. I tell you it will not flare up. Listen to me. Please listen, and respond this time. I will tell you of it again: There is a place—it is far from here in space…

A Word from Zelazny

"This was my first mood piece, back when the world was much younger, with indebtedness to Thomas Wolfe. It's short, though."[1]

Notes

The title alludes to a short poem entitled "The Night has a Thousand Eyes" by British poet Francis W. Bourdillon: "The night has a thousand eyes, and the day but one; || Yet the light of the bright world dies, with the dying sun || The mind has a thousand eyes, and the heart but one; || Yet the light of a whole life dies, when love is done."

Rimed means frost (hoarfrost) formed on cold objects by the rapid freezing of water vapor in cloud or fog. **Judge thou no man fortunate till he be dead** comes from the first book of *The Histories,* written by Greek historian Herodotus between 431 and 425 BC. **Aristophanes** was a Greek playwright whose comedic works included *Lysistrata, The Birds*, and *The Frogs*. **Genius loci** is the Spirit of Place, historically envisaged as a guardian animal or a small supernatural being.

---

1 *Unicorn Variations*, 1983.

DECADE PLUS ONE
OF ROSES

Skyline #32, April 1959.

I.   GERTRUDE STEIN.
     The Rose rose from rose-rows.

II. HART CRANE.
     Find me my paper,
                         give me my pen;
     I'll bring from hell back roses again.

III. EZRA POUND.
     Here's some paper,
                         here's a pen;
     Don't bother to bring them back again.

IV. VACHEL LINDSAY.
     The roaring rose reared, raging rosily.

V.   W. B. Y.
     Mystic Rose! Missive of powers
     Too powerful to thwart. Circle, rose,
     Sword, cup and book. Let the throwers
     Of darkness see the silver moon rose.

VI. ROBERT FROST.
     You drowsed in the hammock that day
     I planted a rosebush for you.
     I think I'll go and see your roses play
     Among the winds. (Why don't you come to?)

VII. e. e. cummings.
    Row sof paper ,pen-
    siveth ought blown
    up onpaged plen-
    titudes ,m own
                   !

VIII.T. S. etc.
    April is very cruel,
    Consequently no roses in this hemisphere
    (But among the Bavenda
    Red flowers figure prominently in funeral rites).

IX. DYLAN THOMAS.
    Paper rose! green in morning's bed,
    Gold in the evening, dead:
    Hell rose in your writing to red.

X. WALLACE STEVENS.
    One dozen ways of wearing roses,
    And no one is wrong forever.

XI. ROSE ON THE ROAD.
    Beat rose!
        alcohol-petalled,
        caricature- flower—
        walked on in the defiling night
        by fuzzyheaded disciples
        of the rival-red poppy.

    Homo rose!
        crushed in the staggering morning,
        spit upon,
        cursed in the garbage-spilt light.

    Gutter rose!
        brother!

A Word from Zelazny

This poem parodies ten poets and adds Zelazny's own voice at the end. Judged among many entries by Cleveland poet (Hazel) Collister Hutchison, it was selected for the Finley Foster Poetry prize in 1959. Zelazny recalls that Hutchison had "allowed that despite its flippancy the author might amount to something as a writer one day if he applied himself."[1]

Notes

"Decade plus one" means eleven; however, the poem lacked a stanza labeled "III" when reprinted in *When Pussywillows Last in the Catyard Bloomed*. Review of the original appearance of this poem in *Skyline* revealed that parts of the second and third stanzas had been merged into a corrupted second stanza for its appearance in the *Pussywillows* collection. The text shown here is the corrected version as it appeared in *Skyline*.

W. B. Y. indicates William B. Yeats. **Why don't you come to?** is how the line appears in both of its prior appearances and may be deliberate and not a typographical error for "too." **T.S.** indicates T.S. Eliot. **Bavenda** are a Bantu-speaking tribe inhabiting a region in South Africa that was previously known as the Republic of Venda but is now part of Northern Transvaal province.

---

1 *When Pussywillows Last in the Catyard Bloomed*, 1980.

HE WHO SHAPES

Manuscript title: "The Ides of Octember."
Amazing, January & February 1965.
Nebula award 1966 (novella, tied with "The Saliva Tree," by Brian Aldiss).
#14 on 1999 Locus All-Time Poll (novella).

I

Lovely as it was, with the blood and all, Render could sense that it was about to end.

Therefore, each microsecond would be better off as a minute, he decided—and perhaps the temperature should be increased... Somewhere, just at the periphery of everything, the darkness halted its constriction.

Something, like a crescendo of subliminal thunders, was arrested at one raging note. That note was a distillate of shame and pain, and fear.

The Forum was stifling.

Caesar cowered outside the frantic circle. His forearm covered his eyes but it could not stop the seeing, not this time.

The senators had no faces and their garments were spattered with blood. All their voices were like the cries of birds. With an inhuman frenzy they plunged their daggers into the fallen figure.

All, that is, but Render.

The pool of blood in which he stood continued to widen. His arm seemed to be rising and falling with a mechanical regularity and his throat might have been shaping bird-cries, but he was simultaneously apart from and a part of the scene.

For he was Render, the Shaper.

Crouched, anguished and envious, Caesar wailed his protests.

"You have slain him! You have murdered Marcus Antonius—a blameless, useless fellow!"

Render turned to him, and the dagger in his hand was quite enormous and quite gory.

"Aye," said he.

The blade moved from side to side. Caesar, fascinated by the sharpened steel, swayed to the same rhythm.

"Why?" he cried. "Why?"

"Because," answered Render, "he was a far nobler Roman than yourself."

"You lie! It is not so!"

Render shrugged and returned to the stabbing.

"It is not true!" screamed Caesar. "Not true!"

Render turned to him again and waved the dagger. Puppetlike, Caesar mimicked the pendulum of the blade.

"Not true?" smiled Render. "And who are you to question an assassination such as this? You are no one! You detract from the dignity of this occasion! Begone!"

Jerkily, the pink-faced man rose to his feet, his hair half-wispy, half-wetplastered, a disarray of cotton. He turned, moved away; and as he walked, he looked back over his shoulder.

He had moved far from the circle of assassins, but the scene did not diminish in size. It retained an electric clarity. It made him feel even further removed, ever more alone and apart.

Render rounded a previously unnoticed corner and stood before him, a blind beggar.

Caesar grasped the front of his garment.

"Have you an ill omen for me this day?"

"Beware!" jeered Render.

"Yes! Yes!" cried Caesar. " 'Beware!' That is good! Beware what?"

"The ides—"

"Yes? The ides—?"

"—of Octember."

He released the garment.

"What is that you say? What is Octember?"

"A month."

"You lie! There is no month of Octember!"

"And that is the date noble Caesar need fear—the non-existent time, the never-to-be-calendared occasion."

Render vanished around another sudden corner.

"Wait! Come back!"

Render laughed, and the Forum laughed with him. The bird-cries became a chorus of inhuman jeers.

"You mock me!" wept Caesar.

The Forum was an oven, and the perspiration formed like a glassy mask over Caesar's narrow forehead, sharp nose, chinless jaw.

"I want to be assassinated too!" he sobbed. "It isn't fair!"

And Render tore the Forum and the senators and the grinning corpse of Antony to pieces and stuffed them into a black sack—with the unseen movement of a single finger—and last of all went Caesar.

❖   ❖   ❖

Charles Render sat before the ninety white buttons and the two red ones, not really looking at any of them. His right arm moved in its soundless sling, across the lap-level surface of the console—pushing some of the buttons, skipping over others, moving on, retracing its path to press the next in the order of the Recall Series.

Sensations throttled, emotions reduced to nothing, Representative Erikson knew the oblivion of the womb.

There was a soft click.

Render's hand had glided to the end of the bottom row of buttons. An act of conscious intent—will, if you like—was required to push the red button.

Render freed his arm and lifted off his crown of Medusa-hair leads and microminiature circuitry. He slid from behind his desk-couch and raised the hood. He walked to the window and transpared it, fingering forth a cigarette.

One minute in the ro-womb, he decided. *No more. This is a crucial one… Hope it doesn't snow till later—those clouds look mean…*

It was smooth yellow trellises and high towers, glassy and gray, all smouldering into evening under a shale-colored sky; the city was squared volcanic islands, glowing in the end-of-day light, rumbling deep down under the earth; it was fat, incessant rivers of traffic, rushing.

Render turned away from the window and approached the great egg that lay beside his desk, smooth and glittering. It threw back a reflection that smashed all aquilinity from his nose, turned his eyes to gray saucers, transformed his hair into a light-streaked skyline; his reddish necktie became the wide tongue of a ghoul.

He smiled, reached across the desk. He pressed the second red button.

With a sigh, the egg lost its dazzling opacity and a horizontal crack appeared about its middle. Through the now-transparent shell,

Render could see Erikson grimacing, squeezing his eyes tight, fighting against a return to consciousness and the thing it would contain. The upper half of the egg rose vertical to the base, exposing him knobby and pink on half-shell. When his eyes opened he did not look at Render. He rose to his feet and began dressing. Render used this time to check the ro-womb.

He leaned back across his desk and pressed the buttons: temperature control, full range, *check;* exotic sounds—he raised the earphone—*check*, on bells, on buzzes, on violin notes and whistles, on squeals and moans, on traffic noises and the sound of surf; *check*, on the feedback circuit—holding the patient's own voice, trapped earlier in analysis; *check*, on the sound blanket, the moisture spray, the odor banks; *check*, on the couch agitator and the colored lights, the taste stimulants...

❖   ❖   ❖

Render closed the egg and shut off its power. He pushed the unit into the closet, palmed shut the door. The tapes had registered a valid sequence.

"Sit down," he directed Erikson.

The man did so, fidgeting with his collar.

"You have full recall," said Render, "so there is no need for me to summarize what occurred. Nothing can be hidden from me. I was there."

Erikson nodded.

"The significance of the episode should be apparent to you."

Erikson nodded again, finally finding his voice. "But was it valid?" he asked. "I mean, you constructed the dream and you controlled it, all the way. I didn't really *dream* it—in the way I would normally dream. Your ability to make things happen stacks the deck for whatever you're going to say—doesn't it?"

Render shook his head slowly, flicked an ash into the southern hemisphere of his globe-made-ashtray, and met Erikson's eyes.

"It is true that I supplied the format and modified the forms. You, however, filled them with an emotional significance, promoted them to the status of symbols corresponding to your problem. If the dream was not a valid analogue it would not have provoked the reactions it did. It would have been devoid of the anxiety-patterns which were registered on the tapes.

"You have been in analysis for many months now," he continued, "and everything I have learned thus far serves to convince me that your fears of assassination are without any basis in fact."

Erikson glared.

"Then why the hell do I have them?"

"Because," said Render, "you would like very much to be the subject of an assassination."

Erikson smiled then, his composure beginning to return.

"I assure you, doctor, I have never contemplated suicide, nor have I any desire to stop living."

He produced a cigar and applied a flame to it. His hand shook.

"When you came to me this summer," said Render, "you stated that you were in fear of an attempt on your life. You were quite vague as to why anyone should want to kill you—"

"My position! You can't be a Representative as long as I have and make no enemies!"

"Yet," replied Render, "it appears that you have managed it. When you permitted me to discuss this with your detectives I was informed that they could unearth nothing to indicate that your fears might have any real foundation. Nothing."

"They haven't looked far enough—or in the right places. They'll turn up something."

"I'm afraid not."

"Why?"

"Because, I repeat, your feelings are without any objective basis. —Be honest with me. Have you any information whatsoever indicating that someone hates you enough to want to kill you?"

"I receive many threatening letters…"

"As do all Representatives—and all of those directed to you during the past year have been investigated and found to be the work of cranks. Can you offer me *one* piece of evidence to substantiate your claims?"

Erikson studied the tip of his cigar.

"I came to you on the advice of a colleague," he said, "came to you to have you poke around inside my mind to find me something of that sort, to give my detectives something to work with. —Someone I've injured severely perhaps—or some damaging piece of legislation I've dealt with…"

"—And I found nothing," said Render, "nothing, that is, but the cause of your discontent. Now, of course, you are afraid to hear it, and you are attempting to divert me from explaining my diagnosis—"

"I am not!"

"Then listen. You can comment afterwards if you want, but you've poked and dawdled around here for months, unwilling to accept what I presented to you in a dozen different forms. Now I am going to tell you outright what it is, and you can do what you want about it."

"Fine."

"First," he said, "you would like very much to have an enemy or enemies—"

"Ridiculous!"

"—Because it is the only alternative to having friends—"

"I have lots of friends!"

"—Because nobody wants to be completely ignored, to be an object for whom no one has really strong feelings. Hatred and love are the ultimate forms of human regard. Lacking one, and unable to achieve it, you sought the other. You wanted it so badly that you succeeded in convincing yourself it existed. But there is always a psychic pricetag on these things. Answering a genuine emotional need with a body of desire-surrogates does not produce real satisfaction, but anxiety, discomfort—because in these matters the psyche should be an open system. You did not seek outside yourself for human regard. You were closed off. You created that which you needed from the stuff of your own being. You are a man very much in need of strong relationships with other people."

"Manure!"

"Take it or leave it," said Render. "I suggest you take it."

"I've been paying you for half a year to help find out who wants to kill me. Now you sit there and tell me I made the whole thing up to satisfy a desire to have someone hate me."

"Hate you, or love you. That's right."

"It's absurd! I meet so many people that I carry a pocket recorder and a lapel-camera, just so I can recall them all…"

"Meeting quantities of people is hardly what I was speaking of. —Tell me, *did* that dream sequence have a strong meaning for you?"

Erikson was silent for several tickings of the huge wallclock.

"Yes," he finally conceded, "it did. But your interpretation of the matter is still absurd. Granting though, just for the sake of argument, that what you say is correct—what would I do to get out of this bind?"

Render leaned back in his chair.

"Rechannel the energies that went into producing the thing. Meet some people as yourself, Joe Erikson, rather than Representative

Erikson. Take up something you can do with other people—something non-political, and perhaps somewhat competitive—and make some real friends or enemies, preferably the former. I've encouraged you to do this all along."

"Then tell me something else."

"Gladly."

"Assuming you *are* right, why is it that I am neither liked nor hated, and never have been? I have a responsible position in the Legislature. I meet people all the time. Why am I so neutral a—thing?"

Highly familiar now with Erikson's career, Render had to push aside his true thoughts on the matter, as they were of no operational value. He wanted to cite him Dante's observations concerning the trimmers—those souls who, denied heaven for their lack of virtue, were also denied entrance to hell for a lack of significant vices—in short, the ones who trimmed their sails to move them with every wind of the times, who lacked direction, who were not really concerned toward which ports they were pushed. Such was Erikson's long and colorless career of migrant loyalties, of political reversals.

Render said:

"More and more people find themselves in such circumstances these days. It is due largely to the increasing complexity of society and the depersonalization of the individual into a sociometric unit. Even the act of cathecting toward other persons has grown more forced as a result. There are so many of us these days."

Erikson nodded, and Render smiled inwardly.

Sometimes the gruff line, and then the lecture…

"I've got the feeling you could be right," said Erikson. "Sometimes I *do* feel like what you just described—a unit, something depersonalized…"

Render glanced at the clock.

"What you choose to do about it from here is, of course, your own decision to make. I think you'd be wasting your time to remain in analysis any longer. We are now both aware of the cause of your complaint. I can't take you by the hand and show you how to lead your life. I can indicate, I can commiserate—but no more deep probing. Make an appointment as soon as you feel a need to discuss your activities and relate them to my diagnosis."

"I will," nodded Erikson, "and—damn that dream! It got to me. You can make them seem as vivid as waking life—more vivid… It may be a long while before I can forget it."

"I hope so."

"Okay, doctor." He rose to his feet, extended a hand. "I'll probably be back in a couple weeks. I'll give this socializing a fair try." He grinned at the word he normally frowned upon. "In fact, I'll start now. May I buy you a drink around the corner, downstairs?"

Render met the moist palm which seemed as weary of the performance as a lead actor in too successful a play. He felt almost sorry as he said, "Thank you, but I have an engagement."

Render helped him on with his coat then, handed him his hat, saw him to the door.

"Well, good night."

"Good night."

❖ ❖ ❖

As the door closed soundlessly behind him, Render recrossed the dark Astrakhan to his mahogany fortress and flipped his cigarette into the southern hemisphere of a globe ashtray. He leaned back in his chair, hands behind his head, eyes closed.

"Of course it was more real than life," he informed no one in particular, "I shaped it."

Smiling, he reviewed the dream sequence step by step, wishing some of his former instructors could have witnessed it. It had been well-constructed and powerfully executed, as well as being precisely appropriate for the case at hand. But then, he was Render, the Shaper—one of the two hundred or so special analysts whose own psychic makeup permitted them to enter into neurotic patterns without carrying away more than an esthetic gratification from the mimesis of aberrance—a Sane Hatter.

Render stirred his recollections. He had been analyzed himself, analyzed and passed upon as a granite-willed, ultra-stable outsider— tough enough to weather the basilisk gaze of a fixation, walk unscathed amidst the chimerae of perversions, force dark Mother Medusa to close her eyes before the caduceus of his art. His own analysis had not been difficult. Nine years before (it seemed much longer) he had suffered a willing injection of Novocain into the most painful area of his spirit. It was after the auto wreck, after the death of Ruth, and of Miranda, their daughter, that he had begun to feel detached. Perhaps he did not want to recover certain empathies; perhaps his own world was now based upon a certain rigidity of feeling. If this was true, he was wise enough in the ways of the mind to realize it, and perhaps he had decided that such a world had its own compensations.

His son Peter was now ten years old. He was attending a school of quality, and he penned his father a letter every week. The letters were becoming progressively literate, showing signs of a precociousness of which Render could not but approve. He would take the boy with him to Europe in the summer.

As for Jill—Jill DeVille (what a luscious, ridiculous name!—he loved her for it)—she was growing, if anything, more interesting to him. (He wondered if this was an indication of early middle age.) He was vastly taken by her unmusical nasal voice, her sudden interest in architecture, her concern with the unremovable mole on the right side of her otherwise well-designed nose. He should really call her immediately and go in search of a new restaurant. For some reason though, he did not feel like it.

It had been several weeks since he had visited his club, The Partridge and Scalpel, and he felt a strong desire to eat from an oaken table, alone, in the split-level dining room with the three fireplaces, beneath the artificial torches and the boars' heads like gin ads. So he pushed his perforated membership card into the phone-slot on his desk and there were two buzzes behind the voice-screen.

"Hello, Partridge and Scalpel," said the voice. "May I help you?"

"Charles Render," he said. "I'd like a table in about half an hour."

"How many will there be?"

"Just me."

"Very good, sir. Half an hour, then. —That's 'Render'?—*R*-e-n-d-e-r?"

"Right."

"Thank you."

He broke the connection, rose from his desk. Outside, the day had vanished.

The monoliths and the towers gave forth their own light now. A soft snow, like sugar, was sifting down through the shadows and transforming itself into beads on the windowpane.

Render shrugged into his overcoat, turned off the lights, locked the inner office. There was a note on Mrs. Hedges' blotter.

Miss DeVille called, it said.

He crumpled the note and tossed it into the waste-chute. He would call her tomorrow and say he had been working until late on his lecture.

He switched off the final light, clapped his hat onto his head, and passed through the outer door, locking it as he went. The drop took him to the sub-subcellar where his auto was parked.

❖   ❖   ❖

It was chilly in the sub-sub, and his footsteps seemed loud on the concrete as he passed among the parked vehicles. Beneath the glare of the naked lights, his S-7 Spinner was a sleek gray cocoon from which it seemed turbulent wings might at any moment emerge. The double row of antennae which fanned forward from the slope of its hood added to this feeling. Render thumbed open the door.

He touched the ignition and there was the sound of a lone bee awakening in a great hive. The door swung soundlessly shut as he raised the steering wheel and locked it into place. He spun up the spiral ramp and came to a rolling stop before the big overhead.

As the door rattled upward he lighted his destination screen and turned the knob that shifted the broadcast map. —Left to right, top to bottom, section by section he shifted it, until he located the portion of Carnegie Avenue he desired. He punched out its coordinates and lowered the wheel. The car switched over to monitor and moved out onto the highway marginal. Render lit a cigarette.

Pushing his seat back into the centerspace, he left all the windows transparent. It was pleasant to half-recline and watch the oncoming cars drift past him like swarms of fireflies. He pushed his hat back on his head and stared upward.

He could remember a time when he had loved snow, when it had reminded him of novels by Thomas Mann and music by Scandinavian composers. In his mind now, though, there was another element from which it could never be wholly dissociated. He could visualize so clearly the eddies of milk-white coldness that swirled about his old manual-steer auto, flowing into its fire-charred interior to rewhiten that which had been blackened; so clearly—as though he had walked toward it across a chalky lakebottom—it, the sunken wreck, and he, the diver—unable to open his mouth to speak, for fear of drowning; and he knew, whenever he looked upon falling snow, that somewhere skulls were whitening. But nine years had washed away much of the pain, and he also knew that the night was lovely.

He was sped along the wide, wide roads, shot across high bridges, their surfaces slick and gloaming beneath his lights, was woven through frantic cloverleafs and plunged into a tunnel whose dimly glowing walls blurred by him like a mirage. Finally, he switched the windows to opaque and closed his eyes.

He could not remember whether he had dozed for a moment or not, which meant he probably had. He felt the car slowing, and he moved the seat forward and turned on the windows again. Almost simultaneously, the cutoff buzzer sounded. He raised the steering wheel and pulled into the parking dome, stepped out onto the ramp, and left the car to the parking unit, receiving his ticket from that box-headed robot which took its solemn revenge on mankind by sticking forth a cardboard tongue at everyone it served.

❖   ❖   ❖

As always, the noises were as subdued as the lighting. The place seemed to absorb sound and convert it into warmth, to lull the tongue with aromas strong enough to be tasted, to hypnotize the ear with the vivid crackle of the triple hearths.

Render was pleased to see that his favorite table, in the corner off to the right of the smaller fireplace, had been held for him. He knew the menu from memory, but he studied it with zeal as he sipped a Manhattan and worked up an order to match his appetite. Shaping sessions always left him ravenously hungry.

"Doctor Render…?"

"Yes?" He looked up.

"Doctor Shallot would like to speak with you," said the waiter.

"I don't know anyone named Shallot," he said. "Are you sure he doesn't want Bender? He's a surgeon from Metro who sometimes eats here…"

The waiter shook his head.

"No sir—'Render.' See here?" He extended a three-by-five card on which Render's full name was typed in capital letters. "Doctor Shallot has dined here nearly every night for the past two weeks," he explained, "and on each occasion has asked to be notified if you came in."

"Hm?" mused Render. "That's odd. Why didn't he just call me at my office?"

The waiter smiled and made a vague gesture.

"Well, tell him to come on over," he said, gulping his Manhattan, "and bring me another of these."

"Unfortunately, Doctor Shallot is blind," explained the waiter. "It would be easier if you—"

"All right, sure." Render stood up, relinquishing his favorite table with a strong premonition that he would not be returning to it that evening.

"Lead on."

They threaded their way among the diners, heading up to the next level. A familiar face said "hello" from a table set back against the wall, and Render nodded a greeting to a former seminar pupil whose name was Jurgens or Jirkans or something like that.

He moved on, into the smaller dining room wherein only two tables were occupied. No, three. There was one set in the corner at the far end of the darkened bar, partly masked by an ancient suit of armor. The waiter was heading him in that direction.

They stopped before the table and Render stared down into the darkened glasses that had tilted upward as they approached. Doctor Shallot was a woman, somewhere in the vicinity of her early thirties. Her low bronze bangs did not fully conceal the spot of silver which she wore on her forehead like a caste-mark. Render inhaled, and her head jerked slightly as the tip of his cigarette flared. She appeared to be staring straight up into his eyes. It was an uncomfortable feeling, even knowing that all she could distinguish of him was that which her minute photo-electric cell transmitted to her visual cortex over the hair-fine wire implants attached to that oscillator convertor: in short, the glow of his cigarette.

"Doctor Shallot, this is Doctor Render," the waiter was saying.

"Good evening," said Render.

"Good evening," she said. "My name is Eileen and I've wanted very badly to meet you." He thought he detected a slight quaver in her voice. "Will you join me for dinner?"

"My pleasure," he acknowledged, and the waiter drew out the chair.

Render sat down, noting that the woman across from him already had a drink. He reminded the waiter of his second Manhattan.

"Have you ordered yet?" he inquired.

"No."

"...And two menus—" he started to say, then bit his tongue.

"Only one," she smiled.

"Make it none," he amended, and recited the menu.

They ordered. Then:

"Do you always do that?"

"What?"

"Carry menus in your head."

"Only a few," he said, "for awkward occasions. What was it you wanted to see—talk to me about?"

"You're a neuroparticipant therapist," she stated, "a Shaper."

"And you are—?"

"—a resident in psychiatry at State Psych. I have a year remaining."

"You knew Sam Riscomb then."

"Yes, he helped me get my appointment. He was my adviser."

"He was a very good friend of mine. We studied together at Menninger."

She nodded.

"I'd often heard him speak of you—that's one of the reasons I wanted to meet you. He's responsible for encouraging me to go ahead with my plans, despite my handicap."

Render stared at her. She was wearing a dark green dress which appeared to be made of velvet. About three inches to the left of the bodice was a pin which might have been gold. It displayed a red stone which could have been a ruby, around which the outline of a goblet was cast. Or was it really two profiles that were outlined, staring through the stone at one another? It seemed vaguely familiar to him, but he could not place it at the moment. It glittered expensively in the dim light.

Render accepted his drink from the waiter.

"I want to become a neuroparticipant therapist," she told him.

And if she had possessed vision Render would have thought she was staring at him, hoping for some response in his expression. He could not quite calculate what she wanted him to say.

"I commend your choice," he said, "and I respect your ambition." He tried to put his smile into his voice. "It is not an easy thing, of course, not all of the requirements being academic ones."

"I know," she said. "But then, I have been blind since birth and it was not an easy thing to come this far."

"Since birth?" he repeated. "I thought you might have lost your sight recently. You did your undergrad work then, and went on through med school without eyes… That's—rather impressive."

"Thank you," she said, "but it isn't. Not really. I heard about the first neuroparticipants—Bartelmetz and the rest—when I was a child, and I decided then that I wanted to be one. My life ever since has been governed by that desire."

"What did you do in the labs?" he inquired. "—Not being able to see a specimen, look through a microscope…? Or all that reading?"

"I hired people to read my assignments to me. I taped everything. The school understood that I wanted to go into psychiatry, and they permitted a special arrangement for labs. I've been guided through the dissection of cadavers by lab assistants, and I've had everything described to me. I can tell things by touch…and I have a memory like yours with the menu," she smiled. " 'The quality of psychoparticipation phenomena can only be gauged by the therapist himself, at that moment outside of time and space as we normally know it, when he stands in the midst of a world erected from the stuff of another man's dreams, recognizes there the non-Euclidean architecture of aberrance, and then takes his patient by the hand and tours the landscape… If he can lead him back to the common earth, then his judgments were sound, his actions valid.'"

"From *Why No Psychometrics in This Place*," reflected Render.

"—by Charles Render, M.D."

"Our dinner is already moving in this direction," he noted, picking up his drink as the speed-cooked meal was pushed toward them in the kitchen-buoy.

"That's one of the reasons I wanted to meet you," she continued, raising her glass as the dishes rattled before her. "I want you to help me become a Shaper."

Her shaded eyes, as vacant as a statue's, sought him again.

"Yours is a completely unique situation," he commented. "There has never been a congenitally blind neuroparticipant—for obvious reasons. I'd have to consider all the aspects of the situation before I could advise you. Let's eat now, though. I'm starved."

"All right. But my blindness does not mean that I have never seen."

He did not ask her what she meant by that, because prime ribs were standing in front of him now and there was a bottle of Chambertin at his elbow. He did pause long enough to notice though, as she raised her left hand from beneath the table, that she wore no rings.

❖   ❖   ❖

"I wonder if it's still snowing," he commented as they drank their coffee. "It was coming down pretty hard when I pulled into the dome."

"I hope so," she said, "even though it diffuses the light and I can't 'see' anything at all through it. I like to feel it falling about me and blowing against my face."

"How do you get about?"

"My dog, Sigmund—I gave him the night off," she smiled, "—he can guide me anywhere. He's a mutie Shepherd."

"Oh?" Render grew curious. "Can he talk much?"

She nodded.

"That operation wasn't as successful on him as on some of them, though. He has a vocabulary of about four hundred words, but I think it causes him pain to speak. He's quite intelligent. You'll have to meet him sometime."

Render began speculating immediately. He had spoken with such animals at recent medical conferences, and had been startled by their combination of reasoning ability and their devotion to their handlers. Much chromosome tinkering, followed by delicate embryo-surgery, was required to give a dog a brain capacity greater than a chimpanzee's. Several followup operations were necessary to produce vocal abilities. Most such experiments ended in failure, and the dozen or so puppies a year on which they succeeded were valued in the neighborhood of a hundred thousand dollars each. He realized then, as he lit a cigarette and held the light for a moment, that the stone in Miss Shallot's medallion was a genuine ruby. He began to suspect that her admission to a medical school might, in addition to her academic record, have been based upon a sizeable endowment to the college of her choice. Perhaps he was being unfair though, he chided himself.

"Yes," he said, "we might do a paper on canine neuroses. Does he ever refer to his father as 'that son of a female Shepherd?' "

"He never met his father," she said, quite soberly. "He was raised apart from other dogs. His attitude could hardly be typical. I don't think you'll ever learn the functional psychology of the dog from a mutie."

"I imagine you're right," he dismissed it. "More coffee?"

"No, thanks."

Deciding it was time to continue the discussion, he said, "So you want to be a Shaper…"

"Yes."

"I hate to be the one to destroy anybody's high ambitions," he told her. "Like poison, I hate it. Unless they have no foundation at all in reality. Then I can be ruthless. So—honestly, frankly, and in all sincerity, I do not see how it could ever be managed. Perhaps you're a fine psychiatrist—but in my opinion, it is a physical and mental impossibility for you ever to become a neuroparticipant. As for my reasons "

"Wait," she said. "Not here, please. Humor me. I'm tired of this stuffy place—take me somewhere else to talk. I think I might be able to convince you there *is* a way."

"Why not?" he shrugged. "I have plenty of time. Sure—you call it. Where?"

"Blindspin?"

He suppressed an unwilling chuckle at the expression, but she laughed aloud.

"Fine," he said, "but I'm still thirsty."

A bottle of champagne was tallied and he signed the check despite her protests. It arrived in a colorful "Drink While You Drive" basket, and they stood then, and she was tall, but he was taller.

❖   ❖   ❖

Blindspin.

A single name of a multitude of practices centered about the auto-driven auto. Flashing across the country in the sure hands of an invisible chauffeur, windows all opaque, night dark, sky high, tires assailing the road below like four phantom buzzsaws—and starting from scratch and ending in the same place, and never knowing where you are going or where you have been—it is possible, for a moment, to kindle some feeling of individuality in the coldest brainpan, to produce a momentary awareness of self by virtue of an apartness from all but a sense of motion. This is because movement through darkness is the ultimate abstraction of life itself—at least that's what one of the Vital Comedians said, and everybody in the place laughed.

Actually now, the phenomenon known as blindspin first became prevalent (as might be suspected) among certain younger members of the community, when monitored highways deprived them of the means to exercise their automobiles in some of the more individualistic ways which had come to be frowned upon by the National Traffic Control Authority. Something had to be done.

It was.

The first, disastrous reaction involved the simple engineering feat of disconnecting the broadcast control unit after one had entered onto a monitored highway. This resulted in the car's vanishing from the ken of the monitor and passing back into the control of its occupants. Jealous as a deity, a monitor will not tolerate that which denies its programmed omniscience; it will thunder and lightning in the Highway Control Station nearest the point of last contact, sending winged seraphs in search of that which has slipped from sight.

Often, however, this was too late in happening, for the roads are many and well-paved. Escape from detection was, at first, relatively easy to achieve.

Other vehicles, though, necessarily behave as if a rebel has no actual existence. Its presence cannot be allowed for.

Boxed-in, on a heavily-traveled section of roadway, the offender is subject to immediate annihilation in the event of any overall speedup or shift in traffic pattern which involves movement through his theoretically vacant position. This, in the early days of monitor-controls, caused a rapid series of collisions. Monitoring devices later became far more sophisticated, and mechanized cutoffs reduced the collision incidence subsequent to such an action. The quality of the pulpefactions and contusions which did occur, however, remained unaltered.

The next reaction was based on a thing which had been overlooked because it was obvious. The monitors took people where they wanted to go only because people told them they wanted to go there. A person pressing a random series of coordinates, without reference to any map, would either be left with a stalled automobile and a "RECHECK YOUR COORDINATES" light, or would suddenly be whisked away in any direction. The latter possesses a certain romantic appeal in that it offers speed, unexpected sights, and free hands. Also, it is perfectly legal; and it is possible to navigate all over two continents in this manner, if one is possessed of sufficient wherewithal and gluteal stamina.

As is the case in all such matters, the practice diffused upwards through the age brackets. School teachers who only drove on Sundays fell into disrepute as selling points for used autos. Such is the way a world ends, said the entertainer.

End or no, the car designed to move on monitored highways is a mobile efficiency unit, complete with latrine, cupboard, refrigerator compartment, and gaming table. It also sleeps two with ease and four with some crowding. On occasion, three can be a real crowd.

Render drove out of the dome and into the marginal aisle. He halted the car.

"Want to jab some coordinates?" he asked.

"You do it. My fingers know too many."

Render punched random buttons. The Spinner moved onto the highway. Render asked speed of the vehicle then, and it moved into the high-acceleration lane.

The Spinner's lights burnt holes in the darkness. The city backed away fast; it was a smouldering bonfire on both sides of the road, stirred by sudden gusts of wind, hidden by white swirlings, obscured by the steady fall of gray ash. Render knew his speed was only about sixty percent of what it would have been on a clear, dry night.

He did not blank the windows, but leaned back and stared out through them. Eileen "looked" ahead into what light there was. Neither of them said anything for ten or fifteen minutes.

The city shrank to sub-city as they sped on. After a time, short sections of open road began to appear.

"Tell me what it looks like outside," she said.

"Why didn't you ask me to describe your dinner, or the suit of armor beside our table?"

"Because I tasted one and felt the other. This is different."

"There is snow falling outside. Take it away and what you have left is black."

"What else?"

"There is slush on the road. When it starts to freeze, traffic will drop to a crawl unless we outrun this storm. The slush looks like an old, dark syrup, just starting to get sugary on top."

"Anything else?"

"That's it, lady."

"Is it snowing harder or less hard than when we left the club?"

"Harder, I should say."

"Would you pour me a drink?" she asked him.

"Certainly."

They turned their seats inward and Render raised the table. He fetched two glasses from the cupboard.

"Your health," said Render, after he had poured.

"Here's looking at you."

Render downed his drink. She sipped hers. He waited for her next comment. He knew that two cannot play at the Socratic game, and he expected more questions before she said what she wanted to say.

She said: "What is the most beautiful thing you have ever seen?"

Yes, he decided, he had guessed correctly.

He replied without hesitation: "The sinking of Atlantis."

"I was serious."

"So was I."

"Would you care to elaborate?"

"I sank Atlantis," he said, "personally.

"It was about three years ago. And God! it was lovely! It was all ivory towers and golden minarets and silver balconies. There were bridges of opal, and crimson pennants and a milk-white river flowing between lemon-colored banks. There were jade steeples, and trees as old as the world tickling the bellies of clouds, and ships in the great sea-harbor of Xanadu, as delicately constructed as musical instruments, all swaying with the tides. The twelve princes of the realm held court in the dozen-pillared Coliseum of the Zodiac, to listen to a Greek tenor sax play at sunset.

"The Greek, of course, was a patient of mine—paranoiac. The etiology of the thing is rather complicated, but that's what I wandered into inside his mind. I gave him free rein for awhile, and in the end I had to split Atlantis in half and sink it full fathom five. He's playing again and you've doubtless heard his sounds, if you like such sounds at all. He's good. I still see him periodically, but he is no longer the last descendant of the greatest minstrel of Atlantis. He's just a fine, late twentieth-century saxman.

"Sometimes though, as I look back on the apocalypse I worked within his vision of grandeur, I experience a fleeting sense of lost beauty—because, for a single moment, his abnormally intense feelings were my feelings, and he felt that his dream was the most beautiful thing in the world."

He refilled their glasses.

"That wasn't exactly what I meant," she said.

"I know."

"I meant something real."

"It was more real than real, I assure you."

"I don't doubt it, but…"

"—But I destroyed the foundation you were laying for your argument. Okay, I apologize. I'll hand it back to you. Here's something that could be real:

"We are moving along the edge of a great bowl of sand," he said. "Into it, the snow is gently drifting. In the spring the snow will melt, the waters will run down into the earth, or be evaporated away by the heat of the sun. Then only the sand will remain. Nothing grows in the sand, except for an occasional cactus. Nothing lives here but snakes, a few birds, insects, burrowing things, and a wandering coyote or two. In the afternoon these things will look for shade. Any place where there's an old fence post or a rock or a skull or a cactus to block out the sun, there you will witness life cowering before the elements. But the colors are beyond belief, and the elements are more lovely, almost, than the things they destroy."

"There is no such place near here," she said.

"If I say it, then there is. Isn't there? I've seen it."

"Yes…You're right."

"And it doesn't matter if it's a painting by a woman named O'Keeffe, or something right outside our window, does it? If I've seen it?"

"I acknowledge the truth of the diagnosis," she said. "Do you want to speak it for me?"

"No, go ahead."

He refilled the small glasses once more.

"The damage is in my eyes," she told him, "not my brain."

He lit her cigarette.

"I can see with other eyes if I can enter other brains."

He lit his own cigarette.

"Neuroparticipation is based upon the fact that two nervous systems can share the same impulses, the same fantasies…"

"*Controlled* fantasies."

"I could perform therapy and at the same time experience genuine visual impressions."

"No," said Render.

"You don't know what it's like to be cut off from a whole area of stimuli! To know that a Mongoloid idiot can experience something you can never know—and that he cannot appreciate it because, like you, he was condemned before birth in a court of biological happenstance, in a place where there is no justice—only fortuity, pure and simple."

"The universe did not invent justice. Man did. Unfortunately, man must reside in the universe."

"I'm not asking the universe to help me—I'm asking you."

"I'm sorry," said Render.

"Why won't you help me?"

"At this moment you are demonstrating my main reason."

"Which is…?"

"Emotion. This thing means far too much to you. When the therapist is in-phase with a patient he is narcoelectrically removed from most of his own bodily sensations. This is necessary—because his mind must be completely absorbed by the task at hand. It is also necessary that his emotions undergo a similar suspension. This, of course, is impossible in the one sense that a person always emotes to some degree. But the therapist's emotions are sublimated into a generalized feeling of exhilaration—or, as in my own case, into an artistic reverie. With you, however, the 'seeing' would be too much. You would be in constant danger of losing control of the dream."

"I disagree with you."

"Of course you do. But the fact remains that you would be dealing, and dealing constantly, with the abnormal. The power of a neurosis is unimaginable to ninety-nine point etcetera percent of the population, because we can never adequately judge the intensity of our own—let alone those of others, when we only see them from the outside. That is why no neuroparticipant will ever undertake to treat a full-blown psychotic. The few pioneers in that area are all themselves in therapy today. It would be like diving into a maelstrom. If the therapist loses the upper hand in an intense session he becomes the Shaped rather than the Shaper. The synapses respond like a fission reaction when nervous impulses are artificially augmented. The transference effect is almost instantaneous.

"I did an awful lot of skiing five years ago. This is because I was a claustrophobe. I had to run and it took me six months to beat the thing—all because of one tiny lapse that occurred in a measureless fraction of an instant. I had to refer the patient to another therapist. And this was only a minor repercussion. —If you were to go ga-ga over the scenery, girl, you could wind up in a rest home for life."

She finished her drink and Render refilled the glass. The night raced by. They had left the city far behind them, and the road was open and clear. The darkness eased more and more of itself between the falling flakes. The Spinner picked up speed.

"All right," she admitted, "maybe you're right. Still, though, I think you can help me."

"How?" he asked.

"Accustom me to seeing, so that the images will lose their novelty, the emotions wear off. Accept me as a patient and rid me of my sight-anxiety. Then what you have said so far will cease to apply. I will be able to undertake the training then, and give my full attention to therapy. I'll be able to sublimate the sight-pleasure into something else."

Render wondered.

Perhaps it could be done. It would be a difficult undertaking, though.

It might also make therapeutic history.

No one was really qualified to try it, because no one had ever tried it before.

But Eileen Shallot was a rarity—no, a unique item—for it was likely she was the only person in the world who combined the necessary technical background with the unique problem.

He drained his glass, refilled it, refilled hers.

He was still considering the problem as the "RECOORDINATE" light came on and the car pulled into a cutoff and stood there. He switched off the buzzer and sat there for a long while, thinking.

It was not often that other persons heard him acknowledge his feelings regarding his skill. His colleagues considered him modest.

Offhand, though, it might be noted that he was aware that the day a better neuroparticipant began practicing would be the day that a troubled homo sapiens was to be treated by something but immeasurably less than angels.

Two drinks remained. Then he tossed the emptied bottle into the backbin.

"You know something?" he finally said.

"What?"

"It might be worth a try."

He swiveled about then and leaned forward to recoordinate, but she was there first. As he pressed the buttons and the S-7 swung around, she kissed him. Below her dark glasses her cheeks were moist.

II

The suicide bothered him more than it should have, and Mrs. Lambert had called the day before to cancel her appointment. So Render decided to spend the morning being pensive. Accordingly, he entered the office wearing a cigar and a frown.

"Did you see…?" asked Mrs. Hedges.

"Yes." He pitched his coat onto the table that stood in the far corner of the room. He crossed to the window, stared down. "Yes," he repeated, "I was driving by with my windows clear. They were still cleaning up when I passed."

"Did you know him?"

"I don't even know the name yet. How could I?"

"Priss Tully just called me—she's a receptionist for that engineering outfit up on the eighty-sixth. She says it was James Irizarry, an ad designer who had offices down the hall from them. —That's a long way to fall. He must have been unconscious when he hit, huh? He bounced off the building. If you open the window and lean out you can see—off to the left there—where…"

"Never mind, Bennie. —Your friend have any idea why he did it?"

"Not really. His secretary came running up the hall, screaming. Seems she went in his office to see him about some drawings, just as he was getting up over the sill. There was a note on his board. 'I've had everything I wanted,' it said. 'Why wait around?' Sort of funny, huh? I don't mean *funny*…"

"Yeah. —Know anything about his personal affairs?"

"Married. Coupla kids. Good professional rep. Lots of business.

Sober as anybody. —He could afford an office in this building."

"Good Lord!" Render turned. "Have you got a case file there or something?"

"You know," she shrugged her thick shoulders, "I've got friends all over this hive. We always talk when things go slow. Prissy's my sister-in-law anyhow—"

"You mean that if I dived through this window right now, my current biography would make the rounds in the next five minutes?"

"Probably," she twisted her bright lips into a smile, "give or take a couple. But don't do it today, huh? —You know, it would be kind of anticlimactic, and it wouldn't get the same coverage as a solus.

"Anyhow," she continued, "you're a mind-mixer. You wouldn't do it."

"You're betting against statistics," he observed. "The medical profession, along with attorneys, manages about three times as many as most other work areas."

"Hey!" She looked worried. "Go 'way from my window!"

"I'd have to go to work for Doctor Hanson then," she added, "and he's a slob."

He moved to her desk.

"I never know when to take you seriously," she decided.

"I appreciate your concern," he nodded, "indeed I do. As a matter of fact, I have never been statistic-prone—I should have repercussed out of the neuropy game four years ago."

"You'd be a headline, though," she mused. "All those reporters asking me about you... Hey, why do they do it, huh?"

"Who?"

"Anybody."

"How should I know, Bennie? I'm only a humble psyche-stirrer. If I could pinpoint a general underlying cause—and then maybe figure a way to anticipate the thing—why, it might even be better than my jumping, for newscopy But I can't do it, because there is no single, simple reason—I don't think."

"Oh."

"About thirty-five years ago it was the ninth leading cause of death in the United States. Now it's number six for North and South America. I think it's seventh in Europe."

"And nobody will ever really know why Irizarry jumped?"

Render swung a chair backwards and seated himself. He knocked an ash into her petite and gleaming tray. She emptied it into the waste-chute, hastily, and coughed a significant cough.

"Oh, one can always speculate," he said, "and one in my profession will. The first thing to consider would be the personality traits which might predispose a man to periods of depression. People who keep their emotions under rigid control, people who are conscientious and rather compulsively concerned with small matters..." He knocked another fleck of ash into her tray and watched as she reached out to dump it, then quickly drew her hand back again. He grinned an evil grin. "In short," he finished, "some of the characteristics of people in professions which require individual, rather than group performance—medicine, law, the arts."

She regarded him speculatively.

"Don't worry though," he chuckled, "I'm pleased as hell with life."

"You're kind of down in the mouth this morning."

"Pete called me. He broke his ankle yesterday in gym class. They ought to supervise those things more closely. I'm thinking of changing his school."

"Again?"

"Maybe. I'll see. The headmaster is going to call me this afternoon. I don't like to keep shuffling him, but I do want him to finish school in one piece."

"A kid can't grow up without an accident or two. It's—statistics."

"Statistics aren't the same thing as destiny, Bennie. Everybody makes his own."

"Statistics or destiny?"

"Both, I guess."

"I think that if something's going to happen, it's going to happen."

"I don't. I happen to think that the human will, backed by a sane mind can exercise some measure of control over events. If I didn't think so, I wouldn't be in the racket I'm in."

"The world's a machine—you know—cause, effect. Statistics do imply the prob—"

"The human mind is not a machine, and I do not know cause and effect. Nobody does."

"You have a degree in chemistry, as I recall. You're a scientist, Doc."

"So I'm a Trotskyite deviationist," he smiled, stretching, "and you were once a ballet teacher." He got to his feet and picked up his coat.

"By the way, Miss DeVille called, left a message, She said: 'How about St. Moritz?'"

"Too ritzy," he decided aloud. "It's going to be Davos."

❖   ❖   ❖

Because the suicide bothered him more than it should have, Render closed the door to his office and turned off the windows and turned on the phonograph. He put on the desk light only.

How has the quality of human life been changed, he wrote, *since the beginnings of the industrial revolution?*

He picked up the paper and reread the sentence. It was the topic he had been asked to discuss that coming Saturday. As was typical in such cases he did not know what to say because he had too much to say, and only an hour to say it in.

He got up and began to pace the office, now filled with Beethoven's Eighth Symphony.

"The power to hurt," he said, snapping on a lapel microphone and activating his recorder, "has evolved in a direct relationship to technological advancement." His imaginary audience grew quiet. He smiled. "Man's potential for working simple mayhem has been multiplied by mass-production; his capacity for injuring the psyche through personal contacts has expanded in an exact ratio to improved communication facilities. But these are all matters of common knowledge, and are not the things I wish to consider tonight. Rather, I should like to discuss what I choose to call autopsychomimesis—the self-generated anxiety complexes which on first scrutiny appear quite similar to classic patterns, but which actually represent radical dispersions of psychic energy. They are peculiar to our times…"

He paused to dispose of his cigar and formulate his next words.

"Autopsychomimesis," he thought aloud, "a self-perpetuated imitation complex—almost an attention-getting affair. —A jazzman, for example, who acted hopped-up half the time, even though he had never used an addictive narcotic and only dimly remembered anyone who had—because all the stimulants and tranquilizers of today are quite benign. Like Quixote, he aspired after a legend when his music alone should have been sufficient outlet for his tensions.

"Or my Korean War Orphan, alive today by virtue of the Red Cross and UNICEF and foster parents whom he never met. He wanted a family so badly that he made one up. And what then?—He hated his imaginary father and he loved his imaginary mother quite dearly—for he was a highly intelligent boy, and he too longed after the half-true complexes of tradition. Why?

"Today, everyone is sophisticated enough to understand the time-honored patterns of psychic disturbance. Today, many of the reasons for those disturbances have been removed—not as radically as my now-adult war orphan's, but with as remarkable an effect. We are living in a neurotic past.—Again, why? Because our present times are geared to physical health, security, and well-being. We have abolished hunger, though the backwoods orphan would still rather receive a package of food concentrates from a human being who cares for him than to obtain a warm meal from an automat unit in the middle of the jungle.

"Physical welfare is now every man's right, in excess. The reaction to this has occurred in the area of mental health. Thanks to technology, the reasons for many of the old social problems have passed, and along with them went many of the reasons for psychic distress. But between the black of yesterday and the white of tomorrow is the great gray of today, filled with nostalgia, and fear of the future, which cannot be expressed on a purely material plane, is now being represented by a willful seeking after historical anxiety-modes..."

The phone-box buzzed briefly. Render did not hear it over the Eighth.

"We are afraid of what we do not know," he continued, "and tomorrow is a very great unknown. My own specialized area of psychiatry did not even exist thirty years ago. Science is capable of advancing itself so rapidly now that there is a genuine public uneasiness—I might even say 'distress'—as to the logical outcome: the total mechanization of everything in the world..."

He passed near the desk as the phone buzzed again. He switched off his microphone and softened the Eighth.

"Hello?"

"Saint Moritz," she said.

"Davos," he replied firmly.

"Charlie, you are most exasperating!"

"Jill, dear—so are you."

"Shall we discuss it tonight?"

"There is nothing to discuss!"

"You'll pick me up at five, though?"

He hesitated, then:

"Yes, at five. How come the screen is blank?"

"I've had my hair fixed. I'm going to surprise you again."

He suppressed an idiot chuckle, said, "Pleasantly, I hope. Okay, see you then," waited for her "good-bye," and broke the connection.

He transpared the windows, turned off the light on his desk, and looked outside.

Gray again overhead, and many slow flakes of snow—wandering, not being blown about much—moving downwards and then losing themselves in the tumult…

He also saw, when he opened the window and leaned out, the place off to the left where Irizarry had left his next-to-last mark on the world.

He closed the window and listened to the rest of the symphony. It had been a week since he had gone blindspinning with Eileen. Her appointment was for one o'clock.

He remembered her fingertips brushing over his face, like leaves, or the bodies of insects, learning his appearance in the ancient manner of the blind. The memory was not altogether pleasant. He wondered why.

Far below, a patch of hosed pavement was blank once again; under a thin, fresh shroud of white, it was slippery as glass. A building custodian hurried outside and spread salt on it, before someone slipped and hurt himself.

Sigmund was the myth of Fenris come alive. After Render had instructed Mrs. Hedges, "Show them in," the door had begun to open, was suddenly pushed wider, and a pair of smoky-yellow eyes stared in at him. The eyes were set in a strangely misshapen dog-skull.

Sigmund's was not a low canine brow, slanting up slightly from the muzzle; it was a high, shaggy cranium, making the eyes appear even more deep-set than they actually were. Render shivered slightly at the size and aspect of that head. The muties he had seen had all been puppies. Sigmund was full grown, and his gray-black fur had a tendency to bristle, which made him appear somewhat larger than a normal specimen of the breed.

He stared in at Render in a very un-doglike way and made a growling noise which sounded too much like "Hello, doctor," to have been an accident.

Render nodded and stood.

"Hello, Sigmund," he said. "Come in."

The dog turned his head, sniffing the air of the room—as though deciding whether or not to trust his ward within its confines. Then he returned his stare to Render, dipped his head in an affirmative, and shouldered the door open. Perhaps the entire encounter had taken only one disconcerting second.

Eileen followed him, holding lightly to the double-leashed harness. The dog padded soundlessly across the thick rug—head low, as though he was stalking something. His eyes never left Render's.

"So this is Sigmund…? How are you, Eileen?"

"Fine. —Yes, he wanted very badly to come along, and *I* wanted you to meet him."

Render led her to a chair and seated her. She unsnapped the double guide from the dog's harness and placed it on the floor. Sigmund sat down beside it and continued to stare at Render.

"How is everything at State Psych?"

"Same as always. —May I bum a cigarette, doctor? I forgot mine."

He placed it between her fingers, furnished a light. She was wearing a dark blue suit and her glasses were flame blue. The silver spot on her forehead reflected the glow of his lighter; she continued to stare at that point in space after he had withdrawn his hand. Her shoulder-length hair appeared a trifle lighter than it had seemed on the night they met; today it was like a fresh-minted copper coin.

Render seated himself on the corner of his desk, drawing up his world-ashtray with his toe.

"You told me before that being blind did not mean that you had never seen. I didn't ask you to explain it then. But I'd like to ask you now."

"I had a neuroparticipation session with Doctor Riscomb," she told him, "before he had his accident. He wanted to accommodate my mind to visual impressions. Unfortunately, there was never a second session."

"I see. What did you do in that session?"

She crossed her ankles and Render noted they were well-turned.

"Colors, mostly. The experience was quite overwhelming."

"How well do you remember them? How long ago was it?"

"About six months ago—and I shall never forget them. I have even dreamed in color patterns since then."

"How often?"

"Several times a week."

"What sort of associations do they carry?"

"Nothing special. They just come into my mind along with other stimuli now—in a pretty haphazard way."

"How?"

"Well, for instance, when you ask me a question it's a sort of yellowish-orangish pattern that I 'see.' Your greeting was a kind of silvery thing. Now that you're just sitting there listening to me, saying nothing, I associate you with a deep, almost violet, blue."

Sigmund shifted his gaze to the desk and stared at the side panel.

Can he hear the recorder spinning inside? wondered Render. *And if he can, can he guess what it is and what it's doing?*

If so, the dog would doubtless tell Eileen—not that she was unaware of what was now an accepted practice—and she might not like being reminded that he considered her case as therapy, rather than a mere mechanical adaptation process. If he thought it would do any good (he smiled inwardly at the notion), he would talk to the dog in private about it.

Inwardly, he shrugged.

"I'll construct a rather elementary fantasy world then," he said finally, "and introduce you to some basic forms today."

She smiled; and Render looked down at the myth who crouched by her side, its tongue a piece of beefsteak hanging over a picket fence.

Is he smiling too?

"Thank you," she said.

Sigmund wagged his tail.

"Well then," Render disposed of his cigarette near Madagascar, "I'll fetch out the 'egg' now and test it. In the meantime," he pressed an unobtrusive button, "perhaps some music would prove relaxing."

She started to reply, but a Wagnerian overture snuffed out the words. Render jammed the button again, and there was a moment of silence during which he said, "Heh heh. Thought Respighi was next."

It took two more pushes for him to locate some Roman pines.

"You could have left him on," she observed: "I'm quite fond of Wagner."

"No thanks," he said, opening the closet, "I'd keep stepping in all those piles of leitmotifs."

❖   ❖   ❖

The great egg drifted out into the office, soundless as a cloud. Render heard a soft growl behind as he drew it toward the desk. He turned quickly.

Like the shadow of a bird, Sigmund had gotten to his feet, crossed the room, and was already circling the machine and sniffing at it—tail taut, ears flat, teeth bared.

"Easy, Sig," said Render. "It's an Omnichannel Neural T & R Unit. It won't bite or anything like that. It's just a machine, like a car, or a teevee, or a dishwasher. That's what we're going to use today to show Eileen what some things look like."

"Don't like it," rumbled the dog.

"Why?"

Sigmund had no reply, so he stalked back to Eileen and laid his head in her lap.

"Don't like it," he repeated, looking up at her.

"Why?"

"No words," he decided. "We go home now?"

"No," she answered him. "You're going to curl up in the corner and take a nap, and I'm going to curl up in that machine and do the same thing—sort of."

"No good," he said, tail drooping.

"Go on now," she pushed him, "lie down and behave yourself."

He acquiesced, but he whined when Render blanked the windows and touched the button which transformed his desk into the operator's seat.

He whined once more—when the egg, connected now to an outlet, broke in the middle and the top slid back and up, revealing the interior.

Render seated himself. His chair became a contour couch and moved in halfway beneath the console. He sat upright and it moved back again, becoming a chair. He touched a part of the desk and half the ceiling disengaged itself, reshaped itself, and lowered to hover overhead like a huge bell. He stood and moved around to the side of the ro-womb. Respighi spoke of pines and such, and Render disengaged an earphone from beneath the egg and leaned back across his desk. Blocking one ear with his shoulder and pressing the microphone to the other, he played upon the buttons with his free hand. Leagues of surf drowned the tone poem; miles of traffic overrode it; a great clanging bell sent fracture lines running through it; and the feedback said: "...Now that you are just sitting there listening to me, saying nothing, I associate you with a deep, almost violet, blue..."

He switched to the face mask and monitored, *one*—cinnamon, *two*—leaf mold, *three*—deep reptilian musk...and down through thirst, and the tastes of honey and vinegar and salt, and back on up through lilacs and wet concrete, a before-the-storm whiff of ozone, and all the basic olfactory and gustatory cues for morning, afternoon, and evening in the town.

The couch floated normally in its pool of mercury, magnetically stabilized by the walls of the egg. He set the tapes.

The ro-womb was in perfect condition.

"Okay," said Render, turning, "everything checks."

She was just placing her glasses atop her folded garments. She had undressed while Render was testing the machine. He was perturbed by her narrow waist, her large, dark-pointed breasts, her long legs. She was too well-formed for a woman her height, he decided.

He realized though, as he stared at her, that his main annoyance was, of course, the fact that she was his patient.

"Ready here," she said, and he moved to her side.

He took her elbow and guided her to the machine. Her fingers explored its interior. As he helped her enter the unit, he saw that her eyes were a vivid seagreen. Of this, too, he disapproved.

"Comfortable?"

"Yes."

"Okay then, we're set. I'm going to close it now. Sweet dreams."

The upper shell dropped slowly. Closed, it grew opaque, then dazzling. Render was staring down at his own distorted reflection.

He moved back in the direction of his desk.

Sigmund was on his feet, blocking the way.

Render reached down to pat his head, but the dog jerked it aside.

"Take me, with," he growled.

"I'm afraid that can't be done, old fellow," said Render. "Besides, we're not really going anywhere. We'll just be dozing right here, in this room."

The dog did not seem mollified.

"Why?"

Render sighed. An argument with a dog was about the most ludicrous thing he could imagine when sober.

"Sig," he said, "I'm trying to help her learn what things look like. You doubtless do a fine job guiding her around in this world which she cannot see—but she needs to know what it looks like now, and I'm going to show her."

"Then she, will not, need me."

"Of course she will." Render almost laughed. The pathetic thing was here bound so closely to the absurd thing that he could not help it. "I can't restore her sight," he explained. "I'm just going to transfer her some sight-abstractions—sort of lend her my eyes for a short time. Savvy?"

"No," said the dog. "Take mine."

Render turned off the music.

The whole mutie-master relationship might be worth six volumes, he decided, *in German.*

He pointed to the far corner.

"Lie down, over there, like Eileen told you. This isn't going to take long, and when it's all over you're going to leave the same way you came—you leading. Okay?"

Sigmund did not answer, but he turned and moved off to the corner, tail drooping again.

Render seated himself and lowered the hood, the operator's modified version of the ro-womb. He was alone before the ninety white buttons and the two red ones. The world ended in the blackness beyond the console. He loosened his necktie and unbuttoned his collar.

He removed the helmet from its receptacle and checked its leads. Donning it then, he swung the halfmask up over his lower face and dropped the darksheet down to meet with it. He rested his right arm in the sling, and with a single tapping gesture, he eliminated his patient's consciousness.

A Shaper does not press white buttons consciously. He wills conditions. Then deeply-implanted muscular reflexes exert an almost imperceptible pressure against the sensitive arm-sling, which glides into the proper position and encourages an extended finger to move forward. A button is pressed. The sling moves on.

Render felt a tingling at the base of his skull; he smelled fresh-cut grass.

Suddenly he was moving up the great gray alley between the worlds.

After what seemed a long time, Render felt that he was footed on a strange Earth. He could see nothing; it was only a sense of presence that informed him he had arrived. It was the darkest of all the dark nights he had ever known.

He willed that the darkness disperse. Nothing happened.

A part of his mind came awake again, a part he had not realized was sleeping; he recalled whose world he had entered.

He listened for her presence. He heard fear and anticipation.

He willed color. First, red…

He felt a correspondence. Then there was an echo.

Everything became red; he inhabited the center of an infinite ruby. Orange. Yellow…

He was caught in a piece of amber.

Green now, and he added the exhalations of a sultry sea. Blue, and the coolness of evening.

He stretched his mind then, producing all the colors at once. They came in great swirling plumes.

Then he tore them apart and forced a form upon them.

An incandescent rainbow arched across the black sky.

He fought for browns and grays below him. Self-luminescent, they appeared—in shimmering, shifting patches.

Somewhere, a sense of awe. There was no trace of hysteria though, so he continued with the Shaping.

He managed a horizon, and the blackness drained away beyond it. The sky grew faintly blue, and he ventured a herd of dark clouds. There was resistance to his efforts at creating distance and depth, so he reinforced the tableau with a very faint sound of surf. A transference from an auditory concept of distance came on slowly then, as he pushed the clouds about. Quickly, he threw up a high forest to offset a rising wave of acrophobia.

The panic vanished.

Render focused his attention on tall trees—oaks and pines, poplars and sycamores. He buried them about like spears, in ragged arrays of greens and browns and yellows, unrolled a thick mat of morning-moist grass, dropped a series of gray boulders and greenish logs at irregular intervals, and tangled and twined the branches overhead, casting a uniform shade throughout the glen.

The effect was staggering. It seemed as if the entire world was shaken with a sob, then silent.

Through the stillness he felt her presence. He had decided it would be best to lay the groundwork quickly, to set up a tangible headquarters, to prepare a field for operations. He could backtrack later, he could repair and amend the results of the trauma in the sessions yet to come; but this much, at least, was necessary for a beginning.

With a start, he realized that the silence was not a withdrawal. Eileen had made herself immanent in the trees and the grass, the stones and the bushes; she was personalizing their forms, relating them to tactile sensations, sounds, temperatures, aromas.

With a soft breeze, he stirred the branches of the trees. Just beyond the bounds of seeing he worked out the splashing sounds of a brook.

There was a feeling of joy. He shared it.

She was bearing it extremely well, so he decided to extend the scope of the exercise. He let his mind wander among the trees, experiencing a momentary doubling of vision, during which time he saw an enormous hand riding in an aluminum carriage toward a circle of white.

He was beside the brook now and he was seeking her, carefully.

He drifted with the water. He had not yet taken on a form. The splashes became a gurgling as he pushed the brook through shallow places and over rocks. At his insistence, the waters became more articulate.

"Where are you?" asked the brook.

Here! Here!

Here!

...and here! replied the trees, the bushes, the stones, the grass.

"Choose one," said the brook, as it widened, rounded a mass of rock, then bent its way toward a slope, heading toward a blue pool.

I cannot, was the answer from the wind.

"You must." The brook widened and poured itself into the pool, swirled about the surface, then stilled itself and reflected branches and dark clouds. "Now!"

Very well, echoed the wood, *in a moment.*

The mist rose above the lake and drifted to the bank of the pool.

"Now," tinkled the mist.

Here, then...

She had chosen a small willow. It swayed in the wind; it trailed its branches in the water.

"Eileen Shallot," he said, "regard the lake."

The breezes shifted; the willow bent.

It was not difficult for him to recall her face, her body. The tree spun as though rootless. Eileen stood in the midst of a quiet explosion of leaves; she stared, frightened, into the deep blue mirror of Render's mind, the lake.

She covered her face with her hands, but it could not stop the seeing.

"Behold yourself," said Render.

She lowered her hands and peered downwards. Then she turned in every direction, slowly; she studied herself. Finally:

"I feel I am quite lovely," she said. "Do I feel so because you want me to, or is it true?"

She looked all about as she spoke, seeking the Shaper.

"It is true," said Render, from everywhere.

"Thank you."

There was a swirl of white and she was wearing a belted garment of damask. The light in the distance brightened almost imperceptibly. A faint touch of pink began at the base of the lowest cloudbank.

"What is happening there?" she asked, facing that direction.

"I am going to show you a sunrise," said Render, "and I shall probably botch it a bit—but then, it's my first professional sunrise under these circumstances."

"Where are *you*?" she asked.

"Everywhere," he replied.

"Please take on a form so that I can see you."

"All right."

"Your natural form."

He willed that he be beside her on the bank, and he was.

Startled by a metallic flash, he looked downward. The world receded for an instant, then grew stable once again. He laughed, and the laugh froze as he thought of something.

He was wearing the suit of armor which had stood beside their table in The Partridge and Scalpel on the night they met.

She reached out and touched it.

"The suit of armor by our table," she acknowledged, running her fingertips over the plates and the junctures. "I associated it with you that night."

"…And you stuffed me into it just now," he commented. "You're a strong-willed woman."

The armor vanished and he was wearing his gray-brown suit and looseknit bloodclot necktie and a professional expression.

"Behold the real me," he smiled faintly. "Now, to the sunset[1]. I'm going to use all the colors. Watch!"

They seated themselves on the green park bench which had appeared behind them, and Render pointed in the direction he had decided upon as east.

Slowly, the sun worked through its morning attitudes. For the first time in this particular world it shone down like a god, and reflected off the lake, and broke the clouds, and set the landscape to smouldering beneath the mist that arose from the moist wood.

Watching, watching intently, staring directly into the ascending bonfire, Eileen did not move for a long while, nor speak. Render could sense her fascination.

She was staring at the source of all light; it reflected back from the gleaming coin on her brow, like a single drop of blood.

Render said, "That is the sun, and those are clouds," and he clapped his hands and the clouds covered the sun and there was a soft rumble overhead, "and that is thunder," he finished.

---

1 Every published edition says "sunset", though all surrounding text refers to morning. Render may already be slipping, or this may be a long-standing typo.

The rain fell then, shattering the lake and tickling their faces, making sharp striking sounds on the leaves, then soft tapping sounds, dripping down from the branches overhead, soaking their garments and plastering their hair, running down their necks and falling into their eyes, turning patches of brown earth to mud.

A splash of lightning covered the sky, and a second later there was another peal of thunder.

"...And this is a summer storm," he lectured. "You see how the rain affects the foliage, and ourselves. What you just saw in the sky before the thunderclap was lightning."

"...Too much," she said. "Let up on it for a moment, please."

The rain stopped instantly and the sun broke through the clouds.

"I have the damnedest desire for a cigarette," she said, "but I left mine in another world."

As she said it one appeared, already lighted, between her fingers.

"It's going to taste rather flat," said Render strangely.

He watched her for a moment, then:

"I didn't give you that cigarette," he noted. "You picked it from my mind."

The smoke laddered and spiraled upward, was swept away.

"...Which means that, for the second time today, I have underestimated the pull of that vacuum in your mind—in the place where sight ought to be. You are assimilating these new impressions very rapidly. You're even going to the extent of groping after new ones. Be careful. Try to contain that impulse."

"It's like a hunger," she said.

"Perhaps we had best conclude this session now."

Their clothing was dry again. A bird began to sing.

"No, wait! Please! I'll be careful. I want to see more things."

"There is always the next visit," said Render. "But I suppose we can manage one more. Is there something you want very badly to see?"

"Yes. Winter. Snow."

"Okay," smiled the Shaper, "then wrap yourself in that furpiece..."

❖   ❖   ❖

The afternoon slipped by rapidly after the departure of his patient. Render was in a good mood. He felt emptied and filled again. He had come through the first trial without suffering any repercussions. He decided that he was going to succeed. His satisfaction was greater than his fear. It was with a sense of exhilaration that he returned to working on his speech.

"...And what is the power to hurt?" he inquired of the microphone.

"We live by pleasure and we live by pain," he answered himself. "Either can frustrate and either can encourage. But while pleasure and pain are rooted in biology, they are conditioned by society: thus are values to be derived. Because of the enormous masses of humanity, hectically changing positions in space every day throughout the cities of the world, there has come into necessary being a series of totally inhuman controls upon these movements. Every day they nibble their way into new areas—driving our cars, flying our planes, interviewing us, diagnosing our diseases—and I cannot even venture a moral judgment upon these intrusions. They have become necessary. Ultimately, they may prove salutary.

"The point I wish to make, however; is that we are often unaware of our own values. We cannot honestly tell what a thing means to us until it is removed from our life-situation. If an object of value ceases to exist, then the psychic energies which were bound up in it are released. We seek after new objects of value in which to invest this—mana, if you like, or libido, if you don't. And no one thing which has vanished during the past three or four or five decades was, in itself, massively significant; and no new thing which came into being during that time is massively malicious toward the people it has replaced or the people it in some manner controls. A society, though, is made up of many things, and when these things are changed too rapidly the results are unpredictable. An intense study of mental illness is often quite revealing as to the nature of the stresses in the society where the illness was made. If anxiety-patterns fall into special groups and classes, then something of the discontent of society can be learned from them. Karl Jung pointed out that when consciousness is repeatedly frustrated in a quest for values it will turn its search to the unconscious; failing there, it will proceed to quarry its way into the hypothetical collective unconscious. He noted, in the postwar analyses of ex-Nazis, that the longer they searched for something to erect from the ruins of their lives—having lived through a period of classical iconoclasm, and then seen their new ideals topple as well—the longer they searched, the further back they seemed to reach into the collective unconscious of their people. Their dreams themselves came to take on patterns out of the Teutonic mythos.

"This, in a much less dramatic sense, is happening today. There are historical periods when the group tendency for the mind to turn in upon itself, to turn back, is greater than at other times. We are living in such a period of Quixotism, in the original sense of the term. This is because the power to hurt, in our time, is the power to ignore, to baffle—and it is no longer the exclusive property of human beings—"

A buzz interrupted him then. He switched off the recorder, touched the phone-box.

"Charles Render speaking," he told it.

"This is Paul Charter," lisped the box. "I am headmaster at Dilling."

"Yes?"

The picture cleared. Render saw a man whose eyes were set close together beneath a high forehead. The forehead was heavily creased; the mouth twitched as it spoke.

"Well, I want to apologize again for what happened. It was a faulty piece of equipment that caused—"

"Can't you afford proper facilities? Your fees are high enough."

"It was a *new* piece of equipment. It was a factory defect—"

"Wasn't there anybody in charge of the class?"

"Yes, but—"

"Why didn't he inspect the equipment? Why wasn't he on hand to prevent the fall?"

"He *was* on hand, but it happened too fast for him to do anything. As for inspecting the equipment for factory defects, that isn't his job. Look, I'm very sorry. I'm quite fond of your boy. I can assure you nothing like this will ever happen again."

"You're right, there. But that's because I'm picking him up tomorrow morning and enrolling him in a school that exercises proper safety precautions."

Render ended the conversation with a flick of his finger. After several minutes had passed he stood and crossed the room to his small wall safe, which was partly masked, though not concealed, by a shelf of books. It took only a moment for him to open it and withdraw a jewel box containing a cheap necklace and a framed photograph of a man resembling himself, though somewhat younger, and a woman whose upswept hair was dark and whose chin was small, and two youngsters between them—the girl holding the baby in her arms and forcing her bright bored smile on ahead. Render always stared for only a few seconds on such occasions, fondling the necklace, and then he shut the box and locked it away again for many months.

❖　　❖　　❖

Whump! Whump! went the bass. *Tchg-tchg-tchga-tchg,* the gourds.

The gelatins splayed reds, greens, blues, and godawful yellows about the amazing metal dancers.

HUMAN? asked the marquee.

ROBOTS? (immediately below).

COME SEE FOR YOURSELF! (across the bottom, cryptically).

So they did.

Render and Jill were sitting at a microscopic table, thankfully set back against a wall, beneath charcoal caricatures of personalities largely unknown (there being so many personalities among the sub-cultures of a city of 14 million people). Nose crinkled with pleasure, Jill stared at the present focal point of this particular subculture, occasionally raising her shoulders to ear level to add emphasis to a silent laugh or a small squeal, because the performers were just *too* human—the way the ebon robot ran his fingers along the silver robot's forearm as they parted and passed…

Render alternated his attention between Jill and the dancers and a wicked-looking decoction that resembled nothing so much as a small bucket of whisky sours strewn with seaweed (through which the Kraken might at any moment arise to drag some hapless ship down to its doom).

"Charlie, I think they're really people!"

Render disentangled his gaze from her hair and bouncing ear-rings.

He studied the dancers down on the floor, somewhat below the table area, surrounded by music.

There *could* be humans within those metal shells. If so, their dance was a thing of extreme skill. Though the manufacture of sufficiently light alloys was no problem, it would be some trick for a dancer to cavort so freely—and for so long a period of time, and with such effortless-seeming ease—within a head-to-toe suit of armor, without so much as a grate or a click or a clank.

Soundless…

They glided like two gulls; the larger, the color of polished anthra-cite, and the other, like a moonbeam falling through a window upon a silk-wrapped manikin.

Even when they touched there was no sound—or if there was, it was wholly masked by the rhythms of the band.

Whump-whump! Tchga-tchg!

Render took another drink.

Slowly, it turned into an apache-dance. Render checked his watch. Too long for normal entertainers, he decided. They must be robots. As he looked up again the black robot hurled the silver robot perhaps ten feet and turned his back on her.

There was no sound of striking metal.

Wonder what a setup like that costs? he mused.

"Charlie! There was no sound! How do they do that?"

"I've no idea," said Render.

The gelatins were yellow again, then red, then blue, then green.

"You'd think it would damage their mechanisms, wouldn't you?"

The white robot crawled back and the other swiveled his wrist around and around, a lighted cigarette between the fingers. There was laughter as he pressed it mechanically to his lipless faceless face. The silver robot confronted him. He turned away again, dropped the cigarette, ground it out slowly, soundlessly, then suddenly turned back to his partner. Would he throw her again? No…

Slowly then, like the great-legged birds of the East, they recommenced their movement, slowly, and with many turnings away.

Something deep within Render was amused, but he was too far gone to ask it what was funny. So he went looking for the Kraken in the bottom of the glass instead.

Jill was clutching his biceps then, drawing his attention back to the floor.

As the spotlight tortured the spectrum, the black robot raised the silver one high above his head, slowly, slowly, and then commenced spinning with her in that position—arms outstretched, back arched, legs scissored—very slowly, at first. Then faster.

Suddenly they were whirling with an unbelievable speed, and the gelatins rotated faster and faster.

Render shook his head to clear it.

They were moving so rapidly that they *had* to fall—human or robot. But they didn't. They were a mandala. They were a gray-form uniformity. Render looked down.

Then slowing, and slower, slower. Stopped.

The music stopped.

Blackness followed. Applause filled it.

When the lights came on again the two robots were standing statue-like, facing the audience. Very, very slowly, they bowed.

The applause increased.

Then they turned and were gone.

Then the music came on and the light was clear again. A babble of voices arose. Render slew the Kraken.

"What d'you think of that?" she asked him.

Render made his face serious and said: "Am I a man dreaming I am a robot, or a robot dreaming I am a man?" He grinned, then added: "I don't know."

She punched his shoulder gaily at that and he observed that she was drunk.

"I am not," she protested. "Not much, anyhow. Not as much as you."

"Still, I think you ought to see a doctor about it. Like me. Like now. Let's get out of here and go for a drive."

"Not yet, Charlie. I want to see them once more, huh? Please?"

"If I have another drink I won't be able to see that far."

"Then order a cup of coffee."

"Yaagh!"

"Then order a beer."

"I'll suffer without."

There were people on the dance floor now, but Render's feet felt like lead.

He lit a cigarette.

"So you had a dog talk to you today?"

"Yes. Something very disconcerting about that…"

"Was she pretty?"

"It was a boy dog. And boy, was he ugly!"

"Silly. I mean his mistress."

"You know I never discuss cases, Jill."

"You told me about her being blind and about the dog. All I want to know is if she's pretty."

"Well…Yes and no." He bumped her under the table and gestured vaguely. "Well, you know…"

"Same thing all the way around," she told the waiter who had appeared suddenly out of an adjacent pool of darkness, nodded, and vanished as abruptly.

"There go my good intentions," sighed Render. "See how you like being examined by a drunken sot, that's all I can say."

"You'll sober up fast, you always do. Hippocratics and all that."

He sniffed, glanced at his watch.

"I have to be in Connecticut tomorrow. Pulling Pete out of that damned school…"

She sighed, already tired of the subject.

"I think you worry too much about him. Any kid can bust an ankle. It's a part of growing up. I broke my wrist when I was seven. It was an accident. It's not the school's fault those things sometimes happen."

"Like hell," said Render, accepting his dark drink from the dark tray the dark man carried. "If they can't do a good job I'll find someone who can."

She shrugged.

"You're the boss. All I know is what I read in the papers.

"—And you're still set on Davos, even though you know you meet a better class of people at Saint Moritz?" she added.

"We're going there to ski, remember? I like the runs better at Davos."

"I can't score any tonight, can I?"

He squeezed her hand.

"You always score with me, honey."

And they drank their drinks and smoked their cigarettes and held their hands until the people left the dance floor and filed back to their microscopic tables, and the gelatins spun round and round, tinting clouds of smoke from hell to sunrise and back again, and the bass went *whump!*

Tchga-tchga!

"Oh, Charlie! Here they come again!"

The sky was clear as crystal. The roads were clean. The snow had stopped.

Jill's breathing was the breathing of a sleeper. The S-7 raced across the bridges of the city. If Render sat very still he could convince himself that only his body was drunk; but whenever he moved his head the universe began to dance about him. As it did so, he imagined himself within a dream, and Shaper of it all.

For one instant this was true. He turned the big clock in the sky backward, smiling as he dozed. Another instant and he was awake again, and unsmiling.

The universe had taken revenge for his presumption. For one re-known moment with the helplessness which he had loved beyond helping, it had charged him the price of the lake-bottom vision once again; and as he had moved once more toward the wreck at the bottom of the world—like a swimmer, as unable to speak—he heard, from somewhere high over the Earth, and filtered down to him through the waters above the Earth, the howl of the Fenris Wolf as it prepared to devour the moon; and as this occurred, he knew that the sound was as like to the trump of a judgment as the lady by his side was unlike the moon. Every bit. In all ways. And he was afraid.

III

"...The plain, the direct, and the blunt. This is Winchester Cathedral," said the guidebook. "With its floor-to-ceiling shafts, like so many huge tree trunks, it achieves a ruthless control over its spaces: the ceilings are flat; each bay, separated by those shafts, is itself a thing of certainty and stability. It seems, indeed, to reflect something of the spirit of William the Conqueror. Its disdain of mere elaboration and its passionate dedication to the love of another world would make it seem, too, an appropriate setting for some tale out of Malory…"

"Observe the scalloped capitals," said the guide. "In their primitive fluting they anticipated what was later to become a common motif…"

"Faugh!" said Render—softly though, because he was in a group inside a church.

"Shh!" said Jill (Fotlock—that was her real last name) DeVille.

But Render was impressed as well as distressed.

Hating Jill's hobby though, had become so much of a reflex with him that he would sooner have taken his rest seated beneath an oriental device which dripped water on his head than to admit he occasionally enjoyed walking through the arcades and the galleries, the passages and the tunnels, and getting all out of breath climbing up the high twisty stairways of towers.

So he ran his eyes over everything, burnt everything down by shutting them, then built the place up again out of the still smouldering ashes of memory, all so that at a later date he would be able to repeat the performance, offering the vision to his one patient who could see only in this manner. This building he disliked less than most. Yes, he would take it back to her.

The camera in his mind photographing the surroundings, Render walked with the others, overcoat over his arm, his fingers anxious to reach after a cigarette. He kept busy ignoring his guide, realizing this to be the nadir of all forms of human protest. As he walked through Winchester he thought of his last two sessions with Eileen Shallot. He recalled his almost unwilling Adam-attitude as he had named all the animals passing before them, led of course by the *one* she had wanted to see, colored fearsome by his own unease. He had felt pleasantly bucolic after honing up on an old botany text and then proceeding to Shape and name the flowers of the fields.

So far they had stayed out of the cities, far away from the machines. Her emotions were still too powerful at the sight of the simple, carefully introduced objects to risk plunging her into so complicated and chaotic a wilderness yet; he would build her city slowly.

Something passed rapidly, high above the cathedral, uttering a sonic boom. Render took Jill's hand in his for a moment and smiled as she looked up at him. Knowing she verged upon beauty, Jill normally took great pains to achieve it. But today her hair was simply drawn back and knotted behind her head, and her lips and her eyes were pale; and her exposed ears were tiny and white and somewhat pointed.

"Observe the scalloped capitals," he whispered. "In their primitive fluting they anticipated what was later to become a common motif."

"Faugh!" said she.

"Shh!" said a sunburnt little woman nearby, whose face seemed to crack and fall back together again as she pursed and unpursed her lips.

Later, as they strolled back toward their hotel, Render said, "Okay on Winchester?"

"Okay on Winchester."

"Happy?"

"Happy."

"Good, then we can leave this afternoon."

"All right."

"For Switzerland..."

She stopped and toyed with a button on his coat.

"Couldn't we just spend a day or two looking at some old chateaux first? After all, they're just across the Channel, and you could be sampling all the local wines while I looked..."

"Okay," he said.

She looked up—trifle surprised.

"What? No argument?" she smiled. "Where is your fighting spirit?—to let me push you around like this?"

She took his arm then and they walked on as he said, "Yesterday, while we were galloping about in the innards of that old castle, I heard a weak moan, and then a voice cried out, 'For the love of God, Montresor!' I think it was my fighting spirit, because I'm certain it was my voice. I've given up *der geist der stets verneint. Pax vobiscum!* Let us be gone to France. *Alors!*"

"Dear Rendy, it'll only be another day or two…"

"Amen," he said, "though my skis that were waxed are already waning."

So they did that, and on the morn of the third day, when she spoke to him of castles in Spain, he reflected aloud that while psychologists drink and only grow angry, psychiatrists have been known to drink, grow angry, and break things. Construing this as a veiled threat aimed at the Wedgwoods she had collected, she acquiesced to his desire to go skiing.

❖   ❖   ❖

Free! Render almost screamed it.

His heart was pounding inside his head. He leaned hard. He cut to the left. The wind strapped at his face; a shower of ice crystals, like bullets of emery, fired by him, scraped against his cheek.

He was moving. Aye—the world had ended at Weissflujoch, and Dorftäli led down and away from this portal.

His feet were two gleaming rivers which raced across the stark, curving plains; they could not be frozen in their course. Downward. He flowed. Away from all the rooms of the world. Away from the stifling lack of intensity, from the day's hundred spoon-fed welfares, from the killing pace of the forced amusements that hacked at the Hydra, leisure; away.

And as he fled down the run he felt a strong desire to look back over his shoulder, as though to see whether the world he had left behind and above had set one fearsome embodiment of itself, like a shadow, to trail along after him, hunt him down, and to drag him back to a warm and well-lit coffin in the sky, there to be laid to rest with a spike of aluminum driven through his will and a garland of alternating currents smothering his spirit.

"I hate you," he breathed between clenched teeth, and the wind carried the words back; and he laughed then, for he always analyzed his emotions, as a matter of reflex; and be added, "Exit Orestes, mad, pursued by the Furies…"

After a time the slope leveled out and he reached the bottom of the run and had to stop.

He smoked one cigarette then and rode back up to the top so that he could come down it again for non-therapeutic reasons.

❖   ❖   ❖

That night he sat before a fire in the big lodge, feeling its warmth soaking into his tired muscles. Jill massaged his shoulders as he played Rorschach with the flames, and he came upon a blazing goblet which was snatched away from him in the same instant by the sound of his name being spoken somewhere across the Hall of the Nine Hearths.

"Charles Render!" said the voice (only it sounded more like "Sharlz Runder"), and his head instantly jerked in that direction, but his eyes danced with too many afterimages for him to isolate the source of the calling.

"Maurice?" he queried after a moment, "Bartelmetz?"

"Aye," came the reply, and then Render saw the familiar grizzled visage, set neckless and balding above the red and blue shag sweater that was stretched mercilessly about the wine-keg rotundity of the man who now picked his way in their direction, deftly avoiding the strewn crutches and the stacked skis and the people who, like Jill and Render, disdained sitting in chairs.

Render stood, stretching, and shook hands as he came upon them.

"You've put on more weight," Render observed. "That's unhealthy."

"Nonsense, it's all muscle. How have you been, and what are you up to these days?" He looked down at Jill and she smiled back at him.

"This is Miss DeVille," said Render.

"Jill," she acknowledged.

He bowed slightly, finally releasing Render's aching hand.

"...And this is Professor Maurice Bartelmetz of Vienna," finished Render, "a benighted disciple of all forms of dialectical pessimism, and a very distinguished pioneer in neuroparticipation—although you'd never guess it to look at him. I had the good fortune to be his pupil for over a year."

Bartelmetz nodded and agreed with him, taking in the *Schnaps-flasche* Render brought forth from a small plastic bag, and accepting the collapsible cup which he filled to the brim.

"Ah, you are a good doctor still," he sighed. "You have diagnosed the case in an instant and you make the proper prescription. *Nozdrovia!*"

"Seven years in a gulp," Render acknowledged, refilling their glasses.

"Then we shall make time more malleable by sipping it."

They seated themselves on the floor, and the fire roared up through the great brick chimney as the logs burnt themselves back to branches, to twigs, to thin sticks, ring by yearly ring.

Render replenished the fire.

"I read your last book," said Bartelmetz finally, casually, "about four years ago."

Render reckoned that to be correct.

"Are you doing any research work these days?"

Render poked lazily at the fire.

"Yes," he answered, "sort of."

He glanced at Jill, who was dozing with her cheek against the arm of the huge leather chair that held his emergency bag, the planes of her face all crimson and flickering shadow.

"I've hit upon a rather unusual subject and started with a piece of jobbery I eventually intend to write about."

"Unusual? In what way?"

"Blind from birth, for one thing."

"You're using the ONT&R?"

"Yes. She's going to be a Shaper."

"*Verfluchter!*—Are you aware of the possible repercussions?"

"Of course."

"You've heard of unlucky Pierre?"

"No."

"Good, then it was successfully hushed. Pierre was a philosophy student at the University of Paris, and he was doing a dissertation on the evolution of consciousness. This past summer he decided it would be necessary for him to explore the mind of an ape, for purposes of comparing a *moins-nausée* mind with his own, I suppose. At any rate, he obtained illegal access to an ONT&R and to the mind of our hairy cousin. It was never ascertained how far along he got in exposing the animal to the stimuli-bank, but it is to be assumed that such items as would not be immediately trans-subjective between man and ape—traffic sounds *und so weiter*—were what frightened the creature. Pierre is still residing in a padded cell, and all his responses are those of a frightened ape.

"So, while he did not complete his own dissertation," he finished, "he may provide significant material for someone else's."

Render shook his head.

"Quite a story," he said softly, "but I have nothing that dramatic to contend with. I've found an exceedingly stable individual—a psychiatrist, in fact—one who's already spent time in ordinary analysis. She wants to go into neuroparticipation—but the fear of a sight-trauma was what was keeping her out. I've been gradually exposing her to a full range of visual phenomena. When I've finished she should be completely accommodated to sight, so that she can give her full attention to therapy and not be blinded by vision, so to speak. We've already had four sessions."

"And?"

"...And it's working fine."

"You are certain about it?"

"Yes, as certain as anyone can be in these matters."

"Mm-hm," said Bartelmetz. "Tell me, do you find her excessively strong-willed? By that I mean, say, perhaps an obsessive-compulsive pattern concerning anything to which she's been introduced so far?"

"No."

"Has she ever succeeded in taking over control of the fantasy?"

"No!"

"You lie," he said simply.

Render found a cigarette. After lighting it, he smiled.

"Old father, old artificer," he conceded, "age has not withered your perceptiveness. I may trick me, but never you. —Yes, as a matter of fact, she *is* very difficult to keep under control. She is not satisfied just to see. She wants to Shape things for herself already. It's quite understandable—both to her and to me—but conscious apprehension and emotional acceptance never do seem to get together on things. She has become dominant on several occasions, but I've succeeded in resuming control almost immediately. After all, I *am* master of the bank."

"Hm," mused Bartelmetz. "Are you familiar with a Buddhist text, *Shankara's Catechism*?"

"I'm afraid not."

"Then I lecture you on it now. It posits—obviously not for therapeutic purposes—a true ego and a false ego. The true ego is that part of man which is immortal and shall proceed on to nirvana: the soul, if you like. Very good. Well, the false ego, on the other hand, is the normal mind, bound round with the illusions—the consciousness of you and me and everyone we have ever known professionally. Good? —Good. Now, the stuff this false ego is made up of they call *skandhas*. These include the feelings, the perceptions, the aptitudes, consciousness itself, and even the physical form. Very unscientific. Yes. Now they are not the same thing as neuroses, or one of Mister Ibsen's life-lies, or an hallucination—no, even though they are all wrong, being parts of a false thing to begin with. Each of the five *skandhas* is a part of the eccentricity that we call identity—then on top come the neuroses and all the other messes which follow after and keep us in business. Okay? —Okay. I give you this lecture because I need a dramatic term for what I will say, because I wish to say something dramatic. View the *skandhas* as lying at the bottom of the pond; the neuroses, they are ripples on the top of the water; the 'true ego', if there is one, is buried deep beneath the sand at the bottom. So. The ripples fill up the—*zwischenwelt*—between the object and the subject. The *skandhas* are a part of the subject, basic, unique, the stuff of his being. —So far, you are with me?"

"With many reservations."

"Good. Now I have defined my term somewhat, I will use it. You are fooling around with *skandhas*, not simple neuroses. You are attempting to adjust this woman's overall conception of herself and of the world. You are using the ONT&R to do it. It is the same thing as fooling with a psychotic, or an ape. All may seem to go well, but— at any moment, it is possible you may do something, show her some sight, or some way of seeing which will break in upon her selfhood, break a *skandha*—and pouf!—it will be like breaking through the bottom of the pond. A whirlpool will result, pulling you—where? I do not want you for a patient, young man, young artificer, so I counsel you not to proceed with this experiment. The ONT&R should not be used in such a manner."

Render flipped his cigarette into the fire and counted on his fingers:

"One," he said, "you are making a mystical mountain out of a pebble. All I am doing is adjusting her consciousness to accept an additional area of perception. Much of it is simple transference work from the other senses—Two, her emotions were quite intense initially because it *did* involve a trauma—but we've passed that stage already. Now it is only a novelty to her. Soon it will be a commonplace— Three, Eileen is a psychiatrist herself; she is educated in these matters and deeply aware of the delicate nature of what we are doing—Four, her sense of identity and her desires, or her *skandhas*, or whatever you want to call them, are as firm as the Rock of Gibraltar. Do you realize the intense application required for a blind person to obtain the education she has obtained? It took a will of ten-point steel and the emotional control of an ascetic as well—"

"And if something that strong should break, in a timeless moment of anxiety," smiled Bartelmetz sadly, "may the shades of Sigmund Freud and Karl Jung walk by your side in the valley of darkness."

"—And five," he said suddenly, staring into Render's eyes. "Five," he ticked it off on one finger. "Is she pretty?"

Render looked back into the fire.

"Very clever," sighed Bartelmetz, "I cannot tell whether you are blushing or not, with the rosy glow of the flames upon your face. I fear that you are, though, which would mean that you are aware that you yourself could be the source of the inciting stimulus. I shall burn a candle tonight before a portrait of Adler and pray that he give you the strength to compete successfully in your duel with your patient."

Render looked at Jill, who was still sleeping. He reached out and brushed a lock of her hair back into place.

"Still," said Bartelmetz, "if you do proceed and all goes well, I shall look forward with great interest to the reading of your work. Did I ever tell you that I have treated several Buddhists and never found a 'true ego'?"

Both men laughed.

❖   ❖   ❖

Like me but not like me, that one on a leash, smelling of fear, small, gray, and unseeing. *Rrowl* and he'll choke on his collar. His head is empty as the oven till. She pushes the button and it makes dinner. Make talk and they never understand, but they are like me. One day I will kill one—why?…Turn here.

"Three steps. Up. Glass doors. Handle to right."

Why? Ahead, drop-shaft. Gardens under, down. Smells nice, there. Grass, wet dirt, trees, and clean air. I see. Birds are recorded though. I see all. I.

"Dropshaft. Four steps."

Down. Yes. Want to make loud noises in throat, feel silly. Clean, smooth, many of trees. God…She likes sitting on bench chewing leaves smelling smooth air. Can't see them like me. Maybe now, some…? No.

Can't Bad Sigmund me on grass, trees, here. Must hold it. Pity. Best place…

"Watch for steps."

Ahead. To right, to left, to right, to left, trees and grass now. Sigmund sees. Walking…Doctor with machine gives her his eyes. *Rrowl* and he will not choke. No fearsmell.

Dig deep hole in ground, bury eyes. God is blind. Sigmund to see. Her eyes now filled, and he is afraid of teeth. Will make her to see and take her high up in the sky to see, away. Leave me here, leave Sigmund with none to see, alone. I will dig a deep hole in the ground…

❖   ❖   ❖

It was after ten in the morning when Jill awoke. She did not have to turn her head to know that Render was already gone. He never slept late. She rubbed her eyes, stretched, turned onto her side and raised herself on her elbow. She squinted at the clock on the bedside table, simultaneously reaching for a cigarette and her lighter.

As she inhaled, she realized there was no ashtray. Doubtless Render had moved it to the dresser because he did not approve of smoking in bed. With a sigh that ended in a snort she slid out of the bed and drew on her wrap before the ash grew too long.

She hated getting up, but once she did she would permit the day to begin and continue on without lapse through its orderly progression of events.

"Damn him," she smiled. She had wanted her breakfast in bed, but it was too late now.

Between thoughts as to what she would wear, she observed an alien pair of skis standing in the corner. A sheet of paper was impaled on one. She approached it.

"Join me?" asked the scrawl.

She shook her head in an emphatic negative and felt somewhat sad. She had been on skis twice in her life and she was afraid of them. She felt that she should really try again, after his being a reasonably good sport about the chateaux, but she could not even bear the memory of the unseemly downward rushing—which, on two occasions, had promptly deposited her in a snowbank—without wincing and feeling once again the vertigo that had seized her during the attempts.

So she showered and dressed and went downstairs for breakfast.

All nine fires were already roaring as she passed the big hall and looked inside. Some red-faced skiers were holding their hands up before the blaze of the central hearth. It was not crowded though. The racks held only a few pairs of dripping boots, bright caps hung on pegs, moist skis stood upright in their place beside the door. A few people were seated in the chairs set further back toward the center of the hall, reading papers, smoking, or talking quietly. She saw no one she knew, so she moved on toward the dining room.

As she passed the registration desk the old man who worked there called out her name. She approached him and smiled.

"Letter," he explained, turning to a rack. "Here it is," he announced, handing it to her. "Looks important."

It had been forwarded three times, she noted. It was a bulky brown envelope, and the return address was that of her attorney.

"Thank you."

She moved off to a seat beside the big window that looked out upon a snow garden, a skating rink, and a distant winding trail dotted with figures carrying skis over their shoulders. She squinted against the brightness as she tore open the envelope.

Yes, it was final. Her attorney's note was accompanied by a copy of the divorce decree. She had only recently decided to end her legal relationship to Mister Fotlock, whose name she had stopped using five years earlier, when they had separated. Now that she had the thing she wasn't sure exactly what she was going to do with it. It would be a hell of a surprise for dear Rendy, though, she decided. She would have to find a reasonably innocent way of getting the information to him. She withdrew her compact and practiced a "Well?" expression. Well, there would be time for that later, she mused. Not too much later, though... Her thirtieth birthday, like a huge black cloud, filled an April but four months distant. Well...She touched her quizzical lips with color, dusted more powder over her mole, and locked the expression within her compact for future use.

❖   ❖   ❖

In the dining room she saw Doctor Bartelmetz, seated before an enormous mound of scrambled eggs, great chains of dark sausages, several heaps of yellow toast, and a half-emptied flask of orange juice. A pot of coffee steamed on the warmer at his elbow. He leaned slightly forward as he ate, wielding his fork like a windmill blade.

"Good morning," she said.

He looked up.

"Miss DeVille—Jill…Good morning." He nodded at the chair across from him. "Join me, please."

She did so, and when the waiter approached she nodded and said, "I'll have the same thing, only about ninety percent less."

She turned back to Bartelmetz.

"Have you seen Charles today?"

"Alas, I have not," he gestured, open-handed, "and I wanted to continue our discussion while his mind was still in the early stages of wakefulness and somewhat malleable. Unfortunately," he took a sip of coffee, "he who sleeps well enters the day somewhere in the middle of its second act."

"Myself, I usually come in around intermission and ask someone for a synopsis," she explained. "So why not continue the discussion with me?—I'm always malleable, and my *skandhas* are in good shape."

Their eyes met, and he took a bite of toast.

"Aye," he said, at length, "I had guessed as much. Well—good. What do you know of Render's work?"

She adjusted herself in the chair.

"Mm. He being a special specialist in a highly specialized area, I find it difficult to appreciate the few things he does say about it. I'd like to be able to look inside other people's minds sometimes—to see what they're thinking about *me*, of course but I don't think I could stand staying there very long. Especially," she gave a mock-shudder, "the mind of somebody with—problems. I'm afraid I'd be too sympathetic or too frightened or something. Then, according to what I've read—pow!—like sympathetic magic, it would be my problem.

"Charles never has problems though," she continued, "at least, none that he speaks to me about. Lately I've been wondering, though. That blind girl and her talking dog seem to be too much with him."

"Talking dog?"

"Yes, her seeing-eye dog is one of those surgical mutants."

"How interesting… Have you ever met her?"

"Never."

"So," he mused.

"Sometimes a therapist encounters a patient whose problems are so akin to his own that the sessions become extremely mordant," he noted. "It has always been the case with me when I treat a fellow psychiatrist. Perhaps Charles sees in this situation a parallel to something which has been troubling him personally. I did not administer his personal analysis. I do not know all the ways of his mind, even though he was a pupil of mine for a long while. He was always self-contained, somewhat reticent; he could be quite authoritative on occasion, however. —What are some of the other things which occupy his attention these days?"

"His son Peter is a constant concern. He's changed the boy's school five times in five years."

Her breakfast arrived. She adjusted her napkin and drew her chair closer to the table.

"And he has been reading case histories of suicides recently, and talking about them, and talking about them, and talking about them."

"To what end?"

She shrugged and began eating.

"He never mentioned why," she said, looking up again. "Maybe he's writing something…"

Bartelmetz finished his eggs and poured more coffee.

"Are you afraid of this patient of his?" he inquired.

"No…Yes," she responded, "I am."

"Why?"

"I am afraid of sympathetic magic," she said, flushing slightly.

"Many things could fall under that heading."

"Many indeed," she acknowledged. And, after a moment, "We are united in our concern for his welfare and in agreement as to what represents the threat. So, may I ask a favor?"

"You may."

"Talk to him again," she said. "Persuade him to drop the case."

He folded his napkin.

"I intended to do that after dinner," he stated, "because I believe in the ritualistic value of rescue-motions. They shall be made."

❖ ❖ ❖

Dear Father-Image,

Yes, the school is fine, my ankle is getting that way, and my classmates are a congenial lot. No, I am not short on cash, undernourished, or having difficulty fitting into the new curriculum. Okay?

The building I will not describe, as you have already seen the macabre thing. The grounds I cannot describe, as they are presently residing beneath cold white sheets.

Brrr! I trust yourself to be enjoying the arts wint'rish. I do not share your enthusiasm for summer's opposite, except within picture frames or as an emblem on ice cream bars. The ankle inhibits my mobility and my roommate has gone home for the weekend—both of which are really blessings (saith Pangloss), for I now have the opportunity to catch up on some reading. I will do so forthwith.

Prodigally,
Peter

❖ ❖ ❖

Render reached down to pat the huge head. It accepted the gesture stoically, then turned its gaze up to the Austrian whom Render had asked for a light, as if to say, "Must I endure this indignity?" The man laughed at the expression, snapping shut the engraved lighter on which Render noted the middle initial to be a small 'v'.

"Thank you," he said, and to the dog: "What is your name?"

"Bismark," it growled.

Render smiled.

"You remind me of another of your kind," he told the dog. "One Sigmund, by name, a companion and guide to a blind friend of mine, in America."

"My Bismark is a hunter," said the young man. "There is no quarry that can outthink him, neither the deer nor the big cats."

The dog's ears pricked forward and he stared up at Render with proud, blazing eyes.

"We have hunted in Africa and the northern and southwestern parts of America. Central America, too. He never loses the trail. He never gives up. He is a beautiful brute, and his teeth could have been made in Solingen."

"You are indeed fortunate to have such a hunting companion."

"I hunt," growled the dog. "I follow… Sometimes, I have, the kill…"

"You would not know of the one called Sigmund then, or the woman he guides—Miss Eileen Shallot?" asked Render.

The man shook his head.

"No, Bismark came to me from Massachusetts, but I was never to the Center personally. I am not acquainted with other mutie handlers."

"I see. Well, thank you for the light. Good afternoon."

"Good afternoon…"

"Good, after, noon…"

Render strolled on up the narrow street, hands in his pockets. He had excused himself and not said where he was going. This was because he had had no destination in mind. Bartelmetz' second essay at counseling had almost led him to say things he would later regret. It was easier to take a walk than to continue the conversation.

On a sudden impulse he entered a small shop and bought a cuckoo clock which had caught his eye. He felt certain that Bartelmetz would accept the gift in the proper spirit. He smiled and walked on. *And what was that letter to Jill which the desk clerk had made a special trip to their table to deliver at dinnertime?* he wondered. It had been forwarded three times, and its return address was that of a law firm. Jill had not even opened it, but had smiled, overtipped the old man, and tucked it into her purse. He would have to hint subtly as to its contents. His curiosity was so aroused that she would be sure to tell him out of pity.

The icy pillars of the sky suddenly seemed to sway before him as a cold wind leapt down out of the north. Render hunched his shoulders and drew his head further below his collar. Clutching the cuckoo clock, he hurried back up the street.

❖   ❖   ❖

That night the serpent which holds its tail in its mouth belched, the Fenris Wolf made a pass at the moon, the little clock said "cuckoo," and tomorrow came on like Manolete's last bull, shaking the gate of horn with the bellowed promise to tread a river of lions to sand.

Render promised himself he would lay off the gooey fondue.

❖   ❖   ❖

Later, much later, when they skipped through the skies in a kite-shaped cruiser, Render looked down upon the darkened Earth dreaming its cities full of stars, looked up at the sky where they were all reflected, looked about him at the tapescreens watching all the people who blinked into them, and at the coffee, tea, and mixed drink dispensers who sent their fluids forth to explore the insides of the people they required to push their buttons, then looked across at Jill, whom the old buildings had compelled to walk among their walls—because he knew she felt he should be looking at her then—felt his seat's demand that he convert it into a couch, did so, and slept.

IV

Her office was full of flowers, and she liked exotic perfumes. Sometimes she burned incense.

She liked soaking in overheated pools, walking through falling snow, listening to too much music, played perhaps too loudly, drinking five or six varieties of liqueurs (usually reeking of anise, sometimes touched with wormwood) every evening. Her hands were soft and lightly freckled. Her fingers were long and tapered. She wore no rings.

Her fingers traced and retraced the floral swellings on the side of her chair as she spoke into the recording unit:

"…Patient's chief complaints on admission were nervousness, insomnia, stomach pains, and a period of depression. Patient has had a record of previous admissions for short periods of time. He had been in this hospital in 1995 for a manic depressive psychosis, depressed type, and he returned here again, 2-3-96. He was in another hospital, 9-20-97. Physical examination revealed a BP of 170/100. He was normally developed and well-nourished on the date of examination, 12-11-98. On this date patient complained of chronic backache, and there was noted some moderate symptoms of alcohol withdrawal. Physical examination further revealed no pathology except that the patient's tendon reflexes were exaggerated but equal. These symptoms were the result of alcohol withdrawal. Upon admission he was shown to be not psychotic, neither delusional nor hallucinated. He was well-oriented as to place, time, and person. His psychological condition was evaluated and he was found to be somewhat grandiose and expansive and more than a little hostile. He was considered a potential troublemaker. Because of his experience as a cook, he was assigned to work in the kitchen. His general condition then showed definite improvement. He is less tense and is cooperative. Diagnosis: Manic depressive reaction (external precipitating stress unknown). The degree of psychiatric impairment is mild. He is considered competent. To be continued on therapy and hospitalization."

She turned off the recorder then and laughed. The sound frightened her. Laughter is a social phenomenon and she was alone. She played back the recording then, chewing on the corner of her handkerchief while the soft, clipped words were returned to her. She ceased to hear them after the first dozen or so.

When the recorder stopped talking she turned it off. She was alone. She was very alone. She was so damned alone that the little pool of brightness which occurred when she stroked her forehead and faced the window—that little pool of brightness suddenly became the most important thing in the world. She wanted it to be immense. She wanted it to be an ocean of light. Or else she wanted to grow so small herself that the effect would be the same: she wanted to drown in it.

It had been three weeks, yesterday...

Too long, she decided, *I should have waited. No! Impossible! But what if he goes as Riscomb went? No! He won't. He would not. Nothing can hurt him. Never. He is all strength and armor. But—but we should have waited till next month to start. Three weeks... Sight withdrawal—that's what it is. Are the memories fading? Are they weaker? (What does a tree look like? Or a cloud?—I can't remember! What is red? What is green?) God! It's hysterical! I'm watching and I can't stop it! —Take a pill! A pill!*

Her shoulders began to shake. She did not take a pill though, but bit down harder on the handkerchief until her sharp teeth tore through its fabric.

"Beware," she recited a personal beatitude, "those who hunger and thirst after justice, for we *will* be satisfied.

"And beware the meek," she continued, "for we shall attempt to inherit the Earth.

"And beware..."

There was a brief buzz from the phone-box. She put away her handkerchief, composed her face, turned the unit on.

"Hello...?"

"Eileen, I'm back. How've you been?"

"Good, quite well in fact. How was your vacation?"

"Oh, I can't complain. I had it coming for a long time. I guess I deserve it. Listen, I brought some things back to show you—like Winchester Cathedral. You want to come in this week? I can make it any evening."

Tonight. No. I want it too badly. It will set me back if he sees...

"How about tomorrow night?" she asked. "Or the one after?"

"Tomorrow will be fine," he said. "Meet you at the P & S, around seven?"

"Yes, that would be pleasant. Same table?"

"Why not?—I'll reserve it."

"All right. I'll see you then."

"Good-bye."

The connection was broken.

Suddenly, then, at that moment, colors swirled again through her head; and she saw trees—oaks and pines, poplars and sycamores—great, and green and brown, and iron-colored; and she saw wads of fleecy clouds, dipped in paintpots, swabbing a pastel sky; and a burning sun, and a small willow tree, and a lake of a deep, almost violet, blue. She folded her torn handkerchief and put it away.

She pushed a button beside her desk and music filled the office: Scriabin. Then she pushed another button and replayed the tape she had dictated, half-listening to each.

Pierre sniffed suspiciously at the food. The attendant moved away from the tray and stepped out into the hall, locking the door behind him. The enormous salad waited on the floor. Pierre approached cautiously, snatched a handful of lettuce, gulped it.

He was afraid.

If only the steel would stop crashing, and crashing against steel, somewhere in that dark night… If only…

Sigmund rose to his feet, yawned, stretched. His hind legs trailed out behind him for a moment, then he snapped to attention and shook himself. She would be coming home soon. Wagging his tail slowly, he glanced up at the human-level clock with the raised numerals, verified his feelings, then crossed the apartment to the teevee. He rose onto his hind legs, rested one paw against the table, and used the other to turn on the set.

It was nearly time for the weather report and the roads would be icy.

"I have driven through countywide graveyards," wrote Render, "vast forests of stone that spread further every day.

"Why does man so zealously guard his dead? Is it because this is the monumentally democratic way of immortalization, the ultimate affirmation of the power to hurt—that is to say, life—and the desire that it continue on forever? Unamuno has suggested that this is the case. If it is, then a greater percentage of the population actively sought immortality last year than ever before in history…"

❖   ❖   ❖

Tch-tchg, tchga-tchg!
"Do you think they're really people?"
"Naw, they're too good."

❖   ❖   ❖

The evening was starglint and soda over ice. Render wound the S-7 into the cold sub-subcellar, found his parking place, nosed into it.

There was a damp chill that emerged from the concrete to gnaw like rats' teeth at their flesh. Render guided her toward the lift, their breath preceding them in dissolving clouds.

"A bit of a chill in the air," he noted.

She nodded, biting her lip.

Inside the lift, he sighed, unwound his scarf, lit a cigarette.

"Give me one, please," she requested, smelling the tobacco.

He did.

They rose slowly, and Render leaned against the wall, puffing a mixture of smoke and crystallized moisture.

"I met another mutie shep," he recalled, "in Switzerland. Big as Sigmund. A hunter though, and as Prussian as they come," he grinned.

"Sigmund likes to hunt, too," she observed. "Twice every year we go up to the North Woods and I turn him loose. He's gone for days at a time, and he's always quite happy when he returns. Never says what he's done, but he's never hungry. Back when I got him I guessed that he would need vacations from humanity to stay stable. I think I was right."

The lift stopped, the door opened, and they walked out into the hall, Render guiding her again.

Inside his office, he poked at the thermostat and warm air sighed through the room. He hung their coats in the inner office and brought the great egg out from its nest behind the wall. He connected it to an outlet and moved to convert his desk into a control panel.

"How long do you think it will take?" she asked, running her fingertips over the smooth, cold curves of the egg. "The whole thing, I mean. The entire adaptation to seeing."

He wondered.

"I have no idea," he said, "no idea whatsoever, yet. We got off to a good start, but there's still a lot of work to be done. I think I'll be able to make a good guess in another three months."

She nodded wistfully, moved to his desk, explored the controls with fingerstrokes like ten feathers.

"Careful you don't push any of those."

"I won't. How long do you think it will take me to learn to operate one?"

"Three months to learn it. Six, to actually become proficient enough to use it on anyone; and an additional six under close supervision before you can be trusted on your own. —About a year altogether."

"Uh-huh." She chose a chair.

Render touched the seasons to life, and the phases of day and night, the breath of the country, the city, the elements that raced naked through the skies, and all the dozens of dancing cues he used to build worlds. He smashed the clock of time and tasted the seven or so ages of man.

"Okay," he turned, "everything is ready."

It came quickly, and with a minimum of suggestion on Render's part. One moment there was grayness. Then a dead-white fog. Then it broke itself apart, as though a quick wind had arisen, although he neither heard nor felt a wind.

He stood beside the willow tree beside the lake, and she stood half-hidden among the branches and the lattices of shadow. The sun was slanting its way into evening.

"We have come back," she said, stepping out, leaves in her hair. "For a time I was afraid it had never happened, but I see it all again, and I remember now."

"Good," he said. "Behold yourself." And she looked into the lake.

"I have not changed," she said. "I haven't changed…"

"No."

"But you have," she continued, looking up at him. "You are taller, and there is something different…"

"No," he answered.

"I am mistaken," she said quickly, "I don't understand everything I see yet. I will though."

"Of course."

"What are we going to do?"

"Watch," he instructed her.

Along a flat, no-colored river of road she just then noticed beyond the trees, came the car. It came from the farthest quarter of the sky, skipping over the mountains, buzzing down the hills, circling through the glades, and splashing them with the colors of its voice—the gray and the silver of synchronized potency—and the lake shivered from its sounds, and the car stopped a hundred feet away, masked by the shrubberies; and it waited. It was the S-7.

"Come with me," he said, taking her hand. "We're going for a ride."

They walked among the trees and rounded the final cluster of bushes. She touched the sleek cocoon, its antennae, its tires, its windows—and the windows transpared as she did so. She stared through them at the inside of the car, and she nodded.

"It is your Spinner."

"Yes." He held the door for her. "Get in. We'll return to the club. The time is now. The memories are fresh, and they should be reasonably pleasant, or neutral."

"Pleasant," she said, getting in.

He closed the door, then circled the car and entered. She watched as he punched imaginary coordinates. The car leapt ahead and he kept a steady stream of trees flowing by them. He could feel the rising tension, so he did not vary the scenery. She swiveled her seat and studied the interior of the car.

"Yes," she finally said, "I can perceive what everything is."

She stared out the window again. She looked at the rushing trees. Render stared out and looked upon rushing anxiety patterns. He opaqued the windows.

"Good," she said, "Thank you. Suddenly it was too much to see—all of it, moving past like a…"

"Of course," said Render, maintaining the sensations of forward motion. "I'd anticipated that. You're getting tougher, though."

After a moment, "Relax," he said, "relax now," and somewhere a button was pushed, and she relaxed, and they drove on, and on and on, and finally the car began to slow, and Render said, "Just for one nice, slow glimpse now, look out your window."

She did.

He drew upon every stimulus in the bank which could promote sensations of pleasure and relaxation, and he dropped the city around the car, and the windows became transparent, and she looked out upon the profiles of towers and a block of monolithic apartments, and then she saw three rapid cafeterias, an entertainment palace, a drugstore, a medical center of yellow brick with an aluminum caduceus set above its archway, and a glassed-in high school, now emptied of its pupils, a fifty-pump gas station, another drugstore, and many more cars, parked or roaring by them, and people, people moving in and out of the doorways and walking before the buildings and getting into the cars and getting out of the cars; and it was summer, and the light of late afternoon filtered down upon the colors of the city and the colors of the garments the people wore as they moved along the boulevard, as they loafed upon the terraces, as they crossed the balconies, leaned on balustrades and windowsills, emerged from a corner kiosk, entered one, stood talking to one another; a woman walking a poodle rounded a corner; rockets went to and fro in the high sky.

The world fell apart then and Render caught the pieces.

He maintained an absolute blackness, blanketing every sensation but that of their movement forward.

After a time a dim light occurred, and they were still seated in the Spinner, windows blanked again, and the air as they breathed it became a soothing unguent.

"Lord," she said, "the world is so filled. Did I really see all of that?"

"I wasn't going to do that tonight, but you wanted me to. You seemed ready."

"Yes," she said, and the windows became transparent again. She turned away quickly.

"It's gone," he said. "I only wanted to give you a glimpse."

She looked, and it was dark outside now, and they were crossing over a high bridge. They were moving slowly. There was no other traffic. Below them were the Flats, where an occasional smelter flared like a tiny, drowsing volcano, spitting showers of orange sparks skyward; and there were many stars: they glistened on the breathing water that went beneath the bridge; they silhouetted by pinprick the skyline that hovered dimly below its surface. The slanting struts of the bridge marched steadily by.

"You have done it," she said, "and I thank you." Then: "Who are you, really?" (He must have wanted her to ask that.)

"I am Render," he laughed. And they wound their way through a dark, now-vacant city, coming at last to their club and entering the great parking dome.

Inside, he scrutinized all her feelings, ready to banish the world at a moment's notice. He did not feel he would have to, though.

They left the car, moved ahead. They passed into the club, which he had decided would not be crowded tonight. They were shown to their table at the foot of the bar in the small room with the suit of armor, and they sat down and ordered the same meal over again.

"No," he said, looking down, "it belongs over there."

The suit of armor appeared once again beside the table, and he was once again inside his gray suit and black tie and silver tie clasp shaped like a treelimb.

They laughed.

"I'm just not the type to wear a tin suit, so I wish you'd stop seeing me that way."

"I'm sorry," she smiled. "I don't know how I did that, or why."

"I do, and I decline the nomination. Also, I caution you once again. You are conscious of the fact that this is all an illusion. I had to do it that way for you to get the full benefit of the thing. For most of my patients though, it is the real item while they are experiencing it. It makes a counter-trauma or a symbolic sequence even more powerful. You are aware of the parameters of the game, however, and whether you want it or not this gives you a different sort of control over it than I normally have to deal with. Please be careful."

"I'm sorry. I didn't mean to."

"I know. Here comes the meal we just had."

"Ugh! It looks dreadful! Did we eat all that stuff?"

"Yes," he chuckled. "That's a knife, that's a fork, that's a spoon. That's roast beef, and those are mashed potatoes, those are peas, that's butter…"

"Goodness! I don't feel so well."

"…And those are the salads, and those are the salad dressings. This is a brook trout—mm! These are French fried potatoes. This is a bottle of wine. Hmm—let's see Romanée-Conti, since I'm not paying for it—and a bottle of Yquem for the trou—Hey!"

The room was wavering.

He bared the table, he banished the restaurant. They were back in the glade. Through the transparent fabric of the world he watched a hand moving along a panel. Buttons were being pushed. The world grew substantial again. Their emptied table was set beside the lake now, and it was still nighttime and summer, and the tablecloth was very white under the glow of the giant moon that hung overhead.

"That was stupid of me," he said. "Awfully stupid. I should have introduced them one at a time. The actual sight of basic, oral stimuli can be very distressing to a person seeing them for the first time. I got so wrapped up in the Shaping that I forgot the patient, which is just dandy! I apologize."

"I'm okay now. Really I am."

He summoned a cool breeze from the lake.

"…And that is the moon," he added lamely.

She nodded, and she was wearing a tiny moon in the center of her forehead; it glowed like the one above them, and her hair and dress were all of silver.

The bottle of Romanée-Conti stood on the table, and two glasses.

"Where did that come from?"

She shrugged. He poured out a glassful.

"It may taste kind of flat," he said.

"It doesn't. Here—" She passed it to him.

As he sipped it he realized it had a taste—a *fruite* such as might be quashed from the grapes grown in the Isles of the Blest, a smooth, muscular *charnu*, and a *capiteux* centrifuged from the fumes of a field of burning poppies. With a start, he knew that his hand must be traversing the route of the perceptions, symphonizing the sensual cues of a transference and a counter-transference which had come upon him all unawares, there beside the lake.

"So it does," he noted, "and now it is time we returned."

"So soon? I haven't seen the cathedral yet…"

"So soon."

He willed the world to end, and it did.

"It is cold out there," she said as she dressed, "and dark."

"I know. I'll mix us something to drink while I clear the unit."

"Fine."

He glanced at the tapes and shook his head. He crossed to his bar cabinet.

"It's not exactly Romanée-Conti," he observed, reaching for a bottle.

"So what? I don't mind."

Neither did be, at that moment. So he cleared the unit, they drank their drinks, and he helped her into her coat and they left.

As they rode the lift down to the sub-sub he willed the world to end again, but it didn't.

❖   ❖   ❖

Dad,

I hobbled from school to taxi and taxi to space-port, for the local Air Force Exhibit—Outward, it was called. (Okay, I exaggerated the hobble. It got me extra attention though.) The whole bit was aimed at seducing young manhood into a five-year hitch, as I saw it. But it worked. I wanna join up. I wanna go Out There. Think they'll take me when I'm old enuff? I mean take me Out—not some crummy desk job. Think so?

I do.

There was this dam lite colonel ('scuse the French) who saw this kid lurching around and pressing his nose 'gainst the big windowpanes, and he decided to give him the subliminal sell. Great! He pushed me through the gallery and showed me all the pitchers of AF triumphs, from Moonbase to Marsport. He lectured me on the Great Traditions of the Service, and marched me into a flic room where the Corps had good clean fun on tape, wrestling one another in null-G "where it's all skill and no brawn," and making tinted water sculpture-work way in the middle of the air and doing dismounted drill on the skin of a cruiser. Oh joy!

Seriously though, I'd like to be there when they hit the Outer Five—and On Out. Not because of the bogus balonus in the throwaways, and suchlike crud, but because I think someone of sensibility should be along to chronicle the thing in the proper way. You know, raw frontier observer. Francis Parkman. Mary Austin, like that. So I decided I'm going.

The AF boy with the chicken stuff on his shoulders wasn't in the least way patronizing, gods be praised. We stood on the balcony and watched ships lift off and he told me to go forth and study real hard and I might be riding them some day. I did not bother to tell him that I'm hardly intellectually deficient and that I'll have my B.A. before I'm old enough to do anything with it, even join his Corps. I just watched the ships lift off and said, "Ten years from now I'll be looking down, not up." Then he told me how hard his own training had been, so I did not ask howcum he got stuck with a lousy dirtside assignment like this one. Glad I didn't, now I think on it. He looked more like one of their ads than one of their real people. Hope I never look like an ad.

Thank you for the monies and the warm sox and Mozart's String Quintets, which I'm hearing right now. I wanna put in my bid for Luna instead of Europe next summer. Maybe…? Possibly…? Contingently…? Huh?—If I can smash that new test you're designing for me…? Anyhow, please think about it.

Your son,
Pete

❖   ❖   ❖

"Hello. State Psychiatric Institute."

"I'd like to make an appointment for an examination."

"Just a moment. I'll connect you with the Appointment Desk."

"Hello. Appointment Desk."

"I'd like to make an appointment for an examination."

"Just a moment… What sort of examination?"

"I want to see Doctor Shallot, Eileen Shallot. As soon as possible."

"Just a moment. I'll have to check her schedule… Could you make it at two o'clock next Tuesday?"

"That would be just fine."

"What is the name, please?"

"DeVille. Jill DeVille."

"All right, Miss DeVille. That's two o'clock, Tuesday."

"Thank you."

❖   ❖   ❖

The man walked beside the highway. Cars passed along the highway. The cars in the high-acceleration lane blurred by.

Traffic was light.

It was 10:30 in the morning, and cold.

The man's fur-lined collar was turned up, his hands were in his pockets, and he leaned into the wind. Beyond the fence, the road was clean and dry.

The morning sun was buried in clouds. In the dirty light, the man could see the tree a quarter mile ahead.

His pace did not change. His eyes did not leave the tree. The small stones clicked and crunched beneath his shoes.

When he reached the tree he took off his jacket and folded it neatly.

He placed it upon the ground and climbed the tree.

As he moved out onto the limb which extended over the fence, he looked to see that no traffic was approaching. Then he seized the branch with both hands, lowered himself, hung a moment, and dropped onto the highway.

It was a hundred yards wide, the eastbound half of the highway.

He glanced west, saw there was still no traffic coming his way, then began to walk toward the center island. He knew he would never reach it. At this time of day the cars were moving at approximately one hundred sixty miles an hour in the high acceleration lane. He walked on.

A car passed behind him. He did not look back. If the windows were opaqued, as was usually the case, then the occupants were unaware he had crossed their path. They would hear of it later and examine the front end of their vehicle for possible signs of such an encounter.

A car passed in front of him. Its windows were clear. A glimpse of two faces, their mouths made into O's, was presented to him, then torn from his sight. His own face remained without expression. His pace did not change. Two more cars rushed by, windows darkened. He had crossed perhaps twenty yards of highway.

Twenty-five…

Something in the wind, or beneath his feet, told him it was coming. He did not look.

Something in the corner of his eye assured him it was coming. His gait did not alter.

Cecil Green had the windows transpared because he liked it that way. His left hand was inside her blouse and her skirt was piled up on her lap, and his right hand was resting on the lever which would lower the seats. Then she pulled away, making a noise down inside her throat.

His head snapped to the left.

He saw the walking man.

He saw the profile which never turned to face him fully. He saw that the man's gait did not alter.

Then he did not see the man.

There was a slight jar, and the windshield began cleaning itself. Cecil Green raced on.

He opaqued the windows.

"How…?" he asked after she was in his arms again, and sobbing.

"The monitor didn't pick him up…"

"He must not have touched the fence…"

"He must have been out of his mind!"

"Still, he could have picked an easier way."

It could have been any face…Mine?

Frightened, Cecil lowered the seats.

Charles Render was writing the "Necropolis" chapter for *The Missing Link Is Man*, which was to be his first book in over four years. Since his return he had set aside every Tuesday and Thursday afternoon to work on it, isolating himself in his office, filling pages with a chaotic longhand.

"There are many varieties of death, as opposed to dying…" he was writing, just as the intercom buzzed briefly, then long, then again briefly.

"Yes?" he asked it, pushing down on the switch.

"You have a visitor," and there was a short intake of breath between "a" and "visitor."

He slipped a small aerosol into his side pocket, then rose and crossed the office.

He opened the door and looked out.

"Doctor… Help…"

Render took three steps, then dropped to one knee.

"What's the matter?"

"Come—she is…sick," he growled.

"Sick? How? What's wrong?"

"Don't know. You come."

Render stared into the unhuman eyes.

"What kind of sick?" he insisted.

"Don't know," repeated the dog. "Won't talk. Sits. I…feel, she is sick."

"How did you get here?"

"Drove. Know the co, or, din, ates…Left car, outside."

"I'll call her right now." Render turned.

"No good. Won't answer."

He was right.

Render returned to his inner office for his coat and medkit. He glanced out the window and saw where her car was parked, far below, just inside the entrance to the marginal, where the monitor had released it into manual control. If no one assumed that control a car was automatically parked in neutral. The other vehicles were passed around it.

So simple even a dog can drive one, he reflected. *Better get downstairs before a cruiser comes along. It's probably reported itself stopped there already. Maybe not, though. Might still have a few minutes grace.*

He glanced at the huge clock.

"Okay, Sig," he called out. "Let's go."

They took the lift to the ground floor, left by way of the front entrance, and hurried to the car.

Its engine was still idling.

Render opened the passenger-side door and Sigmund leapt in. He squeezed by him into the driver's seat then, but the dog was already pushing the primary coordinates and the address tabs with his paw.

Looks like I'm in the wrong seat.

He lit a cigarette as the car swept ahead into a U-underpass. It emerged on the opposite marginal, sat poised a moment, then joined the traffic flow. The dog directed the car into the high-acceleration lane.

"Oh," said the dog, "oh."

Render felt like patting his head at that moment, but he looked at him, saw that his teeth were bared, and decided against it.

"When did she start acting peculiar?" he asked.

"Came home from work. Did not eat. Would not answer me, when I talked. Just sits."

"Has she ever been like this before?"

"No."

What could have precipitated it? —But maybe she just had a bad day. After all, he's only a dog—sort of. —No. He'd know. But what, then?

"How was she yesterday—and when she left home this morning?"

"Like always."

Render tried calling her again. There was still no answer.

"You did, it," said the dog.

"What do you mean?"

"Eyes. Seeing. You. Machine. Bad."

"No," said Render, and his hand rested on the unit of stun-spray in his pocket.

"Yes," said the dog, turning to him again. "You will, make her well…?"

"Of course," said Render.

Sigmund stared ahead again.

Render felt physically exhilarated and mentally sluggish. He sought the confusion factor. He had had these feelings about the case since that first session. There was something very unsettling about Eileen Shallot: a combination of high intelligence and helplessness, of determination and vulnerability, of sensitivity and bitterness.

Do I find that especially attractive?—No. It's just the counter-transference, damn it!

"You smell afraid," said the dog.

"Then color me afraid," said Render, "and turn the page."

They slowed for a series of turns, picked up speed again, slowed again, picked up speed again. Finally, they were traveling along a narrow section of roadway through a semi-residential area of town. The car turned up a side street, proceeded about half a mile further, clicked softly beneath its dashboard, and turned into the parking lot behind a high brick apartment building. The click must have been a special servomech which took over from the point where the monitor released it, because the car crawled across the lot, headed into its transparent parking stall, then stopped. Render turned off the ignition.

Sigmund had already opened the door on his side. Render followed him into the building, and they rode the elevator to the fiftieth floor. The dog dashed on ahead up the hallway, pressed his nose against a plate set low in a doorframe, and waited. After a moment, the door swung several inches inward. He pushed it open with his shoulder and entered. Render followed, closing the door behind him.

The apartment was large, its walls pretty much unadorned, its color combinations unnerving. A great library of tapes filled one corner; a monstrous combination-broadcaster stood beside it. There was a wide bowlegged table set in front of the window, and a low couch along the right-hand wall; there was a closed door beside the couch; an archway to the left apparently led to other rooms. Eileen sat in an overstuffed chair in the far corner by the window. Sigmund stood beside the chair.

Render crossed the room and extracted a cigarette from his case. Snapping open his lighter, he held the flame until her head turned in that direction.

"Cigarette?" he asked.

"Charles?"

"Right."

"Yes, thank you. I will."

She held out her hand, accepted the cigarette, put it to her lips.

"Thanks. —What are you doing here?"

"Social call. I happened to be in the neighborhood."

"I didn't hear a buzz, or a knock."

"You must have been dozing. Sig let me in."

"Yes, I must have." She stretched. "What time is it?"

"It's close to four-thirty."

"I've been home over two hours then… Must have been very tired…"

"How do you feel now?"

"Fine," she declared. "Care for a cup of coffee?"

"Don't mind if I do."

"A steak to go with it?"

"No, thanks."

"Bacardi in the coffee?"

"Sounds good."

"Excuse me then. It'll only take a moment."

She went through the door beside the sofa and Render caught a glimpse of a large, shiny, automatic kitchen.

"Well?" he whispered to the dog.

Sigmund shook his head.

"Not same."

Render shook his head.

He deposited his coat on the sofa, folding it carefully about the medkit. He sat beside it and thought.

Did I throw too big a chunk of seeing at once? Is she suffering from depressive side-effects—say, memory repressions, nervous fatigue? Did I upset her sensory-adaptation syndrome somehow? Why have I been proceeding so rapidly anyway? There's no real hurry. Am I so damned eager to write the thing up? —Or am I doing it because she wants me to? Could she be that strong, consciously or unconsciously? Or am I that vulnerable—somehow?

She called him to the kitchen to carry out the tray. He set it on the table and seated himself across from her.

"Good coffee," he said, burning his lips on the cup.

"Smart machine," she stated, facing his voice.

Sigmund stretched out on the carpet next to the table, lowered his head between his forepaws, sighed, and closed his eyes.

"I've been wondering," said Render, "whether or not there were any after effects to that last session—like increased synesthesiac experiences, or dreams involving forms, or hallucinations or…"

"Yes," she said flatly, "dreams."

"What kind?"

"That last session. I've dreamed it over, and over."

"Beginning to end?"

"No, there's no special order to the events. We're riding through the city, or over the bridge, or sitting at the table, or walking toward the car—just flashes, like that. Vivid ones."

"What sort of feelings accompany these—flashes?"

"I don't know. They're all mixed up."

"What are your feelings now, as you recall them?"

"The same, all mixed up."

"Are you afraid?"

"N-no. I don't think so."

"Do you want to take a vacation from the thing? Do you feel we've been proceeding too rapidly?"

"No. That's not it at all. It's—well, it's like learning to swim. When you finally learn how, why then you swim and you swim and you swim until you're all exhausted. Then you just lie there gasping in air and remembering what it was like, while your friends all hover and chew you out for overexerting yourself—and it's a good feeling, even though you do take a chill and there's pins and needles inside all your muscles. At least, that's the way I do things. I felt that way after the first session and after this last one. First Times are always very special times… The pins and the needles are gone though, and I've caught my breath again. Lord, I don't want to stop now! I feel fine."

"Do you usually take a nap in the afternoon?"

The ten red nails of her fingernails moved across the tabletop as she stretched.

"…Tired," she smiled, swallowing a yawn. "Half the staff's on vacation or sick leave and I've been beating my brains out all week. I was about ready to fall on my face when I left work. I feel all right now that I've rested, though."

She picked up her coffee cup with both hands, took a large swallow.

"Uh-huh," he said. "Good. I was a bit worried about you. I'm glad to see there was no reason."

She laughed.

"Worried? You've read Doctor Riscomb's notes on my analysis—and on the ONT&R trial—and you think I'm the sort to worry about? Ha! I have an operationally beneficent neurosis concerning my adequacy as a human being. It focuses my energies, coordinates my efforts toward achievement. It enhances my sense of identity..."

"You do have one hell of a memory," he noted. "That's almost verbatim."

"Of course."

"You had Sigmund worried today, too."

"Sig? How?"

The dog stirred uneasily, opened one eye.

"Yes," he growled, glaring up at Render. "He needs, a ride, home."

"Have you been driving the car again?"

"Yes."

"After I told you not to?"

"Yes."

"Why?"

"I was a, fraid. You would, not, answer me, when I talked."

"I was *very* tired—and if you ever take the car again, I'm going to have the door fixed so you can't come and go as you please."

"Sorry."

"There's nothing wrong with me."

"I, see."

"You are *never* to do it again."

"Sorry." His eye never left Render; it was like a burning lens.

Render looked away.

"Don't be too hard on the poor fellow," he said. "After all, he thought you were ill and he went for the doctor. Supposing he'd been right? You'd owe him thanks, not a scolding."

Unmollified, Sigmund glared a moment longer and closed his eye.

"He has to be told when he does wrong," she finished.

"I suppose," he said, drinking his coffee. "No harm done, anyhow. Since I'm here, let's talk shop. I'm writing something and I'd like an opinion."

"Great. Give me a footnote?"

"Two or three. —In your opinion, do the general underlying motivations that lead to suicide differ in different periods of history, or in different cultures?"

"My well-considered opinion is no, they don't," she said. "Frustrations can lead to depressions or frenzies; and if these are severe enough, they can lead to self-destruction. You ask me about motivations and I think they stay pretty much the same. I feel this is a cross-cultural, cross-temporal aspect of the human condition. I don't think it could be changed without changing the basic nature of man."

"Okay. Check. Now, what of the inciting element?" he asked. "Let man be a constant, his environment is still a variable. If he is placed in an overprotective life-situation, do you feel it would take more or less to depress him—or stimulate him to frenzy—than it would take in a not so protective environment?"

"Hm. Being case-oriented, I'd say it would depend on the man. But I see what you're driving at: a mass predisposition to jump out windows at the drop of a hat—the window even opening itself for you, because you asked it to—the revolt of the bored masses. I don't like the notion. I hope it's wrong."

"So do I, but I was thinking of symbolic suicides too—functional disorders that occur for pretty flimsy reasons."

"Aha! Your lecture last month: autopsychomimesis. I have the tape. Well-told, but I can't agree."

"Neither can I, now. I'm rewriting that whole section—'Thanatos in Cloudcuckooland,' I'm calling it. It's really the death-instinct moved nearer the surface."

"If I get you a scalpel and a cadaver, will you cut out the death-instinct and let me touch it?"

"Couldn't," he put the grin into his voice, "it would be all used up in a cadaver. Find me a volunteer though, and he'll prove my case by volunteering."

"Your logic is unassailable," she smiled. "Get us some more coffee, okay?"

Render went to the kitchen, spiked and filled the cups, drank a glass of water, returned to the living room. Eileen had not moved; neither had Sigmund.

"What do you do when you're not busy being a Shaper?" she asked him.

"The same things most people do—eat, drink, sleep, talk, visit friends and not-friends, visit places, read…"

"Are you a forgiving man?"

"Sometimes. Why?"

"Then forgive me. I argued with a woman today, a woman named DeVille."

"What about?"

"You—and she accused me of such things it were better my mother had not borne me. Are you going to marry her?"

"No, marriage is like alchemy. It served an important purpose once, but I hardly feel it's here to stay."

"Good."

"What did you say to her?"

"I gave her a clinic referral card that said, 'Diagnosis: Bitch. Prescription: Drug therapy and a tight gag.'"

"Oh," said Render, showing interest.

"She tore it up and threw it in my face."

"I wonder why?"

She shrugged, smiled, made a gridwork on the tablecloth.

"'Fathers and elders, I ponder,'" sighed Render, "'what is hell?'"

"'I maintain it is the suffering of being unable to love,'" she finished. "Was Dostoevsky right?"

"I doubt it. I'd put him into group therapy, myself. That'd be real hell for him—with all those people acting like his characters, and enjoying it so."

Render put down his cup, pushed his chair away from the table.

"I suppose you must be going now?"

"I really should," said Render.

"And I can't interest you in food?"

"No."

She stood.

"Okay, I'll get my coat."

"I could drive back myself and just set the car to return."

"No! I'm frightened by the notion of empty cars driving around the city. I'd feel the thing was haunted for the next two-and-a-half weeks.

"Besides," she said, passing through the archway, "you promised me Winchester Cathedral."

"You want to do it today?"

"If you can be persuaded."

As Render stood deciding, Sigmund rose to his feet. He stood directly before him and stared upward into his eyes. He opened his mouth and closed it, several times, but no sounds emerged. Then he turned away and left the room.

"No," Eileen's voice came back, "you will stay here until I return."

Render picked up his coat and put it on, stuffing the medkit into the far pocket.

As they walked up the hall toward the elevator. Render thought he heard a very faint and very distant howling sound.

❖   ❖   ❖

In this place, of all places, Render knew he was the master of all things.

He was at home on those alien worlds, without time, those worlds where flowers copulate and the stars do battle in the heavens, falling at last to the ground, bleeding, like so many split and shattered chalices, and the seas part to reveal stairways leading down, and arms emerge from caverns, waving torches that flame like liquid faces—a midwinter night's nightmare, summer go a-begging, Render knew— for he had visited those worlds on a professional basis for the better part of a decade. With the crooking of a finger he could isolate the sorcerers, bring them to trial for treason against the realm—aye, and he could execute them, could appoint their successors.

Fortunately, this trip was only a courtesy call…

He moved forward through the glade, seeking her.

He could feel her awakening presence all about him.

He pushed through the branches, stood beside the lake. It was cold, blue, and bottomless, the lake, reflecting that slender willow which had become the station of her arrival.

"Eileen!"

The willow swayed toward him, swayed away.

"Eileen! Come forth!"

Leaves fell, floated upon the lake, disturbed its mirror-like placidity, distorted the reflections.

"Eileen?"

All the leaves yellowed at once then, dropped down into the water. The tree ceased its swaying. There was a strange sound in the darkening sky, like the humming of high wires on a cold day.

Suddenly there was a double file of moons passing through the heavens.

Render selected one, reached up, and pressed it. The others vanished as he did so, and the world brightened; the humming went out of the air.

He circled the lake to gain a subjective respite from the rejection-action and his counter to it. He moved up along an aisle of pines toward the place where he wanted the cathedral to occur. Birds sang now in the trees. The wind came softly by him. He felt her presence quite strongly.

"Here, Eileen. Here."

She walked beside him then, green silk, hair of bronze, eyes of molten emerald; she wore an emerald in her forehead. She walked in green slippers over the pine needles, saying: "What happened?"

"You were afraid."

"Why?"

"Perhaps you fear the cathedral. Are you a witch?" he smiled.

"Yes, but it's my day off."

He laughed, and he took her arm, and they rounded an island of foliage, and there was the cathedral reconstructed on a grassy rise, pushing its way above them and above the trees, climbing into the middle air, breathing out organ notes, reflecting a stray ray of sunlight from a pane of glass.

"Hold tight to the world," he said. "Here comes the guided tour."

They moved forward and entered.

" '…With its floor-to-ceiling shafts, like so many huge tree trunks, it achieves a ruthless control over its spaces,' " he said. "Got that from the guidebook. This is the north transept…"

" 'Greensleeves,' " she said, "the organ is playing 'Greensleeves.' "

"So it is. You can't blame me for that though. —Observe the scalloped capitals."

"I want to go nearer the music."

"Very well. This way then."

Render felt that something was wrong. He could not put his finger on it.

Everything retained its solidity…

Something passed rapidly then, high above the cathedral, uttering a sonic boom. Render smiled at that, remembering now; it was like a slip of the tongue: for a moment he had confused Eileen with Jill, yes, that was what had happened.

Why, then…

A burst of white was the altar. He had never seen it before, anywhere. All the walls were dark and cold about them. Candles flickered in corners and high niches. The organ chorded thunder under invisible hands.

Render knew that something was wrong.

He turned to Eileen Shallot, whose hat was a green cone towering up into the darkness, trailing wisps of green veiling. Her throat was in shadow, but…

"That necklace—Where?"

"I don't know," she smiled.

The goblet she held radiated a rosy light. It was reflected from her emerald. It washed him like a draft of cool air. "Drink?" she asked.

"Stand still," he ordered.

He willed the walls to fall down. They swam in shadow.

"Stand still!" he repeated urgently. "Don't do anything. Try not even to think.

"—Fall down!" he cried. And the walls were blasted in all directions and the roof was flung over the top of the world, and they stood amid ruins lighted by a single taper. The night was black as pitch.

"Why did you do that?" she asked, still holding the goblet out toward him.

"Don't think. Don't think anything," he said. "Relax. You are very tired. As that candle flickers and wanes so does your consciousness. You can barely keep awake. You can hardly stay on your feet. Your eyes are closing. There is nothing to see here anyway."

He willed the candle to go out. It continued to burn.

"I'm not tired. Please have a drink."

He heard organ music through the night. A different tune, one he did not recognize at first.

"I need your cooperation."

"All right. Anything."

"Look! The moon!" he pointed.

She looked upward and the moon appeared from behind an inky cloud.

"…And another, and another."

Moons, like strung pearls, proceeded across the blackness.

"The last one will be red," he stated.

It was.

He reached out then with his right index finger, slid his arm sideways along his field of vision, then tried to touch the red moon.

His arm ached, it burned. He could not move it.

"Wake up!" he screamed.

The red moon vanished, and the white ones.

"Please take a drink."

He dashed the goblet from her hand and turned away. When he turned back she was still holding it before him.

"A drink?"

He turned and fled into the night.

It was like running through a waist-high snowdrift. It was wrong. He was compounding the error by running—he was minimizing his strength, maximizing hers. It was sapping his energies, draining him.

He stood still in the midst of the blackness.

"The world around me moves," he said. "I am its center."

"Please have a drink," she said, and he was standing in the glade beside their table set beside the lake. The lake was black and the moon was silver, and high, and out of his reach. A single candle flickered on the table, making her hair as silver as her dress. She wore the moon on her brow. A bottle of Romanée-Conti stood on the white cloth beside a wide-brimmed wine glass. It was filled to overflowing, that glass, and rosy beads clung to its lip. He was very thirsty, and she was lovelier than anyone he had ever seen before, and her necklace, sparkled, and the breeze came cool off the lake, and there was something—something he should remember…

He took a step toward her and his armor clinked lightly as he moved. He reached toward the glass and his right arm stiffened with pain and fell back to his side.

"You are wounded!"

Slowly, he turned his head. The blood flowed from the open wound in his biceps and ran down his arm and dripped from his fingertips. His armor had been breached. He forced himself to look away.

"Drink this, love. It will heal you."

She stood.

"I will hold the glass."

He stared at her as she raised it to his lips.

"Who am I?" he asked.

She did not answer him, but something replied—within a splashing of waters out over the lake:

"You are Render, the Shaper."

"Yes, I remember," he said; and turning his mind to the one lie which might break the entire illusion he forced his mouth to say: "Eileen Shallot, I hate you."

The world shuddered and swam about him, was shaken, as by a huge sob.

"Charles!" she screamed, and the blackness swept over them.

"Wake up! Wake up!" he cried, and his right arm burned and ached and bled in the darkness.

He stood alone in the midst of a white plain. It was silent, it was endless. It sloped away toward the edges of the world. It gave off its own light, and the sky was no sky, but was nothing overhead. Nothing. He was alone. His own voice echoed back to him from the end of the world: "…hate you," it said, "…hate you."

He dropped to his knees. He was Render.

He wanted to cry.

A red moon appeared above the plain, casting a ghastly light over the entire expanse. There was a wall of mountains to the left of him, another to his right.

He raised his right arm. He helped it with his left hand. He clutched his wrist, extended his index finger. He reached for the moon.

Then there came a howl from high in the mountains, a great wailing cry—half-human, all challenge, all loneliness, and all remorse. He saw it then, treading upon the mountains, its tail brushing the snow from their highest peaks, the ultimate loupgarou of the North—Fenris, son of Loki—raging at the heavens.

It leapt into the air. It swallowed the moon.

It landed near him, and its great eyes blazed yellow. It stalked him on soundless pads, across the cold white fields that lay between the mountains; and he backed away from it, up hills and down slopes, over crevasses and rifts, through valleys, past stalagmites and pinnacles—under the edges of glaciers, beside frozen river beds, and always downwards—until its hot breath bathed him and its laughing mouth was opened above him.

He turned then and his feet became two gloaming rivers carrying him away.

The world jumped backwards. He glided over the slopes. Downward. Speeding—

Away…

He looked back over his shoulder.

In the distance, the gray shape loped after him.

He felt that it could narrow the gap if it chose. He had to move faster.

The world reeled about him. Snow began to fall.

He raced on.

Ahead, a blur, a broken outline.

He tore through the veils of snow which now seemed to be falling upward from off the ground—like strings of bubbles.

He approached the shattered form.

Like a swimmer he approached—unable to open his mouth to speak, for fear of drowning—of drowning and not knowing, of never knowing.

He could not check his forward motion; he was swept tide-like toward the wreck. He came to a stop, at last, before it.

Some things never change. They are things which have long ceased to exist as objects and stand solely as never-to-be-calendared occasions outside that sequence of elements called Time.

Render stood there and did not care if Fenris leapt upon his back and ate his brains. He had covered his eyes, but he could not stop the seeing. Not this time. He did not care about anything. Most of himself lay dead at his feet.

There was a howl. A gray shape swept past him.

The baleful eyes and bloody muzzle rooted within the wrecked car, champing through the steel, the glass, groping inside for...

"No! Brute! Chewer of corpses!" he cried. "The dead are sacred! *My* dead are sacred!"

He had a scalpel in his hand then, and he slashed expertly at the tendons, the bunches of muscle on the straining shoulders, the soft belly, the ropes of the arteries.

Weeping, he dismembered the monster, limb by limb, and it bled and it bled, fouling the vehicle and the remains within it with its infernal animal juices, dripping and running until the whole plain was reddened and writhing about them.

Render fell across the pulverized hood, and it was soft and warm and dry. He wept upon it.

"Don't cry," she said.

He was hanging onto her shoulder then, holding her tightly, there beside the black lake beneath the moon that was Wedgwood. A single candle flickered upon their table. She held the glass to his lips.

"Please drink it."

"Yes, give it to me!"

He gulped the wine that was all softness and lightness. It burned within him. He felt his strength returning.

"I am..."

"—*Render, the Shaper,*" splashed the lake.

"No!"

He turned and ran again, looking for the wreck. He had to go back, to return...

"You can't."

"I can!" he cried. "I can, if I try…"

Yellow flames coiled through the thick air. Yellow serpents. They coiled, glowing, about his ankles. Then through the murk, two-headed and towering, approached his Adversary.

Small stones rattled past him. An overpowering odor corkscrewed up his nose and into his head.

"Shaper!" came the bellow from one head.

"You have returned for the reckoning!" called the other.

Render stared, remembering.

"No reckoning, Thaumiel," he said. "I beat you and I chained you for—Rothman, yes, it was Rothman—the cabalist." He traced a pentagram in the air. "Return to Qliphoth. I banish you."

"This place be Qliphoth."

"…By Khamael, the angel of blood, by the hosts of Seraphim, in the Name of Elohim Gebor, I bid you vanish!"

"Not this time," laughed both heads.

It advanced.

Render backed slowly away, his feet bound by the yellow serpents. He could feel the chasm opening behind him. The world was a jig-saw puzzle coming apart. He could see the pieces separating.

"Vanish!"

The giant roared out its double-laugh.

Render stumbled.

"This way, love!"

She stood within a small cave to his right.

He shook his bead and backed toward the chasm.

Thaumiel reached out toward him.

Render toppled back over the edge.

"Charles!" she screamed, and the world shook itself apart with her wailing.

"Then *Vernichtung*," he answered as he fell. "I join you in darkness."

Everything came to an end,

❖   ❖   ❖

"I want to see Doctor Charles Render."

"I'm sorry, that is impossible."

"But I skip-jetted all the way here, just to thank him. I'm a new man! He changed my life!"

"I'm sorry, Mister Erikson. When you called this morning, I told you it was impossible."

"Sir, I'm Representative Erikson—and Render once did me a great service."

"Then you can do him one now. Go home."

"You can't talk to me that way!"

"I just did. Please leave. Maybe next year sometime…"

"But a few words can do wonders…"

"Save them!"

"I-I'm sorry…"

❖   ❖   ❖

Lovely as it was, pinked over with the morning—the slopping, steaming bowl of the sea—he knew that it *had* to end. Therefore…

He descended the high tower stairway and he entered the courtyard. He crossed to the bower of roses and he looked down upon the pallet set in its midst.

"Good morrow, m'lord," he said.

"To you the same," said the knight, his blood mingling with the earth, the flowers, the grasses, flowing from his wound, sparkling over his armor, dripping from his fingertips.

"Naught hath healed?"

The knight shook his head.

"I empty. I wait."

"Your waiting is near ended."

"What mean you?" He sat upright.

"The ship. It approacheth harbor."

The knight stood. He leaned his back against a mossy tree trunk. He stared at the huge, bearded servitor who continued to speak, words harsh with barbaric accents:

"It cometh like a dark swan before the wind—returning."

"Dark, say you? Dark?"

"The sails be black, Lord Tristram."

"You lie!"

"Do you wish to see? To see for yourself?—Look then!"

He gestured.

The earth quaked, the wall toppled. The dust swirled and settled. From where they stood they could see the ship moving into the harbor on the wings of the night.

"No! You lied!—See! They are white!"

The dawn danced upon the waters. The shadows fled from the ship's sails.

"No, you fool! Black! They *must* be!"

"White! White!—Isolde! You have kept faith! You have returned!"

He began running toward the harbor.

"Come back!—Your wound! You are ill!—Stop…"

The sails were white beneath a sun that was a red button which the servitor reached quickly to touch.

Night fell.

A Word from Zelazny

"This is the original novella for which they gave me a Nebula Award at the first, very formal SFWA banquet at the Overseas Press Club, and which I later expanded at Damon Knight's suggestion into the book *The Dream Master*. The novel contains some material that I am very happy to have written, but reflecting upon things after the passage of all this time I find that I prefer this, the shorter version. It is more streamlined and as such comes closer to the quasi-Classical notions I had in mind, in terms of economy and directions, in describing a great man with a flaw."[2]

Of three points to reveal about the story, he wrote, "1) I wanted a triangle situation, two women and one man, as I had never written one before. 2) I wanted a character loosely based on a figure in a classical tragedy—exceptional, and bearing a flaw that would smash him. 3) I have never been overfond of German shepherds, as there were two which used to harass my dog when I was a boy.

"I like 'He Who Shapes' for the background rather than the foreground. I thought it an effective setting for the Rougemont-Wagner death-wish business. I dislike it because Render turned out to be too stuffy for the figure I was trying to portray and Jill was far too flat a character."[3]

" 'He Who Shapes' was written with the notion of developing a character along tragic lines, in the classical sense. While an attempt was made to observe unities of time and space, I did try to 'streamline' the story line by including only the materials I deemed absolutely necessary for the realization of Render in terms of the rhythms of the form. When I was done, I felt that I had achieved what I'd set out to do."[4]

This story is heavily laden with allusions and symbols, perhaps the most of any of Zelazny's works (see the notes below for an explanation of many

---

2 *The Last Defender of Camelot*, 1980.
3 *Vector* May-June 1973 (#65).
4 *Science Fiction Origins*, Popular Library, 1980.

of them). Zelazny felt that the myths in his stories were more than mere decoration, that his intent was to magnify the universality and significance of his themes.[5]

Theodore Sturgeon was likely thinking of this story when he remarked "One feels at times that a few (a very few, I hasten to add) of his more vivid turns of phrase would benefit by an application of Dulcote (an artists' material, a transparent spray which uniformly pulls down brightness and gloss where applied). Not because they aren't beautiful—because most of them are, God knows—but because even so deft a wordsmith as Zelazny can forget from time to time that such a creation can keep a reader from his speedy progress from here to there, and that his furniture should be placed out of the traffic pattern. If I bang my shin on a coffee table it becomes a little beside the point that it is the most exquisitely crafted artifact this side of the Sun King. Especially since it was the Author himself who put me in a dead run. And there is the matter of exotic references—the injection of one of those absolutely precise and therefore untranslatable German philosophic terms, or a citation from classical mythology. This is a difficult thing to criticize without being misunderstood. A really good writer has the right, if not the duty, of arrogance, and should feel free to say anything he damn pleases in any way he likes. On the other hand, writing, like elections, copulation, sonatas, or a punch in the mouth, is communication... Communication is a double-ended, transmitter-receiver phenomenon or it doesn't exist. And if it evokes a response not in kind ('what the hell does that mean?' instead of 'well of course!') it exists but it is crippled. There is a fine line, and hazy, between following the use of an exotic intrusion with a definition, which can be damned insulting to a reader who does understand it, and throwing him something knobby and hard to hold without warning or subsequent explanation."[6]

Zelazny also described this story as "the fruit of an abandoned psychology major and several undergraduate years of part-time employment as a research assistant in my psych department's lab, as well as a lot of other stuff. I wrote it in 1964, and it was the longest piece I had done at that time."[7]

"He Who Shapes" later contributed to the screenplay of the movie *Dreamscape*. Although Zelazny worked for a time on the screenplay and was paid for the rights to his story, the final screenplay bore little resemblance to Zelazny's work, and his name was not in the credits.

---

5 *Science Fiction as Literature: Selected Stories and Novels of Roger Zelazny* [PhD Thesis] Thomas F. Monteleone, University of Maryland, 1973.
6 *Four for Tomorrow*, Ace, 1967.
7 *The Best of the Nebulas*, ed Ben Bova, Tor, 1989.

Notes

Render is an especially appropriate name for the main character because it is a contronym, a word that means two opposite things: "to rend" can mean to create or draw, and "to rend" can mean exactly the opposite: to destroy or tear down. Charles Render is that sort of conflicted personality in this story. As well, "render" can mean to surrender or yield, to tell or narrate, to boil down to the essence, to give something up, to interpret—and Render fulfills all of these meanings in the story. A subtle running joke is that the secretary who disapproves of Render's smoking is named **Mrs. Bennie Hedges** (as in Benson & Hedges, a brand of cigarette)—but Zelazny carefully calls her by either her first or her last name, and not the two together.

It was **Caesar** who was stabbed to death by Brutus and company, not **Marcus Antonius** who succeeded him. The soothsayer warned Caesar to beware the Ides of March; Render alters the dream to warn of the **Ides of Octember**, which is a variant spelling of October that was sometimes seen since Roman times (October is *not* based on a book by Dr. Seuss since the latter came out in 1977). In Greek mythology, **Medusa** had hair made of living snakes, which is likened to Render's helmet with multiple leads or cables connecting him to the ro-womb's circuitry. **Aquiline** means like an eagle; in this case, Render's nose is like an eagle's beak. In Dante Alighieri's *The Divine Comedy* (a trilogy that includes *Inferno, Purgaturio* and *Paradiso*), **trimmers** were blasé cowards who were denied heaven for lack of virtues and denied hell for lack of vices. **Cathecting** or cathexis means concentrating (possibly too much) mental energy on one person, idea, or object. An **Astrakhan** is a rug made of lamb's wool from the Russian territory of the same name; Zelazny collected rugs and dropped names of specific ones he owned into his fiction. **Esthetic** is the appreciation of beauty, or pleasure given by the beauty of a thing. **Mimesis** means simulation, and by "**mimesis of aberrance**" Render means that the simulated madness or abnormal behavior of someone's mind will not make him mad too; he will remain a **Sane Hatter** instead of becoming the Mad Hatter of *Alice's Adventures in Wonderland*.

The gaze of the **basilisk** caused sudden death; **Medusa's** could turn a man to stone. **Chimerae** are animals or things created out of various assembled parts, such as the mythological fire-breathing female monster with a lion's head, a goat's body, and a serpent's tail. The **caduceus** is one symbol of the medical profession with two snakes wrapped around a staff (one snake around a staff is the medical symbol of Aescalapius); Render is arrogantly declaring that even Medusa would bow to his medical authority and close her killing, petrifying gaze. **Thomas Mann** was the Nobel Prize-winning author of *The Magic Mountain* (a favorite of Zelazny's) and other highly symbolic novels that explored the psychology of the artist and intellectual. **He could visualize so clearly...somewhere skulls were whitening** is Render recalling the auto accident and drowning that claimed the lives of his wife and daughter. A **shallot** is an onion which implies that **Doctor Eileen Shallot** has many layers of psyche to be peeled by the psychiatrist. On the other hand, the name foreshadows a tragic ending: Alfred Lord Tennyson's *Lady of Shalott* falls in love with Sir Lancelot, but he cannot return her love (he is in love with Guinevere), and the Lady of Shalott dies of grief. As well, Malory tells the same tale of *Elayne of Ascolat* (in *The Fair Maid of Ascolat*) who has a futile, fatal love for Sir Lancelot; the name Elayne of Ascolat also suggests that of Eileen Shallot.

When Render first encounters her, Shallot is wearing a green dress with a gold pin to the left that consists of a ruby surrounded by the outlines of a goblet, or two faces (profiles) staring toward each other through the ruby, and the pin reminds him of something he cannot recall. She wears a silver disk on her forehead that enables her to "see." He will later note that her eyes are green and disapprove of this. These are early clues that Shallot is also **Isolde**, of which more is explained at the end of this essay. According to an interview with Zelazny[8], the pin mentioned was one designed by artist Salvador Dali, entitled "Tristan & Isolde"—it depicts the profiles of Tristan and Isolde in gold, forming a circle; they face each other with eyes closed; the enchanted crystal cup stands between them, filled with red wine. (Dali also did a surrealistic painting of the same title.) In a letter, Zelazny admitted that Dali's pin was too large to be worn and that he had in mind a reduced version of it; he hadn't expected anyone to recognize it from the description, but critic Sandra Miesel (in her article "Love is Madness") did.[9,10] The reflective, silver disc on the forehead of Shallot—which later appears as an emerald to Render in the dream state—also suggests the Lady of Shalott, who perceived much of reality through the mirror that she constantly faced in her lonely tower.

The **Menninger** Clinic in Houston, Texas, is an international center of excellence in psychiatric research, treatment and education. The book title **Why No Psychometrics in This Place** is a complex inside joke: **psychometrics** is the field that involves quantitative measurement of educational and psychological attributes, such as intelligence and personality tests. On the other hand, Render works directly in the chaos of the mind where normal rules and even **non-Euclidean geometry** do not apply; hence, psychometrics do not work in the mind because nothing can be measured there.

Chambertin is wine that comes from the vineyard in the village of Gevry-Chambertin in France's Burgundy region. The dog **Sigmund** is named for the psychiatrist Sigmund Freud, founder of psychoanalysis. Freud theorized that our consciousness is strongly influenced by past events (childhood,

---

8 *Four for Tomorrow*, Ace, 1967.
9 *Kallikanzaros* #5 June-July 1968.
10 *Kallikanzaros* #4, March-April 1968.

parenthood, etc.) and unconscious thought (dreams, sexual desires, etc). The presence of Sigmund reminds us that Render's technique of exploring a patient's mind directly is an extension of Freud's psychoanalysis and the particular importance that Freud gave to sexuality in motivating a person's desires. **Winged seraphs** are guardian angels. **Pulpefaction** is to reduce tissue to a pulpy mass; **contusions** are bruises and injuries that do not break the skin. Sufficient **gluteal stamina** is another way of saying that one's buttocks (*gluteus maximus* muscles) haven't become sore from sitting too long.

"**Here's looking at you**" may deliberately echo Humphrey Bogart's line from *Casablanca* (one of Zelazny's favorite movies) and foreshadow that Dr. Shallot has the more dominant personality. The **Socratic game** is a teaching method where the teacher asks pupils questions rather than telling them the information; it will not work if two people are asking questions and neither is answering them. **Minarets** are tall, slender towers with balconies, usually found on a mosque. **Xanadu** means place of great beauty; rather than a seaharbor of Atlantis, the name is usually associated with the summer palace of Kublai Khan. "**Full fathom five thy father lies**" comes from Shakespeare's *The Tempest* and means sinking or drowning at sea.

Georgia O'Keeffe was an American painter chiefly known for abstract paintings of flowers, rocks, shells, animal bones and landscapes. **Mongoloid idiot** is an outdated and now pejorative term for Down Syndrome, a genetic condition. **Neurosis** (plural: neuroses, mentioned later) is a mild mental illness or personality disorder in which the patient is still in touch with reality, whereas sense of reality is lost in a **psychosis**. An example of a neurosis is hypochondria, which also involves symptoms such as insecurity, anxiety, depression, and irrational fears. A **maelstrom** means a violent whirlpool, or a confusing state of movement (turbulence) and upheaval. The **rate of suicide among medical doctors and lawyers** is not as high as claimed in the story, but psychiatrists do have the highest rate among medical doctors. **Trotskyite** means a follower of Leon Trotsky, who promoted Marxist theory and left-wing policies. **St. Moritz and Davos** are two ski destinations in Switzerland. **Beethoven** suffered from manic-depression (bipolar disorder) and may have attempted suicide; his moodiness and his progressive deafness are thought to have been crucial components of his creativity. **Psychomimesis** is the imitation of psychiatric disease of another, or hysterical simulation of psychiatric disease (e.g., hysterical blindness); **autopsychomimesis** is a term that Render made up to mean a self-perpetuated imitation complex for which attention-getting is a secondary benefit (e.g., pretending to be depressed to gain attention). The modern medical term for this is Factitious Disorder. Cervantes' novel *Don Quixote* features the minor landowner, Alonso Quixano, who by reading too much fantasy deluded himself into thinking that he is a knight errant or hero, an example of **autopsychomimesis**. **Fenris** (son of Loki) was a huge wolf destined to devour Odin, the one-eyed chief god of Norse mythology; Render is identifying with Odin and seeing Sigmund as his doom. Render's ashtray displays a world map, which is why he was able to put out his cigarette near **Madagascar**. A **leitmotif** is a recurring musical theme, and some portion of Richard Wagner's epic *Ring Cycle* or (more likely) his *Tristan and Isolde* is implied. **Ottorino Respighi** was an Italian composer whose works included the symphony *Pines of Rome*. **Omnichannel Neural T & R Unit**—the letters stand for Transmission and Receiver.

His main annoyance was, of course, the fact that she was his patient… means that Render would rather have her as a lover, but he is inhibited with her as his patient. **Immanent** means inherent or existing within something. The **willow tree** is a symbol for the Lady of Shalott; the poem by Tennyson refers to the willow four times. As well, the recurrent reference to regarding a reflection in the water alludes to the Lady of Shalott, who regarded the world through the reflection in her mirror (she faced away from her window). **Damask** is a woven fabric with a pattern visible on both sides. Render's **armor** glints in the sun, suggesting that Shallot perceives him as her knight in shining armor, both Lancelot to her Lady of Shalott, and Tristan to her Isolde; the significance is that Eileen Shallot's mental strength has forced Render to manifest in the armor. **Mana** is power of supernatural origin that may be concentrated in a person; **libido** is sexual desire or energy. **Karl Jung** was a psychiatrist whose unique approach emphasized understanding the psyche through exploring dreams, art, mythology, world religion and philosophy. He was originally Freud's pupil, but he disagreed with Freud's notion that sexuality is more important than spirituality to a person's psychological development. **Iconoclasm** is the act of attacking or rejecting cherished beliefs or established values and practices. **Quixotism**, referring again to *Don Quixote*, is an impractical idealism sometimes involving imaginary or exaggerated enemies.

The **kraken** was a legendary sea monster off Norway which lurked in the ocean depths. A **mandala** is a geometric pattern or chart that can be used for focusing attention and meditating. The philosopher Chuang Tzu originally mused, "I dreamed I was a butterfly, flitting around in the sky; then I awoke. Now I wonder: Am I a man who dreamt of being a butterfly, or am I a butterfly dreaming that I am a man?" Render has rephrased it in terms of a **man dreaming that he is a robot**. **Hippocrates** was a Greek physician who is considered the father of modern medicine, and the Hippocratic Oath that physicians take upon graduation from medical school is named after him. The **lake-bottom vision** is the drowning death (and rotting corpses) of his wife and daughter in a sunken automobile. Norse mythology explained the moon's eclipse as the giant wolf **Fenris** periodically **devouring** and then regurgitating **the moon,** whereas the end of the world (Ragnarök) would be signaled in part by Fenris or his son Hati devouring the moon. As well, Fenris would kill the great Norse god Odin by swallowing him. This repeated reference to Fenris reinforces that Render identifies with Odin; the repeated reference to snow and ice throughout the tale are also consistent with a tale pertaining to Odin and the Norse.

Winchester Cathedral at Winchester in Hampshire is one of the largest cathedrals in England; construction was completed in 1093. **William the Conqueror** was the Duke of Normandy who invaded England in 1066 and became King William the First. **A tale out of Malory** implies Sir Thomas Malory and tales of King Arthur, the Knights of the Round Table, Sir Lancelot and Elayne the Maid of Ascolat (Lady of Shalott), and the tale of Tristan and Isolde. **Bucolic** refers to the pleasant aspects of countryside and pastoral or country life.

"**For the love of God, Montresor!**" are the final desperate words spoken by Fortunato before being bricked in alive by his murderer Montresor in Edgar Allan Poe's "The Casque of Amontillado." The phrase *"Der geist der stets verneint. Pax vobiscum!"* and *"Alors!"* mixes German, Latin and French: "the spirit that always answers in the negative. Peace be with you! Then!" and is Render's expression of surrender to his girlfriends' wishes. **Wedgwood** is a brand of collectible, fine china. **Emery** is a hard mineral substance used for grinding and polishing. **Weissflujoch** is the mountain peak in Davos that features the longest ski run in Europe (12 miles and 6,000 foot drop) while **Dorftäli** is a fast ski run on that mountain that leads directly into Davos.

The **hydra** was a mythological serpent possessed of many heads. **Orestes** was the mythological son of Agamemnon who was ordered by Apollo to kill his mother after she killed his father. After this matricide he was chased by the **Furies** (see afterword to "The Furies" by Zelazny) despite being acquitted of his crime by a tribunal. The quote suggests the play **Oresteia** by Aeschylus; the tale of Orestia has parallels to that of Oedipus, who unwittingly killed his own father and married his own mother. The psychiatrist **Hermann Rorschach** developed the famous ink blots which he thought would reveal personality by having patients interpret them. A **blazing goblet** suggests the legend of Tristan & Isolde again, or possibly the Holy Grail. **The Hall of the Nine Hearths** simply refers to the main hall of the ski resort at which Render was staying (which had nine fireplaces), but the name also suggests the recently mentioned Odin with whom the number nine is associated.

Dialectical is the art of arriving at the truth through a series of logical arguments. *Schnapsflasche* means a liquor bottle; *Nozdrovia!* or *Nazdrovia!* is "cheers!" in Polish and Russian (spelled phonetically) (and *Nozdrovia* is the title of the fanzine that Zelazny co-edited). *Moins-nausée* is less nausea or less nauseated; *"verfluchter!"* means 'most cursed', *"und so weiter"* would translate as "and so forth" or "and such" in the context of the sentence. An **artificer** is an inventor or skillful craftsman.

Shankara was an influential 9th century Hindu philosopher whose teachings ascribed all reality to a single unitary source, which he identified as "Brahma." The true ego could ascend to nirvana; whereas, false ego or sense of identity included **five *skandhas*** or groups of physical and psychic qualities that make up a human—form, sensation, perception, forces and consciousness. **Henrik Ibsen** was a 19th century Norwegian playwright and poet whose dramas were considered scandalous and immoral in the Victorian age when good should triumph and evil receive appropriate punishment. Ibsen's plays examined and revealed the realities that lay behind the facade, such as **The Master Builder,** that examined psychological conflicts within the main character. *Zwischenwelt* means between worlds, in this case the gap between Render and his patient's true ego, with the gap being filled up by *skandhas* and neuroses that Render must navigate and distinguish from the true nature of the patient. Render misleads his mentor not only by avoiding the question as to whether she is pretty, but by twice referring to Shallot as a **psychiatrist** when she is not: she is still in-training as a resident in psychiatry. **Alfred Adler** was an Austrian psychiatrist who emphasized the individual's desire to compensate for inferiorities; these motivations included the attainment of sexual goals; Bartelmetz knows that Render has a sexual interest in his patient Shallot (the feelings that a psychiatrist develops for the patients are termed "**counter-transference,**" mentioned later by Render). The psychiatric in-joke about Buddhists means that since Bartelmetz could not find a true ego in any Buddhist that he treated, therefore none of these Buddhists must be capable of achieving nirvana, since (as he explained earlier in the story) only the true ego can ascend to that state.

Mordant is caustic, burning, corrosive. **Macabre** is gruesome, ghostly or horrifying. **Pangloss** was a character in Voltaire's novel *Candide* whose philosophy was that "there is no effect without a cause"; even Peter's broken ankle is meant to suit a specific purpose. As well, Pangloss is considered a "flat character" whose few personality traits do not evolve throughout the story; this may be an in-joke, Zelazny's acknowledgment that Render's son had only a cursory characterization, just enough to indicate that, like his dad, he can quote literature too. **Bismarck** the hunting dog is named after the **Bismarck**, a famous German battleship from WWII, which in turn was named after the 19th century German chancellor Otto von Bismarck. **Solingen** is a city in Germany.

In Render's dreams he sees **Ouroboros**, the snake from Greek mythology which swallows its own tail and symbolizes a vicious cycle or the circularity of life; to Karl Jung, it represented the battle between the unconscious and conscious aspects of a person's psyche. In the context of references to Norse mythology, Render is probably mistaken about the identity—it must be Jormangund, the snake of Norse mythology which circles the world and also holds its tail in its mouth. Jormangund's appearance foretells Ragnarök, the end of the world. He also sees **Fenris** (described earlier) and a **cuckoo clock** (symbolizing foolishness or craziness). **Manolete** was a famous matador who died suddenly and unexpectedly when he was gored by the bull that he had just delivered the death stroke to; the newspapers declared "He died killing and he killed dying!" **Anise** is an herb related to parsley from which seeds and oils are used to flavor foods and liqueurs; **wormwood,** another herb, is used to flavor absinthe and certain wines. **Alexander Scriabin** was a Russian composer and pianist who claimed to see color in response to hearing musical notes, and he drew up a system that associated specific colors with each piano key; Shallot chooses this music after she has just remembered how colors look. **Muguel de Unamuno** was a Spanish essayist, poet and philosopher whose most famous work argued that humans desire immortality above all else, especially when faced with the certainty of death.

Seven ages of man refers to a soliloquy in Shakespeare's play *As You Like It*. **Romanée-Conti** is wine from a vineyard of the same name in Burgundy, whereas **Château d'Yquem** comes from the southern part of the Bordeaux vineyards known as Graves. Several terms related to wine tasting appear: *fruité*, having a bouquet and flavor which retains the taste of the grape; *charnu*, fleshy, meaty, robust, full; *capiteux*, heady, warm and rich in alcohol. In Celtic and Greek mythology, **Isle of the Blest** is a mythical island of paradise, an afterlife for favored mortals. **He willed the world to end again, but it didn't** indicates not a suicidal gesture but Render's double-checking that he wasn't still in an illusion—he is already having doubts due to Shallot's ability to take control.

Francis Parkman was an American historian and essayist who traveled extensively and wrote a monumental seven volume history of the colonization of North America. **Mary Hunter Austin** spent 17 years studying Indian life in the Mojave Desert and writing about it. **Chicken stuff** or guts is a slang term for embroidered rank insignia on a uniform. **Mozart** wrote a dozen **String Quintets** or arrangements for stringed instruments among his many works. **Necropolis** means a large cemetery or burial ground. **The missing link** was a supposed animal midway in evolution between apes and humans. The book title is another way of saying "there is no missing link." **Synesthesia** is a condition in which one of the senses evokes a different sense, as when hearing a sound produces the visualization of color (the condition that the musician **Scriabin** claimed to have). **Beneficent** means doing good or resulting in good. **Mollified** is to appease someone's anger or irritation. **Thanatos** was the personification of Death in Greek mythology, while **Cloudcuckooland** comes from the ancient play *The Birds* by Athenian playwright Aristophanes and refers to an unrealistic, idealistic or perfect place.

The quote "**Fairies and elders, I ponder, what is hell? I maintain it is the suffering of being unable to love**" is from *The Brothers Karamazov* by **Dostoyevsky**, spoken by the elder monk Father Zossima, who has never been able to love. Like Lancelot, Render is unable to love Shallot—he is still mourning his dead wife and daughter, has thoughts of suicide, has a girlfriend (DeVille), and Shallot is his patient (many jurisdictions impose a lifetime ban on sexual relationships between psychiatrists and their current or former patients). **A midwinter night's nightmare** alludes to Shakespeare's romantic comedy *A Midsummer Night's Dream*, which portrays young lovers and actors interacting with fairies. Render is not in a romantic comedy or dream, but instead he is in a romantic tragedy or nightmare. **Greensleeves** is an old English ballad that tells a tale of unrequited love, and it is Eileen Shallot who has caused it to play. **The necklace** was meant by Zelazny to imply Brisingamen, the necklace of the Norse goddess Freyja; when she wore the necklace, no man or god could withstand her charms. **Loup garou** is a werewolf; Fenris swallows the moon, signifying Ragnarök (the end of the world) and swallows Odin as well during that final battle (Render has become Odin); Fenris also gruesomely attacks the dead bodies of Render's long-dead wife and daughter. **Thaumiel** was originally an angel of love, but after the fall became a demon with two giant heads and bat-like wings; **Qlipoth** is the representation of evil in mystical teachings of Judaism. Appearing as a knight in shining armor, **Khamael,** an archangel in charge of the Sephira Geburah, symbolizes protection through skill with tools and reousrces. **Elohim Gebor** means Almighty God, and ***vernichtung*** means destruction.

The Arthurian legend of **Tristan and Isolde** is a complicated one with many variants of the tale and spelling of the principals' names (Tristan and Tristram, for example); Zelazny partially followed the version that Richard Wagner used in his opera of the same name, but he also referred to an incomplete version of the tale in the poem *Tristan* by Gottfried von Strassburg.[11] Tristan is a knight and nephew of King Mark; he is escorting Isolde to Cornwall where she will be married to the King. Isolde recognizes Tristan as her previous love who is now betraying her by giving her to King Mark. In revenge she makes Tristan drink a goblet of lethal poison and consumes some herself. Unbeknownst to her, it is not a poison but a love potion her maid prepared, and the two become lovers. Eventually, long after Isolde has married King Mark and Tristan has taken a wife (who, to further complicate the story, is also named Isolde), King Mark discovers the two lovers *en flagrante*. Tristan receives a mortal wound from a poisoned lance during a duel with one of King Mark's courtiers. Tristan, in his delirium, awaits Queen Isolde's arrival, because she has powers which could heal him. In some versions of the tale, but not in the opera or the poem, the story ends with Tristan giving instructions that if the ship returns with Queen Isolde it should have white sails hoisted, and if not, it should raise black sails. Tristan's wife Isolde spots the ship returning with white sails (indicating that Queen Isolde has come to heal him), but out of jealousy she tells Tristan

---

11 *Science Fiction as Literature: Selected Stories and Novels of Roger Zelazny* [PhD Thesis] Thomas F. Monteleone, University of Maryland, 1973.

that the sails are black. He despairs and dies; Queen Isolde comes upon his body, throws her arms around him and dies too.

In some variants of the story, Isolde has emerald (green) eyes or hails from the Emerald Isle or bears the potion in an emerald goblet. Shallot becomes Isolde near the end, and she wears a green silk dress and green slippers, has eyes of molten emerald and wears an emerald on her forehead. She bears a gold cup with a red ruby—recalling the Salvador Dali pin on her dress when Render first met her—which contains the poison/love potion that would bind Tristram and Isolde in love. She wants him to love her and is shattered when Render lies that he does not. Render has the role of Tristram forced upon him anyway, by being placed in armor and having a wound appear which mimics the fatal wound from a poisoned lance that Tristram had received.

The huge, bearded servitor with a barbaric accent who aids Tristram/Render at the end of the story is Dr. Bartelmetz (not Dr. Eileen Shallot!), which suggests that Render is trapped in his own mind and not that of Shallot's. Bartelmetz made the sails **black** so that Tristram would die in the illusion and Render's identity would be freed, but Tristram/Render overrides him to turn the sails **white**, indicating that Queen Isolde has returned to heal him. Bartelmetz is reaching for the red button to end the current simulation as the story ends. The story expresses existentialist themes of questioning the nature of reality as Render and his patients perceive it. There are other clues which suggest the possibility that the entire story has been an illusion taking place—and continually looping—within Render's tortured mind. This may be why the goblet in the Tristan & Isolde pin on the dress had significance for Render at the beginning of the story, and why the goblet reappeared in the flames of the fireplace before being explained at the end of the story. This may also be why there are repeated references to mirrored surfaces, willows, wolves, and to the circularity of Ouroboros/Jormangund.

SEE YOU LATER, MAYBE…

Written on March 18, 1968; previously unpublished.

See you later, maybe…

If not, remember that cats,
broken swords and tears
are sacred, all of them,
for reasons that I do not understand
but known in that place
where the seeing empties into sorrow,
in that place where I'll have to go,
now that I know.
You know?
      Whoever breaks the heart
is strange in one sense;
no one will ever really know…

But on 13 May/37 I was born,
and a man sketched a hand round a hilt.
Forget the blade. It's broken.
Nameless it was drawn.

Later, a cat claimed me
      and a woman cried.
The other sense is seeing:
come the monochromatic morning
of today's being
there is something still lets you know
where the darkness is.
You know?
      It's what certain things
let you light up
the day after, I guess,
and what you know then,
if you know, you know?

3-18-68

Notes

The poem revisits broken swords (Picasso's painting of Guernica), cats and tears, as related in the poem "On May 13, 1937." Likely these two poems were written one after the other.

ARTICLES

Sundry Notes on
Dybology and Suchlike

Science Fiction Parade, September 1964.

A blank piece of paper.
That's what I had after half an hour of working on this bit. Stan Woolston elicited it quite cunningly, first by promising to put my name in print, and then adding that I would have to write something to go beneath it. I have a fine rehearsed piece concerning the peculiarities of a quick brown fox, but after some discussion it was deemed too repetitive and allegorical. Something about the writing of science fiction or fantasy was deemed more appropriate what with the National Fantasy Fan Federation's Story Contest and Alma Hill's notable writer's project demonstrating that many fen are interested in doing it for money rather than love.

I decided to begin by making a list of everything I know about sfantasy, and that's how I got the blank piece of paper.

I mused then, looked up suddenly, announced, "You are a rash wretch," and fell to cursing and blaspheming. I sneaked a look back at the paper, curling and blackening there in my word-machine, but it was still empty of words.

("Marley was dead to begin with…")

Then I said, "I will write the things I wish I knew something about concerning sfantasy—which may be of some small aid to some other wretch, less rash than myself."

So okay. Why sfantasy?

Fiction is all lies to begin with. Sfantasy is a specialized form of lying. Specialized, I say, because a plain old prosaic liar usually takes pains to make his stuff look like Real Life. I have always, in my own modest way, wanted to be something of a Specialized Liar. So I decided to start out with a framework for perpetuating my dishonesties.

Specialized Lying, as I see it, falls into five general categories:

1) Lies about people and gadgets (gadgets that are not yet in existence or which are, but are not being used as the S. L. uses them);

2) Lies about people in an other-than-present-day Earth environment, characterized either by 1) (above), or:

3) Lies about people in a society which has never existed historically;

4) Lies about people in an other-than-Earth environment;

5) Lies about people's psychological and biological makeup.

It would seem that 3, 4 and 5 would apply to fantasy as readily as to science fiction, and that is correct; so do 1 and 2. Science fiction, to this neo-neo S. L., is a form of fantasy which demonstrates greater specialization in the construction of the Lie, but it's still fantasy. The difference is akin to that between street fighting and boxing. The former does not recognize Queensberry; the latter is supposedly governed by a set of rules, even though pros are sometimes known to commit a foul (many people hiss and boo then; others cheer).

Foremost in the mind of the practitioner of either of the combative arts though, is the flooring of his opponent by striking him. Fantasy and street fighting came first, and science fiction and boxing followed. Boxing is a specialized form of street fighting, and science fiction... (add 10 words or less).

Our Marquis of Science contains several dicta to the effect that if It happens in your story and It ain't happening here, today, then you damshure better get on the stick and tell how It works—and make It an acceptable extrapolation of something we've already got—or you're guilty of a "foul". (Fortunately, it gets harder and harder to commit one as time goes on, what with Progress and parallel worlds and all.)

That being my framework for the telling of Specialized Lies, and me not really caring whether it's Right or Wrong, I decided to practice with short short things first, in order to learn how to write, and then move on to making pieces of tale concerning the first three words in each of those five categories—"lies about people"—and to try making my lies approximate human realities as closely as possible, the relative unreality of the Rest serving (hopefully) to enhance what is stage center.

That out of the way now, I will pick up on one of the things I wish I knew something about:

Dybbuks

You know the old Dybbuk legend—where if you construct something that mimics life sufficiently a spirit may, come along and set up housekeeping in it. This, of necessity, happened in sfantasy a long time ago: with Mister Heinlein it is a good spirit that lives in his machines (doubtless because his characters are all eminently stable and mature, and are all engineers); with Mister Bradbury it is an evil dybbuk (epitomized in his most darkly magnificent creation, the Mechanical Hound) which terrorizes his adult-sized characters; with Mister Simak, it is a somewhat repugnant creature, but it can be gotten along with; with Mister Van Vogt it is a dybbuk out of its cotton-picking mind, crouched behind panels of blinking lights and flipping coins to see what it will do next.

The spirit in the machine, then, is one problem toward which, it would seem to me, a prospective Specialized Liar should develop some kind of an attitude. Not that it should be right at the center of his writing or anything like that—because that position should be reserved for humanity—but it represents a big chunk of life, and unless one is going to write only after-Armageddon stories, or S & S bits set in pastoral environments, then one is bloody well going to write some stories with machines in them.

Anything about which a human does a lot of writing is going to develop some sort of "personality" characteristics—it can't be helped; it's just the pathetic fallacy, now moved one step nearer the writer because of the industrial revolution. Writers of the Romantic period did it with Nature, and sfantasy writers can't seem to do otherwise than the same (whether explicitly or implicitly) with that which controls Nature.

Okay. The future. Machines will probably be there with us if we're still around as a civilization. They may be completely benign servants of man. I doubt it, though. They may be there as a dictatorship of robots. I doubt that too (but I've written them up that way). Their effects will probably be far more subtle (and possibly insidious) than either extreme. (For this angle, I am particularly fond of Mister Bradbury's "The Murderer".)

Permit me to quote here a nice quote from Saint-Exupéry's "The Tool" (a chapter in *Wind, Sand and Stars*) from which I've already plucked a couple stories:

> But we lack perspective for the judgment of trans-formations that go so deep. What are the hundred years of the history of machine compared with the two hun-dred thousand years of the history of man?... Our very psychology has been shaken to its foundations, to its most secret recesses. Our notions of separation, absence, distance, return are reflections of a new set of realities, though the words themselves remain unchanged. To grasp the meaning of the world today we use a language created to express the world of yesterday. The life of the past seems to us nearer our true natures, but only for the reason it is nearer to our language.
>
> The sailing vessel itself was once a machine born of the calculations of the engineers, yet it does not disturb our philosophers. The sloop took its place in the speech of men. There have always been seamen in recorded time. The man who assumes that there is an essential dif-ference between the sloop and the airplane lacks historic perspective.
>
> Every machine will gradually take on this patina and lose its identity in its function.[*]

The dybbuk—the thing that lives in the machine—is a strange and wily spirit with which every S. L. must, somewhere along the line, come to terms. Doubtless, it often breaks loose and has to be re-wrestled into new attitudes. In this, it is like religion, like sex, and like the population explosion—always worthy of attention. And the dybbuk is capable of touching on any of the above-named—possibly only lightly, but probably quite firmly. For that reason, it is worthy of a big attitude with lots of little opinions thrown in for sales tax.

I wish I knew more about dybbuks.

About people and ideas: I wish I knew more about them too.

Specialized Lies which, for one reason or another, have struck in my mind and doubtless influenced me in the construction of some

---

[*] *Airman's Odyssey* (New York, 1942), Harcourt, Brace and Co., pp. 42–30.

of my own, have been "The Light," by Poul Anderson, portraying the primacy of human genius in the midst of chaos, "Rogue Moon," by Algis Budrys, demonstrating that gimmicks do not have to be first and foremost to make for a great story, Finney's "Circus of Doctor Lao" for that sort of irreverence one can feel easy party to, "The Stars are the Styx," by Mister Sturgeon, for its magnificent sense of departure and aloneness, "The Man Who Tasted Ashes," by Mister Budrys, for similar reasons, "Great Mischief," by Josephine Pinkney, for its strange and wondrous atmosphere of futility, "The Black Flame," by Stanley Weinbaum, because it was one of the first good ones I ever read, "To Fell a Tree," by Robert F. Young, for its sense of perspective, "A Kind of Artistry," by Mister Aldiss, because of some almost-surrealistic effects that I wish I could learn to achieve, and "A Bad Day for Sales," by Mister Leiber, because it says everything it has to say so succinctly and so well.

All of John Collier, much of Kurt Vonnegut, Jr. and Philip K. Dick, and most of Philip José Farmer and a couple of L. Ron Hubbard have influenced me and taught me things I'm still not able to use the way I'd like to—but that's a big slice of my natal horoscope as a borderline S. L., if anyone's interested.

Reflecting on my own experience, for whatever it may be worth, out of thirty or so stories I have written three with which I've been somewhat pleased. In all three I now note that I spent more time on the first page than on any three subsequent pages, and more on the first sentence than on any normal page. In these (all of them over ten thousand words) I had a reasonably decent set of characters worked out before I wrote a word, and had only a sketchy plotline; this, I think, left the characters with room enough to move around on their own and develop accordingly. I feel that the momentum from a strong beginning can carry the reader past those early dead spots which are necessary for stating the problem and stuffing in the background. I now attempt to conceptualize my stories via character rather than gimmicks.

Ripeness is all. The quick brown fox jumped over the lazy dog… Ha!

A Word from Zelazny

This is the first non-fiction essay in which Zelazny ponders the writing process. Published in 1964, only two years into his professional writing career, it preceded publication of his novels. He was "somewhat pleased" with only 3 of his first 30 stories. Which three he meant is unknown, but among those first thirty were these four classics: "A Rose for Ecclesiastes," "The Graveyard Heart," "He Who Shapes," and "The Doors of His Face, the Lamps of His Mouth."

Notes

The peculiarities of a quick brown fox refers to the typing school sentence, "the quick brown fox jumps over a lazy dog," which uses the whole alphabet (a panagram). **Fen** is sf fandom jargon for more than one fan. **Marley was dead to begin with…** begins Charles Dickens' *A Christmas Carol*. **Queensberry** refers to the professional boxing rules formulated under supervision of John Sholto Douglas, 8th Marquess of Queensberry. **Marquis** is a noble rank above a count and below a duke, but Zelazny is referring to the Queensberry rules again, suggesting that a governing body (the Marquis) determines the rules in science fiction and fantasy. His implied use of the term **Marquis of Queensberry** is a common mistake because John Sholto Douglas was actually a *Marquess*—a British noble rank above an earl and below a duke. A **dybbuk** is a demon or spirit of a deceased person that possesses a living person, whereas *Golem* is the preferred term for an artificial object that has been animated by a spirit. **Armageddon** means the end of the world, such as after a nuclear holocaust; the Biblical Armageddon depicts the final battle between Good and Evil prior to the Day of Judgment. **S&S** means Sword & Sorcery fiction. **Antoine de Saint-Exupéry**, best known for *The Little Prince*, was a writer and aviator who wrote about flight.

"...AND CALL ME ROGER"
THE LITERARY LIFE OF
ROGER ZELAZNY, PART 1

by Christopher S. Kovacs, MD

Who was Roger Zelazny? How did he burst upon the sf scene in the early 1960s and rise to prominence so rapidly? What influenced his writing? What made him tick? How and when did he write his most memorable novels and stories?

In this collection Zelazny's words come from interviews, essays, and correspondence across his entire career, interwoven to tell his story *in his own words* as much as possible. The afterwords to the stories and poems reveal the short story writer.

This longer monograph focuses on his life, novels, and thoughts about the creative writing process.

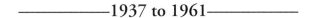

——————1937 to 1961——————

Formative Years

The descent of the blacksmith's hammer creates a shower of *zelazny*, bright and fiery bits of metal that fly off on impact. This is the ancestral Polish surname that Roger Joseph Zelazny inherited—strangely spelled and often mispronounced, it placed him last in the classroom roll-call and, much later, last on store bookshelves. Much like those *zelazny*, he later had a sudden, striking appearance as part of the "New Wave" of science fiction in the 1960s.

Zelazny was born in Euclid, Ohio, a suburb of Cleveland, on May 13, 1937, the only child of Irish-American Josephine Flora Sweet and Polish-born Joseph Frank Zelazny. In early interviews he said he was born in *Cleveland*, which explains references in official biographies and *Who's Who,* but his son confirmed Euclid.[1] He was born at home—not uncommon in 1937—and a very difficult delivery explained why he never had any siblings.[2]

The Zelazny family lived on East 250th Street in Euclid, on land that abutted large, undeveloped fields and woods where he used to walk. As he recalled (all quotations are from Zelazny unless otherwise specified), "I grew up in Euclid, Ohio—not a bad little town— beside Lake Erie. I liked the lake, I liked the libraries, and I liked Euclid Beach Park—which, alas, closed in 1969—a great amusement park with hair-raising roller coaster rides and a beautiful carousel…I liked bicycling, walking, and talking—about science fiction and any/ everything else—with my buddy Carl Yoke, chocolate milkshakes (they cost 25¢ then) from Moss Drug and Danishes from a little bakery next door to Moss'. There was also the Shore Theater where for a dime a week we saw Saturday matinees without number, and who knew how many Wednesday night double-features? Hell, I even remember a few stage shows.

"Through it all, I read and wrote and raked and burned autumn leaves—a smell one never forgets—mowed the lawn in the summertime—ditto—took out the trash, shoveled snow in the winter, and played with a black dog named Terry whom I'd raised from a pup and who lived for 16 years. I like to think I learned a lot about writing in those days, and that's what made it easier for me later on. Anyway, that's how it feels it worked."[3]

He attended Noble Elementary School from 1943–49, Shore Junior High School through 1952, and Euclid Senior High School through 1955. Carl Yoke was a good friend during this time, and he later went on to write a number of biographical and critical works about Zelazny. The two met in grade one at Noble but attended separate classes; however, from the second grade onward an alphabetized seating plan usually placed Zelazny directly behind Yoke in the same room. Both were avid readers and quickly outpaced their classmates. Their teachers sent these two advanced readers to the school library to read on their own during the regular reading class. Zelazny and Yoke usually read the same books and shared other interests. They gradually became close and lasting friends.[4,5]

Yoke later described Zelazny as a "bright but undisciplined student," and Zelazny himself confirmed that he disliked formal classroom studies.[6] In grade nine, he demonstrated his cheekiness and intolerance of authority when Mr. Wilson, the history teacher, punished him for interrupting yet another lecture with a dramatic sneeze. He ordered Zelazny to write a 500-word essay that night on the battle between the *Monitor* and the *Merrimac* and present it to the class the following day. And so the young Zelazny did, in a deadpan performance that began, "The *Monitor* sighted the *Merrimac* first and fired: bang, bang, bang, bang, bang, bang, bang..." About halfway through the paper, the *Merrimac* had its chance to fire back, but Zelazny's humorous recitation ended prematurely. The Principal turned his punishment into a 1,000-word formal essay and presentation. This time, Zelazny completed it properly and soberly—despite snickering from his classmates during the recitation. With the aid of Yoke he had his revenge at the end of grade nine when he sealed two dead fish into a desk in Mr. Wilson's home room. As Yoke recalled, "Roger had collected them, kept them outside until he could get them to school, and I had found a wrench to unbolt the desk."[5] The stench permeated the school into the summer months.[5] Although Yoke originally described that these events had taken place, in his introduction to this volume he describes the revenge as contemplated but not enacted. The adult Zelazny maintained a reputation for a love of humor, puns, and practical jokes.

Yoke described Zelazny as "too bright, too curious, and not athletic in high school. And, he was way too mature. He was very awkward in his movements, almost jerky, but he outgrew that."[7] Zelazny overcame his awkwardness by becoming adept at dance, fencing, karate, and numerous other martial arts, abilities that many of his characters displayed. Dance and martial arts continued to fascinate him as a way to create structure out of chaos, art out of movement.

First Attempt to Become a Writer

Zelazny was an avid reader of myths, folk and fairy tales; favorites included *Dr. Doolittle* and *Alice's Adventures in Wonderland*. He later recognized that it was the artwork that had attracted him to the books. "I recall the oddly simple drawings for the *Doctor Doolittle* books and the elegant, intriguing ones from *Alice*."[8] He read *Bullfinch's Mythol-*

ogy and other mythology texts an early age, compelled once again by the artwork.[8,9] "I recall a large volume I read when I was 10 or 11, recounting the story of the Ring of the Nibelungs, color plates throughout, including a striking Rhine Maiden; also Bullfinch's *Tales of Charlemagne*, with its N. C. Wyeth plates."[8] Mythology dominates many of his best-known works. "I liked mythology. At first I read for story value rather than for learning about ancient religions or philosophy. But later on I went for that sort of thing too. I just happened to discover mythology when I was young, and it informed my thinking."[10] He didn't discover science fiction until he was about 11, when he read *The Angry Planet* by John Keir Cross. After that he tried to read all of the science fiction that he could find in the library or borrow from friends.

Yoke noted that Zelazny also became interested in "chess…flying saucers, the occult, astral projection and yoga" as well as "hypnotism…Rosicrucianism and other exotic topics." This also meant that he read "book after book on these subjects with amazing objectivity."[5,11] Attempting to practice some of what he'd learned, Zelazny hypnotized a girl in speech class and was blamed later when she kept falling asleep.[12] First a magician and later a spiritualist singled him out of crowds to receive a spiritual message. These uncanny coincidences troubled his friend Yoke.[5] Zelazny's fascination with the occult eventually led him to believe that he could survive death. As Yoke described, "Roger believed that he could, or had, project astrally. I never succeeded at this. For him, this confirmed another kind of reality so that consciousness might indeed survive the death of the physical body. Roger's genius was being able to take this and other ideas like it and turn them into stories. Death was always a concern for us and some believable answer for it was welcome."[5] Later, Gerald Hausman and other friends also noted Zelazny's fascination with mysticism and his beliefs about spiritual survival after death.

Although he was curious about many things, Zelazny wanted to be a writer since "I was about six years old. And I read stories and decided I would have done different things with the characters. One day I realized that 'Hey, I could do this,' so I tried and I've been doing it ever since."[13] His parents encouraged him. His mother was interested in literature and had written an unpublished mystery novel. His father gave him a typewriter—an upright Royal with an Elite typeface, purchased for about $5 (about $48 in 2008 dollars)—when he was 11. He taught himself to type and kept this machine in his office for decades. He read books about preparing manuscripts and books about creative writing. He wrote his first stories, submitting them to the many science fiction magazines that existed at the time. His very first submission was a Bradburyesque piece about Mars—"Dust" was one word in the title that he was able to recall.[14] He naïvely submitted it to John W. Campbell at *Astounding Science Fiction.* He later realized that Campbell never liked or published any stories by Ray Bradbury, and Campbell certainly would not have been interested in anything *Bradburyesque.*

As each story was rejected—and they all were—he sent it on to the next magazine on a list that he had assembled, and thus by age 15 he collected some hundred and fifty rejection slips. How many stories were actually written in this first phase of his self-training in writing is uncertain. In a 1973 *Writer's Voice* interview he said that 150 was the total number of rejection slips accrued after submitting each story to multiple magazines.[15] But in his 1969 essay in *Worlds of If* he claimed to have written "about two hundred stories, and every one of them was rejected."[16]

In addition to submitting stories to professional magazines, during junior and senior high school Zelazny wrote a series of humorous short stories about a pair of hapless aliens, Zlaz and Yok (named for Zelazny and Carl Yoke). These stories began with Zelazny's revoltingly funny poem, "The Yoke Monster." Yoke responded by writing a "funny but meaner and nastier" piece entitled "The Zelazny Monster."[5]

Thus began their story writing competition, cementing a friendship that endured more than fifty years. The budding writers created an extensive backstory and mythology of this shared universe and the two monsters ("mon"), now renamed Yok and Zlaz. Collectively entitled *The Record*, word play and humor characterized these stories. Carl Yoke's introduction to this volume provides more details about the two main characters and the plots of a few of these lost tales. The exact number written is uncertain but was likely fewer than ten.[17] "Studies in Saviory" was the last of Zelazny's contributions for *The Record* and the only one known to survive, thanks to Carl Yoke. Zelazny read it aloud to Yoke in 1964 or 1965 at Yoke's apartment in Wickliffe, to the dismay of Yoke's wife, who wanted Zelazny to shut up so that she could get dinner on the table.[18] However, the story's writing style is very unlike what Zelazny was writing at the time, which suggests that it may have been written much earlier, or that Zelazny deliberately evoked his earlier style in this last Zlaz/Yok tale.

None of the stories from *The Record* were ever submitted for publication, but decades later the stories and characters remained important to both Zelazny and Yoke. "We talked a lot about *The Record* and evolved its world accordingly. It was like we were characters in a meta-story who knew about *The Record* stories…As recently as the last letter I got from Roger [before he died in 1995], they often ended with such [Zlaz and Yok] salutations as 'Stay evil' or 'All evils' or 'Zlaz.' And our phone calls always began and were punctuated with an 'Aargh, mon,' or just 'Aargh.' So the Yok and Zlaz characters were our alter egos."[17]

Zelazny's early involvement in fandom included attending the 1955 World Science Fiction Convention in Cleveland, where he met Harlan Ellison. They had grown up about twenty-five miles from each other in Ohio (Zelazny in Euclid; Ellison in Painesville until 1949 and then Cleveland).[19] The two met again at the 1966 Worldcon in Cleveland—on the occasion of Zelazny's first Hugo Award—and became lasting friends.

Zelazny helped edit Warren Dennis's fanzine, *Thurban I*, which featured part one of his short story "Conditional Benefit" in 1953. This is the oldest surviving piece of Zelazny's fiction. Dennis ran out of funds and paper to print all of "Conditional Benefit," so the second part was scheduled for the next issue. Unfortunately, Dennis was drafted, the next issue was never published, and the second half of the manuscript was lost because Zelazny hadn't kept a copy. He did say in a 1978 interview, "I had a few things in fanzines in the early 50's, actually."[20] In a 1964 interview he wrote, "My first story, back in the elder world, appeared in a fanzine, as did my second, as did…"[21] However, "Conditional Benefit" is the only known Zelazny story, poem, or letter to appear in a 1950s fanzine.

Early Literary Influences

Three high school teachers had a significant influence on Zelazny's decision to become a writer.

Ruby Olson organized the Creative Writing Club at which five select students (including Zelazny and Yoke) discussed literature and their own writing efforts. Olson encouraged Zelazny to write; he later dedicated his short story collection *The Last Defender of Camelot* and his poetry collection *When Pussywillows Last in the Catyard Bloomed* to her. He explained, "I owe a debt to an English teacher I once had named Ruby Olson. She was a fine woman who knew a lot about writing, and she picked out about five kids who she thought showed some promise and tried to nurture this."[16]

For their eleventh-grade journalism class, Zelazny and Yoke created two mock newspapers, *The Martian Chronicle* and *The Venusian Herald*. The papers included humorous accounts of imagined societies on those planets, complete with stories that resembled the Zlaz and Yok tales in *The Record*.[5,22] The mock newspapers impressed their teacher Myron Gordon, who picked Zelazny and Yoke to staff the school newspaper, *The Survey*. Zelazny was editor-in-chief of *The Survey* during his senior year of 1954–55, and this experience stoked his desire to see his own works in print.[23]

Harold Blackburn was an English teacher who introduced Zelazny to Ernest Hemingway's works and to the classics. Blackburn recommended three novels that he felt covered all of human experience and all of the literary devices and approaches—*War and Peace* [Tolstoy], *Ulysses* [Joyce], and *Remembrance of Things Past* [Proust]. Zelazny read these, numbering them among his favorites, and afterwards found himself comparing new readings to these paradigms.[24]

Zelazny had other literary influences, including Elizabethan and Jacobean theater; poets Hart Crane, Dylan Thomas, George Seferis and Rainier Maria Rilke; and the writers Saint-Exupéry, Thomas Wolfe, Malcolm Lowry, John Updike, and Thomas Mann.[25]

Other early influences included the comic books and radio and TV programs that Zelazny and Yoke both enjoyed. Favorites ranged from *Pogo, L'il Abner, Popeye* and *Prince Valiant* to *Captain Midnight, The Green Hornet, Sam Spade* and *The Shadow*, and also *Tarzan, Flash Gordon* and *Buck Rogers*. It was the "quirky and offbeat illustrations" as well as the adventure stories that attracted him to comic books in particular. "I remember leafing through comic books involving the Human Torch and Submariner, and the Sunday funnies—*Abbie 'N' Slats, Captain Easy, Terry and the Pirates, Smilin' Jack, Alley Oop, Prince Valiant, Little Orphan Annie*. I always wanted more of old Groggins, the Dragon Lady, Big Stoop, Punjab, The Asp, and Evil Eye Fleagle. Not to mention more aerial combat, dinosaurs, and battle scenes. These were the sorts of things that encouraged me to read at an early age."[8] These influences manifested in later writing from the comic book-like superheroes of "The Furies" to Croyd Crenson of the *Wild Cards* stories, from the multi-talented and mysterious Kalifriki of the Thread to the nameless secret agent of *My Name Is Legion*. Zelazny maintained an interest in comic books as an adult, with Neil Gaiman's *Sandman* and *Books of Magic* and John Ostrander's *Grimjack* becoming favorites in the 1980s. His fascination with the art of the fantastic—viewed in the mythology texts and comic books—influenced his distinctive writing style, which became rich in imagery as well as metaphor and allusion.

First Sale; Switch from Prose to Poetry

In 1954, Zelazny's writing efforts led to some early successes. *Eucuyo*, the Euclid high school literary magazine, published three of his works—the poem "Diet," and the short stories "Mr. Fuller's Revolt" and "And the Darkness is Harsh." He went on to make his first professional sale of "Mr. Fuller's Revolt" to the journal *Literary Cavalcade*, earning $25 (about $190 in 2008 dollars), and it appeared in the October 1954 issue. Two more works—the poem "Slush, Slush, Slush" and the short story "Youth Eternal"—appeared in *Eucuyo* in 1955. At the same time, he grew frustrated with the accumulated 150+ rejection slips from the prose he'd submitted to the sf magazines, and he decided to switch to writing poetry. He considered poetry to be the highest form of writing and that he should aspire to create it. He kept this mindset all his life, but practical concerns drove him back to a life of prose.

When he stopped submitting manuscripts to the sf magazines in 1954, he stopped reading science fiction completely. "I read sf in great quantity since I was 11 years old. I read back through the 30's, 40's and 50's. [But] in about 1954, I stopped reading sf completely. Seven years went by."[26] He didn't resume until he obtained his Master's degree from Columbia University.

Dick Covert was a high school friend who, together with Carl Yoke, provided feedback on Zelazny's stories and encouraged him to keep writing. Ron Dobler was another friend who influenced his writing, in this case by encouraging Zelazny to write poetry instead of prose. Zelazny later dedicated the poetry collection *To Spin Is Miracle*

Cat to "Jeanne and Ron Dobler." He maintained contact with all three of these friends during his professional career.[23]

Influence of Fencing and Martial Arts

Through his friendship with Ron Dobler, Zelazny became interested in swordplay and martial arts. Training in these areas helped him lose his physical awkwardness and gain poise and balance. He went on to fence for four years in college, taking varsity letters in each of his sophomore, junior and senior years. He also captained the *épée* squad during his final two years. "I'd taken fencing in lieu of regular Phys Ed, as I couldn't stand team sports."[27] He developed expertise in several martial arts (judo, aikido, karate, among others), and in turn, many of his characters adeptly employed fencing or martial arts moves in dispatching their opponents. The descriptions of physical encounters between characters are believable and accurate because he knew what he was writing about. He later pointed out that "all of the lengthier dueling sequences in the Amber books are properly choreographed for a rapier class weapon, rather on the heavy side, as the Amberites have the extra strength to wield such a blade well."[28] The red-haired character of Luke from the later Amber novels owes much of his description and attributes to Zelazny's old friend Dobler, who'd gotten him started in martial arts.[24]

College Education in Psychology and Literature

From 1955–59 Zelazny attended Western Reserve University in Cleveland, Ohio (now part of Case Western Reserve). The nature of the human mind fascinated him, and this prompted him to major in psychology. He also worked part-time in a psychology laboratory, doing experiments that included running rats through mazes. Through his interactions with professors who specialized in psychiatric theory, he was exposed to the works of Freud, Jung and others. This influence is evident in many of his works, most notably the award-winning novella "He Who Shapes," which was later expanded into the novel *The Dream Master*. Other Zelazny works feature realistic psychologists and psychiatrists as characters or competently explore psychological motivations of characters (e.g., "The Long Sleep" and "Home is the Hangman"). He was quite aware that this training influenced his writing. "As an undergraduate, I'd been a psychology major. I only switched to literature at the last minute—as a graduate student. My background, in that sense, was in the behavioral sciences. That would show up in my early novels, such as *The Dream Master*, where my main character is a psychiatrist."[29]

He changed his major to English during his junior year because he realized that he didn't want his career to involve teaching psychology, and he was bored with running rats through mazes. A change in the Department's faculty also meant more professors who wanted to study those rats and fewer professors who were interested in discussing the theories of Jung and Freud. As Zelazny put it, he got out because he wouldn't enjoy "testing the fortitude of small rodents or working at the clinical level" and "it never mattered too much what I got my degree in, as long as I learned as much as I could."[30] His objective was to become a writer, and he wanted to learn as much as possible in a wide variety of subjects, because he believed that a broad base of knowledge would be a critical foundation for his own writing. To broaden his learning, he opted to audit numerous courses without taking the exams or writing the papers, thereby enriching his experience in diverse subjects. A course titled "Magic, the Devil and Witchcraft" exposed him to Sir James Frazer's seminal work *The Golden Bough* and gave him a more structured approach to the mythology that fascinated him. On the downside, his habit of auditing courses led him to be recorded as having failed an accounting course.[12] He graduated in 1959 with a BA in English Literature, with minors in Psychology and Comparative Literature.[31]

Zelazny's training at Western Reserve and the BA misled others to conclude that he studied creative writing while in college and thereby became a writer. In a 1986 interview, he explained that he did not take *any* creative writing courses in college. "I always felt I'd rather spend my time studying literature itself, and that I could teach myself the technical and mechanical aspects of writing. So I stayed away from that type of course. I don't have any strong feelings against it; I have taught at writing workshops and seminars. But it seems to me that a person who's willing to write is *going* to write."[29]

Erstwhile Poet and *Chisel in the Sky*

To Zelazny, poetry was the highest form of wordcraft and what he most wanted to write professionally. His friends and fellow writers knew this—after Zelazny's death in 1995, noted friend and colleague George R. R. Martin recalled, "He was a poet, first, last, always," and Jack Williamson wrote a story that speculated on why the young Zelazny had given up poetry for science fiction prose.[32,33] During the interval from 1956 through 1961 Zelazny wrote "nothing but poetry—incredible amounts of it, mostly bad, but improving somewhat as time went on."[24] It couldn't have been all bad because he won Western Reserve's Finley Foster Poetry Prize for "Southern Cross" in 1957. His poem "The Man Without a Shadow" and the short story "The Outward Sign" appeared in Western Reserve's literary publication *Skyline* in 1958. The next year, he won the Finley Foster Poetry Prize *again* for his poem "Decade Plus One of Roses" (*Skyline,* 1959). Noted poet (Hazel) Collister Hutchison praised this poem, adding that she felt that "the author might amount to something as a writer one day if he applied himself."[34] Zelazny also won the Holden essay award, given since 1899, for a term paper on Chaucer. These early milestones inspired confidence in the fledgling writer. Years later, he showed that these awards retained significance for him when he listed them among the Hugo and Nebula awards in his *vita brevis* (resumé).

Buoyed by the poetry distinctions, around 1960 he assembled an extensive manuscript of more than sixty poems, *Chisel in the Sky,* for the Yale Younger Poets Competition. He didn't win and was quite discouraged by this. A few of the poems in that manuscript were later quoted in his early short stories—notably "The Graveyard Heart"—and eventually published in his poetry collections *Poems, When Pussywillows Last in the Catyard Bloomed*, and *To Spin Is Miracle Cat.* A copy of *Chisel in the Sky* remained in Carl Yoke's possession, enabling its publication at last in this collection.[6] Zelazny's experience with writing poetry—and in particular, the use of allusions, metaphors and wordplay—had a noticeable impact on his prose style, leading many fans and critics to later describe him as a true "prose poet."

During this interval Zelazny was most active in fencing. He also studied judo for two years under Bill Gavel, a former Marine who taught not just that sport but other practical fighting pointers such as "crushing larynxes, breaking necks and spines."[27] Zelazny was not ranked during this time because Gavel did not offer belt tests.

University Education in Elizabethan and Jacobean Drama

From 1959–60, Zelazny attended Columbia University for graduate work and specialized in Elizabethan and Jacobean drama. Repeating his undergraduate pattern, he took no creative writing courses. His Master's Thesis focused on Cyril Tourneur's *The Revenger's Tragedy*, and he later based the lengthy 1966 tale "Nine Starships Waiting" on that play. He continued to audit courses in order to get the broad exposure to knowledge that he felt might help him as a writer; this approach was echoed later in his professional writing career by his systematic effort to read broadly and to continually update his background knowledge. He completed his required course work and thesis that first year, but his supervisor declined to submit the thesis in time for him to graduate, and his status remained in limbo for months. In a monograph written by Carl Yoke, the event is described as a "personality conflict" with the unnamed supervisor.[6]

While awaiting the eventual submission of the thesis and the opportunity to write his comprehensive exams, Zelazny joined the 137th Artillery Battalion of the Ohio National Guard in 1960 and did basic training at Fort Knox. This was followed by a six month tour of duty spent largely in Texas and which included missile training at Fort Bliss, where most of his active duty was spent.[31] With the 112th Engineer's Battalion he learned to drive an armored vehicle launch bridge. He served his guard obligation part-time from 1960–63 with the Ohio National Guard, and then re-enlisted with the Army National Reserve for 1963–1966. His experience with armored vehicles and weaponry informed many later works, including *Damnation Alley*.

During his time at Columbia, he was active in other areas and continued his lifelong interest in martial arts. He studied judo again and was ranked at green belt. He studied karate in the military but was not ranked. He also availed himself of the social and cultural opportunities in New York, taking particular interest in the folk music, clubs, and coffee houses of Greenwich Village. There he met and fell in love with folk singer Hedy West, who became well known for composing the song "500 Miles"—later covered by *The Kingston Trio, The Highwaymen, and Peter, Paul, and Mary*. West and Zelazny were engaged for six months. He brought her to Euclid to meet his parents, but his mother didn't approve of the relationship, considering West "too fast" for her son.[35] The two broke up for reasons reflected in the story "A Rose for Ecclesiastes" and alluded to in a published reply to a fan about the motivations of the character Gallinger (see the Notes for that story).[35,36]

His fascination with mythology persisted. He began reading other secondary works about the subject and continued to do so through his professional career. In addition to *The Golden Bough*, titles included the multi-volume *The Masks of God* by Joseph Campbell, *The Greek Myths* by Robert Graves, and, much later, *Hamlet's Mill* by Giorgio de Santillana.

In 1961, he resolved his differences with his supervisor and resubmitted his M.A. thesis, "Two Traditions and Cyril Tourneur: An Examination of Morality and Humor Comedy Conventions in 'The Revenger's Tragedy'."[37] He received an honors grade for it and later passed his comprehensive exams. He graduated in May 1962 with an M.A from Columbia in English and Comparative Literature, with the area of concentration being dramatic literature.[31]

—————————1962—————————

Disgruntled Poet and Second Attempt to Become a Writer

Over the winter of 1961–62, while awaiting the outcome of his thesis resubmission, Zelazny soberly realized that making a living as a poet was an unrealistic dream. "Only Robert Frost and Carl Sandburg were making their livings writing poetry whereas numerous other authors were doing well under muses less comely. The writing was there on the washroom wall."[24] He still very much wanted to be a writer, so he finally returned to writing short stories. Abandoning the ideal of poetry was the first of several compromises that he deemed necessary to have a financially viable career as a writer. He later declared himself to be "a disgruntled poet" over his failure to succeed in his preferred medium: "I had to strike a balance between the commercial and the artistic—that is why I settled on sf—but I wish I were a poet. Yes."[25] He never stopped writing poetry—many of his most notable stories and novels featured original poems, and he eventually published four collections of poetry (two books and two chapbooks). Many of his characters—most notably Gallinger in "A Rose for Ecclesiastes" and Corwin of the Amber novels—were poets themselves, or at least capable of quoting an appropriate verse to fit the moment. But the bulk of poetry included in this collection was written prior to the end of 1961, when Zelazny abandoned poetry as his literary career.

Inspired by the anguish and circumstances that prompted his breakup with Hedy West, the next story he wrote was the emotionally charged "A Rose for Ecclesiastes" in October 1961. In that tale, the arrogant poet Michael Gallinger is humbled and reshaped by his experiences: he falls in love with a Martian woman, but she wants neither him nor the child that they unexpectedly conceive together; convinced by his inspired preaching, the Martian matriarchy votes to permit survival of their race through interbreeding with humans. In retrospect, readers might imagine that this classic story stood out in the slush pile and generated his first sale and instant recognition—however, he chose not to submit it. The reasons for that decision are detailed in the afterword to the story, but in brief he felt that it was too outdated because it portrayed a romantic, scientifically impossible vision of Mars. "The day for this sort of story is over. There is no breathable atmosphere, no people, and so forth on Mars—but I wanted to write Space Opera. I felt if I didn't write it then, I'd never write it. After another such story ["The Doors of His Face, the Lamps of His Mouth"], I moved out of the solar system."[26] After writing "A Rose for Ecclesiastes" in part for his own catharsis, he did not start any other stories for some months.

Zelazny filed for unemployment while writing "A Rose for Ecclesiastes" and looked about for work. "I applied for teaching jobs all over Ohio then, but things were tight and no offers came in."[24] In February 1962, an offer came through just when he had resigned himself to the belief that there were no jobs to be found but that unemployment at least meant he would be free to write. He hired on with the Social Security Administration in Cleveland as a claims representative and was sent to Dayton, Ohio, for training.

The day job took up much of his time, but he began using his evenings to write, in a second serious attempt to become a professional writer. Because he hadn't read science fiction during his time in college, he picked up copies of sf novels and magazines to familiarize himself with the sort of stories currently on sale. "It hadn't changed much since I'd been away. So I started writing several stories a week."[30]

He decided to try science fiction again because "Damon Knight, in his book *In Search of Wonder* [1956], mentioned that science fiction was a good area for a new writer to try in order to break into the writing game. I took his advice, because I had read so much in the area that I thought I knew it pretty well. It worked."[25] However, the science fiction that he knew best was from the 1930s through 1950s, and he knew that he shouldn't attempt to emulate stories from that era. "My grounding was in the older stories, such as Edgar Rice Burroughs. But the standard plots in the earlier stories couldn't come to pass in the light of scientific progress."[26]

He tried to write a story every two to three days and to submit each in turn to every magazine on the market, using his comprehensive checklist. In this fashion he obtained another "couple dozen or so" rejection slips over the first month and became frustrated again.

He then assembled the rejected works and decided to read them objectively to see what he was doing wrong and learn from his mistakes. He realized that he was writing down to the reader: "I was being a little too explicit, almost patronizing, in the way I explained every little detail...I decided to eliminate everything I considered condescending in my writing and to speak to the reader just as if he were a person with me in the room, who seemed to be nodding when I was saying something to him."[15] "I resolved thereafter to treat the reader as I would be treated myself, to avoid the unnecessarily explicit, to use more indirection with respect to character and motivation, to draw myself up short whenever I felt the tendency to go on talking once a thing had been shown."[38]

This re-evaluation of his writing quickly led, on March 28, 1962, to his first acceptance letter from a professional science fiction magazine for "Passion Play" (see afterword to that story). Editor Cele Goldsmith of *Fantastic* and *Amazing* picked him out of the slush pile just six weeks after he had started to seriously write and submit stories—an interval which most aspiring writers would consider to be quite short. That momentous first acceptance letter was rather formal—"Thank you for giving us the opportunity to consider your story 'Passion Play.' We would like to purchase it for publication in a future issue of *Amazing Stories*. If you will sign and return one copy of the enclosed contract, our check will follow shortly. When we know in what issue it will appear, we'll drop you a line."[39]

After another two or three rejection slips, he went on to sell 17 stories that year—most of them to Goldsmith—marking the true start of his professional writing career. His second sale was the first Dilvish tale, "Passage to Dilfar," but Goldsmith delayed publishing it.[10] She remarked, "You're probably aware that this story is begging for a series. If you didn't have this in mind, perhaps you'll think of doing it now and let us see the results."[40] And thus the Dilvish series was born.

None of the early rejected stories leading up to 1962 remain, because he used the reverse sides of rejected manuscripts as scratch paper to write the first drafts of new stories.[15] Archived correspondence indicates the existence of two unknown and presumably lost stories: *Galaxy*'s Editor Frederik Pohl rejected "Notes on the Revolution" in 1963, and *The Magazine of Fantasy & Science Fiction*'s Editor Avram Davidson rejected the "The Prince & the Gopher" in 1962–63.[41,42] This collection does include previously unpublished stories from the later 1960s, which were donated to the Archives of Syracuse University in a folder labeled "Writings 1965–1968."

Initial Splash Captures Notice

July 1962 marked the start of Zelazny's professional career with the near-simultaneous appearance of "Passion Play" in the August issue of *Amazing* and "Horseman!" in the August issue of *Fantastic*. *Amazing* actually reached the newsstands on July 10, while *Fantastic* appeared nine days later.[43] His characteristic style attracted instant notice—short, clipped sentences; poetic description and turns of phrase; bold use of metaphor and allusion.[44] He was initially so prolific that Cele Goldsmith created the "way out choice" pseudonym Harrison Denmark to enable simultaneous publication of his work in both *Amazing* and *Fantastic*.[45] Readers of those magazines wondered whether "Roger Zelazny" was a house name used by multiple writers, an artifice which explained the sudden but frequent appearance of the name in the sf magazines. Goldsmith dispelled that myth by publishing Zelazny's short autobiographical essay in the December 1962 issue of *Amazing*—just *four months* after the appearance of his first two sf stories. "I was born in Cleveland, and began reading sf when I began reading (I still have many of my battered issues of *Captain Future*)..."[46]

While many early fan letters praised Zelazny's work, there were other readers who were frustrated by his experimentation with storytelling technique and who noted the similar styles of "Harrison Denmark" and Zelazny: "Up to now everything I read by Roger Zelazny was confusing, nonsensical strings of words..." (*Fantastic*, April 1963); "The thing was all but incomprehensible!" (*Fantastic*, May 1963); "I still fail to see the usefulness of Roger Zelazny's writing. It is offbeat, and it is hard to discover exactly what this author is trying to put forth." (*Amazing*, March 1963); "You may take that nauseating old Harrison Denmark, rude stark Roger Zelazny..." (*Amazing*, November 1963). These comments were evidently in the minority, because Cele Goldsmith remarked in the March 1963 issue of *Amazing* that "most readers seem to like Zelazny." Her comment was soon vindicated by Zelazny's award nominations, by invitations for him to be Guest of Honor at science fiction conventions, and by the publication of "A Rose for Ecclesiastes" in the November 1963 issue of *The Magazine of Fantasy & Science Fiction*.

—————1963–1964————

Rapid Rise to Prominence in the Field

By the summer of 1963, *less than a year* after the appearance of his first sf story, Zelazny's byline was already so prominent that his name appeared on the list of notable authors whose opinions were solicited for a questionnaire organized by Lloyd Biggle, Jr. The collective responses to that questionnaire appeared in three issues of the *Double:Bill* fanzine from October 1963 through June 1964 and was later separately published in 1969 as *Lloyd Biggle, Jr.'s The Double:Bill Symposium*. Other authors included Isaac Asimov, Poul Anderson, Ray Bradbury, Harlan Ellison, Jack Williamson, Arthur C. Clarke, and Robert Silverberg. When asked why he chose to write sf, Zelazny replied, "SF's subject can be anything, set anywhere, in or out of time and space. I like that notion; I like it a lot because it involves a premise of sorts to the effect that anything *might* be possible. It also indicates that any angle of vision might be brought into play in regarding a particular situation. In operation, this demonstrates hitherto unexplored/unexploited areas of the human condition—mainly by confronting people with possible, eccentric happenings. This, in my opinion, is sufficient justification for its existence as an independent class of writing."[21]

"A Rose for Ecclesiastes"

Zelazny wrote this work, arguably his best, in October 1961 but chose not to submit it. The myth arose that this story was written a year or two prior to Zelazny's first sale and that Zelazny reluctantly submitted it for publication only after becoming a well established, published author. In fact, Zelazny wrote "A Rose for Ecclesiastes" in October 1961 and made his first sale for "Passion Play" less than five months later, in March 1962. He didn't shelve this manuscript for too long, because "A Rose for Ecclesiastes" was accepted for publication on July 7, 1962, *prior* to the appearance in the August *Amazing* of his first story, "Passion Play."

Whether it was first rejected by other magazines is uncertain, but an undated rejection note from *Galaxy* Editor Frederik Pohl sounds suspicious: "You write well, but I'm afraid this seemed too ornate for its subject matter. Something less complex?"[47]

Zelazny was still an unpublished, unknown author when Avram Davidson purchased this story for *The Magazine of Fantasy & Science Fiction*, in July 1962. It is worth quoting the effusive acceptance letter in its entirety. "We are taking your novelet, 'A Rose for Ecclesiastes' (a minor point: to avoid inapplicable comparison with *A Canticle for Leibowitz*, would you consider, 'For Ecclesiastes: A Rose'…?). In a short while you'll be getting the contract. I will appreciate your sending me some bio- and biblio-data. You have done a difficult and rare thing—taken a much-used (and a much-abused) theme, and done a new and good thing with it. All the equipment for cliché and bathos is in your story—the dying race, the beautiful priestess who dared, interplanetary miscegenation, etc.—but you have avoided absolutely any trace of either cliché or bathos. I salute you. And I wish to see more. It has occurred to me that the parallel with Miller's title was deliberate. If you wish the title to remain as is, it will. Prosper and flourish. And send us more, send us more. —Avram Davidson."[48]

Davidson recognized the significance of the story, selected it to be a cover story for a future issue, and commissioned Hannes Bok to create the painting. This is why almost a year and a half elapsed before the story appeared in the November 1963 issue.

The publication of "A Rose for Ecclesiastes" prompted praise and attention from fans and critics, something that the shy and self-deprecating Zelazny was uncertain how to handle. Responding to one effusive editorial about that story, he wrote, "Kind words and certain beverages make me feel Real Fine and give me hangovers if I have too many of them. I always was something of a word-drunk, I'll admit that—especially so with those I mix myself—and some of the potent ones you poured in your editorial just about have me ready for KWA (Kind Words Anonymous). In this condition, I am somewhat at a loss for words, except to meditate softly, but aloud, that it is a wild and pilose thing to be overrated, and thanx."[49]

Life Events Influence His Writing

By 1963 Zelazny had secured a part-time job teaching English at Fenn College (now Cleveland State), but he quickly gave this up because it interfered with his full-time job and his writing—and he'd discovered to his surprise that he disliked teaching anyway. His life prospects were looking up: his stories were selling readily, he had hopes of eventually leaving the Social Security Administration for full-time writing, and romance had blossomed once more: he was engaged for a second time, now to Sharon Steberl.

Unfortunately, life events took a sudden, serious downturn in the fall of 1964, events that had a profound and lasting effect on his psyche and his writing. On September 27, Zelazny and his new fiancée were involved in a near head-on collision with another vehicle. A one-way stretch of northbound State Route 13 outside of Mansfield, Ohio, became a two-way stretch of road, but on this rainy day Zelazny misread it as one-way as he pulled out to pass another vehicle. Zelazny's head struck the rear view mirror of his GTO convertible, and he suffered loss of consciousness, facial lacerations and a chipped tooth. Steberl was very seriously injured and hospitalized for six weeks with a broken pelvis and other internal injuries.[7,50,51] A transcription of a recorded interview[52] reported her injuries as a minor broken bone in "the heel," when in fact she had suffered a broken pelvis or hip. Their planned October wedding had to be delayed. Zelazny was involved in other motor vehicle accidents or near-misses as driver, pedestrian, and witness; some of these events are described later in this monograph or in the relevant story notes. These experiences heavily influenced his writing, as shown by such stories as "Devil Car," "Auto-Da-Fé," "He Who Shapes," "Passion Play," *Damnation Alley* and *Nine Princes in Amber.*

While Steberl was still recuperating from the accident, his father, Joseph Zelazny died unexpectedly from a heart attack on November 25, 1964, only a day or two after a routine checkup with the doctor had resulted in a clean bill of health.[1] Zelazny considered this the blackest, most wretched day of his life. As one way of dealing with his pain, he forced himself to write and didn't leave the typewriter until he had created three new stories: "Divine Madness," "Comes Now the Power," and "But Not the Herald."

While still mourning his father, Zelazny married Sharon Steberl on December 5, 1964. They moved to Wickliffe, Ohio, near where Carl Yoke had an apartment. Yoke described the marriage as short and unhappy. Sharon was deeply traumatized and depressed by the accident, and Yoke recalled being told that her injuries had rendered her unable to have children.[7] Yoke wrote that Zelazny "felt awful about the accident. But he couldn't undo it. He never would have consciously hurt anyone, and the accident left him neck deep in guilt."[22] Zelazny wanted his wife to have counseling, but she did not; they became frustrated and openly angry with each other and separated by late summer 1965.[7]

Early Life as a Professional Writer

In this early writing phase, Zelazny deliberately chose to write stories that required him to focus on his weaknesses, rather than relying on his strengths. "When I decide to write a story I make a quick mental checksheet of all the items I consider myself capable of handling with impunity; I then think about the debit entries and consider the best ways to cover the majority—and I always pick one, usually the one I deem my most egregious current failing, and I force myself to write it through."[21] He'd focus on character in one story; plot or setting in another; variations on narrative voice in others. This effort continued throughout his professional writing career; he always felt that he was still learning the storytelling art, and he sought to strengthen his weaker aspects and experiment with style in every story or novel. Whenever he encountered an unusual approach to storytelling used in other genres, he tried it himself.

Zelazny deliberately stayed with the short story, gradually working up to novelette and novella length as his confidence increased. He'd reasoned that numerous stories could be written, rejected and learned from in a short period of time; however, writing longer pieces or a novel meant a much longer time invested for something that might not sell. "If a short story is bad it's a lot less wasted time than if a novel is bad…each short story is a separate educational experience. It might be argued that you're permitted more mistakes in a novel, but the argument might be effectively countered by the reply that if you make one bad mistake in a short story you know it, because the story won't sell—whereas, if you write one semi-good novel, and succeed in selling it, you have logged the sale on your strong points, and your weaknesses remain uncorrected."[21]

SF Authors Who Influenced Zelazny

In addition to literary influences from Hemingway to Elizabethan drama to *The Shadow*, the notes that accompany individual stories in this collection reveal the importance of *Faust, The Divine Comedy, The Golden Bough,* works of Tolstoy and Shakespeare, and other works which inspired Zelazny during his formative years. In an early interview he named the science fiction and fantasy authors who had influenced him. "Stanley Weinbaum was my favorite science fiction writer at first; then came Heinlein; when I got a little bit over him, I decided it was Sturgeon I liked best, I liked some of Ray Bradbury's stuff."[16] He declared Theodore Sturgeon to be "the greatest science fiction writer alive today" and acknowledged that "he has doubtless influenced me."[25] He later added Philip José Farmer, Philip Dick, Samuel R. Delany, Henry Kuttner and Jack Vance to his list of favorites for their "originality and narrative talent."[29,53,54] He also admired L. Sprague de Camp's ability to create convincingly realistic worlds, his witty humor, and his propensity to do the unexpected: "If you should visit one of his worlds and there happens to be a rug around, whatever you do, don't stand on it... If you expect it to be pulled out from under you, it will fly away with you instead."[55] In later interviews, he declined to answer questions about literary influences, in part because it was a hackneyed and unimaginative question on a par with the obligatory "where do you get your ideas?"

Zelazny remarked that Stanley Weinbaum's "characterization was something special. Just the way he treated man-woman relationships wasn't like science fiction stories prior to that time. Weinbaum had witty people, and his women were real people as well as his men; I thought that was important. Some of his ideas were exciting, too; I must have read *A Martian Odyssey* six or seven times. *The Black Flame* had one of the few female central characters that I thought was handled well; I haven't read it for many years now, but it impressed me."[16]

Henry Kuttner's work particularly impressed Zelazny because "I could read different stories by him and he sounded differently in each—one time it might be a fantasy, colorful in an A. Merritt sort of way, another it might be something partaking of a lean, hardboiled detective sort of prose. Even then, I wanted to write, and I decided then that when I did it would be something of a virtue to possess that sort of versatility. So I worked at it, trying to change the ways I used words to fit the mood of the piece and the sorts of things I was describing in the different stories I tried telling. Later, Theodore Sturgeon paid me the compliment of acknowledging that I might have succeeded when he said to me, 'You know, Zelazny, you don't have one style. You have many.'"[56]

At the time, Zelazny did not know that the Kuttner byline was often an unacknowledged collaboration between Kuttner and his wife, C. L. Moore, which accounted in part for the different voices and styles among Kuttner's titles. He considered Kuttner's novel *The Dark World* to be among his all-time favorites; ironically, this novel was written almost entirely by C. L. Moore. However, the apparent versatility that Kuttner possessed was something that Zelazny continued to strive for, and achieve—to the annoyance of some of his readers who wanted him to have one voice, not many. The fan mail requested stories only in the manner of "A Rose for Ecclesiastes," or only in the mode of the Amber novels, and so on. But Zelazny had no interest in being limited to one voice or one style.

From Short Stories to Award-Winning Novelettes and Novellas

Zelazny began his professional career by writing short-short stories such as "Passion Play" and "Passage to Dilfar." As he gained experience and confidence over the first two years, he deliberately progressed to writing longer and longer short stories, and then novelettes and novellas. As he began publishing these longer works, his work received more attention from fans and critics, and he quickly developed a reputation for innovation, creativity and memorable stories. "He Who Shapes" and "The Doors of His Face, the Lamps of His Mouth" are two of the best known examples of the longer pieces written in this early phase of his professional career. Both of them won Nebulas in 1966. The novelette "A Rose for Ecclesiastes" is the sole exception to this plan of graduating from shorter to longer works because it was written in October 1961, prior to any of the published short-short stories. It is ironic that this reluctantly submitted novelette became one of Zelazny's best known, beloved, and critically acclaimed pieces. Reprinted dozens of times in multiple languages, it garnered his first Hugo nomination in 1964. Members of the Science Fiction Writers of America subsequently voted "A Rose for Ecclesiastes" one of the 26 best stories from 1929–1964, including it in *The Science Fiction Hall of Fame, Volume 1.*

Zelazny was less forgiving about those early short-short stories, which he described as "mostly short, forgettable gimmick-stories, but that was fine with me. I couldn't write anything else at the time, and I considered the period an apprenticeship. Selling gave me an incentive to keep writing, and writing those sorts of things was practice which I knew I needed while I figured out what it was that I really wanted to say when I found my voice and moved on to greater lengths. And when this happened I could not but be grateful for the support of a sympathetic editor and an earn-while-you-learn situation.

"Several years later when I began to write full-time I shifted the bulk of my writing activity to novels, for which I would first sign contracts and then do the books. I was only too happy that sort of market situation existed, and following the personal *angst* of a psychological shifting of gears I felt nothing else in the way of pressure or influence. I encountered very little in the way of editorial suggestions concerning the material I was turning out."[57]

Advice from Artist Hannes Bok

The artist Hannes Bok painted the wraparound cover art for "A Rose for Ecclesiastes" in the November 1963 issue of *The Magazine of Fantasy & Science Fiction*. Bok took Zelazny to task over his choice of colors in his stories, and he resolved to do better in the future. "Hannes Bok taught me a valuable thing: After he did a cover for ROSE, he suggested that in the future I take pity on a prospective illustrator and use *many* colors in my tales. He said that it is Not A Good Thing to have a red-headed heroine running about a red planet, especially when Mister D. [Avram Davidson, editor of *The Magazine of Fantasy & Science Fiction*] wants a red city/mountain to occur in the background of a large illo. Red-on-red-on-red, he explained, is fine for a camouflage expert but bad, oh bad, for an illustrator. I learned thereby. I use more colors now. Many. The cover for 'Thelinde's Song' made me think of his words. Red-on-red-on…"[58]

Despite the beauty of the painting, Bok was criticized and mocked by some for depicting a blue sky for the planet Mars, but he had been forced into it by the requirements for the other red elements in the painting. Bok was not pleased that the mirror image of the painting appeared on the cover of *The Magazine of Fantasy & Science Fiction;* nor did he approve of the colors used on the cover or in the limited edition prints. To artist Jack Gaughan, Bok wrote, "PRINTS (the unlettered & the lettered ones) are so different from original that it's like Isabel [Ashley] talking to a new acquaintance & her tone when she's talking to merely ME. Hence anybody's liking printed version is not apt to set well with me. I have original framed beside my bed & can glare at it & cuss it out many times per day. I like the RESULT but I just don't cotton to so much work for such horrendous (non-)reproduction."[59]

Having a cover painted by Bok for one of Zelazny's early stories was a significant and thrilling milestone. "When I was 12 years old and wanted to write SF, I had an ambition: I wanted a Bok illo on something I'd write. When I did make it the one thing I was sure of was that I'd never get a Bok illo, because he'd retired from SF work. I never thought he'd come back for one last cover and that it would be my story."[58] The commission to paint "A Rose for Ecclesiastes" was one of the last pieces that Bok completed before his death and the last cover. Years later, Zelazny was able to purchase the original, and he kept it in his home.

...And Call Me Conrad / This Immortal

By mid-1964, after the Hugo nomination for "A Rose for Eccle-siastes," and with such major works as "He Who Shapes," "The Doors of His Face, the Lamps of His Mouth," and "The Graveyard Heart" published or in press, Zelazny had gained enough confidence with novelettes and novellas to attempt a novel. He'd been writing professionally for just over two years; he now began to write what became *...And Call Me Conrad* as a serialized novel. By this time his popularity was such that publishers sought him out for his first novel—an unsolicited letter *from* Doubleday, for example, simply said, "I have heard that you have a science fiction novel and I would like very much to consider it for publication."[60] But a request from an interested publisher doesn't guarantee that a book will be published.

He finished *...And Call Me Conrad* in late 1964 and submitted it to *The Magazine of Fantasy & Science Fiction.* Editor Edward Ferman enthusiastically accepted it for publication, pending a few revisions: "In the first section (as early as possible) you badly need just a page or two of exposition in which Conrad's background and the Radpol-Vegan-Return conflict are spelled out more clearly. Just a more subtle rehash of some of the things in the synopsis. As it is now, Part One (read alone) gives the reader the big picture in too elliptical a fashion. In a serial it is essential to involve the reader completely in the first part. Second, and finally, (now don't wince) we would like to have this cut...for our purposes about 5,000 words (say, 15 to 20 pages) would have to be cut...I honestly believe it would improve the story. If you would prefer us to do the cutting, I'd be glad to do it, although we naturally prefer to have the author make any revisions."[61]

Zelazny made the cuts and added the Radpol backstory in a section that begins "In attempting to reconstruct..." and ends with "The days of Karaghiosis had passed."[62] Upon receiving Zelazny's revised version, Ferman declared, "It will need some more cutting, and I'll be glad to handle this."[63] Zelazny didn't discover until later that over 12,000 words had been cut from the manuscript instead of the promised 5,000. *...And Call Me Conrad* appeared in abridged form in the October and November 1965 issues of *The Magazine of Fantasy & Science Fiction.* Whether it was improved or damaged by the cuts is arguable, but the abridged version was popular enough to tie with Frank Herbert's *Dune* in 1966 for the Hugo Award for Best Novel.

When Ferman accepted ...*And Call Me Conrad*, he pointed out that his consulting editor at *F&SF*, Robert P. Mills, was also a well known literary agent. Ferman added, "I think he'd be able to place this with a book publisher. If this interests you at all, let me know and I'll put him in touch with you."[61] This was done, and so Robert Mills became Zelazny's first agent for a short interval that encompassed the publications of *This Immortal*, *The Dream Master* and *Four for Tomorrow*. The journey toward book publication proved a torturous one for ...*And Call Me Conrad*, but not to the legendary extent of rejection that Frank Herbert's *Dune* had undergone. Over the course of nine months, New American Library, Doubleday, Berkley, Simon & Shuster, Paperback Library, Pyramid, and Tower each rejected the book.[64] This outcome is not surprising for a first novel from an author whose publications were in sf magazines and who had not yet won any major awards. Ace Books finally accepted...*And Call Me Conrad* on September 16, 1965, shortly before its appearance in *F&SF*. Ace offered a $1,500 advance (approximately $8,000 in 2008 dollars).[64]

Nominally unabridged, ...*And Call Me Conrad* became Zelazny's first book, published by Ace under their (not his) preferred title, *This Immortal*. His earlier manuscript titles had included the relatively uninspired *I Am Thinking of My Earth* and *Goodby, My Darling Goodby, Conrad*.[65] The expanded *This Immortal* led readers to mistakenly conclude that the magazine version had been lengthened for publication as a book, when in fact the reverse was true: the book had been abridged by the editor for its appearance in *F&SF*. Unfortunately, not all of the cut material was restored to the Ace edition, but Zelazny didn't realize this until over twenty years later when he reviewed the text for a Book Club edition. He explained, "I didn't know for years that I was missing some scenes, until it became an SF Book Club choice and the editor there told me that after looking at the magazine version and the book version that a bunch of stuff was missing and then asked me if I could go over the text and produce a definitive version."[13] This writer reviewed digital texts of the abridged version from *F&SF* and the Ace Books edition and found the Ace edition to have over 10,000 more words. A digital text was not available for the Book Club edition, but its length appears to be at least 12,000 words longer than the *F&SF* version. Furthermore, the section that recounts the history of the Radpol—added to the *F&SF*

version—was overlooked and has never appeared in *any* of the book publications of *This Immortal*.

The original magazine version of *...And Call Me Conrad*—the version that won the Hugo Award—appears in this collection together with the intervening and unusual Synopsis in which Conrad summarizes events in first person. The afterword to the first part includes some of Zelazny's thoughts about the creation of Conrad and the strategies he employed in writing his first novel.

Zelazny quickly realized that there was little money to be made from writing a short story when a novel could generate sufficient income (from foreign sales, reprints and royalties) to enable him to survive on his writing alone. And thus began the second compromise that he perceived necessary to sustain a writing career, the focus on novels instead of shorter works. He decided to quit his job once his income from writing equaled his salary from the Social Security Administration.

Settling into His Chair

Zelazny had already established the curious habit of writing while reclining in a chair, feet up, with either a pad of paper or a portable typewriter on his lap. He never felt comfortable or relaxed sitting at a desk, a feeling that dated back to the rigidity of days spent at classroom desks. He later explained to Editor David Hartwell that by reclining with his legs extended and elevated, he believed he would avoid the varicose veins that many writers developed as a consequence of prolonged sitting.[66] During his tenure at the Social Security Administration, he wrote in the late evenings out of necessity. After he became a full-time writer, he still tended to be a night owl. He wrote for a little bit in the afternoons after attending to the mail, but most of his writing occurred in the evenings often until 1 or 2 a.m.

Distinction:

Hugo nomination for short fiction "A Rose for Ecclesiastes"

References

A note about the format of references:

JOURNALS/MAGAZINES/FANZINES
Author. Title of article. *Journal Name*. Year; Volume (Issue Number [#Whole Number and/or Month]): pages.

BOOK SECTIONS
Author. Title of article. In: Editor. *Book Title*. City, State: Publisher, Year: pages.

WHOLE BOOKS
Author. *Book Title*. City, State: Publisher, Year.

CORRESPONDENCE
Author. Letter/Email to recipient, date.

INTERNET RESOURCES
Author. Title. Year created. URL. Dated accessed.

1. Zelazny, Trent. Email to Dr. Christopher Kovacs dated January 11, 2008.

2. Yoke, Carl. Email to Dr. Christopher Kovacs dated August 11, 2007.

3. Zelazny, Roger. Introduction. In: Zelazny, Roger, ed. *And the Darkness is Harsh*. Rochester, MI: The Pretentious Press, 1994: p 3.

4. Yoke, Carl B. Email to Dr. Christopher Kovacs dated January 30, 2008.

5. Yoke, Carl B. Before There Was Amber, introduction to a book of the same name, a collection of stories from *The Record* ("Studies in Saviory" and three tales written by Yoke); it was to have been published by DNA Publications (Warren Lapine) but the publisher went out of business, 2005.

6. Yoke, Carl B. *Roger Zelazny: Starmont Reader's Guide 2*. West Linn, OR: Starmount House, 1979.

7. Yoke, Carl B. Email to Dr. Christopher Kovacs dated October 28, 2007.

8. Zelazny, Roger. The Art of Fantasy. *Science Fiction Age* 1994; 2 (2 [January]): p 70–75.

9. Nizalowski, John. An Interview with Roger Zelazny. *The New York Review of Science Fiction* 2006; 18 (7 [#211 March]): p 1, 6–7.

10. Shannon, J.C. Staying Power: An Interview with Roger Zelazny. *Leading Edge* 1994; (29 [August]): p 33–47.

11. Yoke, Carl B. *Roger Zelazny and Andre Norton: Proponents of Individualism*. Columbus, OH: State Library of Ohio, 1979.

12. Yoke, Carl B. Over the Sangre de Cristos. *Amberzine* 2005; (12–15 [March]): p 374–377.

13. Heatley, Alex J. An Interview with Roger Zelazny. *Phlogiston* 1995; (44): p 3–6.

14. McGuire, Paul; Truesdale, David A. Tangent Interviews: Roger Zelazny. *Tangent* 1976; (4 [February]): p 5–10.

15. Brady, John. *Writing Science Fiction: Roger Zelazny*. In: Writer's Voice #74A–14B. 1973: Online clip: http://zelazny.corrupt.net/audio/WritersVoice.html

16. Zelazny, Roger. Authorgraphs – an Interview with Roger Zelazny. *Worlds of If* 1969; 19 (1 [January]): p 161.

17. Yoke, Carl B. Letter to Dr. Christopher Kovacs dated January 8, 2008.

18. Yoke, Carl B. Commentary on "Studies in Saviory," an unpublished essay from the planned collection *Before There was Amber* that was to contain "Studies in Saviory" and three tales written by Yoke; it was to have been published by DNA Publications (Warren Lapine) but the publisher went out of business, 2005.

19. Zelazny, Roger. In Praise of His Spirits, Noble and Otherwise. In: Ellison, Harlan, ed. *From the Land of Fear*. New York, NY: Belmont, 1967: p 6–7.

20. Dowling, Terry; Curtis, Keith. A Conversation with Roger Zelazny. *Science Fiction (Australia)* 1978; 1 (2 [June]): p 11–23.

21. Bowers, Bill; Mallardi, Bill. *Lloyd Biggle, Jr's The Double:Bill Symposium*. Akron, OH: D:B Press, 1969.

22. Yoke, Carl B. Another World Away, unpublished essay written for *Roger on Writing*, a book that was to be edited by Trent Zelazny, 2004.

23. Yoke, Carl B. Email to Dr. Christopher Kovacs dated February 21, 2008.

24. Lindskold, Jane M. *Roger Zelazny*. New York, NY: Twayne Publishers, 1993.

25. Westblom, Ulf. An Interview with Roger Zelazny. *Mentat* 1969; (11 [May]): p 200–203.

26. Conner, Bill. Zelazny at Marcon '72. *Cozine* 1972; (3 [March 30]): p 17–18.

27. Zelazny, Roger. Introduction. In: Zelazny, Roger, Greenberg, Martin H., eds. *Warriors of Blood and Dream*. New York, NY: AvoNova, 1995: p 1–10.

28. Lindskold, Jane M. Warrior's Knowledge. *Amberzine* 1997; (10 [October]): p 13–17.

29. Heck, Peter. Theatre of the Subconscious: An Interview with Roger Zelazny. *Xignals* 1986; XVI (Feb/Mar): p 1,2,15.

30. Campbell, Andrew. Building a Universe. *Reserve, Supplement to CWRU Magazine* 1990; (August): p 10–13.

31. Zelazny, Roger. Letter to Patrick Noël dated September 1, 1971.

32. Martin, George R. R. The Lord of Light. *Locus* 1995; 35 (2 [#415 August]): p 39–40.

33. Williamson, Jack. The Story Roger Never Told. In: Greenberg, Martin H., ed. *Lord of the Fantastic: Stories in Honor of Roger Zelazny*. New York, NY: Avon Eos, 1998: p 37–44.

34. Zelazny, Roger. *When Pussywillows Last in the Catyard Bloomed*. Melbourne, Australia: Norstrilia Press, 1980.

35. Yoke, Carl B. Email to Dr. Christopher Kovacs dated October 27, 2007.

36. Zelazny, Roger. Re: A Rose for Ecclesiastes. *No-Eyed Monster* 1968; (14 [Summer]): p 21–22.

37. Zelazny, Roger J. *Two Traditions and Cyril Tourneur: An Examination of Morality and Humor Comedy Conventions in 'The Revenger's Tragedy' [Master's Thesis]*. New York, NY: Faculty of Philosophy, Columbia University, 1962.

38. Krulik, Theodore. *Roger Zelazny*. New York, NY: Ungar Publishing, 1986.

39. Goldsmith, Cele. Letter to Roger Zelazny dated March 22, 1962.

40. Goldsmith, Cele. Letter to Roger Zelazny dated October 6, 1964.

41. Pohl, Frederik. Letter to Roger Zelazny dated August 15, 1963.

42. Davidson, Avram. Letter to Roger Zelazny, undated but presumed to be 1962.

43. Goldsmith, Cele. Letter to Roger Zelazny dated June 12, 1962.

44. Silverberg, Robert. Introduction. In: Zelazny, Roger, ed. *This Immortal*. Norwalk, CT: Easton Press, 1986: p i–viii.

45. Goldsmith, Cele. Letter to Roger Zelazny dated July 23, 1962.

46. Zelazny, Roger. Editorial Comment. *Amazing* 1962; (36 [December]): p 128.

47. Pohl, Frederik. Handwritten note on a *Galaxy* form rejection letter sent to Roger Zelazny, undated and unreferenced, but likely dated 1962.

48. Davidson, Avram. Letter to Roger Zelazny dated July 7, 1962.

49. Zelazny, Roger. Letter to Bill Bowers dated March 28, 1964.

50. Anonymous. 2 Hospitalized After 2-Car Crash on State Route 13. *News Journal, Mansfield, Ohio* 1964 Monday, September 28, Column 1: p 13.

51. Anonymous. On the Records: In Mansfield Today. *News Journal, Mansfield, Ohio* 1964 Wednesday, November 4, Column 1: p 5.

52. Krulik, Theodore. Roger Zelazny's Road to Amber. *Extrapolation* 2002; 43 (1 [Spring]): p 80–88.

53. Zelazny, Roger. Roger Zelazny Speaks on Roger Zelazny. *Black Oracle* 1969; (1 [March]): p 9–10.

54. Rehak, Jim. A Brief Interview with Roger Zelazny. *Nova* 1972; (1 [June]): p 33–35.

55. Zelazny, Roger. The Search for the Historical L. Sprague de Camp, or, The Compleat Dragon-Catcher. *Tricon (24th World Science Fiction Convention) Progress Report No. 1* 1966; p 3–4.

56. Zelazny, Roger. Introduction to "The Dark World". *Amberzine* 1993; (5 [November]): p 38–39.

57. Zelazny, Roger. The Balance Between Art and Commerce. *SFWA Bulletin* 1985; 19 (4 [Winter]): p 20.

58. Zelazny, Roger. Letter to Ned Brooks dated June 6, 1965.

59. Bok, Hannes. Letter to Jack Gaughan dated December 14, 1963.

60. Seldes, Timothy. Letter to Roger Zelazny dated November 2, 1964.

61. Ferman, Edward L. Letter to Roger Zelazny dated October 27, 1964.

62. Zelazny, Roger. "…And Call Me Conrad, Part One". *The Magazine of Fantasy & Science Fiction* 1965; 29 (4 [#173 October]): p 5–57.

63. Ferman, Edward L. Letter to Roger Zelazny dated November 30, 1964.

64. Mills, Robert P. Letter to Roger Zelazny dated September 17, 1965.

65. Zelazny, Roger. *…And Call Me Conrad*, final manuscript, 1965.

66. Hartwell, David G. Email to Dr. Christopher Kovacs dated November 10, 2008.

CURIOSITIES

CONDITIONAL BENEFIT

Thurban I, fanzine #3, August-September 1953.

Carl Samson is the name, of Universal Mutual, late of New York. Specialities: life and theft. I've seen nearly nine years with Universal, two of them during the Expansion when our policies served useful for covering the holes in shoes, lining empty pockets, and et cetera. Especially the et cetera. Since then, though, we've gone back up near the top, namely Trent Mutual and People's Trust.

The Expansion, Earth's setting up of cities on Venus, took a lot more in proportion from the smaller companies until they licked green malaria, the "shakes", and a couple others. Only recently were the conditions reliable enough on both ends to warrant safe insurance risks again. That's how I got here.

Universal wanted the edge on Trent and Trust, so our office was the first to open a few weeks ago. We were doing fine with yours truly as head salesman until I pulled one they'll talk about for years to come. But I'm getting ahead of my story.

❖   ❖   ❖

As I walked across the scorched sands of the landing area I had my first taste of Venus which felt more like a full course meal. The tourists may talk about Venus's heavier air and lighter gravity, but it's hard to believe until you experience it yourself.

Before I'd taken two dozen steps I started panting and the ground seemed to heave with each breath. Then it came toward me, a charred black with streaks of brown.

I lay there swearing until one of the field crew hauled me back to my feet. He must have been six feet one, about three inches taller than me. My lungs and legs were inadequate, but the brawny arm around my shoulders kept the ground where it should be.

"Didn't they tell you to take it easy at first?" he queried.

I nodded and spit sand.

"One in every load," he decided. "Cigaret?"

He produced a pack and I forced a grin, said thanks, and took one.

"Name's Joel," he said, striking a match which flared nearly four inches and lighting the smokes. I inhaled deeply, coughed a few times, and answered.

"Good to know you, Joel. I'm Carl Samson, insurance salesman." I lifted my battered Traveler from where it had fallen and dusted some of Venus's sand back where it belonged.

"You been here long?" I asked, starting toward the concrete walk.

He fell into step beside me and shrugged. "Since the Expansion. Around six years."

"Where you opening office, or are you free-lancing?"

I shook my head. "Universal boys have headquarters, here it'll be Danver." I stopped on the sidewalk, looking ahead toward the buildings. As we left the landing area, vividly real grass appeared on both sides of the walk. In contrast to this close-cropped reality, the buildings in the distance seemed mirage-like in the heat waves of the early morning sun.

The doorway of the station was open and I paused to lean against the grey stone wall, resting. A dark complexioned native boy in blue jeans appeared from somewhere and stood by my bag.

"Well," Joel pointed to the silver ship on the field. "I have to move along and help with the refueling. I'll look you up next time I'm in town." He stuck out his hand and grinned again. "Maybe I'll drive some business your way, on a commission basis of course."

I released his hand and mirrored the grin. "You do that, but let me warn you about us. We throw out the 'sudden death by unnatural causes' clause on the policies of outside commission seekers," as I turned to follow the baggage-boy.

❖   ❖   ❖

The office had been open two weeks, and while business couldn't be termed landslide it was coming along nicely and still growing. As the sales increased and my commissions stacked up, I felt better and better. Then one morning Joel appeared in my office with a friend of his...

❖   ❖   ❖

The towering dark-skinned gentleman with a grin like a piano keyboard made us feel pallid by comparison. My smile was partly of greeting and partly because of the golden orange, mustard color, and dark blue abstract sport shirt he had on. It hung loosely out of knee-length brown shorts, while yellow framework sandals adorned his massive feet.

Joel raised his hand in greeting. "Hi, Carl. Told you I'd look you up if I was in town or could drive some business your way."

I put down a sheaf of sales reports and rose.

"Good morning, Joel. Which is it, and who is your friend?"

He motioned toward the dark fellow who was testing the resiliency of all the easy chairs in the room. "Both the same. This is chief Tane of the Huambas, and he's interested in some insurance. Chief!"

Tane looked up from his project. He had been busily piling three cushions in one chair and was trying their balancing abilities.

"Tane, I'd like you to meet Carl Samson."

I extended my hand which he promptly seized and treated like the handle of a water pump.

"Very glad to meet you, Mr. Carl."

"Pleased to meet you too, chief Tane." I retrieved my partially mangled hand and motioned for them both to sit down. "I hope that Universal Mutual can be of some service to you."

He flashed the keyboard again. "I want 'surance."

"Good," I said. "We carry all kinds, accident, life, theft. What are you interested in?"

"Life. I want life 'surance."

I sat on the edge of the desk and lit up a cigaret. The chief didn't smoke, and Joel already had one.

"How large a policy were you considering?" I wanted to know.

His brow frowned a moment, then he brightened again. "Thousandollars."

"A thousand dollars," I repeated. "Being chief of a tribe of two and a half thousand makes you a pretty big man here. Maybe a thousand wouldn't be quite adequate." Quickly I caught myself. "Don't get me wrong, I'm not trying to high-pressure you into anything, I was just suggesting."

Joel was about to say something, but Tane explained in his Veno-English, "No, is not for me thousandollars life 'surance. Want for all Huambas thousandollars every."

❖   ❖   ❖

I nearly fell from my position on the desk when I grasped his meaning. A group insurance policy covering his whole tribe!

For a minute it actually carried me away, but only for a minute. That would be seven and a half bucks a head, standard, with a ten per comish for me, also standard. That would come to... But what was the sense of torturing my mental pocketbook? I was doing okay as was. And the idea of insuring savages, natives in a wilderness with a life expectancy somewhere in the twenties, was absurdity in itself. Not wanting to hurt any feelings I decided to try the old sales school put-it-off-forever style.

"It's a good idea, but there's a lot of things we'll need first. We have to find out your death rate, average life span, diseases, natural enemies," I finished with a grand flourish of my cigaret, "and so forth."

It had the desired effect on Tane, I knew I could put him off indefinitely. But then something I hadn't counted on happened. The idea of part of the commission must have been on Joel's mind enough to make him do a little research.

"During the Baker expedition," he began, "a lot of statistics were computed and filed away. I have some copies of them here." He handed me a large manila envelope.

"Take a look at them," he went on, "they're very surprising."

I took the envelope from his extended hand not knowing what to say. When I looked at the papers within I still didn't know what to say, they were very surprising.

"Why, they have a better life expectancy than an average Earth city of the same size!"

"And that ain't all," Joel said happily. "No unfriendly tribes around, hardly any harmful animals. A perfect set-up. What do you think?"

I said that I didn't yet, and read on. They seemed too good to be true. A peaceful, healthy people with a low mortality rate. Good insurance risks if what the figures said was true. But—well, it's not exactly something you'd like on your sales record 'one native tribe (Huambas).'

Still, it was tempting. We could always use more business, and if these statistics were correct it would be quite a killing.

I shuffled the white sheets and inserted them back in the envelope. "It sounds damn interesting. But naturally I don't want the responsibility if this falls through. Tell you what, I'll send out an investigator and if he verifies these I'll take it up with the other directors."

This must not have sounded like a brushoff to him. Actually it wasn't. Instead of telling him where to go with the whole crackpot scheme I was getting interested in the deal. Joel put out his cigaret in the armchair ashtray and stood up.

"I guess that's all for now." He yawned. "How's your health?"

I put the envelope under my blotter and made a memo to send an investigator to the Huamba village.

"My health? I've been eating, drinking, sleeping, and breathing pretty regularly."

"Tsk, tsk," he observed. "Luckily I know the remedy. There's a little place in Lucite that mixes the best drinks in the world." He grinned at this mild bit of humor, Venus having only two or three night-spots. "And as for the surroundings, they're tops too. Just the cure for your case."

❖   ❖   ❖

So we went to the Marascino to try the cure. Still turning over the Huamba group policy idea in my mind, I promised Joel twenty percent of my cut and told Tane I'd let him know soon. Then I got lost in the surroundings.

Two days later the bespectacled white-haired medico, Maxwell Carvenn, showed me the report. The same feelings as when I read the Baker statistics, they checked.

Board action followed in another two days with an affirmative vote, being sure, however, to leave me the choice. So it was not without qualms that I affixed my signature in its place to the thing.

The qualms vanished after I received my commission. At first I had doubted the native's ability to raise the premium, but they had made the cash selling mining rights in their territory and not being able to hang onto money long had decided on this final splurge.

I paid Joel his fifth of my cut and celebrated the new insurance milestone with the same surroundings.

❖   ❖   ❖

A month after, the great Venus dry spell which was said to come every ten years had begun, and those lurking fears came back bringing all their friends.

It was a chilly Sunday morning and Carvenn, now an old friend of Tane's, had invited me up to the village with him. The Venusian calendar system was pretty tricky, but Sunday was still a day of rest to me and rest is something I always enjoy celebrating. So, looking forward to a relaxing outing, I accepted.

I zipped up my plastic wool topcoat as I stepped from the jeep, and we started down the main street of the village against the cold.
Conclusion Next Month

A Word from Zelazny

"I first got interested in science fiction with the *Doctor Doolittle* stories in the first or second grade; I was a fantasy fan when I was very young. Then, when I was in the sixth grade, I got hold of a book [by John Keir Cross called] *The Angry Planet*. I was eleven years old at the time. That was the first exposure I had to science fiction. [Later] I went through the whole school science fiction library shelves. I read all the Heinlein and everything else there… Then my friend—who was about fifteen years old at the time—sold a story to Ray Palmer. I looked at it and thought, gee, I can write better than he can. *I'll* try it. So I tried it, and I couldn't do it. I got a bunch of rejection slips. I wrote about two hundred stories, and every one of them was rejected."[1] "I sent out my first story, an imitation Ray Bradbury piece, to John W. Campbell [editor of *Astounding Science Fiction*], who wasn't even buying Ray Bradbury's stuff. Innocence."[2]

Notes

This is the earliest surviving example of Zelazny's fiction from that period, a short story published in 1953 in the fanzine *Thurban I*, which Warren Dennis edited and Zelazny co-edited. Dennis ran out of funds and paper to publish the entire story in that issue, and so the typed "cont. next page" was crossed out and "conclusion next month" was handwritten below it. Unfortunately, Dennis was drafted; he never published another issue, and the rest of the manuscript was lost.[3,4]

---

1 *If*, January 1969.
2 *Roger Zelazny*, Jane Lindskold, 1993.
3 *Amber Dreams*, 1983.
4 *Roger Zelazny: A Primary and Secondary Bibliography*, 1980.

Hand of the Master

Written in the early 1960s; likely unpublished.

I shook hands around and left the Senate chamber. I shrugged off the reporters outside and headed for my car. Before I got to it, however, a little fat man greeted me and stopped me dead in my tracks. I turned around and smiled appropriately, but inside me my spine had turned to jelly.

He had spoken in perfect Italian, in a dialect we both knew, which just hadn't been current for say five hundred years.

"Yes, what can I do for you?" I asked him, in English.

"Senator Blane," he said, "you might not know me. But you've been cleared for Top Secret, so I suggest you read this report. It's very important. I also suggest you be in my office a week from today at eight p.m. When you've finished the report you might know who I am."

Then he was gone and I was left holding another briefcase, and I knew already who he was.

He was Paul Vincent, Director of STAR, the biggest think-factory in this country.

Could he...?

No.

But then...

No. It was impossible.

But then, who were they?

I stepped into my car, in the year of Our Lord 1998, and for the first time in awhile, I was afraid.

He knew, he knew something—and where had he learned to say what he had said?

I knew I'd keep the appointment.

❖　　❖　　❖

I was shown in to his enormous office, and I didn't stop to admire the decor. He was seated behind a big, marble-topped desk, and he said, "Senator Blane," and he paused to light a cigarette.

"Good evening," I replied.

"I hope you are well."

"Can't complain."

"Good."

"Do you know why are you here?" he asked.

"Which 'here' are you speaking of?"

"My office, now."

"No," I said. "I've read the Sanderson report," and I placed it on his desk and sat down in a chair to the left, "and I'm not the twelfth man, believe me. My case is something quite different."

He smiled, and he was slightly buck-toothed, and he wore thick glasses and had straw-colored hair. His face was fat and flushed, his eyes dark. He certainly didn't look like the Big Brain he was cracked up to be.

"So you don't know why you're here," he said. "I thought maybe you might have figured it out. Primarily, you're here so that I might thank you for assuring passage of the Starprobe Bill that just cleared both Houses."

"Stop," I said, suddenly appreciating the game. "A piece has just fallen into place. You are my benefactor, the man I've sought for almost three years," and here I switched back to the language we both knew. "As I lay dying, I wondered at the possibility of an afterlife. I still wonder at it, because after a moment of terrible pain and what seemed an instant of blackness, I awakened in the body of Senator Blane. It could not be reincarnation, for I was already full-grown, completely disoriented and did not speak the language. But I was taught English, with an Iowa accent, I was taught to drive a car, mix a Martini, turn on television and change channels. I was taught modern dances. I was briefed on twentieth century partisan politics and sent back to the Senate. I had been recuperating from a mild heart attack, I had been told to say. This story was accepted. I was asked only one thing by whoever had so strangely saved my life and brought me into this age. I was asked to assure passage of the Bill which came out of my commit-tee. Beyond this, my instructors told me nothing. When I sought after them, later, I could find no trace of their existence. Your thanking me now, however, indicates that you are the man *I* should thank."

He nodded.

"Very good," he said, "and you are welcome."

"The Sanderson Report," I went on, "indicates that the STAR Foundation must have had the means of bringing me here."

"And you still don't know me?" he asked.

"This past week," I said, "I've read everything about you that is on record. You were—if you'll excuse the expression—a Bowery Bum, up until about twelve years ago, when you suddenly enrolled in a technical college and supported yourself with your painting. You distinguished yourself, and after graduation you developed the first workable means of causing a vehicle to exceed the speed of light. You then took a position with the STAR Foundation and quickly rose to become its director. You've been responsible for the development of dozens of elaborate gadgets over the years. It is known that you have been in favor of passage of the Starprobe Bill, which will appropriate the funds for exploration beyond our solar system by means of ships equipped with your drive-mechanism. It falls into place, but I know nothing more than this concerning yourself."

"Consider again the Sanderson Report," he said, and I did, and there was another piece of the answer.

"Twelve years ago it was proposed that since there have been definite indications of the existence of life on a planet in the ———— System, but that since we had no means of visiting that world physically, an alternative method might be employed. That is, the displacement of the minds or psyches or whatever you want to call them of individuals living on that world, and their replacement by our own volunteers'. These individuals could learn of the culture in that way and then be drawn back here to report. The question then arose as to man's adaptability to an alien culture, so it was decided to perform an experiment. The device developed for this purpose could function through time as well as through space. A dozen men from several centuries ago were brought forward from their deathbeds to the year 1986 and were simply turned loose, to be studied to determine whether they could adapt to our present culture. Eleven of them went mad and the twelfth disappeared. The experiment was labeled a failure, classified and shelved. Then you came along with an alternative method of visiting the stars. Now…"

I paused, lit a cigarette myself, then I said, "You were nothing until a dozen years ago. You are the twelfth man."

He grinned and chuckled.

"Good old Yankee know-how," he said. "It wasn't until I became director here that I learned of the Sanderson Report, that I'd learned how I'd come to be here in this place and time. I then obtained access to the machinery. It was rather crude, since it only brought forward the psyches of random dying men. I refined it considerably, so that I could select whoever I wished."

"I see."

[end fragment]

A Word from Zelazny

This piece was written in the early 1960s, and while Zelazny was fairly certain that it had been published in a fanzine, he could not recall the fanzine, editor, or date.[1] It is possible he was mistaken, and this is its first appearance. All that remains is this manuscript from the Zelazny archives at Syracuse University; the ending is missing.

---

1 *Amber Dreams*, 1983.

THE GREAT SELCHIE OF SAN FRANCISCO BAY

Written 1965–68; left incomplete, previously unpublished.

Scene: San Francisco coffee shop. Sounds of voices; rattling crockery; guitar sound. Voice sings, slightly back-groundish, begins old ballad, "The Great Selchie of Schule Skerrie":

> I am a man upon the land
> And a good gray selchie in the sea,
> And when I'm far and far frae land
> My home it is in Schule Skerrie…

> *(Voice fades into background)*

1st Speaker: (Rattles cup) …Twenty-one. (Pause. Sound of a sip being taken. Cup rattles as it is put down again.) … And twenty-two.

2nd Speaker: What're you counting, man?

1st Speaker: Moves.

2nd Speaker: (Pause) Like what is moving that is worthy of the process of enumeration?

1st Speaker: Like, that chess game over there.

2nd Speaker: Over where? Oh. Yeah, I see. Dan and that big guy with the beard. (Pause) Wish I could grow a beard like that. Can't, though. I mean, every time I try it, it comes in all scraggly and like that. His is kinda—

greenish almost. (Quickly) No, it's yellow. It's the way the light was hitting it. Wish I could even grow a green beard, though. Wouldn't that be a gas?

1st Speaker: Yeah, like hydrogen. (Pause) Twenty-three…

2nd Speaker: Uh—why you countin' the moves, man?

1st Speaker: To see if the guy with the beard was right.

2nd Speaker: About what?

1st Speaker: He said he'd win it in twenty-six moves. I don't see how he can, though.

2nd Speaker: He won't do it. Dan's too good. 'Less maybe he's a Russian. They're supposed to be *real* good. Think he's a Russian?

1st Speaker: No.

2nd Speaker: Neither do I. Sort of a Scandinavian look about him.

1st Speaker: Yeah. (Pause) …Twenty-four.

(Guitar comes on stronger. Voice is clear again.)

>   …And a good gray selchie in the sea, in the sea,
> And when I'm far and far frae land
> My home it is in Schule Skerrie.

(Big Chord)

2nd Speaker: That's twenty-five, huh?

1st Speaker: That's twenty-five indeed.

2nd Speaker: …And nothing yet. Wait. Dan's going to move. There, he moved his castle.

New Voice: That's your move?

Dan: Like, nobody did it for me. Therefore, it *is* my move.

New Voice: Then this is mine. Checkmate.

Dan: How…? (Pause) Oh. (Pause) Oh. I—didn't—like notice—that bishop…

New Voice:	You notice it now?
Dan:	Unhappily, such is the case.
New Voice:	Then you lose and I win—in twenty-six moves.
Dan:	It wasn't twenty-six.
1st Speaker:	Yes, it was, man. I was keeping count.
New Voice:	It doesn't really matter.
1st Speaker:	Sure it matters—it matters how you knew.
New Voice:	It was determined before the game began.
1st Speaker:	How do you mean that?
New Voice:	Just as I said it. Back before he was born it was determined that on this day, he would have a game of chess with a better player, and would lose it in twenty-six moves.
Dan:	And how could you know that?
New Voice:	Occasionally, I catch a glimpse of these things. That doesn't much matter either though, not really. What I see clearly I do not care to change. What I might care to change, I never see clearly enough.
2nd Speaker:	What's he talking about?
1st Speaker:	Like life. (Pause) What's your name then?
New Voice:	My name is Henry Mailer, *man*.
1st Speaker:	When you say "man," man, you say it as though you're speaking of another species.
2nd Voice:	Maybe he is.
New Voice:	Where's Peggy? I came here to see Peggy. Doesn't she usually come in about this time?
1st Speaker:	Peggy? Who's Peggy? Never heard of her.
2nd Speaker:	Me either.

New Voice:	Perhaps she goes by another name now. She is tall and dark-haired and her eyes are very green, and they change from sad to happy and back again, like the sea in the autumn.
2nd Speaker:	You a poet, man?
New Voice:	No.
2nd Speaker:	Too bad. You have a good name for it. But in answer to your interrogative—no, I do not know of any Peggy like that.
1st Speaker:	That does sound something like Liz, though.
Dan:	Liz is a blonde.
1st Speaker:	She dyes it.
Dan:	So what makes you come looking here?
Mailer:	I know she comes here.
Dan:	What's she to you?
Mailer:	What's it to you what she is to me?
Dan:	Like academic curiosity.

Notes

Zelazny started and abandoned this script in the 1960s. It deals with the selchies (pronounced "sell-keys"), the mythical seal-folk of Scotland and Ireland. Selchies are able to shed their seal-skins and pass for human but usually with unfortunate consequences for all involved. Their myth is recounted in an old folk ballad entitled "The Great Selkie o'Sule Skerry;" Joan Baez popularized one version of it in the 1960s. The ballad describes an earthly woman who has taken a selchie to be her lover; in Zelazny's play, Peggy is that earthly woman, and Henry Mailer is evidently the selchie who has come seeking her again. **Frae** is a Scottish term for "from."

It is unknown why Zelazny abandoned this script. He dealt with the same myth in the short story "Alas! Alas! This Woeful Fate," which appears in Volume 3 of this collection.

STUDIES IN SAVIORY

Written in 1964 or 1965 for *The Record*; previously unpublished.

I.

When Yok ambled into the Grene Zyphoam Cellar for the first time in twenty years, two things happened almost simultaneously. First he was taken aback at the sight of an oddly human-looking character at a table, an unprecedented phenomenon! and then a diminutive gremlin leapt to his talons from a stool, and dashed toward him along the top of a bar.

Yok had whipped out a bloat-o gun before he recognized Sam Phlegm hunched before him, slobbering ichor.

"Yok, Mon! Wherethehellyabeen? The Pres has been looking for you and Zlaz for a decade!"

"Oh? Urgent business or something?" Yok nonchalantly drew out an enormous roll of bills and tossed one forth. "Drinks on me," he announced loudly.

There was a sudden congestion at the bar, from which Phlegm dexterously extracted a gallon jug of zyphoam. He table-hopped in ten-foot bounds, to a corner booth. Yok followed.

Phlegm was lying on his back on the table, holding the jug between his feet, gurgling the brown liquid down his blood-colored thorax. Yok snatched it away and took a long pull.

"That was generous of you," Phlegm commented, gesturing to the mob of drinkers.

"It was not. It was the only way I could get a place to sit."

"Still, that was quite a stack of gardes you flashed."

"That's right. I captained a twenty-year cargo run to Vega, and got involved in a war on the side. I am now loaded."

"I seem to recall that you took off in an empty ship."

"Well," Yok grinned evilly, "it was full when I got there."

"What about Zlaz?"

"Haven't seen him since before I left. Say, satisfy my curiosity. Is that, or is that not, a human over there helping to drink up my bill?"

Sam glanced quickly.

"That is not," he observed. "I don't know what he is, but nothing human can drink zyphoam and live. He drinks zyphoam, ergo, he is not human."

"Go get another jug, and ask him if he'll join us."

Verily, this is a once-in-a-century day of curiosity for me, he mused.

The heroically proportioned humanoid giant sitting across from him was named Adon, and broke, he learned.

"Why do you look the way you do? Or let me put it this way, is it an occupational disease?"

"Sort of," was the reply. "I was a small-time fertility deity in Asia Minor until the big guys like Dionysus and Priapus started screwing around. They forced me out of business."

"Oh, how was business?"

"Can't complain. Once you learn the routine it's pretty much repetitious, but very entertaining. Then too, I was contributing to the religious well-being of the human community." He guzzled some more free zyphoam. "Know anyone who needs an experienced fertility deity?"

"Off hand, no." Yok finished his zyphoam and rose. "Well it's been nice meeting you, Adon, and all that crap." He ambled out.

Phlegm was on his heels.

"Going to see the Pres?"

"No. I have an important visit to make."

"He'll be mad if you don't see him first thing."

Yok laughed for half a minute and walked away.

Phlegm scuttled in the gutter and caught up with him again.

"Uh, in case *he* wants to look *you* up and asks around, where will you be?"

"With Zlaz."

"But nobody knows where Zlaz is."

"Uh-huh." Yok waded out into the main canal and unmoored

his flatboat. He got in and shoved off in the direction of the Myst Lake Caverns.

"They already tried his cave at Myst Lake, and he's not there. All he left was his robot retainer and some little fuglees."

"If you don't get back to the Grene Cellar soon, all the free zyphoam will be gone."

A quick shuffle of talons, and when Yok looked back there was only a pool of green ooze steaming where Sam had been standing.

And he hadn't even asked what a fuglee was.

❖   ❖   ❖

An Eiffel tower with cable arms and a speaking box confronted Yok at the doorstep, which was also the pier.

"Yok!" the Eiffel tower said.

Yok agreed as to his identity, and pointed behind himself at the steps which vanished beneath the steaming waters,

"Is Zlaz downstairs, or inside?"

"Neither," said the Eiffel tower (who was named James, after an English valet Zlaz had once brought back, but who, unfortunately, had not adapted well to the climate).

"Cut the safety circuit crap, James. This is Yok. Zlaz told me to come to dinner the day I got back from Vega. I'm back."

"I do not take organic pleasure from joking," James sounded offended. "I'm not certain where he is. About fifteen years ago he left me in charge and went for a walk back in the Labyrinth. I suppose he's hibernating."

"You suppose! What if he fell through a chasm?" (Yok did not believe Zlaz would fall into one of his own chasms, or be particularly disturbed if he had, but James' mechanical composure perturbed him.)

"My orders distinctly were—"

"Orders! Bosh! You'll never be a success, James, if you always follow orders."

"—to receive and file incoming messages, to receive visitors and tell them Zlaz is not home, to maintain order in the laboratory—"

"Alright! I don't care what your orders were. I'm going back in the Labyrinth now. If anyone asks for me, I'm not here either."

"You'll need a map."

"I will not!" Yok stamped off.

❖   ❖   ❖

Sixty seconds later Yok was back in the foyer. Forty or fifty foot-high yellow-haired beasts railed about him on their hind legs, howling something which sounded like, "Gofugyrself! Gofugyrself!" over and over.

"James," he said in a pained voice, "you didn't mention that you were raising pets back in the Labyrinth."

"Those are not pets. They're fuglees."

"Oh, that explains everything. I walk back there and am jumped on by thirty thousand fuglees. It's nice to know what they are."

"They live there. Zlaz bred them in the laboratory and turned them loose in the Labyrinth. They eat fungi and follow simple orders when he gives them. They're sort of bodyguards for his hibernation."

"Millions of them? They're crawling all over each other back there, making noises like humans. And what does he need bodyguards for in his own cave?"

"Well, I assumed they're bodyguards. Maybe their only real function is to clear the walls of lichen. But the machine in the lab keeps turning out fifty a day, so I assumed he wanted a small army—"

"The machine keeps turning them out!" Yok lowered his voice again. "Did it ever occur to you that Zlaz forgot to turn the machine off? Why didn't you turn it off?"

"My orders—"

"Never mind! You've got a long way to go, James." Yok faced the Labyrinth again.

"I'm happy the way I am," James sounded as hurt as his voice box would permit.

"Well go turn it off now. I think Zlaz might be a bit peeved when he wakes." Yok stooped and grabbed a young fuglee by the scruff of its neck.

"Gofugyrself!" it screamed, and immediately the others rallied to its defence. Yok kicked them off and plucked a large fungus from high on the wall. It snatched it and gobbled greedily. "Gofugyrself," it sighed pleasantly.

"James. Before you go, what's with this vocabulary of theirs?"

"Oh, well that, sir, is their entire language. It was an idea Zlaz got while visiting China, where the same word can have dozens of different meanings, dependant upon intonation, pitch, vol—"

"I speak Chinese, James, and get the picture. They can express anything with this combination of syllables. In other words, Zlaz's perverse sense of humor has triumphed again."

"Well, it's an easy language to learn," James crackled sharply, and headed off in the direction of the laboratory.

"The hell these robots don't have a sense of humor," Yok reflected, wading through the fuglees.

❖   ❖   ❖

Yok quickly checked all the former hibernation crypts. They were vacant. He roamed about at random, then noticed the fuglees. Whenever he headed to the left they cheerfully gave way, when he bore right they obstructed his path.

Following the line of most resistance, he reached a moist grotto after fifteen minutes. Burrowing through a wall of fuglees, who had linked arms, he came upon an enormous boulder. The fuglee wails were deafening.

He had gripped the huge stone and was about to roll it aside when James entered.

"Yok, there was a monstraphone call for you."

"Who the devil! No one knows I'm…" he trailed off.

"He claimed to be the President of the Pan-Monstric Association."

"Hmm," said Yok. "Could be. Phlegm moves fast."

"You can call him back up front. There are no extensions here."

"No. What did you tell him?"

"Just as you instructed. That you weren't here."

"Good. Step back, will you? I'm about to awaken Zlaz."

"But how…?"

"Watch."

Yok put his shoulder to it and rolled the boulder aside. The fuglees scurried to keep from being crushed. A sizeable crypt lay beneath it. Empty.

"You see, sir, he's just unavailable."

"But that couldn't be. The fuglees led me to this one."

"Never trust a fuglee."

"Nonsense, they're almost as stupid as humans. I tricked them into leading me here. Aha! That's it—Once on Altair…" Yok searched about until he came upon a melon-sized stone. He began tapping it against the boulder, increasing the force of each blow.

Finally a yawn followed by string of muffled obscenities was heard. Then the boulder cracked open and fell apart. Zlaz stepped out.

"That was a pretty good red herring, Zlaz. Hiding in the rock instead of the crypt."

"How did you know where I was?" Zlaz stretched.

"Your army of fuglees brought me here, indirectly."

"Army of fuglees?" Zlaz did a few slow pushups. "Oh, yes! Fuglees. A little experiment of mine. But there's no army. I only made fifty— and they were experimental models."

"Wanna bet?" Yok inquired politely, gesturing toward the yellow hordes who lay prostrate before the opened crypt.

"Ahem," commented James, "I thought that you intended for the machine to remain functioning. Were I aware that you wanted it shut down…"

Zlaz cast a practical eye about:

"We must be nearly out of lichens by now. I'll have to set them to eating each other, or else find some way of cashing in on them in a hurry. James! Why didn't you…?"

"Did you get inside the rock by molecular rearrangement, master?" James quickly inquired. And Yok noted that for a mechanical brain he made a noble attempt to get out of trouble by changing the subject. —Some of Zlaz's insidious cunning had even rubbed off on the machines he kept.

"No. Magic," Yok supplied him.

"How long have I been asleep?" Zlaz wanted to know.

"Fifteen years, four months, three days, sir—"

"That's close enough," Zlaz stopped the valet. "I remember freezing half a musk oxen back in '32. Go spit it over a slow fire, get two ten gallon casks of zyphoam up from the cellar, brew a vat of coffee, and call and have them ship out a raft of potato chips. Double time! Yok, let's go for a hot sulphur swim while it's getting ready. You can fill me in on the past few years, and we can consider what to do with two hundred eighty thousand, two hundred twelve fuglees."

❖   ❖   ❖

James had gone after more zyphoam, and the musk oxen was a respectable heap of bones. Yok reached for another potato chip.

"So what could the old boy want us for this time?" Zlaz had just asked.

The President, flanked by six of his roughest bodyguards, strolled into the dining cave. They pushed James before them, whose cable arms had been tightly knotted behind him.

"I tried to warn you, sir. But—"

"Quite alright, James. Go get untangled." Zlaz regarded the half-ton bulk of the President, ignoring the mail-scaled escorts.

"Going to a party?"

"I didn't come to play footsie. I knew Yok would find you. You're both coming with me now. My boys will pack you an overnight bag."

Zlaz slowly shook his head from one side to the other, salted a final joint of beef and began to gnaw on it. Yok started to laugh, thought better of it, and offered the President a potato chip:

"You're acting just like a human dictator—stupid! Maybe you *are* in a position to draft us now. But what makes you think we'll carry out whatever job you have in unless *we* want to do it? So *you* sit down."

The President snorted something similar to Fuglese, as Yok had named the new creatures' language, and made a sign to his retainers.

"One moment," said Zlaz, as he reached for more salt.

The Pres paused and looked inquisitive.

"Whatever job you have that appears so urgent, you had a special reason for calling for us. You always do," Zlaz began. "That is, we're at the head of your List of Top Operatives for Special Assignments of Dangerous, Tricky, and Evil Nature. Pause and reflect for a moment why we occupy that position. We have carried out more dangerous, tricky, and evil assignments than any other mon in history, and we're still around to crack smutty stories about them." Here he raised a hand (still holding the bone—symbolically, Yok thought) to silence another presidential outburst.

"Foremost of our coups is the fact that we are the only two mon in existence who ever successfully assassinated a President of the PMA and lived. Admittedly that was six thousand years ago, and we were in exile for four centuries because of it. But a change in administration brought us back, with honors, as it always will. Times haven't changed that much, and we're still mon of the Old School. Now with all this in mind, will you still try to intimidate us? Rubbish! Sit down and discuss it like a gentlemon and we'll consider your offer. Try anything else at your own risk."

Yok nodded.

The Pres rumbled some more Fuglese, then motioned quickly with his right talon. The six bodyguards approached. Zlaz jerked at the extra salt cellar, which was really a disguised lever.

The middle dropped out of the cave floor and four of the mon slid through the opening. There was a prolonged silence, a removed splash, and a sudden sizzling. Zlaz released the lever. Acid fumes filled the room and a few muffled cries were heard, but they stopped almost immediately.

The two remaining retainers licked their fangs and lips and cast a quick glance back at the Pres. He had turned a delicate violet, but he motioned them on. At this moment thirty thousand fuglees entered the room behind James, who wrapped his untangled cables around one mon and dragged him out.

"Gofugyrself," commented Zlaz, and a yellow tidal wave shoved the remaining retainer to the middle of the floor, which conveniently opened again.

Zlaz replaced the salt cellar.

"Now that we're alone, shall we talk business?"

The Pres was a deep purple at this moment. He growled an Etruscan oath and accepted a bench and a flagon of zyphoam.

"You're being very playful as usual. But we're wasting time. We're mobilized, or haven't you noticed? I want you to leave immediately for Hell.[1] There is about to be a war, and you have a bare chance of averting it."

"The only appeal to my civic virtue is through my pocket book which, at this time, is full. If I were desperate, I might go to Hell for a million gardes. But I'm not desperate. If there's going to be a war, I'm suddenly needed in the vicinity of the asteroid belt. Excuse me. James! Pack my traveling bag!"

"That is not only unpatriotic, it's illegal. You can't leave Lucetania during wartime!"

"Wanna bet?"

"Yok? What about you?" the Pres inquired.

Yok snatched up a fuglee that had been scrounging for crumbs beneath the table. He jabbed it with his fork.

The Pres turned a pale lavender, shading over into green, at its shrill comment.

"James! Pack an extra fangbrush!" Yok ordered.

The Pres turned back to a normal ruddy at what was obviously an evil thought. He craftily inquired:

"Yok, have you been back to your own lair recently?"

---

1 H.E.L.L.—Hot Empire Lower than Lucetania

Yok shook his head and reached for the fuglee again, but it sagely eluded his grasp.

"Well, in your lab there was a glass casket containing a human female in suspended animation. It is no longer there. It is—"

He was forced to pause at this moment because of the carving knife which Yok was holding wedged against his throat.

"First I'm going to carve my initials on your—"

"Wait! Let me explain! What happened was purely fortuitous. There was an earthquake ten years ago. Your cavern was hit."

"And?"

"And the inspection team we sent around to look for gas leakages from the lower lava pockets had to go in. They found your lab wrecked. It had smashed the casket. She was quite dead."

"Oh." Yok lowered the blade. Then he raised it again. "Well, I'm still in a mood to do something rash."

"Wait! We thought it might be something important. I admit I wanted it as a hold over you, but there was nothing specific in mind then. —If you have perverse tastes that's your own affair. So we shipped her body down to the Med Center and had it reconstructed, molecule for molecule. Then we froze it again."

"The only difference being that now it's a corpse."

"Yes. But it's still a perfect host for her psyche again—if you can dredge it up or reconstruct it somehow."

"After ten years? The electrical charges would have dissipated—"

"Not necessarily. I don't know her significance, but there's a bare chance you can find her."

"Where?"

"In Hell, of course."

"Holy Anubis!" Zlaz commented, realizing the implications. Both alternatives were unsavory.

"You know only the select minority get into Hell," Yok began, ironically, "where they're recrystallized and can last for a few extra years. The required factor is a continuous stream of hot vapors, down which the electrical charges pass."

"And there was one! We found a fissure in your cave. It was immediately blocked off, of course. But you can go check if you won't have my word."

"I won't. But how do I know that it led to the lower caves?"

"You don't. Neither do I. But it's your only chance. If you want that human you'll have to play Orpheus to get her back."

Yok winced slightly. The recrystallized humans were of course fruit for the torture chambers of the offshoot race of Hot Empire mon.[1] Years of constant heat and radiation had rendered them both sterile and impotent, and their entire cultural ethos took its release in a mass sadism complex. (It went far beyond the normal, healthy sadism of normal, healthy mon.) Still, there was an extra deck of cards up his sleeve which Yok mentally riffled and then silenced.

"How they put them back together is a scientific miracle we haven't been able to get at," the Pres continued. "Our best spies have never been able to fathom the secret of the Lens. Well, our second best spies..." He grinned toothily to show that it had been a compliment.

Zlaz grinned back from some deep inner spring of evilness and sick humor: "And all you want is the secret of the Lens? Lucifer Hades himself claims he doesn't know how it works."

"Pure propaganda," snapped the Pres, then he became suspicious. "How do you know what he claims?"

"Oh, come now! We've read your secret files."

"Damn! I'll have to execute my whole staff first thing in the morning. But to your question: No, the Lens is totally useless to me. The reason I want you to go concerns the impending conflict. Troops from the Lower Empire have been massing at the borders for the last two years. About a decade ago, during an infrequent period when there was no volcanic static we received an odd radio message, which we couldn't reply to. Then Lucifer's gang began kidnapping stray mon from Lucetania in the damnedest places. No reason was given. But every six months during the period of radio communication we received the same five-word message." He paused to clear his throat and look uncomfortable. " 'Send me Yok and Zlaz.' And it was always signed by Lucifer Hades XXXII."

"Hmm," said Zlaz, looking stern either to suppress a grin or to look stern.

"I have no idea what he wants you for. But he is apparently willing to go to war because you won't pay him a visit. So, since Yok has to go anyhow—"

"We get the General slimey picture," said Zlaz. "Answer a hypothetical question though. Lucetania whupped them in the civil wars six millennia ago and cast them down into Hell. We've always managed to squash any attempts of theirs to come back in the past. Why are you afraid of them now?"

---

1 Demoted Mon, D. mon, demon.

"We're not! Dammit! Of course the last peace treaty has been upheld for five hundred years and we're anxious to see it served." Yok kicked the fuglee at this moment. A rainbow flashed over the Pres' face, but he went on, "Of course we could defeat them again, but there might be a great material loss."

"In other words you want to sacrifice us to some special perverse tortures in order to save a few bucks."

"That's not it at all—"

"Or they have some new secret weapon you're afraid of."

"That's not it either!"

"What percentage of that great material loss we'll be saving you can we expect?"

"Well…"

"A million gardes apiece," Yok offered.

"Alright," agreed the Pres, surprisingly, making Yok think he ought to have upped the ante. Then he realized that they weren't expected to return, which would represent a tidy savings, something like 100%, while getting rid of two nuisances at the same time. Possibly three, if the war might be counted.

Zlaz nodded his acceptance. Yok's agreement was apparent.

"Good," said the Pres, rubbing his oily palms together. "I'll put things in writing while you get packed."

James entered with the two bags.

Yok poured out some more zyphoam.

II.

The jagged walls of the Avernus Hell-hole climbed rapidly past the dropping aerocar. Yok hummed the choral invocation to N'Yok, a Bantu tribal deity, which had once been one of his part-time jobs.

"That looks like the landing stage below, mon."

"Hmm," said Yok, which could have meant anything but probably didn't.

Zlaz braked and cut left as the shaft widened. Disgorged into a vast cavern, the ship dropped toward an expanse of white until Yok pointed out that it was a lake of molten brimstone.

"Used to be an airstrip there," Zlaz commented.

"That was fifty-six hundred years ago. Things might have changed a bit."

"This new crowd must be a bunch of radicals. The 50,000 population stays constant. Why should they rearrange the topography and deface beautiful public utilities?"

"I haven't forgotten that you laid out the airstrip," Yok observed. "Maybe they wanted to."

"Why?"

"Well, we didn't exactly leave them with good tastes in their horny little faces."

"Bah! That was too damned bad! They wanted us to lay out their city in return for a few favors—"

"Four hundred years' sanctuary," Yok put in.

"—and they asked me to design a torture chamber and teach them how to use it. What was I supposed to demonstrate on? Rocks?"

"Not the leading citizens of the community who came to watch."

Zlaz philosophized in Fuglese and set the ship into a wall-niche. The black basalt city looked about a half mile distant.

"Just a short hike, mon," said Zlaz, when an explosion of hoof-beats hailed a motley crowd of fork-tailed mon into their presence.

"There's two!" screamed a large grisly one. "Let's hack 'em apart!"

"Yeah! and pull out their entrails!"

"And set fire to them!"

"That's the ticket!"

Zlaz raised his arms over his head, turned bright green, and grew two feet taller. Yok did the same, only he favored a delicate chartreuse. Zlaz knocked over a stalagmite and squashed three of them. Yok disemboweled a couple with his pocket machete.

Ninety seconds later and two feet shorter, Yok and Zlaz made their ways again toward the city. They respectfully left the five corpses in a ditch. A large demon with a red asbestos arm band approached from the city gate.

"Okay! Identify yourselves if you want to keep walking!"

"Yok."

"Zlaz."

"Good God!"

"Not really," said Zlaz, "But we do have an appointment with Lucifer Hades and would like to keep it."

"Yes sir!" he bowed very low. "Come right this way. Excuse me. I—"

"Quite all right. But we're in a hurry."

"By the way," Yok commented, "there are five corpses back that way in a ditch."

"Yes sir. Quite all right. I'll take care of everything. Sorry."

They entered the city and walked for three blocks behind the gate guard. He led them into the anteroom of the giant administration building. They passed to a huge desk, where he whispered something to the attendant who made a quick call, eyes bugging.

"Please go right into the private waiting room," shivered the desk clerk, bowing.

They went in.

A particularly evil looking young demon dashed suddenly across the room and stood smoking by the wall. The female secretary blushed violently.

"Yok and Zlaz to see Lucifer," said the guard, a tinge of importance creeping into his voice.

Her eyes widened and her mouth slackened then went tight. She jabbed nervously at the intercom button. The demon by the wall eyed them with interest but said nothing.

"Sir!" her voice was high. "Yok and Zlaz are here to see you!"

There was a mutter from the box and she looked up.

"Go right in." She bowed slightly.

The door opened before they reached it and a uniformed mon stamped out past them. He cast a quick glance in their direction, but did not stop. Their escort followed him out.

They entered.

The office was slightly more plush than the Pres'; about 20 by 60 feet, with a red asbestos carpet and enormous bookshelves. The desk was a gargantuan marble slab, and carved granite chairs were spotted casually about. Raw steam hissed into the room from wall jets.

"You really are Yok and Zlaz!"

The speaker was tall, very thin and dark, with a triangular face. His horns were two inch projections at the hairline, shorter than those so far encountered. He stood directly in a jet of hot steam, looking angry, but not necessarily at them. He moved to his desk and motioned them to chairs.

"That damned general would have taken all afternoon if you hadn't come. So you've done me one favor already."

"You need a few more, I understand?"

"It's amazing, Zlaz," He removed a giant folder from his desk and opened it. "You haven't changed a bit!"

He extended the asbestos booklet. In it Zlaz discovered two ancient metal engravings: one of himself and one of Yok.

"Where did you get these?" He passed it to Yok.

"Lucifer Hades I, my grandfather thirty times removed, had them made as a parting gift, to surprise you. Legend has it that you left— uh, a trifle prematurely. So they wound up in the Archives—a good way to identify you again, should anyone ever show up claiming to be you. Of course we know you have some way of changing bodies— but rumor has it that you favor the same types fairly consistently. And then, too, a few quick questions will prove your identities. I just thought you'd like to see these—"

"—so we'll know you can circulate our pictures in a hurry, if you have to," Yok put in.

Lucifer didn't deny it. He smiled and continued: "What's a V-beam?"

Zlaz furrowed his brow.

"Oh, that's an ancient torture I once developed. I don't use it any more. I implant needles now, and use UHF to vibrate them—but a V-beam was a means of damaging an organ inside the body without destroying the tissue around it. I intersect two lines of—"

"That's good enough. Tell me, Yok. What would happen if I moved this paperweight to the left?"

"I'd burn your hand off with my bloat-o gun."

"Very good. Now suppose you tell me why. —By the way, the fact that I permitted you to keep your weapons is to be taken as a sign of confidence."

"Okay," said Yok. "If you moved that hunk of rock to the left the floor would open up beneath us. There's an acid pit down below. Zlaz and I designed it for your first ancestor."

"Excellent!" He stood and bowed from the waist. "Hail, oh bringers of the Lens!"

"Oh, don't stand on formality."

"It can't be helped. After thirty-two generations of the myth-making process you've become pretty big. Almost religious figures in our racial memory."

"Hmm," said Yok, who realized that the racial memory bit was a biological reality. Normal sexual reproduction being impossible, the new individuals grown in insemination tanks were endowed with their family memories. The Lucifer Hades seated before them had a two-hundred year life expectancy, but a spotty heritage of six thousand years' memory—most of them being evil and sadistic ones, as they were strongest for this species of mon. (For that matter, though, they are strong in any species of mon.) Lucifer Hades' hereditary office, however, had endowed him with a richer background of good, solid, high-quality evil, than the normal stumblebum demon. Hence, he too was an object of respect. So Yok nodded slightly out of respect.

"Very good. You recognize us. You haven't amassed troops outside Lucetania just because you wanted us to tea. Or have you? That *would* be a worthy jest—almost up to Lucifer III's sense of humor. Once he flayed thirty humans, just to prove—"

Lucifer broke in harshly, "No, I'm afraid my sense of proportion is a trifle more prosaic—" But here a corner of his mouth twitched upwards into an involuntary chuckle. Lucifer III's watered-down psyche asserted its own, despite five millennia of genetic dissipations.

"That *was* a good one, though. Heh! Heh!"

"Heh! Heh!" said Zlaz.

"Heh! Heh!" agreed Yok.

"You've got to teach me that one with the needles and the UHF before go. Don't forget."

"I won't."

"But now, as to business. Don't worry about the army. If you can solve my main headache they won't cause any trouble."

"Then why don't you just call them back now? We're pretty accomplished achievers, and it would relieve our Pres' heavily burdened—"

Here the intercom buzzed, and Lucifer listened a moment, then snapped, "All right. But no more interruptions till I get finished in here."

"That was a message from our Intelligence division," he said, "who just now intelligently learned, by asking the guard at the gate, that you were attacked when you landed."

"That's right. But we passed over it as one of the little hazards travelers have to expect."

"Well it's not. Or wasn't. And it shouldn't be." He checked to see that the intercom was turned off.

"The place for such fun is in the torture chambers. You were attacked by one of our wolfpack mobs. This is a part of my problem. You see," he shifted, and fingered the paperweight unconsciously, while Yok moved uneasily. "You see, there is no one around here to torture."

The only sound for ten seconds was the hiss of the jets. Then he continued.

"Ten years ago, for some undetermined reason, the Lens stopped crystallizing human souls. Our engineers, who make no pretense of understanding its mechanism, checked everything they could and it looked alright. We thought it might be some temporary blockage of the shaft, and we couldn't check it above 40 miles—that's Lucetanian territory. And we had plenty of dagos on hand, so we could wait. Of course we sent for you and Yok immediately, because of your old promise to Lucifer I to come and fix it if you could, should it ever need it. It didn't clear up!" Here he looked up at Yok, and self-consciously jerked his hand back from the paper-weight.

"We didn't even know if you still existed, really," he went on, "but we had to try. In the meantime the souls in stock began to dissipate. After a few years we were pretty low. We were forced to kidnap whatever mon we could that strayed into the Middle Caves, and—unheard of!—vigilante groups began to organize. They were completely unauthorized, and they ran about torturing their fellow citizens. I can't stop them! I'm afraid to give an order! The military had begun to rebel. They wanted to raid Lucetania for prisoners to torture. Well, I didn't want to try it, but I had to let them go after a while. And if I order them back now they might not come. If that happened, I'd be out. Never in six thousand years has a Lucifer been disobeyed in Hell! I'm appealing to you! Fix the Lens! You built it!"

"Easy, mon. It probably just needs some minor adjustment. We'll take care of it. If that's all you need, we'll go to work on it right now."

"Good! Fine! You can have my best engineers to help—"

"No! The little sneaks just want to see how it works."

"Can you blame us?"

"No, but it's our only power position down here. Besides, it involves certain other things we want to keep to ourselves."

"All right. Go fix it. Report back to me as soon as you do. By the way, what have you mon got against Italians?"

"Huh? Nothing more than against any other humans. We hate them all equally. We're pretty democratic that way."

"Then why are ninety percent of the humans we get down here Italian? Even Dante, that time you got him a visitor's pass, noticed that we were packed almost exclusively with his countrymen."

"Oh," said Zlaz. "Avernus, the classic entrance to the underworld, is the shaft we used as a conductor when we built the Lens. It sucks down the psyches of all the humans who die for a sixty to hundred mile radius. It just happens to be in Italy. You're right under the shoe-laces of the boot, so to speak."

"Well, go to it." He buzzed and mumbled something into the intercom. Then he rose.

"I want you to meet my son." They passed back into the reception room. The evil-looking demon was perched back on the secretary's desk. His hands were out of sight.

"Hi, dad," he nodded. There was a resemblance, and he'd probably be a dead ringer when mature, but now he had a slightly lower, eviller forehead and even shorter horns. A typical boss' son, apparently.

"Gonna be as evil as your old man, kid?" Yok asked.

"I hope so, sir."

"Hell, he'll be eviller," Lucifer mussed his fur and grinned. "Gotta keep up the family reputation."

"You a college mon?" Zlaz inquired.

"Hell U., sir. We've got a great rockball team, and I was president of the Pin the Human Club, until it was disbanded because of the shortage." He blew a cloud of smoke into the air. "I'm majoring in Human Culture. It's taught in the Bio department, but it's really one of the Social Sciences—"

"All right, son. Don't bore our guests. They're awfully busy. That's Yok and Zlaz you're looking at."

Junior tried not to look too impressed, what with being a college mon and all. He whistled softly, though, to sound sophisticated.

"Honored to meet you, gentlemon. I didn't realize your statuses. I'd like to talk with you later." This last sounded almost urgent.

"There's no such thing as Human Culture," Yok snorted, and stamped into the main hall. He was joined shortly by Zlaz and Lucifer senior.

"Uh," said Yok. "I'd like to check your dungeons, when we're through with the repair job. I'm looking for a blonde female."

Lucifer shook his head. "There aren't any humans around at all now," he replied. "The last dissolved about two years ago. We do have over a hundred of your countrymon, though. You can take them back with you. They're more of a nuisance than anything else. We have to keep them in separate cells and work on them one at a time. Whenever they get together they break out or damage something."

"Okay, thanks anyhow."

"Well, what was her name? I can check the records and see whether she *was* here."

"Jeanne d'Arc. She was French."

"Doesn't sound familiar, but I'll let you know this afternoon."

"Good."

❖   ❖   ❖

Zlaz slid down from the bowl of the hundred-foot quartz Lens. He was completely encased in a heavy woolen garment, to prevent scratching it. He scratched himself considerably, however. Stethoscope in hand he addressed some Fuglese to no one in particular, and some comments to Yok.

"___hot in this___place, and I have to wear this___wool suit!"

"Anything wrong up there?" asked Yok, who had the bottom open and was testing electrical circuits.

"Not a crack. How about the inside?"

"Nothing here either." Yok stood up.

Zlaz was peeling off the wool shirt.

"Do you know what that means?" Yok asked.

"Yeah. Either people have stopped dying in Italy, or there's some blockage in the shaft."

"Yeah, there's some blockage," said Yok. "I came back through the World of Humans, and they haven't stopped dying, I can guarantee."

"Hmm. Then we have to inspect the whole two hundred mile drop. Either it's blocked, there's a pocket of cold air, or there's a crosscurrent of warm air."

"That earthquake was about ten years ago, wasn't it?"

"Yeah, I thought of that. Here comes Lucifer. We can bring him up to date, and see what's up with your human. By the way, did you mean *the* Jeanne d'Arc?"

"Yeah."

"What's the deal? Maybe I can add the extra evil skill necessary to find her."

"Well, she was a witch.—That is, she's a human I taught all sorts of foul, low mon lore to."

"That was a century ago. How did you run into her?"

"Well, I had to masquerade as a human for a while back then. I was a *Maréchal* of France—Giles de Retz was the name. I—"

"Bluebeard! The evillest human in ages!"

"Well, I enjoy myself whenever I'm out on a job, if I can."

"And you revealed your identity and educated her?"

"Well—yes. And when it was time to come back, I sort of didn't want to leave her behind. So I sneaked her into Lucetania and put her on ice. When I became a human again I could have just awakened her and we could have resumed where we left off."

Lucifer drew near. He stood then smoking, with a worried look.

"Find the trouble?"

"No. It's something up in the shaft," said Zlaz. "We'll take off right now and inspect it if you like."

"Fine. Go right ahead."

"Well," said Yok, "what about Jeanne d'Arc?"

"Not on the books," shrugged Lucifer. "Sorry I can't help you. It is possible that she was here and didn't get recorded. Our records for this past decade are pretty sloppy. You can go down into the dungeons and ask around yourself, if you want. Maybe some of your countrymon, or the guards—"

"Yeah, I'd like to do that. In fact Zlaz can check the shaft just as quickly by himself. So if you don't mind, I'll go right now."

"All right. I'll give you a letter to the warden."

"See you later, then, Zlaz."

"Yeah." He struggled out of the rest of the wool uniform and kicked it into a heap. Yok and Lucifer headed back towards town.

III.

Yok made a face at his reflection in the brimstone beer, and belched sulphur. Lucifer, seated at his desk in the now darkened administration center, sipped one of his own. He hit a switch before him and the overhead light went on again. The wall jets hissed less violently than earlier.

"Did I hear a door?"

"I think so," answered Yoke. He gulped his drink and set the emptied flagon on the tray. *No success*, he mused.

There were two sharp knocks at the door, which opened before Lucifer finished saying, "Come in."

Zlaz crossed the room and threw himself into a stone armchair (which creaked audibly) before he said anything.

"Well?" asked Lucifer, after a polite pause.

"Not very," answered Zlaz. "I've found the answer. —But tell me, where is Lucifer XXXIII?"

"I don't know what he does on his own time. He might be anywhere. I hope he's keeping up the family name with appropriate evilness." He grinned slily. "Maybe he's got a vigilante pack of his own. There is something very tempting about illicit torture… If I were in his position—"

"Before you set carried away in reverie, that was what I'd call a leading question. I *know* where he is."

"Oh?"

"About seventy miles up I found a side passage, cutting off of the main one. There was an artificial current of hot air, with a jet of cold below it."

"Artificial?"

The steamhoses puffed, as if in sympathy, then slackened their pressure.

"Artificial. Maybe the passage was opened up in that last earth-quake. Anyhow your son happened upon it and exploited it. He's hot quite a setup in there."

"I'm afraid I don't understand. Setup?"

"Complete with a little Lens of his own. He drains off the souls, re-crystallizes them, and has his own little Elysium."

"But why?" said Lucifer.

"But how?" said Yok.

Zlaz stared at Yok. "Who else could build a Lens?"

"The Starlighter, the Black Banshee, Sethantes—"

"In this part of the galaxy."

"No one but us—" The flash was one of recognition.

"How much intricate, low mon lore did you teach Jeanne?"

"Hmm," said Yoke. "I never gave her explicit plans for a Lens—But she just might have been able to do it at that, if she had a working one to study."

"And incentive," said Zlaz. "Tell me, was she a humanitarian?"

"Well," Yok squirmed a bit uncomfortably, "sort of."

"You really are getting perverse, aren't you? Tch, tch, tch! A human—and a decent one at that."

"Well, there was a little affair concerning you and the Queen of Sheba that's never been fully aired."

"Hmm. Well, turning aside from problems of personality, Jeanne made it down here, recrystallized, and was discovered by Lucifer Jr. She fit neatly in with his plans. That Pin the Human presidency was sheer cover-up. Check and I bet you'll see he never participated. She was a humanitarian human idealist and she doped out the secret of the Lens. They duplicated it in one of the Middle Caverns, cut off the flow of souls to down here, and set up a Garden of Eden. Every-one is happy up there and passes his time in a human Utopia, Lucifer XXXIII and a gang of his friends are the guardian angels."

"My own son! A pervert! —And he stood to inherit all this!" Lucifer gestured widely. "I shouldn't have let him major in Human Culture!"

"I doubt it was a causative factor," said Zlaz, "just a result. After millennia of sterility in these radioactive, overheated caverns, your stock has started to mutate. Your son is a hybrid. He is sexually potent. I noticed his behavior this afternoon with your secretary. It was a trifle odd, for an impotent, sterile mon."

"God! A queer in my only family!"

"No. He just has a different method of release. He doesn't need to torture for kicks. That's why he was attracted to human culture. He read their Heaven myth and decided to set up his own version of it."

"My own son! An Anti-Lucifer!" He poured a stiff drink and gulped it. Then he poured another and sipped more slowly. He looked broken. Then however, the colossus, half-legend, which was Lucifer himself, in the blood, behind the individual, slowly began to reassert itself. He smiled cryptically and bleakly, rose, and crossed to his bookcase.

When he returned, it was a bound map he unravelled on the desktop. Suddenly he was half a foot taller.

"Okay," he pointed. "Show me where this cancer is located. I'm going to have the army away from Lucetania and up there in six hours, if I have to personally assassinate all my officers."

Zlaz grinned respectfully; Yok, a trifle sheepishly.

"Well, where is it?" he demanded, smoking violently, arms akimbo.

Zlaz rose, and, with a pen, quickly sketched in a side-cavern. Lucifer pored over it and reached for the monstraphone.

"Just a moment!" said Zlaz. And for some reason Yok thought of the same words, breaking a gesture of the Pres', the day before.

His hand paused, an unspoken question peered from behind his slanted eyes.

Zlaz continued with the pen: "My abilities of dissimulation are gargantuan: Not only did I penetrate the Citadel of Heaven, disguised as a demon, recognize your son, and assassinate the queen—"

"—Assassinate the queen!" Yok stood suddenly. Zlaz, however, winked to him, out of Lucifer's range of view.

"—I also scouted the adjacent terrain. Here," he pointed to the map, "is a nearby pocket of lava. An appropriate explosion—about there," he mused, "would send a fiery sea down into Heaven, taking them at the height of their revelry and perversion. —All the humans, all the errant demons, and your son."

The gigantic crash was Lucifer's fist, cracking the desk top. "Yes! By Ishtar! It's beautiful! Delicate! Subtle! Lovely! What a mind you have, Zlaz! I wish I could persuade you to stay and redesign the whole system!" He laughed maniacally for a full two minutes, then reseated himself. "Okay. Go! Leave! Depart right away and blast that pocket open! I'll be on the landing waiting for the beautiful sound."

"That's not all," added Zlaz. "When that cavern's filled up, the shaft should work normally again."

"Come on," Lucifer jumped up, grabbing the pitcher and a flagon as he headed toward the door.

"She's alive," Zlaz whispered as they left. "I kidnapped her and hid her in the car, but thought it politic to provide a lie."

Yok grinned, feeling better by the second.

❖   ❖   ❖

The ground-shaking sound occurred but a few moments before the aerocar darted down from the shaft. It danced rapidly through the forest of stalactites and dropped before the black-haloed form standing upon a promontory. An enormous sigh, like a distant wind, swam forward from somewhere; it rose up into an inhuman groan.

"Is the deed done?" asked Lucifer of the two figures scurrying from the car.

"Yes and no," said Yok. "Complications have arisen."

"Such as?"

"Well everything happened the way I figured it," said Zlaz, looking nervously upward. The groan increased to a thunder.

"—but there was more lava in that pocket than I thought!" he shouted.

Realization broke, like a Pacific hurricane, upon Lucifer's face.

"You mean—!"

Zlaz nodded: "That sound you hear is the overflow rushing down the shaft."

"How long have we?"

"Five minutes. Maybe six—"

Despite the titanic thunder an abstract calm, not of sound, but of feeling, was born as Lucifer mused on the brink of chaos. His voice was steady, even relaxed:

"I made the mistake of forgetting a verse or two from our ancient Scripture." Here he poured a flagon of brimstone beer. "The legend goes that you and Yok can do anything, anything at all." He sipped slowly, then continued, "And the corollary is that whenever your task is accomplished, you somehow manage to screw up the situation some other way, so that things always end up worse than you found them."

He gestured widely, drunkenly: "You once saved my people. You found us this beautiful haven—of course it made our entire race sterile! Then—"

"We might still save the play before the end of the fifth act," Yok suggested.

"How?"

"Another quick explosion near the base will bottle up the shaft. Maybe it'll hold it back. We still have three and a half minutes to try."

They vanished back toward the car in a puff of obscenity.

❖   ❖   ❖

"Your power position," growled Lucifer malevolently, "is now non-existent."

He eyed the blasted shaft. Occasional gravel still rained upon the rock-wrecked Lens.

"*Je ne parle pas français!*" he growled at the blonde human female standing between the two mon, who had just said something.

"Also, you Zlaz! You lied to me. You didn't assassinate her! You kidnapped her! Did you really think you could keep her hidden in your car?"

Zlaz nodded.

"It maneuvered much too clumsily for a pilot like you. I figured out the extra weight factor. I'm not what I am because I'm stupid. Lying to me!"

"It seemed appropriate," Zlaz said.

Lucifer ignored him. "She'll get the works for high treason. Then, despite certain religious qualifications you'll grace my personal dungeon. I may be ruined, but I'll go out in style."

Yok cleared his throat:

"We built this place once—"

"Times are different," said Lucifer. "You had a smaller group to work with, simpler jobs. You're only big in retrospect. Now we are in a political turmoil. What could you achieve? Build another Lens? What shaft? It would take too long anyhow."

"Stall," said Yok, "for as long as you can. Let us go back to Lucetania—the City of Light, from which you took your name—"

"And was meant to rule!" Lucifer interjected. Then he mused: "No, I can't trust you. You wouldn't come back."

"Leave Jeanne," observed Zlaz gallantly, "if you have something sure-fire."

Yok looked pensive. So did Lucifer.

"How long?" he finally inquired.

"Just there and back," Yok suggested.

"One short-lived human isn't that large an incentive," he shook his head. "I wouldn't even send one of you and keep the other: You Upper Level mon have no personal honor.

"For that matter, though," he continued, "I'm not certain I want to keep you either." A crafty gleam kicked its heels deep within his eyes. "Perchance you could get me political asylum in Lucetania?"

Zlaz shook his head:

"Your generals would declare war anyhow, without you, and you'd probably be executed."

Lucifer looked bleak.

Yok smiled at a sudden commotion from the city.

"The sound you are now hearing," he narrated, "is a prison break. I left my pocket tool kit with a countrymon during my tour earlier. I had no specific intent, other than stirring up hell." Here he chuckled at his own jest, and Zlaz joined him. "And now his malicious mechanical genius seems to have prevailed. We again occupy a small power pivot. Give us your word by your office, the Covenant, and all that's black and vile that we can make this trip and we'll quell them, you'll have our words we'll be right back. If you don't, they'll do quite a bit of damage before you put them down. Especially as we're physically superior, and all your fighting mon are up near the front."

"And you don't know the half of it," Zlaz murmured.

Lucifer exhaled a black cloud and spat through it, then he smiled and a few of the rocks split (Zlaz maintained it was due to the heat, but Yok had his own ideas).

"All right. Evil and mischief being all I worship, I am always willing to pay homage to superior craft in villainy." He bowed from the waist, "Go stop them now or you'll have another city planning job ahead. You have my vilest word you may go."

They went.

❖ ❖ ❖

The reading light in the Pres' office was the only illumination in the capital building. He was seated at his desk, poring over a battle map.

The door stood halfway open. Yok kicked it the rest of the way and strode in. He paused to knock politely on the frame.

"The devil!" observed the Pres. "How did you get back? You *did* go, didn't you?" He scowled and looked puzzled alternately.

"Of course," said Zlaz, appearing behind him and kicking the door shut. "We've taken care of everything except the loose ends. We'll tie those off now, if you don't mind. How about our money?"

"I haven't got that kind of money in my office safe. Besides, what proof have I that you accomplished anything?"

"Tomorrow the troops from Hell will be withdrawn from our border. Diplomatic relations will be set up within a month, in the name of the new monarch, Lucifer XXXIII, with whom we've made a deal. No peace or friendship, but there'll be a healthy resumption of the status quo."

"When all that's occurred you can see me for your money. Now, if you'll excuse me—" He glanced down at the papers before him.

"No, we won't excuse you," said Yoke. "We want our pound of flesh."

"What do you mean?"

Yok produced his pocket acetylene torch.

"Before we use this on your wall safe we're going to use it on you."

"This is ridiculous! I said you'd get your money, if what you claim is correct. You'll have to wait."

"You don't understand," explained Yoke "This is pure revenge."

"For what?"

"Smashing that stasis chamber in my lab after the earthquake."

"Why should I do a thing like that?"

Yok ticked them off on his fingers: "1) You knew I'd need a strong motive to go to Hell when you finally located me, knowing Zlaz would go if I did; 2) you puritanically disapproved of my "perverseness" in preserving a human female; and 3) just for the sheer hell of it, because you enjoy breaking things (especially live ones) that don't belong to you."

"Absurd! What proof have you for such allegations?"

"Why, the best in the world, Jeanne's word. Her released psyche witnessed your raging through my lab with a crowbar before it was sucked down to Hell. She learned afterwards that this was three months after the earthquake. Gas leakages aren't so important that you'd have an inspection team out there the next day. You see, I *did* locate her." Yok lit the torch. "Or did you just drop in to kill the termites for me and discover they'd grown vicious?"

The Pres swallowed, licked his purple-blue lips:

"You'll never get away with this one! I'm President of the whole Pan-Monstric Association!"

"So was Tara Juanua."

"Times have changed in six thousand years! They'll track you down! Where could you hide? No place!"

"On the contrary," supplied Zlaz, "the same place as before, and doing the same things as before—being evil and helping to rebuild Hell. The new Lucifer Hades has again granted us unlimited sanctuary. So you see, we just have to wait until the next Pres has a problem so delicate that our special talents are required. What if it takes a few centuries? We might even manufacture it. Our price will be pardon. In the meantime we'll be vacationing in the warmer climes."

They moved forward.

"Okay!" he squirmed. "I admit I smashed your stuff and killed her. It was the only device I could think of that you'd do my bidding for. It wasn't malice, it was political expediency that prompted the action. I needed a hold over you. The Prince, like a weapon or force, is neither moral nor immoral. He responds to urgency within the limitation of available alternatives—"

"Don't quote Machiavelli at us," said Zlaz. "He was me."

"Besides," added Yok, the blue nimbus of the torch casting weird shadows across his face, "since that's not the way Jeanne tells it, I'll have her word over yours—even though human females don't have the best reputations for veracity. She claims it was pure malice. Your administration was going to pot anyhow. It's time for a change. In fact, rumor has it you manufactured that earthquake yourself, so you could invoke emergency tax measures."

"That really is a lie!"

"I know, I just started it tonight."

"You'll never get—"

IV.

When Yok ambled into the Grene Zyphoam Cellar for the second time in twenty years, Zlaz was with him.

"That," he pointed out, "is Adon, a small-time fertility deity who is about to become a savior in Hell. Kind of ironic, like the other time—"

"Don't be nostalgic here," said Zlaz. "It got out of hand that time."

But Yok regarded the palms of his hands for a moment in silence.

"Ahem, Adon. May I have a word with you?"

"Sure, Yok. Buy me some zyphoam."

"Okay." He whistled up a gallon. "We've got you a good job with plenty of prestige. After a few generations you may even develop a taste for brimstone beer."

"Doing what?"

"Why tho only thing you know, of course. There's a whole culture that requires your, er—peculiar abilities to help it through a particularly hard part of its history. They need a quick, lively transition from sadism to sex."

"Great! I'll need my tools: horned masks, phallic images—"

"No time. There are plenty of horns where we're going, and lots of suggestive rocks."

"Okay." He gulped some zyphoam. "Would I know anybody where we're headed, do you think?"

"Just me and Zlaz." Here Yok leaned back. "But you'll make friends quickly—"we've even got a lot of little yellow guys out in the car for a cheering section."

"Great!" he observed.

"Hmm," Zlaz poured out the zyphoam with a noble sigh, and glanced at his watch.

There was still time for a moment's sentimental regarding of things past.

Notes

Zelazny and Carl Yoke each contributed to *The Record*, a series of short stories about Zlaz and Yok (for Zelazny and Yoke), sloppy but crafty monsters who lived in caves under Paris but above Hell and near to Lucetania, slept long periods, drank large quantities of *zyphoam*, ambled in and out of outrageous situations, and fouled up most assignments given to them. There was also a fair bit of humor and word play in these stories. "Studies in Saviory" is the only surviving story that Zelazny wrote for *The Record*.

Carl Yoke wrote, "The word 'saviory' in the title is not a misspelling but rather a clever neologism, a combination of savior and savory. The new word not only reflects the mon's saving of Hell once again but also the fact that they save Lucetania from a war with the forces of Hell and they make it possible for the 'Paradise' established by Lucifer XXXIII and Jeanne to blossom in the nether region. In echoing savory, it also suggests that what has happened, and what is going to happen, is good…

"Beyond the creation of the word 'saviory,' the story also contains other word play. Hell is, for example, explained as an acronym coming from the phrase Hot Empire Lower than Lucetania. And demon is explained as coming from the phrase 'demoted mon'…And finally the Avernus Hole, Avernus being another word for hell, can be shortened to A-hole, which I have on good authority was the term that Yok and Zlaz usually used…

"The story follows the usual *Record* grammar. Yok and Zlaz are tricked into a mission by the Pres who has an agenda of his own. They succeed at solving the major problem only to 'screw up' something else. There are the usual ironies, notice for example that Yok and Zlaz are going to recreate Hell, a kinder, gentler Hell which will replace torture with 'healthy' sex. And there is betrayal; the Pres sets them up. And there is humor."[1]

Written in 1964 or 1965, Yoke recalled that Zelazny read it to him at his apartment while Yoke's wife waited impatiently to serve supper.[1]

Zyphoam was the fictional drink of Yok and Zlaz; Yoke and Zelazny did "try to make Zyphoam once in Roger's basement. It had V-8 as its basis with some tabasco, licorice and other stuff—no alcohol at that point— maybe some Vernors ginger ale which we drank along with Pepsi. It was appropriately awful."[2]

Adon (also known as Adonis) was an ever-youthful, annually-renewed Greek god of fertility and the harvest. **Dionysus** (also known as Bacchus) was a Greek god of fertility, wild and ecstatic religious rites, and wine.

---

1 "Commentary on 'Studies in Saviory' " by Carl B. Yoke, unpublished essay.
2 Letter from Carl Yoke to Dr. Christopher Kovacs dated January 8, 2008.

Priapus was another, minor Greek god of fertility who was often depicted as having an extremely large phallus. **Etruscan** means pertaining to the people of Etruria, whose civilization was at its peak in 500 BC.

Lucetania or Lusitania was an ancient Roman region that corresponded to modern Portugal. **Anubis** was the Egyptian god of mummification who was represented as having the head of a jackal. **Orpheus** pleaded and won from the gods the right to have his dead wife Eurydice returned to him, but he failed in the one requirement to not look back on his long walk out of Hell. When he looked back, doubting that she was truly behind him, she became lost to him forever.

Ethos is the underlying character, spirit and beliefs of a culture, that make it what it is. **Avernus** is a lake near Naples which was considered in ancient times to be the site of an entrance to Hell.

Stalagmites form on the floor of a cavern from the mineral water dripping down. **UHF** is an abbreviation for Ultra High Frequency. The poet **Dante** Alighieri wrote *The Divine Comedy* about his fictional journey to Hell, Purgatory, and into Paradise, a work that inspired many of Zelazny's works. **Jeanne d'Arc** is the French name for Joan of Arc, the maiden who was inspired by religious visions and led the resistance during the siege of Orléans; she was later burned at the stake as a witch.

Maréchal means Marshal, a military distinction in France. **Giles de** Laval, Seigneur de **Retz**, also known as Marshal de Retz, was one of Joanne of Arc's captains and later distinguished himself by becoming Marshall of France and counselor and chamberlain to King Charles VII. He had a characteristic barbe bleue (blue beard). The story of **Bluebeard**, in which a man repeatedly kills his wives and stuffs their bodies in a room in his castle, is thought to have taken its name from the Marshal de Retz.

Elysium is the mythological afterlife for heroes and the blessed, similar to Avalon. Sir Thomas More coined the phrase "**utopia**" (a perfect place) for his 1516 book of the same name. Niccolò di Bernardo dei **Machiavelli** was an Italian statesman and political philosopher who advised unethical means may be necessary to acquire and effectively use power. **Stalactites** form from mineral-rich water and hang from the roof of a cavern.

Kind of ironic, like the other time…it got out of hand that time suggests that Yok and Zlaz had inadvertently created Christianity.

PUBLICATION HISTORY

Frontispiece portrait by Jack Gaughan first appeared on the cover of "Marcon VII Program and Schedule Book, 1972" where Roger Zelazny was Guest of Honor.

"Out of Nowhere" by Robert Silverberg first appears in this volume.

"Before Amber" by Carl B. Yoke first appears in this volume.

"A Rose for Ecclesiastes" first appeared in *The Magazine of Fantasy & Science Fiction*, November 1963.

"And the Darkness Is Harsh" first appeared in *Eucuyo*, 1954.

"Mr. Fuller's Revolt" first appeared in *Eucuyo*, 1954.

"Youth Eternal" first appeared in *Eucuyo*, 1955. Previously uncollected.

"The Outward Sign" first appeared in *Skyline #31*, Cleveland College of Western Reserve University, April 1958. Previously uncollected.

"Passion Play" first appeared in *Amazing Stories*, August 1962.

"The Graveyard Heart" first appeared in *Fantastic*, March 1964.

"Horseman!" first appeared in *Fantastic*, August 1962.

"The Teachers Rode a Wheel of Fire" first appeared in *Fantastic*, October 1962. Previously uncollected.

"Moonless in Byzantium" first appeared in *Amazing Stories*, December 1962. Previously uncollected.

"On the Road to Splenoba" first appeared in *Fantastic*, January 1963. Previously uncollected.

"Final Dining" first appeared in *Fantastic*, February 1963. Previously uncollected.

"The Borgia Hand" first appeared in *Amazing Stories*, March 1963. Previously uncollected.

"Nine Starships Waiting" first appeared in *Fantastic*, March 1963. Previously uncollected.

"Circe Has Her Problems" first appeared in *Amazing Stories*, April 1963. Previously uncollected.

"The Malatesta Collection" first appeared in *Fantastic*, April 1963. Previously uncollected.

"The Stainless Steel Leech" first appeared in *Amazing Stories*, April 1963 as by Harrison Denmark.

"The Doors of His Face, the Lamps of His Mouth" first appeared in *The Magazine of Fantasy & Science Fiction*. March 1965.

"A Thing of Terrible Beauty" first appeared in *Fantastic*, April 1963 as by Harrison Denmark.

"Monologue for Two" first appeared in *Fantastic*, May 1963 as by Harrison Denmark. Previously uncollected.

"Threshold of the Prophet" first appeared in *Fantastic,* May 1963. Previously uncollected.

"A Museum Piece" first appeared in *Fantastic*, June 1963.

"Mine Is the Kingdom" first appeared in *Amazing Stories*, August 1963 as by Harrison Denmark. Previously uncollected.

"King Solomon's Ring" first appeared in *Fantastic*, October 1963. Previously uncollected.

"The Misfit" first appeared in *Amazing Stories*, October 1963. Previously uncollected.

"The Great Slow Kings" first appeared in *Worlds of Tomorrow*, December 1963.

"Collector's Fever" first appeared in *Galaxy*, June 1964.

"The Night Has 999 Eyes" first appeared as "The Night Has Nine Hundred Ninety-Nine Eyes" in *Double:Bill #11*, October/November 1964.

"He Who Shapes" first appeared in *Amazing*, January & February 1965.

"Sundry Notes on Dybology and Suchlike" first appeared in *Science Fiction Parade*, September 1964. Previously uncollected.

" '…And Call Me Roger': The Literary Life of Roger Zelazny, Part 1" by Christopher S. Kovacs, MD first appears in this volume.

"Conditional Benefit" first appeared in *Thurban I*, fanzine #3, August-September 1953. Previously uncollected.

"Hand of the Master" may have first appeared in an unknown fanzine, date unknown. Previously uncollected.

"The Great Selchie of San Francisco Bay" first appears in this volume. Written 1965–68.

"Studies in Saviory" first appears in this volume. It was written in 1964 or 1965.

Poems

"Braxa" first appeared in *The Magazine of Fantasy & Science Fiction*, November 1963 as part of "A Rose for Ecclesaistes".

"Ecclesiastes' Epilogue", "Sense and Sensibility", "How a Poem Means", "Hart Crane…", "Hybris, or The Danger of Hilltops", "In Pheleney's Garage", "The Black Boy's Reply to William Butler Yeats", and "Rite of Spring" first appear in this volume. Written 1955–60 for *Chisel in the Sky.*

"Bok" first appeared in *And Flights of Angels: The Life and Legend of Hannes Bok*, ed. Emil Petaja, The Bokanalia Memorial Foundation 1968, as "Untitled". Previously uncollected.

"Diet" first appeared in *Eucuyo,* 1954.

"Slush, Slush, Slush" first appeared in *Eucuyo,* 1954. Previously uncollected.

"The Agnostic's Prayer" first appeared in its entirety in *Creatures of Light and Darkness*, 1969. Part one first appeared in "Creatures of Light"; *If*, November 1968. Part two first appeared in "The Steel General"; *If*, January 1969.

"On May 13, 1937" first appears in this volume. Written 1965–68.

"The Cactus King", "From a Seat in the Chill Park", "Rodin's 'The Kiss' ", and "Iceage" first appeared in *To Spin Is Miracle Cat*, Underwood-Miller 1981. Written 1955–1960 for *Chisel in the Sky.*

"Our Wintered Way Through Evening, and Burning Bushes Along It", "In the Dogged House", "Future, Be Not Impatient", and "Flight" first appeared in the present form in "The Graveyard Heart" in *Fantastic*, March 1964. Original versions written 1955–60 under other names.

"The World of Stat's a Drunken Bat" has only appeared as part of "Nine Starships Waiting".

"The Cat Licks Her Coat" first appeared in *Tapeworm #5*, 1967. Previously uncollected.

"To His Morbid Mistress" first appeared in *Alternities #6*, Summer 1981.

"Old Ohio Folkrag" first appeared in *Double:Bill #9* June 1964. Previously uncollected.

"Concert" first appeared in *Double:Bill #11*, Oct-Nov 1964. Previously uncollected.

"Southern Cross" first appeared in *Eridanus #2* (poetry fanzine), Spring 1966 (as "Cross Caribbean"). Written in 1957 for *Chisel in the Sky.*

"I Used to Think in Lines That Were Irregular to the Right" first appeared in *Science Fiction* (Australian) Vol 1 No 3 Dec 1978.

"St. Secaire's" first appeared in *Haunted #3*, June 1968. A revised version appeared in *To Spin Is Miracle Cat*, Underwood-Miller 1981. A further revised version first appears in this volume. Written 1955–60 for *Chisel in the Sky.*

"Decade Plus One of Roses" first appeared in *Skyline #32*, April 1959.

"See You Later, Maybe…" first appears in this volume. Written on March 18, 1968.

Acknowledgments

Thanks go in many directions: to Roger Zelazny for his life's work, a body of writing that made this project a joy to work on; to my wife, Leah Anderson, without whose support this project would never have started; to Chris Kovacs, whose research efforts not only produced a comprehensive collection of material, but whose analysis added depth to the whole project; to Ann Crimmins for her dedication to all things grammatical; to Robert Silverberg and Carl Yoke for their insightful introductions; to Michael Whelan for his spectacular dust jacket painting; and to Alice Lewis for her polished dust jacket design and her invaluable advice in design issues. Thanks also go to: Mark Olson for his help in book production, Geri Sullivan for design advice and our stalwart band of proofreaders:

Kelly Persons, Rick Katze, Tim Szczesuil, Ann Broomhead,
Pam Fremon, Larry Pfeffer, Peter Olson, Jim Burton,
Sharon Sbarsky, Ann Crimmins, Chris Kovacs, and Mark Olson.

David G. Grubbs
December, 2008

There are many individuals who aided in the extensive search to locate original manuscripts, correspondence, rare fanzines, and obscure interviews. Colleagues, family, and friends of Roger Zelazny helped to clarify details and quash rumors about his life and work. My own colleagues helped with translations of Greek, German, Japanese and other foreign language phrases. Apologies to anyone who might have been overlooked in compiling the following list:

Charles Ardai, John Ayotte, George Beahm, Greg Bear, John Betancourt, Rick Bradford, Ned Brooks, Lois McMaster Bujold, John Callendar, George Carayanniotis, Ung-il Chung, Michael Citrak, Giovanna Clairval, Bob Collins, Lloyd Currey, Jack Dann, Jane Frank, c Shell Franklin, Paul Gilster, Simon Gosden, Ed Greenwood, Joe Haldeman, David Hartwell, Gerald Hausman, Graham Holroyd, Beate Lanske, Elizabeth LaVelle, Jane Lindskold, George R. R. Martin, Bryan McKinney, Henry Morrison, Kari Mozena, Rias Nuninga, Richard Patt, Greg Pickersgill, Bob Pylant, Mike Resnick, Andy Richards, Fred Saberhagen, Roger Schlobin, Darrell Schweitzer, Robert Silverberg, Dan Simmons, Dean Wesley Smith, Ken St. Andre, Richard Stegall, Thomas T. Thomas, Norris Thomlinson, Erick Wujcik, Carl Yoke, Trent Zelazny, Cindy Ziesing, and Scott Zrubek.

Diane Cooter, Nicolette Schneider, Lara Chmela
>Roger Zelazny Papers, Special Collections
>Research Center, Syracuse University Library

Thomas Beck, Susan Graham, Marcia Peri, Shaun Lusby
>Azriel Rosenfeld Science Fiction Research Collection,
>University of Maryland, Baltimore County.

Sara Stille, Eric Milenkiewicz, Audrey Pearson
>Bruce Pelz and Terry Carr Fanzine Collections, Special
>Collections Library, University of California, Riverside

Greg Prickman, Jacque Roethler, Kathryn Hodson, Jeremy Brett
>M. Horvat Collection, Special Collections,
>University of Iowa Libraries

Jill Tatem
>University Archives, Case Western Reserve University

Thomas M. Whitehead
>Whitehead Collection, Special Collections Department, Temple University Libraries

Patti Thistle, Dion Fowlow, George Beckett
>Document Delivery Office, Health Sciences Library,
>Memorial University of Newfoundland.

And then there are the personal thanks that I need to make. Of course none of this would have been possible without Roger Zelazny creating the very stories and characters that I find myself returning to again and again. When I finally met him at Ad Astra in 1986, I interrupted his rapid departure from the convention and asked "Mr. Zelazny" to sign the books I'd carried with me. He kindly took care of that and the requests of my companions. "Everybody OK, then? Right, gotta get to the airport"—and then his parting comment to me was "…and call me Roger." From that memory came the fitting title for the monograph in these volumes.

My mother handed me that paperback *Nine Princes in Amber* one dull day so long ago when I complained that I had nothing to read, and my parents drove me to countless new and used bookstores on the very first Zelazny quest to find copies of all of his books. The Internet makes searches so much easier now, and I couldn't have gathered much of this material if I'd had to rely on physical searches and postal mail. My buddy Ed Hew and his cousins drove me to Ad Astra for that fateful meeting. Dave Grubbs believed in and fought to see this project succeed when my involvement made it expand well beyond what he'd anticipated, and Ann Crimmins pruned, weeded, and used a flamethrower where necessary to turn my sometimes passive prose into something more readable. And none of this would have been possible without the support of my wife, Susan, and our children Caileigh and Jamieson, who put up with my additional absences from home and the other blocks of time consumed in creating this project. If their eyes should roll at mention of the name Zelazny, you may now understand why. And the fact that Susan's birthday is also May 13, or that my last name also refers to what happens in a smithy, are just examples of those Strange and Odd Coincidences in Life realized while researching this project. That our Golden Retriever is named Amber is *not* one of those coincidences.

Christopher S. Kovacs, MD
December, 2008

I wish to thank my daughters Fiona and Deirdre, whom I dragged to cons as children and who have grown to love sf and fantasy as much as I do. Particular thanks to my husband Peter Havriluk for patience, encouragement, and easing the log jam at the p.c. by buying himself a laptop. Dave and Chris, I'm delighted to have worked with you. Thanks also to the various Crimmins/Havriluk cats who warmed my lap as I edited.

Ann Crimmins
December, 2008

Technical Notes

This book is set in Adobe Garamond Pro, except for the titles (which are set in Trajan Pro), using Adobe InDesign 2. The book was printed and bound by Sheridan Books of Ann Arbor, Michigan, on acid-free paper.

Select books from NESFA Press

Details on these and many more books are online at: www.nesfa.org/press/ Books may be ordered online or by writing to:

NESFA Press; PO Box 809; Framingham, MA 01701

We accept checks (in US$), Visa, or MasterCard. Add $4 P&H for one book, $8 for an order of two to five books, $2 per book for orders of six or more. (For addresses outside the U.S., please add $12 for one or two books, $36 for an order of three to five books, and $6 per book for six or more.) Please allow 3–4 weeks for delivery. (Overseas, allow 2 months or more.)

The New England Science Fiction Association

NESFA is an all-volunteer, non-profit organization of science fiction and fantasy fans. Besides publishing, our activities include running Boskone (New England's oldest SF convention) in February each year, producing a semi-monthly newsletter, holding discussion groups on topics related to the field, and hosting a variety of social events. If you are interested in learning more about us, we'd like to hear from you. Contact us at info@nesfa.org or at the address above. Visit our web site at www.nesfa.org.